The Firekeeper is a story of the Mohawk Valley at the time of the first settlements, when the settlers and the natives first learned each other's ways. It is the tale of a forgotten giant of the American frontier; Billy Johnson, who founded a kingdom in America, and who saved the British colonies by convincing the Iroquois to fight against the French.

It is also the story of two powerful women, Catherine Wissenberg, who fled the horrors of the war in the Rhineland and became Bill's wife, and Island Woman, the Iroquois shaman who recognizes Billy as the fulfillment of a prophecy. *The Firekeeper* is an American epic with classic scope.

ROBERT MOSS is the author of a number of bestselling spy thrillers, including *The Spike* and *Monimbo* (with Arnaud de Borchgrave), *Moscow Rules*, and *Carnival of Spies*. His last novel was an American historical adventure, *Fire Along the Sky*. He lives in Troy, New York.

"I found it an exciting read! The clash of early colonists and cultures, romance, and the mystery of the spirit world have been interwoven masterfully with dreams as the underlying force bringing meaning to *this* story and *history*.

—Rita Dwyer, π executive officer,
Association for the Study of Dreams

FORGE BOOKS BY ROBERT MOSS

Fire Along the Sky
The Firekeeper

THE
FIREKEEPER

A NARRATIVE OF THE EASTERN FRONTIER

ROBERT MOSS

TOR®

A TOM DOHERTY ASSOCIATES BOOK
NEW YORK

This is a work of historical fiction. Any resemblance to living persons or contemporary events is coincidental.

THE FIREKEEPER

A Forge Book
Published by Tom Doherty Associates, Inc.
175 Fifth Avenue
New York, N.Y. 10010

Forge® is a registered trademark of Tom Doherty Associates, Inc.

ISBN: 0-812-54847-7
Library of Congress Card Catalog Number: 95-15452

First edition: July 1995
First mass market edition: September 1996

Printed in the United States of America

0 9 8 7 6 5 4 3 2 1

With this book, I return love and thanks
to my wife and daughters
to my teachers
to my friends of the Six Nations
and to all dreamers

and I requicken the memory of William Johnson,
champion of all that is human.

Ni bheidh ár leithéidi an arís

CONTENTS

PART THREE: THE LIVING BONES

The different tribes of Indians . . . say there never was such a man and never will be another.
> —Tench Tilghman, Washington's aide,
> on Sir William Johnson

The soul of Indians is much more independent of their bodies than ours is and takes much more liberty. It leaves the body whenever it deems it proper to do so to take flight and go to make excursions.
> —Father Joseph-François Lafitau, S.J.,
> *Customs of the American Indians* (1724)

Know this well: no woman wants to rub shoulders in your heart with the dead you are keeping there.
> —Honoré de Balzac

THE FIREKEEPER

PART ONE

A WIND OUT OF IRELAND

Nothing is more real than the women's superiority. It is they who really maintain the tribe, the nobility of blood, the genealogical tree, the order of generations and conservation of the families. In them resides all the real authority: the lands, fields and all their harvest belong to them; they are the soul of the councils, the arbiters of peace and war; they hold all the taxes and public treasure; it is to them that the slaves are entrusted; they arrange the marriages; the children are under their authority; and the order of succession is founded on their blood. . . . The Council of Elders which transacts all the business does not work for itself. It seems that they serve only to represent and aid the women in the matters in which decorum does not permit the latter to appear or act. . . . The women choose their chiefs among their maternal brothers or their own children.

—Father Joseph-François Lafitau,
*Customs of the American Indians
compared with the Customs of
Primitive Times* (1724)

CHAPTER 1
WOMEN OF POWER

1.

It was the time of dream-telling.

In the longhouse, in the ruddy glow of the new fire of Midwinter, the clanmothers dressed the heralds in buffalo robes and bearskins. The women crowned them with wreaths of cornhusks that fanned out around their blackened faces. They fastened braids of cornhusks, like dance rattles, to the Bigheads' wrists and knees. They knotted corn cobs into the thong ties of the animal hides. They armed the dream heralds with huge wooden paddles, shaped like corn pounders, to stir the ashes in the firepits and make the earth tremble under the elmbark lodges of the Upper Castle.

"Now you are complete," the clanmothers told them. "You will leave the Longhouse by the men's door and return by the women's door. You wear the skins the animal masters have given our men on the hunt and the fruits of the earth that the Mother has entrusted to the care of our women."

The women released the Bigheads, each chosen by his dreams, to the Speaker. They had supped at midnight and kept vigil until dawn, while the village dreamed.

They had seen the last stragglers coming home from the hunting camps, threading the deep drifts on snowshoes.

"You will run through all the fires," the Speaker instructed them. "This is the time when minds are turned inside out. This is the feast of dreams." Island Woman's children had barely slept, for all the noise and excitement, although she thought they might have been worn out by now, because the Mohawk village had been astir for days. Even before the dream-prophet saw the Seven Dancers rise to the zenith in the night sky and announced the coming of the moon of Midwinter, the women had been busy sewing costumes, boiling up great kettles of corn soup, pooling tobacco and crushed straw- berries for the doings in the Longhouse. It was already four days since the heralds had raced through the lodges, kicking out the fires, and the new fires were kindled with a bow and a spindle, in the way of the ancestors. Day and night since then, the Upper Castle had vibrated to the thud of the water-drum, the snap of turtle rattles, the high, nasal whine of the singers, the thump of dancing heels coming down hard on the frozen earth.

But Snowbird, Island Woman's seven-year-old, was fizzing with energy. He jumped out at his sisters in a grotesque clown face he had made with bark and old sacking.

Snowbird scared Bright Meadow, who had been walk- ing less than a year. She put her fists to her cheeks and screamed until Island Woman caught her up in her arms and fed her a scrap of maple candy.

Swimming Voices, Island Woman's eldest, was all of thirteen and far too grown-up to pay attention to her little brother's antics. She seemed detached from all of them.

She's got something on her mind, Island Woman thought. *Maybe she has a dream to share. I hope it's not about a man.*

Swimming Voices had her mother's height and looks. The same high cheekbones and huge dark eyes, the raven hair. The child's face was rounder, but some of that was puppyfat that would wear away. The older boys, and

some of the warriors, had started sniffing around since
Island Woman had taken her daughter out to a cabin in
the woods, when the moon-flux came on her for the first
time.

That stuff can wait, Island Woman told herself, watching Swimming Voices wrapping a warm blanket over her
doeskin kilt and leggings. *I still have many things to
teach her, and she has many things to learn. If she is the
one.*

Island Woman frowned, because even with the passing
thought, a veil seemed to fall between her and her elder
daughter.

She had felt this often, especially in dreaming. *There is
something that separates us. Something that hides her
from me. I must know what it is.*

But perhaps not today.

Bright Meadow fanned her fingers against her
mother's bottom lip, making it give out a plopping,
gurgling sound.

"Where is my father?" Snowbird demanded.

"It's a secret."

The truth was Island Woman had no idea what had
happened to her husband. Blackbuck had been gambling
wildly at the bowl game the day before. He had come
blundering through the lodge like a bull moose in rut,
trying to steal the beaverskin blanket off the children's
sleeping mat so he could wager that too. She had hit him
with a corn pounder. When that failed to stop him, she
had hit him with a cast-iron pot. Blackbuck was a good
man when he wasn't gaming or drinking, but that was
not often, not when he was home from the trails and
had something to trade. She guessed he had stayed up
drinking with Hendrick Forked Paths, who had seemed
to be piling up most of the winnings at the game.

"Is my father one of the Bigheads?" Snowbird persisted.

"I told you. It's a secret. Go scare somebody. Go
dream of something good to eat."

Snowbird ran out through the doorflap to find his
friends and start collecting tolls around the village.

The rules of the dream-guessing contest were simple.

The dreamer mimed her dream, and the others tried to guess what she was showing them. Once the content of the dream was discovered, the guesser—and sometimes the whole village—was required to help the dreamer to enact it or, in rarer cases, to avoid it.

The Real People believed this was vital to the health and well-being of the dreamer, because dreams reveal the secret wishes of the soul. The soul speaks through dreams, and if its desires are not honored it may depart from the dreamer in disgust, producing sickness or death.

This was what had been taught from generation to generation.

But what was mimed in the public dream-telling was often what someone had dreamed while waking. Like Snowbird acting out a craving for popcorn or a new lacrosse stick. Or a woman miming her need for a new kettle. Or that shameless lecher, Dragging Antlers, playing out his desire to put a new woman in his bed.

This was understood by everyone, except the white men who sometimes came to the village when they were not wanted and hung about slack-jawed, round-eyed.

Big dreams are told in a different way. They come from spirit guides or from journeys of the soul. They come from the Real World, where all the events of the Shadow World of waking life are born. They are shared only with those who need to know, or whose counsel was required. With the *atetshents*, the one who dreams, or the *arendiwanen*, the woman of power.

Island Woman knew these things because she was a dreamer.

Before I even belonged to the Flint People, I dreamed of living here, in their Valley. I saw the Mohawks coming. I saw their warriors slipping across the frozen lake. I saw them scaling the palisades of our village in the hollow of night, when we were defenseless because the snowdrifts were as high as our walls. My grandmother heard me, but our elders did not listen. My grandmother took our women and children to the island, to keep us safe. But

*hey came for us there, when they had finished with the
*illage. I died that life. Now I belong to the Wolf Clan of
*he Flint People. This is what I am. Before this life, I
*dreamed it. Nothing happens that is not dreamed, before
t comes into the Shadow World.

The day of dream-guessing mocked everything, including the dreaming.

It was not a day for big dreams. It was a day for people
to let out their feelings, to be as stupid or greedy or
obscene as they needed to be, to take the piss out of
other people's pretensions. It was a big thing among the
Real People—especially the men—to hide your emotions, never to get mad in public, never to show you were
vulnerable. This was a day when it was fine to let go of all
that. You could put on a mask if it helped; it was a day
for a blow-out.

Island Woman intended to have some fun.

□

She had made herself a special necklace. She had made it
with hickory bark and a snakeskin, and decorated it with
little pinecones, broken shells and grayish tubular objects that proved, on close inspection, to be elderly dog
turds.

She put it on over her oldest blanket, the one the dog
that produced the turds generally slept on.

In case anyone failed to get the message, she added a
crown. It was torn from a colored print, produced in
London, that had been delivered to the village in large
quantities when Hendrick Forked Paths came back from
visiting Queen Anne. The print was taken from a portrait by Verelst, the court painter. It depicted Hendrick
in theatrical garb, which was highly appropriate, since
his outfit had been provided by a playhouse costumier.
The accompanying text described the warchief as an
Indian King and as Emperor of the Six Nations. These
terms had not translated well into Mohawk, since the
world of the Longhouse knew neither kings nor emper-
ors. The chiefs of the Six Nations, the *rotiyaner* or "men
of good minds," were chosen by the clanmothers and

served at their pleasure. And Hendrick Forked Paths was not among their number. He was a good talker and a seasoned killer and valued for both talents. But he was not welcomed home in his London dress as an "Indian King." The ensuing stink had forced him to abandon his lodge in the Lower Castle and move up the Valley.

With a bit of Hendrick on her head and a pair of cornhusks—a crazy parody of a white society lady's fan—in her hand, Island Woman sallied out among the lodges.

Her immediate target was not Hendrick himself, but the warchief's daughter.

Hendrick's daughter Redbird was the snootiest girl in the village. She thought she was better than the others, because her father had been to London and was courted by the governors of three English colonies. Hendrick was soft on her, bringing her back expensive baubles every time he went to a council at Albany or Boston or Philadelphia. He brought her new calicos every spring, in the brightest prints. He even gave her a quilted silk gown, which she had worn until the brambles and spruce twigs ripped it to pieces.

And he gave her the Necklace. It had been the buzz of the village girls for two whole seasons and was still the focus of envy. The necklace was sterling silver, encrusted with gemstones. Hendrick said he had taken it from a Frenchman, but it was widely believed the necklace was part of the booty from London that he had reserved for himself and his family, instead of turning it over to the clanmothers for the benefit of all.

Redbird wore the necklace on the Sundays when she went down to Fort Hunter to attend Anglican services in the little stone chapel inside the stockade. They called her by a newcomer's name in church. The minister had written it in his book. They called her Margaret. At least it was a name Mohawks could say without screwing up their faces. English was full of sounds Mohawks didn't make. Real People spoke with their mouths open. They did not make noises like B or P, which required you to close your lips. Yet because the newcomers complained

hey couldn't get their tongues round Mohawk names,
Mohawks like Hendrick and his daughter were quick to
oblige them by borrowing white men's names.

Island Woman did not have an English name. She had
changed her skin name once, when the Mohawk family
that adopted her had decided to call her Tewatokwas—
She Comes From The Water. Changing your skin name
once in a lifetime is enough. Unless a dream tells you
different.

Now, where were Hendrick and that fat-assed Margaret Redbird?

The village was in an uproar. Sun Walker, a warrior
about the same age as Island Woman's husband, ran up
making violent motions with his arms. He looked like he
was paddling a dugout through white water.

"A new canoe?" she guessed, laughing.

Sun Walker scowled and blew a hard spray of water
into her face. The droplets froze at once, forming tiny
icicles on her skin and hair.

Island Woman laughed again when she saw Fruitpicker, her own clanmother, waddling about clutching
her belly, with her cheeks puffed out. She was the image
of a fat-bellied pot, big enough to feed the whole
women's council. How like Fruitpicker to ask only for
something simple, something to be shared with the rest
of her clan.

Fruitpicker's plump cheeks collapsed in hoots and
giggles when she noticed what Island Woman was
wearing.

"Bad!" the clanmother whooped. "Bad, bad, bad!"
Then, with a wriggle of uncertainty, "Are you really
going to do it?"

Island Woman twirled the frozen dog turds as if they
were the brilliants the newcomers' fancy women wore at
New York and Philadelphia. Or the gemstones in Redbird's silver necklace.

"It is my *ondinnonk*," she announced solemnly. "It is
the secret wish of my soul."

Fruitpicker spluttered, and a knot of enthusiasts began
to form. Clowns and beggars capered and postured

around Island Woman as she continued her search
making it hard for her to see everything that was goin
on.

She was drawn by another crowd to the clearing i
front of the council house, where a big man was whirlin
and stamping. She thought the crazy man was Hendrick
but as he wheeled, she saw it was White Owl, a younge
warrior who had already brought home many scalps
White Owl was stripped to a beaded breechcloth and
slick of bearfat, indifferent to the chill. Now he wa
cupping his hand over his eyes, as if trying to se
something far off, on the other side of the river, in th
glare of the sun. Now he flapped his arms like a warbird
beating pinions. He snatched up a stick and stabbed th
snow, outlining a triangular, headless figure with stic
limbs.

He wants a war party, Island Woman thought. *Mayb
he wants to go south, against the Flatheads. Or north
against the French and the Bark-Eaters. There is alway
an enemy to kill when the blood-frenzy is on a mar
When he is ridden by the hungry ghosts.*

The bignose clown who was bouncing along in he
entourage turned a cartwheel and screamed, "I am th
upside-down, inside-out, backward-forward, yes-and-n
man, and I am the wisest of the wise!"

That was part of it, Island Woman recognized. Th
Feast of Dreams was not only fun, sometimes not eve
fun. It was the overthrowing of everything right an
proper, everything you were taught about how to behav
and what to expect. There was terror in that too.

She strutted on, swinging her rump, still on th
lookout for Hendrick and his daughter.

Her entourage got bigger and bigger. When people go
a look at her necklace and paper crown, they ran alon
whistling and crowing, clapping their hands.

She beat her fan faster. The bignose clown sniffed th
dog turds and cooed.

You had to expect the unexpected during the Feast o
Dreams, but Island Woman was still shocked by wha
came crawling toward her through the moving legs. /

little old woman, the age her own grandmother would have been. Island Woman knew her, but had never seen her like this.

Deermouse had thrown off her winter blanket. She was as naked as White Owl, with just a rag between her legs and a coat of fish oil or bearfat on her skin.

The old woman clutched at Island Woman's ankles, babbling like a baby. She made wet sucking noises, begging for her dream to be told.

A new granddaughter? Island Woman knew she was right, but did not speak the thought, because this was a dream she could not—*would not*—undertake to fulfill.

She knew that Deermouse had lost her daughters and their children to the white man's plague of spitting sores. They had died like rotting sheep, their skins faded to the color of burned bones. Now Deermouse depended on her surviving brother for food and skins to clothe her. But her brother lived in his wife's lodge, as was expected, and his wife had no use for extra mouths. The brother's wife drove Deermouse away from her fire with her curses, leaving the old woman to scrounge for leftovers from other fires.

I can't give you a granddaughter, old woman.

Only the warriors could do that, if they brought back a captive for adoption no one else claimed. *A child as I was.*

Only the warriors can give you your dream wish. Only the Burned Knives. Maybe you and White Owl are dreaming the same dream. Maybe that is why you are naked together in the snow.

She saw a cocked hat, trimmed with silver lace, bobbing above the heads of the dream-guessers and clowns.

Hendrick Forked Paths was a hard man to miss, even without the hat. He was the biggest man in the village, bigger even than White Owl. He cut off his hair in all seasons, leaving only a ridged scalplock—now hidden by the fine beaver hat—to show he was always ready for war. The white scar of an Abenaki hatchet ran from the corner of his mouth to his ear. He was solid muscle, apart from the hard round belly that stuck out like the ball-head of his killing club through the folds of his scarlet mantle.

Hendrick was smoking a pipe, watching the revelers without joining in.

Island Woman spotted Redbird behind him, peeking out through the doorflap. Redbird's flat face vanished the moment she saw Island Woman moving toward the lodge, at the head of her retinue.

Hendrick creased his face in a sociable smile, but his eyes were cold. He had not forgotten that Island Woman had been one of those who had jeered when they showed the magic lantern pictures of his visit to London. Maybe he had heard that she had spoken against him before the women's council, accusing him of selling the land the women tilled for the white man's hard liquor and of leading Mohawk warriors to their deaths to fight wars that profited only the newcomers.

Whatever his feelings, Hendrick did not move to deny Island Woman and her troupe passage as they skipped toward the entrance of his mother-in-law's longhouse. No house was spared from the Feast of Dreams, no place—except the burial grounds—was taboo.

But Redbird was not playing the game by the rules.

"What do you want?" she hissed. Her fingers stiffened into claws when she saw the things Island Woman had hung around her neck.

Rolling her hips, flapping the cornhusks in front of her face, Island Woman tripped through the firepit, scattering hot coals across the floor of the lodge. Redbird squealed and rushed about, stamping out flames, rescuing baskets and rush matting.

Island Woman saw a gilt-frame mirror and pounced on it.

She blew kisses at her own image, fondling the circlet of dog turds and broken shells.

"Tell the dream!" the bignose clown screamed right in Redbird's face.

"Tell the dream!" they all echoed.

Redbird's mouth tightened as if drawstrings had been

ulled. She looked ready to claw Island Woman's eyes
ut.

But they were all tormenting her, poking and prod-
ing.

"Tell the dream," came the clown's singsong.

Redbird was bound by the custom. She pulled down
ie beaded pouch that hung from the pole behind her
eeping place. She wrenched it open and took out the
lver necklace.

She held it in her palm for a long moment, until it
egan to seem that the cold had grafted the metal to her
kin.

Then she made a fist and flung the necklace into the
repit.

Island Woman snatched it up, sudden as a hawk,
npervious to any surface burns.

"*Tsitak!*" Hendrick's daughter spat at her. "Eat shit."

"You eat." Island Woman dropped the mock-necklace
n the dirt floor of the lodge, and Redbird's dogs ran to
laver over it.

□

sland Woman had not made Redbird tell the dream
ecause she coveted silver. She had done it because
Hendrick Forked Paths was selling out their people to
he newcomers who were killing the forests, driving the
leer and the beaver away. And because Margaret Red-
ird needed to be pulled off her gilded perch, brought
ack to the earth where Real People lived.

It was not right to keep the necklace, Island Woman
new; it would make a path for Redbird's evil thoughts
o follow.

She could trade it. She could fill her larder against the
tarving time ahead, when the corn in the bark silos ran
ow and the hunters could not follow the deer through
he melting snow, before the pigeons came back and the
naples started to give sugar again.

Then she saw Deermouse. The old woman was shak-
ng and wailing in earnest now. The chill was eating into
ier marrow.

She pulled the old woman's thumb out of her mout
and pressed the necklace into her palm.

"Here, Aksotha. Let this be your granddaughter."

□

Though her Anglican minister would not have approved
Redbird found a way to get even before the Feast o
Dreams was over.

Night came down like a shutter, over a day that ha
never seen the sun, and Island Woman took her childre
back to the lodge to eat. She had fried up a heap o
cornbread, sweetened with dried blueberries and a littl
maple sugar. There was jerked venison and a fat slab o
bearmeat left over from the hunt. She had thawed out
goose from the snow barrel and boiled it up. Real Peopl
did not use a lot of seasoning. A little ground sumac i
place of salt, a blade of mint.

What Snowbird liked best about the meal was th
okarita, the popped corn. That was something you go
only at festivals. So part of Snowbird's dream had bee
fulfilled. He wasn't too happy about the other part. H
had mimed his dream wish to White Owl, his herc
White Owl was the best lacrosse player in the Uppe
Castle, a man who could shoot the ball so hard and fast i
would take your head off if you didn't get out of its way
White Owl had guessed the dream, of course. Bu
instead of rewarding Snowbird with a full-size lacross
stick—Snowbird was hoping for the one he had used t
beat the Senecas when they played the Mohawks a
Onondaga—White Owl had fobbed him off with
miniature bat, a toy for infants. White Owl said it was
charm that would make Snowbird a champion playe
Snowbird was not consoled; he was grumpy, munchin
stolidly through the popcorn, staring into the fire.

Fruitpicker had joined them, with her young husban
Swampduck, a River Indian only recently adopted b
the Flint People. Island Woman wondered how the ol
clanmother always managed to get a younger man. I
wasn't her looks, though Fruitpicker was a strikin
woman. She was stocky, but moved with a confiden

xuberant rhythm. Her face was broad and flat and oily, with a dusting of freckles like scattered pumpkin seeds. he could have been as homely as a hunk of cornbread, ut wasn't because of her vibrant energy. She was full of *orenda,* full of soul. You could see it in the shining ntensity of her eyes, in the way her broad shoulders hook with laughter.

Fruitpicker was eating soup from her own ladle. Its owl was as big as a white man's soup dish and the andle was a carved figure of a she-wolf suckling a man.

Fruitpicker licked the ladle clean, belched content-dly, and lit up a pipe.

She then asked Island Woman, "Where is your hus-and?"

"I haven't seen him all day. He won't be in a hurry to ee me. He stole my copper kettle and lost it on the bowl ame."

"It wasn't him," Swampduck spoke up for his fellow nale. "He was drinking the hard water. I saw him. He vent away and an *otkon*—a wild spirit—got into his ody. He doesn't know anything about it."

"Don't talk shit." Fruitpicker nipped her husband's neck, like a she-wolf calling an unruly pup to order. "Every time a man makes a mess," she said to Island Woman, "he makes out it's not his fault. He doesn't remember. Something got into him. *Whooo*-ooo!" She let out a spooky noise that made Snowbird laugh and set Bright Meadow howling again.

Island Woman had not seen her eldest all day. Well, that was natural. Swimming Voices was thirteen. She wanted to explore the no-man's land between childhood and getting settled. Island Woman had been just the same at that age.

She heard shouts and drunken laughter just outside the lodge. She jumped up from the fire, recognizing Blackbuck's voice. She was going to give him hell over that kettle. She would have hit him harder with the cast-iron pot if she had seen it was missing the day before.

She found Blackbuck sprawled in the snow, half-covered by a filthy buffalo robe that stank of piss and

spilled rum. A woman was on the ground with him. She
was down on all fours, shaking her butt like a bitch in
heat.

"Get away from him!" Island Woman yelled.

Her anger grew white-hot when she saw that the
woman who was throwing herself at Blackbuck, in the
eyes of the whole village, was Redbird.

Hendrick's daughter rose to her feet, a twisted leer on
her face and eyes of pure hate.

She had something in her hand. Long and silvery, pink
on the underside. What was it? A rainbow trout, from
one of the snow barrels.

Redbird pointed the frozen fish at Blackbuck, then
slid it between her legs. Squalls of laughter were coming
from Blackbuck.

When Island Woman flung herself on Redbird, wrestling her for the fish, Blackbuck laughed so hard he
almost choked.

"Tell the dream!" cackled the bignose clown, who
came skipping around them. "Tell the dream!"

Island Woman broke from the grapple, with flakes of
Redbird's skin under her nails.

The clown was right.

Redbird was claiming Island Woman's husband according to the same rules that had allowed Island
Woman to claim the silver necklace.

It had happened before. Island Woman had seen it.
Dragging Antlers had done it three years running, claiming a night or a whole season with another man's wife or
daughter. Until some of the men followed him out in the
woods and left him too sore to think about his fish for a
while.

Island Woman rushed back through the moosehide
doorflap. She ran past the three firepits of the longhouse,
out the sunset door. She worked the lid off the smallest
of the snow barrels. There were a few carp and walleye
inside. She picked them out of the ice, breaking a nail.

She ran back round the side of the lodge and found
Blackbuck shambling along after Hendrick's daughter
like a dog on a leash.

Island Woman let out a long, wordless howl.

Redbird and Blackbuck stopped in their tracks. When he howl died, the whole village was silent.

"You want fish?" Island Woman did not need to shout, in that sudden calm. "You want fish?"

She bounded forward and started throwing the frozen fish. The first whipped across Redbird's mouth, cracking her lip. The second was deflected by the huge bulk of Hendrick Forked Paths, thrust between his daughter and Island Woman.

Hendrick said, "We will dream no more tonight."

Island Woman was asleep, her feet to the fire, when Blackbuck pressed his body against her, under the beaverskin blanket. The sight of the women fighting over him had excited him. He grunted, trying to shove his thing into her without asking.

"Sehnekakeras," she growled. "You stink of liquor."

He kept on butting, so she hit him where it got his attention.

He did not fight back. He whimpered and coaxed, trying to get round her another way.

She told him, "You owe me a new kettle."

He complained that he would not have any more peltries to trade until the spring.

"Iotkennisotsen," Island Woman said, nestling her head in the crook of her arm. "May your fish rot right off."

It was about the worst thing you can say to a man in Mohawk.

2.

Dreams that are wishes of the soul (when they are true dreams as well as wishes) can tell you that you need something you didn't know you needed or something you denied wanting because you felt ashamed for wanting it.

Big dreams tell you more.

When you go walking in your dreambody, you can see things that are many looks away, things that can save your life. You can find where the deer are yarding in the starving time. You can see where your enemies are lying in ambush along the trail.

When your dreamsoul goes flying, it visits the future and brings back memories of things that haven't happened yet, in the Shadow World. Sometimes you can stop those things from coming to pass. Sometimes you just have to live them out. Blackbuck dreamed once that he was captured by enemies and burned to death at the stake. He woke up terrified. He went to the elders and asked for help. One of the grayhairs dreamed on it. He told them to tie Blackbuck to a stake and burn him with red-hot knives and hatchets. They hurt him a lot, but did not kill him. They thought that by playing out Blackbuck's dream, but changing the ending, they were taming the future he had seen.

Life is filled with crossroads. Often you don't even notice them until they are behind you, unless you know how to dream. Dreaming, you can scout out the different trails you might follow and see where they lead. Dreaming, you are already choosing the events that will take place in your waking life.

The more conscious you are, the more practiced in hunting and catching dreams, the more you can accomplish.

You can even find out who you are.

Without a big dream, it is impossible to know this. In the day world, you are mostly asleep. In big dreams, you wake up. That is when your dreambody goes wandering and your guides can speak to you.

You might visit your teachers, or one of them might drop in on you, which is usually the way it happens the first time. Your guide might send an animal or a bird to get you out of your body so you can start to *see*. You might be called to a place of power, a place in the dreaming to which you can return, to learn and receive counsel.

You will start to learn that you have counterparts in the Real World. These powerful beings appear in different forms. When you have changed your eyes and your hearing so you can see and hear the great ones as they

ruly are, they will give you power songs to help their
nergy to flow through you.

When you start living with that energy in waking life,
ou are no longer like other people. You see their second
odies. You see the colors of their feelings. You see when
part of their soul is missing, or when something has
een shot inside them that is causing pain and sickness.
And then you want to help them. Because, although you
re no longer like other people, you know that every-
hing is connected.

Orenda—soul-energy, the power of life—flows
hrough everything, it binds the universe. It gathers in
ome places that are natural accumulators: an old oak
ree, or a mountain, or a stone. Some people are charged
with it; they light up a whole lodge. You can feel their
energy fields before you see them. They are not blocking
hemselves, their power centers are all connected. They
can put the day mind, with all its noise and clutter, on
one side, and let the great ones through. They can make
hemselves hollow bones for the spirit to work through.

This is what Island Woman was told by her teacher,
the dream-prophet whose name was never spoken aloud:

"You must visit the upper and lower worlds. You must
journey to the Land of Souls and speak with your
ancestors. You must know your spirit guides and your
animal guardians, and how to summon them. You will
be required to confront and overcome many powerful
opponents. You must never forget that the Real World
cannot be seen with ordinary eyes, and that in the Real
World there is only *now*.

"When you have done this, when your courage is
proven, you will be an *atetshents*. One who dreams.

"When you know *who you are,* you will be an *arendiwanen*. A woman of power."

3.

The palisades of the Upper Castle were formed by three
rows of stripped pine logs, sharpened to spearpoints at
the top. They had been hammered down deep into the
hill, angled so they crossed each other nearly twenty feet

above the ground, forming a bristling rampart that could tear out an attacker's entrails if he fell on it with any force. Native ladders—unstripped pines with the stub of the branches left on—led up to the platforms from which warriors could shoot down at an approaching enemy.

Only a single sentry was posted today, although there was word of new raiding parties of Mission Indians moving on snowshoes through the Endless Mountains with their French advisers. It had been almost a generation since an invader had dared to attack one of the strong-walled Mohawk Castles. It would take a bold attacker to try it, unless he was marching with white men's cannon or was certain the bulk of the Mohawk warriors had left the village. The Flint People did not treat defeated enemies gently. And the caresses of the Mohawk women were more feared than the warclubs of the Burned Knives. Mohawk women had been known to slit open a captive's belly and measure the length of his intestines; they always left a captive alive to return to his own people and tell what had happened. Every enemy deterred by the terror of what he could picture was an enemy who did not need to be killed.

The village was only half awake, when the lone guard gave a hoarse cry at the sight of a slim figure loping along the top of the palisades.

The cloud-roof was gone. Beyond the Noses, where twin limestone cliffs pinched the Valley, the eastern sky was red as a cock cardinal. The fading moon hung pale at the sunset end of the world. The juxtaposition was powerful, but the horns of the moon were turned down, which was a bad sign. Island Woman noticed as soon as she came out of her lodge, pulled from her dream by the sentry's cry.

The runner was halfway around the palisades when she halted and squatted, her arms dangling between her knees, like the wolf's.

Then she tipped back her head and opened her jaws. Her howl changed pitch and then hovered in the air in a long tremolo. All the dogs in the village joined in. From

omewhere beyond the hemlock ridge, a timber wolf
answered.

Island Woman walked through the snow in her calf-
high moccasins, stuffed with dried moss, and stared up
at her daughter.

Swimming Voices watched her for a long moment,
making sure she understood. Then she made her spring,
landing lightly in the snow on all fours. She greeted her
mother with a high squeaking noise, then rubbed her
nose against Island Woman's neck.

Tell the dream. Swimming Voices spoke with her eyes
and her body, hitting her mother with flanks and shoulders in a kind of rolling dance. She was wearing a
wolfskin and the snout lolled over her head.

Island Woman seized her daughter's wrist, to make
sure of the dream.

This was not another game for the Feast of Dreams.
This came from the beating heart of their lives.

Island Woman felt the tides of her daughter's blood
under her fingers.

The *atetshents*—the one who dreams—does not interpret other people's dreams. She enters them and ex-
plores them. She can even find dreams you lost.

Island Woman picked up her daughter's trace. She
followed its scent, moving faster and faster, through
landscapes she knew to a place in the dreaming.

*I do not know this place. It is a clearing in the woods,
no wider than a little-used trail. Hot coals are glowing in
a line that runs all along the center. On both sides of me,
women are drumming. I smell cedar and sweetgrass and
the real tobacco. I throw off my blanket. I stand naked
before my sisters. I was born for this.*

*Now I am running. My muscles are firm, my blood is
strong. The pads of my feet are hard. They have been
toughened by long seasons of running over flints and
stinging nettles. My mother made me do this. To run like
a wolf, you must be intimate with pain.*

*I am running on fire. I touch the coals and feel only joy.
I run so fast I become something other. My shape is no
longer that of women.*

The pack is waiting for me. I run with them, over the mountains. We hunt together. With their eyes, I see the one who is ready to give me his life. I know pride when they offer me the heart of the fresh kill.

Now my mother will know me. Now I am Okwaho.

Island Woman released her daughter's hand.

Swimming Voices was trembling, waiting for her mother's word.

"Wakateriontare," Island Woman confirmed. "I know this matter. I will speak with our clanmother."

4.

Fruitpicker prepared a fresh pipe. She added a few pieces of dried sumac to the native tobacco, lit the mixture with a splint from the fire, and passed the pipe to Island Woman.

We ride to the skies on a cloud of tobacco.

After a long silence in the smoky lodge, the clan-mother said, "Your feelings are not clear."

"This is true."

"Speak to me from your heart. You are a gift to us, my daughter. The power of dreaming has been reborn in us through you. It is natural that it should be passed on, through your bloodline."

Island Woman said nothing.

"Swimming Voices is young. She is proud. Life has not yet taken her by the throat. Is this the root of your misgivings?"

"There is something more. Something I cannot see."

"What is it you fear? Your child has the gift. We knew that when she was still inside your body."

"It is the use she could make of it." Island Woman did not need to complete the thought. Both women knew that the power to heal is also the power to harm.

The clanmother spoke, "My daughter, we have shared many things, many hardships. Don't bite me if I speak as I must. Is it possible that a part of you is afraid to relinquish something of your own power?"

"It is possible," Island Woman agreed.

"We will wait until the Sugar Moon," Fruitpicker
ruled. "We will wait until the maple leaves are the size of
a squirrel's foot. Then we will make the tests that are
necessary. But Swimming Voices is impatient. Therefore
we will bring her before the women's council. She will
learn what she might become. And what will be required
of her."

□

"Fruitpicker looks different," Swimming Voices whispered to her mother.

"She *is* different."

The girl had seen Fruitpicker hoeing the cornfield,
picking lice out of a child's hair, rooting for the Wolf
Clan boys in a lacrosse game, trading bawdy jokes while
she smoked a pipe or added a pinch of potash to a pot of
cornsoup to make it good and slick.

Now Swimming Voices saw Wahiakwas—She Who
Picks the First Fruits—as *ka'nihstensera*. Clan mother.

Fruitpicker was wearing her cleanest doeskins and
holding a fourteen-row wampum belt. The white and
purple shells had the patina of great age. In one of the
designs Okwaho—the she-wolf—was suckling a pair of
human figures, male and female. Swimming Voices
could not make out the other designs clearly and might
have wriggled deeper into the circle for a better look, but
she was daunted by the voice in which the clanmother
began to speak.

Fruitpicker's voice was quite soft, as she chanted the
thanksgiving. She started, as always, by returning thanks
for the living, and thanks to the Mother for the blessings
of earth.

The power was in the rhythms, with words washing
back and forth like waves, carrying her audience deeper
into the meaning beyond the words. Her voice was more
song than speech.

This was the voice of power.

And it seemed to Swimming Voices, as Wahiakwas
went on and on, that the clanmother was speaking to *her*.

This is what Fruitpicker said:

"Women give life. Men can only take it. Women are the life-bringers, and we must always be reverenced. Before male and female, there was She.

"She Who Fell from the Sky danced this world into being, on the turtle's back.

"Women must always *choose*. We choose our husbands. We choose whether to return a soul to this earth. We choose the land that we plant so our people may be fed, honoring the Three Sisters and all of our life supporters. We raise up the men of good minds to wear the living bones of the Confederacy. We remind them that a chief is to live as a walking stick that the people may lean on. We teach them that they must consider the consequences of all their thoughts and actions, down to the seventh generation. When they forget, we de-horn them. We bring them down very close to the earth, so they may recover the Mother's wisdom.

"You see how the newcomers use their women. They use them as slaves, or like trade women to be bought and sold.

"The Peacegiver taught us that all the races of humankind are related. That Sonkwaiatison, our Creator, made all of us. That when he forged us, with clay and sunlight, with the foam of the waves and the wind of his spirit, our Creator gave all of us the same songs and the same drums, so we could speak with him. So we would remember.

"My grandmothers told me that we, the Real People, are the youngest of all the races of humankind, and that our Creator made us because he was not satisfied with the others. My grandmothers said that because we are the youngest of the races, we remember better than the others how our Creator wishes us to live.

"The newcomers have forgotten. They say that woman was made from the bone of a man, and lives only to serve him. They say that the bird tribes and the animal nations do not have souls. Instead of honoring the Mother, they rape her body.

"Now they have come among us, and we walk where the earth is narrow.

"When Forked Paths crossed the great water, to visit

he court of the English Queen, I gave one of his companions counting sticks. I wanted him to count the Tiorhonsaka—the People from the Sunrise—so we would know how many of them we have to face. He broke the counting sticks. He returned sick in his soul. He told us that the People from the Sunrise are as many as the leaves of the forest. We knew then that we could not fight all of them. We had to find a way to live beside them.

"It is hard, because the newcomers move among us like Whirlwind. They spread madness with their hard water. They send death among us with many faces. They kill us with the plague of spitting sores that our medicine cannot heal, because it comes from a different dreaming. They make our men greedy for their rum, and for things we cannot make for ourselves. They set brother against brother, bribing our warriors to fight our kinsmen in wars between white men.

"Because of this, the Dark Times are returning. I have seen this. The Real People will come close to dying this life. But the shadow falls over all. The elms will die. Then the maples. The fish will float belly-up in poisoned waters. Then the strawberries will begin to die, until we have only a few leaves and scrapings for the sacred rituals that restore the earth and call back our brother sun."

"This world has died four times before.

"It will die again, within seven generations.

"But our greatest dream-prophet has told us it can yet be saved. For this to be done, dreamers and women of power must rise among all the nations. They must recall the peoples to the songs and the drums our Creator gave us all. They must bring back the dreaming.

"We who remember are charged with a duty beyond all others. We must keep the fire burning within our lineage, so that the souls of the great ones will return to us and a great dreamer will walk among us in times to come.

"We must reach out in dreaming, even among our enemies, to those whose souls can be wakened.

"We can do this, as long as we can dream, as long as we can think with the heart.

"We are keepers of the earth. We are the life-givers. We are one heart, one mind. This is our power. This is the only power that is true."

CHAPTER 2
TARA'S SHADOW

1.

The spring melt came late in the Valley. But when the pigeons flew back, they covered the sky in mile-long flocks. The children could take them easily off the maples, with nets or clubs. Blackbuck, with a debt to pay, went off with the hunters, to where the beavers were trying to tame the swollen creeks with new dams. Island Woman worked with her neighbors—burning undergrowth, clearing a new field for corn, beans and squash. She kept close watch on her daughter Swimming Voices, who joined her for the digging and hoeing, waiting for a sign. Her boy sat up in an elm, honking and throwing stones to scare away the crows, when the women put in the seeds.

On the far side of the ocean, in a green valley of County Meath where no Mohawk had ever trod, the bluebells were out. And an Irish farmer with a face as ripe as a plum was about to lose his temper.

Christopher Johnson limped back and forth under the weeping beeches that flanked his stone coachhouse. The bluebells were a dream of beauty among the soft greens. On another day, they might have soothed Squire Johnson's red-flecked eyes and made him give thanks for the land in which he was rooted. Instead, he swung his blackthorn viciously at a young thistle and cursed when the stalk jumped back. A stab of pain in his belly took his breath. He had to rest for a moment, leaning his weight on his stick. The old war wounds pained him on these soft spring days.

The broadcloth weighed heavy on his shoulders, soaked through with the damp he never minded unless he had been kept waiting in it for an hour. Where *was* Anne? His wife's fetchings had grown intolerable. First the night cravings, for ginger root and berries out of season. Now the demand for a sudden gallop to a pagan well.

"Mick!" he barked at his tenant, who was pacing the gray mare, already hitched to the shay. "Will you go and see what is keeping Mrs. Johnson?"

Mick Flood entered the hip-roofed stone house by the kitchen door. He came back to report that Mrs. Johnson had decided to change her dress for the third time.

"It's the way with the ladies, when they are in the family way," Mick apologized for his landlord's wife. "In her season, Mrs. Flood don't abide nothing but buttermilk and raw liver, and liver is a hard thing to come by, to be sure. As your honor well knows."

"You would know, Flood. How many do you have now? Twelve, is it?"

"Paddy made it thirteen," Mick informed him proudly.

A baker's dozen. *And the country cannot feed the people it has already.* High summer, between the potato crops, was the worst time for the cotters, who lived on buttermilk and spuds. When the potatoes ran out, they tumbled out of the bogs and the mean tenant farms and went begging for their food. They sprang from the ditches, pestering travelers, pecking like crows around the stables and chicken coops. Squire Johnson had installed metal bars on the ground floor windows of Smithstown House to keep them off. Though he counted himself a fair man in his dealings with his own tenants, he resented the demands of others, not least because the starving tribes of beggars were closer kindred than he cared to acknowledge.

Squire Johnson was the master of two hundred acres of rolling pasture, with a fine stone house and servants. But he was not one of the owners of Ireland. He rented his acres from the Earl of Fingal. His lease had a term of thirty-one years, because Catholics were allowed neither to buy land at freehold nor hold leases for life, and Christopher was still a Catholic when he came home from the wars. He had been persuaded to change his faith, to escape the brutal provisions of the Penal Laws, that made many crimes out of following the old religion. He had not managed to improve his title, even by changing his family name from MacShane to Johnson. In spurning his Irishness, he had not succeeded in becoming English. To the great English landlords, who enjoyed Ireland as a private estate, and their hard-drinking agents, who abused it as a conquered nation, Christopher Johnson would remain a teague and a bog paddy.

Uncertainty about his status made Squire Johnson irritable. But he had recently advanced his claims to social rank by marrying Anne Warren. She was no great beauty, with that long, pale face and narrow, awkward body, and overtall for a woman. But she was a Warren of Warrenstown and, in this section of the Pale, that counted for a good deal.

If he combed back far enough through his MacShane forebears, Johnson could claim a connection with the great O'Neills, the tribal kings of Tyr-Owen—but so could half of Ireland. The Warrens were more recent, but more authentic, nobility. They traced their descent from a Norman knight who came with Strongbow the Conqueror. Unlike the English, the Normans had gone native in Ireland. Anne's father, Michael Warren, was Irishman and Catholic enough to fight for King James in the bloody field beside the River Boyne. He remained a Catholic to the day of his death, three years before, when he left his wife and his three children an estate of seven hundred acres, sinking in debt.

Anne's mother, Catherine Warren, had made it her mission to repair the family fortunes. She leaned on the advice of her brother, Sir Matthew Aylmer, whose spectacular rise in the Royal Navy had been newly crowned by his appointment as Admiral of the Fleet.

"You must have the children raised as Protestants," the Admiral had counseled her. "Then I can take the boys and make sailors out of them. Who knows?" He smiled, hinting that his own brilliant career proved the merit of joining the Church Established.

His sister, who feared the hellfires and prayed each day to the Virgin, had not taken this with good grace.

"We must live in the world as it is," said the Admiral.

Catherine took the advice, but remained true to her own faith, and prayed for the souls of her children.

She found precious little money was to be won from the mortgaged lands of Warrenstown, and closed up part of the house. The Admiral would provide for the boys— Oliver and Peter—but what was to be done for Anne? The girl was too plain, and too whimsical, to make a grand alliance. Her finespun, coppery hair was her best feature, but she made no effort to tame it. She ranged the countryside like a tramp, visiting ruined abbeys and fairy-forts. Or she sat in a window with her nose in a book, usually something quite unsuitable, a rogue's progress or a book of Celtic rhymes. Her mother loved her—but would any man?

Enter Christopher Johnson. He made his first advances in the Anglican church, and then outside the rustic store that sold little except spirits, tea and tobacco. When he asked Catherine for permission to call on Anne, she said he must ask her daughter.

"I don't mind," Anne had said.

Nor had Catherine any objections to the suitor. There was a difference in age: Christopher was thirty-five, Anne only eighteen but this was common in the best society. And it was no bad thing for a young girl to marry a man who had knocked around the world a little. The suitor was a fine-looking man of substance, as sober as could be expected, able to provide. But his conversation tended to wander between old war stories and bloodstock and then run out. Catherine Warren had doubted whether her fanciful daughter would settle for a bore from some horse artillery barracks with a gimpy leg.

When Christopher made his formal proposal, Anne heard him out on her window seat, looking across the fields to the turrets of the Castle of Killeen.

Asked if she would marry, Anne said, "I don't mind."

□

She was always flighty. Christopher resigned himself to wait a little longer. *Flighty and difficult, with moods that swirl up out of thin air and knock a man sideways.*

They did not quarrel, because Anne did not oppose her husband head-on. Instead, some part of her just slipped away. Then she was quite unknowable.

She had a passion for wandering in deserted places. It troubled Christopher, because of beggars and thieves along the lanes. And because it reminded him that a vital part of her being always escaped him.

When she had first announced she was with child, he had expressly forbidden her to leave the Smithstown estate. She had defied him, stealing away when he was picking heifers for market. He had suffered the embarrassment of sending tenants and farm laborers to hunt for her. They had found her at last, idling away the hours in the graveyard of a ruined monastery. Anne had looked at him as if he was some form of hedge life, a badger poking its snout where it did not belong. She had had nothing to say to him for the rest of the day. This had taught him prudence.

"Don't go off by yourself," he had implored her, when she told him she was again with child. "If you must go, let me come with you."

Thus he had brought today's expedition on himself. The fierce country roads between Smithstown and Navan were no place for a pregnant woman. But Anne had set her heart on visiting the holy well at Ardmulkin, and there was an end of it.

Here she was at last, coming down the front steps. A little sway-backed, her great height accentuated by the parasol.

"Top of the morning, milady," Mick greeted her. "Are you quite well today?"

"Quite well. Thank you for inquiring."

The tenants were all fond of her. She got more from them with a smile than Christopher could get with a threat of eviction or the butt-end of a whip.

He handed her into the shay, and they set off at a good clip down the back country lane, running parallel to the river. At the end of the lane was a stone mill. Over hedges of blackthorn and whitethorn, Johnson could see his cows at pasture. His spirits lifted a little, as he contemplated a world he could manage. He was trying to persuade his mother-in-law to give him the management of the Warrenstown estate. With the use of the Warren lands in addition to his own, he would be a man to be reckoned with.

Yellow gorse was aflame under the high hill of Tara. On the green slopes above, sheep grazed where the high kings of Ireland once sat in counsel, where their druids communed with the spirits inside the circle of double trenches.

"Christopher, let's stop."

Anne's eyes were wandering the heights of Tara. Johnson despaired of ever knowing what went on in that head.

"You shall have to choose," he told her. "It is a long ride to Ardmulkin, and that's the truth." Indeed, the Tobar Patraic, the well she was so bent on visiting, lay in the ruins of a Norman church, two rough miles north of Navan, where the Black Water joined the Boyne. "Besides which, you are in no state to go scrambling over hills like a tomboy, my darling."

He saw she was bent on this diversion, and his face darkened. Was it to be his lot to humor all her whims, all his days? She must learn that the mistress of Smithstown House had obligations.

He declined to accompany her up the rise of the hill. His irritation returned as he waited, and he took a few nips from his flask.

The flask was empty by the time she returned. She

floated, more than walked, down the hill, her arms outstretched. She was unusually flushed, and her eyes were fever-bright.

Her brother Peter looked something like, when he came back from the sugar islands with the malaria upon him. Too many sailors in her bloodstock. Brushing their rods with nigger women and bumboys and bringing home God-knows-what.

"You look in a heat, my dear. Is it a fever you have taken? Shall we go for a doctor?"

"My poor Christopher. I am such a penance for you."

He helped her back up into the shay, liking her appearance even less. There was a touch of the crazy woman. But this time it hadn't carried her off somewhere remote. She was intensely with him, in a way that disturbed him even more.

"Christopher."

"What is it?"

"Something happened to me. Up there on the hill of Tara. I believe I had a vision. It was like a dream, but I was entirely awake. I have never been more awake."

Christopher shook the reins, wanting nothing more than to get the day over with and settle in by the fire with a bottle or two.

"It is something I wish to tell you."

The woman would not leave off. He grunted, "I know you will have your way whatever I say."

"I was giving birth."

"Ah." Squire Johnson relaxed a little. Perhaps it was not so bad. He had heard that women sometimes go through childbirth in their minds, or their dreams, before they are brought to labor. Dr. McBride, a no-nonsense sawbones and a sound man with a bottle of Madeira, had expressed the opinion that these imaginings might actually shorten the time of labor.

"It was tiny," Anne went on. "It was bright pink and hairless, and so small it would fit inside the palm of my hand."

Christ Jesus. Not a defective.

"It looked very like a fattish worm. Yet it was not

repugnant to me. Then its blind eyes opened, and it grew faster than I can tell, into a shape like a man. Yet larger than any ordinary man and covered with fur."

"Fur?" Christopher groaned. Either his wife was off her head, or she was carrying some abomination only the Old Church would know how to deal with. "What kind of fur?"

"A lush thick pelt. Christopher, he is so *strong."*

"Let me know if I understand you. You fancied you gave birth to an *animal?"*

"A bear."

"A *bear?"* Johnson squalled. "I will have—nothing—to do with bears!"

"But Christopher—don't you see—"

"Hold your tongue, woman! I am sick to the gills of you and your moony notions. It is more than a man can do to keep his sanity."

Enraged, Squire Johnson set his whip to the rump of the gray mare, and the shay rattled forward, much too fast for the road.

Anne saw faces, smooth and sooty as potatoes pulled from the ashes, rising from the ditch.

Christopher cracked the whip again.

"Stop it!" Anne screamed. "Can't you see them?"

"Bloody vaguing paddies," Johnson snarled.

"Christopher!"

As they rounded the bend, he saw, later than his wife, that some of the impudent scoundrels were lounging in the middle of the road. They were a sorry bunch, scarecrow figures; the ash of the peatfires would never wash off them. Perhaps they purposed to stop the shay and rob its owners. His rage found a new focus.

I will teach the rascals a lesson.

He drove hard on down the road, sending dust-clouds flying, and the peasants scattered before him. All save a tattered, black-haired boy. *Damn him for his insolence.*

"Christopher! He's a cripple! Do you mean to kill him?"

Now Johnson saw the crutch—just a spindly stick with a knob at the end—and, sickened by the sight, he dragged at the reins, forcing the mare over to the right.

The shay bounced and lurched. Anne cried out in panic or pain. Then horse and cart went bounding into the ditch. Johnson clutched at his wife, trying to cushion her fall.

He felt the shock at the base of his spine. It drove a splinter of exquisite pain up into his brain. He was lost to the morning.

When he came round, he was laid out at the side of the road, as if for burial. The right wheel of the shay was in the ditch. Crows flapped overhead, a traveling umbrella that shut out the sun. The air was clotted with the stench of blood and ordure. Pale shadows flitted by, carrying burdens.

"For God's sake," Christopher called. "Where is my wife?"

An old man's eyes flicked sideways, then away. Painfully, Johnson got to his feet and stumbled after him.

"You, man! I am addressing *you!* Where is my wife?"

He received no answer. He grabbed at the old man's shoulder, compelling him to stop. The fellow kept his head down, eyes low, like a dog that would bite if it dared. He stank like a slaughterhouse.

"Holy Mother of God." The squire of Smithstown House retreated into the language of his fathers, because he now saw that the old man was holding a ragged stump. It leaked blood through his fingers, down the front of his filthy smock. There was still a patch of skin and gray hair attached.

"You've murdered my horse!" Christopher bellowed. "You hellions shall pay for it!"

He went for his pistols, but found they were gone. Maddened by rage, heedless of danger, he rushed at the stick-men who were hacking at the dead horse, tearing them from their dinner, shoving them into the bushes. They would not fight him, but they would not give up. One by one, they crept back to rip at the carcass. There were dozens of them. Their eerie silence smothered his anger and his hope.

I am fighting the dead.

Something nudged him, under the ribs. He turned and saw the blackhaired boy with the crutch.

"My mother said I am to bring you to the lady."

"Merciful God."

Johnson blundered along behind the boy, over stone walls and neglected fields, to a tenant's house no better than a bird's nest, slathered together with clay and straw. There was no chimney, not even a hole in the roof. Inside, the acrid smoke from a fire in the middle of the dirt floor made it difficult to see, even to breathe.

"Anne!" He could see her dimly, laid out on a heap of straw against the wall.

"Give me your hand, Christopher."

"Are you hurt? Is the baby—"

"Our baby lives. But he is impatient. I told you he is a bear." There was a beauty in her face her husband had failed to see before. Her face shone, not with the fever-light, but with an inner radiance beneath her fine translucent skin.

"I will send for a doctor and a carriage. We must get you between clean sheets. Who will go?" He peered about, at the circle of muddy faces in the hut. "I will pay well."

No one moved to oblige him.

"Must I go myself?" His relief was doused at the prospect of his wife enduring the pains of labor in that squalid, unsanitary hut. "Must I leave my wife?"

"Don't leave me, Christopher," she squeezed his hand. "Be still. I am where I am meant to be."

He turned from those smoky eyes, whose puzzle he would never read, and found those of the crippled boy's mother. She was a horror to look at, deathly pale, her face gouged and grooved like a blasted rock. But her gaze had an astonishing effect; it reached inside him and sucked out all the violence of his emotions, leaving stillness and peace.

"I am Maire," she said. "Your child is safe in my hands. You must bring water from the spring. Cormac will show you the way."

He obeyed her. When he came back with the pail full of spring water, the labor had begun. Maire knelt at his wife's side, speaking words of the ancient tongue. He

saw waves of pain beating across Anne's face. Then her
eyes rolled up into her head, and he gasped, because it
seemed there was no life in her except where the child
was raging to be born.

"What is happening?" he demanded of Maire, who
continued to chant. "You must do something!"

"Be still."

In the smoky room, he held his breath until his lungs
hurt. When the child burst from Anne's womb, it
seemed enormous, though it came a month before its
time.

"It's lucky she is he comes early." Maire added, *"Dia
leat.* Praise God for the soul that returns to us."

CHAPTER 3
WOLF CAPTIVE

Island Woman's elder daughter was quick at everything. She could swim farther and run faster than any other girl in the Upper Castle. She could beat some of the boys. She could talk to the newcomers in their own language, though her mix of chapelhouse English and the frontier pidgin of Dutch traders and lobsterback soldiers made some of them smile.

But there are things that cannot be rushed.

The Sugar Moon had long come and gone. Planting time was over. Soon it would be the Moon of Strawberries, the time when the Real People returned thanks for the first fruits of the earth. A favored time for rituals of naming and initiation.

Yet the clanmother had not revealed whether she would honor the dream Swimming Voices had enacted on the ice of the palisades during the Feast of Dreams.

"We never take from the tree until the fruit is ready to fall," Fruitpicker had told the girl's mother. "This must never be forgotten in affairs that are sacred. We must never give power to one who is not ready. When the time reveals itself, I will put this matter into the fire."

Island Woman knew Fruitpicker was right. Her own reservations were even greater than those of the clanmother's, because of the thing in her daughter that remained hidden from her, like a bird that hides in a hollow tree.

She felt the force of Swimming Voices' rising anger and impatience each day, in gusts of temper and savage mood swings.

"I am going berrying," Swimming Voices announced, snatching up a basket.

Island Woman noticed she had put on her finest blouse and her silver earrings and nose-bob. She had scented her body with sweetgrass, and the smell of wildflowers clung to her hair.

She's going to meet a man, Island Woman thought. *Maybe that Spotted Wolf. He came back early from the hunt. He gave her a pair of minkskins, to make a pouch. He smells her, all right.*

It wasn't much of an excuse. The strawberries were still mostly white.

Island Woman gathered up the trade blankets in the lodge and pushed the bundle into the girl's arms.

"Here. You wash these. Then we'll see if you still want to pick berries."

"We have no soap," Swimming Voices objected.

Island Woman pursed her lips and made a rude blowing sound.

"We'll have soap just as soon as you move your butt. Get the ashes."

Swimming Voices moved stiffly, taking tiny steps, as if her legs were hobbled. She took her time bringing the hardwood ashes from the firepit. Island Woman put them into a pot of water she had set to boil. When the lye had separated, she added some scaps of coonfat.

She let the mix stand for an hour. She made Swimming Voices change the toddler's diaper of dried moss, which did not improve the girl's humor.

When the soap was done, Island Woman called Snowbird and they all set off on the path that wound down to the creek, below the falls.

Snowbird had made himself a new bird trap, with a strip of elmbark the length of his mother's hand. He had cut an eye in one end and tied a piece of bark twine that curled into a noose to the other. When they got to the cliff, he squatted down and weighted the trap with a heavy rock. He dropped a few kernels of corn into the hole, the trap was set. If a bird tried to get the corn, her ruff of feathers would snag in the string, bringing the noose around her neck. The moment she tried to fly, the noose would be drawn tight. She would be strangled or captured, depending on the force of her struggle.

"It works pretty good," Snowbird announced, with maker's pride. He would stay up on the cliff to see what he caught.

Island Woman was carrying Bright Meadow in a cradleboard, secured by a burden strap, bright with dyed moosehair, that ran around her forehead. When they got down to the water, Island Woman looped the strap over the limb of a hickory, so Bright Meadow could watch them work. The child was getting too big for the cradleboard, but it saved Island Woman from having to watch over her every second, and it was still helping her to learn to run and to walk as one of the Flint People. There was a little block of wood wedged between the toddler's heels, to make sure her feet would turn inward, helping her avoid protruding roots and boulders along the forest trails. And to prevent her from walking in the awkward, ducklike gait of the newcomers.

Island Woman and her elder daughter used a pot the earth had given them—a rounded hollow in the rocks along the riverbank—to make a soapy solution and soak the blankets in it, spreading them on a flat rock and pounding them with a board before rinsing them in the stream. The wet blankets were heavy. Soon their arms were aching.

They rested in the shade, waiting for the wool to dry in the sun.

"How long is Fruitpicker going to make me wait?" Swimming Voices demanded.

She was chafing for life, in all its dimensions.

She wants a man between her legs. She wants to trade

*with the Dutchmen at the Net, like a matron. She wants,
most of all, to be joined in the mysteries that are forbidden to men and held secret from ordinary women.*

"Only our clanmother can say," Island Woman repeated. "She says the signs must be clear."

"But I have dreamed this!" the girl protested. "You
both know I have the gift! It was known before I
was born. I am no longer a child. Why am I kept waiting?"

Island Woman sat quiet. She saw a wary muskrat poke
its whiskers out of a hole among the cattails.

Swimming Voices complained that three moons had
passed since the sugaring.

"Maybe waiting is your test," Island Woman said
firmly.

She took her daughter's hand. She could see nothing,
feel nothing, except the tempest of anger that threatened
to blow.

*Again, she escapes me. What is it in her that will not
show itself to me?*

These feelings were familiar. But the sudden fear that
came to her was new.

She was startled by a harsh, downward-slurring squeal
from the heights behind her.

Keeer-r-r-r!

She looked up, expecting to find a redtail hawk sailing
across the gap in the forest cover.

Instead, she saw Snowbird. He was flailing his arms.
His open mouth was a scream.

She was halfway up a steep deerpath, the washing
forgotten, when Snowbird choked out, "My father is
dead."

□

Newcomers from across the river had brought the body
over in a boat. Island Woman knew their faces.

She saw their mouths move as they fumbled words of
regret, words of apology. They wanted the Flint People
to know this death was not their doing. They were ready
to prove that by going out with the Mohawks, to hunt
down the killers.

She pushed through the words, past the sturdy, whiskery Germans.

She saw her husband. Blackbuck stared up at the sun with wide open eyes. His body and clothes seemed to be unscathed, except that he had lost the otterskin bag he always carried on the trail, containing the vocabulary of his dreams.

When she closed his eyes and pulled his torso against her chest, she saw they had killed him from behind. They had shot him in the back. She touched the black powder burns around the hole at the base of his neck.

She looked at the hair.

They must have been interrupted or been too cowardly to finish the job. They had scraped off only a tiny circle of skin, no bigger than the ball of her thumb. But it was enough.

They had taken his *onononra,* his spirit-head.

Now his burned bones will call us to war.

Hendrick Forked Paths loomed up beside her. For once, she did not resent his domineering mass, the hard edge of cruelty in his eyes and features.

"Sister, we are going after them," Forked Paths announced. "The Germans say they are Mission Indians. There is a Frenchman with them. If we are swift, we will overtake them. We have paths they cannot see. Their paths will be cut off. This is our promise to you."

Island Woman nodded her consent.

The Germans gathered around the warchief. They were brothers. Their name was hard to say; it began with an F. The tall, thoughtful man was a friend of Weiser, who had led these people westward into the Valley after they had been robbed and cheated by the English who lured them across the great water with promises of land and a life free from hunger and war. They had befriended the Mohawks. The Flint People had given them corn when they were close to starving in their first hard winter. In turn, they had shown the Flint People their ways of farming, puzzled by the fact that only the women attended this instruction. They were decent, sturdy people who lived close to the earth. Island Woman had no quarrel with them.

They were offering to go on the warpath with Forked Paths, to show their friendship.

White Owl, listening in silence, glanced at Island Woman, then at the warchief. They understood each other.

Hendrick Forked Paths said to the Germans, "We will not take you with us, because white men move as if they have logs tied to their feet. When you have learned to run like us, you will be ready to take our trails."

□

Island Woman crouched over the fire. She reached into the coals and brought out fistfuls of ashes and embers. She tossed them over her head and shoulders, not caring about the acrid smell as holes were burned in her clothes. She rubbed the charcoal into the pores of her skin.

She grabbed up her skinning knife and sliced her kilt to ribbons.

She plunged her fingers into the roots of her hair and pulled as if she meant to scalp herself. Her hair came out in bleeding hanks.

All the while, she raised the death-wail—an eerie, ululating cry that made the dogs whine and stirred fear and vengeance in every lodge.

Fruitpicker was waiting for her when she stepped back into the sunlight.

Island Woman's eyes were dull. The soul-energy in her had been trampled down, like a fire on the first day of Midwinter.

She said, "I die this lifetime."

The clanmother did not step across the path of grief. For ten days, Island Woman would wear ashes and walk with her dead. Then she would join in the ritual of parting, so that her soul would not follow her husband to the villages of the dead, so that Blackbuck would not remain to trouble the living, sitting on the roof of her longhouse, drinking the smoke of her fires. Blackbuck's name would not be spoken aloud—because the dead are always listening—unless another came to requicken his name.

The wall between the dead and the living must be tended carefully. It is precisely the width of the edge of a maple leaf.

They laid Blackbuck in the ground—his arms wrapped around his knees, his face, painted blood-red with the holy paint, pressed to his chest. They buried him with his pipe and his warclub and a pair of maskettes that were part of his dreaming. They placed crystals beside him and a statuette that would be a resting place for the part of the soul that remains close to the earth, if the bones were stolen or disturbed.

They buried him facing the rising sun, his body flexed, ready to be reborn.

His clanmother said, over the snap of a gourd rattle, "Now we fold him in the blanket of our Mother Earth."

Island Woman broke from the circle of mourners. She flung herself full-length on the earth beside the grave. She rubbed her face in the dirt. She wormed her fingers deep down into it.

"Kia:tat." The word issued from her as a dragging groan. The syllables fell like the clods of earth that were being tossed into the open grave.

"Kia:tat. I am in the womb of the Mother. I am buried."

□

Hendrick Forked Paths returned from the trail two nights after the burial. He blazed a white pine with his hatchet, in a place where all would see it. He carved the rough outline of a head. He scratched the figure of a sunburst on it—the figure of the gunpowder tattoo on his left temple. Then he carved the shape of the clan wolf, behind the head and very close to it: his counselor. He added three upside-down figures, stick-limbs protruding from wedge-shaped torsos. One for each enemy he had killed on the hunt for Blackbuck's murderers.

He left this warpost unfinished.
There was a further act to be played out.

□

At dawn, Fruitpicker huffed breath from her belly into a conch. Its seagull scream brought the people of the Upper Castle running, Island Woman and her children among them.

The clanmother announced, "We have Wolf captives."

There were two of them. The warriors dragged them by rawhide leashes knotted round their necks.

One was a Nipissing, a Sorcerer. Island Woman tensed at the sight of him; the Nipissings were blood enemies. Many of them lived under the protection of the black-robes at the Lake of Two Mountains, near Montreal. But in the shadow of the cross, they kept their magic. Their shamans were renowned and feared as shapeshifters, stealers of souls, ones who killed from afar with a bone and a song. It was not only their enemies who called them the Sorcerers.

This Sorcerer was slender, with a long narrow face and close-set eyes. He wore his hair long, dropping to the small of his back. His captors had removed his earrings and nose-bob, the heavy gorget on a flame-colored ribbon. They had stripped him to his tawny-yellow skin, to run the gauntlet.

The second captive was a newcomer. Island Woman did not inspect him closely, because the men and boys had already formed two lines, and Forked Paths was shoving the Sorcerer between them. The newcomer had startling corn-yellow hair, she noticed that. Also that he was young and did not want to face the scene inside the gate. And that his knees kept buckling under him.

"You are dead!" the Mohawks screeched at the Sorcerer. "You will be burned!"

The Sorcerer, freed from the leash, walked tall and straight between the lines, his face a mask of indifference.

"Tsihei!" White Owl yelled. "Die!" He jabbed the butt of a fishing spear into the captive's ribs.

The Sorcerer staggered on. He was singing his death-song.

Sun Walker ran out and hit him with a fist-sized iron knob. The Sorcerer's whole body shook under the force of the blow. He staggered, gasping for breath, but recovered and walked on.

Now the blows came thick and fast, from old and young. Island Woman saw Snowbird hopping out from the lines, whacking the captive over the shins with his father's warclub.

The Sorcerer was down.

The Mohawks hooted. Forked Paths screamed, "I will eat your liver without salt!"

When the Sorcerer got back on his feet, his whole body was streaming blood. Only the whites of his eyes showed pale through the mess of mud and gore.

He found the strength to finish his deathwalk.

The warriors whooped. They admired a man who endures.

The Flint People rewarded the courage of enemies. This was well known. They had a reputation to uphold. And the blood-frenzy was building between them. The warriors closed on the Sorcerer like wolves at the end of the starving time.

A scaffold had been raised, on a platform of earth and boughs. They tied the captive to the stake. Now they held knives or hatchets, some of them heated in the fire.

Hendrick raised his hand, restraining them.

He asked Fruitpicker for permission.

The clanmother said, "It is Island Woman who must choose. It is her man who has been cut down like green corn."

Island Woman looked at the bleeding captive, who was still singing his song. She felt no pity, no mercy, for this blood-enemy who had taken her husband.

But she found no joy when Forked Paths cut off his thumb and shoved a splint into the incision, all the way to the elbow.

She turned her face from the rest of the men's entertainments.

□

Soon it was the turn of the women.

Forked Paths raised the cry. "Let our women caress the whiteface!"

The women and girls of the Wolf Clan replaced the men, making the path for the yellowhair to walk.

Island Woman stood near the end, holding a corn pounder half her height.

The yellowhair did not know what is expected of a man on the deathwalk.

He fell again and again. He shook and quivered, even before the first blow. Before he had suffered any real injury, he played possum and had to be dragged to his feet.

He whimpered and begged, as if he did not know there is a life beyond this one.

When he came abreast of Island Woman, she clubbed the huge pounder and brought it down hard, aiming for his head. His legs gave way and he fell into her, so the blow glanced off his shoulder, dislocating it.

His face rested on Island Woman's foot. She contemplated him with disgust. His abject submission reminded her of a puppy, the runt of the litter, begging for food and warmth.

Swimming Voices kicked him. "Let me kill this one," she urged.

Island Woman put her foot on the yellowhair's back. He looked strong enough, even if there was a coward in his heart, and she was sure he would mend soon enough.

She looked at Fruitpicker. She said, "I claim this dog for my fire."

The clanmother nodded her agreement.

□

Island Woman fed the yellowhair very small amounts of corn, boiled in water without meat or seasoning. She gave him a piece of bark to lie on at night, when she bound him by rawhide thongs to four stakes hammered into the earth.

The first days, Swimming Voices and Snowbird took turns tormenting him, pressing hot coals into the skin of his belly and buttocks. Bright Meadow joined in, learning from her elders.

When Swimming Voices set out to shave his foreskin with the edge of an oystershell, her mother said, "Enough. We must keep him strong enough to earn his food."

Island Woman set him to carry firewood and clear scrub. She found he was useful with his hands. He had some of the skills of a carpenter. When he made a little chair for the toddler, she began to warm to him.

She wanted to know if he could make a wagon. Only a few of the Mohawks had them. Before the newcomers came, the Flint People had no use for wheeled vehicles, since they had no beasts of burden to pull them. But now there were horses and oxen, and the English were widening and smoothing a road along the river. With a wagon, Island Woman could trade for others. She was good at it; this was recognized.

Women make the best traders. We don't leave Albany with a thick head and nothing else to show.

It was hard to communicate with Yellowhair. He had only a few words of English and the little Mohawk he had picked up in Island Woman's lodge. Stranger, his French was no better than that of Spotted Wolf, who had lived with the Caughnawagas at the mission at the Sault St. Louis. And his accent was so uncommon it mystified Spotted Wolf when Island Woman asked him to interpret.

"Polognais," Yellowhair kept saying.

"What is he saying? Is it his name?"

Spotted Wolf could only shrug.

"Moi. Polognais." Yellowhair punched his chest. *"Non français."*

"Says he's not French."

With time, they got the gist of it. Yellowhair said he came from a country called Poland. His father, forced by hunger to join the army of the French King, had brought him to Canada. He had gone out with a party of Mission Indians and *coureurs du bois* to hunt and trade. It was not a war party, he claimed. His companions had not been able to resist the temptation of ambushing a small band of Mohawk hunters bringing in a fat load of beaver peltries.

He told them his Polish name. *Czeslaw.* The Mohawks laughed at each other's attempts to get their tongues round it.

"Tsiokawe," was Snowbird's version. It was the Mohawk word for crow.

The others cawed at him. "Kahr, kahr, kahr!"

"His name *is* Crow!" Snowbird insisted.

While they were arguing, the smokehole above Island Woman's fire was closed off, as if a sheet of bark had been pulled over it. She looked up, and saw a huge black bird contemplating them. Its shaggy neck feathers puffed out like a goiter.

A chill ran down her spine.

She thought of the Sorcerer who had died, very slowly, at the stake.

Is he flying now on the flat wings of Raven?

The black bird croaked its mocking laughter.

Island Woman said to the captive, "You are no longer a dog. You are Laughing Crow."

The bird on the roof made a metallic sound—*tok, tok*—and flapped away, to kite over the Valley toward the Endless Mountains and the country of the Sorcerers.

□

The matter of Poland troubled Island Woman. She talked about it with Fruitpicker, who talked with the elders.

No one had ever heard of Poland. Not even Forked Paths, who had journeyed across the great water.

It seemed Poland was between Germany, of which the Flint People knew something because of the newcomers across the river, and a wilderness empire of snow and ice, ruled by bears.

First the Dutchmen. Then the French and the English. Now men with yellow hair from a country called Poland.

"How many white men are there?" Island Woman asked Fruitpicker. "How many will come to the Valley?"

"I told you the word of my son," the clanmother reminded her. "The People from the Sunrise are as many as the stars in the sky or the leaves of the forest. To live beside them, we must find strong ones who speak from the heart. We must make them half ours, half theirs. Is this not what our dream-prophet showed you?"

"Yes," Island Woman agreed. *But he never mentioned men from Poland.*

CHAPTER 4
STRENGTH OF A UNICORN

1.

The German settlers who had brought home the body of Island Woman's husband were survivors. They had been tempered by fire.

They had washed up in the Mohawk Valley in the wake of the largest migration North America had yet seen.

They were Palatine Protestants, born subjects of the small principalities along the Rhine.

In their native land, they had lived on intimate terms with all the horseman of the Apocalypse. Their destinies had been broken and scattered as the armies of greater powers, especially the French, marauded across their fertile valleys in wars that were always hatched somewhere else. In the years they had been spared war, the Palatines had been lashed by hunger and plague. They shared memories of the terrible winter that killed their vineyards and fruit orchards, and of the mysterious hot fever, unknown to their physicians, that had claimed tribute from every house. They remembered wives or daughters who had drowned themselves in the Neckar to avoid giving birth to the bastard children fathered on them in violence by French dragoons or nationless dogs of war. Others had saved themselves, drowning only their unwanted babies.

In the rare intervals of peace, the madness of their condition took possession of their rulers. Eberhard, the whimsical, licentious Duke of Württemberg, had ordered the streets of his capital covered with salt in midsummer, to the height of a horse's knee, because his mistress fancied a sleighride out of season.

In this depth of suffering, the risks of crossing the Atlantic in ships like floating coffins and the prospect of having to fight hostile scalpers in a howling wilderness had in no way daunted the spirits of the hardiest. Their leaders were men of faith, steeled by scripture, open to the power of direct revelation. They knew that the wisdom of God is the folly of men, unknowable to all but the elect. They read in their Book that the chosen will be subjected to the cruelest trials, because of their election, but will be given the strength of a unicorn to survive all their ordeals.

The three thousand Palatines who had made the crossing in the time of Queen Anne had been deceived, penned in forced labor camps, fed rotten provisions by the greatest magnates of the Hudson Valley, cheated of the land they had been promised, and pursued by bailiffs, sheriffs and redcoat soldiers as they struck out for freedom, deeper and deeper into the forests of New York and Pennsylvania.

Yet they endured, not like trees that bend with the prevailing wind, but like a granite mountain, that stands on its own terms.

Their kinsmen and countrymen knew now that Protestant monarchs lied as others did and that the New World was no land of milk and honey. Yet the promise of the New World had not died in their hearts.

It was four years since Anne Johnson gave birth to the bear she insisted would be called William in a hut of clay and wattles on a fierce back road in County Meath. And since Island Woman had asked her husband's clanmother to adopt a yellow-hair captive from an unknown country into the Mohawk nation.

In Germany, in the little valley of the Klöpferbach, another child was about to be born; she would join their destinies and open a path that would require the strength of a unicorn to complete.

2.

The conception was brusque, in a farmhouse that was no more than a kitchen and a sleeping loft, shared with the animals in the depth of winter.

Johann rammed his wife, with his thick, hard body, impervious to any need except his own, until he was spent. Then he rolled off her, emitted a noise between a fart and a belch, and started to snore.

Johann Weissenberg was a stiff-necked man who calculated profit and loss but rarely succeeded in bringing any of his calculations to market. He despised all talk of values that could be expressed in a currency other than coin. He could not bear his wife to finger the lute, an instrument handed down from a distant ancestor from a more leisured, mannerly environment. He thought that music of any kind, save hymn-singing in church, would put notions in the head of his flighty wife and any children they were fortunate enough (in the case of sons) or unlucky enough (daughters) to keep.

He smashed the lute in his daughter Catherine's third year. He'd been drinking beer, trying to get his mind off his rising debts. He prided himself on being a practical man, but he was sinking. It was the war, and the weather, and the lunacy of their mad Duke Eberhard, who applied himself to pleasuring his favorite mistress while the people starved.

With enough beer under his belt, Johann had felt lion enough to go on with his drinking mates to Frau Hagemann's and pay for an hour with a big, bouncing Bavarian girl who would do it in the raw, in plain view, like his prize pigs. But the beer was working, or perhaps it was the shock of a woman bared from head to toe. He failed to rise above half-mast. His humiliation turned to anger, and he tried to take it out on the whore with his fists. She called her brothers and they drove him out with staves and whips.

Torn and muddy, he staggered home. Before he opened the door, he heard the moonlight shiver of the lute strings. It set him to frenzy. His wife's face, smooth as a river stone, turned to him as he burst into the kitchen. He greeted her with his bully fist, breaking her nose, splitting her upper lip. He pawed the lute away from her. He smashed it into kindling against the bricks of the hearth and dropped the pieces onto the grate.

"It's more use now," he yelled, "than your damned daughter will ever be!"

Daughters were always *hers,* not theirs. But rarely for long. Catherine was the first of their children who had survived two whole winters.

The year Johann destroyed the lute was the year Margret Weissenberg slammed up against her limits.

There is a limit to endurance. If a woman is halfway lucky, she never gets right up against it. She may feel she has been pushed farther than flesh and blood can be pushed. She may feel life has opened her wrists and bled her dry. But she's got something left. If she's lucky.

Margret hit her limit in that autumn of the French. She reached the point at which there are no reserves of heart or nerve or sinew left.

For people in Württemberg, or more distant cities, this was the result of a minor incident in the perennial war between Catholic France and the Protestant rulers of Germany. All Margret understood about the fighting was that it was about grabbing and using, and that no man in uniform was to be trusted. Friend or foe, when the soldiers were finished with a town or a farm, it looked the same: stripped and burned.

Johann wasn't home when the dragoons came.

Margret stopped counting after the eighth stuck his rod into her. Her infant daughter stopped howling, but never turned her eyes away.

Some of the dragoons, heated by the sweat and spurt

and boasts of prowess, came at her a second time, even a third.

They left her for dead, gouting blood, in a mess of blood and puke, the prey for swarms of buzzing flies. The pigs were licking her when Johann came home, and little Catherine had vanished. A neighbor found her the next day, hiding in an abandoned barn.

For a long time, nobody could find her mother in the heap of ravaged flesh Margret had formerly inhabited.

To help her live, to get her through, her mind had gone somewhere else.

Under the savagery inflicted on her body—once so shapely, with a small-boned elegance unusual in a farmer's wife—she had stopped feeling the pain. She had even stopped worrying about her daughter.

She found herself floating around under the rafters. That sack of meat into which rough brutes were sluicing and jabbing was a curiosity, something she'd shrugged off like a soiled dress. It was distasteful to look at it. So she sailed off across the valley. She started falling upward, through a hole in the sky. Up became down, or the other way round. There was a roar in her ears like the sound of a waterfall. Then a tunnel, and nasty things that plucked and slithered before she found the light. There were people waiting to welcome her, faces she knew and loved. Some she had prayed, but never expected, to see. She was safe. She was at home. Nobody was going to hurt her.

"She's not all there," people said of Margret, as time passed. They said it in whispers, to begin with, but later in normal voices, because Margret did not seem to hear or care.

Her eyes were dull. She moved slowly and was forever bumping knees and elbows. She spoke little and forgot what she said as soon as it was out. She sucked her thumb until it was puckered white.

As little Catherine grew, she started leading her mother around by the hand, as if Margret was her baby sister. As her vocabulary grew, Catherine spoke up for her mother, interpreting. For all she had witnessed, Catherine seemed to be intact. Except that a certain shade of military blue would send her scurrying for cover in a doorway or behind a hedge.

Years passed, and old busybodies muttered that Catherine was budding too fast and should not be left alone with a drunk and a halfwit.

Johann despised his wife. He might have despised her less, but would certainly have hated her more, if she had retained the spunk and wit to stand up to him. Her survival, her mere presence in the house, was a threat to his manhood.

When he looked at her, he sometimes felt as if someone was threatening to snip off his cock with a pair of shears. Then he would think, Why didn't *she* use the shears? Why didn't she fight? *The slut.*

He would not look Margret in the eyes. They sat at table in stony silence, apart from the slurping of both adults. Johann had always been a guzzler, and now Margret sucked and played with food like an infant.

He touched her only out of unbearable hunger, always with her outer clothes on and her face covered.

They had nothing to give Catherine, nothing to teach, except perhaps by negative example.

She learned more from the cat, the stray her father didn't want.

It came in the depth of winter, a winter that struck early, killing the vines, stealing the last fruit from the orchards along the shallow valley of the Klöpferbach. A winter that brought wolves out of the Black Forest, and men who were worse than wolves.

Catherine was fetching logs from the pile behind the pig slurry. She knocked them to the ground before making up an armful, to shake off the heavy coating of snow.

She heard a thin mewling, from low down, near her feet. She looked for its source, peeking through the gaps in the woodpile.

The cat slipped from hiding and rubbed itself against her leg. But when she reached down for it, the cat fled back into the woodpile. It was pure white, all but invisible against the snow. Catherine crouched down to see it better. Gray-green eyes, pink nose. It did not look like a farm cat, even less like an alley cat from town. Its hair was long and silky. A storybook cat, the kind that was supposed to ride in a carriage on a satin cushion.

The shivering cat did not respond to her coaxings, and when she groped after it, the cat hissed and clawed at her tattered mittens.

She carried a load of wood into the house.

"Stop daydreaming," her father growled. "We'll freeze to death waiting for you to get the wood in."

When his back was turned, she stole half a cup of milk and smuggled it out in the folds of her blanket-coat.

"Here, kitty, kitty."

She held out the cup. The cat stuck its head out of its hole. She backed away a few paces, still holding out the milk. She saw fear and hunger struggling for ascendancy.

Finally hunger won out. The cat came to her and started tonguing up the milk. Swiftly, Catherine moved her hands from the cup to the animal's thin flanks. It trembled violently and tried to run. But she had it now. She cradled it to her chest. The wretched thing was almost fleshless under its extravagant pelt. Someone must have hurt it very badly to make it so terrified of humans it would risk starvation rather than eat in their company.

She put the cat under her coat and kept it there while she ferried in a few smaller armfuls of wood. Her mother was lying on the straw mattress, staring at the ceiling and sucking her thumb.

When Catherine brought in the last load of wood, her father banged out of the house to relieve himself.

Catherine squatted beside her mother and opened her coat.

"Look."

Her mother's eyes were pale and vacant, like a blind person's. But then she put out her fingers and stroked the cat's hair, with surprising tenderness.

"Silky," Margret murmured.

"Yes, Mama," Catherine said eagerly.

"Silky." Margret smiled. Something was coming back. "Like you, Cat."

A pet-name was born.

"What the fuck is that?" Johann Weissenberg bellowed. "I need no more mouths to feed in this house. Two useless women and now—Here, give me that!"

He pushed his brawn between them and seized the cat, which hissed and clawed at him, drawing blood. Margret screamed—a single, piercing note that hung in the air and made Cat shudder.

"Papa—"

"Shut up!"

He threw the cat outside and bolted the door.

"There's enough of it," Johann ruled.

Cat lay awake half the night, hating her father, thinking of ways of escape.

She had watched the emigrants crossing the valley. They came year after year, season after season. They carried their possessions on their backs, or yoked themselves like oxen to high, two-wheeled carts, stuffed with food and clothes and bedding.

One spring, she had followed them all the way to the customs post, where the little Klöpferbach joined the Murr. She had prayed that they would take her with them. She had even asked a man who looked kindly, with grown sons well able to provide for themselves, if he would include her in his family.

"Are you an orphan then, child?"

She had mumbled the lie, then flushed red with the shame of denying her mother. She could abandon her father and never look back; he would miss her less than one of his sows. But the burden of her mother lay on her young shoulders and she could not shrug it off.

She had run from the puzzled man with lines of laughter at the corners of his eyes, run back to the pig farm and the woman who sucked her thumb and rolled her eyes back till only the whites showed.

But she had never stopped thinking about the walk to the sea. She knew little of maps and charts, but she had memorized the names of rivers. The Murr flowed into the Neckar. The Neckar poured its waters into the Rhine, queen of rivers, which flowed all the way to the sea.

Beyond the sea were the realms of the English Queen, peaceful lands with neither French nor German dragoons. Catherine had seen the Queen's portrait in a picture-book. *The Golden Book,* they called it. Besides the Queen's thoughtful, slightly melancholy face, there were pictures of nodding wheatfields and gentle parklands in a country of plenty called America, where emigrants who were willing to brave the Atlantic passage were promised farms and freedom. The book was old, and some said the Queen had died and England and its empire were now ruled by a King. If true, this could be no obstacle to an emigrant from the Palatinate, because this King was born German, a prince of Hanover.

Johann Weissenberg said the promises about America were lies. He had heard of Germans who had been fettered and lashed like slaves, making tar for the Royal Navy. When they were not being worked to death, they were slaughtered by savages who were worse than the wild men who came down off the Lowenstein Mountains.

Cat had overheard her father saying these things to his friends. She did not believe him. She thought her father wanted to stay in his mudhole, like a frog.

She was different.

She would follow the rivers to the sea and the life beyond it. She would watch for her time. And she would take her mother. Because, whatever God intended for her in this lifetime, she was sure it must include the woman who had brought her into it.

CHAPTER 5

BURDEN STRAPS

The yellow-hair captive's Mohawk name did not stick.
The girls called him Dandelion, because of that impossibly yellow thatch, and that was the name everyone,
including Island Woman, came to use.

In his first months at the Upper Castle, he was a
curiosity. Mohawks came up from the Lower Castle and
the Floodwood Valley, and from as far as Oquaga and
Oswego, to stare at the prodigy.

The girls were especially curious, wanting to know if
his nether hair matched the hair on his head, and if his
fish was as pale as the rest of his skin, which never
tanned but merely sprouted freckles and unhealthy pink
spots. The spots worried people until it was established
that they came and went without touching any of the
Flint People.

Even after four years among the Mohawk, Dandelion
was still hard to understand in any language, and Island
Woman began to believe that her protégé must be dim-
witted. But he had made her a wagon, thick-wheeled and
strong-timbered, like the carts from Schenectady. She
broke an axle on her first ride down the Valley, but had

little trouble after that. Soon she was playing middleman
for several families at the Upper Castle, and for some
Oneidas and Onondagas as well. At Widow Veeder's, on
Pearl Street in Albany, she kept a sharp eye on the
entries in the account books, where debts and credits to
Indians were figured with drawings of beavers and deer.

Dandelion was a fair shot, and at eleven, Snowbird
was already an accomplished hunter. With the meat they
brought in, and the profits from her trading runs, Island
Woman felt under no compulsion to marry again to put
food in the mouths of her family.

Her main worry was her elder daughter.

Swimming Voices ought to be married by now.

But she scared away the dependable young men, with
her moods and her wildness and her appetite for white
men's finery.

The men she toyed with were ones Island Woman did
not want under her roof.

Bright Meadow was now big enough to join with gusto
in the game of nesting—hunting for couples making out
in the woods—always a favorite with Mohawk girls. She
told her mother she had seen Swimming Voices bare-
assed in the high grass with Spotted Wolf—news that
put Island Woman in a spitting mood. Spotted Wolf was
trouble, furtive and sly, still too mixed up with the
Burned Knives from Caughnawaga to be trusted. There
were little birds that said Spotted Wolf had a wife at the
Caughnawaga mission; that would not stop him from
taking a new wife—though it was a little harder for a
Mohawk man to drop his wife than the other way round.
But wife or no wife, Spotted Wolf was not Island
Woman's idea of a suitable match.

Worse than any dalliance with Spotted Wolf, Swimming Voices was spending too much time hanging
around the trading posts and grogshops where the newcomers made Mohawks lose their minds.

She is spoiling herself, Island Woman thought. *She is
acting like a trade woman. She is not making babies, as
she should be at her age. She must be stopping them from
coming.*

Swimming Voices knew enough about *ononkhwa*—medicine—to do that. Unfortunately, her greatest affinity with plants seemed to be with the dangerous ones, the ones that are poison more than medicine.

Swimming Voices forgets everything Fruitpicker and I have tried to teach her. That women are the life-bringers. What it means to be born a woman of power. She sells herself to stinking newcomers for trinkets.

Island Woman confronted her difficult daughter.

Swimming Voices told her, "If there is anything wrong with me, it is your doing. I had a dream that was not fulfilled, by those whose duty it is to fulfill it. You and our clanmother decided to shut me out."

It is true, thought Island Woman. *Fruitpicker put the matter in the fire, as she said she would do. She saw terrible consequences if we accepted Swimming Voices into the secret society. She saw our mysteries profaned, our medicine power abused. She saw evil worming its way into the heart of our villages. She saw all this in the flames of the fire she lit with her mind.*

Fruitpicker had ruled that the matter was closed.

But Island Woman would risk her anger by asking again.

□

The clanmother said, "Bring her to me. Make sure she is *wrapped.*"

Island Woman led her daughter at a fast clip for more than an hour, down little-used trails, before she stopped and explained Fruitpicker's instructions.

It was long after dark, and the light of the moon did not reach below the upper canopy. The night goers were out. A snowy owl flew low overhead.

Swimming Voices mocked and scolded when her mother wound the black cloth over her eyes. "I know where you meet! I'll get us there faster than you can!"

"*Serihokten.* Stop the words. Even when you are not speaking, I can hear them banging around in your head. If you can't stop the chatter, you don't have a place from which to operate. You don't have a center. That's what we have been trying to tell you, but the chatterers in your head won't listen."

Stumbling blindly beside her mother, Swimming Voices' willful self-confidence began to slip a little.

Now they could hear the crash of the falls, below the place where the two creeks joined their waters.

Island Woman stepped out onto the high, slippery ledge along the rim of the limestone gorge, forcing her daughter to step behind her, toe to heel. She felt Swimming Voices' deepening uncertainty.

This is not what she expects. Good. Before she can learn, she must stop believing she knows anything. I had to learn this lesson too.

The entrance to the caves was an egg-shaped hole, barely wide enough for Island Woman's shoulders.

"Let me take off the blindfold," her daughter begged, horrified to find her hips snagging on the rough edges and nothing to step on or cling to below the hole. She might be crawling into empty space.

"Stop the words! Come *on!*"

Island Woman brushed a few small brown bats away from her face, and felt Swimming Voices shudder at the unseen flapping of a leathery wing against her skin.

The way down was a sloping shelf that tilted almost to the vertical. Island Woman dropped down the black shaft.

"Ihstenha!" Swimming Voices squealed as her feet skidded off moist flowstone and skittered down into the void. She closed her eyes and let her arms drop to her sides. She fell two or three times her own height, onto the balls of her feet. The shock jarred her bones.

From somewhere to her left, her mother laughed. "Come on! You move like a blind woman."

□

The clanmother waited for them in a chamber at the heart of a warren of caves and passages. The roof of the cavern was domed, the walls gently rounded. It was like being inside a bowl.

In a smaller, alcove-like cavern, a cascade of water

from far above fell to an underground river. A pale blue light flickered in the deeps of the water. A stone figure stood sentinel over the hidden river. From where Island Woman sat, it looked like a primal mother, half-human, half-animal, squatting with her legs apart, in the act of giving birth.

All the women in the circle around the fire were masked, except for Island Woman and her daughter.

What remained of Swimming Voices' assurance was slipping into doubt, edged with fear. She alone was standing, in the midst of the circle of eyes.

She had been certain she would know the initiates, even if their faces were hidden. But as they moved and spoke, she was less and less sure. The savage figure across the fire—the wolf face ringed with cornhusks, the body cloaked in fur and feathers—*had* to be Fruitpicker. But the voice was different, hard to understand. The words came out of a different time, when women knew the language of the birds and the four-leggeds, when shamans journeyed to the Upper and the Lower Worlds in their meat and bones as well as their dreambodies.

The shapes that danced on the walls in the flickering firelight were even more ancient. They danced life into death, death into rebirth.

"Only one man has come to this place that is sacred." Wolf-face changed to the lilting rhythms of power that Swimming Voices had heard in the women's council. "But when he came here, to leave us his dreaming, he was neither man nor woman. For what he had become, there is no name.

"We are here because there is one among our people who is putting trees across our paths. She troubles our peace. She disturbs our dreaming. We have all felt her. She brings a gusting in the force that protects all our people.

"She must be cleansed and healed. Only through the way of sacrifice and purification can she join us, because she has strayed far from our path.

"I speak for the order that is forbidden to men and must be held secret from the uninitiated.

"You have asked for admission." Now she spoke directly to the young woman. There was rolling thunder under her words. "Are you ready to be cleansed and made new?"

"Yes." Swimming Voices was gripped by a sudden panic. Her stomach turned over.

"Your flesh will be stripped from your body. Your bones will be numbered. Are you ready for this?"

"Yes." But her legs fluttered under her. She realized her mother had vanished; Island Woman had hidden herself in the circle of masks. Was she behind the one that stared with the great disc-eyes of the snow owl?

"Understand what waits you if you are accepted. You will take up the burden. You will be poorer than any, because the weight of their need will be on your back all your days and nights.

"You will become the *ahsha:ra.*" The speaker raised her arms, letting the ends of a very ancient burden strap trail from her hands.

The burden strap had been woven from the bark of the slippery elm, which is durable, soft to the touch, and can be closely braided. Its maker had twisted the bark filaments into twenty cords and laid them side by side to make the warp. In the cross-weave, she had placed the fine long hairs that grow near the rump and between the shoulders of the moose, working with a bone needle. The hairs were dyed red, blue, and yellow, and formed sacred patterns. The preparation and weaving had consumed a great amount of time and required extraordinary patience.

All women of the Real People knew the meaning of the burden strap. It was passed around the forehead, lashed to a pack, a litter, or a cradleboard. It was used to carry all that was precious, all that supported life, all that was women's work. No article made by women's hands commanded such skill and dedication. None—except the wampum belts—was more precious.

But Swimming Voices was shocked to hear the secret name of the members of the secret order she had dreamed of entering and one day ruling. She had come in search of *power*. She was being told that the price of that power was to become the burden strap for the whole community. To carry its weight.

Her panic returned. She wanted to run from the cavern, but she had no idea which of the many openings led back into the night.

She was stripped and bathed in the underground river. The women smudged her. She smelled the fragrance of the sage and sweetgrass. They brushed her from the soles of her feet to the crown of her head with a white wing. They sang over her. They drummed for her spirit guides to return to her and state their wishes.

Fear never left her.

She began trembling violently when the speaker said, "Now we take this matter into the fire. Let us look together."

"I don't want to look!" Her fear rebelled, though she had looked many times for the future in fire and for truth in still water.

"You must look."

"I cannot."

Naked and shivering, she began running blindly, toward one of the passages. Her legs grew heavier and heavier. Her blood ran thin. Her heart was caught up in her throat, like a bird trapped in an angle of the roof. She felt she was going to faint. Something was blocking her exit—she could see it only as a massing of the air. She had the overwhelming sensation that if she persisted in trying to escape, she would die.

You can go. The voice that spoke inside her head might have been her mother's. *But if you go, you will not return to us in the Valley.*

She drifted back into the circle, a dead leaf blown on shifting winds.

"Look into the fire."

She looked.

I see a man. His eyes are knifepoints in a mask of black paint. He is powerful, but fearful.

This is not the guide I met in my vision quest. This is not one of the ancients who have come to me in my dreams.

He wants me to look lower. There is a hollow below his ribcage. A bird is nesting there. It is huge. It is Raven. He ruffles his feathers. He is coming for me.

□

"You see why she will never be one of us." The clan-mother spoke gently to Island Woman, who had seen her daughter crumple like an empty cloak.

"I have always known it."

"The Dark One has claimed her. She made herself open, because she has used power without heart."

"I blame myself. She is so young."

"You are not to blame, my daughter. Remember what our grandmothers taught us. The Dark One was fighting his twin inside his mother's womb, before they were even born. The shadow was born with her. We must make room for it. We cannot fight half the universe. We must also build walls around it. We must guard the one who is returning, the great soul the dream-prophet told us would come again through your lineage. I think it is not in Bright Meadow."

"No." Bright Meadow was a happy, larksome child, but wholly of this world. She did not see what can only be seen with closed eyes.

"Then it will come through a child of one of your daughters. It is hard to know which. We must keep watch for it. And over it."

CHAPTER 6
A LAKE OF BEER FOR GOD

1.

Denis Rahilly was singing as he went swinging along the lanes beside the strapping Johnson boy.

"I'd like to give a lake of beer to God—" Billy Johnson picked up the old Gaelic tune, and echoed the last verse in his fluting alto:

I'd make Heaven a cheerful spot
because the happy heart is true.
We'd be drinking good health forever
and every drop would be a prayer.

Rahilly flung back his shaggy mane and laughed, for the beauty of the morning and the joy of the singing and the drop of poteen—none better than Maire's—that had lightened his breakfast of oatcakes.

"But whissht!" Rahilly put a finger to his lips, admitting the nine-year-old boy into his conspiracy. "Not a breath of that hymn around Smithstown House, do you hear? It is not for the unbelievers."

Especially not for Squire Johnson, Billy's father. The master of Smithstown House had made it known he was less than satisfied with the boy's tutor, and not merely

because Rahilly's brogue made the county name—
Meath—sound like something for dinner.

"You're not telling me that is a hymn, Mr. Rahilly,"
Billy Johnson spoke up.

"Sure and it's a hymn."

"It is about drinking beer. Quite a lot of it."

"And isn't that a most religious subject? If God did
not love ale, why would he make us love it so? The spirit
works in various and mysterious ways, Billy, and that is
the best that can be said."

They had skirted the manor of Killeen, where the
Earl's great gothic castle loomed like a thunderhead—
deserted in this season, as in most, except for the
apartments of Gerald Tracy, the English estate manager,
who collected the rents in his lordship's absence.

"We are ruled by men who do not even care to view
the source of their annuities," Rahilly said, not minding
that the bitterness showed. "And the best of us that love
the land are forced to fly off like the geese in winter."

*The boy must know these things. This is the best I can
do for his education. To remind him who he truly is.*

Rahilly's destination was the church of Saint Mary at
Dunsany, only three centuries old, but already a ruin.

*Gone like all the holy places our Established Church
has no use for. A place for a couples beggar—a furtive
priest of the old religion—to marry believers by night,
shielding the light of their candles, the gleam of the altar
vessels, from hostile eyes.*

*I have performed the trick myself, when no priest could
be found or was willing. I have the words, and when the
Latin fails, the common people cannot tell when I make
them up.*

The entrance to the churchyard was all but invisible
among overgrown hedges. Rahilly knew it by the way-
side cross.

The nave was open to the sky, filled with tall grass and
brambles. The stone features of St. John on the medieval
font were blurred by weathering, like a face glimpsed
across a taproom.

Rahilly let Billy discover the marble slab by himself. It
had been carved the year after the boy's own birth, with

the arms of a local branch of the O'Neills, Billy's kinsmen.

How our great names are fallen! They are struck from the books by the hired scribes of our rackrents. Yet among us, without clamor, with only the music of the harp and the fiddle, only the protection of a tongue our owners never troubled to learn, the keepers of the names still honor the high ones.

Billy Johnson had found it. He stared at the headstone of O'Neills made baronets for accepting the English men's terms.

He was puzzled by the great fish on their coat of arms. He searched his tutor's face, for the reason.

"The salmon!" Rahilly exclaimed. "Mark it well Billy. Your O'Neill kinsmen knew what they were doing when they took it for their badge of power. If you make your name, you could do worse than borrow it."

"But why the salmon?"

"Ah. Did no one tell you that is how Fionn got the sight? You are a wonder to me boy, with all it is you do not know. Take your rest now, in the shade of the stone. A story is the quickest way between a man and his soul, and that is God's own truth. That is why we must keep telling stories. If we lose our stories, we lose our souls."

So Rahilly talked, in the cool of the ravaged stone, of the boy Fionn, the son of Mairne, a chief druid's daughter, who was instructed by a druid who bore the same name as himself to cook a salmon that was fished in a deep pool along the River Boyne. The boy was forbidden to taste the salmon. But as Fionn was turning the fish in the pan over the fire, he burned his thumb. When he put his thumb in his mouth, to suck at the pain, he received the gifts of the seer and the wizard, because the salmon had swallowed nine hazelnuts from the tree of wisdom.

Rahilly talked and talked while Billy, drowsing under closed eyelids, drifted in and out of the tale.

"We can talk the stars out of the sky, we Irish," Rahilly laughed, though only he had been speaking. The tutor dusted the grass from the shiny seat of his breeches.

Rahilly contemplated the boy. "There are stories that wait for people to tell them," he declared. "Maybe the story of Fionn and the salmon was waiting for you, Mr. O'Neill-MacSalmon-Johnson."

"It is a fairytale," the boy shrugged.

"It is a tale of *faerie*," Rahilly corrected him, serious now, even sober-seeming. "We are more than we seem, Billy Johnson. Do not forget that Fionn was serving a master who bore his own name. Do not neglect that he gained the sight, and the power to kill or create with a thought, from a power of nature."

"From a tree and a fish." Billy wrinkled his nose.

"Only in seeming."

"I don't understand." Billy's tone suggested he did not choose to hear more.

Rahilly heard the father's voice in the son's. *Whisky-dreamer*, Squire Johnson had called him, to his own face. The tutor's eyes lost their glint of intent. The lashes came down, the pupils slid sideways, downward. He was hiding himself, as he had learned to do in the presence of men like Billy's father, who could take the food off his table and the sunlight out of the morning.

He took his disgust out on Billy by making him conjugate Latin verbs for the whole of the walk back to Smithstown.

But as he leaned on the gate to the stableyard, watching the boy bounding to greet the chestnut colt, Rahilly called after him, "Do you have any liking at all for salmon? I am meaning the eating kind."

"I don't mind."

"Well, then. Since you're so eager I'm thinking we will go fish along the River Boyne, where the hazel shed and your grandfather bled and all Ireland mourned."

□

They waited to go fishing for a day when Billy's father had gone to Dublin on business. Mick Flood, who had charge of the stables, made no objection to letting Billy take the brown mare, but refused Rahilly a better horse than old Phoenix, worn out from years in the traces. This pleased the tutor well enough, because he was a

man who had never managed to post on a horse's back
without feeling that a tender part of his person was in
direst jeopardy.

John Johnson, Billy's stolid elder brother, came up
from the pastures to ask where they were going.

"Mr. Rahilly means to improve my Latin by teaching
me Mr. Linnaeus' new classifications for plants," Billy
said straight-faced.

"Never heard of them," John growled.

"Never heard of Linnaeus?" Billy shot up his eyebrows. "When he is such a gift to agriculture? Is that not
so, Mr. Rahilly?"

"Truly the farmer's friend," Rahilly agreed gravely.

"Very well." John would always accede to an argument of *practicality,* but remained suspicious. He indicated a thistle. "So what does Mr. Linnaeus call *that?"*

Rahilly said with supreme confidence, *"Phlogiston
superiorus."*

John's eyes moved from one face to the other. Finding
no evidence of humor in either, he grunted and went on
his way.

□

Rahilly cut fishing poles for them both from an old hazel
tree, above the place where the Black Water joins the
Boyne. While he worked, he told stories of the battle in
which the cause of the Stuarts and the old Ireland was
lost.

He had lines and hooks ready. Berries would be good
enough for a fish that was tired and hungry from the
spawning runs, he said.

They settled in to wait. In the intervals between
Rahilly's stories, the only sound was the drone of bees
and cicadas. Rahilly pulled in a trout, then a dead
branch, drifting with the current.

Billy was bored with waiting and ready for lunch when
a tug on his line came so strong that it set him tumbling
off his perch on the bank. Rahilly was after him, quick as
an eel. He got hold of the boy's ankles and dragged him
out of the stream.

Billy never relaxed his grip on the rod, not even when he saw the gleaming arch of the monster he was fighting. Even with Rahilly's weight added to his, it seemed a losing battle. The line, or the hazel stick, must surely break.

Then something changed. Billy moved like a dancer, toward the fish, then spinning away. With a flash of pink and silver, the salmon leaped from the water onto the grass.

When he got his breath back, Rahilly said, "Will you just look at him now. You have hooked a knight in armor. The knight of the waters."

Billy stared at the powerful fish, at the tough skin, stengthened by bony plates, laid row on row like chainmail. It was nearly as long as he was tall.

Now its life force was ebbing, its thrashing reduced to a dying tremor.

"We salute you." Rahilly had a bottle. He splashed a drop on the salmon's nose before he took a deep swig and offered the bottle to Billy. The boy hesitated only an instant before he tossed back a quantity of raw liquor equal to his tutor's. It burned a hole through his chest, down to the pit of his belly. He came up coughing and spitting.

Rahilly slapped him on the back, roaring his laughter. "You are one of ours, Billy, though your name be Johnson."

"*Johnson!*" Another voice echoed. It was clipped and cool, with a sneer.

Billy looked up and saw Andrew Tracy, mounted on the black stallion from Killeen.

"We saw you drinking." Tracy added a note of menace. The estate manager's son was four years older than Billy, and lorded it over boys his own age or younger as though he owned the county, because his family came from Dorset and his father worked for an Earl. He was almost too pretty for a boy, with that snub nose and white skin, framed by brown curls. He slapped his riding crop against his thigh, an assertion of masculinity and pretended power.

He said, "Give that bottle here."

"It is not mine to give." Billy saw now that Andrew Tracy had come with other riders. Three—no, four of them. Sons of half-mounted gentlemen and noblemen's agents, mostly English. How like Andrew Tracy. He never issued a challenge unless the odds were altogether in his favor.

Rahilly saw the fight coming, noted the odds, and calculated the consequences for a tutor who took a stick to the back of a youth under the protection of an Earl. He came to a rapid conclusion. "Well now. It is my pleasure to share a drop with your honor, you being a fine gentleman of mettle."

Andrew Tracy took the stumpy brown bottle. He and his companions emptied it in a quick round. Tracy tossed the bottle into the Boyne, not caring that Rahilly would have to pay for another before he went back to Maire's still.

"Are you actually going to *eat* that?" Tracy sniffed at the salmon.

Billy balled his fists. He was not going to part with his prize without leaving blood on the field.

An instinct of danger led Tracy to choose a different ground. "I cannot abide fish," he declared. "Besides, we are on our way to Newgrange, for better sport. Some oaf of a farmer has found an old grave, and has all his neighbors spooked with tattle of banshees and the like. We mean to lay these ghosts to rest. What of you, Johnson? Are you brave enough to join us? Or are you afeared of things that go bump in the dark, like all bog paddies?"

Rahilly darted Billy a sideways look, of warning, not evasion. *Don't go.*

But Billy's blood was up.

"I am scared of nothing you will face, Andrew Tracy. Or of many things you will not."

"Not even of getting between a whore's legs?" Tracy goaded.

"Aw, Johnson is only a baby," one of his companions chortled.

"I may be younger than you." Billy looked steadily at the youth on the black stallion. "But, I have more between my legs than you will ever have."

Rahilly groaned inwardly. *In a mood, the boy will leap at a waterfall. Like the salmon. It is his strength and his peril. And, God help him, the ladies will know it.*

Andrew Tracy's face whitened even more. He spurred his horse forward, raising the crop, as if he meant to slash it across Johnson's face. At the last moment, he wheeled the horse away. Billy had stood his ground, raising the fishing pole across his chest like a falchion.

"Follow us!" Tracy cried. "We will see what a cow herder's vaunts are worth."

"Don't go," Rahilly said out loud.

"I have never refused a dare."

"That is a poor sense of honor, Billy. And if it were not, it would put a low valuation on life and health. Think beyond your temper, boy."

"I will go. They may do that farmer some injury."

"What about the fish?"

"Cook it for both of us. Don't worry. I will not forget to put my thumb to it."

Billy galloped the mare harder than she was used to, along the post road through the town of Navan, north by east to the round hill bright with gorse where a sheep farmer digging stone for a wall had discovered something older that the invasions and occupations of Ireland, older even than the tale of Fionn and the salmon.

2.

In the sunlight, the yellow gorse that covered the flanks of the ancient burial mound smelled like sweet oil. Coconut oil, Uncle Peter said. Billy Johnson had never seen or smelled a coconut. According to Peter Warren, who was now a captain in His Majesty's Navy and would know such things, coconuts grew on a hot coast of Africa, on a tree that stood taller than any tree in Ireland or England.

It was not the gorse that Billy was looking at now. It

was the great ring of standing stones that stood sentinel over the mound. Only a few of the guardian stones had been completely freed from the rubble around the passage grave. They towered over him. It would have taken a dozen strong men, at the least, to carry one of them more than a few paces. Yet they had been fetched from somewhere far distant, perhaps from across the Irish Sea. Had the stone giants been brought to Newgrange to keep trespassers away from the mound? Or to keep something in?

"We are waiting, Johnson," Andrew Tracy said coldly.

"Johnson's scared," chirruped one of his hangers-on.

"Phew!" A carrot-headed youth held his nose. "The paddy's gone and done it in his breeches!"

Billy ignored them. He would save the next fight for something that mattered. He squinted into the mouth of the tomb. Just a chink in the hill, a patch of darkness largely concealed by the farmer's efforts to board it up. As Tracy had claimed, a farmer had stumbled on the passage by chance, quarrying stone for a wall to keep his sheep in. On either flank, the hillside was scored white, where the diggers had peeled gorse and earth back to the quartzite shell of the tomb.

"Get on with you, then," Tracy prodded, making no move to enter the tomb himself.

Chaffinches hopped away as Billy scrambled the last few yards. For miles around, across the valley of the Boyne, the day was shining, the blue sky flecked with only a few fleecy, fair-weather clouds. Yet it seemed to Billy that there was a change in the air when he penetrated the circle of standing stones. The breeze seemed to shift.

He yanked at the timbers jammed into the mouth of the tomb. They were firmly set, but Billy had strength far beyond his years, and the confidence won from wrestling the knight of the waters out of the Boyne.

He is built like a scrapper, his father complained grimly.

Was that why he always seemed to be the one against whom others—even much older youths, like Andrew Tracy—needed to score?

His freckled face reddened with his efforts. His fingers were bleeding before the stubborn beams tore loose.

Billy pushed his reddish hair out of his face and stuck his head into the hole. It was pitch-dark inside. And cold. The air smelled stale and rank, like a fox's earth.

"Give me the torch."

Tracy nodded, and one of his henchmen obliged, striking flint to steel to light the tar-soaked cloth around the stick. The wind picked up from a new direction and swallowed the flame. The youth swore and lit it again. Billy wriggled behind it, on his belly, into the bowels of the hill.

"It don't count except you go all the way!" Tracy shouted after him. "You must prove it, Johnson! Or else the penalty is a flogging!"

"And if I win the dare?" Billy called back. He could not hear Tracy's response, if there was one. It was of no account. He was not doing this to win a dare. He was doing it so he would have a story to match Rahilly's.

Rahilly says these hills belong to the sidhe. That princes of the earth and warrior-druids are trapped here, in a state between life and death, lured by the beauty and the siren calls of women who are not women.

These, of course, were a wild man's drunken maunderings. Billy would tell him how it *really* was.

Rahilly says the standing stones were raised by a race of men older than our own, not to keep people out, but to keep the spirits in.

He wormed his way along the narrowing passage. Something brushed his cheek, and the torch was snuffed out as suddenly as a candle.

He struggled on, in the dark, willing himself not to go back to face Tracy without something to end his jeers.

At last the passage widened and he was able to crawl, then walk. At this depth, the place was cool, but not uncomfortably chilly, and the air was bone dry.

He entered a vaulted chamber. As his eyes adjusted to the grainy dark, rings of stone were set high above his head: circles within circles, like ripples in a pool. For some reason, men who had not had the use of the wheel had clambered up there, in darkness or guttering light, to lay the slabs with aching precision, making a corbelled roof, as precise in its design as a church dome.

There was a different smell here, in the vault. It reminded Billy a little of the spermaceti candles that were lit at Warrenstown Hall on special occasions.

Groping around the walls, Billy found smaller chambers or passages that opened out like the arms of a cross, and he chose one at random. He stumbled against a great boulder, hurting his shin. He felt his way around it. It was hewn stone, squared off and hollowed out on top, to form a shallow trough or basin.

He grubbed inside it. His hand closed on smaller stones.

No. They are bones.

They were strangely warm to his touch. Not dry, but faintly moist.

Moist and sticky.

He dropped them, feeling a froth of revulsion rising from his belly.

But maybe I should take one of them for a trophy. They will not challenge me then.

While he considered this, another idea came to him. If he got up on the hewn stone, he could carve his initials high up, on the walls or ceiling of the tomb. He would challenge Tracy and his cohorts to find them. He would not only prove himself beyond all dispute; he would set the standard for future dares. It was an easy thing to do, even in the dark, with his keen-edged pocket knife.

He clambered up on top of the hewn stone. And slipped, in the stickiness he had felt on the bones.

I am falling.

I am not falling under my own weight. I am in the talons of a great bird. I am in his grasp yet I see myself plain. I am a dead man in his claws. If he drops me, my skull will break like a gull's egg.

Now I am lying on wide stone steps. They are slippery with blood, also a white liquid that smells like candles.

This is a throne room. A Queen is seated above me. Perhaps she is more than a Queen. I cannot see her distinctly. She is tremendous and never still. The shadow thrown from her leap like dancers, like lovers, like joyful killers.

There is a woman who comes to me now. She is naked, except for the strip of animal fur about her loins.

Her eyes are whirlpools or windstorms. They contain the birth and death of galaxies.

□

"He fainted," Andrew Tracy said. "Johnson swooned like a girl."

The others sniggered and giggled, though they had not cared to venture inside the tomb when Billy had failed to come back.

"Take it back." Billy moved forward into Tracy's space. Though four years younger, he stood eye to eye with the agent's son.

"Whooo!" Tracy held his nose. "The pig slurry is mighty ripe today."

Billy feinted with his right. He hit the older boy just once, below the ribcage, with his left. It was enough to send Tracy skittering backward, whimpering.

The others grabbed Johnson from behind, pinioning his arms. Billy heard, before he saw it, the whine of the leather crop, slicing air. It ripped across his cheekbone.

His rage gave him the strength to break free from his captors. He surged at Tracy. He pummeled him again and again, in the face, the chest, the belly. Then the kicks and blows to his kidneys knocked the wind from his body.

Tracy staggered back. He had abandoned his crop in favor of a large chunk of fieldstone, jagged at the end.

"You shitten dwarf," Billy spat through his own blood.

Tracy teetered, in danger of losing his balance as he raised the heavy rock above his head. He was ranting wildly, about making an end of pretend-Englishmen. He scared some of his own companions, who started backing away, giving Billy a final chance to break free.

He catapulted off his heels, under the arc of the stone, hurling Tracy backward with the force of his spring.

Breathing hard, the veins pumping against the skin of

his neck and arms, he straddled the older boy, then reached down and gave a savage twist to the thing inside his breeches.

Tracy screamed, his voice breaking upward, into a shrill.

The other boys did not oppose Johnson when he walked, stiff-legged, to reclaim his father's mare. Not even when, on reflection, he cut Tracy's black stallion loose, and gave it a hard slap on the rump.

"You should belong to a man who can serve a woman!" he shouted after the horse.

He did not linger to hear Andrew Tracy say he would drink a toast at Billy Johnson's wake.

3.

"You do not take to bridle and bit," Rahilly told him, as he nursed Billy's wounds with whisky and a damp cloth in his thatched cottage.

"I will not be ridden by fops and cowards."

Rahilly was secretly appalled by the size of the purple-black bruises over the boy's torso and buttocks. It was a wonder no bones were broken.

He was outnumbered four to one, by older boys, on top of the fall he took inside the tomb. There is something that fights on his side. There is no accounting for it otherwise.

Rahilly brought out a swag-bellied bottle, to drink his pupil's health. Maire had lent it to him, making him promise not to lose this one as he had lost the other.

"They'll not tolerate you in the county, you know," Rahilly reflected after a few swallows. "Not unless you find a cleverness to match your pride. Otherwise you'll be off to the Wild Geese, my boy. Or trooping around with the woodentops for the King's shilling. For you are not made out for a quill-driver, and I think you will never take to the cloth. My own confessor told me that a man that cannot mind his own morals should not mind the morals of others."

"Give me that bottle."

"By all the saints, Billy. You are nine years of age! Your father will take a whip to me with more certain aim than Master Tracy, if he hears anything of this."

"I am blooded," Billy said grimly.

They drank together, and presently Rahilly got out his fiddle and sang a few of the old ballads, of pirate-queens and druid-warriors. When the hush fell between them, Billy said, "What *was* it I saw, in the tomb?"

Rahilly sighed and folded his hands over his stomach.

"Ah, Billy, Billy." He smiled. "You saw the breasts of Herself."

The boy flushed bright crimson.

Rahilly nodded. "You saw the breasts of the Goddess. There is no call for shame. What I would not give for the sight!"

Billy squirmed on his hard seat.

Rahilly reached for the pouch that hung next to his fiddle on the cracked and discolored wall. He took out a thing of metal, on a leather thong. Three whirling shapes, cast in bronze.

"You saw this." It was not a question. "This is part of it, the whirling in and out of life."

He let the boy handle the ancient triskele. It weighed heavier than seemed possible, in the palm of Billy's hand.

"So you *feel* it, too." Rahilly's breath was expelled in an odd kind of whistle. "It is a gift, Billy. There are not many left to us who see with their feelings, as you do."

"Why me?"

"Because you were in a holy place. Because She *wanted* you to see. Because the world hasn't taught you *not* to see. Not yet, anyways. *She* took you into her. She touched you in your immortal soul, and that is the only thing we are required to love in another human being. What is the rest of us? Seawater and the dust of dead volcanoes, warmed by moonshine."

Billy gasped, at the pain that seared through his head, and the dizziness that came after.

"Listen to me, boy. You will not speak of this to them that don't know and can't understand. My sainted

mother always said it is no use teaching a pig to sing. You
will lose your time and irritate the pig. Oh, you will meet
them that see, as you did today. Most like, they'll be
women. Or drunken poets. And you'll be able to talk to
them, if you remember. But I expect you'll forget. That's
the way with us men. We take a drink, and another, until
we forget."

"I won't forget."

"Go on with you, you great roaring boy. You'll forget
all of it. Breasts of the Goddess!" Rahilly snorted and
capered around the room, making the shape of a woman
of ample endowments with his fluttering hands.

"You'll *forget!*" Rahilly repeated at the top of his
lungs. Then his voice dropped. "Unless something in
this life takes you by the throat and thrusts you into a
larger story."

CHAPTER 7
TIME OF POWER

1.

Billy Johnson had never heard of the Mohawk Valley. He knew the word "Mohawk" only as a synonym for bold revelers, the careless Dublin rakes who broke window glass, terrorized the watch and all beddable women, and supped with the devil in the ruined abbey up on Mount Pellier.

On the other side of the Atlantic, his mother's brother, Captain Warren, had never set eyes on Mohawk country. But as Billy grew to manhood, a dream of a fortune to be made in the Mohawk Valley blazed in Peter Warren's mind.

Uncle Peter counted himself a fortunate man.

Born the younger son, he had run off to sea at the age of twelve, to serve on the *Rye*, a thirty-gun ship of the line, as an ordinary seaman. He had found himself among a different species of men, who talked and walked in a different way, swinging their bodies like pendulums to keep their balance in the roll and pitch of the waves. The influence of *his* mother's brother had plucked him out of the ranks soon enough. His rise from midshipman to lieutenant to command of his first ship was hastened by other men's deaths: a first mate blown apart by the Spanish *guarda-costas,* a captain spitted by black men in leopard skins along the Slave Coast, another taken by the bloody flux. His wealth grew with the prize-ships he seized from the King of Spain in the West Indies. It was doubled when he married into one of the richest merchant dynasties in the Province of New York, in the greatest society event of the year. He built himself a palazzo at the head of Broadway, and a private race course at his Greenwich farm. But on land, as on deck, Peter Warren kept the swinging gait of an ironsides who has yelled defiance into the heart of the storm, and a sovereign contempt for all mealy stay-at-homes.

Billy Johnson had grown into a young man with a rage for life; he was banging around County Meath like a moth in a bottle—as his father complained—when Peter Warren took a plunge into the Mohawk Valley he had never seen.

Captain Warren had been newly appointed to command of the *Squirrel,* the twenty-gun station ship at Boston. One of his first tasks was to escort the doughy widow of Governor Cosby from New York to Boston on the first leg of her homeward journey.

Peter Warren's voice was an instrument he valued. It could be used to order a man flogged through the fleet or to wrap around a lady. He tucked Mrs. Cosby inside it.

She had just buried her husband, a puffy, arrogant bully who had made himself most hated Governor in the memory of New York. Governor Cosby had spent his last months in a drunken delirium, imagining he was other people, including a dead Queen. In his moments of clarity, he was much preoccupied with the health of his bribes. There was only one reason an Englishman of breeding came to the American colonies, with their insufferable climate and fractious assemblies, and that was to make a fortune. Governor Cosby's chief contribution to colonial governance had been to increase the take. He insisted on a one-third share in the patents for Indian land that he confirmed. He had no interest in improving the vast tracts of wilderness he acquired in this fashion or even in inspecting them. The trick was to

urn the titles into ready cash, money to be spent at
ome in England.

But the manner of the Governor's passing—which
roduced scenes of feasting and jubilation in the streets
f the city—had left his affairs in disarray. He be-
ueathed deeds he had failed to convert into cash. Some
f them read obscurely. Straw men were made out to be
wners. There was reference to a "square oblong." The
imits of one parcel were described as a "crooked tree"
nd a "standing stone." The compass references were
qually impenetrable to Mrs. Cosby.

The widow needed counsel. She waxed tearful as she
old pleasing, patient Captain Warren how cruelly she
ad been used and deceived by the vipers of New York
ommerce.

"I allow I know something of business," Warren told
Grace Cosby. "Though I am only an old sea-dog. Busi-
ess, now, is a dirty, dreary, unpleasing subject. I would
hat no lady should ever need to soil herself by contem-
lating it."

Mrs. Cosby was so grateful when Captain Warren
volunteered to look through her husband's papers she
orgot protocol and gave him a peck on the cheek.

Warren withdrew to his stateroom for several hours.

When he dined with the widow, he wore a face of deep
concern and regret, like the chief mourner at a wake.

It was dreadfully difficult, he apologized, pouring the
widow little thimbles of canary wine. Some of the deeds
overlapped with other claims. Some were blemished by
he names of the front men the Governor had used to
mask his dealings. In any event, most of the lands
defined were utterly inaccessible.

"The Mohawk Valley, now." Captain Warren put his
fist on the deed he had singled out. "I am told it is lost in
a forest-sea, ruled by wolves and savages who will eat a
white man as soon as look at him."

The deed was to 13,000 acres, on the south side of the
river, along the Chuctenunda Creek. Warren had heard
the surveyor-general, the dour, scholarly Mr. Colden,
praise the Mohawk flats as the most fertile farmlands in
the Province.

They will be our chiefest granary. There will be a day when the Mohawk Valley will feed the West Indies and all His Majesty's fleets. You may lay money on it.

Captain Warren helped the widow to another serving of partridge pie.

"I loathe to see a lady of quality put at any inconvenience," he assured her.

"Mohawk land is a drug on the market," he apologized again. "But in honor—if I may be so bold, milady—in honor, I say, of the tender sentiments you have inspired in me—"

"Oh, Captain Warren."

He was not a handsome man, short and stubby, tending to a paunch, and high in color. But he used his voice like a master violinist. And his eyes were the blue of fair-weather skies.

By the end of the voyage, Captain Warren was the owner of 13,000 acres in the Mohawk Valley, and the Governor's widow had a note of hand for £110. The purchase price was the equivalent of four cents an acre, provincial money.

Captain Warren deliberated whether he would call his new estate Warrensbush or Warrensburgh. And who would manage and improve it for him.

He gave no thought to the Flint People, except to affright Mrs. Cosby.

But Captain Warren's sway with a widow would join the destinies of Island Woman, Billy Johnson and Carl Weissenberg. And for the Real People, nothing would be the same.

2.

Island Woman remembered the day the lands that would be Warrensbush had been sold.

Mohawk men had put their clan emblems on many deeds without consulting the women who tilled the earth and were its keepers.

The men of the Flint People thought this was a great game when the newcomers first arrived, because they did not believe that the land could be sold.

The land is the body of our Mother. It may be used to support our lives, so long as we live in balance with the plants and the trees, with all our sisters who share it.

The Real People thought the newcomers were crazy to pay for what could not be traded.

Then they saw what happened to the people to the north-east. The Mahicans, the people among whom Hendrick Forked Paths had been born, were reduced to itinerant broom-sellers—those who did not take shelter among the Mohawks, their former enemies. Kannono, the island at the mouth of the great river, was no longer home to the River Indians who had traded with Dutchmen for beads and rum; now the River Indians called it Manhattan, The Place Where They Got Us Drunk.

The Mohawks saw that the newcomers enforced deeds that few of them could read and fewer could understand; they saw white men with surveyors' chains, probing deeper and deeper into their hunting grounds.

Then the clanmothers spoke to the chiefs, and they sent speakers to the Governor of New York. The Mohawks denounced the papers signed by men who spoke for no one but themselves—not even themselves, since they were drunk and their spirits had left their bodies in disgust. They warned that unless these lying deeds were buried, the Flint People would turn against the English. And the Governor was afraid, because the Mohawks held the passes. At their choosing, the Mohawks could open or close the greatest warpaths of America, the water-roads to Canada and the Great Lakes. They could squeeze off the fur trade. They could bring a French army into the Hudson Valley.

So the Governor took counsel with the Lords of Trade, and held an Indian council at which some of the fraudulent land deeds were burned in the sight of the Six Nations. One of these deeds encompassed the bottomlands near Tiononteroken, the Lower Castle, that Peter Warren purchased, years later, for four cents an acre.

But it was impossible for the Mohawk women to know how many deeds their men had signed, or into whose hands they had fallen. Sober, the men said they could not remember what they had done. And their partners among the newcomers were deceitful, none more so than the Commissioners of Indian Affairs, who met at Albany. The Commissioners, charged with handling all relations with the Six Nations, were traders and land barons who drew no line between public interest and private greed.

The flow of rum, and the newcomers' insatiable appetite for land and profit, ensured that, when a fraud was detected and undone, it was quickly committed again.

Governor Cosby—whose widow was charmed by Peter Warren—had publicly burned a deed in favor of the Albany cartel that included the fertile bottomlands near the Lower Castle that were to become Warrensbush.

Then Lieutenant Walter Butler, the hard-drinking commandant of the little garrison of Independent Fusiliers at Fort Hunter, gave a party for the Mohawks. The rum-kegs were opened, and a pipe of claret, and Walter Butler proceeded methodically to drink all his guests— natives and newcomers—under the table. By the end of the revels, Spotted Wolf had a chunk missing from his nose, bitten out by one of the women. Island Woman's son Snowbird—a seasoned warrior now, who asked no one for permission to go on a drinking spree—had stomach cramps and fell into a black dog sulk. And fourteen Mohawk warriors and chiefs had put their marks on a new deed, one the Governor would not burn, since Lieutenant Butler had already assured his blessing by promising him thirteen thousand acres for the favor of a signature and a wax seal.

"This will not stop," Fruitpicker said in the women's council. "The tide from across the great water flows among us like a powerful river. We cannot halt it. We must learn from beaver and shape its course."

"How can we do this?" Island Woman asked.

"We must find true friends among the newcomers. We must make them our own. We must bind them to the Real People so they are one mind, one heart with us."

It is not impossible, Island Woman thought. *There are those who say the People from the Sunrise do not have souls, that they are hungry ghosts who have taken on flesh. But this is not true.*

She had found friends among the newcomers, especially among the Germans, who lived close to the earth and came to her people both to learn and to teach. They worshiped their God in high, stony places. They were interpreters like Conrad Weiser, who had moved through the Valley and down into the Pennsylvania colony, and neighbors like the Freys and the Laucs, from Stone Arabia, who had brought home the body of Island Woman's husband.

She had even found traders at The Net who treated her fairly.

But none of these were powerful enough to serve the clanmother's purpose. For this, what was needed was a man—among the newcomers, women were treated as slaves or concubines. He must be not only high in rank, with the ear of the chiefs of the English, as far as London. He must carry *orenda*, the force of soul.

□

Dreaming, Island Woman journeyed to her guide to seek counsel. She returned in her dreambody to a place of teaching he had opened to her in childhood visions.

She addressed the great dreamer as *raksotha*. Grandfather.

She never called him by a personal name, even in dreaming, though sometimes she called him by a title of respect: *Sakowennakarahtats*, "he who digs up the words and plants them anew." The Interpreter.

She asked the Interpreter if Fruitpicker's path was the right one.

"Can a man be found among the newcomers who will defend our people as well as his own?"

"He will come." The Interpreter's face glowed like polished basswood.

"How will we know him?"

"He will know your ways as if born to them. *Rarenye's*. This one spreads himself. You will feel the soul-force in him. It will make the earth tremble. He will dance with you, run with you, sing with you. He will know your women. You will fear him and distrust him when he comes, and you will be right to do this, because friendship must be cultivated. When he comes, he will be like the other newcomers, except more powerful and therefore more dangerous. Until you make him your own."

"But how can we do this, Grandfather?"

"There is one who is the way."

In the patterns of light on stone, she saw a sun-bright face, the face of a girl with almond eyes.

3.

If he came, the newcomer Fruitpicker hoped for would not be like the men Swimming Voices was using up.

Island Woman's elder daughter went after men as a wolf goes at meat at the end of the starving time. She bled them and sucked them dry. She had even toyed with Dandelion, her brother by adoption. This ravening hunger was not natural among the women of the Real People. The old women muttered that Swimming Voices had a bad spirit inside her. Some sprinkled salt around their living areas when Swimming Voices came near. As she grew older and stranger—as the clouded part of her into which Island Woman could not see grew darker— she took pleasure in feeding the gossips.

Swimming Voices moved out of her mother's longhouse—outside the palisades of the Upper Castle. Men came to build her a sturdy frame house above the creek, like the houses of the white men across the river. They brought her sawn planks from Clements' mill, and oiled paper to cover the windows against cool breezes, and shutters for the hard times. The gossips whispered that she bought these luxuries—and her silks and calicos of midnight blue, hung with silver—with her body and her sorceries.

Swimming Voices no longer joined the women of the village to till the fields where the Three Sisters grew together. While Island Woman took dried cornstalks to make little tubes for her powdered medicines, her daughter wound the husks into dolls. She dressed the cornhusk mannequins in scraps of skin or cloth. Rumors went flying that she was singing over them, to harm or entice people in the village.

Spotted Wolf's wife came down from Caughnawaga, to reclaim her man. Pretty soon she got sick. The gossips said the night before she collapsed, a black bird flapped low over her lodge, croaking her name. Again, suspicion turned on Swimming Voices. Everyone knew she had been fooling with Spotted Wolf, leading him on a dance among her other admirers.

Now Swimming Voices was in danger.

There are things that are without forgiveness. If she was witching Spotted Wolf's woman, and the woman died, not even the clanmother would be able to save her. The Real People killed witches, like they killed rattlesnakes. There was a cleft between two great rocks, on the edge of a spruce bog, where several had been buried alive. There was another hole, in the side of a low ridge, whose edges were charred. It was not much bigger than a woodchuck hole. The old ones pointed it out to the children. They said that was where a witch was trapped, in the shape of one of her animal familiars, and burned to a crisp.

Island Woman went to warn Swimming Voices.

She hesitated at the door of her daughter's house. She had a bad feeling about the place. There was a smell of old, decaying meat.

There was worse inside the house. There was a False Face on the wall, in plain view. That wasn't right. The Faces were to be kept secret. Women fed them, but never used them in the public rituals of healing. If you mistreated a Face or abused it for dark purposes, it could turn into a poison mask, driving the owner and all around her to madness and crimes of blood.

Island Woman felt a cold puff of wind against her neck.

Do you feel me, mother?

The wind swirled inside the room lifted her hair.

Something unseen but substantial pushed up against her.

Do you feel me? You always knew I had the gift.

"Stop it!" Island Woman commanded.

Now she could see her daughter. Swimming Voices was perched on the window sill, between her mother and the brightness of the day. She had not been there when Island Woman had walked into the room.

"Stop it!" Island Woman repeated. *Wahetken.* It is shameful."

"Whatever I am is what you made me." Swimming Voices dropped lightly to the floor and crouched for a moment, her arms swinging between her knees.

You know my weakness, Island Woman acknowledged mutely. *We shut you out. You have proven we were right to do this. But by shutting you out, we left the force that is working in you unbound.*

"Leave Spotted Wolf and his woman alone." Island Woman spoke of the talk in the village.

We must cut out the heart of this black bird, Spotted Wolf's sister had demanded in the women's council.

Swimming Voices laughed. She said she was no longer interested in Spotted Wolf. She had found a new man, a better prospect. She was moving west with him.

Island Woman guessed this must be the half-Frenchman who had turned up in the Valley after the spring melt, spying out the territory for his masters at Niagara. She had smelled a perfume on her daughter that came neither from the flowers and grasses of the field, not from the Dutchmen's truck houses at Albany.

She made no effort to dissuade Swimming Voices; she told herself her daughter would be safer out in Seneca country, that she would come back if she was meant to.

If the way lies through her.

Island Woman felt no pain in parting, no tug of love. Was something missing in her, as a mother?

Why do I feel this is not my daughter?

She knew one thing. Everything she had to give—all her love, strength and knowledge—must be passed on to Bright Meadow, the daughter who remained to her.

In the new moon, Bright Meadow's time of power was coming.

Island Woman knew this, in the tides of her blood.

4.

Women need to be strong. Their bodies must be toughened like fire-hardened wood.

From infancy, Island Woman had schooled her younger daughter in endurance. As soon as her legs were strong enough to carry her, she made Bright Meadow run until she was exhausted, and beyond exhaustion. She made her run underwater, with creek water lapping her thighs. She made her run backward. She made her run through the woods without breaking a twig, without stirring the leaves.

When Bright Meadow was three, Island Woman had taken her down to the river, tied her by the waist to a tree stump, and ordered her to swim upstream, defying the powerful currents.

Sometimes Snowbird, the girl's older brother, was put in charge of her training. Bright Meadow was happy on those days, because Snowbird was softer. He did not expect her to push herself harder and farther than any of the boys, as her mother did, because she was born to be a woman.

When Bright Meadow gave up, or disobeyed, or answered back, Island Woman never beat her. That was unthinkable among the Real People unless the parent was drunk. Island Woman might raise her voice. She might even yell hard enough to shake the sheets of bark around the smokeholes in the roof of the lodge. Sometimes she took a swallow of water and blew it in a fine spray over her daughter's face, to cool her off, when she was little; to shame her, as her body grew straight and tall.

She was careful never to scare the girl more than was needed. If you went round scaring children, the way the newcomers did, you could frighten a child's soul right out of its body. It might back off just a few paces, or maybe hide out behind the house. If you scared it badly, that soul might wander many looks away, and not come back at all. Then the child would develop that dull look in the eyes, the soul-gone look of a person who wasn't

really there. Island Woman had seen it. Then you needed
an *atetshents* in a hurry, to go hunting that soul through
the neverlands to try to bring it back.

Now Bright Meadow's moon-change was coming.

Island Woman had been waiting for it, clocking the
cycles of the moons on a curved piece of elkbone, incised
with thirteen vertical marks and thirteen crescents.

Bright Meadow had seen her mother and her elder
sister go off together to the shelter in the woods at the
time of the new moon. She knew that the women kept
apart from the men for four days in each moon, eating
from sacred vessels, because this was their time of
power, when they returned their blood to the Mother.

All the same, the girl whimpered when the cramping
seized her, low down in her belly, and she smelled her
own blood.

The older girls snickered, "Now the bucks will come
sniffing after you."

Bright Meadow crouched close to the earth, fearful of
what was happening in her body. She sobbed, "I want
ihstenha. I want my mother."

□

Island Woman led her daughter out to a round cabin
among fir trees. She gave Bright Meadow the bowl she
must use to eat, in this special time. She showed her how
she must sit, with her back against a post, to make it
straight, and her knees pressed up against her belly, to
make it flat.

She gave her soft strips of moss, and a fat little clay pot
with a bulge like a belly button.

After nightfall, they heard hoot-owls and the howl of
far-off wolves.

"Why must we stay apart from the village for four
whole nights?" Bright Meadow asked. "Is is because we
are unclean?"

Island Woman laughed, stroking her daughter's hair.
"Men say such things, because they are afraid. This is
our time of power. You now own the power that allows
women to bring new life into the world. We give thanks

to the Mother for this power by returning our blood to the place from whence it comes.

"You will give your first blood to the Three Sisters, on the hill, to thank them for supporting your life.

"This is the beginning of all sacrifice. This offering is sacred and acceptable to the Mother beyond all others, because it comes without killing.

"This power is something that belongs only to women. That is why men are afraid, why they say we are unclean. Men can offer blood only by hunting and killing our relations that walk or creep or fly. This is why we keep our power separate from them, when the moon-flux comes."

Island Woman showed her daughter how to catch her blood in the rounded pot, to return it to the earth among the seeded rows of corn, beans and squash.

They sat together late into the night, and Island Woman retold the stories that explained the nature of birth, and why the bloodlines of the Real People were always traced on the mother's side.

"Ataensic is falling from the Earth-in-the-Sky. She is already with child. This child is a daughter. She is the first woman to give birth in this world, after her mother dances it into being. A power of our Creator comes to her in the form of a cloud. He looks like the mist that rises from the river in the morning and vanishes when the sun is high. He places crossed arrows on her belly. In this way Sky Holder and his brother, the Dark Twin, were conceived."

Bright Meadow listened to the whole of the story without interrupting, without asking, *Is it true?*

Like the story of the Peacemaker, like so many of the sacred stories of the Real People, its heroes were born of woman and spirit.

Where is the father?

Bright Meadow, like all Mohawk children, had spied on lovers and spouses coupling in nests in the woods, or among the shadows of the longhouse. She knew all about the parts of the body and how they worked. She saw that a woman needed a man inside her before she conceived.

Her mother's stories drew her into the Real World, where things worked in a different way.

But her curiosity remained, as the succession of virgin births was recounted.

Where is the father?

"Woman is the life-bringer," Island Woman declared. "Man helps to make the path into the body for the soul that comes home to us. But the true father is the spirit guide that escorts the returning soul and introduces it into the body. *Sehiarak.* Remember this."

□

Island Woman left her daughter to dream alone, when the new moon was low in the sky. The most powerful dreams came with the moon-flux. Bright Meadow must enter them alone. Dreaming, she would face the ordeals that awaited her in the Shadow World. She would learn to see them through. She would meet the allies who would help her to do this.

Island Woman picked her way along the trail to a larger cabin where several of the other women of the Wolf Clan were sleeping by the fire. They bled together, all but the few who were with child or lost, by something dark or diseased in their own souls, to the rhythms of the women's circle.

As she rolled herself in a blanket, feet to the fire, near Fruitpicker, Island Woman acknowledged the fear that had snaked inside her and lay coiled in her stomach.

She was frightened of losing this daughter, as she had lost Swimming Voices.

I am teaching her in the old way, as our grandmothers have always taught us. But is it enough?

Bright Meadow would need to be able to survive in the world of the newcomers as well as that of the Real People. To do this, she would need to be able to number and to read and write.

Protestant missionaries had taught a handful of Mohawks the rudiments of book learning, and there was talk of a new school in Connecticut. More had been taught to read by the blackrobes in Canada.

But the Flint People who sought this knowledge were made to run the gauntlet.

Other newcomers steal only our land. The blackrobes have come to steal our souls.

Still, a way must be found for Bright Meadow to learn. New seasons demanded new tricks. Maybe Island Woman would swallow her scruples and take her down to Fort Hunter, to talk to the Anglican minister.

The newcomers would tell her different stories about the beginnings of things and the process of birth.

□

Bright Meadow tossed and turned for a long time before sleep came for her. She had been told by her mother that what was happening to her was beautiful, but she felt pain.

And the old stories left troubling questions roiling in her head.

If fathers counted for so little, why did the other girls make sneering remarks about Swimming Voices' parentage, calling her "the Frenchman's daughter," long before they started whispering that she was a witch? Wasn't the fact that she and her elder sister were as different as night and day connected to the fact that they had different fathers?

Bright Meadow woke into a terrible dream, filled with the violence of men and horses. Strangers with guns and axes were marching up the Valley, laying waste to the women's cornfields, burning the elmbark lodges, killing the forests.

She tore herself out of this dream.

In that hour before dawn—the twilight of the wolf—it seemed to Bright Meadow that the woods were unnaturally still. She strained for the sound of a night hunter, the rustle of a marauding raccoon, the screech of the owl she had heard before. She heard only the sigh of the wind. A gust from the east brought her something else: a pungent smell, like the salt pork the white men ate.

She sat upright, suddenly aware that newcomers were in the woods.

They could be enemies, preparing a surprise assault on the village. Or casual looters, who would fall on the defenseless women in the waiting places.

I must find out who they are and warn the others.

Bright Meadow crept up the slope of the ridge. She counted four or five strangers, moving in a line along the crest on the far side of the creek. They had guns, but they did not look like soldiers.

The white men seemed to be tied together by chains. Their leader carried a burning torch. He dipped it close to his chest to examine a paper and a round object that gleamed in the light. He made a mark on his paper and tramped on.

Bright Meadow did not know what this meant. But she was sure it flowed from her dream, which warned of possible destruction for all of her people. She must go to her mother.

□

Island Woman was roused by her daughter's cold body pressing against the small of her back, under the blanket.

In whispers, Bright Meadow reported what she had seen.

Island Woman yelped once, and the women of the clan were instantly alert.

"Despite their promises, the newcomers have come here to take the earth that feeds our people. We must send for the warriors. We must scare them so bad they won't dare to come back."

The clanmother agreed this must be done, and done quickly.

But Fruitpicker and Island Woman both knew what would not be said aloud this night, in Bright Meadow's time of power.

The Real People could scare away the newcomers—

settlers, soldiers or surveyors—or kill them. This time, and the next, and the time after. Then a time would come when the Real People could no longer do this, and Bright Meadow's dream would become their life in the Shadow World. Unless they found the one Island Woman's teacher had promised, and bound him to their ways.

CHAPTER 8
WELCOMED BY LARKS

1.

In the petty principalities along the Rhine, the cycle of famine and flood, drought and hot fevers, rolled on. A mad duke was succeeded by a myopic scholar-duke who had no better notion of how to provide for his people and no better prospect of shielding them from the armies of stronger monarchs. There was talk of another great war, growing out of a looming vacancy on the imperial throne of the Hapsburgs. And the New World was a dream across an aching distance.

But hardly a week went by in the valley of the Klöpferbach that failed to bring a traveler, a gypsy hawker or even a letter with news of America. Cat Weissenberg fed on these stories; it was these, more than the solid fare at her father's table, or the pastor's words from the pulpit, that gave her the strength to carry on.

Old Anna Laucs received a message from her son Adam, who had sailed for America when Cat was still in swaddling clothes. The message came in a letter from a minister in Pennsylvania to the pastor of the Lutheran church in the village, wrapped between fierce quotations

from scripture about the election of the Chosen People
and the ordeals prescribed for them. Adam had his own
farm now, on the border of the New York colony. He was
doubling his wheat crop every year. The soil was wonderfully rich; with the application of modern principles
of fertilization, unknown to the natives and older-
established settlers, it gave in abundance. The Indians in
the vicinity were feared for their savagery, even among
the other tribes. But they had been good neighbors to the
little German community at Stone Arabia.

Stone Arabia.

What a wild, beautiful name! When Cat said it aloud,
she pictured the sun glinting on terraces of polished
stone.

There was a caution in Adam's message. If others were
to come, they must at all costs *stay out of the hands of the
soul-drivers.*

Many of those who had signed deeds of indenture in
exchange for their passage had been greatly abused. An
indentured servant, bound for five or seven years, was
regarded as no better than a white slave, and was often
treated worse than African slaves, whose masters had a
greater interest in their longevity, since they were bound
for life.

There were many other tales of America: of new
fortunes to be made in tobacco, which Cat thought a
noxious, foul-smelling weed; of wild men viewed at a
traveling circus at Amsterdam or Cologne. The wild men
of America, it was said, were hairless even between their
legs, and built of compacted muscle. They went about
naked except for their tattoos, ran on four legs as fleet as
deer and ate the flesh of their enemies. Yet at Stone
Arabia, the savages were counted friends.

Cat spoke of America with the neighbors for whom
she sewed and mended, and within the circle of women
who were learning to read Bible stories at the church on
Sundays, when the men could hardly object to their
absence from home.

But her father would not tolerate talk of America
under his roof.

"It will set off your mother," he complained, though Cat thought what her mother needed was to be "set off," whatever that meant. Margret Weissenberg drifted about with a perennial, vacant smile that frightened and infuriated her daughter. She paid no mind to Johann's infidelities. He had a new woman, whom Cat detested, pink and shiny and brimming over, trotting about in her low-cut gowns like a pig on its fat hind legs.

But Fat Bertha was less offensive to Cat than her father's repeated threats to marry her off. These threats had taken on concrete form since Karl Zimmer's wife died of a colic. Karl was a man her father's age, well-off, because he was a cabinetmaker as well as a farmer; he claimed to have made a sideboard that was in the ducal palace in Württemberg. But he was old and warty, and his hands trembled before the first drink of the day. And he smelled.

"I won't have him," Cat announced. "Not even if I have to starve."

Her father snarled but went off to his Bertha, that first time. But Cat knew he would try hard to make her bend. Karl had promised a handsome dowry: four cows and a team of horses.

In a rare moment of lucidity, her mother said, "No one escapes pain."

That was very true, Cat thought. *I can live with pain. But I will not agree to be dwindled, to be shrunk by men.*

She had heard reports of the customs of another savage tribe that put heavy weights on the heads of its girl children, to flatten their skulls to conform to their idea of beauty. Cat had felt that weight, pressing down on the brain, crushing thought and imagining, softening the bones.

I will not let them do this to me.

Helga Zee, one of the women in the reading group, said her family was planning to immigrate to America by way of Ireland. It was possible to find work in Dublin, to save money to pay for the passage and escape the souldrivers. In England, Palatine refugees were no longer welcome, because of mob protests against the competi-

tion for work. But across the Irish sea, restrictions were
laxer. There was already a community of emigrants from
the Rhineland in Dublin, their minds set on America.

When the women left the church, Cat hurried after
Helga.

"I want to come with you."

There was sympathy in Helga's face. There were no
secrets between their families.

"You're not old enough, Cat."

"I am old enough to be married. Besides, my mother
comes with me."

Helga's face clouded. Where they were going, there
was no room for dead weight.

"I can support both of us," Cat said quickly. "I am the
best seamstress in the village, and you know I can make
anything to order. There will always be work for me."

Helga did not dispute this. She said, "What about
your father?"

"He doesn't believe in America."

Helga frowned. "My Friedrich doesn't believe in
breaking up families."

"I will talk to my father again," Cat promised. She felt
that crushing weight, pressing down on her brain. *I will
not give in to it. I will not be broken.*

2.

Anyone could see, Billy Johnson's father insisted, the
boy was not made to be a quill-driver. But Anne Warren
Johnson was adamant: Billy would have his chance at
Trinity.

Denis Rahilly's appointment as Billy's tutor had been
cancelled abruptly, when the two of them were discovered sleeping off a drunk in the hayloft. But Rahilly had
remained Billy's mentor and spiritual director in most
of the areas the boy cared to know about, other than
horses and women—and Rahilly had made himself
useful in the latter domain too, covering for Billy when
he kept secret assignations with Georgina Tracy. She was
a fetching, frisky girl with gray eyes that seemed lilac in

half-light. She was Andrew Tracy's sister and shared his snobberies, but would throw precedence to the wind for a lover readier than the bloodless dandies her family considered suitable admirers. Part of the thrill of meeting her was in the stealth and the ruses required. They met in shut-up apartments of the great house her father managed. Billy would steal through hedgerows, like an American Indian, hiding from gardeners and gamekeepers, round the edge of the lake where swans glided.

"There is no game like it," he had avowed to Rahilly, who was curiously shy about affairs of the bedroom, and would silence Billy with a jest or a song when he reported too vividly on what he was learning from the older girl in those vast rooms where the furnishings were draped in white sheets.

Rahilly, the coy bachelor, went on playing lookout for Billy in his amours, lying when necessary. When one of them was caught, it was Rahilly who had to face the Tracy family, and he stuck to his story that he had been after a rabbit, even when they told him he would be horsewhipped.

"I shall miss you most," Billy told him, when he was packed to leave for Dublin.

"Go on with you, boy. What about the filly?"

"There will be others."

Yet he was more grateful to Georgina Tracy than he would admit. Just as Rahilly had been his first teacher in matters of spirit, the Tracy girl was his first teacher in the art of pleasing a woman.

It is an art that will take you far, she had promised, when he had succeeded at last in sating her formidable appetites.

What Billy had learned from these teachers was not widely recognized as the stuff of scholarship. Fortunately for Johnson, academic merit was held in no exaggerated regard at the Faculty of Law of Trinity College. The members of the faculty applied themselves stoutly to defending their title as the hardest drinking school in Ireland. What was required of a Trinity man was a

nominal adherence to the Protestant cause, a readiness
to blaze—to duel with pistols—and the means to sustain a life of organized debauchery. Either Trinity's
reputation had not reached to Smithstown, or Anne
reasoned that her favorite son would be exposed to no
worse temptations in Dublin than at home.

Billy applied himself to new lessons. He learned how
to box with the Orchard Street butchers' boys, who often
laid in ambush for Trinity scholars as they trooped back
from compulsory Sunday services at Saint Patrick's. He
learned how to blaze at nine paces, according to the
Tipperary Rules. He learned to knock the stem off his
wineglass, and drink without setting it down until there
was no more left to swill. He learned more about the art
of pleasuring women. One useful tutorial was conducted
in the upstairs room of Meg Ryan's, with several genial
ladies of the town, whom he serviced in order of
seniority. They were so pleased with his promptness they
decided, without dissent, to forgo payment.

He explored more arcane corridors with a new drinking crony, Jemmy Fitzsimmons, an initiate of the Hellfire Club. This society conducted midnight sessions in a
stone lodge up on the brow of Mount Pellier, where a
place of honor was always set at table for the unseen
guest, Prince Lucifer. If there was madness in all of this,
it was the madness of Ireland, whose tribal kings had
been displaced by foreign users who saw the natives as
inferior. Rakery was a diversion from the misery of the
land. For Billy, this studied oblivion was perhaps more
necessary than for those of his fellow-scholars who were
English by race as well as manners and ambition. His
roots were in this land. The beggars that florid foxhunt-
ers chased away with cries of "View Halloo" were the
same people who had dragged him out of a ditch to be
born. Yet he could do—or so he convinced himself—
little or nothing for them, except when he had blunted
the edge of his father's wrath against a dilatory tenant, or
when he returned to Rahilly's hut in the shut-up times
with a gift of a bottle, to listen to his stories till they
drove the stars out of the sky.

3.

Cat Weissenberg dreamed of a chrysalis.

I am caught inside gauzy wrappings. The light filters through, but I can see nothing distinctly. It is stifling in here. I must have air. I must see what is outside the cocoon. I must have the world.

I am butting and pushing. The wrappings are sticky. They enmesh me like a spider's web. But I am growing bigger, more powerful. The wrappings stretch. They are yielding to me. There is a place where the light is stronger. I am working my way through it.

This is as hard as being born.

Now I am in the light. But I recognize no clear shapes. Everything is blurred. And I move slowly, slowly, as if motion is unnatural to me. I am soft and sluggish and afraid. I am scared of falling, terrified of things that spring and rip and devour.

I am falling. I am lost.

No.

Down is up. I am sailing on air. My wings hold yellow fire, like the sun. A whole world opens below me. It has been washed clean. The colors are brilliant.

The brightness of flowers welcomes me. Someone comes to guide me.

He leads me into the heart of the flower, through silky veils that shiver and part. We dance in a shower of golden pollen.

Waking to the barnyard sounds of her father's pig farm, Cat ran her tongue across her lips to taste the sweetness.

She found she was moist between her thighs. And tender, as if a strong lover had come to her in the night.

She felt bruised in many places. Her sensations were pleasurable more than painful. Though she could not find the marks, the strength of a dream lover's hands and the sharpness of his teeth lived with her.

□

She thought of the new boy in the village, the blacksmith's apprentice. His name was Otto. He was tall and well-made, with strong, knowing hands. He did not look at her furtively, as other men did, stripping her breasts and buttocks with their eyes, avoiding her face. He had a trade for which there was a market anywhere. In the New World, a 'prentice would surely be worth as much as a master tradesman in the old.

She would ask him to walk with her, among the hollyhocks. Maybe he would be the one to brave the passage to America with her. She must take care not to speak too boldly, in case she scared him away. In case he was not the one in the dream.

She let him kiss her chastely, with her lips closed, during the third of their rambles at dusk. He was quite good-looking, and he touched her with gentleness, even respect, despite his strength and her forwardness. But nothing stirred inside her. He was not the one from the dream.

Her father was waiting for her by the stile, flushed and angry.

"Karl Zimmer must have an answer," he puffed. "Karl is a serious man, a man of property. He won't want you if he knows you go shaking your ass at any young runt. You'll be spoiled goods."

She tried to avoid argument, walking around the stile, swinging over the low wall. Her father rushed to block her path. He had been drinking. A deep brick red had spread from the sides of his neck up to the cheekbones. The skin of his face was stretched too tight, like the skin of a sausage about to burst under heat.

"Bitch-dog!" Johann Weissenberg muttered. "I'll teach you to defy me!"

He swung at her. She ducked and the first blow whistled above her head. But the speed and accuracy of his next movement surprised her. He rammed his great fist into her chest, above the heart. She dropped straight down on her bottom. A driving pain shot from her pelvic bone.

A woman's voice shrilled, *"Unanstandig!* Indecent! Shameful!"

Johann turned and stared at his wife. She was running toward him, and the vacancy of her eyes had been replaced by focused hatred. She was carrying a pitchfork longer than her body.

"You'll never touch our daughter again!" Margret screamed, thrusting the prongs of the hayfork straight at her husband's swag belly.

He rolled out of the way.

His jowls shook with his laughter.

"Noch einmal!" he bellowed. "Do it again!"

Her father could not stop laughing. His belly shook. He turned a jig.

Margret hit him with the butt end of the hayfork. It glanced off his skull, and he stopped capering. The red flush spread across his whole face, drowning the tracery of broken capillaries. His eyes bulged. A thick curse plopped from his swollen lips.

Then he gasped and clutched at his throat like a condemned man pulling at the noose. His muscles stood out. His neck stretched. His tongue bulged between lips blue and swollen.

The women watched him fall.

They watched until they were sure the life was gone. By that time, a soft rain was falling over the valley. Cat took her mother's arm and led her the long way back to the house. The gentle rain settled in their hair.

At the house, they shook the damp and the hateful memories from their hair and their clothes, like wet dogs.

Cat said, "We are free."

4.

Billy Johnson was in his second year at Trinity College when Jemmy Fitzsimmons took new lodgings, near Saint Stephen's Green, and became infatuated with a housemaid. She was foreign, he told Billy, one of the

German refugees who seemed to pour off every ship from the Continent. Fitz had fallen hard. By his own admission, he had come at the German girl from all directions—with a show of guineas, even hints of marriage. But she would have none of him.

Billy watched Fitz's obsession decoct into a dank fever.

Johnson hardly knew his friend when Fitz staggered into the Eagle before noon, his hair loose as a scarecrow's, red-eyed, in a shapeless old hunting coat.

Billy worried the meat from the last of his breakfast chops and pushed the pitcher of ship's beer across the table.

"I must have the bitch!" Fitz stared like a madman. "She swears she is intact, but I saw her at close quarters with Foley on the stairs!"

"You are not yourself, man. Abstinence is making you ill."

"Last evening, I rang the bell for tea. She came in her wrapping-gown, the doxy, tempting me beyond all pity. I begged her to sit, and she agreed, but kept the door open. I made to kiss her, and she let me. But when I got the door closed, the trollop slipped through my hands, smiling all the while. She makes sport of me."

"What of it? *Nil admirari.*" Billy remembered something of Rahilly's dog-Latin. "Stare at nothing. There is plenty more game to be started in Dublin."

"I told her I was going to Wexford for a few days. I said a gentleman friend, a visitor from Navan, would take my rooms while I am away. I wish you to go to my lodgings and try your luck with her."

"You are not yourself, Fitz."

"You must say you will go!"

Billy was astonished by his friend's intensity even more than the strangeness of his request.

"You say I am to try my luck with her?"

"That is the nub of it."

"May I know the lady's name?"

"It is Catherine. Catherine Weissenberg."

For Johnson, the name conjured up a big, buxom woman, pink as a geranium, with that shouting good

health he associated with Germans. Well, what of it? H
was catholic in his tastes in women, if not in his religio

"I wish to understand you perfectly. You ask me t
offer the lady a rudeness. Very well. But what if sh
complies?"

"Then you'd best put it home to her, Billy." Fitz
simmons' attempt at a smile made him look ready t
heave up his beer.

□

Billy hired a chair and arrived at the house off Baggc
Street like a lord, in his long green coat and his shirt c
finest cambric. A dark-eyed, slender girl, brown as
Spaniard, showed him up to the front room on th
second floor. It reeked of Fitz's Virginia shag, althoug
the windows were open.

"Is Catherine in the house?" Billy asked the girl, as sh
laid out the clothes from his traveling-bag.

"She might be." There was something foreign in th
girl's speech, but the evasion was flawlessly Irish.

"Would you be good enough to ask her to fetch me
dish of tea?"

The girl did not respond immediately. She turned t
him with an absent, languid expression. He found some
thing keenly appealing in this languor—though, in
servant, it bordered on impertinence—and tried t
picture her without the cap and apron. He wanted t
catch her eyes, but they drifted lazily over the gol
threads in his waistcoat, half-hidden by the lashes.

"Is it only Cat's tea that will do for you then, M
Johnson?"

"Cat. Is that what you call her?" There was promise i
the name. "You may tell Cat," he said formally, "that
have a message from Mr. Fitzsimmons."

"Oh. Mr. Fitzsimmons." The eyelids drooped lower
She yawned and stretched, so the fabric tightened acros
her chest. She lived in her body without inhibition, lik
an animal, and there was no servility in her at all.

He gave her a shilling, and in full view of him, sh
tucked it away inside her bodice.

He admired the easy roll of her hips as she left the room. *Fitz, the slow mule, has his eye on the wrong one.*

Twenty minutes later, there was a tap at the door.

"Come!"

It was the black-eyed girl, returning with the tea things.

"Is Cat not below?"

"No, sir. Cat is not below."

It was the mockery in her voice that gave her game away.

"You are Cat!" he exploded, both astonished and delighted. "You must forgive me. You are not what I expected."

"I am sorry if I fail the gentleman's expectations."

"That is not it, at all. I mean to say—I understood you were German."

"Not all Germans are fair. Not all Irishmen are small." She stared at the big man boldly.

God's pistols, Johnson swore inwardly. *You are playing with me. I shall teach you a game or two.*

"You must sit and take tea with me."

"It would not be proper. Besides, there is only one cup."

"Then you must take some brandy with me." He got out his flask.

"No, sir. My mistress does not tolerate drinking among the servants. Mrs. Carlow gave the cook the sack last week for stealing a cup of sherry."

"Then sit with me, at least."

"Only if we leave the door open."

On these terms, he got her onto a padded settee.

"You said you had a message from Mr. Fitzsimmons."

"Only that he is your ardent admirer. Now I see the reason."

He expected her to blush, and sensed the warmth of the blood beneath her skin. But whatever her emotion, it did not betray her in her cheeks. To be near her made him think of sunlight on ripening grapes in a summer vineyard. He moved to join her on the settee, but she slipped away from him. She said Mrs. Carlow would be wanting her tea-cakes, and would only permit him to squeeze her hand. When he attempted to take her by the waist, she evaded him, smiling.

He told her, "You are a girl that is made for loving."

"No girl, sir."

"How old are you?"

"Seventeen." Her eyes flashed. "There was not time for girlhood, where I was raised."

"A woman then," he saluted her with his cup. "A woman made for love."

Her reply stung lightly, like a grass-whip in the fields of boyhood sport.

"I think that you, Mr. Johnson, can give a woman anything except love."

5.

For a hunter, the sport is in the chase. Seized with a violent desire for this slight, olive-skinned girl of seventeen, Billy Johnson stalked and laid traps. Late and early, under Mrs. Carlow's roof, he would pull on the bell-rope, summoning Cat with transparent requests to set a fire or brush his clothes, showering her with favors from the market and gold sovereigns that she accepted as her due, without thanks. On the third day, she allowed him a dry kiss on the lips when he blocked her path on the stairs.

That same evening, when he returned from the tavern to find her making his bed, he managed to catch her up into a tight embrace. He found her mouth, and it opened to him. Her body yielded, but her eyes denied him. Then she pressed a hand to his heart, pushing him away.

"You are ready for me. I can always tell."

"You flatter yourself, Mr. Johnson."

"It's no lie. I can smell it."

"You do not speak like a gentleman, sir."

"I speak what is in me. Do you deny me for that?"

He watched as she smoothed her dress and gathered up the soiled linen. The plain domesticity of the scene and the glow of her skin under candlelight, increased his desire. He set his hands to her waist. It was so narrow he could almost circle it. He wanted to test the springiness of her hips, but she leaped away, toward the door he had bolted behind them.

He laughed and bounded after her. He sucked on her full lower lip. He hoisted her so they stood belly to belly, so she could feel the power she stirred in him. *She will scratch and bite,* he thought. *But she will not cry out, for fear of her mistress. Once I kindle the woman in her, she will not wish to deny me.*

Cat said softly, "It would be a gallant conquest, Mr. Johnson, to impose on a poor serving-girl, a foreigner without friends in this town."

Chastened, he set her free.

"I was not made for a monk," was all his apology. "And Cat, I think you are no bride for a convent."

She said, with a smile that did not reach her eyes, "You make a jest of life, Mr. Johnson. I do not have that privilege."

□

She was damnably clever for a serving girl, Billy reported to Jemmy Fitzsimmons. Clever and self-possessed. She must have ambitions far beyond a place in Mrs. Carlow's house. The key, no doubt, lay there.

Each day, at the Eagle Tavern or in the courtyard of Trinity College, Fitz accosted him, anxious for news of the progress of the siege. Fitz's prurience and suspicion soon grew wearisome. How many times had he kissed her? Where had he placed his hands? What hope had she given him of a full engagement?

"You are not telling me the whole of it," Fitz accused him.

"If you have no faith in me, you had best find another accomplice."

"No, no, Billy. But you must swear to tell me *everything.*"

Johnson began to fear his friend had lost either his mind or his manhood. What man in his prime makes love by proxy?

But he was now less interested in Fitzsimmons' condition than in Cat.

He learned that the maid had Wednesday afternoon off and volunteered to escort her to Phoenix Park.

"I shall hire a carriage. You will be grander than any lady in Dublin."

"I cannot," she told him.

"There is no such word as cannot."

"Then I will not."

"Why? Do you like me so little?"

"I go to my mother on Wednesdays," she explained "She is alone. She has only me."

Cat told him she had lost her father to a hot fever.

"I'll escort you to your mother," Johnson volunteered

She refused him abruptly. She said she would not have her mother know she was reduced to working as a servant in a boardinghouse for single men. Billy would have argued, but fell silent because—for the first time—he read real fear in the girl's face.

He did not use that Wednesday afternoon for his usual pastimes, at the Eagle or Meg Ryan's or a cockfight, or a rarer visit to the college library. He stalked Cat from Mrs. Carlow's house through the Dublin streets past the cathedral into the low warren of working men's hovels huddled in the lee of slaughterhouses and distilleries below the south embankment of the Liffey. It was the first time Billy Johnson had set foot in this corner of the Liberties and, in his gentleman's finery, he drew street boys and beggars as dung attracts flies.

"Plaze your honor!"

He looked down at the pale round face of a young girl cradling a baby, limp as a rag doll, and dropped a farthing into the outstretched palm.

The chorus rose from a dozen throats. "Plaze your honor! Plaze your honor!"

He hurried on, jumping brown puddles, anxious not to lose sight of Cat's pink shawl in the narrow, winding alleys. The low houses crushed together were worse than the birds' nests of the cotters. Through glassless windows, he saw whole families fighting drunk, or vying for space on a dirty wad of straw. A jiggling, drunken bawd hailed him from a doorway, scrolling her shift up to her waist. The stench of raw sewage assailed him on all sides; it came from great heaps of ordure, rising window-high behind the houses. Loosened by the morning rain, the filth oozed under back doors and trickled out into the streets. Worse smells were emitted by the slaughter-houses and the soap factories. Billy took a pinch of snuff, to shut out the stink, and nearly lost the silver box when he was obliged to swing his cane to ward off a light-fingered boy who had already made one try for his watch.

He rounded a corner and saw the arrogant battlements of Dublin Castle above the rooftops. Twenty feet away, Cat turned into one of the houses. It was as wretched as its neighbors, except that it had shutters, and even a window box with yellow flowers—a breath of country air in those fetid stews.

He decided he would risk walking past and wait for Cat at the far end of the street. As he idled along, his escort of beggars dropped behind. The voices that gusted out of the houses spoke a foreign tongue, presumably German. It seemed he was now in a Palatine ghetto. When he positioned himself at the corner, two rough-looking, round-headed men came out of one of the houses and stood staring at him. They did not respond to his casual greeting. They lit their pipes and watched.

Billy, feeling distinctly uncomfortable, sought shelter below the wall of the corner house. But when Cat slipped out the door of her mother's house, she pounced on him in his place of hiding, eyes blazing.

"Are you happy, now you see how we live? My grandfather built an orangery for an Emperor! Are you satisfied, to shame me in front of my own people?"

"I wanted to protect you." Once the words were out, he realized they were truer than he had intended.

"I am safer here than at Mrs. Carlow's, under the same roof as you!"

"Are those jolly fellows your bodyguards, then?" He waved his cane at the silent watchers.

"They are friends. They want to go to America."

"America! I have an uncle in America. His name is

Captain Warren. He has made himself a great man by bearding the King of Spain and taking his treasure ships among the Caribees. I have heard many of your countrymen have gone to the New World. Is it in your mind to go?"

"I had some thought—" She left the rest of it unspoken.

"It would not be a thing to be ventured without friends."

There was something new in her eyes, something fierce and intent. It seemed to him the wind nudged them both, at that moment, bringing a whiff of clean salt air into that diseased hollow.

"Take supper with me," he proposed, "and I will tell you all there is to know about America."

□

He plied her with wine and with stories of Captain Warren in an upstairs room at Finn's Tavern—not the Eagle, because he did not wish to encounter Jemmy Fitzsimmons or his usual crowd. She drank sparingly, he noted, and paid little attention to his tales of how Uncle Peter had fought with cannibals on the coasts of Africa and had almost certainly discovered the North-West Passage. She asked pointed, practical questions about daily wages, land titles, and the price of grain that quite overpowered the slender knowledge of conditions in America that Billy had gleaned from his uncle's infrequent letters and gossip around the table at Smithstown.

If the girl were a paid doxy in a bordello, she would soon be the madam of the house.

Billy was obliged to improvise. He told Cat that Uncle Peter, as the ruler of the Royal Navy in the American plantations, most definitely had the power to grant lands for settlement all the way down the great Mississippi Valley.

"Is the Mississippi in New York? I thought it belonged to the French."

Billy's confusion was swallowed by his smile. "I was referring, of course, to the *top bit*. My uncle's influence is rather extensive."

"What of the wild men? The Mohawks?"

Mohawk—or *Mohock,* as it was rendered with some frequency—had become a household word in England and Ireland since the visit of the Four Kings to London five years before Billy was born. Some of the hell-raisers of Billy's vintage, the ones who roamed the streets by night, blowing out the lamps with gunpowder squibs and terrorizing the watch, called themselves Mohocks. These were the only Mohawks about whom Billy Johnson could speak with authority.

"I'll teach you something of wild men," he announced, and plunged his hands into her petticoats.

That night, she did not deny him. Though it may have crossed his mind, as he made free with her body, that she acted—or failed to react—out of calculation more than concupiscence, this did not interfere with his pleasure. She was deliciously tight, which made him suspect, at the outset, that she might still be intact. Then she took so spirited a role in the game that he found it hard to believe she had not had a seasoned trainer. When they had learned something of each other's needs, she worked her inner muscles to wonderful effect. "I am welcomed," he gasped, "by a hundred larks' tongues."

6.

He was not Cat's first. She had learned that her body enabled her to use men, while they thought they were using her. She had needed to know this, during her first cruel winter in Ireland. There had been no work for a seamstress, let alone a custom tailor, because the rulers of Ireland—at the behest of the mill owners of Manchester—were engaged in crushing the local manufacture of linen and fabrics, and master cutters now vied with simple sewing women for work. To survive, Cat had done things she preferred to put out of her mind, even as her body moved on the bed. Her mother had taught her how to be absent; it was the one thing her mother had to teach.

But it was different with Billy.

She had felt the force field between them when he first

crossed the threshold of the house with bay windows on Baggot Street.

She had felt him inside her before he first offered to kiss her.

It is the dream.

She had known it instantly, though she feigned indifference.

When he touched her bare skin, his hands praised her.

I am a silk flower, she said without speaking. *I am a closed bud, opening layer upon layer, circle within circle.*

She did not want him to stop.

She said nothing of this to Billy, because it would seem like surrender.

She did not want to love him.

But love is dangerous. It comes like a pickpocket, stealing your heart before you know what you have lost.

7.

In the morning, Billy strolled north along Dawson Street. Chaffinches hopped about the pavement. There was a song on his lips, an old ditty about Grania Waile, the Irish she-pirate who dared to divorce her warlord husband, Richard-in-Iron. It came lilting out of his past, out of a smoky evening at Rahilly's, where a blind harpist, revered among the Gaels, had come in quest of an answering spirit.

The soft morning rain seeped into the heavy wool of his coat. It did not dampen Billy's mood. He threw back his head and boomed out the chorus of his song, to the alarm of respectable passers-by:

Sing didro, sing bobro,
Sing Grania Waile—

Then Jemmy Fitzsimmons jumped out of nowhere and grabbed him by the shoulder.

"Where have you been?" Fitz demanded, his lip trembling, his voice shrilling dangerously high. "You have avoided me for two days!"

"Get a bridle on yourself, sir. You prate like a jealous housewife. People will begin to suppose there is an unnatural affection between us."

"By God!" Fitz erupted, peering into Billy's face. "You've done it, haven't you? You've had her!" Bright points of color flamed in his cheeks.

"I will not speak with you unless you calm yourself."

"Damme, you put it home to her, by God!"

"You begin to vex me, sir. You are speaking of an honest woman, worthy of the addresses of a better man than you."

"Damn you and your tainted trollop! I would not touch the bawd if she came to my bed, now you have poxed her!"

This drew coarse laughter and shocked hisses from various of the passers-by.

Billy lost his normal high color and grew deathly pale. What his friend had spat at him should be answered with dueling pistols. But he tried to make allowance for Fitz's condition. Jealousy, liquor and thwarted lust had turned his mind.

"I want you out of my lodgings today!" Fitz shouted.

"You would do well to stay elsewhere," Johnson told him. "As I said, Cat is an honest woman."

"You can go to the devil. I shall go where I please."

□

When Billy told Cat he was moving out, she said only, "It is for the best. Old Carlow has already started sniffing after me."

But she agreed to meet him the following Wednesday, and he promised to write to Captain Warren on behalf of her family.

He pressed money into her hand. She took it matter-of-factly. But later, when he passed her on the stairs, he saw her eyes glisten. It was difficult for a man of Johnson's upbringing to conceive of an affection for a woman of her class that operated above the level of the solar plexus. Yet he resolved in his heart, at that moment, that he would look out for Cat Weissenberg.

□

Past midnight, two days later, Billy was crouched by the fire in his room at Mrs. Brady's across the river, a musket-shot north of the humpbacked bridge. He had one hand on a book—Virgil, because his college tutor was after him to improve his Latin—and the other on the poker he had stuck into the fire. When the poker glowed red, he thrust it into a hearty bowl of bumbo—rum, sugar-water and nutmeg—and stirred until the potion steamed.

He had barely wetted his lips with the toddy when there came a scratching at his door, like a stray cat begging for entry.

He opened the door and saw the girl. She might have fallen in the river. Her matted hair stuck to her forehead. She was shivering under her light coat, clutching a sorry bundle of clothes.

At her heels was Mrs. Brady in her wrapping-gown, red-eyed and anxious.

"Upon me conscience, Mister Johnson," his landlady reproached him. "This is no hour to be bringing in company, not in any house of good report. Whatever will people say?"

Billy salved Mrs. Brady's conscience with a half-sovereign and sent her back to her bed grumbling.

He made Cat take off her outer clothes and set them to dry by the fire when he had her wrapped snug inside a blanket.

Her sentences broke over each other, to end in sobs, as she tried to explain what had happened. The picture leaped at him from the tumble of words. Jemmy Fitzsimmons had called for tea. When she had fetched it, he had locked the door and attacked her like a rabid animal, cursing her for a whore and telling her that if a bog paddy who gave himself airs was good enough for her, then she could not deny a true English gentleman. She fought him, and he hurt her so badly that she could not stifle the screams. The clamor roused Mrs. Carlow, who came beating on the door, threatening to see both of them in Marshalsea prison. When Fitz came to his senses and let her go, Mrs. Carlow threw Cat's things in the street and ordered her to follow.

"I could not go to my mother like this." Cat shivered. Johnson pressed the toddy to her lips.

"Drink it down. It will warm you."

"What am I to do?"

"Rest." He turned down the bed and motioned for her to lie in it. Her hair spilled over the pillow. She tensed when he smoothed an errant lock from her cheek but managed, with a tight smile, to indicate that she would offer no protest if he chose to have his way with her. He drew the covers up to her chin and kissed her forehead.

"You no longer want me?" she frowned up at his reserve, lapsing back into the slight stiltedness of expression that was the only clue that English was not her native tongue.

"You're not ready for me tonight. I know these things."

He blew out the candle and sat on the floor beside her in the ruddy light from the fire.

She traced the contours of his face with her hand like a blind person, from the cheekbone along the firm line of the jaw to the sensualist's cleft in the chin.

"Mister Johnson," Cat murmured drowsily, "you are a sweet, sweet man."

8.

He went looking for the Honorable James Fitzsimmons after breakfast and found him at the Eagle, engaged in ridding himself of one hangover by drinking up another. Billy made an appointment with Jemmy by knocking him off his bench with a blow to the shoulder and another to the ribs.

When the two men met in Phoenix Park, in a cold dawn, Billy had enlisted Mick Tyrrell for a second. Mick was his cousin, sandy and wiry, a practiced ball-driver who was frightened of nothing on God's earth. As a boy, Mick had run off from home to enlist in the Royal Irish, and his father had had to pay good money to buy him back.

A watery sun lacquered the instruments the surgeon had laid out on the grass. Fitz's lugubrious second delivered the Code of Honor in a nasal bray. Then the seconds walked out the prescribed nine paces, and instructed the principals to remove their coats, take their positions and load.

Fitz's hands shook badly as he tried to put the balls in the mouths of his pelters. There was a delay while he engaged in a muffled exchange with his second, who shook his long horse's face in evident disgust as he stepped back to address Johnson and Tyrrell.

"Mister Fitzsimmons says he is prepared to forgive the slight to his honor and withdraw his challenge, if Mister Johnson will tender his apology."

The offer was directed, as etiquette required, to Johnson's second. But it was Billy who snapped back, "No apology. Mister Fitzsimmons has impugned a lady's honor."

The second went back to confer with Fitz and returned at once.

"Will you look at this trotter?" Mick Tyrell complained to Billy. "Why don't they get on with it?"

"Mister Fitzsimmons says he is ready to make an apology for any imagined slight to Mister Johnson's honor." Fitz's second cleared his throat, patently embarrassed.

"Mister Fitzsimmons is plainly a man who is high in his blood for honor," observed Billy. "Remind them of the rules, Mick."

"Rule Seven," said Mick Tyrrell, solemn as a judge. "No apology can be received *after* the parties meet, without a fire. I am surprised you need reminding."

This ended the parleying. Fitz at last got his pistols loaded. He appeared to have trouble keeping his balance as he waited, ashen-faced, for the starting signal.

"Blaze away, boys!" cried his second.

But Fitz's nerve was gone. Before the first word was out, he had pulled the trigger—on a flash in the pan. His face was less than human as he realized his situation, staring into the mouth of the pistol Billy had yet to fire. His bowels rebelled. Mick Tyrrell held his nose as he growled, "Have at him, Billy!"

"Stand your ground, damn you!" Fitz's outraged second yelled at him as he lurched toward the nearest beech, hugging his belly.

When Fitz staggered back, his second apologized formally to Billy and Mick.

"It is still your turn to fire, Mister Johnson."

"That is no matter to me. We will begin again."

"Very well."

The man was still having trouble with his principal. *"Medio tutisimus ibis,"* Billy heard him urge Jemmy Fitzsimmons. Johnson had learned enough from Rahilly to recognize the old tag from Ovid. Freely translated in blazers' language, it meant "You're safest going for the middle." The second added, "Hip the fellow! Hip, my boy, *hip!*"

This time, when the signal came, the two duelists fired simultaneously.

Johnson was untouched. But he heard his opponent gasp, "I'm hit!" and saw him drop his pistol and clutch his hand to his chest, before he crumpled and the dark stain flowered across his shirt.

The surgeon came running with his tools.

Having taken a hard look at his principal, Fitz's second marched over to Johnson and stuck out his hand. "My congratulations, sir. You are a gentleman to the backbone, whatever others have said. But you had best get away quickly. This has turned out a bad business."

9.

Whether the bullet or the surgeon claimed Jemmy's life could not be cleanly established, but the consequences were plain and rapid. The Provost of Trinity, who frowned on dueling, expelled Billy Johnson. The Fitzsimmons family pressed for a criminal prosecution. This had little chance of prospering, since the Irish judges were themselves much addicted to blazing—the Attorney-General himself had stood his ground at nine paces—but the family had influence enough to cause a good deal of trouble for Billy if he remained in Dublin. In any event, an angry summons to return to Smithstown came from his father on penalty of being cut off without a penny if he refused.

Turning his back on Dublin was no hardship; he was no longer entirely at home in the singular world of the Dublin rakes. But he had a dependent to consider. He acknowledged an obligation to Cat, less as man to woman than as one of his O'Neill forbears, in the days when the land was still ruled by native-born Irishmen, might extend his protection to any who took his hand in friendship.

How would he break the news to Cat? How would he discharge his promise to protect her—a promise that weighed more because it was freely given?

Billy borrowed money from Mick Tyrrell and put it together with what was left of his allowance, and the gold watch his father had given him on his twenty-first birthday.

Cat did not look at the purse he set before her when he returned to his lodgings. She sprang into his arms, gripping his hips with her knees. They fell into bed together, and he plunged deep inside her. She slowed his powerful thrusts to her own rhythms, raising a slim brown hand when he threatened to peak too soon. Even when she shuddered and moaned her delight, she held him in check. "Not too fast. Not yet. You don't know how voracious I am."

"It is exquisite torture," he told her, staying himself at the edge, "this exaltation of larks."

He was fierce when she released him. His spasms carried her halfway off the bed. She received him with answering ferocity, knitting their bodies together with knees and ankles, taking all of him.

"You are a gift of life to life," he told her, when he had recovered speech.

She put a finger to his lips.

"Has any man ever spoken to you like that?"

"Have you ever spoken like that to a woman?" she countered.

"No."

She studied his gray-green eyes. "You will," she told him. "You are fond of words, and women love a man who can make love to them with his tongue. I think there is no woman who will tame you, Billy Johnson. You will never be leashed."

"We know each other, Cat."

She kissed the knob of his member. "This is the last time, isn't it?"

"I cannot say." His eyes fled to the window, to the failing light over the slate roofs. "My father has called me back to Meath."

She touched the purse he had left on the table. "What is this?"

"It is the most I can do. It will help pay for your passage to America, if you are determined to go. You would land as a free woman, not a bound servant in the charge of the soul-drivers. There are those who would help you."

"Am I to go?"

"I cannot choose for you, Cat."

"But for yourself?"

"I would wish us to be together. It will not be easy here. There are too many eyes. Too many hedges."

"And in America?"

"I have thought on it. A person goes to live in another country because he is not wanted at home or because he must breathe a larger air. In America, I have heard, the sky is vast. A man makes his own boundaries, according to what he can take and hold."

"How would we find each other, in this vastness?"

"I will listen for the larksong."

She traced a line with her forefinger from the cleft of his chin to the root of his member. She said, oddly, "I fear for you, Mister Johnson."

"For me?"

"You have not known enough adversity. You have

looks, and words, and money—" he tried to deny the latter, but she would not let him interrupt "—and ways to please a lady." She squeezed the shaft of his member which revived at her touch. "The gods are jealous. Is that not what the Greeks say? I think they must be preparing a terrible trial for you."

CHAPTER 9
SOUL-DRIVERS

1.

Island Woman drove her younger daughter down to Sunday school at Fort Hunter in the wagon Dandelion had made for her. It had stood up well to the rigors of the rough, cratered road that turned to a trough of sucking mud in the spring thaw.

Bright Meadow did not like going to the church, and she scrapped with the Mohawk kids from the Lower Castle who made up most of the class.

"They are apples," she complained to her mother. "Red on the outside, white on the inside."

And they would not say boo to the minister, the formal, pompous Mr. Barclay, whom she disliked most of all.

Island Woman counseled her to stick it out. Bright Meadow was quick; she was making good progress with her lettering. "When you've finished your schooling," her mother promised, "you can stop being an Anglican."

Island Woman started over to Two Rivers to look for her friends while Bright Meadow sat through the lesson in the stone chapel near the gate of the fort. A white man with a big chest and a flying jaw, in a buckskin jacket and native leggings, ran out to greet her. She recognized

Walter Butler. He was not playing commandant of Fort Hunter; he was dressed for trade.

"Hoop kam je on?" he asked in frontier pidgin, a savagely mutilated form of Dutch. "How's it going? Got anything for me?"

Island Woman had a fisher pelt and a few martens Snowbird had brought in. Whenever she traveled, she took something that could be traded. Prices fluctuated wildly, and you never knew when you might run into a greenhorn who did not know what things were worth.

Lieutenant Butler was no greenhorn.

He offered her an insulting price for the furs—a tiny pannikin of his watered rum or a couple of tawdry brooches.

"You'll not do better," he told her. "Since our boys started going up to Oswego and bringing back all them peltries from the north, prices are going nowhere but down. Law of supply and demand. This peace with the damned Frogs makes it worse. You can trust old Walter, anyone will tell you."

"Sehnsonhsaksen," she said with a tight smile. "You have crooked fingers."

She left Walter Butler to look for a thirstier customer. At the Lower Castle, her friend Windweaver was waiting for her. Windweaver was a matron of the Turtle Clan, which was powerful at Two Rivers; once the whole village had belonged to her clan.

"Let's walk," Windweaver said.

She had something to show Island Woman. The trail wound back through virgin forest, then picked up the line of the little Chuctenunda creek, which the Mohawk women crossed by a log bridge.

Windweaver motioned for Island Woman to move softly.

Through the trees, Island Woman saw cleared land, a twist of smoke from a rough cabin with gaps between the logs. White children with smudged faces, chasing a hen. A gaunt woman with her hair tied up in a kerchief. The white woman froze, sensing danger in the woods. She could not see the Mohawk women who moved like arms of the forest. But she shooed the children back inside the house.

"There are nine families like this one," Windweaver told Island Woman. "They use our land without asking permission. Without even hanging a deerskin for us to see."

The reference was to the Great Law of the Confederacy, instilled in every man and woman of the Real People through constant recital and discussion. The Peacemaker's law required that a traveler who needed to use the lands of the Real People to support his life was permitted to do so, as long as he honored their rights. If he killed a deer to feed himself, he must hang the skin where the Real People could find it easily, because it belonged to them.

Island Woman thought about the scared, dirty faces and ragged clothes of the squatters hidden in the deep woods, a long way back from the river and the King's Road.

She said, "They took the land without permission from anyone."

"Hen." Windweaver grunted her agreement. "We sent pine tree chiefs to Albany. They sat with the Commissioners. They were told there is a new paper for this land, a paper we never heard about. They were told this land belongs to a man called Captain Warren, who is a stranger to us. They were told that if this Captain Warren will pay, the Commissioners will send armed men to drive the newcomers out of the woods."

"It's a trick," Island Woman judged. "The Albany men want to take the land for themselves, as they tried before. Besides, you do not need white men to remove the newcomers from the woods." She told Windweaver how the Mohawks of the Upper Castle had scared off a party of surveyors.

Windweaver nodded, but said, "I think this would not help us. The newcomers in the woods are weak and frightened. If we send them away, others may come who are stronger. This Captain Warren is said to be a great warchief among the English."

"What will you do?"

"The minister at Fort Hunter says we must deed some of our lands to him, so he can guard them for us."

"Don't trust him."

"But you send your own daughter to his school."

"We must use the tools that are given us. This is different from allowing these tools to use us."

Windweaver considered this as they walked back to the Lower Castle. Then she changed the subject, as Real People often did when they could not find agreement.

Windweaver said there had been visitors from Caughnawaga, the blackrobe mission near Montreal where many kinsmen of the Mohawks were living. They brought news of Island Woman's elder daughter.

"They say Swimming Voices lost her husband."

"What do they say?" Island Woman was suddenly cold.

"They say he fell into the slow madness. They say he was throwing live coals around his own lodge. They say—"

"Tell me all of it." Island Woman held her breath, waiting. She knew in her gut that something terrible had been done, something that could mark her daughter indelibly.

"They say he took the witch root."

Island Woman let out her breath. *At least they do not say Swimming Voices made him do it.* Or maybe her friend was sparing her the worst. Either way, the news that Swimming Voices was coming home to the Valley brought no joy to the morning.

2.

Christopher Johnson stalked from the fireplace to the foxhunting prints above his favorite armchair.

"Strength!" he bawled, his back turned to his son, who had been left standing just inside the door, like a schoolboy called before the headmaster. "Give me strength!"

Squire Johnson grabbed a cut glass decanter from the

sideboard and tossed down a serious quantity of spiced rum.

"Drummed out of Trinity!" He rounded on Billy. "Damned waste of money!"

"My mother's, sir."

"Don't talk back to me, you damned coxcomb! Why in God's name did you go killing a Fitzsimmons?"

"It was a matter of honor, sir."

"Honor!" The words came fizzing out of his mouth, in a spray of rum and saliva. "They have brought a complaint to the Lord Lieutenant! There will be no future for you in Ireland, none at all."

"I can farm as well as John, if needs be."

"Not here, you can't. You make enemies as fast as you bed women. The Tracy girl is in the family way and says you are the father."

"Not possible."

"Don't lie to me, boy!"

"It is the simple truth, sir. I have not bedded Georgina in more than nine months."

"You spoiled her, though. Is that not a fact?"

"The lady was spoiled from birth."

Christopher Johnson spat curses and replenished his glass. "You gallop among the ladies like a wild colt. I am telling you there are men who will not stand for it."

"Does Tracy say I must marry his daughter?"

"Quite the contrary. Tracy wishes to hush the connection. He is paying for a suitable bridegroom, a man from Sussex, I believe. He wants you away from here, out of sight and sound of the girl. By the way, Andrew has vowed to kill you on sight."

"I am not scared of Andrew Tracy."

"You are not scared of enough, William Johnson. If you do not learn your place, you will be broken to it. I know whereof I speak."

Billy tried to hold down the hot words that sprang to his lips. *I must not feed my father's rage.*

A light tap at the door brought welcome relief from the confrontation.

Anne Johnson entered in her riding habit, without waiting for permission.

Christopher groaned. Billy had always been his wife's favorite. She was forever finding ways to soften the blows the boy needed for his guidance.

"I have a letter from Peter," she announced cheerfully, as if the escapade at Trinity and the Tracy affair were of no consequence. "My brother has bought himself a fine new estate in America. He is seeking a lively young man to settle it for him, with tenants from home. He is good enough to think of us first. What do you think, Christopher?"

"John is the one he wants. John is reliable. I cannot spare him."

"You are mistaken, Christopher. I believe the one Peter wants is Billy, though he does not know it yet. He needs a man who is ready to change with the currents of life, not one who treads a straight line, never looking to left or right. And Billy needs a larger air."

She looked at her son, reading his emotions.

Billy thought of Cat, and her hopes of the New World.

There are things that like to happen together. Perhaps Cat's departure is a message to me.

□

"I'll miss you," his mother said, stroking his auburn curls, when they had shared Peter Warren's letter and come to decision. "But I have known, from your birth, that you would be the one to leave us. There is something calling you. A purpose that awaits you, though I cannot say now what it is.

"You must not think harshly of your father. He lives in the world as he sees it. This is not the same world that you inhabit. It has very little sky. My brother Peter will understand you better. He will recognize something of himself in you.

"But he will not value you right if you cross the ocean as his dependent. You must go as your own man, Billy."

"You taught me to always be that."

"In heart, yes. But money speaks also. It speaks louder than rank and titles in America, I am told. I have something left of my own inheritance. Peter says there is a market for our linen in America. We will invest in good Irish linen and you will use it to make your own way."

Billy protested when he learned how much she planned to give him. This would rankle his father, even more than the cost of his abbreviated education, and draw the jealousy of his brothers.

"Hush. This is my gift to you. You must fly from us as an eagle, not a crow."

□

Peter Warren wanted a dozen Irish families to people his estate on the Mohawk. Billy sought out likely recruits. His cousin Mick Tyrrell said he would come, though no one believed Mick was made for a farmer.

"I'll earn my passage," Mick pledged. "Then I'll take the first ship bound for the Spanish Main. Why should Uncle Peter have all the plunder?"

His father and his brother John grumbled over the number of tenants' sons who were eager to go.

The last person on Billy's list was his former tutor, Denis Rahilly.

"Ah, you'll never get me out of Ireland," Rahilly told him. "It is slicing a piece of bread off the loaf where it belongs."

"I cannot get Ireland out of you," Billy corrected him. "But I can get you out of Ireland."

"What use am I, on your uncle's estate?"

"No more use than Mick, but he is coming too."

"But why do you want me, Billy?"

"To keep you from drinking yourself to death in poor company. And to keep the stories that will remind us who we are, whatever comes to pass."

3.

Cat Weissenberg and her mother crossed the Atlantic in a floating coffin, despite the promises of the smiling man at Wexford who had pocketed their money.

There was not headroom to stand between decks, in a space less than five feet deep.

The captain had improved the accommodations for his passengers. He had brought in carpenters to make sleeping berths by dividing the space vertically with two rows of wooden slabs.

"Put your things up there. Lively, now," a sailor urged Cat, thumping an upper shelf with the flat of his hand.

"It is a chicken coop. It is for poultry, not people." She measured the space with her arm. It was exactly the length of her forearm, from elbow to fingertips. The hutch was just wide enough for Cat and her mother to lie side by side.

"Hurry up, little chickadee." The sailor's hand moved to her rump. "You'll be thankful later."

"For what?"

He brought his hot, stubbled cheek next to hers. "For being able to *breathe.*"

This, at least, was no deception. During storms, when Captain Briggs ordered the candles extinguished and the hatches locked, the only light and ventilation came from the cracks in the deck immediately above her face. That was when seawater was not sloshing through.

The four hundred of them—bondsmen, redemptioners and manacled felons—were packed in like herrings.

For two weeks becalmed in port and three weeks at sea, the diet was the same, day after day. Cold oatmeal for breakfast, a scrap of brisket or cheese with peas and biscuit for dinner, molasses for supper. All that varied was the condition of the food. The weevils thrived in the biscuit, the beef sprouted a yellowish mold.

After the first big storm at sea, these provisions seemed like luxuries.

"There's a hard gale coming," Captain Briggs bawled into the wind. The ship started to pitch and roll, dwarfed by the thunderheads massing at its stern, the vastness of the ocean ahead. "Get the cargo below! Douse the lights! Bolt the hatches!"

By evening, the sea was running mountain high.

Cat shivered in her hutch, drenched by seawater and her mother's vomit, gasping for air.

The dark magnified everyone's fears.

Cat pictured the wild gusts ripping the sails to shreds,

men cursing as they fought to control the helm, sodden ropes snapping. There was terrible thunder overhead as something huge broke loose and cannoned across the deck. The ship leaned over so far Cat was sure the sea must swallow it.

"Oh, Lordie, we're drowned," a woman screamed as a great wave sloshed into the hold, sweeping trunks and bags from one end of the passage to the other. The passengers who had gathered under the hatch door, straining for air, were thrown about like jackstraws.

People sobbed and prayed, hacked or babbled in fever-dreams. Most of them had been sick for weeks, with dysentery, jaundice, pleurisies and putrid fevers. Many now bore the marks of scurvy: large, uneven spots and fungal growths on the skin, swollen legs, rotting gums, a general lassitude and distemper of spirit. All of them had spewed out whatever their stomachs held.

Her spasms of nausea over, Margret Weissenberg lay calm. So calm, in that roiling pandemonium, that Cat feared she had left for good. She tried to clean her mother's face and neck with a rag.

When she kissed her mother's forehead, Margret sighed and smiled and started crooning a lullaby.

"It's going to be all right," Cat promised.

"Where are we?"

"We are going to America, remember?"

"I remember. Where is your father?"

"He couldn't come. Don't worry. You'll be safe in America. I'll keep you safe."

"I know. I am always safe with you."

Cat squeezed her mother's hand. *She'll come back,* Cat promised herself. *She goes away when she's afraid. She'll be back.*

Someone clutched at her shoulder. A foul smell, like fishguts left standing for weeks.

Cat tried to prise the fingers loose.

"Take my child!" A woman's voice. The gray, mushy features swam out of the dark, close to Cat's face. "Don't let him drown," the young mother begged.

Touched, Cat reached for the child, but recoiled from its cold, lifeless skin. The ship sawed again, and the woman and her dead infant were borne away, crashing into the berths of the hard-eyed men with irons on their legs and brands on their thumbs, condemned convicts spared from the gallows because they were able to read. The felons repelled the crazed woman with oaths and blows.

When the storm receded and the holds were opened, they found her drowned in two feet of water, still clutching her child. Captain Briggs had the bodies thrown overboard, without ceremony.

Why do the priests seek to command us with threats of hellfire and damnation? Cat asked herself. *Hell is here, on this earth.*

She watched the scorbutics rotting and dying. They lay down like sheep. They forgot their dreams of the New World. They gave up and let death take them.

I will not die like a sheep, Cat pledged.

She focused, in her mind, on the world she hoped to find on the other side of this watery hell. She found a place of extravagant colors, a rose garden blooming in clean sunlight at the edge of a grove of ancient oaks. She saw pheasants rise from cover, swans on a mirror-bright pond.

She dared to find Billy Johnson. His skin smelled of a warm, dark spice. When they embraced, his enveloping strength filled all of her senses. She opened to him like a silk flower. Her joy was an exploding sun, deep within her being.

"Eh, chickadee."

She woke from her reverie to find the coarse-skinned sailor bending over her. He thrust something dripping in front of her face.

"Nice piece of slat beef, duckie. Keep you nice and plump. You save something juicy for old Pat, and he'll give you a piece."

Cat's nose twitched. The meat was tolerably fresh, cut from one of the shanks the sailors trailed in the ocean from a line.

Daydreams would not keep Cat and her mother alive for the rest of the voyage. Since the terrible storm, they had been given only foul slops and filthy water, full of worms. Nine hogsheads of water had been lost in the storm, all the molasses, and the greater part of the salt brisket and ship's biscuit. The survivors were living on starvation rations. Captain Briggs—it was rumored—was selling off his private stock to passengers who could pay gouger's prices, two shillings for a bottle of Bristol beer.

There was uglier talk. One of the men with a thumb-brand had muttered, in Cat's presence, that it was time to start eating the dead instead of tossing them overboard.

Cat inspected the sailor. He might be her father's age. There was a saurian cast to his features, his skin leathery as an old turtle's.

"I'll want water," she said briskly. "And bread."

"Right you are."

When he pushed a meaty hand down her front she did not resist. "Old Pat will give you a choice gallop, never fear," he murmured.

She agreed to meet him behind the surviving lifeboat, after dark.

She carefully sifted through the contents of her trunk before she kept the rendezvous. The clothing was spoiled. The old copy of Queen Anne's *Golden Book,* about the delights of America, and the family Bible she would save and dry out. The watch Billy had given her no longer kept time, but the gold casing would still fetch a price.

She found what she needed at the bottom of the trunk—one of a pair of bone knitting needles.

She concealed it between her breasts when she went to meet the sailor after dusk.

He dragged her under the dinghy, grabbing at her bust, her thighs.

"Wait. I have no other decent clothes."

She saw, in the half-light, that he had kept his promise. He had brought a pannikin of lobscourse—boiled up from the slat beef, with potatoes and onions, for the crew and paying passengers—a waterskin, and a hunk of stale black bread. Saliva rushed through her mouth. She was famished. It was all she could do not to fall on the food and stuff it into her face like an animal.

She willed herself to go ahead with her plan.

Fight or die. That was the only rule she had observed on this ship.

She fumbled with the neck of her blouse, while the seaman rolled down his breeches. He had his thing out. It was very dark, and pointy-ended, like a dog's pizzle, and it seemed to bend to one side. Under different circumstances, Cat might have laughed at it.

She pulled out the bone needle. With her next movements, she grabbed the sailor's balls with one hand and jabbed the point of the needle against his throat, behind the windpipe, with the other.

A sewer of curses bubbled from between his lips.

Cat pushed the point of the needle through the skin.

The sailor yelped, and grabbed at her wrist.

She twisted her other hand, as if forcing a stubborn doorknob. The seaman turned pale and gave up fighting.

"I am taking the food to my mother." She gathered up the things he had brought. "If you seek to do harm to either of us, I will tell the Captain how you use his stores and his passengers." ·

He gathered himself up, as if to hurl himself on her again.

She held the needle like a dagger in her raised fist. He called her a German pig, but only his muffled oaths followed her as she picked her way along the deck.

"You'll pay. Trust old Pat Knapp. You'll pay."

□

There was one consolation amid the fear and the hardship—she was coming to America as a free woman, not a bound servant.

True, she had been twenty pounds short of the price the agent at Wexford had demanded for the transport of two passengers from Bristol.

But that was no problem at all, he had assured her. All she need do was sign the contract he had ready.

She had flinched from the paper in his hand; she had

heard too many stories of what had happened to previous emigrants who had signed without understanding.

"It's all quite in order," the agent had insisted. "See, this is not an indenture. It is just our ordinary business arrangement. You agree to redeem your debt in a reasonable period of time. No obligation of labor. You say you have kinfolk in the colonies? Well then, where's the risk?"

She had peered at the difficult words. She had asked, "What is a redemptioner?"

"Why that's you, love. Nothing like an indentured servant. More like a gentlewoman who makes an arrangement with her dressmaker for a wee bit of credit. No worries at all."

4.

From the outer bay, New York was only a lump of rock against the skyline, with a little fort in the foreground. The spires and cupolas of the churches, the bulk of warehouses and the more substantial townhouses—some four and five stories high—came into view only as the ship rounded the island and headed up the East River, toward Hunter's Quay.

The larger quays were set parallel to the shore, because ice floes in winter and high tides in spring made short work of piers that jutted straight out. This severely limited the number of ships the port could accommodate at any given time. The *Derwent* dropped anchor in the deeper channel, and Captain Briggs had the emigrants mustered on deck, with much piping.

Cat's heart lifted at the sight of a blue heron—its wings gilded by the sun—soaring above the press of oysterboats about the slips. The air smelled so *clean,* redolent of pine resin.

"America!" She patted her mother's arm. "I told you we'd do it."

Margret was keenly focused, drinking in the whole view. She had lost much weight during the voyage, and her legs were very weak; she walked propped on her daughter's arm. But she had come back.

"Is it Philadelphia?"

"It is New York. I must speak to the Captain about our onward passage."

She had chosen Philadelphia because she had been told their distant relations—the Weisers—had moved from New York to the Pennsylvania colony. But she had a connection in New York too, though not one she felt she could count on. She had a letter to Captain Warren, Billy Johnson's uncle. It was blemished and water-stained now. But perhaps she should try to deliver it. If Billy ever had thoughts of her, it would be a way for him to find her.

Perhaps he will cross the ocean too. He is not a man for shut-up spaces.

She crushed the hope that leaped in her heart.

I will harbor no false expectations. Billy had his way with me, as he has had his way with many women. I think I pleased him more than others, as he pleased me. He was more than generous, he was gentle. He owes me nothing. I can ask nothing of him except what he will give freely. When I go to him, it must not be as a petitioner but as a free woman.

She sighted Captain Briggs, running his thumb down a list, his ample chins lapping over his stocks.

"Captain Briggs. May I have a word with you?"

He pursed his lips, looking at the Palatine girl who spoke better English than many of his crew. Her speech and her manners must be worth something in hard coin. Not to mention her looks, once he got her scrubbed up. All the emigrants came up from the hole below decks stinking like hogs from a slurry, with lice in their hair.

"Mister Knapp!"

The sailor who responded was the one who had tried to buy her with a piece of raddled meat. He was dressed quite nattily, in a blue jacket and red check trousers. Cat realized, uneasily, that he was something more than an ordinary seaman—a bosun's mate, at the least. And he was carrying a blunderbuss.

She noticed, at that moment, that all of the sailors on deck were armed. Captain Briggs had tucked a brace of

istols into a sash around his middle, in addition to the
word that hung from its sling.

"Aye, sir!"

"Bathtime for our guests, Mister Knapp."

"Captain—"

She did not know what was happening. But she
refused to believe that, after all they had survived at sea,
anything could interfere with her salvation now. America was *there,* in plain view. A chance to start over, free of
memory, free of fear.

Captain Briggs cocked an eyebrow at her. It arched its
back like a woolly caterpillar.

"I presume you are taking on supplies here. How long
before we sail for Philadelphia? I would like to go on
shore."

"You'll be going on shore, no worries."

Cat did not like the way the ship's master leered at her,
before running his thumb back down his list. She saw
columns of numbers, expressed in pounds and shillings.
The list ran on for pages and pages.

"Let's see now. You signed on as a redemptioner. Is
that right?"

"Yes." Cat's heart was pounding. The blood rose in
her face. Pat Knapp's tongue flicked in and out of his
chapped lips, like a lizard's.

"You agreed to pay the balance owing, for passage for
you and your mother, within three months of landing in
the colonies. Correct?"

"Yes."

"That balance would be sixty-eight pounds eight shillings and threepence."

"That is impossible!" Cat stared. She had paid all but
twenty pounds of the costs of passage. It was a simple
round number, she pointed out. There could be no
mistake.

Captain Briggs cleared his throat. "You have over-
looked the additionals."

"What additionals?"

"Insurance, interest—"

"That is preposterous!"

"Provisions removed from ship's stores." The Captain brought his eyebrows down in a darkening scowl. "At a time of general want and hunger. Count yourself lucky you are not being punished with something worse than the market rate."

Pat Knapp winked at her, making her wish she had driven the needle in all the way.

"You can't do this!" she protested. "I am not a felon. Nor an illiterate. I know I have rights under English law."

"English law, is it?" The Captain tugged on his earlobe, and the bosun's mate guffawed. "That might be well enough in Bristol, missie, but I am the law on my ship. Do you tell me you will not pay?"

"Will not and cannot!"

"You hear that, Mister Knapp?"

"Aye, sir."

"You have said, before witnesses, that you renege on your contract." Captain Briggs spoke to Cat like a hanging judge under the silk. "There is a law for violators of your ilk, and I am obliged to serve it. You will be put up for sale at auction, on board my ship."

"After I give you a bath," Pat Knapp grinned wide, exposing the roots of his cratered teeth.

"Quite right, Mister Knapp. The soul-drivers are most fastidious gentlemen."

5.

Cat was scrubbed with salt water and vinegar, in front of the crew and many of the steerage passengers. Pat Knapp handled her body as if it were to be sold off by the pound, publicly commenting on various features of her anatomy. Then he took a shears to her lice-infested hair.

She did not dare to search for her mother's face among the crowd on deck. She was terrified that, when she found Margret, the vacancy would have returned.

I can take this too, she told herself. *I will not yield. I will not break. If I go on long enough, fortune must turn.*

They rowed the soul-drivers out from the common dock on a sturdy passage-boat, built to weather the wells on the longer journey to Staten Island and the Jersey shore.

The crew issued clumsy gowns and smocks—patchwork or canvas—to Cat and the indentured servants who were to be put up for sale.

The soul-drivers ranged the deck, peering at teeth, probing into orifices, with the casual brutality of cattle-buyers. They were wholesalers. They would resell the white slaves whose contracts they bought wherever there was a going market for their skills. By selling off part of his stock to them, Captain Briggs—and his unseen partners—sought to avoid the costs of feeding and sheltering all of his cargo for an undefined period.

"Any smiths?" the shout went up from one of the buyers. "Tinsmith? Silversmith?"

"Blacksmith, sir." A youth with a withered leg stepped forward.

The soul-driver turned down his mouth. "They'll never look at you, with a leg like that. You're too young for a blacksmith, anyways."

"Prentice, sir."

"You can pad the leg, Dick," Captain Briggs volunteered. "They'll never see the blot."

The buyer grunted and moved on to Cat. He had curly black hair, and sharp, narrow features. A blue shadow ran up to his cheekbones. She met his gaze and saw only darkness.

"What can you do?"

Cat said nothing.

"I reckon that one for a prime mantua-maker," Pat Knapp snickered. "She's a dab one with a needle, to be sure."

"Mantua-maker!" Dick Langdon snorted. "If she was anything like, you'd be saving her for Napthali Levy or another of our sharks on shore." They all believed it was the truth. There was always a demand for a dressmaker who could keep up with the fashions.

Cat was about to protest that she was as good with a needle as any, when the soul-driver put his hand under her chin and tilted her head back.

"Pretty enough, if you weren't bald. I wager you can

turn a trick on your back, not so? Alas, we have mor
doxies about the town than—"

He was interrupted by the sting of Cat's palm acros
his cheek.

He wiped it away slowly.

"Shall I whip her?" Pat Knapp moved in.

"No, I like a woman with mettle. Strip her. Let me se
what I am buying."

The bosun's mate hastened to oblige.

Dick Langdon sucked in his breath when he saw Cat'
naked body. Then he drew a line, very deliberately, fron
the root of her throat down to the pubic bone.

"I think I will keep this one for myself," he an
nounced. "If the price is acceptable. Mrs. Langdo
needs more help about the house."

Pat Knapp slapped his thigh, treating this as a goo
joke.

Naked and cropped, exposed to the eyes of coars
strangers, Cat forgot her shame in her urgent need t
locate her mother.

She called out in German. She called as if to a los
child. *"Margret! Liebchen!"*

"Stop that squalling!" her new master commanded
having concluded a brisk trade with Captain Briggs, fo
colonial paper and rum from the islands.

"I will not leave without my mother!"

"I did not buy your mother. Old bones are no good t
me." Dick Langdon manhandled her—in her canva
gown, bereft of belongings apart from a small bundl
tied up in her old cloak—toward the gangway.

"Mother!"

There was no answering call.

When she fought, they tethered her hands behind he
back and half-dragged, half-kicked her into the passag
boat.

She entered America as a slave, stripped of family an
possessions. She had seen war and famine and plague i
the Old World. But she had never known anything as ba
as this.

A desperation seized her, when they threw her into

art with iron tires, whose driver raced like a madman
through the noisy, cobbled streets, routing passers-by.

Beyond hope, beyond reason, she screamed his name.
"Billy!"

She yelled until Dick Langdon felled her with a blow
to the side of the neck, nicely calculated to leave the
goods unspoiled and unblemished.

CHAPTER 10
NEWCOMERS

1.

Three months after Cat was sold like a tethered ewe, Susannah DeLancey Warren sat late over her toilette in the house at the head of Broadway.

Arrayed before her was a legion of jars and vials containing Mr. Lillie's waters and scents—musk and ambergris, sandalwood and citron, essence of orange flowers, attar of roses, oil of cloves and coriander—as well as batteries of marbled washballs, pearl powders, rouges and ointments. Mrs. Warren had a sensitive skin, with tendency to rashes and spots, especially under the pricking confinement of a gauzy head-dress built up with pads and puffs of false hair, powdered and ornamented with lace and ropes of pearls. Though she ordered generous quantities of Royal milk-water, guaranteed to take off spots and scurfs, she was often reduced to composing a mask of Italian paste and Spanish red.

This morning, however, Mr. Hayes had sent round a boy from Bayard Street with a novelty, described in the pharmacist's hand as The Bloom of Circassia. Mrs Warren scanned the accompanying advertisement, printed at London.

It is allowed that the Circassians are the most beautiful women in the world. However, they derive not all their charms from nature. A gentleman long resident there in the suite of a gentleman of distinction, became acquainted with the secret of the Liquid Bloom, extracted from a vegetable, in use there with the most esteemed beauties. It differs from all others in two essentials. It instantly gives a rosy hue to the cheeks, not to be distinguished from the lively and ornamental bloom of rural beauty, nor will it come off by perspiration, or the use of a handkerchief.

The pharmacist had assured her that a moment's trial would prove that the lotion lived up to the claims that were made for it.

Susannah Warren smelled the contents of the jar. There was a touch of ginger, she thought. The scent of rosemary did not disguise something astringent that made her nose wrinkle.

I must not be weak, she told herself severely. *Mr. Hayes says it is the height of fashion, that Lady Halifax swears by it.*

"Portia."

Her maidservant stepped forward. All the slaves in the Warren household had names out of Shakespeare. It was the same in the house of Mrs. Warren's brother, Chief Justice DeLancey. As their wealth and the size of their retinues increased, Susannah Warren and James DeLancey vied with each other to unearth exotic sobriquets from the works of the bard.

Portia was round-faced and placid, a quality that was indispensable in attending Mrs. Warren in her dressing room, where she was known to spend five hours at a sitting when the barber came to repair her head-dress.

"You may apply the Bloom," Susannah said through her long Van Cortlandt nose. "Be careful now. It is more costly than liquid gold."

She pouted as Portia's deft fingers smoothed the ointment into her skin.

"It stings worse than Hungary water," Mrs. Warren complained.

Nonetheless, as the operation proceeded, she was pleased to see a pink glow spread over her cheeks. It masked the blemishes without aid of powder and rouge, and drew the eye away from the doorknocker nose.

The burning sensation grew sharper. Mrs. Warren touched the side of her cheek. She felt a sponginess under the skin.

"Give me the hand mirror!"

In the oval inside the silver frame, she saw her worst fears confirmed. Her skin was starting to blotch and bubble.

"I have been boiled!" she shrieked, hurling the looking-glass at the yellow damask of her favorite settee.

She vowed the direst revenge on all pharmacists and purveyors of novelties.

□

Portia was wonderfully able with Venetian paste and white lead paint, and soon made Mrs. Warren a new face. But Susannah's rage had not cooled when Caliban came up with a letter on a silver salver.

Captain Warren complained that Caliban was wasted as a house servant; he had learned something of the art of working metals in his own country and had a real gift with horses. But Mrs. Warren valued the African for his native elegance—his features were finely chiseled, and he carried himself with unstudied dignity—and his command of English. She had insisted on making him her majordomo.

"What is this?" Mrs. Warren stared at the envelope. It was soiled and watermarked, with a great tear across the middle. It looked like something that had fallen off a night soil cart. The address, scrawled in tall, looped letters, was all but illegible.

"The lady says it belongs to Captain Warren. Says it is from his nephew."

"His nephew?"

Peter had told her about his arrangements to bring his sister's boy, William Johnson, out to the colonies to manage his Mohawk Valley estate. *Billy is a bit of a boyo,* Captain Warren had said indulgently. She interpreted this to mean that the young man was a scrapper and a womanizer. *But dukes do not emigrate.* Perhaps young Johnson would thrive on the roughness of the colony. He would find no worse among the Mohawks than here in New York town, Mrs. Warren thought. A respectable woman was not safe alone in the streets in broad daylight, between speeding coachmen, footpads and grogshop gallants. It was all jostling, pushing and brawling. Six public markets already—more than Boston or Philadelphia—and talk of opening a new one. The din of hammers and saws, day and night. The town was bursting at the seams. The population was already pushing ten thousand, her brother calculated. *And Peter says it will double in a decade if we ever finish our business with the French.* There was room for another Irish tearaway.

"Portia, bring me the letter-knife from the secretary."

Captain Warren would be in Boston until late in the season, if he was not away privateering on the Spanish Main or at the mouth of the St. Lawrence. Mrs. Warren thought she had best see what Mr. Johnson intended.

She scanned the brief missive and scowled. Young Johnson commended an "honest and industrious" woman named Catherine Weissenberg to his uncle's protection. He presumed to suggest that Captain Warren would wish to concern himself with this woman's employment and lodgings.

One of Billy's cast-offs, Susannah Warren judged.

She glanced at Caliban. "You say a lady brought this?"

"Yes ma'am."

"Well, let's have a look at her. I will receive her in the yellow parlor."

□

Cat sat on a rush-bottomed chair near the door of the yellow room. She was neatly but simply dressed in a homespun striped waistcoat and petticoat, blue stockings, and a calico wrapper. Though her hair had grown back in springy curls, she covered it with a blue bonnet that fastened under the chin. On her lap was the basket in which she was supposed to bring back the provisions Mrs. Langdon had ordered her to fetch from Hanover Square.

This was only the second time her mistress had trusted her to go on a shopping expedition, though Captain Langdon's fears she would run away had diminished since they had brought her mother into the old Dutch style house that stood gable-end to the street.

Her reunion with her mother had been Cat's only triumph, and it had cost her dearly.

She had made this her condition for entertaining Captain Langdon in the garret room when his wife was away or otherwise engaged.

Times were, when Langdon took her in the dark stinking of liquor, emitting hoarse grunts and a sawing snoring wind through his nose, when she had told herself the price was too high. There had been nights she had wished herself and her mother dead.

God help me.

Now she sat staring dully at the strange cast-iron stove between the windows, wondering if any help awaited her in the house of Billy's uncle.

The previous Thursday, she had walked to this same corner, circled the block, and swung back and forth between the boy selling cobs of Indian corn down by the water and the lime tree across the cobbled street from Captain Warren's front door, without quite daring to mount the steps or to try the knocker at the servants' entrance.

The tall black slave came in and looked at her. He seemed quite grand to her in his powdered wig and sky-blue coat with shiny brass buttons. He wore knee buckles over spotless white hose.

She went on staring at the stove.

"Six-plater," the black man said. "Came from Philadelphia. I put the exhaust pipe in myself." He showed her how it led out the window. "Keeps you good and snug in the winter. You been through a winter here?"

She shook her head.

He blew on his fingers. "New York winters can freeze your ends off."

He did not look or talk like any slave she had ever seen, black *or* white, except maybe the bookkeeper in Mr. Franks' trading house, who had two years left on his indenture.

"What is your name?" she asked him, curious.

"They call me Caliban. They tells me it's the name of a cannibal in a play. I don't mind what they call me," he added, reading her confusion. "I got my own name."

Further conversation was interrupted by the entrance of Mrs. Warren, resplendent in a dazzling quantity of white satin, embroidered with vines and twining flowers, picked out in green and gold.

Only the eyes showed true in the mask of paint and powder, capped by the gauzy head-dress. The eyes were cold and inquiring. They made a brisk inventory of Cat's homespuns and cottons.

Cast-offs, Mrs. Warren judged. *Like the wearer.* She especially disliked the girl's smooth, unblemished skin, glowing with natural good health, untouched by powder. The sight revived the humiliating experience with the Bloom of Circassia, and inclined Mrs. Warren against her visitor before they had exchanged two words.

"You are in service," she addressed the German girl.

"I am being held against my will."

"Yet you are here at liberty."

"I am here by subterfuge." She began to tell the story of how she had been deceived and sold illegally on the deck of the brigantine, but Mrs. Warren brushed the words away with her fan.

Servant class, Susannah judged. *Every last one of them has some complaint. If one were to entertain their stories, there would be an end to precedence and the dissolution of order.*

Her brother James had said this often.

Mrs. Warren wavered in her resolve to close her ears to a common servant's complaints when Cat mentioned the name of her master. Dick Langdon had an evil reputation. There had been charges that he sold free men as slaves, though they had come to nothing; no court in the land would hear a black man's testimony against a white man.

Cat sensed her hesitation and felt a change in Caliban too. The African tensed at Langdon's name. He was standing stiff as a board.

"Enough!" Mrs. Warren beat down whatever was troubling her. "We cannot hear gossip about how others manage their houses. You come here with a note from my husband's nephew. How do you know Mr. Johnson? What are you to him?"

Cat looked at the six-plate stove. "Mr. Johnson was kind to me, ma'am."

"Kind to you? Do you mean you were his whore?"

Cat looked through the slits in the painted mask. "We may have loved each other a little. I believe it is no crime, ma'am."

"You dare—you *dare*—" Mrs. Warren was beating her fan. "You are not the same class!" she shrieked. "Do you dare insinuate Mr. Johnson owes you anything?"

"Nothing, ma'am. He was more than generous. I know there is no future in it, ma'am. I came here only because he asked me to come. He says Captain Warren is a kind and a fair man."

They said the Palatines were a stiff-necked people. Susannah was rattled by the way the German girl held her ground. *She speaks to me as if we are equals, though she calls me ma'am. She looks me in the eye. We cannot risk having her anywhere within view when Billy comes. If she gets her claws into him, she could ruin him for decent society.*

Mrs. Warren rose, declaiming that she would dearly love to be of assistance, but her husband was detained abroad indefinitely on the King's business, and the master of the house must rule.

"Perhaps I should see the lady safe home," Caliban suggested discreetly.

Cat began to protest that she had errands to run at Hanover Square. The African silenced her with a glance. He walked a pace behind her on the street, as society demanded, though the relative quality of their dress might have suggested she was waiting on him.

He spoke just loud enough for her to hear above the clatter of wooden and iron wheels, the banging of builders, the cries of the hawkers.

"I know something of Langdon. He is a devil in flesh. If you need help, you come to me."

The squall of a seagull took away the next phrase.

He repeated it. "My name is Ade Awotunde."

She could not get her tongue round it.

"Ade is enough. Ah-day." He made the syllables equal length. "Say it to my friends and they will know you are invited."

"You are kind. But—"

"But what can a black slave do for you? Listen up. You can find me at Trinity Church on Sundays, after first communion. The Warrens are Anglicans."

And the Anglicans have been taught we may have souls as long as they do not make us free men.

As they came in view of the recently opened Bowling Green, the first public park in the city, the African said, "It is best if you look for me at Hughson's."

He gave her the address. She recognized a neighborhood of low grogshops and worse, along the North River.

"I am let out on Tuesday and Saturday nights."

She turned to face him.

"Why are you doing this?"

He read her unspoken thought. *Do you want this body too?*

He smiled. "You are too skinny."

2.

Captain Langdon came home early from the tavern on Saturday night, because his luck had ran sour at the dice. His wife was away to her sister, who was expecting another baby.

He swarmed up the stairs, hauling himself along the railing, arm over arm.

He shouldered his way through the low door of the garret.

"Get out!" he bulled at Cat's mother, who sat knitting in the light of a tallow candle. He showed the women the belaying pin he had used on them before.

"It's all right." Cat kissed her mother's forehead. "Go down to the kitchen. I'll come for you."

Langdon put the club on the windowsill and took Cat by the hair. He wound it tighter and tighter against her nape, making it the living rope with which he bound her and hurt her. His lizard tongue flicked in and out, as he enjoyed her breathing pain.

She held back the scream. Her mother must not hear.

Now he was spinning her like a top. He bit deep into the flesh around her nipples, puncturing the skin.

The fighter in her took charge.

She struck at him with fists and knees, aiming for the groin. He laughed and wrenched at her hair violently, forcing her down onto the bed.

She fought him with raking fingers, seeking the eyes. One of her nails hooked the stubbled skin below his cheekbone, and tore a shallow trench to his chin.

He cursed and relaxed his grip.

"I'll take the whip to you, like a slave mare," he promised.

She reached for the belaying pin on the window ledge. With her arm extended full-length, her fingertips just brushed the wood.

As Langdon swung back at her, she made a desperate lunge. With one movement, she snatched up the club and swung her arm upward and outward. She saw her target, Langdon's bony jaw. She moved so quickly that Langdon did not appreciate his danger until the dark object whirled up into his face. He turned from the blow, exposing his neck. The club collided with the back of his skull with the thwack of splitting hickory, and Langdon dropped to the floor.

Cat did not pause to weigh the consequences as she rifled her master's pockets and threw a few articles of clothing into a bundle. She grabbed her mother's cloak and hurried down to the kitchen.

3.

Bent over his work, the African did not hear the drunken laughter from the tippling shop or the loud curses of its owner as he tried to clip another coin or a filched piece of property for the services of Fireship Peg or Jiggle Sue on the straw mattresses upstairs.

Hughson's was open day and night, and John Hughson did not mind whether a customer was black or brindle, slave or free, as long as he could pay. More often than not, payment was offered in kind—in tubs of butter or sides of bacon from a master's storehouse, or a candlestick off a mahogany dinner table.

The African had spread a finely woven mat under his work table to catch any filaments of silver that fell. By mutual agreement, these were part of his fee for his services in melting down stolen silver and hammering it into plate or the semblance of Spanish pieces of eight.

"You're a strange one," Hughson had told him, when he had named the remainder of his price. That he would be allowed to work metal on his own account in the makeshift smithy. And that he would be allowed to entertain those of the slaves that were willing with his own song and dance, an unwholesome jabber in Hughson's ears.

But Hughson could tolerate black men prating of wind and thunder and croaking chickens in his yard so long as they did not eat into his profits. Whatever objections he might have voiced stayed in his throat when he saw that the fancy Negro from the Warren mansion was not thieving what had been thieved already. Ade's purposes were a mystery.

Ade sang to himself now, in Yoruba, as he worked with fire and wind to turn metal into liquid. He saw the charcoal consumed. He watched silver flow into the hollow of the brick, fluid as water.

And in that moment, he heard the voice of the praise-singer in the village, as his father worked the blood of the earth. He saw his father rise to his full height and roar his pleasure, dancing with the hammer of Ogun, lord of metal, in one hand, and a ram's horn filled with magical substances in another.

Tears glistened on his cheeks.

He wiped them off with the back of his hand and pulled his leather apron straight as the noises from outside the shed grew louder. Someone was banging at the door, rattling the bolt.

"Open up, you crazy bastard!" Hughson called.

Ade pulled back the bolt.

"There are white women here that want you. You crazy nigger! I knew you'd bring me trouble."

Behind Hughson's greasy leer, Ade saw frightened faces. Cat, and an older woman. Black men spilled out after them from the grogshop, mistaking them for new talent.

"I show you good time, missy," one of them beamed, clutching at Cat's petticoat. "Nothing like nigger love."

"Let them pass." Ade stood in the door frame, the hammer raised in his right hand.

"This is no part of our bargain," Hughson warned.

"Later."

Ade pulled the women inside the shed and fastened the door. Cat blinked at the silver hardening in the mold, not understanding. The African looked different, without his powdered wig and his livery. His short, crinkly hair fitted his head like a tight cap. He had a circlet of shells around his neck. His rough costume did not diminish him. He looked stronger.

"I broke the leash," she told him. "I am sorry to inconvenience you. I did not know where else I could go."

He stopped her when she began to tell more of what had happened in Langdon's house.

"We crown our own heads," he said oddly. "I expected you."

He contemplated the silver cooling in the brick, as if coming to a decision.

"I have some money," Cat told him. "I have relatives in Pennsylvania."

He shook his head. *Too far. Too many ferries, too many checks.*

"Some of my countrymen live in the interior of the province, beyond Albany. They will help one of their own."

Ade considered this, which spoke more closely to a dream of his own. He had been told that there were limitless prospects for a man who knew metal on the frontier of the colonies. And that few questions were asked.

Someone was rattling at the door again.

Ade opened it and found Fireship Peg's slack face. Her plump breasts bulged like heaped pillows.

"Hughson says you got to go now." Peg sent a withering look to Cat, a possible rival. "There's men here looking for the women. Hughson says if they search the place, we's all for the noose."

"Tell him to hold them. We'll get out the back way."

When Peg was gone, he said to Cat, "It can be done. Do you know Coenties Quay?"

"On the East River?"

He nodded. "Meet me there in two hours. I know of a sloop captain who is no more particular than Hughson."

He showed the women the gap in the fence and the alley behind it. Then he took off his apron and put on his blue coat. He gathered up his tools in a leather bag. On reflection, he slipped in the silver brick.

4.

Geese winging south in V formation honked as they crossed the bow of the *Squirrel,* the station ship from Boston, off the western tip of Long Island. A south wind snapped the canvas as bluejackets in red, baggy breeches clambered among the ratlines. Captain Warren, the commander of the *Squirrel,* swelled with proprietary enthusiasm as he pointed out the sights of New York's Lower Bay to his Irish nephews, William Johnson and Michael Tyrrell, two young peacocks set to charm the birds out of the trees, in their fancy waistcoats and silk hose.

"That is the Sandy Hook," Captain Warren boomed in the voice of a man who had bellowed orders to fell the

mainmast in the teeth of a hurricane. "Old Frog De-
Lancey made a pile there, smuggling gin and gunpowder
from Holland. He had his skippers offload by the Hook,
with wagons in wait to spirit his goods to York or Philly.
His ships rolled into port in ballast, not a shilling in
duties to be paid."

"Were the customs men asleep?" asked Johnson.

Peter Warren laughed at the boy's greenness. "There is
nothing in New York that cannot be had for money. And
Stephen DeLancey is the richest man in the province."
He threw an arm around Billy's shoulder, which had an
odd effect since Johnson stood nearly a head taller. "I
would have you mind your manners about the De-
Lanceys. Not the least of Old Frog's distinctions is that
he is my father-in-law."

Captain Warren pointed out the half-moon battery
below the ramparts of Fort George to Mick Tyrrell,
whose fancy ran to soldiering more than commerce.

As the *Squirrel*'s bow came about, Billy saw a score of
merchantmen tied up at the long wharves that jutted out
into the East River below warehouses, sugarhouses and
distilleries.

All the way from Boston, Uncle Peter had talked less
of things Billy could see than of values he was just
beginning to learn: of how Adolph Philipse had trebled
his money in a year, with two building lots on Pearl
Street; of how Jacob Franks had made a packet, cornering the market in flour and peas for the Islands; of
Captain Warren's land speculations, including the tract
of farmland he had recently purchased at Greenwich, on
the northern edge of the city. Warren imagined his
Greenwich orchards filling with houses and tenements
to accommodate new tides of immigrants.

Eager to learn, Johnson had plied his uncle with
questions about how the great fortunes of New York had
been made. Warren indulged him with gossip about
shady deals with the Indians, bribes to Governors, and
the contraband trade with the French in Montreal and
the Islands. It was plain that, in the Province of New
York, money was not to be had through a surfeit of

scruples. And that here money, not breeding, was the patent of nobility.

"A man who has money here, no matter how he came by it, is better than a lord," Warren advised his nephews.

Captain Warren gave a quick, appraising look at Billy as they threaded the Narrows into the Upper Bay. Johnson's arrival in the colonies had been preceded by some ripe rumors of scandal involving women of high and low degree. "A man who lacks money here is nothing. You will not go amiss to bear that in mind in all dealings with Americans."

American. The word was novel, even exotic, to Billy Johnson. His uncle used it somewhat disparagingly, as an Englishman might call an Irishman a paddy or a Scot a loblolly. Yet it was plain, even from the water, that the little city on the tip of Manhattan Island, surrounded by an untamed wilderness of forest and stone, was thoroughly different from the Europe Billy knew. Boston might have passed for a tidy English port. New York, with its brick houses standing gable-end to the street, looked more Dutch than English. But, with its polyglot population of Dutchmen and Germans, Scandinavians and Ulstermen, English and Irish, Sephardic Jews and African slaves, with its great river-road to the Indian country and its beckoning frontier, New York was more than Dutch, or English, or European. It was a new kind of society, with a new kind of promise, and perhaps the word for that was the one Peter Warren let fall as a friendly insult: *American.*

□

The Warren house was built in the new style, with a balcony where Susannah DeLancey Warren sat with her Tenerife wine on close summer evenings, to view the sunset over the Jersey shore. It was grander than the DeLancey house, at the corner of Broad Street and Pearl, which conformed to the old Dutch manner, gable-fronted and pantiled. Lime trees and water beeches, leafless in this season, lined the cobbles of Broadway.

No expense had been spared at Number One. The

house even had a bathtub, imported from Holland; a luxury not only almost unheard-of at New York, but generally unenvied. A slave had to haul fresh water for Mrs. Warren's ablutions from a spring more than a mile away, because water from city wells was brackish and smelled of raw sewage. The Warrens were never short of slaves, although they had recently lost Susannah's favorite. Slaves were part of the Captain's share in the spoils he plundered from the Spaniards and the French. And Captain Warren could spend what he liked on a house to pleasure his wife.

His prize money, shrewdly invested in land and building lots, had ranked him with the richest men in the colony even before he landed New York's most coveted heiress as his bride. On the day of their wedding, Susannah had brought him a dowry of £3,000 in cash and £6,000 in trust funds, invested in safe New York bonds, though regrettably under the guardianship of her clever brother James. If Frog DeLancey ever agreed to die—and he was not a man who was easily persuaded of anything against his interest—Captain Warren could look forward to a generous slice of a fortune he estimated at better than £150,000. Enough to hold up his head among the best of society in England or Ireland. To buy himself a seat in Parliament, perhaps, or a small peerage.

□

From ten in the morning, the traffic on Broadway increased as manservants jostled their way through the crowd, bearing Susannah's lady guests aloft in their *chaises*. Mrs. Clarke, the Lieutenant-Governor's wife, arrived from the Fort in a coach and four, complete with military escort. Anne Heathcote DeLancey, Susannah's sister-in-law, did not feel obligated to make any show of her rank. She was an heiress in her own right, and the wife of James DeLancey, who was not only the Chief Justice but the eldest of the seven DeLancey children, and the principal heir to the Huguenot enterpriser that Captain Warren called Old Frog behind his back. Anne DeLancey walked over the cobbles from her own house, wrapped in her shawl, with a feathered umbrella over her head and a single black slave to attend her.

In the blue parlor, Susannah watched critically as Titania, the new maid, offered her guests a selection of tea, Madeira and Tenerife wine. She had kept a keener eye on the slaves since Caliban had gone missing. *That is what happens when you pamper the niggers.* She could already hear her husband's reproach.

Nancy Clarke, a Governor's daughter who thought herself too grand for New York society, bragged of her villa on Hempstead Plain and whined about the burden of maintaining a household befitting the dignity of the King's representative on the grudging allowance the Assembly provided. Susannah Warren heard her out with a frozen smile. It had not escaped the Warrens' attention that George Clarke had grabbed a dozen fat sinecures for himself and his son since he became Acting Governor. And no doubt His Excellency had wasted no time, during his recent visit to Albany, in grabbing deeds to Indian land.

Anne DeLancey shifted the conversation to a more suitable topic, chatting about a musical entertainment in the Italian style she was planning to hold over the Christmas season.

Puck, a black footman, interrupted this with the news that Captain Warren's ship had been sighted in the East River.

The news caused a stir among the ladies. In the small world of New York a new arrival was always an event.

"The Governor heard—" Nancy Clarke announced tartly "—that Captain Warren recruited a choice pair of hell-raisers."

"Your husband must be very well-informed." Susannah's mouth tightened. She added mentally, George Clarke isn't Governor *yet*.

"I am told that William Johnson is the talk of Dublin," Mrs. Clarke pursued. "It is said that he ruined a lady of quality, and fought and killed her brother in a duel in Phoenix Park. I believe it was the Earl of Fingal's daughter, or the Lord Lieutenant's. The man is notorious as a rake and a skirt-chaser."

Martha, Recorder Horsmanden's spinster daughter, darted a quick, hopeful look. She reminded Susannah of a mouse poking its head out of a hole.

"Such things are said of men who turn women's heads," Anne DeLancey spoke up, a soft smile playing over her lips. Mrs. Warren's sister-in-law was ironical and oblique, difficult to know. "Men who are shaped for the ruin of the sex," she mused, and the smile deepened. "Who can say where is the blame?"

The Recorder's daughter raised a pale hand to her lips. Mrs. Clarke flushed crimson.

Susannah Warren made an effort to retrieve the situation.

"There will be no cause for scandal in New York," she said firmly. "My husband has engaged his nephews to manage his estates on the Mohawk River. I am sure they will find more than a match for their wildness there."

She thought she saw Titania sniggering and would have spoken sternly to the girl but for a loud rattling, rumbling noise from the street. It sounded as if several coachmen were racing their masters' horses. Why was the watch never out when it was needed?

The tray bounced in Titania's hands and scalding tea sloshed over Nancy Clarke's quilted dress.

"You idle hussy!" Susannah yelled at the maid. "I'll send you to Jamaica, to work in the fields!"

Titania fled from the parlor.

Susannah started after her, but found the floor pitching under her feet, like a ship's deck during a storm at sea. The windows shook. Her delftware banged against the wall and flew into pieces. Her father's portrait came tumbling off its place of honor above the mantel, bowling over her flower arrangement.

As suddenly as it had come, the tremor receded. All was calm, except for the shouts and the pad of running feet outside the windows.

"I believe the earth moved," said Anne DeLancey. "And we are told the town is built on solid rock."

Susannah marched out to the kitchen, in search of her maid.

She found Titania down on her knees, chanting some mumbo-jumbo in a foreign tongue.

"Speak English, girl! Or I'll see you on the auction block!"

"It's a sign," Titania moaned. "Oh Lordy, it's a sign."

"Stand up at once! I won't tolerate this heathen tomfoolery under my roof! Go and lay out some brandy for the Captain and his guests."

□

It was a very small earthquake, less daunting to Billy Johnson than a squall off Rhode Island. He drank in new sights and sounds through the window of the carriage and wondered if somewhere in this jostling traders' town—stinking of shellfish and skinners' yards, pig slurry and tarpits—he might find Cat Weissenberg.

He had asked after the girl within hours of his first meeting with Captain Warren in Boston, sooner than was prudent. Peter Warren had denied any knowledge of Cat, or the letter Billy had written on her behalf, and cocked a sandy eyebrow at this fresh evidence of his nephew's weakness for the ladies.

"I did not fetch you across the sea before time," the Captain had observed. "I suspect your father was right. He said you were banging around in Ireland like a moth in a bottle."

Billy had grinned at this, acknowledging the truth of the charge. He could turn on a smile that skipped across his whole face. It gave him an unfair advantage in life; it made men more tolerant and women more complaisant than was altogether good for them. It triumphed over even the cool, practical Dutch streak in Susannah Warren. But not to the point that she shifted in her resolve to say nothing to Billy about the German servant girl who had come looking for him.

□

Mrs. Warren arranged a banquet to celebrate the Captain's homecoming and to introduce his Irish kinsmen to *le tout* New York. She placed her sister-in-law, Anne DeLancey, next to Billy at table.

Anne DeLancey arrived in full warpaint, rouged and powdered, with a patch on her cheek and her hair piled up in the height of London fashion. Her saffron silks framed a dazzling expanse of neck and shoulders. As liveried servants brought platters of bay oysters and guinea-fowl, turkey and Westchester beef, Anne amused herself with Billy in a manner that made Mrs. Clarke twitter.

"I imagine, Mister Johnson, that you must have left more than one pretty colleen sighing over a hedge in Ireland."

"I find, Mrs. DeLancey, that the beauties of Europe are flown to the New World."

"You flatter us, sir. Come, you must make your confession. Is there no lady who has won your heart?"

"There is one here for whom it would be an easy conquest." Billy smiled his winning smile, but a shadow passed across his eyes.

From the far side of the table, James DeLancey turned an appraising eye on the young Irishman with whom his wife was diverting herself. Subtle and watchful, this grandee of New York measured men by only one rule: their usefulness to the cause of Chief Justice DeLancey. He had bought the last Governor and been rewarded with the post of Chief Justice, the second most powerful office in the province. He had read law at Corpus Christi and preened himself that there was no man better-educated in New York.

"Do you read, Mister Johnson?" he addressed Billy. "I am told that in Ireland, the talk is mostly of hounds and horses."

"The art of reading is not wholly unknown to us."

"You must read Newton. It will be a consolation to you, living among the hairdressers of the Mohawk. Newton teaches us that man is not the center of the universe, but only a minuscule cog in an infinite mechanism created by a God who is not especially concerned about us. Newton encourages humility."

"That must explain his appeal to you, James," Anne DeLancey said archly.

"Humanum est errare," mumbled the Rector of Trinity, mildly shocked by the possible blasphemy in Newton's view of the creation.

"If I am not mistaken," Billy spoke up, "Doctor Newton also compares himself to a child on the seashore, casting pebbles into the waters of a vast unknown."

"You surprise me, Mister Johnson," said DeLancey. "I had not thought to encounter an Irish philosopher. What do you say, Peter?"

"More sail than ballast in all of it, if you want my opinion." It amused Captain Warren to play the part of sea-dog. A man spared himself many difficulties in life by taking care not to seem too clever.

"When you tire of felling timber and consorting with savages," DeLancey smiled at Johnson, "you must come to me. I can find a place for a man who knows Newton."

"Now James," Peter Warren rebuked him, "don't turn the boy's head with your fancy talk. He has honest business to attend to."

"Not overly honest, I trust."

5.

Captain Warren and Ade, his runaway slave, were in full agreement on the power of money in the colony of New York.

The sight of silver had silenced any questions the skipper of the Albany sloop might have asked when the African had bearded him in the smoky taproom of a tavern near the Meal Market. But Captain Van Schaik was sensitive to his other passengers, some of whom might have taken objection to the phenomenon of a black man traveling with two white women in conditions other than obvious subjugation. Ade had agreed to sleep on deck with the other servants.

The sloop was wide-beamed, with a bottom of sturdy white oak, strong enough to survive frequent altercations with sandbars, with five hundred barrels stowed on top.

"Oak will bend but not crack," Captain Van Schai]
observed to Cat, as he did to all first-timers on Hudson'
River. "And red cedar—" he had stomped his foot dow
hard on the deck "is slow to rot, unlike some gentry
could name you."

The speed of the journey upriver was in the gift o
wind and tide.

It had taken them five days—with pauses to wait out :
hard blow in a safe anchorage—before they reachec
Kinderhook.

Cat had grudged none of the delays. The whole voyag
was a spectacle. Near the mouth of the river, she hac
gaped like a child at schools of porpoises gambolin
around the boat. Then the cliffs rose high and grand, lik
castle walls. And then came the dreaming hills, the wilc
tang of unspoiled forests.

Cat felt her lungs open wider and wider as she travelec
deeper into the continent. Her countrymen had sailec
this river-road before her. Somewhere beyond the hill:
were friends who spoke her native tongue and woulc
welcome her and her mother into their world.

Would she ever see Billy again?

If our paths cross, will he still wish to know me?

She had no answers; for now, the escape from bondag
was enough.

On deck, watching the swooping flight of a crane, she
asked the African what he had meant when he told her
"we crown our own heads."

"You have a double in heaven who is watching you,"
Ade told her.

"I do not understand."

"There is a place in you where you know what I an
saying. Each one of us is born with a character and :
destiny. These are not the same. Your destiny is easier tc
change than your character."

Cat had frowned, more puzzled than before by the
strangeness of this black man whose eyes seemed tc
reach inside her and number the bones.

"Who are you?" she had challenged him.

"In my own country, I would have been a *babalawo*. A

father of mysteries. I came back for this. Here, I am nothing. Unless my paths are opened."

They had talked, after that, until some of the cabin passengers became suspicious.

Before the sloop reached the Kinderhook landing, Captain Van Schaik had taken Ade out of hearing of the others. He had said, "I'm going to drop you off before we reach Albany. It is for your own good. I don't like the mood of some of the gentry on board. I believe they are on to you, son. Not a word. I wish to know nothing more of you, and your lady friends, than I already know."

"Then how will we get to Albany?"

"I have kin at Kinderhook. Good Dutchmen, like me, who don't care for English rules and taxes. They will hire you a wagon."

□

On the rutted wagon-road from the Dutch settlement on the Hudson, Cat watched a blue heron break from the mist and sail into a white-gold sun.

On either side of the track, the red crests of the staghorn sumac tossed and swayed.

Then the Mission Indians rose from the thickets. Their scalplocks bristled among the cones of the sumacs, dyed the same blood-red.

The mist clotted about them. It billowed out toward Cat like a physical thing, a sheet spread wide about her head.

Caught in its net, she lost movement and volition.

As in a dream, she saw Ade grapple with their attackers and fall beneath them. She reached for her mother, pulling her face against her breast.

She heard the African gasp as the rawhide noose was fastened around his neck. She saw the veins stand out on his forehead as the noose was pulled tight.

The yell of protest that rose in her throat was cut off as a face out of nightmare loomed in front of her own and her wind was cut off.

6.

They followed the path of sun on water. Their faces and chests were painted red and blue. They wore silver armbands and strings of red and black beads and deerskin moccasins that held up better over rough ground than Cat's new shoes, which were scarcely broken in.

She begged them to slow the pace.

Their only response was to pull harder on the rawhide noose around her neck, or to whack her shins or buttocks with the wiper sticks from their flintlocks.

When she fell, grabbing at the leash to stop it from choking her, one of them hit her with the flat of his hatchet.

They did not slow for her even when she lost one of her shoes and was reduced to kicking off the other and running in her bare feet. Thorns and flinty rocks gashed her skin. When they reached the canoes the French Indians had concealed among the bushes along the creek bank, Cat's feet were bloody and swollen. They no longer looked human.

They look like bear paws, she thought. *Or something a bear has gnawed and discarded.*

Her captors worked their paddles at a dizzying speed, sending the light birchbark canoe skimming over the water.

Cat could see her mother's pale face in the second canoe. The one thing she could give thanks for was that these savages had been gentler with the old woman. When she had fallen, instead of beating her, they had tied her in a makeshift litter and dragged her along with them. This was not what Cat had expected. The stories of Indian captivity that circulated among the servants of New York told of the instant execution of anyone who could not keep up with her captors—of babies whose skulls had been crushed like quail's eggs, of the elderly and the inform hewn down and scalped. But for some reason unknown, these Indians were tender with Margret Weissenberg.

Not so with the African. They had loaded him up with

packs of stolen goods and outsized powder horns on the trail, driving him like an ox with their clubs and wiping sticks.

Cat had no idea what tribe had taken her. She knew only that her captors must be French Indians, because some of them wore the double-barred silver cross, and she thought she heard French words in their speech. She counted eleven of them. Two appeared to be white men in Indian dress.

They made camp for the night beside a natural stone archway. A rivulet coursed below it, making the dead-hollow sound of a kettle drum. They made no fire, and sentries took up posts in a tall tree and atop the stone vault.

They lashed Cat's arms behind her and tied her by the neck to a tree, out of speaking distance from her mother and Ade. They spread-eagled the African on the ground, binding him to stakes by his ankles and wrists. Her mother, she saw, was again treated more gently. They sat her under an evergreen, and tied a cord round her waist. The other end was knotted into the belt of one of their captors.

A warrior brought Cat a scrap of dried venison the size of an egg.

"Venez, rafraîchissez-vous," he encouraged her in clumsy French.

She found it hard to get the meat down, even with swallows of water from the tin cup he offered her. It had the texture of willow bark.

She looked at the warrior's face. He had shaved off all his hair except for a small topknot, dyed red and dressed with feathers. A nose that could split firewood poked out of a mask of midnight blue, with red lozenges around the eyes and mouth.

"Where are you taking us?" she asked.

"Lac des Deux Montagnes."

Lake of Two Mountains. She could get that much. The rest of his words were lost on her.

His eyes were like smooth pebbles, shiny and impenetrable. They traveled over her.

Does he want this body? Are they going to rape me?

She did not think she had the strength left to resist them. *I will lie like the dead, like a corpse in an open grave. Let them use me and go quickly.*

But the warrior did not molest her. He was pointing at her mutilated feet. Later, when the tree frogs shrilled, he brought her a poultice of crushed leaves or roots. It smelled like wild balm, clean and sweet. It soothed her pain.

She could not sleep.

The seeming randomness of her life oppressed her as much as the fear and suffering. She thought of a boy she had once seen destroying an anthill. He had chopped off the top, flooded the passages inside, and pinned and dissected each of the insects as they came out, leaving some to stagger on one or two legs before he finished them off.

My mother and I have been used like that. As live toys for cruel boys. Will it ever stop? Can we choose anything that matters in this life?

She dozed off when the moon was low in the sky. When she snapped awake, with a violent ache in her neck, it was still dark.

She could see ripples in the black water of the creek below. There was something pale beside the stream. A man? No, smaller. As her eyes adjusted, she saw it was a white owl, stretched lengthwise at the very edge of the water. It appeared to be sound asleep. Maybe one of the Indians had killed it noiselessly, with an arrow.

In the next instant, a fish broke surface. With amazing speed, the owl shot out its talons and plucked the fish from the water. Astonished, Cat watched the huge, staring eyes in the enormous head as the owl flew off, carrying off its supper.

PART TWO
THE FLINT PEOPLE

The Wolfe never values how many the Sheep are, and it is a very unequal war between us & them; let dog eat dog & Indian fight with Indian, for the tame People of America, notwithstanding all their vaunts are not a Match, the French know it by dire Experience.

—William Johnson to Sir Peter Warren
July 24, 1749

CHAPTER 11
THE OCTAGON

1.

Cat's journey north proceeded by forced marches. The Indians roused their captives long before dawn and stopped for a hasty breakfast at sunrise. Their food was parched cornmeal or dried venison, because the warparty would not linger to fish or hunt, and lit no fires until they came out of the drowned lands into a narrow bay at the head of Lake Champlain.

The prisoners were kept moving, by land or water, until long after nightfall every day. They were driven past endurance.

Cat feared their captors' curious affection for her mother would end grimly when Margret Weissenberg sat down on a rock and flatly refused to go any farther. But the Indians rigged up a litter, stretching a moosehide over poles, and dragged her along like a load of firewood.

They were less patient when Cat's strength gave out. The muscle spasms in her calves felt like great talons snatching and tearing, ripping flesh from bone.

A gaunt nightmare with a mask of black paint around his eyes and a headdress rigged together from a bobcat skin, black feathers and the bodies of dead birds, capered in front of her, brandishing his warclub. He croaked like a crow bent on picking the eyes out of carrion.

Cat looked for the blue-painted warrior who seemed to be the leader, who had spoken to her in French and might be a Frenchman under his terrifying mask.

Blue Paint shrugged and loped ahead of them, along the trail, abandoning her to the man-crow. The bones in his necklace might be human, she thought. There was one that was jointed, like a little finger.

"I take her," Ade moved between them, unshouldering his load, letting it fall to the road.

The man-crow swung at the African with his club. Ade ducked, and the steel fang set in the ball-head sliced the air above his neck.

"You!" the African called to Blue Paint. *"Ecoutez!"*

Blue Paint paused and turned back.

"I take her," Ade repeated, pointing at Cat, then himself.

Blue Paint spoke sharply to Crow, who made a slurring noise of disgust, ending in a gobbet of spit, but jogged on through the firs.

"Save yourself," Cat whispered to Ade, when he had slung her across his shoulders. "You do not have the strength."

"You're not so heavy. And if I save you I save myself."

"How can that be?"

"They see I am no slave."

They were led on a long circuit, around a fortified house on the bend of a river, where Cat saw white men and horses in the distance. The Indians moved with special care from this point, concealing their tracks.

Blue Paint walked behind the others with a long stick, poking up grass and weeds the others had flattened in their passing.

After their next rest, Cat found her legs were sturdy enough to carry her, even at the fierce pace the Indians set.

The body can always be stretched a little farther.

When they made camp that night, the Indians lit a fire with flint and steel and relaxed their security a little. Cat was permitted to talk to her mother.

"They are a gentle people, I think," Margret Weissenberg said. Her eyes were cornflower blue. The lines of her face seemed to have been wiped from the skin.

She is become the complete child, Cat realized.

"Is that why the Indians are kind to her?" she asked Ade.

"I guess they think crazy people are close to the spirits. Think a body that's touched is sacred."

"What do *you* think?"

"Think if I can figure a way to make out I'm crazy, I'll do it."

There was fresh meat that night. Crow brought in a rabbit on the end of a stick he had sharpened into a spear. The rabbit was still alive. It quivered and squeaked as he held it to roast over the fire. Its gouting blood hissed on the coals.

Cat shuddered.

With a leer, the man in the mask of black paint offered her a piece of his kill. A clump of singed fur, trailing shreds of bloody meat. Cat gagged and pushed this dinner away, though her stomach had been aching to be fed for hours past.

Crow—Le Corbeau—croaked his mirthless laughter.

He would burn any one of us alive with no more compunction than he killed that poor rabbit, and relish it more.

She realized, with that thought, that the ornaments slung from Le Corbeau's belt were not painted shields. They were circlets of skin and hair, dyed red and stretched on willow hoops.

□

They moved on in the hollow of the night, skirting a bald mountain that rose sheer above the black waters of a lake. They had left their canoes far behind, but the Indians had a fresh set concealed in the bushes here; they were skilled in the logistics of forest fighting and confident of their ground. They paddled down the lake, keeping close to the shore.

When the sun rose, it was screened by a dense fog,

white and opaque as lambswool. As the fog burned off,
Cat gasped as a dark tower, huge and oppressive, reared
against the sky at her left hand. The cold fear that
touched her now was older than the brass cannon she
saw glinting in their embrasures. This black tower came
from the Old World, not the New. It rose out of the Dark
Ages, on tides of blood and ambition.

2.

The French stronghold stood on a neck of land the
English called Crown Point, commanding the narrows at
the southern end of Lake Champlain. It rose from a
rocky hill of black limestone, above a narrow beach
where sand the color of steel or charcoal flashed with
garnet lights when the sun cut the fog. The high stone
walls of the fort were built thick to withstand assault by
mortars and field-guns, if the English ever managed to
haul them through the fir-woods to take possession of the
wilderness they claimed on the maps. The fort had been
dubbed St. Frédéric by the Governor-General, but many
called it The Octagon, because of the shape of the grim
keep that loomed over the canoes and dugouts of the
Indians and the stone windmill, east of the fort, where
guards kept watch for spies or smugglers who slid quietly
down the lake, hugging the shore, as Cat's captors had
come.

The shadow of The Octagon fell deep into the provinces of New York and Massachusetts. It was the forward base and the sanctuary for scalping parties from
many nations allied to the French. Diplomats might sign
treaties in distant countries, across the Atlantic, but
there was never peace here.

The Sieur de Landriève, the commandant of Fort St.
Frédéric, was an elongated, melancholy man. Since the
savage loss of his wife and children to Mohawk raiders,
he had wrestled with eternal questions—Why does a just
God allow suffering?—until he had felt obliged, for the
sake of his nervous health, to focus his energies on the
fulfillment of two ambitions.

The first he held secret from the cocky gallants, hard-living voyageurs and buckskin-clad Indian agents who were his company at the fort, men who read little when they could read at all. It was to complete the masterwork that Euripides, prince of tragedians, had left unfinished. This project towered over the Sieur de Landriève like a physical thing. A bald mountain of schist, flecked with bright points of mica when the lightning flashed. A place for desperate lovers and wounded souls, a place that beckoned to madness and self-annihilation. Aulis was like that. Who cared if his vision matched the physical reality of the physical Aulis, just a speck on the map in the Mediterranean sea?

Landriève saw a country of the mind. A place where a desperate, despotic father flinched from his brutal intent to offer up his daughter to his gods as the blood-price for his intended conquests. Landriève *saw* the grim man in clanking armor, Homer's strong-greaved Achaean, falter in the presence of his daughter's radiance of body and soul. He saw the girl, Iphigenia—so noble, from the fine high forehead to the white shapely knees—deliver herself to her father's savage gods, a willing sacrifice to male fury and ambition. Man the ravager, woman the yielding martyr. Why had the great Euripides stopped short in his ascent? Why had he failed to complete *Iphigenia at Aulis,* which would surely have been the shining summit of his life's work? Because it required him to go deeper into the heart of woman than his world—a world where heroes and philosophers were always men—would license?

There is no greater theme, Landriève thought, than the mystery of woman.

But Landriève had a more personal reason for climbing the rock of Aulis in his mind.

He believed that he had sacrificed his favorite daughter to his own appetite for titles and military honors. She had gone willingly, without bitterness or protest, with love in her eyes and a smile on her lips. But the guilt was on his neck, and it weighed heavier than the bronze armor of mighty Agamemnon, or his cursed crown.

Landrière wrote in the hollow of the night, scratching and cancelling with the quill of a crow or a goose. When he described the ancient tyrant's daughter, he saw his own. Félice appeared to him as she had looked on the last day he had seen her living. Yoked by a noose no civilized man would set to a beast, dragged backward into sunless woods by a troop of painted horrors. Rattlesnakes. That was the meaning of the word Iroquois in another Indian tongue. The Iroquois struck like rattlesnakes. The worst among them were the Mohawks, the Man-Eaters. Mohawks were worse than rattlesnakes. The rattlesnake warns once, but Mohawks. gave no warning at all, and they waged total war. To a Mohawk war-party, nobody was an innocent, no one a civilian.

Landrière had lost his wife and sons to a Mohawk raiding party in the last war. He had lost Félice, his surviving child, because he had brought her into this country of man-monsters, over-confident of his ability to protect and to conquer.

His work on the play progressed very slowly. He was often diverted by his second ambition: to exact the most thorough and painstaking revenge on the savages who had taken Félice and on their English allies.

The view from the narrow slit in the massive stone walls of Landrière's monk-like cell was of a mountain very different from the Aulis of his waking dream. Or rather, of twin mountains, slumped together like sleeping bears lying head to head. They lay across the narrows of the lake, toward the east. Beyond them was a howling wilderness of primal forest; beyond that, the nervous, vulnerable forts and settlements of Massachusetts. Where the sun had not yet touched them, the waters of Lake Champlain were tar-black. The rose-colored glass in the embrasure—a faulty piece, rejected by a church—did not soften the scene. It made everything look faintly burned.

Landrière's glance turned to the huge fireplace that filled most of the wall opposite his writing table. He must have wood brought up, pine knots for color and heat, oak logs for constancy in the lengthening nights ahead. Winter was speeding on. He pulled his pelisse tighter over his bony chest. However much he ate, he could not manage to put on flesh. His ribs stuck out like an image of the martyrs.

There was a scratching at his door, then a more resolute knock.

"Venez!"

An ensign of the Troupes de la Marine came to attention. His oversized coat hung from his shoulders in loose folds. What father's pride and pull—or mere necessity—had sent this child to The Octagon, to be blooded by Rattlesnakes?

"What is it?"

"Casse-Pierre has come in with a war-party. There are captives."

□

Cat's clothes hung in rags from the relentless march through the brambles and spiked trees. She pulled the tattered fabric tighter around her, conscious of the lewd grins of soldiers in gray uniforms and hairy bushlopers in greasy skins and socklike red caps. The uniforms brought back a nightmare from infancy. It moaned inside her head.

The French commandant towered over her. He had left off his wig; his skull showed through gray bristles, shorn to within a quarter-inch of the skin. He inspected the captives carefully. His eyes lingered on Cat's moose-hide moccasins, stuffed with scraps of rabbit fur she had saved from the fire, to fill out the gaps and keep out cold and damp.

She had known by instinct that the gift of these moccasins was a sign her captors would let her live.

Would this sad, lanky Frenchman give her freedom?

He was speaking to Blue Paint and to Crow in their own language. She saw his tongue vibrate in his open mouth like the reed in a flute. From time to time, he made a noise at the top of his throat as if he was gargling.

"Vous parlez français?" he turned to her.

Cat shook her head.

His eyes were intelligent, even sensitive. There was something wounded in them, that recognized her and felt for her. They gave her hope.

"Moi, je parle." It was Margret Weissenberg who spoke.

Cat was astonished by her mother's revival.

Margret was not only able to sustain a brisk dialogue with Commandant Landrième, but to translate for her daughter and the African.

The Frenchman wanted to know if they were Dutch, if they came from Albany.

When he learned they were German, newcomers to America, his face tightened. He said to Blue Paint, "The English want to drown us in new immigrants." He called Blue Paint by a name Cat could not understand. Casse-Pierre. She learned later that it meant Stonebreaker.

Cat spoke to the Commandant through her mother. "Tell him we place ourselves at his mercy. That we are innocent civilians that can do no one harm."

"Je le regrette beaucoup, mesdames." Landrième gave a little bow. "There is nothing I can do for you. If we were at war, I might offer you my protection, as prisoners of war. But in peacetime, our law maintains that captives taken by the *domiciliés*—our friendly Indians—are their absolute property. I am not permitted to intervene."

"But that is monstrous!" Cat erupted. "These savages clearly answer to *you!* That one there—" she pointed at Blue Paint—"speaks and acts like a Frenchman. Do you tell us you give these people license to kidnap and murder at their own discretion?"

"These savages, as you call them, are our allies. They behave no worse than the Indians allied to our enemies, and they serve a better cause."

"But what will become of us?"

"You should count yourselves fortunate, Madame. Your captors have found the true faith and will take you to their mission at the Lake of Two Mountains. They may choose to adopt you or to offer you in trade. Perhaps you have friends or relatives who are willing and able to ransom you. It is also possible that some of our Canadians will purchase you. There is a shortage of labor in New France."

"Commandant—" Cat again found that answering sadness in the eyes. "I beseech you. You are an officer and a gentleman. A white man. We are not slaves, to be bought and sold. Do not abandon us to these demons."

The one they called Le Corbeau strolled by at that instant, across the *terreplaine* of the fort. He had erased his mask of black paint, but this did not improve his looks. An emerald-bright bird, no bigger than Cat's thumb, hung in the air on shimmering wings. With a sudden, predatory throw, the Crow-man caught it in a net and pulled it into his fist. He grinned at Cat as he twisted the hummingbird's neck between his middle fingers.

A darkness came down over Landrième's face.

What mercy did my Félice know? Or my wife and sons?

Landrième said, "You place too much trust in the accident of skin. I can do nothing for you. Your servant, *mesdames.*"

3.

The Lake of Two Mountains was a bulge in the Ottawa River, a dozen leagues north-west of Montreal. The Sulpicians had recruited three nations of Indians to live in the bark lodges inside the stockade: the Nipissings, or Sorcerers; the Algonquins; and the Iroquois, who were mostly Mohawk, Oneida or Onondaga. The distinctions between these tribes were lost on Cat until she had spent several weeks at the mission, and found a friendly trader—in an Indian store stuffed with contraband goods from Albany—who spoke English.

The wind made drumsnaps around her head, blowing her matted hair into a spiked halo, as they disembarked. Their party was saluted by the swivel guns mounted on the ramparts of the mission and by volleys of musketry from Indians lined up along the shore.

With its blockhouses, guns and parade ground, the

place resembled a fort more than a mission. But there was a large stone church, shared by all the tribes. And two blackrobe fathers stood with the welcoming committee. Cat tried to speak with them, but was dragged away by her captors.

Blue Paint took her to a lodge where an old native woman—his mother?—examined her teeth and pinched her breasts, before sending her out, under guard, to haul firewood.

Again, Cat's mother received different treatment. The old woman gurgled over her, tickled her, and made her sit with her by the fire, feeding her corn gruel from her own cup.

The second night, the old woman painted Cat's face and hair red and led her by a rawhide noose into a lodge that was several times larger than the others. The flames of a central fire and a few grease candles cast gigantic shadows above scores of squatting Indians. The place looked to Cat like a witches' cavern. Meat simmered in pots over the fire.

Cat, her mother and Ade were paraded in a slow circle around the ranks of watchers.

Cat thought, *I am a slave again.* It was almost as bad as being displayed to the soul-drivers on the deck of the brigantine in New York harbor. But there was no sexual menace. And a wary solemnity among the witnesses in the council house.

The old woman who had sent her to fetch firewood raised an eerie, whistling plaint. It sounded like the wind in dry leaves. Like the call of wandering souls.

Then the old woman broke into a sighing, singsong chant.

She placed her hands around the neck of Cat's mother. Lovingly, tenderly, like a solicitous lover. Or parent.

To Cat's dismay, she saw her mother go with the old woman gladly, her face beaming.

Then Blue Paint raised the song.

Cat did not know the meaning. She did not know that her hosts were singing for the dead, that they were calling on the souls of departed relatives to take up residence in the bodies of their captives. That these were the rare words of requickening.

But she felt the force of violence in that place, threatening to burst the walls of custom and ceremony, when Le Corbeau rose to defy Blue Paint's claim to the younger woman.

The two warriors faced each other for a moment, circling and stamping the dirt floor, eyes hard as knives.

Then a white-haired matron, older even than the ancient who had claimed Cat's mother, moved with fluid grace to separate them.

Cat could not follow the words of the negotiation, but she tracked its intent and saw its consequences. Ade was turned over to the Crow-man, who again spat his disgust and affected to scrub at the African's skin.

She was smudged with tobacco and sweetgrass, and taken by women to be washed and dress in fresh doeskins, and led back to Blue Paint's lodge.

She lay alone that night, expecting Blue Paint to come under the blanket they had given her and maul her as other men had done. But he did not come.

□

Cat tried to keep track of the time, by scratching little vertical marks on the burden strap they gave her to haul wood and provisions on a litter rigged up from branches and a hide. It was December, she calculated, when the Canadian winter set in hard and fierce, bringing a white light off the snowfields that stung her eyes, and ripping winds that scorched exposed skin like firebrands.

Canadian voyageurs and traders stopped at the mission, hauling goods on sleds drawn by dog-teams, muskets strapped to their backs.

She approached one who looked less rough than the others; he was a handsome boy, with a face tanned by wind and sun that lit up when he saw a fresh girl. It clouded over when he learned she was living with Blue Paint's family.

"Casse-Pierre is a bad one to cross," the young man muttered. "You'd best talk to old Adhémar."

"Who is Adhémar?"

"He might come with the melt. You can find out at the store. But you'd best be quiet about it."

She thought about ways of escape. Then the new moon brought a storm of sleet followed by harsh frost and freezing rain, glazing the trails with ice, so it was difficult to walk downhill, even in moosehock boots. And the cold was so bitter she felt her exposed flesh would come off in strips. She huddled by the fire, swathed in a beaver robe and as many blankets as she could purloin, waiting for a better time.

CHAPTER 12
WINTER GAMES

1.

That first winter in New York, Billy Johnson saw the mercury in the port thermometer that hung by the tradesmen's door to the Warren house sink below the lowest markings on the tube. As he walked home from Todd's, under a clear night sky, muffled to the cheekbones in his cloak, the deep, dry chill in the air pricked his eyes. It puzzled him that the cold could be so severe in a town that lay at a latitude lower than Dublin or London. At the bustling Albany Coffee-House, where gentlemen gathered to swap news and petition the grandees of the town for favors, Mr. Colden explained to Billy that the vast forests to the north worked as a bellows, sucking in the frigid winds off the Great Lakes, and blowing them out again with renewed force. As the forest succumbed to the axe—so Mr. Colden maintained—the climate of the province would become more bearable.

This was not all that Billy gleaned from the Surveyor-General. Short and ill-favored, sharp-tongued and pedantic, Cadwallader Colden viewed the great men of the colony with sovereign contempt.

"Does James DeLancey own you?" he challenged Billy, in the style that accounted for his unpopularity.

"He is my connection by marriage," Billy responded, surprised by the malice in Colden's tone. "He has been a good friend to my uncle."

"Be careful of DeLancey," the Scotsman warned. "He incarnates the worst passions of this province, where men change sides according to their interest, not the country's."

"You are less than generous, sir."

"Indeed? I find you are a stranger to politics, Mister Johnson. The DeLancey family has made its fortune by trading with the enemy. When this province was blessed with a Governor who tried to ban the evil commerce with the French and restore our influence with the Indians, the DeLanceys moved heaven and earth to destroy him, and at last had their way. When the King sent us a weak fool in his place, James DeLancey played majordomo to him. Now we are ruled by a Lieutenant-Governor who declines to be led by the nose, James DeLancey poses as the chief of the popular party and sets himself up as a little god in the Assembly. Thanks to your uncle's friend, our forts are in ruins, our soldiers without ammunition, and our influence with the Indians diminishes daily."

"But we are at peace with the French!" Johnson protested.

"Peace! DeLancey's peace will lose us this province! Let me show you something."

Colden left the table and moved to the wall, where a map of the colonies hung above the reading-stands for the newspapers from London and Philadelphia. The Scotsman was oblivious, or uncaring, that his remarks were drawing a good deal of interest from the habitues of the coffee-house, and that James DeLancey himself held court at a table across the room. Billy glanced across. James paid him no heed, but his younger brother Oliver, a fat, jovial rake with a face that would ripen cucumbers, gave a lewd wink and, rising from his place, raised up his coat to expose his broad backside.

"Here!" Colden jabbed his finger at the river that joined the Hudson above Albany. "These are your uncle's lands. The soil exceeds any I have seen. It will grow anything that can survive our damnable winters."

"Then our enterprise should prosper," said Billy, encouraged by the Surveyor-General's report.

"Ah, but consider your neighbors." Colden's finger slid west, along the shore of Lake Ontario. "Here is Jean Coeur's stone fort at Niagara. Beyond it, French soldiers command the Great Lakes and the river-roads, all the way down to the Bay of Mexico. Now look here." His hand moved back, to indicate a point on Lake Champlain, well within the borders of the territory the English claimed for their province. "Here, at Crown Point, the French have put up Fort St. Frédéric, commanding the great warpath from Canada that leads into the very heart of this province. The self-interest of your friends in this town allowed them to build it, though self-interest may be too nice a term for what some would call treason. Niagara and Fort Frédéric are the points of the Frenchman's shears. The day will come when we will have to drive them out, or be cut very badly."

He thrust his small, speckled hand over the vast sweep of wilderness between the two French posts. "Neither we nor the French are the masters of this land, whoever may hold the deeds. If you have read history, Mister Johnson, you will know that the strong hold the passes. The strongest men in the forests of this continent are the Five Nations. The Six, we will learn to call them, now they have taken Tuscaroras from the Carolinas into their Confederacy. Without the friendship of the Mohawks and their sister-nations, this colony is nothing more than a puny island trading-post, and a dirty Dutch town at the head of navigation on the Hudson. With it, New York is the key to an empire greater than any the world has seen. But I fear my words would be wasted on your friend DeLancey and his money-dropper cousins at Albany. I fear their negligence will lose us both the Six Nations and the war that is surely building."

The only Indians Billy had seen, other than in prints,

were a few ragged families from Long Island, reduced to hawking brooms and baskets. He was eager to know more about the people who would soon be his neighbors.

"When sober," Colden told him, "they are quite as subtle as James DeLancey, and infinitely more principled. If they give their friendship, it is no mean thing. But it carries heavy obligations, and it is not given lightly."

He broke off, because Oliver DeLancey came stumping over, tankard in hand, looking for sport.

"Have you taken the oath of temperance, Billy?" Oliver roared. This was aimed at Colden, who was drinking tea. "Or are you trying to get Uncle Cadwallader to beat up a nice plump patent for you?"

After the way he had expressed himself, it was startling to be reminded that Colden, too, was related to the DeLanceys, having consented to marry his daughter Elizabeth to another of James' brothers. Billy detected a strong odor of incest in New York society, ripe as the stink of the tanning-pits down by the eastside wharves.

"Mister Colden has been good enough to teach me something of the Indians," Billy said carefully, anxious not to take sides in a feud he had not initiated.

"Indeed! Uncle Cadwallader is an authority on the subject. But he has an hereditary advantage."

"What might that be?" Colden asked.

"Why Uncle, you are a Scot, and one savage is always at ease with another."

"I find your hereditary principle most illuminating," Colden responded, his eyes glinting wickedly. "It discovers to me the reason why you and the Chief Justice enjoy an influence with our Assembly that I, alas, am sadly lacking. I have the misfortune of not being born the son of an alehouse keeper."

Oliver DeLancey glowed purple at this reference to the early career of his immigrant father.

"That, sir, is an infamous slur on the noblest citizen of this province," he thundered.

"No, indeed, for I believe there is no man born in New York who is more noble than a publican."

With a thin smile, Cadwallader Colden excused him-
elf. He murmured to Billy, "Read my book. It is better
ompany than any you will find here."

2.

The Surveyor-General escaped upriver by sleigh, to his
manse in the woods, leaving behind what he was pleased
o call the dunghill of human passions, and was soon
mmersed in his ruling obsessions, scrutinizing dried
plants, struggling with a grand work of scientific theory
hat would expand and correct Newton's work on gravi-
ation. With Oliver DeLancey as a frequent guide, Billy
Johnson and his cousin Mick explored the groggeries
and tippling-houses of the town, wagered on games of
shuffle-board and backgammon, and inspected the
haunts of the shady ladies. The last included the turf-
opped stoneworks of the half-moon battery, where
bawds denounced by Oliver as fire-ships floated their
wares beside thirty-two pounders of cold iron.

"There's one to fill a girl up, Tess," one of them cried
o her accomplice, stroking the barrel of a gun as she
admired the tall, broad-built stranger from Ireland.

In the parlors of DeLanceys and Philippses, Billy
delighted daintier ladies with teasing games of forfeits.

"You must kiss the one you love without revealing
who she is!" he announced to a giggling throng in Anne
DeLancey's ballroom.

"That is too much for the feeble wits of us poor
rustics," James DeLancey's wife simpered, finding herself powerfully drawn to the young man. "You must
show us how it is done."

Billy Johnson took his time, making a lingering inspection of each lady in the room, which produced much
fluttering of fans and not a few blushes. Anne Heathcote
DeLancey found her own heart beating harder as Billy
drew near. She felt his breath on her cheek, drew in the
warm, manly odor of leather and tobacco. He was
bending over her. In the shadow he cast, all the juices in
her body rushed to meet him, as if they were in some
place other than this brilliantly lit room, under the eyes

of New York. Anne's skin had become a fine-spun web of nerve endings.

"No," she gasped, as he planted a kiss at the corner of her mouth. Around Billy's shoulder, she saw the frown settle on her husband's face.

"I want you alone," he whispered in her ear.

"No," she protested softly, sensing the ripples of excitement this embrace was causing. Soon those ripples would froth into gossip and scandal.

He released her. James DeLancey opened his mouth to break the spell with one of his endless store of cynical aphorisms. But what was this? Billy Johnson was hanging on the neck of Phila Franks, the wife of the colony's leading Jewish merchant, a beauty with jet-black hair and bright, flawless skin, untouched by powder. Now he was paying homage to Martha Horsmanden, that bloodless spinster. Anne DeLancey wanted to stamp her heel in disappointment and jealous irritation. Billy Johnson was toying with all of them. He proceeded to kiss every lady in the room, not forgetting Anne's elderly Dutch mother-in-law.

"I claim my forfeit!" Billy cried, the color high in his cheeks, his stock in disarray.

"You did not say what it would be," Anne DeLancey reminded him.

"That I should have the honor of leading my hostess into dinner."

There was no arguing with the boy's smile or his mannerly invitation, which brought polite applause from the rest of the ladies.

But when the DeLancey butler summoned them for dinner, Anne dug her nails into Billy's arm and hissed, "You trifle with me, sir."

"I only trifle with that which I value most highly," Johnson countered. "You must consider how I may call on you without exciting rumor."

□

Billy Johnson found time, among his diversions, to read Cadwallader Colden's brief *History of the Five Nations,* printed a decade before to support Governor

Burnet's efforts to stamp out the Canada trade and build British forts on the Great Lakes. Colden's book, the only one on its subject that existed in English, was also the first—and only—history of New York; the citizens of the province were much too busy making money to record their activities outside the pages of ledgers and business letters.

Billy had borrowed the book from James DeLancey, who kept a well-stocked library at his country villa, The Bowery.

"I don't know what you expect to learn from Colden," James DeLancey had sniffed, when he gave him the book. "He praises the savages because he hates his fellow men. Had he been born six inches taller and somewhere other than Scotland, his judgment might be sounder. You should see the son! He is the true fulfilment of the father. A hunchback, with shingles to boot!"

Then his eyes had narrowed, as he added, "No doubt you expect, Mister Johnson, to find easy morals in the colonies. There are many ladies of the town who will not disappoint you. But my wife is not among their number. I have asked her not to receive you. Oliver informs me that you two have frequented certain low houses along the river. If you compel me, I shall share this information with Mrs. DeLancey. Do we understand each other?"

"Perfectly," Billy responded, reasoning that James DeLancey's friendship was more valuable than a dalliance with his spirited wife. But Johnson was not easily intimidated. Given opportunity—and the lady willing—he would yet have his way with Anne.

Reading Colden's *History,* Billy was struck by the author's sympathy for the Indians, whom he described as "the living images of our Earliest Progenitors." At the Warren and DeLancey dinner tables, the red men of America were dismissed as subhuman brutes, wallowing in filth and superstition—rather the way a certain type of Englishman referred to Billy's Irish countrymen. Colden wrote of a society ruled by shockingly democratic principles, in which the authority of the chiefs depended entirely on the opinion of the common people, and the chiefs themselves were generally poorer than the rest of their tribes. He recounted the birth of the great League of the Iroquois, with its guiding metaphor of a tree of peace whose top reached to the sun, and whose white roots spread deep and wide. He presented sachems as skilled in diplomacy and statecraft as in forest warfare, triumphing in both through cunning and stratagem rather than brute force. He was not embarrassed to liken the orators of the Iroquois to Roman senators, and bemoaned the fact that rude frontier interpreters were quite unable to convey the beauty and the power of the metaphors in which their thoughts were couched. Colden insisted that the alliance between the Confederacy of the Longhouse and the English—envisioned by the Indians as a covenant chain of bright silver—was the key to the security of New York and the expansion of the British Empire in North America. Daringly, he praised the French Jesuits, who labored tirelessly to break that chain. "One cannot but admire the Zeal, Courage and Resolution of these Jesuits, who comply with all the Humors and Customs of such a wild people." The last phrase stuck in Billy's memory. It was a stinging, if oblique, judgment on the negligence and standoffishness of the men who ruled New York. Colden ended his narrative in the 1680s, about the time Old Frog DeLancey had landed in the colonies. But there was promise of a sequel.

Billy returned the book at an hour of the late morning when he knew that James DeLancey was presiding over his courtiers at the Albany Coffee-House. The lady of the house received him in her wrapping-gown, coy as a virgin girl.

Anne allowed him to steal a kiss, but when he pressed his advances, she called for her maid.

Having secured a hiatus, she sent the girl away immediately, ordering tea and sherry.

She said to Billy, reproachfully. "James is an extraordinary man."

"I believe you have an appetite for such men."

"Whatever they taught you in Ireland, Mister Johnson, it did not include modesty."

"Forgive me," he smiled. "I was not myself."

"I fear you were only too much yourself."

He renewed his assault and, weakening, Anne DeLancey was thankful for the return of her maid.

She said to Billy, "Whatever will they make of you, among the Mohawk?"

3.

Frustrated, for the moment, in his siege of Mrs. DeLancey, Billy roamed the town, asking for Catherine Weissenberg. Robert Todd, the tallow-faced landlord of the tavern next to the DeLancey townhouse, counseled him to make enquiry of the sea captains who brought immigrants to the colonies.

"Give me some names," Billy coaxed him, leaning to one side to avoid the spume of tobacco-juice and foul hair from a seasoned toper across the table.

"Damn ye bitch, wherefore winna ye fetch a man a drink?" the landlord called to one of his girls.

"A name or two," Billy reminded him, smiling.

"Well, there's Jarvis and Waterman."

"There's Langdon, too," cried the toper squatting opposite.

"Aye, there's Langdon," Landlord Todd agreed. "But he is a slaver. White slaves and black slaves. You willna find an honest girl with him."

Billy visited all the captains mentioned and discovered much that was interesting, but not the object of his quest.

However, his reception at Captain Langdon's house, near the ferry, intrigued him. On his first visit, he found the captain away from home, and when he asked after Cat, a surly housekeeper shut the door in his face. He heard a considerable stir and commotion in the house with voices raised, but as if from below ground, in a cellar. When he returned, Captain Langdon received him in person and welcomed him inside for a mug of beer. Billy's host expressed high admiration for his uncle, Captain Warren, and hopes of a new war with Spain that would bring honest profit to any God-fearing sailor.

But when Billy mentioned Cat's name, Langdon's face tightened.

"You ought to know, sir," he informed Johnson, "that hired servants fetch a high price in New York."

"Hired servants? Do you mean indentured servants?"

"What else would I mean?"

"But the lady I spoke of is a free woman, of independent means."

"Ah well, there I can't help you."

Billy went away with the suspicion that Captain Langdon had something to hide, and resolved to call on him again. But his inquiries would have to wait on another season. The river ice was breaking up; fortune beckoned from the Mohawk Valley.

□

A week that began in freezing cold changed to steaming summer heat. Above the city, the ice on the river cracked with the dull thump of coehorn mortars. The ice cliffs tore apart, exposing the dark swell of the water. The sun glittered on the white crests of the Endless Mountains, to the west, and the stubborn drifts along the river, but the land between was soon the color of old, well-rubbed copper. The post-road to Boston turned to treacherous slush, snatching and sucking at hooves and carriage wheels. Billy was roused in the morning by the tapping of woodpeckers and the calls of bluebirds and low-flying geese. The bay was full of oyster-boats, and fresh shad appeared in the market. The DeLancey brothers entertained their gentlemen friends at a great outdoor feast and roasted a dozen turtles.

Captain Warren sent men with cudgels to range the tippling-shops in search of replacements for deserters from the *Squirrel;* it was time to take her back to her post at Boston. On a smoky day, with a warm wind gusting from the south, Peter Warren saw his nephews on board the high-decked sloop for Albany. He gave Billy letters of introduction to his relation by marriage, the Patroon, and to Lieutenant Butler at Fort Hunter.

"I expect you to write regular and keep strict accounts," Warren reminded his nephews. "See that my fields are laid out in orderly fashion. You might plant some hedgerows, to make everything tidy."

He made Indian country sound as tame and manageable as County Meath.

CHAPTER 13
THE NET

1.

The port where Billy and his companions disembarked after several days on the Hudson River had worn many names. The Indians who crossed the pine barrens from the Mohawk River to trade their peltries inside its stockades called it the Place Beyond the Pines. Early Dutch traders called it Beverwyck, in honor of the furry animal that had lured them so far upriver. The town had worn the names of Dutch princes: Orange (the name the French still preferred), Nassau, Willemstadt. The English called it Albany, in honor of the Duke who gave another of his titles to New York.

Island Woman's people called it The Net. They saw the traders' town as a net spread to catch their furs and their lands.

A scuffle was in progress at the landing when Johnson waded ashore, wishing he had been warned to wear something less vulnerable than his best hose, because this was a port without wharves. Denis Rahilly splashed after him, singing a ballad. Mick Tyrrell, more solicitous of his hose—or less impatient for the sights of Albany— delayed to negotiate with a burly porter and rode to the grassy shore, shaded by water beeches, on the shoulders of his human horse.

It was an unfair fight that Johnson found being waged. Three sturdy white men who looked serviceable with fists or knives were struggling with a native woman and her small boy. As Billy clambered up onto the bank, drenched and mud-spattered to his groin, the biggest of the white men laid hands like smoked hams on the Indian boy and tore him from his mother's arms. She raised a weird, ululating scream as the other white men grappled with her, trying to restrain her. They were not choosy about where they pressed her flesh.

"Good morning, gentlemen," Billy said pleasantly. He swept off his hat in a theatrical greeting to the native woman. "May I be of any assistance, ma'am?"

"Mind your damned business," growled the red-faced brute who was straining to keep his grip on the boy.

"I see you like short odds. Is it your custom here to fight women and children?"

"I'm doing my job," the bully spat. "The trade squaw owes money. I'm paid to collect."

"Is that why you are manhandling a child?"

"The brat is a pledge, damn you. Don't you know nothing? It's the one way to make these bush niggers pay their debts."

The boy was wild as a ferret. He turned and slithered in his captor's arms, then sank his teeth deep into the man's meaty forearm. The big man yelped, and the boy slipped free, hurling himself on the men who were holding his mother. The big man cursed and went after him.

Billy coolly interposed himself, toying with his blackthorn stick.

"I believe the boy has the better of the engagement. I would be glad if you would honor his courage."

"Lick my ass." The big man whipped out a knife half the length of Billy's forearm. The other river-rats abandoned the woman to focus on their new antagonist.

Mick Tyrrell dismounted and took a stand at Billy's right hand, loosening his coat to reveal its peach silk lining and the silver-chased butt of the long pistol he had acquired in Manhattan. Denis Rahilly flanked Billy on his other side, unarmed but bouncing on the balls of his feet, cocky as a gamester.

The Indian woman and her boy were moving at a rapid jog along the river bank, under the palisades of the town.

The river-rats hesitated between the newcomers and their quarry. One of them turned as if to give pursuit.

"Let them go," Johnson said.

The native woman glanced back at him, but made no gesture of recognition, not even a nod. A silver nose-bob quivered against her upper lip.

"You will pay for your meddling," the man with the knife promised Billy. "Livingston Huyck don't take kindly to them that interferes with his business."

"I have not had the pleasure of meeting your Mister Huyck. But if our paths cross, I shall most surely compliment him on how he is served. May I know your name."

"Bratt. Andries Bratt. You will remember it."

"Bratt. It will be hard to forget a name that suits its owner so well."

□

"To take a child as surety for a debt," Rahilly said, wondering. "Is that the morals of this town?"

"I cannot say," Billy responded. "But if it is so, I think there is a great deal to be accomplished simply by treating the natives with a little good humor."

□

Albany was a Dutch town, more even than the city at the other end of the river. Billy saw this in the houses, slated with Holland tiles, offering their stepped gable-ends to the street like memories of Amsterdam. The front they presented to the public view was faced with bricks, the other sides shingled with white pine.

The cloying smell of chocolate, from Wendell's factory, hung over the town. The cobbled streets were ripe with steaming cowpats. Even the grandees of Albany had their cows brought up at nightfall from the pastures on the south side of the stockade and quartered in the street outside their doors.

The Dutch merchants on Market and Barrack Streets sold sterling silver of quality and quantity that Billy had never seen, even in the smartest emporiums of New York. Watches as fat as turnips, tobacco boxes embossed with florid designs, charming footed *knotjes*—or bride's boxes—to be filled with coins and presented by a suitor to his lady.

"Why don't you buy this as an investment against the future?" Mick teased Billy, removing the lid from a *knotjes* engraved with ships in full sail and buxom ladies in full hooped skirts.

"You first."

When Johnson looked more closely at the silver box, he noticed a flaw—a runnel along one side like the track of a musket ball.

He pointed this out to Douw Volkert, the proprietor.

"A lady with love in her eyes would never notice it," Volkert winked at him.

"But that is a bullet mark, is it not?"

Volkert winked more broadly. "We don't ask provenance in these parts. You'll catch on soon enough, if you have trading in your soul."

Billy inspected the rest of the stock more closely. He noted family initials and crests, sometimes whole marriage vows engraved on many of the pieces. There was a scrolled W on a fine set of dessert spoons.

"Deerfield," Volkert said curtly, in response to Johnson's cocked eyebrow, declining any more specifics.

"It is an interesting scene," Billy remarked to Mick as they walked up the hill to pay their respects to the Patroon, Jeremiah van Rensselaer. "It seems the Mynheers are dealing in silver looted by French Indians from our New England neighbors."

Mick Tyrrell muttered imprecations against "treacherous banditti."

"That is perhaps too harsh," Johnson told his cousin. But he had the feeling that they had moved beyond the bounds of Britain's empire, whatever was shown on the maps. And beyond the rule of any law save that which flowed from a man's force and cunning.

□

At the Patroon's mansion, they were made to wait in a room filled with immense, dark furniture. Vault-like cupboards almost touched the ceilings. There was a pervasive tang of tobacco, and Johnson readily added to it by accepting a pipe from the big case that had pride of place on the wall, and a pinch of shag from a silver box like those in Volkert's store. A jambless fireplace stood out from the wall, with a big hood to catch the smoke and a display of delft and majolica dishes above the mantel.

A fresh-faced girl with hair the color of wheatsheaves and bright blue hose that traveled a long way up before they vanished under a short petticoat and a jacketwaist came in to tell them the Patroon was indisposed. But because his guests came from Captain Warren and Mr. DeLancey, Jeremiah van Rensselaer would receive them briefly in his bedchamber, if they would pardon the informality.

Billy found the Lord of Albany in a corner bedstead raised up like a full-rigged galleon, groaning on goose feathers. He parted the heavy curtains of camlet long enough to give his guests a glimpse of a waxy face under a nightcap. He had them served a glass of genever, and counseled Captain Warren's nephews that—while they had his sympathy, indeed admiration—they could never prosper.

"There is no money to be made west of Albany," the Patroon informed them. "I caution you strongly to avoid trade unless you decide to return to Albany and live with us here. We are not easy with outsiders, I admit it, but something may be done for a man who is vouched for by a DeLancey. Now, I must conserve my strength. Is there anything I can do for you?"

Johnson described the episode at the landing.

The Patroon flatly refused to believe that a merchant of the standing of Livingston Huyck—"a prince of our commerce, a member of the Commissioners of Indian Affairs"—could be embroiled in such a low incident.

"It is our policy to treat Indians fair," the Patroon insisted. "Our survival, in all senses, depends on it. There are vulgar ruffians to be found on any frontier. You had best put it out of your mind."

Johnson agreed to let it pass. He also agreed to the Patroon's offer to supply him with horses and wagons for the journey west.

□

Albany was no city on a hill. It was squeezed between the river and the western bluffs where the fort made a show of imperial might—an empty show, since the fort's magazine was empty. Captain Rutherford, the commander, had no balls for his cannon.

John Rutherford complained to Billy, over a glass or two, that the state of his defenses was no secret to the French.

"When the gates are not open, French Indians hop through the gaps in the stockade like locusts in summer. Sometimes they come fresh from scalping parties over the Massachusetts line. That is no matter to the masters of this town. Its chief business is treason. Your friend the Patroon made a secret visit to Montreal that might well be the source of his sickness. I hope it rots his vitals. I am reliably informed he made a treaty with the Frogs, like the prince of an independent power. They will not fight each other, even if war is declared and the Praying Indians lay waste to our frontiers."

"I find that hard to believe," Johnson said quietly.

"The only outsiders that are welcomed here are those that are enemies of the King. Mark my words."

The commandant of the Albany garrison was plainly not one of those rare outsiders—like the famous Scots enterpriser, Robert Livingston—who had made themselves useful enough to the masters of the town to be accepted as having the right to live among them. On the table beside the bottles, Billy noticed a copy of Leibniz's *Theodicy* with dog-eared pages. Difficult reading, he thought, for a difficult, lonely man.

Rutherford took a pull on his mug. "Even the dogs bark in Dutch. Those that do not bark in French. You had best watch your back in Albany, Mister Johnson."

Billy picked up the *Theodicy* and opened it at random.

"'The best of all possible worlds,'" Captain Rutherford quoted, smiling without joy. "It taxes a man's brain to sustain that thesis in these parts."

2.

If Albany was a net spread to catch profits, the blackrobe missions around Montreal were nets cast to trap souls.

Father Luc Nau, the superior at the Jesuit mission at Sault St. Louis, on the south bank of the St. Lawrence, was not a soldier-priest. Unlike the Abbé Picquet, the Sulpician in charge of the Iroquois at the Lake of Two Mountains—where Cat Weissenberg had been taken—or fellow-Jesuits who had led Abenaki war-parties against New England, and other tribes against the Foxes, far to the west, Father Luc took no delight in the smell of gunpowder or the death rattles of the heathen. He had winced at the sight of a Caughnawaga war canoe, returning from the western wars with the heads of enemies impaled on spears in the prow.

But in his struggle for souls, Father Luc found himself obliged to adapt to the customs of the country. He protected the Desaunier sisters and other traders who used his mission as the hub of a profitable contraband traffic with Albany, despite dark threats from the Governor-General, who damned the independence of the blackrobes at the Caughnawaga mission as hard as Captain Rutherford had damned the treachery of the merchant princes of Albany to Billy Johnson. The constant movement of Indians between Caughnawaga and Mohawk country brought new recruits for the mission. Several Mohawks had come in that winter, including a proud young woman called Swimming Voices, who had taken the name Louise at her baptism in Father Luc's stone church.

The Jesuit did not deceive himself that the motives of the Indians who sought sanctuary at his mission were altogether Christian. Or that those who accepted the chrism changed all their ways and beliefs.

The Indians came to escape war and hunger and imported disease. And the madness spread among them by liquor.

But Father Luc could not give them a safe haven from any of these. Not even alcohol, though he purged the faithful who returned to the demon drink. He had them flogged on his parade ground; he made them kneel for long hours in penance in the sight of all, outside his church, which was a harder punishment for a grand old warrior like Red Squirrel, the paramount warchief of the Caughnawaga Mohawks.

Some Indians sought conversion on their deathbeds, or in fear of the death of children or loved ones, believing that the white men who brought diseases the native shamans could not heal must be able to take them away. Or simply that the God of conquerors who came with cannon and horses must be stronger than the spirits of lakes and woods.

Father Luc baptized these desperate people and watched them die. He hungered for miracles, but was not allowed even one. Some of his converts recanted, even with their dying breaths. He worked long hours with one old reprobate who had agreed to be baptized, in fear of the hellfire Father Luc had promised for unbelievers. Then the ancient warrior fell into a dream or a vision. When he came back, he told his family that he had traveled the Path of Souls, to the worlds beyond this one, and seen nothing that resembled the talk of the blackrobes. He had his face painted red, dressed in his finest regalia, took up his dish and his spoon, and died with a smile on his lips as if he was going to his wedding.

Father Luc tormented himself, with hairshirts and fasting, with midnight vigils, for the lapses and deficiencies he observed among his flock.

He did battle for souls. He said his first mass at daybreak, for the women going out to the fields. One hour later, he said mass again, for the whole village. After breakfast, he gathered the children, to teach them the prayers he had set to music. He found their voices strangely mellow and sonorous. They sang better than nuns or cordeliers, never missing a half-tone. Later, he assembled the adults who were not yet baptized to rehearse the answers to the catechism. In the evening, there were more prayers. He celebrated the festival days with pomp and color, which the savages loved. At the feast of Corpus Christi, the warriors paraded in feathers and paint, as if going to battle. When the Sacrament was laid down at the shrine of the Blessed Kateri, the Mohawk woman revered as a bride of Christ, the Caughnawaga Mohawks fired off musket volleys, answered by a salvo of French mortars.

Father Luc was vigilant for signs of backsliding and increased his penalties. He made drunken Indians do penance by kneeling outside the church during service, for ten or twelve days at a stretch. He reserved harsher penalties for those who were obstinate in their pagan practices, gathering in the woods at night to celebrate obscene rituals, smuggling charms and amulets inside his church, consorting with familiar spirits. The Jesuit knew that, for all his efforts, the eternal Enemy was busy among his flock. Banished from the waking lives of the faithful, he visited them in dreams.

The blackrobe was appalled by the power of these dreams over the minds of even the most dutiful of his converts. They appeared to be in the grip of a collective delusion, that when they lay down at night their souls went journeying to far places. In their ignorance and superstition, they believed that powerful spirits—even the demon their sorcerers held to be the creator of this world—appeared to them in these fantastic imaginings.

Father Luc, believing himself the servant of a unique revelation accessible only through the Church of the Apostles, made war against the ancient heresy that revelation is to be found in each human soul.

He had persuasive weapons: gifts of food and tools and warm blankets, the apportionment of choice fields to be worked along the river.

He was a man of reason as well as faith, but he did not scruple to play on the teleological fears of his charges, in language plundered from their own folk beliefs. He old the Indians:

"We are all possessed of an immortal soul. If you lead ,ood lives, your souls will migrate after death to a happy and toward the setting sun, as your grandmothers have old you. In this happy land, your men will hunt beaver ind elk and your women will bring in the corn without ffort, and you will all dance together and sing songs of raise. But this reward awaits only those of you who are edeemed through our Saviour. For it is certain that nighty archangels stand guard at the portals of the next vorld, and that all souls shall be judged. And that those imong you who have spurned the Risen Lord and stayed esolute in sin will be cast down into a hell of burning ire where your punishment will serve the evil you have erved."

When Father Luc delivered such homilies, his congreɛants usually heard him out in silence, collected the rifling gifts with which he rewarded regular attendance —little mirrors for the women, jew's harps for the nen—and went on their way. Because they did not ontradict him, Father Luc reassured himself that he was naking headway.

Until a visitor presumed to debate him in his own :hurch.

This had happened many winters past, but the memo- y lived with him now. It stung worse than poison oak.

She was a Mohawk woman, come to trade with the Desaunier sisters or visit relatives at the mission.

They called her Tewatokwas, Island Woman, though ιe had not known this until he had made inquiries after he incident.

A tall, strong, handsome woman of uncertain age, :tanding up straight as an alder in the back pews of the :hurch.

Not one of the baptized. He had seen that because she ιad presumed to wear fetishes and medicine pouches— hings forbidden to the faithful, things of the demon— nto the house of God.

Nonetheless, Father Luc, hunter of souls, had welcomed the chance of making an important convert. The woman had natural presence and carried authority among the other Indians. They seemed to create a special space for her.

And there had been something else about her. A kind of radiance. As if light fell around her from a skylight that did not exist in his steep-angled roof.

She spoke slowly in Mohawk, in the accent of the Valley. It was hard to understand her. She used ancient words that were not in Father Bruyas' lectionary, and they came as song more than speech.

"Niawen," she had told him, speaking as if for all.

"We thank you for reminding us that the soul is immortal. The Real People know this is true, because at our choosing, our souls leave our bodies to talk with our ancestors and our spirit guides, and to travel to places many looks away. This is how our hunters find where the deer are herding in winter. This is how our warriors know where our enemies are hiding in ambush. This is how we discover who we are and what we are meant to be.

"Since our souls take flight from our bodies in our dreams, we know very well that the soul does not die with the body. As for your place of fire, our dreamers have seen this too. But we think this place is not for us, but for white men. You killed the Son of your Great Spirit. We are not responsible for this. When white men die, they go to a different place from us."

Outraged, Father Luc had begun to protest. "Be careful, lest you burn in hell for your pride."

She had defied him to his face. "You speak much of this hell of Christians. Have you seen it with your own eyes? Have you felt the heat of its flames?"

"Good Lord! I hope never to see the fires of damnation."

"Then how do you know what they are like?"

"I have it on the authority of scripture." He had placed his hand on the Book, solid, indomitable.

And the Mohawk woman had presumed to say, "I do not know your book. But I know what I have seen in my dreams, and what the spirits teach me. So I think you will keep your book, and we will keep our dreams. For we trust only what we can see and live for ourselves."

Besieged in his own church, under the eyes of his congregation—some of whom he saw wavering, even smirking—Father Luc had rallied all his strength for a ally.

"What are these spirits of which you dare to speak?"

"They come in many forms, to those who are ready."

"Do they appear to you as birds or animals?"

"It can happen."

Smelling sorcery, Father Luc had struggled to respond in a measured way, telling himself, *This Mohawk witch gives me the chance to expose the deceits of the Adversary before all her kinsmen.*

He had chosen the armory of logic, asking slyly, "How do you know the soul leaves the body? How can you prove this?"

"We know this because we dream."

"Then tell me this. When you dream, is your body dead or alive?"

"It is alive."

Father Luc had pounced. "Then it cannot be true that the soul quits the body when you dream, or else the body would surely be dead."

"What remains with the body is the breath-soul. After the body dies, the breath-soul dies also. Then the true soul is released."

"Where does this true soul go?"

"It goes to the Real World. It may come back, to learn something it failed to learn. To finish something left unfinished. Or to guard the people and the land it loves. But if it has listened to false words, or lived a false life— or died suddenly, without preparation—it may become lost and bewildered. Then we can hear it keening on the wind, drinking the smoke of our cooking fires."

The breathing silence in the church had weighed on Father Luc. He had felt it crushing his lungs.

He had gasped, "How can you *know* these things? Unless from Satan himself?"

The Mohawk woman had not answered, except perhaps with her eyes. The intensity of that gaze had produced an odd hallucination.

As if she had flown the whole length of the nave and pressed close against my face. There seemed to be something soft and glossy about the eyes. Like feathers.

Crossing himself, Father Luc had resolved to regain his grip on the situation. *The heart of their superstitions is their dreams.* He had bent all his reserves on dealing with this.

"You say you see all these wonders in your dreams. Do you sleep with your eyes open?"

"No." Her lower lip had made a spout of derision.

"Then these wonders you report are figments of the mind," Father Luc had pressed his advantage. "For how can you see with your eyes closed?"

"A man who sees only with his eyes open is blind."

Father Luc had conceded then, in his own mind, that his sword of logic was forged from soft metal.

From the depths of memory, a new weapon had leaped to his hand, the fierce words of Ezekiel against the eternal Adversary:

> Wherefore thus saith the Lord God: Behold, I am against your pillows, wherewith ye there hunt the souls to make them fly, and I will tear them from your arms, and will let the souls go, even the souls that ye hunt to make them fly.

He had laid his hand on the Book, to hurl this lance at the Tempter. But to his bafflement, he had found the stranger gone. How could he have failed to see the Mohawk woman travel the twenty paces from her place to the door?

Not a week had passed, since this encounter, when he had failed to think about it. The Mohawk woman had returned to him in dreams, and he blamed her arts for dreams even more troubling, in which brown, nubile girls tempted his chastity with the play of their limbs and breasts.

Most troubling was the inner voice that taunted him n the long nights of his spiritual exercises, which neither is hairshirts nor his austerities would quiet.

This voice said to him: "If your soul has not walked with Christ in this world, how will you find him in the next?"

□

So Father Luc welcomed the news that Island Woman's daughter, spurned by her mother and her own kind, had fled to the sanctuary of his mission.

There were evil rumors about this Swimming Voices, whom the blackrobe had christened Louise. That she, too, was a sorcerer, driven from the Valley because she had used the black arts against her own people.

But Father Luc was resolved to trust only the evidence of his own senses. The savage mind was not easily enlightened, and his flock was rife with superstition. Many of the faithful begged to be buried under the church itself, not trusting to the holy ground of the cemetery, for fear their remains would be disturbed by necromancers.

Then, too, he had seen how charges of witchcraft masked other jealousies. There was friction between Swimming Voices and one of the Caughnawaga women over a man called Spotted Wolf, a wild, feckless character who came and went at whim between the mission and the Mohawk country, bartering furs and information. This Spotted Wolf was forever starting fights, especially after rolling home drunk from one of the Indian grogshops across the river, where everything breakable was kept out of throwing range and the barkeeps doled out watered Nantes brandy from booths constructed like miniature blockhouses. Father Luc would have expelled him from the mission, but for the fact that he had some pull with the government's Indian agents, and relations between the Jesuits at the Sault and the government were already strained.

Louise Swimming Voices was regular in her church attendance and had even hoed and weeded for the

Jesuits in their kitchen garden. So Father Luc was disposed to dismiss the stories against her as black bile spewed out by the mother. Or perhaps by Hortense Whistling Birch, the woman—the blackrobe would not dignify her with the term *wife,* since she was unmarried in the sight of the Church—who claimed Spotted Wolf as her man.

Hortense, by contrast, had not been in church for nearly a month. Father Luc decided to check on her. The boom of the rapids was deafening as he approached her lodge, on the brow of the hill, just inside the stockade. He caught sight of a woman's naked back and turned away in hot embarrassment. But looked again, to confirm his troubling first impression.

Hortense had not seen him coming. She reached into a bark container and brought out a clod of raw, dripping meat. The priest stared, revolted, as she reached behind her back and stuffed the bloody meat into a huge, suppurating hole below her right shoulderblade. As she craned around to inspect her work, her eyes met Father Luc's.

The priest cleared his throat as the woman gathered up her clothes and covered her breasts.

"Forgive me, Hortense. I do not mean to intrude. You clearly need doctoring. Perhaps I have something that can help."

The size of the red, gaping crater in the woman's back had shaken him. Was it an ulcer, or a wound?

"I know what doctoring I need," Hortense said flatly.

"What do you hope to accomplish with the meat?"

"I am feeding this thing so it does not feed on me."

Sympathetic magic. Is there no end to their delusions?

"You are treating the symptoms, after a fashion. Perhaps we would do better to treat the causes."

"I know where this comes from. Your pet, Louise Swimming Voices, put this one on me. We are going to send it back."

"What are you talking about?"

She closed up tight.

He set off in search of Swimming Voices.

3.

While Father Luc sought proof of witchcraft—a dese-
crated grave, a devil-doll dressed in the intended victim's clothes or hair—new visitors were on their way to
his mission.

With the spring melt, the beavers left their lodges and
swam around in their ponds, basking in their liberation
from the ice. They made themselves easy prey to a man
like Blue Paint, who knew the right place to hide a trap
and had a steady aim with a firelock. Beavers were
smart. They would spot a trap unless it was carefully
concealed, at the end of a fresh-padded trail, where the
jaws could be hidden under the water and the trapper
could rake up bits of dead wood to make everything look
natural.

If you wanted to shoot beaver in the water, you had to
kill with a head-shot; a wounded beaver would swim to
the bottom and die where you couldn't find it. When the
ice broke, you had no time to waste, because the rivers
rose fast. You had to get to the small, spring-fed streams
the beavers loved to dam before they flooded.

Cat Weissenberg learned all of this, when Blue Paint
and his family took her up the muddy Ottawa River in a
sleek birchbark canoe into beaver country. The hunters
sat watching at dusk for the telltale bubbles of a beaver
coming up to feed. They pegged the pelts of their kills of
frames and set them facing the sun to dry. When they
saw that Cat was deft with her hands and a quick learner,
they entrusted more and more of the skinning and
drying to her. When she was not doing this, she was
bringing in firewood or helping Blue Paint's mother with
the cooking pots, which simmered all day long, because
the trappers were voracious and any stranger who
dropped in expected to be fed.

She watched Blue Paint discussing her with one of
these strangers, a whiskery *coureur du bois* whose skin
had acquired the texture of beef jerky. After a while,

Blue Paint made a curt gesture of dismissal. She understood that she had been offered in trade, but had not raised a sufficient price. With this, she began to see her present status in its true light. Despite the ceremony in the council house, she was not treated as a full member of Blue Paint's family; he had not even approached her as a woman. Yet she was something more than a slave, better used, in all senses, than in Captain Langdon's house.

I am an article for trade, she realized. *Blue Paint negotiates for me as he will do for a pack of beaver plews.*

It was easy hunting, up north. After a few weeks shooting and trapping, they filled three canoes with their peltries and headed back downriver. The men crouched in the thwarts, paddling fifty strokes to the minute, laughing at the swirl of white water.

Traders came out to meet them, at the Lake of Two Mountains. But to Cat's surprise, they did not stop at the Sulpician mission, but followed the yellow waters of the Ottawa downstream, to where they vanished into the cold, clear flood of the St. Lawrence.

Her captors did not explain to her that they were going down to Caughnawaga because the profits would be greater here, closer to the great merchant houses of Montreal. And to Albany.

Blue Paint knew the Mohawk women at Caughnawaga. They were picky. Their men might prefer cognac to rum, and French powder to the English version, but the women usually got the final say in business matters, and they wanted copper kettles from Birmingham, not the clumsy, heavy French pots. They wanted strouds from Leeds and Manchester, dyed a good, deep scarlet, or a midnight blue, for their skirts and leggings, not the rusty, scrappy *écarlatines* from France.

And the Jesuits at this mission on the south side of the St. Lawrence were indulgent. They smiled on the illegal trade, to the extent of allowing the Desaunier sisters—Marie and Magdalene—to set up a store on mission ground, between the church and the bark lodges of the Indians, on condition that they did not sell brandy.

A man with a boatload of prime winter furs could usually find things worth trading for at Caughnawaga. And if not, the water-roads to Albany were always open.

Blue Paint did not care much for the Desaunier sisters. They went to church three times a day, to satisfy the priests, but would haggle all day over the price of a needle.

But there would be plenty of white men at the mission this spring. Bawdy, open-hearted *voyageurs,* looking for a girl and a good time; shifty brandy peddlers who sat out in the woods, whistling for trade; officers of the Troupes de la Marine, recruiting killers; nervous burghers who called themselves seigneurs, terrified of being caught smuggling to the English colonies, but incapable of resisting the lure of a profit; Albany pirates; double agents and spies.

Someone would pay well for the white woman who had wintered with his family.

He had considered making her his own woman, but there was something in his heart that resisted this. And his mother had turned her face against Cat, though she spoiled Cat's mother like one of her own brood.

□

They hauled the canoes on shore and walked up the slope to the mission. Cat stared at the wooden image of a rooster—a flightless bird—atop a cross with a slanting bar across the shaft, close to the ground. Then at the spare figure of a priest in a broad-brimmed, flat hat and trailing cassock, moving at a half-run between Indian lodges, bent on some urgent business.

She paused to admire the light slanting across the white mountain of Montreal.

Then Blue Paint's mother jabbed her in the kidneys, reminding her that this distant beauty was not something she could possess.

I am a coin that is passed from hand to hand, until its shine is gone, its markings worn smooth and dull. Or a piece of eight, that is clipped and shaved. A thing that

*dwindles with use and could recount only the uses men
have made of it.*

 We crown our own heads, Ade had said.

 But how could this be true, except in dreams?

 Will I ever be permitted to claim my own fate?

CHAPTER 14

FOREST KILLER

1.

Island Woman saw that the rhythms of the newcomers' lives were unlike the rhythms of the Real People. In the country of her grandmothers, before the whites came, the cycle of each year was the same. It turned with the seasons, with the fish-runs and the mating of the deer, with the seeding and harvesting of the corn, with the rituals of thanksgiving. What was expected of a person was known to all: to honor the ancestors, to bring new life into the world, to share the gifts of the Mother, to walk in balance between earth and sky. The life of a person, or a whole nation, followed a spiral course endlessly turning on its beginnings.

The Real People did not have a history as the newcomers conceived of history: relentless forward motion down a straight road. The great events relived by the winter fires—the descent of She Who Fell from the Sky, the coming of the Peacemaker—did not happen in time. They happened in the Real World, where it is always *now*, where dreamers walk with the spirits.

The newcomers were different. They made the future different from the past and hurried after it. Island Woman knew that her people must learn how to do this;

the rhythms of their lives could never be the same now the newcomers had imposed their history on the forest-sea. But changing was not easy; it was not natural.

□

Island Woman met a white man in a hurry on the road through the pine bush, between Schenectady and Albany.

She was riding in her own wagon, with Bright Meadow and Fruitpicker and a fat heap of beaver plews and raccoon pelts for trade in the Dutchmen's town. Snowbird walked ahead. Dandelion and White Owl brought up the rear.

White Owl said he had business of his own at Albany. But Island Woman had noticed that the Bear Clan warrior was taking a keen interest in Bright Meadow since she had become a woman. She would not discourage the match, if it was what her younger daughter wanted. Despite his youth, White Owl had won a reputation as a war leader that was second only to that of Hendrick Forked Paths, and the women noticed that the men who took the warpath with him came back alive. White Owl was solid and steady, modest in his comportment with women and elders, and there was always plenty of food in his mother's lodge.

Snowbird stopped in the road, making a quick snatching motion with his fingers.

Far ahead, Island Woman made out a crowd of newcomers struggling with a wagon that had run into a ditch or mudhole. In the distance, they looked like white ants working to shift the carcass of a beetle.

□

Billy Johnson was down on the ground in his shirt-sleeves, cursing because the spring rains had turned the road into sucking mudholes interrupted by rocks.

One of his wagons had sunk to the axle-trees, while the team struggled knee-deep in the muck. The horses were wretched, scrawny beasts—Albany horses, left to fend for themselves in the woods in the depth of winter. He had found that at least one of them was infested with botflies under the saddlecloth. The nasty hooked things would have to be winkled out one by one at the point of a knife; until it had healed, the little stallion would not be able to bear weight.

Billy cursed himself for not having made a thorough inspection. He had allowed the Patroon to presume on his station and a remote family connection; Jeremiah van Rensselaer was an in-law of Uncle Peter's DeLancey in-laws. Most galling of all, Billy knew if he made any public complaint, he would suffer worse.

If word gets out that I have allowed myself to be rooked by the Patroon of Albany, his inferiors will vie with each other to treat me even worse. Word will run from here to Oswego that a prime greenhorn is here for the taking.

Mick Tyrrell slipped in the muck. His flying boot spattered mud over Billy's face and shoulders.

Johnson threw back his mane and roared, "Jeremiah van Rensselaer, may you melt off this earth like snow off a ditch!"

"Amen to that, Billy!" Denis Rahilly shouted. Billy's sometime tutor had done a disappearing act in New York. The night before he boarded the sloop, Billy had found Rahilly holding court in a tavern near the customs house, with a tally written up in chalk on the blackboard he had no prospect of paying—at imminent risk of being invited back to sea by a press-gang. Rahilly had agreed that departure was prudent. He had brought with him a fiddle, an Irish harp in need of restringing and a new batch of improbable stories about the Governor's cook.

"Hear me, Patroon!" Billy boomed louder. "May the grass grow high before your door!"

"And above your head!" Paddy Groghan volunteered.

Mick Tyrrell interrupted the flow of verbal invention. "Billy, will you take a look there. I believe these are some of our new neighbors."

Wiping mud from his face with a handkerchief, Johnson strolled into the middle of the road and inspected the advancing party of Indians.

He was not accustomed to looking up to other men.

But the Mohawk who walked ahead of the women in the wagon stood nearly a head taller and was half as broad again. The Indian was naked except for a scarlet blanket that he wore draped like a toga and two flaps of buckskin, tucked into a beaded belt, that covered his nether parts.

Billy had never seen anyone, male or female, adorned with so much jewelry. A blue stone bobbed against Snowbird's upper lip, suspended from his nasal septum by a silver loop. His earlobes were pierced in several places. They sprouted bright sprays of turkey down. They jangled with little silver bells. Silver and brass gorgets, circlets of claws and stone fetishes, jounced over the gunpowder tattoos on his massive chest. Over the heart, he wore a disk of stiff white buckskin or buffalo hide, beaded and laced with dyed porcupine quills in the design of a circle-cross. The snout of a wolfskin hung over his forehead. The tail drooped to the small of his back, decorated with dozens of gleaming bits of silver that looked like women's thimbles to Billy. When Snowbird spread his arms in greeting, he tinkled and clanged like a tinker's wagon.

Rahilly clapped his hands in delight.

"*Sekon,*" Snowbird offered the newcomers the customary greeting. "*Skenakowa.* Peace be with you."

"How do you do." Johnson extended his hand. "I am William Johnson and these are my friends. We are on our way to Fort Hunter. Perhaps you have come from there?"

Snowbird's glance moved from the proferred hand to the wagon the white men had been struggling with. He grunted to Dandelion, who came at a brisk jog, drawing curious looks from the newcomers, who had seen few Mohawks, let alone a blond one. Dandelion caught the firelock Snowbird tossed to him, then the red blanket he pulled from his shoulder.

"Lord, Billy," Rahilly called in a stage whisper. "Do you see the fellow's cloak? It would do credit to a Henry the Fifth at Smock Alley."

Snowbird motioned for the white men around the wagon to stand aside. Then he dipped low to get a firm grip on the axle. When he raised himself to his full height, the muscles stood out in his arms and neck. The front wheels of the heavy wagon tremored in mid-air. With a single, rolling motion, Snowbird dislodged the rear wheels from the mud and pushed the huge cart, loaded high with trade bundles, onto solid ground.

"I will study long before I wrestle with you," Billy said admiringly.

Snowbird's breathing was still regular. He started poking about under the canvas cover of the wagon. He found bolts of fine Dublin linen and Scottish checks, pieces of cambric and lace.

"I hope you will let us show our appreciation." Billy dug into one of the bundles and produced a leather cap. Uncle Peter had included a couple of gross of caps and bonnets in the consignment, having been assured by one of his suppliers that they were all the rage with the natives.

Snowbird turned the cap inside out. "What for?"

"You wear it on your head, man," Mick volunteered.

Snowbird turned down his mouth. "You Scottish?"

"Absolutely not. Why do you ask?"

"Scottish wears piece of shit on his head."

Mick blushed to the roots of his ears. Billy started laughing. Snowbird's face was quite expressionless.

"You got steel traps?" It was a woman who spoke.

Billy turned to look at her. She was tall and sinewy, of uncertain age. She moved with natural grace and absolute assurance. Her hair was tied back in long braids. She wore a pair of luckenbooth brooches at the collar of her scarlet blouse. Her eyes were sharp as obsidian knives.

"I'm not sure," Billy faltered.

"You *handlaer?*" Island Woman used the Dutch word for trader.

"Yes and no. I brought goods for trade. But I mean to stay. My uncle has bought land on the Mohawk River." He looked at the other women in the wagon. A proud old matriarch, a likely girl with a pleasing softness in her figure and eyes that avoided him.

Island Woman followed his glance and frowned. *Another user.*

"Funny kind of *handlaer,*" she commented. "With no steel traps."

She walked over to Snowbird. He had found a ruffled shirt and some boxes of gunflints that pleased him better than the fabrics.

Island Woman ignored the bolts of linen.

I have everything to learn, Billy realized.

"You Scottish?" Snowbird asked him.

"Not me."

"Where you come from?"

"I was born in Ireland. It is a small country surrounded by water, on the edge of Europe. You are our nearest neighbors to the west." Billy had rehearsed this statement, thinking it would please the Indians.

But Snowbird grunted, "I know Irish." He tipped back his head and mimed the action of drinking. "Lieutenant Butler is Irish. Irishmen all great drinkers, damn-me-to-hell. You got drink?"

"He's got our ticket, Billy!" Rahilly cackled.

A little crestfallen, Billy produced his traveling flask.

Snowbird spat out a strange, snaky word as he raised it to his lips. *"Snekira!"*

Island Woman uttered a short, barking sound. And the man-mountain changed. He sniffed at the flask and said, "No good." He handed it back to Billy.

"By God, you'll not find better in the colonies!" Billy cut off his protest as he became alive to the strange chemistry between the warrior and the older woman.

Among the Six Nations, the women rule. That was what Cadwallader Colden had told him. Could it be true? *Surely not to the point of coming between a man and his drink.*

Island Woman, joined by the other women, had found a few things she liked. Some bright Gloucestershire strouds, a gleaming copper kettle, mirrors and knives.

She drove a hard bargain, and the men in her party stood aside from the negotiations.

These Mohawks were from the Upper Castle, some distance upriver from the Warren estate. Billy consoled himself with the hope that the Indians at the Lower

Castle, near Fort Hunter, would be easier to deal with. And he was cheered by the fact that Snowbird responded with a palpable wink when he murmured, at their parting, "If you change your mind about the drink, you must not forget to call on me."

2.

The frontier began at Schenectady.

The town fronted the Mohawk River, at the end of the wagon road through the pine bush from Albany. It was still haunted by the memory of a massacre in midwinter, when French Indians had crossed the northern wastes on snowshoes.

Lodges for Indian visitors stood just outside the stockade, their elmbark roofs banging in the wind. Billy saw curious animals depicted in charcoal on the walls. A thing like a monstrous lizard with devouring teeth. He was told this was called a crocodile, and was found far to the south. The shaggy bull was a buffalo, at home on the seas of grass in the vast interior of the continent. The pictures testified to the boldness and range of the warriors of the Six Nations. It seemed they thought nothing of walking a thousand miles to bring home a trophy.

At the Mohawk landing, hard-eyed, whiskery men inspected Billy and Mick, their servants and their trade bundles. They watched Billy lead his damaged horse to the farrier's.

When Johnson threw off the saddlecloth, the farrier spat out a foul rivulet of tobacco juice and confirmed, "Bots."

He jabbed the business end of a long hunting knife into the stallion's hide and twisted out a nasty black bug. He held it up on the knife-point for Billy to examine. The botfly's legs were quivering hooks. Dozens of the ugly things were nesting in the horse's back.

"Never looked, did you?"

"I was pressed for time." Billy was resolved not to mention the name of the Patroon. *It will make me look like a snob as well as a fool.*

"Can you do something for him?"

"How much time you got?"

"Not much. We are going upriver."

"Best leave him here. He'll not make a saddlehorse. No way." The stable man allowed he might be able to get Billy a quarter what he had paid the Patroon.

"I'll think on it." He paid for food and water for the horse, and a good scrub-down. But his mind was already made up. He patted the long gray neck. *I'll keep you,* he promised. *I'll call you Fergus. I'll get you well again and we'll show the Patroon I got the best of the bargain after all.*

◻

Beyond Schenectady, with its slit-eyed traders and quick-tempered river jockeys, there were only a few scattered beachheads of white settlement in the forest-sea. On isolated farms or in the small, huddled communities at Stone Arabia, Burnetsfield and along the Schoharie, Dutch and German families worked the land with sickles and hoes; like the Israelites of the Old Testament they loved to quote at mealtimes as well as at services. There was a busy traffic on the Mohawk River, but it was seasonal: fur traders shipping their cargo west on long, shallow bateaux to the tiny post at Oswego, the only toehold of the English colonies on the Great Lakes; Indians canoeing downstream to try their luck in the truck houses of Albany.

Billy Johnson found himself riding into the thickest woods he had ever seen.

The Warren estate fronted the river for more than three miles on the near side of Fort Hunter, the sole British garrison between Albany and Oswego. The land ran back into the woods for five miles along the winding course of the Schoharie. What greeted Billy Johnson was not the vision of open, arable farmlands that Mr. Colden had conjured up—the "natural granary" where you had but to scratch the topsoil to bring up a bumper crop.

As he began to probe the limits of the estate, Billy's path was blocked by fallen trees piled so high the woods seemed to grow sideways. Thorns and brambles ripped at his clothes and skin. He was plagued by deerflies the size of the top joint of his finger, and by swarms of mosquitoes and invisible, pricking things. You could walk for hours in those woods without seeing the sun. Ghostly things thrived in the shadow—fungus the size of dinner plates that grew out from the trunks of dead trees, ether-white plants whose heads curled like pipe bowls and never touched the earth, drawing their life from rotting vegetation. The woods were full of life that did not welcome newcomers: with black bear and brown bear, timber wolves, shy deer and shyer squatters who fled from their new landlord like Smithstown tenants who had missed a payment or two. Billy inspected the squatters' dirt farms with interest. There was good loam over the clay where they had scratched a clearing among the trees. But it was far less fertile than the deep black bottomlands on the other side of the Mohawk River, and every inch of it had to be won by axe and fire.

"It is not a job for the drinking class," Mick Tyrrell observed, openly dismayed by the prospect of all the sweat that would have to be expended to plant Captain Warren's dream of a genteel estate in this wilderness.

"Uncle Peter bought the wrong side of the river." Billy stared enviously at the open farmlands on the north side. The road on the Warrensbush side petered out at Fort Hunter. But on the north side, the King's Road ran west through Little Falls to the Oneida Carry. It was the main artery of commerce between the settled areas of the province and the fur trappers of the Great Lakes, other than the river itself. Taverns and truck houses, sawmills and the first grist mill west of Schenectady were already springing up along it.

A man with an eye for land or an eye to trade would look there, not here, Billy thought.

They girdled and burned enough timber to sow ten acres of wheat on what was to be the home farm on the Warren property. Before summer's end, Billy and Mick moved from a rough log shelter to a good-sized frame house, with two airy rooms and a sleeping loft above.

Denis Rahilly came calling when Billy was sitting out on the stoop after supper with a pipe, gazing across the river to the King's Road and the high country beyond it, rising in the purple dusk to the spires of the Adirondacks.

"It is a sight and a half," Rahilly avowed. "And I know what is in your mind, Billy Johnson."

"What do you know, Mister Rahilly?"

"I know you mean to make some of that your own. You mean to put down your roots here."

"My agreement with my uncle is for three years."

"Ah, that was made in a city. And you are not made for cities, Billy, though you have sampled their pleasures. You are like the oak, which must have room in the earth to spread his roots, so mighty does he rise. And you are that type of Irishman in the story. Sure and you remember. He was dragged down to hell and when they opened his heart the first thing they found writ on it was *land.*"

"Maybe you do know me, Denis. Will you stay with me?"

"I am the other sort of Irishman, Billy. I must hop about like a sparrow and sing in all seasons. And I think I must fly before winter."

3.

Billy worked with the teams in the woods, girdling and felling trees. And he studied his neighbors.

There were only a few hundred newcomers in the Valley: Palatine refugees, hardy Dutch pioneers—Wemps, Clements, Van Pattens—and a spattering of Anglo-Irish. Kast's farm, at Little Falls, marked the western boundary of settlement in the Province of New York. Beyond it, the Iroquois Trail—a shallow trench pounded deep by numberless moccasined feet—wound west through the lands of the Oneida and Onondaga to the trading post at Oswego on Lake Ontario.

Fort Hunter, on the rise where the Schoharie joins the Mohawk, was the hub of the white community and the only visible sign of the British presence. The fort had been built in Queen's Anne's time, reflecting the grand design of carrying the boundaries of Empire into the interior of America, and challenging the French influence over the nations to the west. The fort did not inspire confidence. Its defenses were a rude stockade of hewn logs, laid horizontally, with chunky blockhouses at the corners. They would not withstand an assault by fieldguns or coehorn mortars, and there were gaps in the walls where wind and ice had taken their toll.

In meeting his neighbors—newcomers or natives—Johnson had the advantages of a natural joiner, ready to engage in any sport that was on offer. He mud-wrestled with the generally somber German farmers along the Schoharie. He smoked with the Dutchmen at Fonda's tavern and brought them across the river for a pig roast at the home farm. He drank with Walter Butler and his sons at the fort. Lieutenant Butler, ever wary of interlopers, plied the boys from County Meath hard their first evening. He told them, "We must know the wheat from the chaff." When the night was done, only Billy still had the use of his legs. Even Denis Rahilly, who had trained well and long, had to be carried home.

"No man ever died of drink," Rahilly counseled Billy when he had made a partial recovery. "But there is many that have died learning to drink."

Johnson earned the Butlers' respect at some risk to his liver. The Mohawk made him run the gauntlet in other ways.

They turned up unannounced at all times of day and night. Sometimes, out in the fields, he would turn to find an Indian standing right behind him. They would lounge or squat for hours—men, women and children—saying little or nothing, watching his men clearing land, observing the thin business of his little trading post.

He had written to his uncle that many of the trade goods he had brought with him were of no interest to the Indians. Captain Warren, grumbling, had allowed his nephew to order things that always seemed to be in demand at the Mohawk castles: strouds in bold colors, gaudy paints, knives and steel traps, and ruffled shirts. And liquor.

Billy ordered four hogsheads of rum from Bayard's in New York. The day after they arrived, Snowbird turned up at Warrensbush with a dozen warriors and a sachem built to his own heroic proportions, grandly rigged out in a Prussian blue coat, trimmed with silver, and a matching hat.

Hendrick swept off his hat, lordly as a courtier at Versailles.

"I am Tehayanoken," the warchief announced. "He Whose Paths Fork."

"You are welcome."

Hendrick Forked Paths removed a great ball-headed warclub, with a steel blade set in the ridge, from its sling. He pointed to the notches incised on the side. He said, "I have eaten the hearts of many enemies of my brother the King."

"Your courage is known throughout the nations." Billy slipped easily into the theatrical style.

"Let us smoke together."

One of the warriors produced a long pipe-tomahawk, decorated with figures, and it passed from hand to hand. Billy found the native tobacco harsh. It burned the roof of his mouth. He swallowed, trying not to cough.

Hendrick smiled for the first time. "The old ones say man rides to the skies on a cloud of tobacco. But maybe this is thirsty work for you."

Billy was not slow to follow the hint. He called for Jane Watson, one of the serving girls he had brought over from County Meath, and asked her to bring refreshments for his guests.

"Snekira!" The Mohawks raised their strange, sinuous toast.

Hendrick sampled the rum punch and smacked his lips. "Iawekhon. This tastes good. But I like cognac better. Or claret."

Johnson asked Jane to oblige.

By nightfall, when Billy had set a young calf to roast on a spit for his visitors, more than thirty Mohawks had gathered at the farm and were punishing an impressive array of bottles and kegs.

They drank so many toasts that Billy, who prided

himself on his repertoire of rhyming versions, found himself back at the beginning. Lieutenant Butler had warned him of the violence that could explode from Indians in liquor, as dangerous and arbitrary as a whirlwind. But nothing serious had been broken as yet, and the fighting had been only a little harmless cuffing between Snowbird and a couple of the younger men.

After a burst of war stories and a series of complaints about longer-established traders—especially aimed at an Albany merchant who was said to water his rum with his own product—Hendrick Forked Paths had fallen silent.

Billy paced himself, watching for the next mood shift, the one that could be dangerous.

Hendrick shifted his bulk. Then he jabbed with his forefinger, pressing the root of Billy's neck through the loosened collar of his ruffled shirt.

"Why do you drink?" the warchief demanded.

"It is a natural pleasure. Why do we smoke tobacco? Why do we eat?"

"It is not the same. It is not natural to us. It eats our minds and our bellies." Hendrick twisted the thick-bottomed firing-glass in his hand.

"So why do *you* drink?" Billy risked the question.

Forked Paths turned on him with killer's eyes.

He looks at me as if he means to pluck out my liver and eat it without salt.

Hendrick did not answer the question. And the new-comer did not know enough of the Real People to answer it for himself. Not yet.

"What do you want from us, Tiorhenshere?"

Tiorhenshere. Man from the Sunrise. A pretty name for a newcomer. But not when spoken by a man with the eyes of a hawk.

"I want to know you. I want to be your friend."

Hendrick removed the finger from his throat. His fist tightened around Billy's upper arm, nails biting into the flesh.

"You speak from the lips, not the heart, whiteskin. *Where is the paper?*"

"I do not know what paper you mean." Billy was genuinely confused.

"When white men give us hard water, it is always because they want to steal something from us. They say there is a paper for this land, with our marks on it. If we signed this paper, we were drunk and not ourselves. Where is your paper?"

"I have no paper for you to sign."

"Then what do you want from us? We come without gifts."

"I told you. I wish to know you."

"You cannot know me unless you walk in my moccasins, and do this for many moons."

"I am ready."

Hendrick Forked Paths stared at Billy Johnson with different eyes.

He thinks I am crazy.

□

Arent Stevens, a veteran Indian interpreter, came visiting at Fort Hunter and heard about Billy's long night with the Mohawks. Stevens rode down to Warrensbush to introduce himself to the newcomer.

"Certainly old Hendrick thinks you are crazy," the interpreter advised Johnson. "It gives you an edge. The Indians respect crazy people because they think they have a special connection with the spirits.

"That's not all they respect in you," Stevens added. "They told me at the Lower Castle they have given you a Mohawk name."

"That's an honor, isn't it?"

"Sometimes."

"What name have they given me?"

"Yehatson."

Billy practiced the alien syllables. "What does it mean?"

"Don't get too cocky. It means, He Finishes the Bottle. Or something like. I gather you got the better of Hendrick's crew, as you did of Lieutenant Butler's. Your hollow leg had harder exercise at Butler's, because the natives have no tolerance for liquor. I never met one who could hold his rum as good as a middling Quaker. The Woodland Indians never tasted alcohol until we came among them, and there is something lacking in their bellies that makes them unable to transform it. You were fortunate to escape some serious broils when you got them drinking."

"We had to tie down two of them to stop them from killing each other."

"That is nothing. I have seen them do it, husband to wife, mother to son when the drink is on them. You were lucky on this occasion, Mister Johnson. But make no mistake. Before the Mohawk accept you, they will make trial of you on their own ground. Hendrick will test you before he takes to you, and he will do it stone cold sober."

"How do you mean?"

"Difficult to predict. I expect they will make you run with them. You seem fit enough, but I doubt you are ready for this. These fellows can run down the deer. They might take you hunting. You don't know Indians till you've been out in the woods with them." Stevens gave Billy a sly look, running a finger down the side of his nose. "I wouldn't put it past old Hendrick to use a woman. They will fasten on a man's ruling weakness. As the wolf courts the member of the herd that is ripe for the harvest."

4.

Snowbird came home to the Upper Castle with a splitting headache that did not prevent him from telling admiring stories about the hospitality of the Irish newcomer to the Valley.

Island Woman was disgusted by her son.

Yehatson, Snowbird had nicknamed the newcomer. He Finishes It Up. Snowbird claimed this man Johnson could drink with any man in the Valley until he was the only one still conscious, and then walk away fresh as the morning.

This was not an accomplishment that won Island Woman's respect. It made the white man dangerous.

He spreads the evil of the hard water that steals our dreams as well as our lands, and he suffers nothing.

Yet this was not at the heart of Island Woman's misgivings about Billy Johnson.

Her suspicions found a focus and a name when she was traveling home from Schenectady with Bright Meadow in the last slanting rays of the sun.

They saw a purple-black column of smoke rising high above the Valley. With it came the squeals of panicking animals and the crackle of blazing underbrush and thorn bushes, fierce as musketry.

The air was filled with the pungent tang of green or half-seasoned timber. As Island Woman and her daughter drew closer to the source of the fire, they found it hard to breathe.

They saw men with black faces—slaves sent up from New York by Captain Warren—and men with faces blackened by fire and cinders moving through the windows, working with handspikes of ironwood or ash. They were rolling half-burned tree trunks into huge bonfires. There was a hellish sight behind them: a vast man-made furnace, consuming acres of hardwoods and evergreens that were dead or dying, girdled by axe-teams earlier in the year.

A stand of hemlocks exploded with a great *whoosh* that sent up plumes of flame and a sooty cloud that swallowed the lowering sun.

Billy Johnson trotted down the slope of the hill, dressed for the work in hand in his coarse osnaburg shirt and leather breeches, with a handkerchief over his nose and mouth. He pulled the cloth away from his face and called a cheery greeting to the Mohawk women.

"Sekon! Kwekwe!"

His accent was not bad. Island Woman wondered which of the Mohawk girls might have been coaching him in the sleeping loft of his new frame house or a love nest out in the woods. He had an open hand and a ready smile—too ready in the company of women. He made them fidget and giggle. Fruitpicker had noticed this too. *Elk dreamer, she calls him.*

Island Woman grunted a curt response to Johnson.

The speed with which this newcomer was killing the forest gave her bad feelings.

The white men's greed for beaver pelts—the "soft gold" of the colonies—and the greed for liquor and imported goods they inspired among the Flint People had already driven beaver from the streams and ponds of Mohawk country.

The rattlesnakes were migrating farther and farther west, away from the clamor of steel axes.

Soon there will be no place here for Wolf and Deer. Soon there will be room only for tame things, born to collars and sties. Wherever the newcomers walk, with their axes and chains, the Mother cries out in pain. The four-leggeds and the winged tribes flee. The wildness and beauty of the earth die, and what remains is the wildness and cruelty in the minds of men.

Island Woman heard the rattles before she saw the snake.

The rattlesnake warns only once.

Johnson's descent down the slope turned into a vigorous jig. He hopped to avoid the rattler's strike, then came at it with his blackthorn stick. He hit it again and again, until long after it was dead, the scales torn open to reveal the pink flesh.

"There are no snakes in Ireland," he said to the Mohawk women, with a trace of embarrassment, when he was done. "Can't stand the buggers."

"Then why don't you go back where you came?" It was Bright Meadow who spoke, using her Sunday school English.

"I'm sorry if I have offended you." Billy was surprised by this open hostility from a young, attractive native woman. Several Mohawk girls Bright Meadow's age—or a few years older—had approached him in a very different way, often with a pleasing directness.

This one is prime meat, Billy thought, stripping Bright Meadow with his eyes. *She smells wilder, yet cleaner, than our women. Musk and sweetgrass, flowing together.*

His eyes became gentler, his voice softer. "My wish is to please you."

"Then stop it." Bright Meadow was trembling.

Island Woman watched her intently, not sure what was coming.

"Stop what, exactly?"

"Don't you hear it? Don't you hear the trees crying?"

Island Woman could hear it. *The scream of the heartwood.* The groan of an ancient oak, taken by the flames as they leaped through the first-growth forest. The deathsong of a tree that had survived the lightning.

"I—" Johnson was at a loss for words. A rare occurrence.

"Warragiyaguey," Bright Meadow snapped at him as her mother whipped up the horse.

"I don't understand!" Billy called after them.

Warragiyaguey. The name Johnson had failed to recognize was the one that would stick to him. It means, They Chop Down the Woods for Him. Forest Killer.

It is the right name, Island Woman thought.

This was not just another settler, nibbling at the edge of the forest, or another trader, content to take his hides and pelts without changing the land. This was a man who was slashing and burning his way through the Valley, claiming more land for the plow that all the villages of the Real People could till.

Hendrick Forked Paths has begun to favor him. Snowbird and the Burned Knives come to sit by his fires. Our elders are inclining toward him because they say he is a fair man in trade. Our women laugh when he comes to our villages.

This Johnson had no army at his back, no title from his King, yet he was bending his neighbors to his purpose, because the life-force in him was strong. He was killing the forest. And he had come to stay.

CHAPTER 15

GIFTS OF IRON

1.

Cat tried to talk to the Jesuit priest at the Caughnawaga mission, the one with kind, tired eyes, when Blue Paint was busy at the trading post.

Father Luc's English was fractured, hardly sufficient to ask the question she had become inured to: "Are you Dutch?"

When she explained she was the captive of Indians from the mission at the Lake of Two Mountains, Father Luc's face darkened. "You must address yourself to the Abbé Picquet. I cannot interfere with his converts."

"A man spoke of a merchant called Adhémar. Someone who might help me. Do you know him?"

"He is a grasshopper out of hell. Stay away from him if you can."

The blackrobe walked away from her.

Cat followed him. "Surely you will not deny help to a Christian woman."

"Are you of our faith?"

"Christ is my teacher."

"Then I will pray for your soul."

When he saw her stricken face, Father Luc relented a little. "Who brought you?"

She pointed at Blue Paint, who was haggling over the price of his peltries.

"I know him," the blackrobe acknowledged. "He is not a bad man, I think. I will see what may be done. You must come to church."

At that moment, her knees weakened, because she saw the crow-man they called Le Corbeau. He was dressed in a Frenchman's coat, with lace at the seams. He had washed off his warpaint, but this hardly improved his looks. The hooded eyes were still those of a killer who enjoyed prolonging the act. Le Corbeau was leading Ade by a leash.

"You know them?" the blackrobe followed her gaze.

"The African was kind to me. The other—" She faltered, remembering how Le Corbeau had come within an inch of killing her.

"The other," Father Luc completed her thought, "is no friend of God. Or this mission. Half Sorcerer, half Caughnawaga. It is an evil mix. Be happy you are not in his charge."

The priest's face closed down tight, and he moved on resolutely toward the stone church.

"Father!" Cat called after him, when she saw that Le Corbeau was leading Ade down to the trading post. "Is everything for sale in your mission? Is it a slave market you are running here?"

"Address yourself to your immortal soul, my child."

You are in the province of the demon. When he was driven from the Old World, he found sanctuary among these savages.

Father Luc did not speak this thought. In part of himself, he denied it, though he had found similar musings of despair in the papers of those who had preceded him at the mission.

He was not without sympathy for the slim, almost waiflike, German girl. But the fate of a Protestant heretic could not command his energies. Protestant captives from New England, indeed, seemed to thrive among the natives of this mission as among the Abenakis at St. Francis. Red Squirrel, the paramount warchief at Caugh-

nawaga, had a white mother, taken from a border settlement in Massachusetts as a child.

It was strange how white captives—with rare exceptions—lived happily among the Indians, while the
Indians sickened and churned like caged leopards in
captivity among whites.

The German woman would learn to be happy among
the natives. She would be better off with them than with
a man like Gaston Adhémar, who sold women as well as
rum and powder, to the highest bidder.

Father Luc entered the cool sanctuary of his church.
He knelt before the high altar, seeking guidance. The
altar was hung with native offerings—wampum belts,
bracelets, women's hairbows. Some of the collars were
finely wrought, with holy names in Latin picked out in
black beads against the white ground, finished with
fringes of red-dyed porcupine quills. Some of the objects
were more troubling to the Jesuit, shields and talismans
designed to guard against witchcraft or the evil eye,
smacking of the sorcery they intended to avert.

He was troubled by the feud between two of his female
converts, Louise Swimming Voices and Hortense Whistling Birch.

Hortense had openly accused Swimming Voices of
witchcraft. This was like issuing an invitation to a
lynching, since the Indians feared nothing so much as
sorcery.

Yet there was no evidence against Swimming Voices,
except that she had the bad taste to commit adultery
with Hortense's husband, if a scoundrel like Peter Spotted Wolf could be dignified with such a term. Father Luc
would have pressed Swimming Voices to make a public
penance for the sin of adultery, in the hope of ending the
wretched business there—if Hortense and Spotted Wolf
had been married in the eyes of the church, which they
were not.

Sinners accusing sinners. An old story. And when it
came to witchcraft, the proof, such as it was, weighed
against Hortense. Louise Swimming Voices was the one
who was most often seen at Mass. When he had visited

her lodge, unannounced, he had found no witch's cauldron, no foul potions; only a missal and gilt-framed pictures of the saints. Indeed, it had been Swimming Voices who had directed him to a place where she said Hortense concealed the impedimenta of her own black practices. And in a midden behind Hortense's cabin, the priest had discovered an ugly thing, a cornhusk doll swathed in snakeskin and smeared with feces. Hortense had denied all knowledge of this, shrieking like a wheel that needs oil.

Father Luc did not know whom or what to believe, except that the faith that he sought to promulgate ran off as fast as a flash flood in the desert in the face of more ancient fears and imaginings.

2.

Blue Paint was a good man, as Father Luc said, when he wasn't drinking. But there was a blind pig just a whistle away from the border of the mission precinct, and when Blue Paint had finished bartering with the Desaunier sisters or sporting with his Caughnawaga friends, he liked to go down there and forget his worries, one of which was that he was a long way from the country of his ancestors, the Hill People, or Seneca. Another was how to get a fair price from Gaston Adhémar or one of the other dealers for his white captive. Blue Paint thought she was a fine-looking woman, slender and brown as one of the Real People, but Adhémar complained she was too scrawny for his customers and that there was not much prospect of extracting a good ransom for a penniless German serving-girl without friends in the English colonies.

Blue Paint might have defied his mother's disapproval and kept the white woman for himself, except for the dream. In this dream, he had seen a white eagle trapped in a cage. The beautiful bird was miserable in captivity. It was beating its wings against the bars, hurting itself in its efforts to get free. Finally it started gnawing off its own talons. When this happened, the house of the people who kept it caged burst into flame and was reduced to ashes.

Blue Paint knew this dream was about his captive and a threat to his own family. It had come like a warning scream in the night, the kind of dream from which you wake with your heart in your throat.

So he had to get rid of the woman, so different from her mother, who seemed to welcome her life among the Real People and possessed—according to his own mother—the gift of healing hands. Blue Paint thought it was best to return the woman to her own kind. Or else trade her to blood enemies. Because he would not wish the fulfillment of his dream on his own people.

Cat was cooking meat and corn soup for him now, with some of the Caughnawaga women, while he drank and diced with the mixed crowd at the grogshop within spitting range of the mission. The blackrobes had pleaded with the Governor of Montreal to close down this Indian tavern, but the Governor's soldiers were boozing there with the natives and ogling their women.

When the drink was on him, Blue Paint would wager on anything—the rise of a sturgeon, the throw of a hatchet, the number of pigeons in an apple tree. Tonight, they were casting the bones. These were small disks carved from the knucklebones of a deer, blackened on one side.

Blue Paint was ahead. He had won back as much beaver as he had bartered with the Desaunier sisters, and a fine plum-red shirt with ruffles beside. Then smooth, jowly Gaston Adhémar eased his bulk into the circle and asked to play.

Blue Paint's luck continued, and the watered brandy flowed faster and faster. His head spun with the excitement of the game. He hardly cared when his pile of winnings began to dwindle. Even when one of his companions yelled "Cheat!" and was pinioned by rough men in Adhémar's pay and dragged away from the game, Blue Paint would not leave off.

The first time Adhémar told him he was bust, he did not comprehend.

Then he offered to fight.

They were ready for that. Strong arms restrained him when he flew at the fat Montreal trader.

"There is no need for trouble," Adhémar said softly. "You have something left to play. The German girl, against all you have lost."

The bones flew.

Blue Paint remembered dimly that this game was once sacred. He recalled his father, at midwinter, speaking of a cosmic battle between Sky-Holder and the Dark Twin, relived with the casting of the bones. The Dark Twin was well ahead tonight.

He had lost everything, including the white eagle that gnawed off its talons in his dream.

As in a dream, he heard Adhémar's men laugh when the merchant said, "Tie the poor bastard up and let him sleep it off."

□

Blue Paint came back stumbling drunk to his wife. She was the one who warned Cat she was someone else's property, before the trader turned up to collect his winnings. She twitched her lips toward the gate of the mission, making it plain no one in the lodge would prevent Cat from leaving.

Cat hesitated only over the means of escape.

She had been held twice against her will. She would not suffer a third master.

There were soldiers at the gate who might stop her. And the risk of running into Adhémar and his men on the road. Or Blue Paint, who might wish to reclaim his stake, since the game was no doubt fixed, and in any event—the Indians said—a man in liquor is not accountable for his actions.

The stone church was no sanctuary. In the way he had spoken to her, Father Luc had belied his kind eyes.

There was a splendid elm, the shape of a perfect, fluted vase, near the stockade of the mission. Cat had admired it each morning since she had been brought to the Sault. The branches overhung the wall. It was a way out no one would notice, unless they had a reason to look.

She had few possessions. She threw them inside her blanket roll and used a beaded burden strap to fasten it to her shoulders.

She had had no trouble shinnying up trees as a girl, to get to a bird's nest or a neighbor's apples. Her time in the wilderness had hardened her muscles and made her limber. In an instant, she was up the trunk of the elm and perched on a limb that extended out over the stockade toward the river.

The city of Montreal was across the water. Would she find help there, or only a new kind of prison?

Rough laughter carried from somewhere below her. White men and Indians, moving together along the road.

Cat froze, flattening herself against the branch, willing herself invisible.

The laughter stopped. The footsteps halted.

A man said, in clumsy English, "Damned big for a squirrel."

Then, in French, *"Qui êtes là?"*

"She don't know if she wants in or out," came another voice.

"That's the trouble with women."

"Venez ici," the first voice coaxed. "Let's have a look at you."

Cat looked back. Strangers were prowling around the cabin she had left.

"Who are you?" she whispered to the men below.

"It speaks English." One of them sounded genuinely surprised.

"You are English?"

"Ssshh! We are whatever it pleases us to be. Or what pleases you, if we like you. Are you coming down or not?"

Cat heard baying behind her, of men who called like hunting dogs.

She made her choice.

The men below the stockade cushioned her fall, catching her up in their arms.

She instantly regretted the choice she had made. The man who seemed to be the leader of the group was huge and ill-favored, with one eye that glinted at her and another that sat glassy and dead in its socket. He was powerful but awkwardly made, jointed like a wooden marionette.

"What are you?"

"We asked first," the one-eyed man responded. Then with a greater show of sympathy, "Was it Northampton, where they took you? Or along the Hoosic?"

She struggled to remember the name of the Dutch village on the Hudson where she had disembarked from the Albany sloop.

"Kinder—I think it was Kinderhook."

"Kinderhook," another man echoed in a flat voice Cat would only later identify with the accents of New England. "That's your neck of the woods, John Henry. It seems Yorkers are in this with us after all."

"This is no place to talk about it," John Henry said. "Let's get the lady back to our foxhole and see what we have caught."

3.

"If you can see something clearly," Island Woman instructed Bright Meadow, "you can change it for the better."

Island Woman lay shoulder to shoulder, hip to hip, ankle to ankle, with her daughter in a cave high up in the limestone cliff on the north side of the river. Rattlesnakes were sunning themselves on the hillside above their heads. There were more of them every summer, driven farther up the Valley by the axes and plows that were steadily chewing up the land. Island Woman lived at peace with the snakes. They kept casual visitors away from the dreamers' cave. And though the Longhouse People feared rattlesnakes and often killed them on sight, Island Woman taught Bright Meadow what her mother's mother had taught her. That the snake energy, which comes from deep in the earth, is one of the secret tools of a woman of power, an *arendiwanen*. It brings the power to transform: fear into courage, poison into medicine, medicine into poison.

The women lay together on a cornhusk mat. The rhythms of the turtle rattles they had used to summon the spirits still moved through Bright Meadow's mind.

"Let's go check on Fruitpicker," Island Woman said.

They flew together, through a window of light that opened in the darkness of the cave. Bright Meadow dipped too low, coming down over the Upper Castle. Island Woman whistled to her, and she corrected her flight to catch an updraft of air that carried her over the sharpened poles that bristled from the high palisade.

Bright Meadow saw the clanmother bent over, hobbling on a stick. Fruitpicker groaned as she settled her backside on a blanket in the sunlight that streamed from the roofhole in her corner of the lodge. A younger woman came to brush and plait her hair, which she could no longer do for herself.

Bright Meadow felt the old woman's pain as she performed the simple motion of raising a pipe, filled with dried sumac and native tobacco, to her lips. To lift her right arm above waist height caused Fruitpicker savage aches. She had not raised it above the level of her shoulder for many seasons.

"You see her."

"Yes," Bright Meadow agreed.

"See her another way."

Where Fruitpicker had squatted, like a child that needs an adult to fix her hair, Bright Meadow now saw a silver birch. One of the limbs had been all but severed. It hung down from the trunk, held to the tree only by a few threads of wood.

"Make it different," Island Woman directed.

The girl tried to see the branch springing up like a sapling, joined to the trunk by young wood, in a fresh skin of paper-bark.

She went into the roots of the tree. She willed new sap to rise. She saw it flowing up through the heartwood to the injured shoulder, healing, renewing. Making strong.

She worked with the force of her intention, as Island Woman had taught her. She flooded the whole scene with colors of healing and fresh growth with yellows and greens that were more vivid than any seen in the surface world, with colors that have no names in human language because they cannot be seen with the outer eye.

Now she saw Fruitpicker standing straight and proud, not scuttling like a crab. She saw the clanmother stretch her arms to the sun, whirling them above her head in the pure joy of being able to do it. She saw Fruitpicker showing off to the niece who had been braiding her hair and to her husband Swampduck when he returned from drinking and talking with Forest Killer at his stone house. She saw the old woman sitting up on a buckboard, grand as any merchant's lady at Albany, riding down to Johnson's trading post to pick herself gay calico for a handsome new dress, bright as midsummer, to celebrate her release from pain and disability.

"Is it done?" she asked her mother when she came back.

"It is done," Island Woman confirmed. "I think Fruitpicker will not tarry long in this life. But she will live better. You did good. Nothing you do from the heart is ever wasted. Whenever you feel something with your whole insides and you send that feeling to someone, it reaches that person. It doesn't matter how far away that person might be living. Unless they have done something to block you out, you're going to reach them, to heal or to harm.

"It's easier to heal," she smiled at her daughter. "Because when we try to do something good, something that supports life, then the whole universe leans toward us."

□

Island Woman was pleased with this daughter. She had worked hard and long to develop the gifts of dreaming and healing. She had learned the medicine of plants. She knew the herb that stopped bleeding, when ground and boiled into tea. She knew the herb that made someone throw up when she chewed it and spat it out over the back of her head. She knew the roots that relieved aches and fevers, that assisted childbirth or prevented the baby from coming. Bear had taught her some of these medicines. She had watched the roots and berries that Ohkwari picked in the deep woods. She had learned to dry the leaves and roots of one of these plants and mix them with beargrease to make a poultice that relieved swollen limbs and helped fractures to heal.

Bright Meadow is not as powerful as her sister Swimming Voices. But she has heart. She will not abuse her gifts.

But the great dream-prophet had not revealed himself to Bright Meadow.

Was this because her mind was cluttered with the newcomers' thoughts and appetites, since she had gone to Sunday school?

Or was it because she was frightened?

The dream-prophet set terrible tests.

He revealed himself only to those who confronted and overcame the legions of hostile beings that stood guard at the gates of dreaming.

He has chosen to stay close to the Real People. He is the guardian of this earth, and those who walk it in balance.

He needs warriors, and warrior-women.

He put stakes through my body.

I did not die.

I did not even cry out.

If Bright Meadow flinched from these ordeals, her fear was natural.

But Island Woman knew that whoever was fit to succeed her must have the courage and the cleverness to conquer anything that opposed her, inside the dreaming.

She is not the one, Island Woman reminded herself. *But I think that the one we are waiting for will come through her.*

She saw something undulating in the shadows of the cave. A black panther, the size of a grizzly.

She knew that her teacher was close and put her hand on her daughter's wrist, to discover whether Bright Meadow could also see his messenger.

She caught her breath as a thing of hooks and claws bobbed out, mocking and jeering, obscuring the vision.

She felt something more terrible. A wild gusting in the flow of Power.

She went to the looking pool and waited for clear images to form. She saw a face contorted with hate. It resolved itself into the features of Swimming Voices.

Stop it, she spoke to her elder daughter with her mind.

Mocking laughter brushed her inner ears like bats' wings.

Darkness always walks with light. But the darkness in Swimming Voices was growing stronger and stronger.

4.

Father Luc was a Jesuit. He did not confuse the interests of the Faith with those of His Most Catholic Majesty, King Louis, as he suspected his Sulpician rivals at the Lake of Two Mountains of doing. He did not object to the fact that the Desaunier sisters—pious ladies who were regulars at Mass—ran a trading post on mission property that trafficked every day in contraband goods from Albany, 225 miles to the south, in flagrant violation of the laws of New France. He was perfectly sanguine about the secret contacts between his Caughnawaga flock and their Mohawk kinsmen, who were either pagans or Protestants, and were known to scalp his French neighbors along the St. Lawrence. Father Luc turned a deaf ear to accusations from Governor-General Beauharnois that he and his colleagues had founded an "independent republic."

Kingdoms rise and fall.

Our purpose is constant.

We are fishers of souls.

Father Luc was a zealot only on two issues: alcohol and pagan practices. Sometimes he found them to be connected, as in the disturbing case of Spotted Wolf and his two women.

Why Spotted Wolf—known at Albany as French Peter—should excite the jealousies of two halfway attractive females was an utter mystery to Father Luc. The rogue had a piece missing from his nose, the result of some drunken brawl. But then, Father Luc admitted to himself, he was no expert on women.

He had been trying to keep a lid on the tensions between Louise Swimming Voices and Hortense Whistling Birch, the two women in this squalid love triangle.

But when Spotted Wolf returned from a spring visit to Albany, loaded up with the best scarlet strouds and copper kettles, the pot boiled over.

Spotted Wolf moved out of Hortense's cabin and lived openly with Swimming Voices.

Father Luc was perfectly aware that, in native custom, this might equal the ceremonies of divorce and remarriage. Since he did not acknowledge the right of divorce, the only way he could hope to regularize the situation, on mission ground, was to induce Spotted Wolf to enter into Christian matrimony with one or the other of his women. The blackrobe's sympathy was divided between them. Hortense was the mother of Spotted Wolf's children. On the other hand, Louise Swimming Voices was a dedicated member of his congregation and her adherence to the Faith was a powerful example to those—like Island Woman, her Mohawk mother—who clung to pagan superstitions.

Making his parochial rounds, Father Luc was shocked to find that Hortense had relapsed into the blackest savagery. He found her engaged in a filthy ritual—in the woods behind the graveyard—involving a painted doll and a captive blackbird. She and her female accomplices were dancing around the doll, howling imprecations. They had slit open the bird's chest and were using its heart as a prop in their ceremonies.

Hortense pleaded for his understanding.

She said this was not as it seemed. That she and her coven were seeking only to turn back the witchcraft directed at her, by her rival in love.

Father Luc, in righteous anger, excommunicated Hortense. This punishment affected body as well as soul, since it drove her from the mission, and her rights in the cornfields and cattle that were shared among the faithful.

The blackrobe thought this would settle matters.

He sought out Spotted Wolf, assuming he would now welcome the chance to legitimize his relationship with Louise Swimming Voices.

To his horror, Spotted Wolf accused him, to his face, of siding with dark forces.

"I have been under a spell," Spotted Wolf babbled. "I must break it for the sake of my children. I must do this under the protection of the Church. Give me a penance, Father."

"Your penance is to marry in the sight of God."

"Not to the witch! Never to her!"

This outburst was incomprehensible to Father Luc. Though he saw other Indians cross themselves in the presence of Swimming Voices, he saw constant evidence of her piety, not only in her regular attendance in Church, but in her private devotions, in front of the marble statue of Saint Sebastian.

Spotted Wolf moved on. He took up with yet another woman.

Then he turned yellow. His disease looked like jaundice, but did not respond to any treatment.

And something came to pass that tested Father Luc's faith as sorely—he reflected—as Isaac Jogues and his brother-Jesuits had been tested in the Valley of the Mohawk, that factory of martyrs.

During a normal Sunday Mass, Spotted Wolf burst into the stone church.

He seized the statue of Saint Sebastian, bristling with arrows. He raised the statue up in his arms and marched resolutely toward the pew where Louise Swimming Voices was kneeling.

Her head swiveled. She fixed him with her gaze.

Seeing this in profile, Father Luc did not grasp the full force of the woman's emotion, but he sensed it.

Spotted Wolf staggered. He toppled backward. If Newton's laws of physics held any truth, the Indian should have dropped the statue at his feet, possibly shattering it. Instead, it rolled back on top of him, crushing his chest.

The congregation howled and twittered.

When the priest got to Spotted Wolf, the man was dead.

An old woman, normally quiet as a lamb, spat at Swimming Voices and ripped at her dress. Under the torn fabric, against the coppery skin, Father Luc saw something unholy. A fetish that should never have entered a house of God.

When he found words to rebuke the woman who had brought this evil into his Church, Swimming Voices was gone.

5.

While Father Luc warred for souls, Cat Weissenberg enjoyed a condition closer to freedom than anything she had known since her days on the Hudson—a brief idyll, seemingly eons ago—with a runway slave.

In a farmhouse near Chateaugay, her one-eyed escort had made more elaborate introductions.

"John Henry Lydius. Or Johann Hendrick. Or Jean-Henri. Make your choice. I am known in all three tongues and several more. But I prefer that you call me something other than Lydius while we are in Canada. The French booted me out of Montreal a few seasons back. They were so fond of me they shipped me all the way to Europe, which I had never hoped to see. Even so, I got out of their stinking prisons only by persuading a villain at Quebec that I had a rich uncle at Amsterdam who would pay a good penny to see me again."

"Then why are you here?"

Lydius winked, out of his one good eye, at his New England companion.

"I am a man of business, Mistress Catherine. And, alas, there are less profitable businesses in these colonies than the hostage trade. Elkin and I have New England customers who are keen to get back their loved ones. Frankly, we had hoped you were one of them. See, in peacetime the French allow their Indians to buy and sell whatever white captives they can get."

"I was informed of that fact by the French commandant at the fort on Lake Champlain."

"You met Landriève?" Lydius whistled noiselessly. "Now, *he* is one I give a wide berth to. No business with a man like Commandant Landriève. A man with a ghost sitting between his shoulderblades.

"Now—" he pushed bread and cheese across the table "—the question is, what are we going to do with you?"

"Take me back with you," Cat said without hesitation.

"Where might that be, I wonder?"

"Is it Boston?"

Lydius smiled. "It is a damn sight closer to where you started. My trade house is on the carry between Hudson's river and the lakes. You can't miss it if you know how to get from Montreal to Albany without undue formalities. It might cost a penny or two to get you that far, though. The Frogs on the lakes are not altogether asleep."

"I have no money. But I can earn my keep."

Lydius' smile was less wholesome. "I could be interested, but I have a wife that watches me close. Half-native, sharp and jealous as needles."

He let this stand for a bit, then asked, "You know anyone in New York?"

He shrugged when she mentioned some distant relations, far up the Mohawk Valley. Then she added, "I came with a letter of introduction to Captain Warren. Not that it did me much good."

"Captain *Peter* Warren?" Lydius sawed at the loaf with his knife. "That is quite a grand name. Now what would a poor girl like yourself have in common with him?"

When she mentioned Billy Johnson, Lydius chewed his bread and cheese for a good while, then leaned back, rubbing his belly.

"Eggs is what I mostly favor," he came back. "Hard-boiled eggs. Nothing like them for promoting a man's endurance, if you take my drift."

Cat said nothing.

Lydius swiveled his good eye. "William Johnson," he repeated. "That might bear looking into."

6.

Billy Johnson sat out on his porch in the cool of the evening, watching redtail hawks riding a thermal over the mountains. There was a girl at the Lower Castle he had not tried, who had made it plain to him, with a bold look and a sway of her hips, that she might be available. The casual attitude of the native girls—at least the unmarried ones, with the exception of Bright Meadow—was an unalloyed pleasure to him.

This was not the romantic love of the troubadours.

He knew that the women who lay with him came to him for what he had to give. They saw him as rich and powerful. But he flattered himself that they returned to him for satisfaction of a very personal nature.

There were some that were insatiable. Sarah Little Canoe, in defiance of her name, had left him gasping like a beached salmon. She was generously endowed, brimming over like a barmaid, with an unusual physical feature—an appendage almost large enough for a man, which set her off in a most gratifying way when he chafed it. He could turn her on readily enough. The problem was in turning her off.

He was still sore from the previous night's engagement.

Perhaps he would give the new filly a rest tonight, after all.

Denis Rahilly, normally circumspect in such matters, had teased that unless he had a bone in his member, he would soon be sending for cantharides—the celebrated Spanish fly, a decoction of the blister beetle—to keep it up, because a man could only stretch so often in one lifetime.

Billy chuckled, catching the distant scraping of Rahilly's fiddle.

Then an arm of the forest reached out to him in the massive shape of Hendrick Forked Paths.

Johnson tried to conceal his passing alarm, conscious that his Mohawk neighbors took delight in demonstrating how newcomers were impaired in sight and smell and hearing.

"Drink with me," Billy proposed.

"Iah." The warchief shook his head. His refusal of drink, and the fact that he had come alone, suggested serious business. He was dressed informally, in an old crimson shirt and a blanket. He rested his firelock against the wall of the house and squatted on his heels next to Billy.

"Tell me about your childhood," he said. "Tell me about your people."

So Billy talked of Ireland and scenes from his youth.

Hendrick listened in silence for a time, puffing on his calumet.

Then he said, "Why did you come here?"

"It was a chance to live a larger life."

"Because you were born into a conquered people."

Johnson frowned, unsure how best to play this.

"The Flint People have never been conquered," the warchief went on. "But my father's people were conquered. They were driven from their lands and turned into a nation of drunks and wandering broom-sellers. This is why you see me here."

"You were not born a Mohawk?"

"My father's people were Stutterers." This was the Mohawk name for the Mahicans, a nation of River Indians who spoke differently.

Hendrick spoke for a time of the fate of the River Indians, at the hands of both the saints of New England and the Dutch masters of the early New York colony. He spoke of white soldiers who had burned native villages, and fired the underbrush when they believed native families were hiding there, making a circle of death so none could escape. He spoke of a Dutch governor of New York whose men had thrown Indian children into a river. They had permitted the parents to swim out to them but allowed no one on shore until all were drowned. The heads of their victims had been displayed in the streets of the city; the governor's mother had kicked one of them around like a football.

Hendrick's narrative made all these events sound like things he had witnessed. Yet although the warchief was old—Billy's guess was that he might have been born sixty years before, around 1680—he could surely not have witnessed atrocities from the time when New York was New Netherlands.

"You speak of these crimes—these abominations." Billy was not immune to a disturbing sensation of shared guilt with the white men who had done these things. "Yet you are a friend of the English. You have even been to London."

"The English are too many to fight. I saw that in England, before the last war. They showed me their ships and their cannon. Our clanmothers gave us counting sticks, so we could number the English and see how many we might have to fight. They are beyond numbering.

"Besides—" Hendrick stretched and blew out a great cloud of smoke "—the French were our enemies before the English came. The first time the Real People met the French, they shot lead into us from firesticks we had never seen before. The Real People have long memories."

A silence fell.

Then Johnson said, "I hope to be a good neighbor. I trade with you fair. I will take no land except at a fair price, with the agreement of all."

Hendrick grunted. Then he spoke of the first white man he had trusted in matters of land.

He was a man of religion, a Dutch Reformed minister called Godfrey Dellius. He had picked Hendrick—only recently adopted into the Wolf Clan of the Mohawk and living in the Schoharie Valley—as a likely lad. He had lured Hendrick and his brother Abraham into church with promises of gifts and education, and claimed him for the God who speaks through a Book.

This minister had a very this-worldly interest in Indian land.

Dellius and his business partners persuaded a number of Mohawks to put their marks on a deed to their hunting grounds north of Albany. The compass references, obscure to the Indians, embraced a vast tract extending all the way to the borders of New France. The Mohawks were told—on the solemn word of a man of the cloth—that the document appointed Dellius and his friends as guardians and trustees for the Mohawk nation. But in plain English, it was a bill of sale, quickly approved by a crooked Governor. The Mohawks who signed had been liberally warmed with rum at the minister's house or at Peter Schuyler's before the deed was thrust in front of them.

Hendrick had stood before Lord Bellomont, the new Governor of the Province, to protest the fraud. He was not yet twenty, but he already had the headless figures of half-a-dozen slaughtered enemies incised on the side of his warclub. And he was already being assiduously courted by the French; they had invited him to a council at Montreal and heaped him with presents.

His imposing physique and the power of his oratory had engaged the new Governor's fullest attention. Lord Bellomont had promised to destroy the offending deed. Though Dellius and his fellow-speculators appealed to London, and the shadow of the Dellius Patent still hung over the Mohawks, Hendrick had scored his first political victory.

"But they come again and again, settling on our fields like crows," Hendrick continued.

Billy had already heard numerous complaints of fraudulent land deeds, of surveyors chased from the woods by howling Mohawks.

"I do not understand how you can give away so much, so cheap," Johnson commented. "You say your own mark was on the Dellius deed."

"You want to know how it came to be there?" Hendrick jumped to his feet, towering over the strapping Irishman.

He grabbed the bottle from Billy's elbow, swung it over his shoulder, and hurled it toward the river.

"That is my mark!" he shouted.

When his calm returned, Hendrick said, "I did not

know what I was doing. When a man is drinking, he is not himself."

The silence fell between them again, and Billy let it grow, sensing that the Mohawk was feeling him out on a level deeper than words.

Then Hendrick said, "You will run with our young men. We will see if you are good only for running with women."

CHAPTER 16

BUGLING ELK

1.

Hunting is dangerous, because everything you kill has a soul. If you kill without asking permission, without returning thanks, then the Animal Masters will prevent the souls from coming back. The dreamers will no longer be able to find where the deer are yarding in winter, because their power animals will leave them and they, will be sightless. Then the hunters will return from the trail empty-handed, and the people will starve.

This is what Snowbird's father had taught him.

When he had made his first kill, with a blunt arrow fired from a miniature bow, his father had shown him how to give thanks in the proper way. They had made a ritual feast for their kinsfolk, at which the young hunter was required to give away every part of the game, saving nothing for himself—though the kill was only a gray squirrel. They had painted the skull in a sacred way and set it up to greet the rising sun.

When we cease doing these things, the old ones said, *the Earth Turtle will shake us from her back in anger and our world will end as it has ended before.*

Snowbird said nothing of this to Billy Johnson when

he invited him to go hunting that fall, because the newcomers did not know these things.

In the Moon of Shining Leaves, Snowbird went down to Warrensbush and took Billy by surprise, looming up through the drifting fog from the river.

Snowbird said, "We might go hunting."

Mick Tyrrell was eager for sport, and Denis Rahilly asked to come too.

Snowbird was traveling light. He showed the white men the contents of his food pouch: parched cornmeal, a little venison jerky, dried pumpkin flowers to thicken the gravy of the meat they would take on the trail. A light kettle, a skinning knife, his weapons and a pair of steel traps made up the rest of his kit, apart from a little deerskin bag and a bobcat pouch he did not explain.

"I wager it contains the vocabulary of his dreams," Rahilly whispered to Johnson. "I have heard that the Indians look to dreams for guidance on where to find the game."

"Best save your wind for the trail, Denis," Mick advised him. He had less patience than Billy with Rahilly's agreeable nonsense.

Johnson added as many bottles and jugs to their salt beef as he thought they could comfortably carry. Snowbird was vague about exactly how long they would be camping out in the woods and responded to questions about where they were heading with a wave of his hand toward the whitening Adirondack ranges. Snowbird spurned the offer of a jug of liquor for himself.

"It's a long trail with no spirits on it," Rahilly observed.

"It is my understanding a native hunter indulges only the other sort," Johnson commented as they strolled down to the river landing where Snowbird had left his elmbark canoe.

"No female company, either, eh?" Mick winked at his cousin. "You'll never make one of them, Billy. You will never take to their taboos."

They fished for their dinner. After nightfall, Snowbird tied a pine knot in the cleft of a fire-hardened stake with strips of birch bark, and leaned it from the prow of the canoe. In the glow of the blazing torch, the men could see the fish swimming in the water, while they remained invisible to their quarry. They took turns to try their skill with Snowbird's spear. Billy caught an ugly, whiskered fish that drew jibes from Mick. It was Johnson's turn to laugh when Mick, lunging too far after a trout, lost his footing and fell headlong into the cold stream.

In the morning, Snowbird spotted muskrat lodges along a creek flowing out of a cranberry bog. He motioned for the white men to rest quiet while he set one of his traps. The Mohawk placed the trap in the shallows. Then he took a whitish paste from his deerskin bag and smeared some on a tall splinter of wood. He planted the stick upright, inside the jaws of the trap, so the pulp was above water level.

Billy assumed Snowbird would leave the trap in place, to be checked on their return journey. But the Mohawk said they would wait.

Mick got bored within half an hour and went off to try his luck with his gun in the woods.

"I think Mick has the right idea," Billy remarked a few minutes later.

"Wait," Snowbird said in a tone that would not be countermanded.

He's trying to teach me something, Billy realized.

With a squeaking, snuffling sound, a pair of muskrats burst from their lodges and rushed at the stick in the water. The lead muskrat leaped at the point of the stick, where Snowbird had smeared the paste. Then the trap snapped shut and the furry animal and his prize became a thrashing heap in the water. Instead of taking flight, the remaining muskrat hurled itself into the melee. Billy thought it was trying to help its partner, then realized it was fighting the other for whatever they had smelled on the stick.

Snowbird jogged lightly down to the creek and dispatched the muskrats with two deft flicks of his knife.

Snowbird chanted some formula of thanks, holding

the slain animals by the tails, looking up at the sun.

"Jesus and Mary," said Mick, returning empty-handed. "The savage does his mumbo-jumbo even for rodents."

Johnson told the Mohawk, "Whatever you put on the stick would seem to have a fatal compulsion, at least for muskrats. I presume it is a scent lure of some kind."

Snowbird showed him more of the pulp. He gave Billy to understand that it was a chewed root from a native dogwood.

"There is nothing in these forests that is alien to them," Billy said to Rahilly and Mick by the fire that night, when Snowbird had gone out among the trees to relieve himself or to scout for night-goers. "Everything has a name and a purpose. Look at us." He gestured at the immensity of the woods around them. "How many of these trees and bushes can any one of us name? One in ten? Snowbird is showing us how little we *see.*"

"I vouch he is doing something more," Rahilly contributed. "He is taking us back to the way his people lived before any of us came. Notice he has yet to fire a gun."

"You are a romantic, Denis." Mick mocked. "And you show traces of the disease yourself, Billy."

"If you mean dragging women around by the hair, I plead guilty."

"And what is wrong with a romantic?" Rahilly defended himself.

"We must live in the world as it is," Mick said stoutly.

"Ah, that is the thing of it. Which world is it we must live in? You cannot call Snowbird and his people romantics. In their way, everything is sacred and everything is down-to-earth."

"Even shitting?" Mick kept up the attack as he watched their Mohawk guide returning between the trees, adjusting his breechcloth.

"Especially shitting," Rahilly said, grave as a church-warden.

□

In a fold of the Endless Mountains, Billy was roused by a call between a scream and a trumpet.

He rolled from his blanket and crawled on his belly to where Snowbird squatted among the pines.

The Mohawk motioned for him to be silent and pointed at the forest wall beyond the cranberry bog.

Now Billy saw him. The huge bull elk had broken from his forest cover. His breath whitened in the cold dawn. His dark shoulders and tawny flanks were slick with the morning dew.

He stomped the wet earth, kicking up mud. He tilted his black muzzle and threw back his splendid, many-tined rack until the points seemed to rest on his back. He quivered, curled his lips, and called again. His call rose in a piercing, vibrating bugle that pained Billy's ears, and ended in grunting roars.

The bull elk ripped open the stillness of the dawn. His high-pitched, grunting squeal laid claim to the world around him and to every female within it.

"By God," Mick Tyrrell gasped. "Look at the rack on that bugger!"

He aimed and cocked his firelock.

"Tohsa," Snowbird hissed at him. "Don't."

Billy put his hand on the gun barrel, lowering it to point at the ground.

"I thought we came to hunt," Mick complained.

"Will you look at that great beast." Rahilly had finally dragged himself from his sleeping place.

As they watched, the bull elk's movements grew wilder. He was wallowing in the bog, rolling and kicking. He stopped to raise himself to his full height, bugling at the woods on the other side of the clearing. He racked the soggy ground with his antlers and came up dripping black ooze. He tossed back his rack and shrieked his challenge again.

"I believe the old boy has a rival," Billy whispered to Rahilly.

They saw a second bull elk emerging from their side of

the woods. The newcomer threw his head back and made his own sound attack with menacing gutturals and ear-bursting whistles.

The bulls eyed each other and stood frozen for a moment, like duelists waiting for the starter's signal. Then they dropped their heads and charged. Billy saw now that their antlers were more than a testimonial to male potency. Their points jutted like quartz knives.

They pulled up twenty paces away from each other, grunting and stamping. The older one, dripping mud, began to describe a heavy circle dance around his adversary.

"The old boy's no fool," Rahilly commented. "He wants to see the other off without a fight."

But the newcomer stood his ground.

Furious, the old bull hurled all his weight at his rival, behind the spikes of his antlers that could shear through to the vital organs. The newcomer came to meet him, tipping his rack from side to side. Their antlers locked. They shoved and rocked together in a battle without blood. It took only minutes before the old bull's superior weight and cunning told. The racks disengaged smoothly, and the young bull trudged away through the wetland. The old bull bugled his victory, and his rival broke into a run.

"He's coming straight for us," Mick exclaimed, snatching up his firelock. "Don't tell me I can't take this one," he muttered in Snowbird's direction.

"That one you may kill," the Mohawk said. "That one is chosen."

□

Mick was a good shot. His ball took the elk cleanly. He was gouting his heart's blood when the men went down to take the kill.

As they left their place of concealment, Snowbird described a marking on the elk's hind leg, like a gourd.

Before they started skinning the animal, Johnson looked for the mark and found it exactly as described.

"You have keen eyesight," he complimented the Mohawk.

Snowbird just grunted, intent on the business of letting nothing of the kill be wasted. Then he must honor the Elk Master and set up the skull to face the rising sun, to make sure the soul would come back.

Johnson returned to the theme that night when they rested after gorging themselves on elkmeat roasted over the fire.

"It is a pity," Denis Rahilly remarked, "that we cannot make war like the elk, without bleeding."

"And fight only for something worth taking," Billy volunteered. "Our friend the old bull was doing battle for a whole harem of ladies."

He passed the bottle. Snowbird again declined. "Is it being sober that keeps your eyesight so keen?" Johnson asked the Mohawk.

"I dreamed that one," Snowbird said curtly.

Rahilly perked up at this. "You mean you dreamed about an elk with a mark on its leg?"

Snowbird nodded.

"That is extraordinary."

Snowbird shrugged and walked off among the bushes.

He had dreamed the kill. How was it possible that the newcomers did not understand that nothing happens until it is dreamed?

2.

On a mild night in the husking time, Island Woman and her clanmother sat together by a roaring fire of sumac brush, stripping corn. They worked with wooden pins secured by loops to the middle fingers of their right hands.

Fruitpicker picked a fresh ear of corn and gripped it firmly, butt downward, in her left hand. She thrust her pin into the nose, under the husk. With a sideways, shuttling motion, the clanmother's thumb closed quickly over the pin and tightly against the husk. With a jerk of the arm downward, toward the body, Fruitpicker tore the husk free.

She tossed the husk into the basket, ready for braiding. With the same unconscious rhythm, she was propping

the stripped ear up against the others when she saw it
was different.

"You owe me!" she told Island Woman.

"Show me."

The clanmother passed her the ear of corn. Only two
of the rows of corn kernels had filled out, on opposite
sides, leaving broad trenches in between. It was the
pattern the Real People called the Roadway. In some of
the stories the old ones told, it was called Whirlwind's
Road. They said the Dark Twin had licked the ear with
his tongue. Whether it was lucky or unlucky for others, it
was a happy sight for its owner. By custom, any other
women who were present had to hand over a stripped
ear of corn to the one who had found it.

Island Woman paid up with good humor.

Fruitpicker stretched and yawned and reached for her
pipe. "I've had enough for tonight. I am getting old."

Island Woman crouched behind her, massaging the
shoulder that was causing her pain.

"I think Bright Meadow is ready," Fruitpicker observed. "Have you spoken with her?"

"Yes. My daughter says she has no objection to White
Owl."

"That is good. White Owl is a good provider. And I
believe it will not be long before he is raised up as a
chief. Is everything agreed with his mother?"

Island Woman frowned. "She wants a horse."

"What did you tell her?"

"I told her she is greedy. I told her cornbread and corn
soup are what are always given. But because White Owl
is her only son, I said I would find her a calf."

"It is fair," the clanmother agreed. "I will speak to
her. I think this marriage will take place in the new
moon."

This was the way it had always been, among the Flint
People. Marriages were arranged by the mothers. And
since the husband was expected to live with his wife's
family and to hunt for them, it was reasonable for his
mother to demand compensation for the loss of a
provider.

"Bright Meadow should be married before her sister comes back," the clanmother added.

"Yes," Island Woman agreed quickly. Dark stories were circulating about Swimming Voices and the half-Frenchman who had died. Even if they were untrue, Island Woman did not want to run any risk that Swimming Voices might do something to blight her sister's marriage.

"That feels good." Fruitpicker purred as Island Woman's fingers worked deeper into her shoulder and neck. "But not even your touch can keep this bag of bones together for long. I'm getting ready for the path of strawberries."

"Totek! Don't say that!"

"We are not snakes, that shed their skins and go on. The sleepmaker is getting ready for me, and I'll be happy to see him. I want you to be good to my husband. Swampduck has looked after me. He's not that bad-looking, and you are of an age—"

"I'm not looking for a man!"

"Hush. A clanmother should have a man to lean on, like a walking stick."

"What are you saying?"

"My only fear is for our people." Fruitpicker looked at her steadily. *"Sakkwaho.* You are a woman of the Wolf Clan. Okwaho speaks to you. When I am gone, she will speak through you, as the Mother of our Clan."

"I am not worthy." Island Woman was trembling.

"It is not true. When you first came to us, I saw that you had the sight, but I was not certain you had the heart. Now I know you have both. Trust your dreaming. You know the power is already passing to you."

3.

A light snow was falling on the day of the wedding, in the first quarter of the Moon of Popping Trees, when the fish swim close to the shore, before the rivers freeze.

White Owl's family had sent the gifts that were expected to Island Woman's lodge: belts of wampum strung by his mother, furs and skins the hunter had brought back from the trail, with a fresh-killed deer, to show that he would provide. Acceptance of these gifts meant that the marriage contract was sealed.

At dusk, Bright Meadow sat on a cornhusk mat by her mother's firepit, dressed in her softest doeskin and waited for her husband to come to her. Her mother sang over her songs from the cradleboard, from when the world was fresh.

White Owl walked through the village with all his kinsfolk of the Bear Clan around him, enjoying the ribald laughter and the envious stares. He had not yet made up his mind whether he wanted to stay with his wife's mother, in the traditional way. Maybe he could persuade Bright Meadow to move out and live in a small house, apart from the rest of her family, as some of the Mohawks had learned to do from the newcomers. It was not a matter of privacy. Real People knew how to make space for each other under the same roof. If curious children wanted to peek at grown-ups having sex, well, that was natural and a useful part of their education. No, the problem was different. Island Woman was a forceful woman; White Owl had seen strong men wilt under the lash of her tongue. She was also, it was said, an *arendiwanen,* a woman of power. White Owl was not sure how much of his life would belong to him once Island Woman got working on him. But these were questions for the future.

Shadows moved between White Owl and Island Woman's elmbark longhouse, with its painting of a baying wolf over the sunrise. A tall woman, booted and caped in the French style in a flowing black mantle lined with scarlet, with two children beside her, swept through the moosehide doorflap of Island Woman's lodge.

Island Woman smelled crushed flowers, of a kind that were foreign to the Valley.

Then the doorflap flew open and two children, frisky as wolfpups, rushed in, followed by a tall woman in European dress.

"You—"

Island Woman recognized her eldest daughter as Swimming Voices unfastened her hood and shook out her long black hair. She held out her arms to her mother and sister. Bright Meadow rushed into her embrace.

"I've come to bless you," Swimming Voices told her. "Look, I have presents. Something old, something new."

White Owl's mother peered under the doorflap.

"Soon," Island Woman called to her.

She looked at the children. Two boys, not more than five or six, dressed alike, in little French jackets with lace at the seams, and otherwise as similar as two corn kernels.

"Who are you?" Island Woman asked them.

"I am Earthdiver," said one.

"I am Firewalker," said the other.

"Brave names," Island Woman told them, not displeased to hear herself called *Aksotha*—Grandmother—by her own blood. The boys were very fair, and their eyes were hazel. *The mark of the French is on them*, she thought.

"Mother."

She turned to her elder daughter. There were dark circles of fatigue around Swimming Voices' eyes and something akin to desperation inside. She was still beautiful, but worn to an edge. She made Island Woman think of a raccoon trapped among the roots of a tree.

The cornered animal is most dangerous.

"I brought you your grandsons," Swimming Voices skimmed the ice of reproach.

"Mother—" it was Bright Meadow who spoke. "It is my wedding day. And see what my sister brought me."

Island Woman glanced at the gifts. A comb carved from moosebone in the Seneca style, with a trickster-spirit on top, holding a pair of geese. A little silver cup that looked as if it belonged in a communion service.

Why are you always against me? Swimming Voices said with her eyes.

And Island Woman felt her hardness crumble. Whatever Swimming Voices had done—or might do—today they should be one family, one heart.

Island Woman opened her arms to her elder daughter. She hugged her even though she felt, before their skins touched, something cold and slick around her daughter's body. Even though, once again, she felt the darkness fall between them.

It was a relief to turn from the mother to the boys. Island Woman scooped them up in her arms.

"There is nothing wrong with you at all," she told them. "Except those big names you have to live up to."

□

White Owl had been kept waiting for longer than was seemly. Island Woman shooed her grandsons out of the way and signaled to the people that all was ready. Then she withdrew with Swimming Voices and the boys to the central chamber of the lodge.

White Owl came in alone and sat down on the mat that Bright Meadow had vacated for him. He squatted facing the fire, not looking at the supple young girl who was to be his wife, while she busied herself with the cooking pot. She filled a bowl-sized ladle with the corn soup she had boiled for her prospective husband. She had made it nice and greasy, with man-sized chunks of bearfat.

White Owl wolfed down the whole bowlful. *"Ia-weken,"* he said solemnly. "Tastes good."

Now Bright Meadow brought him tiny loaves of cornbread she had wrapped in cornhusks and tied in the middle with threads, giving them the shape of gourds.

White Owl sampled her bread and pronounced it equally good.

The groom's formal consumption of the gifts of corn was the whole marriage ceremony. It would be left to the mothers of the newlyweds to remind each of their obligations to the other's family. It would be Bright Meadow's duty, for example, to supply White Owl's mother with firewood for a whole year.

Before White Owl withdrew for the evening—as was considered proper—to return in the morning with his possessions, Island Woman added a ritual of her own to the wedding. She would have done this under any circumstances, to protect Bright Meadow and the great one that might return through her. It was essential now that Swimming Voices had come back to her lodge, bringing trouble Island Woman could almost *hear*, like the whirr of angry wasps.

Island Woman swept the lodge clean with a white wing. She chanted formulas of protection over Bright Meadow and her husband while she smudged them with the smoke of sage and sweetgrass and the real tobacco.

The boys closed in, curious to watch. But Island Woman noticed that Swimming Voices drifted further and further away, into the dark at the fireless end of the longhouse.

4.

That winter, the ink froze in Billy Johnson's inkwell as he tried to write a letter to Captain Warren explaining why there were no profits to report from his trading activities. Johnson's back ached from helping to shovel away drifts of snow that rose as high as the roofline. He learned why there were so many words for snow in the native languages. It came at him in a fine dry powder and in hard freezing rain. It lay in wet heaps that could hardly be crossed even in snowshoes. It melted and froze over, piling up like a wedding cake, layered by ice.

Soldiers of the Fort Hunter garrison, sent to fetch firewood, returned with toes and fingers turned purple-black that snapped off like icicles when they tried to warm them. In bed, Billy shivered beneath a bearskin and a dozen blankets, listening to the creaking of the frozen trees in the woods, which became rolling thunder when the big ones fell.

He looked hungrily across the river, where the land was sheltered from the worst of the arctic gusts by the high country rising to the north. When the snow packed down, the King's Road along the north bank of the river was ideal for sledding, and was busy with traffic all winter long, while Johnson's own trading post was

deserted except for the occasional tenant asking for flour
or dried peas on credit.

Not a week passed without one of them—Mick, or
Rahilly, or Paddy Groghan or Billy himself—saying, yet
again, "We are on the wrong side of the river." When
little green-eyed Jane Watson said it, Johnson decided to
act. Uncle Peter would not approve, but he would not be
consulted.

Billy had learned quickly that the frontier was not a
place where a man sat on his hands, waiting for permission. Here a man claimed his own fate or retired broken
and defeated. The life of a retainer, however cushioned,
was not in Billy's plans. And he did not consider the
possibility of defeat.

He still had the bulk of the Irish linen his mother's
money had bought. There was no market for it in the
Valley, where his white neighbors had neither the taste
nor the money for luxuries, and the Indians preferred
gaudier colors and splashier fabrics. But the linen would
still fetch a decent price at New York or Philadelphia. It
was negotiable currency, especially for a man who had
had his fill of the frontier and was minded to move to a
milder climate and tamer neighbors.

Over tankards at Fonda's tavern, Johnson sought men
on the north side who had failed to prosper or were
jittery about the talk of a new war with the French. He
talked with them quietly, one by one.

For bolts of linen and kegs of rum, he bought several
parcels of land along the creek bordering Joseph Clem-
ent's property. For the equivalent of £180, he cobbled
together a tract that extended for a quarter of a mile
along the north bank of the Mohawk River and ran back
a mile into the woods. His property included several
small islands in the river, and a house built of freestone
in the simple style of the German settlers.

The stone walls of the house had been carefully laid,
without mortar, and plastered inside up to the ceiling
line, barely eighteen inches above Billy's head. But the
steepness of the roof—pitched to slough off snow and
ice in the harshest of winters—allowed room for a high

garret that rose fifteen feet from the wide boards to the ridge pole. This was reached by a narrow enclosed stairway, as steep as a ladder, which would test the resolution and sobriety of Johnson's guests and retainers.

The house faced south, toward the river, with three rooms, including the kitchen, on the ground level. The axis of the house was the massive chimney, fed by enormous back-to-back fireplaces in the parlor and the kitchen. There was a summer kitchen twenty paces east of the house, with a big round beehive oven and a low brick building beyond it with a fireplace in the basement that would do for the servants.

There was not a pane of glass in any of the windows. When the cold weather set in, the previous owners—like their neighbors—had simply nailed pieces of linsey-woolsey across the openings.

The rustic German house was not Billy's idea of a manor, though it was a long step up from his cabin at Warrensbush. In his mind's eye, he saw the house that would one day be his. It was compounded of memories of Smithstown and Warrenstown. Nothing pompous, nothing soft and mannered. An armed stone house, strong enough to overawe potential rivals and enemies, elegant enough to accommodate a visiting Governor or commander-in-chief.

He would call his new home Mount Johnson, in honor of the hill behind the house, and the man he intended to be. The King's Road was at his front door, and along it flowed the black gold of North America. His fortune or failure would depend on whether he could divert the flow of furs from the Oswego gang and the Albany cartel to his new truck house.

He had a dozen tin sconces fitted to the elk antlers Mick had preserved as a trophy and hung the rack over his dinner table as a chandelier. Beyond this, he gave little thought to interior decoration. A woman would attend to all that, if the right one presented herself.

5.

Swimming Voices listened to her brother's stories about the Irishman who had moved across the river, the one her family called Forest Killer. He had promised the Mohawks that he would beat any price other traders offered them for their furs, at Albany and Oswego. He had said he would reward anyone who brought Indians from the other nations of the longhouse or the western tribes to trade with him.

Swimming Voices heard Mohawk girls whispering and giggling about this newcomer and his appetite for sex.

After the spring melt, she went down to Mount Johnson with Snowbird and Hendrick Forked Paths to look at Billy Johnson and what he had to offer. She put on her best dress from Montreal—a glossy bombazine, dyed bottle green—and carried a little parasol.

The white man's trading post was busy. The bins in his storehouse were spilling over with beaver plews, deerskins and raccoon pelts. A narrow-built man in a gray suit and pebble glasses sorted the furs and had them bound in tight bundles, each with a paper stamped with Johnson's mark. Slaves carried the bales down to the waiting bateaux at Johnson's new wharf, which was already crowded with barrels of flour, tubs of butter, and bags of dried peas.

Swimming Voices studied these signs of wealth. Then she looked for the owner.

There was no mistaking which of the newcomers was Forest Killer. He greeted his Mohawk guests with a rolling laugh and a carrying voice that wrapped itself around you.

He greeted Swimming Voices formally, speaking of his friendship for her brother. He gave her sons candy and toy whistles.

He doesn't see me yet, Swimming Voices realized. *He sees Snowbird's elder sister, a matron with a family of her own.*

She watched Johnson strip off his clothes, in response

to a challenge from Snowbird, and plunge into the river
His skin was the color of stripped white oak. His
shoulders were very broad, his chest deep. His bottom
did not bulge or droop, as was common with the
newcomers. He kept up with the Mohawk warriors all
the way to the island, trailing behind only after the turn

Swimming Voices reflected on the fact that, though
Forest Killer seemed to take women whenever it pleased
him, there was none that had a claim on him. By any
definition, he was the most marriageable man in the
Valley.

I will make him see me, Swimming Voices resolved.

□

At Walter Butler's urging, Johnson agreed to take command of the Valley militia. The musters he assembled
were community parties rather than exercises in military
discipline.

Billy and Mick were always to the fore in the point-to-
point races. Late one summer afternoon, the riders
received their instructions.

"The prescribed distance," Johnson shouted, "is from
my stableyard to Fonda's tavern, where each gentleman
shall consume one quart of beer and one gill of rum
without dismounting, the same to be accomplished on
return to my house!"

Walter Butler fired off a charge of birdshot, and the
horsemen galloped up the road, sending up dust devils.

Billy was thirsty when he reached Fonda's and
claimed a decisive advantage over the other riders from
the speed with which he drained the tin mugs.

He was just picking up speed on the return sweep
when the high grass along the road rippled like a wave
and a tawny shadow leaped straight at his mount.

"God's triggers!" He fought to control the frightened
stallion as it bucked and reared. He felt a slim, firm body
pressed taut against his own, a woman's arms cinching
his waist.

"Let me see how you ride," she breathed.

Her skin was honey-colored, hardly darker than her
soft doeskins, hung with little silver ornaments and

jingling bells. She smelled wild and gamy. He craned round to see her face. When she laughed, her eyes flashed and her lower lip made a deep V, like the beak of a calling hawk.

He dug his spurs into the flanks of his stallion, and they shot forward after the other riders.

He came in last, but his place had improved to second by the time the drinking was done.

He leaped off his mount and turned to assist his lady passenger. But she laughed again, jumping up to stand on the horse's back. Knees bent in a half-crouch, she galloped the horse in a swift circle around the stone house. Then she leaped back into the grass, leaving the horse to canter back to its master, trailing its reins.

"She is magnificent," Johnson exclaimed. "Who is she?"

Mick and the others shrugged. But Robert Adams, the bespectacled Dublin bookkeeper who had left the store to watch the games, came up and said, "You met her just the other day."

"This is not a lady I would forget."

"She came with the Indians from the Upper Castle. Isn't she Snowbird's sister?"

Billy was puzzled. He remembered the matron in the fancy French dress, with two kids at her side. Handsome in her way, but showing her years. The feral girl who had leaped up onto his horse appeared young enough to be her daughter.

"By God," he swore to anyone who cared to hear, "whoever she is, I mean to have her."

□

Swimming Voices led him a chase. At dusk, in the smoke of guttering woodfires, when he had been out with the men cutting and burning, she let him find her down by the creek. He washed off the ash and sweat that gleamed on his skin like potblacking, and called to the others that he was going to walk for a bit to cool the fire in his head. He waded upstream, his feet slithering on the mossy stones of the creekbed, to the deep cleft in the earth through which the water bubbled. There was a natural pool inside, almost closed to the sky. In the grainy half-light, he saw the gleam of wet skin, the long curve of her body, quivering like a bowstring as she rose on her toes for the dive off a protruding shelf of rock. He was after her in an instant, and thought he had her when he saw her braids bob once above the surface. Then she was gone, lost in the black deeps of the pool. He waited for her to come up, for longer than anyone could breathe underwater, and finally concluded she had a secret way out.

He spoke to Snowbird about her.

Snowbird agreed to talk to his sister, but warned, "She is her own woman. Whatever comes of it, don't blame me."

When Snowbird came back, he said, "My sister dreamed you will visit her house in the dark of the moon. And I dreamed you will give me a small keg of rum for telling you this thing."

"I have a dream too," Johnson said.

Snowbird looked uneasy. Dream-sharing could be expensive.

"I will save it for now," Billy reassured him. *That man is truly rich,* he added mentally, *who is owed more favors than he owes others.*

□

He found Swimming Voices living in a log house of her own, outside the palisades of the Upper Castle. A nervy white dog yapped at him, showing thin yellow teeth like a racoon's, and would not stop until Swimming Voices hushed it, although Billy prided himself that he had the confidence of most canines. The twins gawked and sniggered until their mother shooed them away.

Billy noticed that the house was furnished with an eclectic mix of native curiosities—masks and dried roots, rattles and snakeskins—and European goods.

Swimming Voices offered him tea. It tasted like nothing he had ever sampled.

"It has the juice of the deereye," she told him. "Good for the blood. Makes you strong."

"I am not as feeble as I look," Billy teased.

He was used to native women who gave—or received—sexual favors without protocol or lengthy flirtation. This one was different. She plied him with a hundred questions. She wanted to know every detail of his family history. She asked directly about his relations with other women.

"I confess I was once an out-of-the-way animal with women."

"I knew it as soon as I saw you."

"But that was in my former life, my dear. Before I met you."

"I can always tell when a man is ready for me."

"How is that?"

"I can smell it."

Her sudden candor excited him, but at the same time he felt sluggish. The effect of the tea?

She came to him, working expertly with buttons and ties. Her tongue darted over him. She grabbed his swollen penis and pulled it inside her without further preliminaries.

Her face was alternately smooth and radiant, then contorted as if in the extremities of physical pain—teeth clenched, lips stretched back, eyes pinched tight. Her breathing came in harsh, rasping draughts. Then she was clutching at him, clutching to hold and receive life. He responded to the fierce, compelling suction of her inner muscles. Her grip became painfully tight. It denied him release. When she finally let him come, she brought a caged explosion.

She murmured, *"Khenoronhkwa.* I want your soul."

□

She became a frequent visitor at Mount Johnson. She brought more of her herbal teas and potions, which he might have poured out the window except that she watched to see that he took them according to her instructions.

He found she was remarkably well versed on the politics of Mohawk life. She advised him on which chiefs and matrons could be influenced most easily, and which needed to be pulled out of their stirrups. She mocked native taboos, and talk of the Great Law and the Peacemaker.

"My people are like children," she told him. "Maybe you were sent to make them grow up."

Unlike her younger sister, she shed no tears for the falling trees. She told him he need feel no guilt for living on what was Indian land; the law of the forest said the land belonged to the strongest.

"You will be the strongest of all," she promised him. "But you cannot do it without me. I will show you the way."

Sometimes she talked dirty in bed, as dirty as Meg Ryan back in Dublin. She told him he had a good hard fish and she liked to feel it filling her up. He had never heard talk like this from a native women; it shocked him and excited him.

He dreamed differently. Her face appeared to him, in the nights they were apart. He saw it glow in the dark with a dull, blue-gray light, at the foot of his bed. Sometimes an animal came. It scared him the first time, pushing its snout up against his face. He could smell its wild tang. It was so real he lit a candle, to drive the thing out, but found it dissolved in the circle of light.

He had other kinds of dreams, in which he was drawn through the air to a cabin in the woods where a woman sat chanting over a circle of bones or shells. He woke with his heart thumping from a dream in which he seemed to be *inside* this woman's body, and heard her voice praising it.

See how I am beautiful.
You will have no eyes for other women."

He spoke of these dreams to no one. They were only night fancies, that faded before the substance of the day.

6.

People started talking.

"Maybe some good can come of this," Fruitpicker remarked to Island Woman, when she got to hear about it. "What does Swimming Voices say about it?"

"She doesn't talk to me about it. Snowbird put her together with Forest Killer, but he won't talk about it either. I think he has bad feelings."

"She's a bad one, your daughter," the clanmother went on. "But at least she can stop the other girls fighting over this newcomer. He's an elk dreamer." She tipped her head back, flared her nostrils, and mimicked the bugle of a bull elk in the rutting season. She jumped up and started pawing and kicking at the earth, delighted by the game.

Island Woman did not smile.

"Don't give me those ice-eyes," Fruitpicker chided her. "Swimming Voices could do worse. And she's not like you and me. She wants a rich life. She needs a rich man."

"The white man won't stay with her. She's lived twelve winters longer than he has."

"Never stopped me," the clanmother cackled.

□

Little Jane Watson, who had warmed Billy's bed on a few chill evenings, had a shouting match with Swimming Voices that was occasioned by more than jealousy.

Jane came in to clean house and found the Mohawk woman prying about under the sleeping loft.

"What are you doing here?" Jane demanded.

Swimming Voices gave her an evil look, so sharp and devouring that Jane crossed herself and brandished the broom.

Then she saw the Mohawk woman trying to conceal something in the folds of her dress.

"Thieving bitch!" she shouted. "Show us what you've got there!"

Swimming Voices held her ground until Rogers, Johnson's personal servant, came in from the yard and warned Jane she had better go easy on the master's favorite.

"Let her show us what she's thieving then."

Swimming Voices finally dropped it on the floor in disgust and leaped out the door.

"Why, it's nothing more than an old shirt, ruined in the field," Rogers commanted, holding up the garment, which was soiled with mud or blood. "The master probably said she could have it for rags."

Jane Watson was not content. "She has an evil, witchy look about her, does that one," she complained.

"Hell hath no fury—" Rogers grinned, and she went for him with the broom in earnest.

□

It was a few days later that Jane found the little figurine that had been stuffed into a crack in the wall, under Billy's bed.

She gave it to Johnson, saying, "I figure that Indian woman is fixing to put a hex on you."

"I'm grateful for your concern, Jane. But you really mustn't trouble yourself. She probably imagines she is protecting me."

Johnson mentioned the incident at the farewell dinner he gave that night for Denis Rahilly, who had announced that his wanderlust could be curbed no longer; Rahilly was to return to New York to try his luck there and perhaps in the southern plantations.

"What exactly will you do?" Billy asked, ever protective of his former mentor.

"Latin master, musician, dancing-master, tutor in topery to the sons of the great—" Rahilly raised his glass. "As long as my wind holds, I will have bread and beer."

Later, they passed the statuette Jane had found around the table. It was a curious thing, with round, empty eyes and a round, blowing mouth. An arm and a leg appeared to be deformed. There was a tiny belt of snakeskin around the middle.

"It is a mystery to me," Rahilly spoke. "But you remember the saying in the old country. If you go looking for the spirit world, you will find you are already inside it. I believe that is as true for Indians as it is for us Irish. And Lord knows what you will find when you go stirring up the spirits of a different tribe."

"I do not believe it is spirits that Billy is after stirring," Walter Butler remarked, drawing chuckles.

Rahilly, for once, had no share in the merriment. He put the figurine down quickly and inspected the skin of his palm as if the thing had scalded him.

CHAPTER 17

WOLF DREAMING

1.

Cat Weissenberg re-entered Johnson's world at the tail end of winter, just before the thaw. Lydius brought her sledding up the frozen Mohawk, muffled to the eyes in a beaver blanket.

"The lady insists she knows you," Lydius told Johnson. "But pretty eyes can be great deceivers. I would not wish to burden you in any way, Mister Johnson. A nephew of Captain Warren deserves better consideration. Say the word and I'll disencumber you."

"No, no." Billy was unsure what to make of this odd, one-eyed man dressed all in black, like a crow, with his insinuating airs. He struggled to understand the scene at his door. He might not have recognized Cat in a bustling street. Her face was stronger and leaner, the skin pulled tight against the skull, the cheekbones sharply defined.

"Don't you know me, Billy?"

Mick leaned in the doorframe, whistling an Irish air, waiting to be introduced.

"Of course I know you," Johnson said stiffly, taking Cat's hand. "You are welcome."

The formal handshake hit her like a slap across the face.

Now he receives me as a servant, in front of his gentleman friends.

A retching pain rose from the pit of her stomach to her throat. Johnson's eyes slid away from her.

Did I expect more from him than a place of safety, a shelter from the cold?

No, but I dreamed it.

Billy turned to a pretty young Irish girl with a snub nose and green eyes.

"Jane, perhaps you'll be good enough to find Catherine a place to sleep with you. I'll warrant she'll be glad of hot food and a change of clothes."

Cat went, unprotesting, to the servants' quarters while the men settled in by Johnson's fire to talk business. She saw that, though the master's house was not grand, it was the center of a whole community.

She found herself sneaking sidelong glances at the Irish serving girl, then noticed she was being inspected the same way.

Each of us is wondering if the other slept with Billy, and both of us know the answer. A woman can always tell.

2.

Johnson was intrigued by his principal male guest. He had heard something of Lydius from visitors, none of it favorable. Some of the Albany crowd muttered that the man was a papist and a secret agent of France, citing as evidence his half-breed wife, Genevieve Massé. Others said Lydius was in the pay of Massachusetts, a no less serious charge in the minds of the jealous, territorial Albany Commissioners. *Doubtful in his loyalties, risky as a debtor,* Arent Stevens had said of him. Lydius had gone bust in New England—so the story ran—and skipped off to Montreal, where he proclaimed himself a Catholic and prospered under the skirts of the Desaunier sisters until the priests had him deported.

Yet Lydius announced, "We have much in common," when he had settled his long legs in front of Billy's fire.

"Not at table," Johnson countered. Lydius drank tea in place of wine or rum punch; he had shocked his host

by requesting the cook to boil him a half-dozen eggs
instead of a respectable beefsteak.

"I have a willful stomach." Lydius patted his flat belly.
"I must listen to what it tells me. But I do not speak of
our tastes in food and drink. I am thinking of our
common enemies. The gentry at De Fouck."

In the frontier pidgin, Albany was The Net.

Lydius rolled up one of his shirtsleeves. He was sitting
in his vest, with his coat off, as if it were high summer.
The man's constitution was a puzzle to Johnson. The
long Dutchman was missing an eye; one of his legs
appeared to be withered, so that he walked with a
swaying limp; and he was easily fifteen years Billy's
senior. Yet all his motions were brisk and robust, and he
appeared impervious to cold, on a diet of hardboiled
eggs and hot tea.

"Look here."

Lydius displayed an ugly raised scar on the inside of
his left arm.

"An assassin's sword did that. It happened on a foul
night in the courtyard of my town house, on Pearl Street.
I believe that Livingston and the Commissioners are at
the bottom of it, though they put word about it was the
Jesuits."

"Why would the Commissioners try to kill you?"

"Why?" Lydius echoed, with a wicked gleam in his
good eye. "Because I am sitting between them and their
soft gold. My trading post is on the upper carry of
Hudson's river, the last post where English is spoken
before you get to Montreal. The Albany ring does not
like competition, Mister Johnson. And I might observe
that just as I flank them to the north, you are flanking
them to the west. From the size of your storehouse, I
believe you are beginning to know your business. If you
prosper, the Albany gang will be out for your blood too."

"There may be something in what you say." Billy had
not forgotten how he had been cheated by the Patroon
on his first visit to Albany. On his most recent, a Dutch
trader had set dogs on him; he had been obliged to take
refuge in Hogan's tavern.

"There will be war," Lydius pursued. "I can smell it. My counsel to you is, Be ready for it. War offers opportunities to a man who is willing to stand when others cut and run. Especially when he stands athwart the warpaths of a continent, as do you and I, Mister Johnson. Come war, the Albany gang will weasel and chisel. The Mohawks won't fight for them, and they won't ask them to fight. So the powers that be will need new men. Bolder men. You and your uncle have connections that reach back to London. I have a certain influence at Boston. It may be we can serve each other."

Billy expressed cautious interest. He was more immediately concerned with the travelers Lydius had delivered at his door—and what Lydius wanted for his trouble.

"As for the girl—Well, now. She is a likely wench, and serviceable in many ways in a gentleman's house. And she has cost me more than a trinket or two, as you would suppose."

"How much?"

"Shall we say fifty pounds?"

"I don't have anything like that amount in ready money."

"A credit with your factors will serve just as well. Which raises a larger question."

"I am listening."

"I believe you are being robbed blind by your partners at Albany." Lydius spun a lurid tale, of barrels tampered with and bundles switched. Billy thought there might be something to it, because Bayard at New York had complained of mold in peltries that had been in perfect condition when they left Johnson's wharf.

"I do not mean to be pushy," Lydius went on.

"No indeed."

"But I believe you need a man who knows the scene to make sure your goods board the Albany sloops in the condition they left your dock."

As the result of Cat's return, a business partnership was sealed that night. The men who made it could hardly begin to guess its consequences. The relationship between Johnson and Lydius would never run straight. But its snaking course would guide the fortunes of the bloodiest—and ultimately decisive—conflict between European empires for the possession of North America.

3.

Cat did not speak to Billy again for days. He left it to others to show her what her duties would be.

She saw him at a distance, talking with traders and Indians. Once she saw him walking with a tall native woman, his arm around her waist, and felt the pain drive deeper inside her belly.

One morning, when she was washing clothes in a tub by the stream with some of the other female servants, Jane Watson said slyly, "You know our Billy has any one of them he wants."

"I don't know what you mean."

"Had you too, didn't he?"

Cat scrubbed furiously.

"He's a lovely man," Jane went on, relentless. "But you know he doesn't give a damn about any of us. One of these days he will marry a grand lady from York or the old country. She'll have her work holding him down, though."

Cat finished her washing quickly, without waiting for the clothes to dry, and walked back to the brick house where she shared a bed with Jane.

I'll go away, she promised herself. *I will find my own people. And I will get my mother back.*

But she needed time to get her bearings, to recover her strength.

I must have a place where I can think.

She looked around the loft where she had slept since she came to Fort Johnson. There was room for another bed, a small one. She spoke to Rogers, who had been kind to her, and he spoke to Mr. Adams, who had charge of the store. They found her a straw mattress and an old rope bed, some pieces of coarse osnaburg no one wanted, and a few iron hooks.

The ceiling in the loft was so low Cat could reach it

with ease, balancing on top of a blanket chest. She hammered inside the curve of the iron hooks, so as not to bend them out of shape. Then she hung the first sheet of coarse linen. She had measured well. The hem quivered six inches off the floor. She dragged the rope bed behind it, and threw the straw mattress on top.

She put up the rest of the curtains, then flung herself down on the bed. The half-light inside the screen she had made reminded her of tunneling down between the sheets on lazy days in childhood—days when she feigned sickness or was truly ill, since idleness had always required an explanation. She laughed like a little girl, delighted by the small world she had made. For the first time in her life, she had a space that belonged to her alone.

A broad hand yanked one of the curtains aside. "What are you playing at, Cat?"

Billy did not look well. His skin had a yellowish, jaundiced look, and he was puffy under the eyes.

"May I join you?"

"I am sure you will do as you please. It is your house."

"That is a hard way to speak to me, Cat."

"It is less hard than saying nothing at all. You have avoided me since I came."

"I'm sorry. I have not been myself."

He sat beside her on the bed and pulled the improvised curtains shut.

"There now. A world to ourselves."

When he smiled, the wall she had built up brick by brick to preserve herself from being hurt by him again collapsed in an instant.

He kissed her eyes, her mouth.

He touched her secret places.

I am a silk flower, opening wave upon wave.

She took his hands. She said, "You have another woman."

"I have no wife, Cat. My life is my own."

"I saw you with an Indian woman."

Billy shrugged. "The natives have a saying. 'A man in a strange country takes a woman of the hill.' It carries no obligation. The woman is nothing to me."

When he said this, the pressure above his eyes pounded like a soldering iron.

"What's wrong?"

"Damn headaches. Overdid it last night, I dare say. Not sleeping well. Listen to me, Cat. I'm sorry I did not speak to you sooner. There's been no end of business, with Mick going off to the wars."

The news of the war with Spain had arrived with an express to Fort Hunter the day Lydius left. An English sea captain had had his ear clipped by the Spaniards. It was a good enough excuse for a fight, with all the prizes to be taken among the Spanish treasure ships. Mick Tyrrell had started packing immediately and would take five or six fellow-Irishmen with him in pursuit of El Dorado.

"The house needs a woman's touch," Johnson went on. "You can imagine what it's been like, a pair of Irish bachelors roughing it together. I'd like you to manage things for me, Cat."

"Your housekeeper. Is that it?"

"You will have charge of all the female domestics."

Jane Watson will love that. The shadow of a smile brushed Cat's lips.

She said, "Is that all?"

He kissed the slope of her neck. "You'll have me, my love. If it is your pleasure. You can move your things to my room."

"I'll come to you tonight," she promised, when he touched her again, under her petticoat.

But I will keep my rope bed, and my curtains. Because I must have a place that is mine alone.

4.

The owl called again. Its call was soft, but strangely intimate. It might have been on the windowsill, or inside the room. A feathery gust of air brushed Cat's neck. She shivered and buried her face in the pillows.

Billy slid from the canopied bed and pulled on shirt and breeches.

Cat groaned and reached an arm toward him.

"Go to sleep, my love," he murmured, stooping to kiss her hair. "I must see to the horses."

Outside, Billy heard only the squall of the crickets.

The owl hooted from the old oak at the edge of the cornfield.

Billy stepped out in the clear moonlight. The horned moon was tipped on its back.

A shadow separated itself from the oak. He saw the gleam of silver against dark calico. In the moonlight, the Mohawk woman's skin was the color of pewter.

"Kawennotie, is it you? God love us, it's the middle of the night."

"I missed you." Swimming Voices waited for him to touch her. He took her by the fingers, holding his body apart. There was a soapy smell on his skin. The smell of the German woman.

Rage and hunger were in her eyes. Johnson felt their violence. Her hands tightened over his, the nails pressing into his flesh.

He had shamed her in front of her people, showing off his new woman, without even a smile for Swimming Voices. The Mohawk girls had flayed her raw with their tongues. They said she was getting her reward for putting on airs, for making out she was better than her own kind. When a white man took a wife, he abandoned his Indian family. The wife made sure of that. To white men, an Indian woman was good enough until something better came along or for a poke on the sly. Forest Killer was no different from the rest. "We told you, we told you," the girls chanted. "You wouldn't listen." If Swimming Voices got a big belly, she would cry by herself.

Island Woman had talked to her about it, worried about the force of her elder daughter's emotions. "Let him go," her mother had counseled. "Men come and go. A woman endures."

Swimming Voices did not want her mother's advice. She wanted Johnson. She was not going to give him up to a stranger—a pale-eyes as skinny as a rabbit at the end of winter—without a fight.

"Did you miss me?"

"You know I missed you." Always the gallant, Johnson raised her hand to his lips.

"Who is that woman?" Swimming Voices demanded. "Is she your wife?"

"Of course not."

"Does she sleep in your bed?"

Billy looked around nervously. The horses were restless, the dogs strangely quiet. "We cannot talk here."

She tugged him by the hands, leading him into the corn. The silvery tassels waved high above their heads. The leafy stalks parted for them and closed behind them, a rustling curtain.

She unfastened her dress and let it fall to her ankles. She was naked underneath, except for her necklace of bright beads and bird fetishes, her silver bangles and leggings that tinkled softly when she moved her legs.

She threw her long braids over his shoulders. An act of possession. He did not resist it. She pressed against his chest. She rubbed her hard belly against his groin, and felt him rise.

"Do it to me now," she said gruffly.

"It's cold."

She fumbled with the brass buttons on the front of his breeches. His cock was purple-dark in the pale light and stood up like a warclub. She smiled. Whatever the stranger in his bed was doing for him, it was not enough.

"Lie with me."

"We can't," Billy protested, scowling at the thickets that surrounded them.

She laughed and sprung up into his arms. He swayed with the new weight. He yelped with pain when she sank her teeth into his neck, and toppled backward. The cornstalks snapped under their joined bodies, falling in diagonal rows, making a springy mattress. In the morning, it might look like a place where a buck had lain in hiding from the hunters.

5.

In the Moon That Beats Down the Bushes, Fruitpicker walked the path of strawberries and Island Woman was raised up as the Mother of the Wolf Clan.

Swimming Voices came to her at sunrise, when her mother was brewing acorn coffee over the fire.

She said, "I have a dream."

Island Woman reached for her wrist, to see clearly, but her daughter pulled her arm away and squatted on the far side of the firepit.

Swimming Voices said, "I dreamed a newcomer gave me a gold ring. It glowed like the sun, and it had a sunburst on it. The ring was too big for my finger, so I put it on my thumb. What does it mean?"

"You can put that right out of your head," Island Woman snapped. "You have no business messing with another woman's man. You bring shame on your family."

"My dream does not lie!"

"Not all dreams speak true. You say the ring in the dream is too big for you? How do you know it belongs to you?"

"Because—because—" Swimming Voices touched her belly. She was sure now. It had been three moons since the dark blood had returned to the earth, since she had taken Forest Killer's seed in the field of waving corn.

"What do you care?" Swimming Voices spat at her mother, remembering all the winters of rejection. "All you've ever done is spoil things for me. You never cared about me. You give all your love to Bright Meadow."

She threw her coffee into the fire. It hissed angrily.

"Careful," her mother warned. "The rattlesnake warns only once."

Swimming Voices spoke to Snowbird, who paddled downriver to Mount Johnson.

"It's time you played lacrosse with us," Snowbird told Billy.

"I won't be any good," Johnson demurred. He had watched a game between Mohawks and Senecas. The players ran like deer and wielded their ball bats like machetes.

"We're a man short," Snowbird told him. "And we're playing Onondagas. They're not so hard to beat. Anyway, it will be like a family game. Men and boys playing together. Do you want me to tell Hendrick Forked Paths you are fearful of children?"

This was quite a speech for Snowbird, and it gave Billy a hint of a further agenda. He assumed that Hendrick was looking to do some business. And of course both Hendrick and Snowbird would be hoping to win something in the betting, which was usually fierce at lacrosse games.

□

Rogers always went on the road with his master. But when Paddy Groghan, Billy's overseer, got wind of what promised to be the native equivalent of a day at the races, there was no keeping him out of it. They packed a trade bundle with showy items—bangles and brooches, beads and mirrors—and the inevitable supply of rum. Indian wagering, like Indian trade, was done in kind.

Billy was greeted warmly by Hendrick and the warriors and sachems of the Upper Castle. Island Woman acknowledged him formally, keeping a distance.

Every inch the new clanmother, Johnson thought. *And a power to be reckoned with.*

Island Woman's face was scored by hard living and the burdens she carried, but her eyes blazed with life and intelligence.

Had I but known you in your prime.

He looked around for Swimming Voices, but did not find her. Bright Meadow, the younger daughter, was walking with her husband, White Owl.

I am glad that man-mountain is on my team.

Snowbird escorted him over to his mother's lodge to prepare for the game. Above the eastern door, a red wolf bayed at an unseen moon.

Inside the longhouse, Billy stripped to the buff. He circled his waist with a deerskin belt, then reached for his breechcloth—a strip of broadcloth dyed a rich scarlet, with beautifully beaded fringes, patterned in a design of oak leaves and antlers. A gift from Swimming Voices. He passed the cloth between his legs and reached down to fold the ends over the belt so they hung down, front and back, like aprons.

He heard squeaks and scratches overhead.

Looking up, he saw two small brown faces framed in the smokehole. Swimming Voices' kids.

"Come down, little squirrels." He crooked a forefinger.

The boys squealed and scrambled off the roof.

Outside, Island Woman settled herself in the shade of a maple, with her friend Windweaver, now the Mother of the Turtle Clan.

"That white man has got something," Windweaver chuckled. "See how the girls fidget, wherever he goes? They can't sit still."

"He's got silver," Island Woman said curtly.

"He's got a nice ass." Windweaver jabbed her in the ribs. "Not a big sloppy butt like most of those newcomers."

Island Woman said, "Bull elks get gored in the rutting time. They get so weak from doing it even a scrawny old wolf can take them."

Billy came back into sunlight, the red lights in his hair shining as it streamed loose about his bare shoulders.

There were seven players on each side. Snowbird gave Billy a fire-hardened bat, fitted with a rawhide net, and showed him his position in line, between White Owl and Hendrick Forked Paths.

Johnson saw familiar faces among the Onondagas. A grand old man with a mane of flowing gray hair, still vigorous, known throughout the Six Nations as The Word. And a visitor from the north who had come to Mount Johnson with Lydius and dined in Billy's own kitchen: the hook-beaked Caughnawaga Lydius had called Le Corbeau.

Johnson saw no children in the opposing teams. Some of the men looked capable of going head-to-head with a buffalo.

The object of the game was to carry the ball through

your own gate—two poles set three rods apart. You were not permitted to touch the ball with hands or feet. This was the only prohibition that was strictly policed. Jabbing the butt of your stick in your opponent's ribs or groin was a venial infraction, much enjoyed by the crowd.

Billy had suffered a few bone-jarring blows—mostly from Le Corbeau—by the end of the penultimate round. The score was now four–four. The ninth round would be the tie breaker.

The howls of the spectators rose to a crescendo. The women's voices shrilled highest and most savage.

The heaps of wagered goods rose higher and higher. Paddy Groghan was active among the punters. Mohawk men were betting their pipes, their hatchets, even their bedding. An outraged woman fought with her husband to reclaim a three-point blanket he was trying to add to the pile. The delirium was fueled by liquor. It infected the players.

The hard deerskin ball was in play.

Billy saw it flying straight at his head. He caught it in mid-field and bolted. The goal seemed impossibly far.

The Onondagas swooped after him.

He skidded round the rock-hard bulk of The Word, who ran interference. Billy jumped higher than he had known he could to escape the slicing thrust of another player's stick, looking for a teammate to whom he could pass the ball.

Le Corbeau leaped at him. Billy tried to dodge the hammer-blow, angled to break his arm. It knocked the stick from his hands. He scrambled after it.

A woman's voice rose in a hellish shriek. "Kill him! Eat his liver without salt!"

The Caughnawaga slammed into him again. Billy was down. He saw Le Corbeau's glinting, close-set eyes, the whites of his knuckles as he swung his stick.

This bugger isn't playing a game, Johnson realized. *He has it in for me.*

Billy rolled to escape the scythe-like sweep of the Caughnawaga's stick.

His fumbling on the ground would not save him.

At the last moment, White Owl thundered across the field, shouldering Le Corbeau aside. With his next motion, he scooped up the ball and drove away through the Mohawk gate.

The Mohawks raised the scalp-yell.

□

Paddy Groghan had done well with his bets, though Billy was a little miffed when he discovered that his overseer had laid long odds that his master would not score a goal.

"Traitor!" Billy rumbled. But Paddy had a drink ready and another.

After several toasts, Billy noticed the woman moving among the trees.

When he went to her, Swimming Voices slipped away.

"Hey!" he called after her. "Whose side were you on? I thought I heard you calling for my blood."

Her laughter rippled in the cooling air.

"Tonight," she called back. "By the horned tree. When the moon is below the hills."

She had kept away from the stone house these two or three months past. And Billy had not sought her out. She had become difficult, jealous and grasping. And when she was in the neighborhood, he was disturbed by evil dreams.

But he thought, *There is no harm in ending the game with a little gentler sport.*

□

She wore soft doeskin, worked until it was white, because he liked her best in native clothes. She flaunted her body as she pulled at the strings.

He had been drinking too long.

Although he flattered himself that it rarely affected his stamina, she needed to work on him with her lips and her fingers.

There was something else amiss. He could not put his finger on it.

In their breathing silence, he ground into her monotonously, dutifully.

When he pulled out and started to apologize, she cut him off. She knew in her gut he was about to cut the cord between them. She would not let this happen.

She pinched the skin of his chest, above the nipple.

"Forest Killer, I am carrying your child."

Billy swallowed. It was on the tip of his tongue to say, *How do you know it's mine? How do I know?*

But he would not cast a child of his body away like soiled clothes.

He said, "I honor my obligations. If the child is mine, it will be well provided for."

"What about *me?*"

"What do you want of me?"

Her eyes glistened. "I told you. I want your soul."

Billy laughed. "I fear you must ask for something easier to deliver."

His laugh turned brittle, because the passion in her face and in her voice quivered on the edge of hatred.

"I think it would be prudent," he went on soberly, "to curtail these—ah—assignations, delightful though they are."

Her fingers stiffened into claws. She looked ready to tear off his face.

"You think you can use me like a bone you pick over and throw to the dogs?" she snarled.

Billy took a step backward. He became a little afraid of her.

"You got away from me this time," she told him. "Next time, you won't get away."

6.

When he washed, Johnson found rust-colored smears on his undergarments and concluded that Swimming Voices had lied to him about a child. The thought that she had lain with him in the time of her moon-change made him uneasy. The taboo against having sex in a woman's time of power was strong among his own people as well as the Six Nations. He remembered Jane Watson's talk of a hex, the odd things hanging from the beams in Swimming Voices' house, the bad dreams. He wished he could talk to Denis Rahilly about this. Rahilly would never mock a man for speaking of witchcraft. On the other hand, Denis could be as much the credulous fool as a Mayo dairymaid blaming the evil eye or the pooka every time the buttermilk in her churn turned sour.

Billy resolved to put the affair with Swimming Voices out of his mind. He had plenty to attend to. He had sent one of the Butler boys to Oswego, to trade for him there. He was negotiating for a new tract of land, running back into the woods for several miles. He had a notion he might be able to corner the winter market for peas and flour.

There were mornings when he woke with a shudder, feeling he had been split apart.

This is how an oyster would feel when it has just been shucked.

He suspected, some of these mornings, that his debility was a hangover from evil dreams, as much as the drink.

But he did not look back into his dreams. At breakfast, he hurried their escape with a pitcher of beer or heart-starters of brandy.

He shut out the singsong voice of the dreams, that chanted the same things over and over:

> *Listen to me.*
> *Let me in.*
> *I am beautiful.*
> *With all other women, you are lonely.*
> *Other women are becoming dull and ugly*
>   *as miserable crows.*
> *Now your soul is rising.*
> *It is walking toward me.*
> *It is coming into me.*
> *Listen.*

One night, lying beside Billy in his canopied bed, Cat was wakened by a sound like a strong wind shaking the leaves of the locust grove.

The sound came from Billy.

It was unlike the snores that came from him naturally, when he lay sated, sprawled shameless on his back. This was not snoring at all. It came on the breath of his mouth, in a sawing of the air through his teeth.

It formed words.

She could hear the same phrase, repeated over and over:

Let me in. Let me in.

She did not know whether to wake Billy or let him lie. But the wind-words filled her with a crawling dread. Finally she shook him and he raised up. Billy stared about blindly, as if there was a screen between him and the room. Then he rolled over and fell back into sleep.

Billy was now snoring hard enough to shake the bed. Cat felt a little better, because this was familiar, even if it was likely to cost her sleep.

Then she saw the pale shadow sliding along the wall toward the window. It was almost a substantial thing, bluish-gray, like a faded pearl. It vanished into the wan moonlight.

Cat slipped from the bed and looked out the window.

An owl-like bird, bigger than any owl she had seen, flapped away into the river mist.

□

Cat took to wearing the little cross Sister Mary had given her. Billy did not comment, but Jane Watson did, when she caught a glimpse of Cat dressing.

"Can't do any harm," Jane whispered, giving Cat a glimpse of the Celtic cross she wore around her own neck. "But you're not our kind, are you? Is it because of the Indian witch?"

The Irish serving-girl told Cat about her previous run-in with Swimming Voices.

"I found her trying to hide a devil-doll under Mister Johnson's bed. She gave me a look like she wanted to pluck my heart out with her bare hands."

"What did Mister Johnson say?"

"Oh, he laughed it off, as you would expect. Said the Indian superstitions have no power over white people.

Or else we wouldn't be here, with all the enemies we have made."

Cat wondered whether it is necessary to believe in something in order to be vulnerable to it.

The question became urgent after she discovered she was pregnant.

When she told Billy, he took her by the waist and swirled her around the kitchen.

"You make me a very happy man, Cat. The Valley needs more Johnsons. If it is a boy, we will call him John."

"Must it be a boy?"

"You know I love girls. If it is a girl, we must call her Anne, after my mother."

No talk of marriage, but she would never ask for that. It was enough that the child would have Billy's acknowledgment and protection. And the Johnson name.

It did not take long for the news to circulate up and down the Valley. There were few secrets in the small world of Mount Johnson.

And strange things began to happen to Cat.

There was nothing threatening, to begin with. She found her personal things disturbed. Her place settings at the table in the stone house were reversed, so the spoons were where the forks were meant to be. The soap balls in the sleeping loft were replaced by greasy gobbets of baconfat.

Then, one morning, she could not find the ginger cat that came to the kitchen door for milk and scraps. She looked for it in the barnyard, but no one had seen it.

In the afternoon, she walked to the little herb garden Billy had allowed her to clear, where she was experimenting with native plants as well as Old World varieties. There was a nasty buzzing of flies from the back of the garden. She pushed through a knee-high patch of celandine. Horrified, she saw the cat splayed against a bush. Its entrails wormed from its slit stomach, crawling with flies. There was a collar round its neck that the cat had never worn before.

Outraged, gagging, Cat recognized her own garter.

□

"It is native trickery," Jane insisted. "It is that Indian whore, trying to get in your head and scare you off."

The Irish girl's jealousy evaporated in the face of a common rival.

Cat thought Jane was probably right about the Mohawk woman, but there was no proof, nothing to take to Billy. She spoke to Rogers. He allowed he might have seen Swimming Voices the day before, but that counted for nothing; Indians were always hanging about the house, forever poking their noses into things.

Then Cat's dreams changed again.

She dreamed of a horrible, twisted face, with a lolling tongue and eyes that gleamed like brass. A masklike thing, dancing around her.

She heard the hiss of rattles and woke inside the dream. The rattles became writhing serpents. She wanted to crush them, to shake them off. But they were coiling inside her own belly.

She fought to get out of the dream, but she was stuck in a place between dreaming and waking. She seemed to be meshed in sticky wrappings. She could see nothing beyond them except a darkness like the cold between the stars.

She struggled harder. She tore free from the sticky substance that bound her, but as she did so she felt something ripped away from herself, like a second skin.

When she opened her eyes, she saw only the same dark.

She wanted to scream, but no sound came from her throat.

Then she heard birdsong from the fields, and the power of movement returned to her.

But she was utterly depleted. The simple act of dressing was like climbing a mountain.

During the morning, things from the dream bobbed back into memory, menacing but indistinct.

What did I lose?

Why were the snakes inside me?
She was chopping vegetables when it came to her.

Her hand shook as she brought down the knife, and she sliced a corner of her finger. She moved slowly toward the pail of water, her shoulders slumping forward, as if to protect her heart.

Not the baby. I can endure anything but that.

7.

She bandaged her finger and applied herself to the household chores.

What you imagine can make you sick. The best preventive, she thought, was to keep busy. She had to keep a watchful eye on the new house girl, one of the slaves Captain Warren had recently sent up from New York. The girl acted like she had never seen a broom and did not know one end of a skillet from the other.

Cat reserved Billy's room for herself. She would never conquer his roving eye, but she could try to keep the maidservants out of his bed.

When she entered the bedroom, she sensed she was not alone.

She quivered beside the bed, a pile of fresh linen over her arm, as the terror of the night walked over her bones.

The Indian witch wants to get inside my head, Jane had said. *I won't let her.*

She marched resolutely to the bed and threw back the covers.

The rustle of dry, leathery scales rose to an angry rattle.

The serpent in the bed shone as its muscles contracted, tightening the scales.

Cat threw the folded sheets at it and turned for the door.

The rattlesnake whipped out at her. She felt the fangs sink into her forearm.

Sobbing, she shook it loose and stamped on it until it lay still.

Her face was drained of color when she reached the

top of the stairs. The African girl caught her at the bottom. Cat was covered by a slick of sweat. Her head was swimming. She could no longer stand unassisted.

The house slave ran out into the yard and came back with a chicken. She twisted its neck and wrapped it around the wound. She said fresh-killed meat would drink up the poison.

Cat could not understand one word in three.

She drifted in and out of consciousness as men hurried in and out of the kitchen. One of them cut her with a razor.

"Billy—"

He leaned over her, kissing her eyes.

"Our baby—"

"Rest easy, my love. You are both in good hands."

She did not see the harried look on Johnson's face when the doctor came upriver and told him, "She has the snake spots. You don't see many people come back when they have got the spots."

□

She rolled in the coils of a dream that would not let her go. She was no longer human. She kept changing forms.

She was a broken willow, hanging low over the green-brown river. She was a rotting log. Her limbs splintered and floated away with the current.

She was a tawny spotted animal, mired in a sucking mudhole. She tried to shed her skin, but her flesh came away with it in bloody clumps.

This dream is not in my head, part of herself was saying. *I am inside this dream.*

A tall, regal woman walked into this dream.

She looked like Swimming Voices, but she was older, and there was no darkness in her heart.

She showed Cat a plant on which small white flowers grew in clusters on stalks that bristled with spiked leaves. She made Cat touch the roots and stem of this plant, the small scalelike leaves that grew close to the ground, so she would always know it.

She showed Cat how to dry the roots, and the exact amount that must be used for a healing potion.

She cautioned, *This medicine is also poison.*

She communicated all this without speech, mind speaking to mind.

Cat took the potion from her hands.

□

When the fever broke, Cat said, "Was someone here?"

"You were never alone, duck," Rogers told her. "Half the county has been fussing over you."

"I mean a native woman."

"You was honored, I reckon. The master sent to the Mohawk for one of their medicine people, seeing as how they know the rattlesnake better than any. The woman who came was a clanmother, no less. She gave you a drink that seems to have broken the sweat."

"The baby—"

"I expect Mister Johnson will want to tell you himself. The doctor says there are no worries."

8.

Dark and solitary as Raven, Swimming Voices kited over the Valley. She saw the joy at Mount Johnson at Cat's reviving health and spirits, and her jealousy sharpened into a killing hate.

They do not know my power yet. I have not finished with them.

The wind currents changed, and suddenly she was losing height, dropping low over the Upper Castle. She beat her pinions to catch an updraft and saw her shadow skimming the river like a flint arrowhead. A larger shadow moved behind it, coming on fast.

She looked for the source and found a huge white eagle swooping down at her, talons outstretched. She tried to outdistance it, but it was faster. She worked frantically to regain height, to fight it on equal terms. But it knocked her off course with a furious blow that crippled her wing, and she flapped frantically toward the shelter of her cabin in the swale.

The eagle screamed, and she knew its meaning.

Her mother had come to warn her off.

□

When she rose from her bed, her arm ached and she could not bend it at the elbow. She told the boys to bring her splints from the woods.

While she waited for them, she put her questions to the looking water, angling the pot so she had a clear, silvery surface.

She was calling on her ally, the dead sorcerer for whom she burned tobacco and offered blood sacrifice in the dark of the moon.

Another face appeared in the water.

Swimming Voices flinched from the blazing eyes in the mask of Okwaho, the She-Wolf.

Your path is becoming black, Island Woman walked through her mind.

"I won't listen to you," Swimming Voices defied her. "I won't look. You have always been against me."

You will see this.

Against her will, Swimming Voices looked. She saw the circle of women, in the firelight of the cave. Island Woman was holding something. A black bird. She was cutting its chest open with a knife. She touched its beating heart with the tip.

Swimming Voices' heart jumped against her ribs.

"No!"

Go back, her mother cautioned. *There will be no more warnings.*

In her fear and despair, Swimming Voices overturned the pot. She gasped at the pain from her broken arm.

Where is my ally? He promised I would be stronger than any. Now I am outcast by all.

She heard a movement at the door. *The boys, back with the splints.*

Instead, Le Corbeau walked into the room. He still wore the scalps in his belt, stretched on their little hoops. He had painted a mask of black paint around his eyes.

The sorcerer's close-set eyes battened on her.

He cawed, "We are two of a kind."

He made a fist of his hands and ground it into his solar plexus.

She watched intently as he moved his palms slowly apart. There was a ball of dull light between them. It grew bigger and bigger as he stretched his arms apart. It assumed shape. It was half-bird, half-man.

"You see?" Le Corbeau croaked. "We are the same. I am the only one who can protect you."

CHAPTER 18
DEVILS OF NEW YORK

1.

Cat's baby opened her lungs and howled so long and hard that Juba, who had assisted as midwife, clapped her hands and sang out in pure celebration, "This chile wants *life!*"

Cat lingered over every detail of this new life as if she had just been given the gift of sight.

My nose and skin, she thought.

There was more of Billy about the generous, sensual mouth, the dimpled chin, the tassel of red-gold hair.

But the eyes are your own.

The eyes astonished her. They were sea-gray, changing color with the light. They seemed fully focused, as if the newborn was already drinking in the world around her, though Cat thought this was not possible.

"Wise eyes," Billy said when he came in. "I think we have drawn an old soul, my love. It must be your goodness."

He kissed her hands, her hair. He smelled of the sun and tobacco and warm spice. She ignored a fainter, sweeter scent. Though Swimming Voices had left the Valley, there were other women. There always would be, she thought. But on this day, she could forgive Billy anything.

Pleasure shone in his face as he held his daughter in his arms. Then he whisked the infant out into the garden, to show her off to the servants and tenants.

"This day brings us a new laughter!" Cat heard his rich, carrying voice as she lay back against the pillows. It had not been an easy labor. The baby—big enough at close on nine pounds—had a head that seemed enormous in proportion to the rest of her.

A head that goes with those wise eyes.

She will have the best teachers, Cat promised both of them. *She will read any book she likes. She will choose her own life, and her own partner. She will not walk in the shadow of any man. They will not be allowed to soften her bones.*

Outside, the baby's father called for his biggest punch-bowl.

"Let the world know—" Cat heard Billy roar "—that a flower of Ireland has come into our field. Let us welcome Miss Anne Johnson! Here's to you, little Nancy!"

2.

The winter after Nancy was born was the hardest in the memory of anyone living in the Province of New York.

In the Valley, blizzard blasts from the north had the effect of snow-bearing hurricanes. They piled drifts as high as the tops of the palisades at the Upper Castle. The powdery snow would not bear the weight of man or beast. Yearling deer, yarding in their evergreen hollows, could not reach the spruce and balsam tips, and perished by the thousands. The hunters from Island Woman's village waded after them on snowshoes, sharing the meat with the wolves with sinking hearts, knowing that all of them would go hungry before the melt.

Sledding home from Schenectady along the King's Road, Billy was knocked from his seat by a driving gale that hit like a giant's fist and left him foundering, snowblind, among the drifts. It was his wolfhound, Favour, that got him out, whimpering for his master in the white night. Billy groped after him, even hanging from his tail, until they found shelter at a neighbor's farm. After that, the wolfhound was given the run of the house. He liked to lie under one of Billy's kegs of Madeira, swiping the spigot with his paw until the wine ran into his mouth. Billy did not mind a dog that drank, and would allow Favour anything. But he complained that it was impossible to teach the wolfhound the trick of turning off the wine-tap.

□

On Manhattan island, the terrible winter exacted an appalling toll, especially among the poor and the old. Men gathering firewood on the Jersey shore came back missing fingers or toes. In the markets, vendors asked extortionate prices for the scraps of meat they sawed off frozen carcasses.

Denis Rahilly tried to stave off the cold by traditional methods. But the winter was not kind to Billy's former tutor. Rahilly had a falling-out with the Governor's cook, whose affections were now inclined toward a sergeant of the garrison. Denis was reduced to sleeping in a low dosshouse and earning his dinner by coaching thick-headed merchants' sons and scraping his fiddle in taverns.

On Christmas Eve, he played at Hughson's grogshop, near the North River. Hughson's drew the scum and swill of the town, but the rum was cheap and plentiful, served in raw drams. And Rahilly, as a student of human nature, was intrigued by the variety of the customers. More than half were black men: slaves in fancy livery from the houses of the great, Spanish negroes with the languid manners of hidalgoes, taken as prizes in the West Indies. Supplying slaves with liquor in a public house was no doubt against the law, but the Constable, one of Rahilly's fellow-countrymen, was a tolerant fellow who was paid to look the other way. Indeed, Constable Kennedy stopped in at the tavern to drink a bumper with Denis on the night before Christmas. The white clientele included water-rats and soldiers whose talk was as salty as ammonia. But there were also distressed scholars with whom Rahilly found much in common; men like John Ury, an itinerant schoolteacher who could debate politics and theology and was known to read and write at the common table. Hughson's was safe enough for a man with an empty purse, like Rahilly, as long as he kept clear of Fireship Peg and the other bawds, who were no more particular than the proprietor about the company they kept.

Rahilly's supper that Christmas Eve was no better than a lump of wheat cake and a piece of boiled fish. But it came with a jug of hard cider. And when Rahilly got up to play a sprightly jig, the crowd picked up the festive air and started dancing and singing along.

At midnight, Rahilly was in high spirits.

He called to the crowd, "A great day is dawning! Will you hear me, lads? It is Christmas!"

There were groans and catcalls. But enough expectant faces, black and white, were turned to Rahilly for him to share a new song that burst from his heart unrehearsed:

Today we give thanks to the Risen Lord.
Mary knew you through dreams and the comfort of
     the angels.
The shepherds knew you through the instinct of
     creatures that live close to the earth.
The wise men knew you by prophecy and the flight
     of a star.
The disciples knew you through wonders and the
     winds of your soul.
Sinners may know you through the miracle of
     grace.

This brought more hoots and catcalls. "Not in here!" a seaman jeered.

"Does that mean Hughson will give us a drink on the house?" someone else shouted.

"All of us may know you—" Rahilly pursued "—through the love that brings our world into being and daily preserves it."

He swallowed. Fireship Peg, spilling out of her décolletage, was raptly intent. Rahilly thought she might have posed, at that instant, for a painting of the Annunciation. The Africans whispered to each other. An Irish soldier, deep in his cups, wiped tears away with the froth of his beer.

"Papist."

The word was spat by a man sitting in shadow against the wall. Rahilly could not make out his features. He saw the man catch Mary Burton, Hughson's indentured servant, by the wrist.

Something in this exchange struck a damp into Rahilly's spirits.

He made an effort to recover himself, scraping a bawdy tune. Before he had finished, several of Hughson's customers were fighting each other, and the man by the wall had slipped away into the night. It was not the way Rahilly would have chosen to see in Christmas.

3.

Spring in the city brought violent fevers, rumors that the French and the Spanish were readying an attack on the colony, and a series of mysterious fires.

Shortly before noon, the morning after St. Patrick's Day, Susannah Warren heard hoarse shouts of "Fire!" in the street. Getting only confused accounts from the servants, she swept up to the widow's walk on top of her house.

She saw a column of smoke rising above Fort George. As she watched, tongues of flame leaped from the roof of the Governor's house to the chapel, the barracks and the secretary's office, above the gate. Like most of the houses in New York, these buildings were all roofed with wooden shingles. They ignited like dry punkwood.

Mrs. Warren heard urgent drum-rolls from inside the fort. Soldiers and civilians were forming a chain, passing water in leather buckets from hand to hand.

Her brother Oliver galloped up to the house, wild-eyed, his wig awry.

"You must come away!" he called up to her. "The fire may reach the magazine!"

Susannah Warren refused to leave her house. Mercifully, the blaze did not reach the powder magazine. However, it did inflame the imagination of the town. Over the next days, Susannah heard rival theories about the origins of the fire debated in every house she visited.

Being of a practical bent, Susannah put most reliance on her husband's opinion: that a careless artificer, soldering a gutter, had let sparks fly from his fire-pot.

"If he was any sort of Irishman, native born or honorary," Captain Warren opined, "he can have been none too steady the morning after Saint Paddy's night."

But there were wilder theories. Major Van Horne, a parade-ground martinet who was Major Drum to his men, put it about that the fire was the work of black slaves. There was a dark conspiracy afoot, according to Major Drum. The slaves were plotting to burn the city, cut the throats of their masters, and bed their wives. The ringleaders were supposedly "Romish priests" and "Spanish niggers," including the slaves Captain Warren had recently seized as prizes in the West Indies.

Captain Warren dismissed this as a drunken delusion. Susannah sniffed at all such stories as specimens of the boorish superstition that still prevailed in the colony.

But as fires spread through the town, so did Major Drum's version of causes.

To Mrs. Warren's extreme discomfort, the second fire broke out in her own house, exactly one week after the first. There were those who whispered that this was God's own justice, because of those Spanish negroes. Susannah could see for herself that it was nothing more than a common chimney fire. If anyone was to blame, it was only herself, for being laggardly in fetching the sweeps. The fire had done no serious damage, thanks to the promptness of a relay of volunteer firemen.

But Judge Horsmanden came in person and insisted on interrogating Mrs. Warren's slaves.

"There is much amiss," Daniel Horsmanden informed Susannah. "Your footman Caesar has a way of turning his eyes inward. Those who are familiar with the African race, as I am obliged to be, recognize that this is a certain reflection of conscious villainy."

Susannah defended her slave stoutly. Having lost one favorite—Caliban—she had no intention of parting with another.

Then Van Zandt's warehouse, by the East River, was gutted by a new fire. At Murray's stables, live coals were found under the haystacks. A row of mean houses by the North River was burned down. A witness claimed to have seen a black man running from one of them, whooping with joy.

The town needed someone to blame for all the maladies that had settled on it—not only the fires, but the bitter winter, the poisoned air, the soaring prices in the markets. So the Great Negro Conspiracy of New York was born.

A mob attacked Caesar, the Warrens' slave, when he was sent to water the horses at the spring.

Slaves found out of doors were arrested at random.

Terrified men and girls, quaking in fetters in the bowels of Horsmanden's jail under City Hall, gave him the evidence he needed to launch a witchhunt to rival Salem's.

In the wake of the fires came a rash of burglaries, including the theft of a large quantity of merchandise from Hogg's store. Reports flowed in that some of the stolen goods had been sighted at Hughson's grogshop. Though Hughson had long held a reputation as a fence, a preliminary search by the placid Constable Kennedy turned up no proof. A subsequent search—guided by a reliable informer—led to the arrest of Hughson, his wife and daughter, and a white indentured servant, Mary Burton.

Mary was an interesting study for Judge Horsmanden, trembling between fear of punishment and righteous wrath. She told scandalous tales of black men being entertained by white women. She whispered that one Margaret Kerry—otherwise known as Fireship Peg—had kept up a regular courtship with a swaggering

Spanish negro called Antonio, who clambered up the side of a shed to her bedroom window and set the bedpost banging until it gave those below wicked headaches. Mary Burton confided uglier things. That sinister white men held sway at Hughson's, inducting the slaves into the mysteries of the Pope and the devil. These were not ordinary sailors or chandlers; they were men who could read and write. One of them scraped a fiddle and sermonized over it in praise of popery and sedition.

Mary's testimony grew more alarming and more detailed when Horsmanden quizzed her with the aid of other material that fell to hand, especially a letter from General Oglethorpe, chief of the King's men in the Georgia plantations. Oglethorpe had written to the Acting Governor, warning that he had sure intelligence that the Spaniards were hatching a plot to burn New York and the other principal towns in the colonies in order to divert the English from the war at sea. The organizers of the plot, according to Oglethorpe's information, were Roman priests camouflaged as teachers and dancing masters.

Judge Horsmanden glowed when Mary Burton helped to pinpoint these agents of Rome who had held court at Hughson's knocking-shop.

The ability to read and write, in a man of no rank who frequented low taverns, was already suspect in a town where few of the citizenry could write presentable English. A command of Latin smelled strongly of popery, especially in an Irish fiddler.

Horsmanden's men dragged Denis Rahilly from his foul bed—shared with three others in no better circumstances than himself—on a warm May morning.

Judge Horsmanden, confident in his mastery of physiognomy, found incontrovertible proof of Rahilly's guilt in his shifty way of avoiding his inquisitor's eyes.

He announced triumphantly that he had unmasked "a scheme that must have been brooded in a conclave of devils, and hatched in the cabinet of hell."

The public needed devils to blame for the province's misfortunes. Seized by the popular fervor, every lawyer

in town begged to assist Horsmanden when he made it
known that the conspirators would be tried by the
Supreme Court.

Only Susannah Warren's brother, Chief Justice
DeLancey, stood aloof. He could indulge in this posture,
at least at the outset, because he had been absent from
the colony for several months on a mission to the
government of Rhode Island. When he returned to
Manhattan, he could plead the pressure of family business; Stephen DeLancey, the patriarch, died that summer, leaving a will that divided his enormous estates
among his five surviving children, including the wife of
the fortunate Captain Warren.

But not even the new head of the powerful DeLancey
family could stand above the Manhattan witchhunt for
long. Two of his brother Peter's slaves were named as
members of the fiery cabal. Then a terrified informer
named Othello—Anne DeLancey's favorite manser-
vant—as one of the ringleaders.

4.

Billy Johnson sailed down the Hudson that summer. He
did not come on account of Rahilly; he had not heard of
his friend's misfortunes. Billy came because his uncle
had blood in his eye.

Johnson had addressed several of his recent letters to
Captain Warren from "Mount Johnson." He now had a
place on which to stand. If he owed anyone for it, he
believed, it was his mother, and he had expressed his
gratitude and love for her in naming his daughter. To put
the name of his own estate at the head of his letters was a
very mild assertion of independence, Billy thought. He
had made every effort to assure his uncle that the
Warren interest in the lands across the river was fully
protected; hardly a day passed when Johnson did not
cross the Mohawk to check on the tenants and supervise
work on the home farm.

But Captain Warren's angry summons—penned as
soon as he returned from making war on the Spaniards

at Port Royal—left no doubt that he believed his nephew was stealing his money.

But, thanks to the improvements Billy had initiated, the Warrensbush estate would be worth vastly more than Captain Warren had paid for it at the end of the three years he had agreed to manage it. Peter Warren's profit from the sale of the property—if he chose to sell—would more than absorb his outlay on trade goods.

Besides, with his prize-taking on the Spanish Main and his wife's inheritance from her father, Captain Warren was in no need of cash. He was well on his way to making himself one of the wealthiest men in the colonies. Rich enough to buy himself a tame, landscaped estate in the Pale of Ireland or even the Home Counties. Or to buy himself the governorship of New York, if his tastes turned that way.

Billy hoped to appeal to his uncle's sense of humor and his taste for a wager. Though he was no soldier, he knew that attack is the best method of defense. With all the rumors of a land war, the merchants of Albany were pulling in their horns. Billy intended to persuade his uncle to help him take advantage of the nervousness upriver by underwriting a far deeper plunge into the Indian trade. And how would he talk Uncle Peter into throwing good money after bad? He counted on both his invisible allies—charm and luck—and on highly visible companions.

Johnson did not board the Albany sloop alone. He brought Mohawks with him: Hendrick Forked Paths, Snowbird and White Owl. They would prove to his uncle the influence that he had developed among the natives of the Valley. This was the key, he would argue, to victory or defeat in another land war with the French. And to profits beyond the imaginings of even a DeLancey or a Van Cortlandt.

☐

When Billy's party disembarked at Coenties Quay, an African slave followed with a bundle of presents for Uncle Peter and Aunt Susannah. Johnson had collected

native curiosities calculated to startle and delight—
feathered pipes and headdresses, the medicine pouch of
a Potawatomi chief, killed in a skirmish near Oswego, a
painted buffalo robe—as well as the first plums and
apples from Warrensbush. The slave's name was Cuffee.
He was a sturdy young field hand, booty from one of
Captain Warren's prize-ships, sent upriver before Susannah Warren had a chance to shackle him to one of her
Shakespearian appelations.

The idlers and hustlers at the quay were used to
Indians, though they gaped at the physical stature and
splendid array of Johnson's Mohawks. Their hostility
was reserved for Cuffee.

A tight knot of men formed at the end of the wharf,
barring Johnson's way. Some of the men were armed.

A short, officious fellow stepped up.

"Mister William Johnson?"

"You have me at a disadvantage, sir."

"Clerk of the Court. His Honor requires your negro
Sandy for examination."

"There is some confusion here. My boy's name is
Cuffee."

"It is all one. None of the brutes can letter anywise."

Johnson wondered how this fellow could have received such precise news of his traveling arrangements
prior to his landing. His suspicions centered on the
Albany Commissioners. He had made the mistake of
paying his respects to them, in company with the Mohawks. There were several who would stop at nothing to
put an obstacle in his path.

Snowbird inspected the dead hair on the clerk's head.
It sat up high above the forehead, then bulged out at the
sides, above the ears, waved and whitened with powder.
Snowbird whispered to Hendrick, "Pigeon wings."

"May I know what this is about?" Billy asked.

"You come from the back settlements, so you may be
excused your ignorance. There is a plot afoot to burn the
town, and half our negroes are embroiled. The Pope and
the Catholic kings are at the back of it."

"I believe this plot must be the effect of either the
fever or the drinking water."

"You had best mind your tongue, sir. This is New York. We are dealing with a villainous coven of latent enemies, and your negro stands accused."

"Really? May I ask by whom?"

"By a negro called Quack, formerly his fellow-conspirator."

"Quack? Quack!" Johnson mocked him. "Would that be a duck or a Dutchman?"

"By Ged, sir—" Pigeon Wings was elegant in his expletives as well as his headgear "—you speak like a damned Irishman."

"I am Irish-born and make no apology for it. What is it to you?"

"Then you may also be acquainted with an Irishman called Rahilly."

"Denis Rahilly?"

"So you do know him."

"Rahilly is an excellent man, a friend to all humanity."

"I warn you, Mister Johnson. You are in deeper waters than you wit. Your friend Rahilly is mired in this foul plot. We have it on oath that he swore the niggers to burn the town and rape the women and promised them absolution for their sins in the name of the Pope."

"That is a damned lie!"

Billy raised his blackthorn stick. Men rushed forward, leveling their firelocks. The Mohawks casually took up position on either side of Johnson. Hendrick tested the weight of the warclub with many notches.

The clerk of the court was uneasy in the presence of the Indians, not only because of the physical threat they posed, but because Hendrick Forked Paths was a great man in the colonies, wooed by Governors.

"We will get to the bottom of this in our own time," Pigeon Wings said hastily. "For now, I will merely caution you to serve the law, Mister Johnson, or risk being charged for an accomplice in this bloody business. You will deliver your nigger to me at once."

One of the Yorkers leered, tapping a cudgel against the palm of his hand, and Cuffee panicked. He dropped his bundle and ran back along the wharf. When he saw other men blocking his path, he plunged into the water, forgetting that he could not swim.

"This is intolerable!" Johnson exclaimed, as he watched the Yorkers fish Cuffee out of the East River with boathooks.

"The villain shows his guilt by his behavior," said Pigeon Wings.

"You have stolen my property," Billy told him, as they put Cuffee in chains. "You may expect to account for it. My uncle is Captain Warren, and his wife is the sister of Chief Justice DeLancey."

"No disrespect, sir," said Pigeon Wings, with a smile more offensive than his scowl. "But one of Mister DeLancey's own slaves awaits the gibbet. When it is a matter of treason and murder, the law is no respecter of personages."

The Mohawks remained impassive. Snowbird could not grasp the cause of the altercation, but he knew that it was foolish to take sides in a squabble between white men over things that meant nothing to the Real People. Among the Real People, there were no slaves. Captives were adopted or killed; they were not made to go through life in bits and collars. Snowbird felt no particular affinity toward Cuffee and his people, although white-men-with-black-faces were no longer strangers in the country of the Six Nations. Runaway slaves had moved into the Seneca country with the Tuscaroras, when they made their long migration from the southern plantations, to be joined by a handful of free mulattoes from Albany. They had been adopted into the Longhouse, receiving its identity as completely as any captive white or Huron or Pani. They were Real People. For the thousands of Africans in the Province of New York who remained slaves, Snowbird and his Mohawk companions felt no special sympathy. Unlike the Mohawks, these were a defeated people. The Flint People were not in the habit of losing fights and wasted no tears on the vanquished. But no man should be put in irons and used as a tame animal. So, though he showed no emotion, Snowbird felt a sour disgust as he watched them drag

Cuffee away, and he saw that Forked Paths and White Owl shared his feelings.

□

Instead of going directly to his uncle's, Johnson rushed to James DeLancey's house at the foot of Broad Street, demanding immediate admittance to the Chief Justice.

Anne DeLancey received him. She was in mourning for her father-in-law, but her dress was a sacque in the new French style, with pleats at the back that swelled into billows over her large hooped petticoat. The rounded décolletage, above the long-waisted bodice, showed off her collarbones to perfection.

Anne was alarmed by the noise Billy made at the door and the sight of the three Mohawks.

"Mister Johnson! What is all this commotion? Are the French at our door?"

"I must speak to the Chief Justice."

"You are distracted, sir. Your face discovers it. Have you forgotten your manners?"

"Forgive me." Billy brushed her hand with his lips. "A pack of scoundrels has taken my boy Cuffee."

Anne put a finger to her lips. "Cordelia," she addressed her maid, "pray take our Indian guests to the kitchen. I am sure they are hungry after their journey."

When she was alone with Johnson, she touched his arm and said, "Tread softly, Billy. There is scarce one family that is not missing a negro. It seems this plot goes very deep. Yesterday, our boy Othello made his confession. He is to be hanged on Saturday."

Johnson insisted again on seeing her husband. Anne DeLancey took a mischievous pleasure in showing him up to the powder closet, which opened off the Chief Justice's bedroom. Inside, James DeLancey sat up on a rush chair. On his head was the wig his valet had fetched back from the barbershop, freshly curled on hot clay rollers. A vast white cloth extended from his chin to his shoe-buckles, protecting his clothes. James DeLancey held a paper cone in front of his face as his valet dusted his wig with powder. He resembled a monstrous chicken.

"Damnation!" he greeted Billy. "Can a man have no privacy in his own house?"

DeLancey threw off his half-powdered wig, exposing his shaved pink scalp, and pulled on the floppy silk cap he wore at his ease in the house. Under his dustcloth, the Chief Justice was draped in a loose silk banyan, a garment of oriental origins that New York gentlemen found suited to the summer heat.

When Johnson explained his business, the humor of the Chief Justice did not improve.

"Horsmanden is making a bonfire of our negroes," DeLancey grumbled. "This affair is ruinous to men of property. The one man who stands to profit is your uncle Warren. This must end by driving up the value of slaves—unless people fear to have a negro under the same roof."

"Then why do you not intercede? Mrs. DeLancey tells me your own man Othello faces the gallows."

"Many witnesses have sworn against him, both negro and white. It is charged that he plotted to murder us in our beds."

"Othello? I cannot believe it. He was devoted to you, and you showed him unusual liberties."

"He has made a confession," DeLancey said grimly. "He denies that he planned to murder us, but he admits he attended villainous meetings with Hughson and others. He must be made an example to the rest of them."

"Your attitude toward the treatment of your own slave is your business, Mister DeLancey. But I must insist that my slave Cuffee be released immediately. This is patently a case of mistaken identity. Why, your clerk of court was asking after a fellow of a different name. All he was sure about was my name. I suspect this craze is being used by certain parties to wage private wars—"

"What do you mean by that?" The color rose in James DeLancey's face.

"I was insulted by your clerk because I was born in Ireland. And I am given to understand that one of my countrymen, a schoolteacher named Rahilly, is also held on trumped-up charges."

"Rahilly has not served his own interest," DeLancey said darkly.

"Denis Rahilly has the soul of a poet and the heart of a meadowlark. He is quite harmless except to those who insist on living with their snouts in the mud."

"Very pretty, Mister Johnson. But try those words in front of a jury of Yorkers and see what they get you. Rahilly is known to have consorted with negro prisoners at the low dive where the plot was hatched. He defends himself with jests. He is known for a jeerer and a fleerer at the King, and he has stated in public that our Established Church is a public convenience."

"Is a man to be persecuted for the truth?"

"You had best command your tongue in this town, Mister Johnson. There are rumors abroad that people in ruffles are behind this plot—" the Chief Justice eyed Billy's snowy shirt-front "—and our witchfinders would love to find an Irishman of quality to nail for it."

"So you admit it is a witch-craze."

"I admit nothing. Except that the passions of this colony, in these times, require subtle management."

"Who gives witness against Denis Rahilly?"

DeLancey recited the improbable names of several slaves, starting with the ubiquitous Quack.

"Forgive me," Billy interrupted. "I am no man of the law. But I was not aware that black men can give testimony against white men in any court of English law."

"Your understanding is exact. There is a white witness. A woman called Mary Burton. She was a servant at Hughson's, where the plot was hatched."

"Just the one witness?"

"One *white* witness." DeLancey lost his lips.

"So. You propose to hang Denis Rahilly because he loves a song and a jest. On the word of one white slave and the gossip of black slaves rotting in irons. I won't have it."

"*You?* Who are *you* to teach law to me?"

"I brought Rahilly to this country. He is part of my family, and he is under my protection."

"Those are prideful words, Mister Johnson. For a— family retainer. And a squaw man, I hear."

"Does what you hear come from the people at Albany who inspired the arrest of my man Cuffee?"

"You are impertinent, sir!" DeLancey sprang out of his chair. "You have presumed on my patience too long!"

"Allow me to presume one moment longer. You may not have the resolution to defend your man Othello, and I will not dispute your motives when it comes to the safety of your household. But Denis Rahilly and Cuffee are members of *my* household. When I return to my home, I will take them with me. Whatever is required."

"I can hear no more of this! I will thank you to leave my house."

"I can no more advise you on protocol than on law. But sachems and warriors of the Mohawk are waiting to condole you for the death of your father. I suggest it would be politic to receive them."

James DeLancey's veneer of smooth superiority was intact when he met the Mohawks in his parlor. Madeira and canary wine were served. Hendrick Forked Paths presented the Chief Justice with several strings of wampum and the skin of a fisher.

"With these strings," Hendrick said formally, "we open your eyes, that you may see clearly. We open your ears, that you may hear truly. And we open the path from your heart to your lips, so you may speak only from the heart."

The Chief Justice thanked the Mohawks and found some morocco-bound hymnals to return the gift.

"We think you should listen carefully to what our brother Forest Killer tells you, because he sees many looks away," Hendrick continued. The Mohawks had evidently conducted some private consultation while Billy was upstairs. Hendrick spoke more words of commendation for Johnson, with such quiet authority that the Chief Justice took Billy aside before his party left the house.

"I respect power when I see it," DeLancey said, with the semblance of candor. "You seem to have ingratiated yourself with the Mohawk, and in this province that counts for power. Thus I will overlook your hasty words in my dressing room. I will undertake only to review the depositions against Rahilly and your slave. I can make no promises. I am not the engine that drives this affair. Do you know Horsmanden?"

"I believe I have met the judge's daughter." Billy had a slight memory of a mousy girl who had blushed to the roots of her hair when he walked into a room.

"Daniel Horsmanden is no fool," DeLancey asserted. "He knows we must give the people devils to hate. Or they will end by hating their masters."

5.

Peter Warren inspected his nephew as if he had it in mind to order him flogged around the fleet. The Captain's skin was an unhealthy color, like beaten dough, covered by a moist film. He was recovering from a fresh bout of the quatern ague that had troubled him since his blighted expedition against Cartagena. The expedition that saw his sailors die of scurvy and the flux on storm-tossed ships while the marines were dumped on the beach, under the walls of the enemy fort, to be knocked down like skittles.

Well or ill, Peter Warren had a hearty appetite for figures. He had his business ledgers open in front of him now, in his private study, while his wife endeavored to entertain a trio of unwanted Indians who had to stoop to get in the door and looked capable of emptying both the larder and the wine cellar. Captain Warren had no doubt why his nephew had brought these barbarous guests down the river. This was a transparent ruse to deflect the Captain from his purpose. Peter Warren was not so easily put off the chase.

"Well, sir," he addressed his nephew. "I see you now consider yourself grand enough to write to me from Mount Johnson."

"I engaged to manage your estate for three years," Billy reminded him. "I have kept my undertaking."

"I suppose you have taken my tenants across the river with you."

Billy explained that only his household staff and his slaves had removed with him to Mount Johnson. Warrensbush remained in the care of a capable overseer, working under his own supervision.

"I have received not a shilling in rent," Uncle Peter complained. "Indeed, I find I am paying for the support of my tenants."

"Sir, the Mohawk country is not County Meath. It is the hardest country you ever saw, and the thickest wooded. No man would be willing to endure the weather, girdling trees and grubbing soil for another man's profit, without inducements. I give your tenants tools and seed and livestock. In return, they clear your land and support themselves. You could not have the work done any cheaper way."

Uncle Peter let this go. He had a larger bone to pick.

He consulted his ledger and started reading off numbers.

"Your first year in the colony," he announced to Billy, "I advanced you £1210, New England currency, in trade goods from Boston and £350, York money, in drafts on DeLancey & Co. for the same. Your second year, I advanced you better than £800 for goods from Boston and London. This spring past, profiting from my distraction with the war, you drew heavily on my credit with Messrs. Baker at London. I have laid out thousands to fit you out as a trader—" he slammed his ledger shut "—and where is my return? All I have had from you are a few planks and a handful of Indian gewgaws! Do not give me excuses, Billy! I am informed by other gentlemen that the profit from the Indian trade is above one hundred percent. What do I have to show for this hemorrhage of money?"

Johnson sat with the impassivity he had learned from Hendrick, waiting for his uncle's rising anger to peak.

"This is not an ordinary undertaking," he said mildly, when Warren paused to draw breath. Billy wanted to explain his vision of a trading empire dominating the whole country west of Albany. That vision required vast resources, vaster than those he yet deployed, to over-whelm competitors and to secure the lasting friendship of the Indians.

But Peter Warren burst out, "Ordinary? I suppose it is not ordinary for a man to abscond with his uncle's money! If you were not my sister's son—"

He bit off his last words and took up a paper.

"You will sign this."

Johnson examined the document. It was a bond for more than a thousand pounds, payable in three years' time.

"You will have nothing more from me until this is paid."

Billy Johnson set his large, looping signature to the bond and left Uncle Peter's study in easy spirits. If called in, the obligation could ruin him. But he resolved to put it out of his mind. In three years, anything could happen.

☐

"You use black men like cattle," Hendrick informed the Chief Justice over quail and roast mutton at the Warren house. "But you kill cattle only when you are ready to eat them. Are you going to eat your slaves?"

Embarrassed, James DeLancey referred the question to Daniel Horsmanden, the moving spirit in the conspiracy trials.

"This matter touches our very survival," Judge Horsmanden asserted, nettled at having to answer to a painted savage, but warming quickly to his theme. He described how a band of slaves had been recruited by a grogshop keeper named Hughson and a secret coven of Irish Catholics to reduce the city to ashes. Hughson had plied them with egg-punch and promises of wealth and white women; papist agents had promised to save their souls from hell. Meeting at the spring where slaves were sent to fetch tea water for their masters, they recruited others for the diabolical plot. They stood within a chalk circle and swore dreadful oaths, on thunder and light-ning and the powers of hell, that Satan should fetch and burn them if they discovered their secret to any outsider.

Hendrick was impressed by Horsmanden's description of the secret covenant. Had the plotters hoped to prevail by witchcraft?

"Where popery is involved," Judge Horsmanden responded darkly, "the infernal power is always present."

"Since we arrived at this town," Billy Johnson interposed, "we have heard a great deal about loose talk over a punch bowl. Do you have proof of arson, other than servants' gossip?"

"I take offense at your tone, sir."

"I take offense that one of my negroes is being held in your pest-ridden jail on no better grounds than these chimaeras. And that my friend Denis Rahilly, who would not bruise the wings of a moth, is charged with being a prime mover in an incendiary plot."

"Chimaeras!" Horsmanden shrieked. "I have a score of confessions!"

"They appear to come from people neither of us would trust, under other circumstances, to give us the time of day. I asked if you had proof of arson. If I am not mistaken, this sorry business began with a fire at the fort."

"On St. Patrick's Day," Horsmanden narrowed his eyes.

"A festive occasion, to be sure."

"Only to Irishmen of a certain persuasion."

Billy felt the warning pressure of a foot against his calf and looked across the table into Anne DeLancey's troubled eyes.

"If that is a reference to me, sir," he said evenly, "I think I may say I am as good a Church man as any present."

"I am sure Mister Horsmanden meant no disrespect," Captain Warren hoisted his pennant. "I am myself an Irishman."

"No disrespect, to be sure," Horsmanden beat a retreat.

"Then perhaps you will answer my question," Johnson pursued.

"Certainly. The fire at the fort was set by a negro called Quack—that is to say, Roosevelt's Quack. He climbed up into the garret with a firebrand from the servant's hall after dinner and set it to lie on a beam under the shingles."

"You say he did this after dinner? I had received the impression that the fire broke out at midday." Billy looked at Aunt Susannah, who nodded.

Horsmanden fiddled with the silk ribbons of his solitaire. They wound round his throat from the drawstring at the nape of his neck that confined a prodigious quantity of hair in a squarish bag that covered most of his narrow shoulders. Snowbird leaned forward in his chair to inspect this curious apparatus, and Horsmanden's irritation increased.

"The villain set the fire at midnight, sir," he said to Billy, "but it took hold only at noon."

"How can that be?"

"This dusky Guy Fawkes set his fire on St. Patrick's Eve—" the Judge's expression invited the table to applaud his patience "—according to the papist calendar. When he saw that by morning his attempt had come to nothing, he climbed up to the garret once more to examine his handiwork. He found that his firebrand had failed to set the shingles alight. So he blew on it and went away. Within an hour, the fort was ablaze."

"I beg your pardon," said Billy. "You say he *blew* on it?"

"Certainly he blew."

"You mean to tell me that a firebrand set twelve hours before was still alive?"

"Our American hardwoods, sir, are marvelously durable."

"So you instruct me. I must allow, Mister Horsmanden, that your intelligence of this business appears admirably complete. May I inquire where you received this news about the firebrand?"

"From the villain himself," said Horsmanden, sucking at a glass of good Madeira. "He made his confession at the stake."

"At the stake. I see. I suppose the poor wretch would say anything to save his skin."

"You trifle with us, Mister Johnson. On the brink of

eternity," he added piously, "the villain sought to save his immortal soul through confession."

"Were you ever instructed in the tenets of Rome, Mister Horsmanden? I fear I detect a papist flavor in your doctrine of confession. I hope you do not propose to persecute Denis Rahilly or my poor man Cuffee on the substance of such testimonials."

"By God, Johnson!" Judge Horsmanden's cheeks darkened to an alarming damson hue. "You try me beyond all endurance! You would do well to recollect that in this colony, no man is above suspicion, whatever his family connections."

"Felix quem faciunt aliena pericula cautum," James DeLancey interposed, with a sharp look at Billy Johnson. "He is a happy man who learns caution from other's dangers."

Horsmanden was fairly frothing. "There are *people in ruffles* at the back of this. So says the Burton wench."

This last salvo was too much for the Chief Justice. "You are not running for election, sir," he reminded Horsmanden. "And we neglect our Mohawk guests."

6.

Now Johnson stood with the Mohawks on Gallows Hill, to see how black men died. Below them, Fresh Water Pond was yellow in the thick summer haze. Lime was stewing in a gaping hole down there, at the edge of the negro burial ground, ready to receive fresh corpses. Nearer than the bittersweet reek of the limepit were hot odors of sweating fear. They were drumming chained men up the hill, forcing the pace so the irons clanged in time with the beat. The names of the victims were Fortune and Frank, Galloway and Othello, Venture and Walter's Quack. The heavy man who came stumbling last, far behind the others, with a bayonet at his back, was Doctor Harry, who was supposed to have manufactured firebombs. They were saving Doctor Harry to the end to please the crowd, which liked a hanging, but loved a burning.

Venture's death was the messiest. He came giggling and making faces, sticking his tongue out at the jeering, heckling crowd, clowning with death. When they put the halter round his neck, he flung himself off the cart before the hangman was ready, and they had to string him up again.

Othello died in silence, looking at the sky.

Doctor Harry's turn came at last. It was said that his firebombs were designed to be thrown up on the shingled roof of Trinity Church during divine service, while the exits were blocked so the congregation would roast inside. The prosecution had produced no evidence that his "blackstuff combustibles" had ever been made, but intended to improve the record by extracting a graveside confession. Doctor Harry did not oblige. As the flames from the pyre licked his feet, he sang a song of the islands. The Mohawks grunted their approval. A man should die with a song on his lips.

Forked Paths had killed enemies more slowly than Doctor Harry died. He had pricked their flesh with burning splints. He had measured the length of their intestines. In his youth, he had eaten the hearts of valiant opponents to capture their strength and spirit. If it had been his fortune to fall into the hands of his enemies and endure the same lingering caresses, he would have sought to die a warrior's death, without complaint, singing his song of farewell.

The mob hooted and gawped as the captive writhed on the stake. Johnson averted his face from the spectacle. Snowbird watched without show of emotion. He had no tears for the white-men-with-black-faces. But he thought their deaths shamed the executioners more than the victims. Real People killed for a reason—to eat, to survive, to appease a hungry ghost. The white men of New York were killing for no reason, and this was beyond forgiveness.

7.

Johnson boiled with rage. Neither of his powerful relatives was ready to exert himself to stop the madness that had seized the town, or to secure the release of either Rahilly or Cuffee, who might soon follow Othello and Doctor Harry up Gallows Hill. Billy suspected that his uncle was shackled by fear that the conspiracy-mongers could turn against his own family. Peter Warren was also an Irishman, and some of the "Spanish negroes" who had already gone to the stake had come from Warren's prize-ships.

"I must consider my household," Captain Warren told Billy when he pleaded for his uncle's intervention. "Thus far, Susannah and I have been able to preserve our own servants. If the mood of the mob turns against us, the sheriffs will come for them too. Horsmanden already talks as if every slave in New York is infected."

James DeLancey's calculations, as always, were more convoluted, and Billy did not understand them fully until he sought the counsel of Cadwallader Colden.

"Here," said Colden, thrusting a letter into Johnson's hand. "You had best read this if you wish to fathom our affairs. I have not seen the mind of our town described better."

The superscription on this missive, in Colden's neat hand, identified it as a "Letter from a Person Unknown, in the Province of Massachusetts-Bay." Billy read the following:

Sir,
    I am a stranger to you & to New York, & so must beg pardon for the mistakes I may be guilty off in the subsequent attempt; The Design whereof is to endeavour the putting an end to the bloody Tragedy that has been & I suppose still is acting amongst you in regard to the poor Negros & the Whites too. The horrible executions among you puts me in mind of our New England Witchcraft in the year

1692 Which if I dont mistake New York justly
reproached us for, & mockt at our Credulity about.
I suspect that your present case & ours heretofore
are much the same, and that Negro & Spectre
evidence will turn out alike. We had near 50 Con-
fessors, who accused multitudes of others, alledg-
ing Time & Place, & Various other circumstances
to render their Confessions credible, that they had
their meetings, form'd confederacies, sign'd the
Devils book &c. But I am humbly of Opinion that
such Confessions are not worth a Straw; for many
times they are obtain'd by foul means, by force or
torment, or in hopes of a longer time to live.

Possibly there have been some murmuring
amongst the Negroes & a mad fellow or 2 has
threatened & design'd Revenge, for the Cruelty &
inhumanity they have met with, which is too rife in
the English Plantations. And if that be all it is a
pity there have been such severe animadversions.
And if nothing will put an end hereto till some of
higher degree & better circumstances & Characters
are accused (which finished our Salem Witchcraft)
the sooner the better, lest all the poor People of the
Government perish in the merciless flames of an
Imaginary Plot.

I intreat you not to go on to Massacre & destroy
your own Estates by making Bonfires of the Negroes & perhaps thereby loading yourselves with
greater Guilt than theirs.

There was no signature at the foot of this epistle. The
anonymous correspondent described himself only as a
"well-wisher to all humane beings."

Cadwallader Colden inspected Johnson over the rims
of his spectacles.

"Admirable!" Billy exclaimed. From the twinkle in
Colden's eye, Johnson formed the opinion that the
author of the letter lived a lot nearer than Boston. "Will
you publish it?"

"I shall try," Colden sighed. "But I am afraid our

printers will not risk having their heads and their windows broken, while this frenzy rules the city. I blame your relative DeLancey above the others. He is too intelligent not to read the true features of our insanity, and too ambitious to use his intelligence for the common weal. The Chief Justice thinks first and last of power. He hopes to use these bonfires to increase his power and his popularity with the mob at the expense of Governor Clarke. But he is careful to let his creature Horsmanden walk first, for fear of a pitfall in the road. If they are not curbed, they will end by finding Romish arsonists on the Governor's Council. I advise you to stay among the Mohawks, Mister Johnson. The Indians conduct their public business with greater philosophy than we do."

Billy explained his fears for Rahilly and Cuffee. According to the Chief Justice, both men would be found guilty by any New York jury and the best that could be hoped for was transportation in place of execution. One of Cuffee's cellmates swore he had heard the slave boast of taking an oath to murder white men before he was shipped upriver. At this swearing-in, Cuffee had supposedly removed his left shoe and placed his toes inside a chalk circle, while the wife of Hughson, the tavern-keeper, held a punchbowl over his head.

According to Mary Burton, the lone white witness for the prosecution, Rahilly had preached to the slaves that they would be rewarded for their crimes in heaven.

Colden snorted. "If James DeLancey could tell you that with a straight face, I must give him credit for being a better dissembler than I had dreamed. You must go to the Governor, Mister Johnson. George Clarke is too timid to blaze with DeLancey and cares little if another man is fool enough to allow his property to be burned. But you may look to him for assistance, because you are in a position to do him a service. Governor Clarke is a deep speculator in Mohawk lands. Since you appear to have found favor among the Mohawks, you may also hope to find favor with him."

8.

Billy talked about his problem with the Mohawks. Hendrick said they would sleep on it, to give the matter their best thoughts.

In the morning, Hendrick Forked Paths said, "I have a dream."

Snowbird and White Owl sat on either side of the tough old warchief, faces expressionless, arms folded.

"We dreamed together once before," Johnson remarked. "I remember it cost me my favorite coat."

"I have another dream."

Billy was obliged to make room for it.

"I dreamed that a wild goose was caged. Its feet were bound by iron chains. But flight was in its heart. It was so unhappy it started to tear at its feet. It was gnawing them off, striving to be free."

The word-picture was vivid. It tugged at Billy's heart. He had not thought of Rahilly in leg-irons. But men who burned others at the stake would not flinch from chaining a drunken poet.

"I dreamed that this bird is close to Forest Killer's heart. My dream showed me that the one who can free it is Corlaer." This was the old Mohawk word for the Governor of New York. "But he will do this only if Forest Killer's brothers of the Flint People tell him to do it."

Johnson could not fault the analysis so far, whether it came from a dream or a private chat between the Mohawks and the quietly effective Mr. Colden.

"This is a powerful dream," Snowbird spoke up.

There was more coming. But Hendrick paced his delivery, filling and lighting a pipe which he proceeded to pass around the room.

In a different life, Billy thought, *Hendrick would be a master of the stage.*

"I dreamed that if we make right the wrong that is done to Forest Killer's friends, Forest Killer will make right the wrong that is done to us."

Hendrick proceeded to list several of the more egregious swindles by which Mohawk land had been deeded to comfortable gentlemen at Albany and New York.

Billy pointed out that he could promise only to defend the Mohawks' cause. He had no authority to overturn these deeds, and could only hope for allies who did.

"Forest Killer's stone house sits on land that was stolen from us."

"Do you ask me to give up my own house?" Johnson exclaimed. He protested that he had bought his property from white men, not Mohawks.

"Receiver of stolen goods," Snowbird volunteered in English. The phrase had become familiar in discussion of the plot allegedly concocted at Hughson's.

"What exactly are you asking?" Johnson demanded, wishing that just once his Mohawk neighbors would make a plain show of emotion.

"I dreamed Forest Killer paid us again."

"How much were you paid?"

Hendrick passed little colored sticks to the other Mohawks. Memory sticks. They took turns to recite items from the list of trade goods they had allegedly received for the deed that covered the Mount Johnson property.

Billy did some rough mental figuring. The market cost of the goods, at prices inflated by the war and the bitter weather, might run close to £100. He had almost that much left over from his mother's parting gift. If Captain Warren went along with his new schemes—and Uncle Peter was starting to lean—he could draw on a new line of credit.

It was a steep price for a favor. But how did one compute the value of a man's life?

Will they think me a pliable fool if I agree to this? Johnson asked himself, studying the unreadable Mohawks. *No. I think that giving something of value to save a friend is an act they will respect. It is something they will tell others. They will say that William Johnson is generous to the Indians and stands with his friends.*

He said to Forked Paths, "I like your dream."

□

The Mohawks escorted Johnson to the Governor's temporary lodgings, outside the fort.

Hendrick remarked to Billy, "I have yet to meet a British official who cannot be rolled up in a beaver blanket."

Cadwallader Colden sat in attendance on Governor Clarke. Billy saw the ghost of a smile travel across Colden's thin lips when he walked in with the Mohawks.

George Clarke suffered the long litany of ritual greetings and received the gift of a beaver robe, to condole him for the death of a young British officer in the swamps along the Oneida Carry.

Then Forked Paths said, "I ask for a living soul to replace sister's son, who has gone the long trail."

Discomforted, Governor Clarke asked for time to confer with his adviser.

"It is a perfectly normal request," Colden assured him. "It has long been the policy of the Six Nations to adopt strangers or enemy captives to replace their dead. Indeed, but for this policy of adoption, the Mohawk and their sister-nations might long since have melted away like the snow in summer. The French understand this better than we do. They encourage the Mission Indians to take white captives along our borders, and present them with Panis taken in battle in the west."

It would be prudent to humor the Mohawk sachem, Colden counseled.

"But who am I supposed to give him?"

"We do have a number of Spanish prisoners in our jails."

"Are you suggesting I should turn over a Spanish naval officer to these—savages?"

"Perhaps not a naval officer. Why not a Spanish agent?"

"I don't understand you!"

"Young Johnson can explain it to you. The Mohawks have developed some affection for Rahilly, the music teacher who was taken by Horsmanden to feed our witch-craze. I understand this Rahilly lived with them for some time."

The Acting Governor was distraught. "Rahilly is to be hanged for high treason! What will people think?"

"They will no doubt think—" Colden cleared his throat "—that being turned over to *savages* is not a kindlier fate."

The Surveyor-General took the opportunity to remind Governor Clarke that his hopes for improving his vast estates around Lake Otsego—purchased under the names of dummy partners—rested on the good will of the Mohawks.

"I am gravely distressed by your sister's loss," Clarke announced to Hendrick when the meeting resumed. "I am happy to tell you I believe we will be able to relieve her sorrow."

Hendrick accepted this with full solemnity.

Then he said, "My brother Snowbird has also suffered a great loss. He asks for a living soul to replace his father, who has gone the long trail."

"This is a mockery!" Governor Clarke complained to Colden, hardly muffling his words with his hand.

"My brother Snowbird asks for the white-man-with-a-black-face who was stolen from my friend Forest Killer."

□

The court recorded a sentence of transportation for both prisoners, without specifying their destination.

"I don't know how you do it," Billy's uncle told him. "I believe there is an imp in you that plays tricks on all of us. You should take care how often you let him out of the bottle, because there are powerful men who do not care for his antics, and my wife's brother, the Chief Justice, is foremost among them. You have made James DeLancey look like a fool or a coward, and that is not something he will forget or forgive."

"I will stand with the Mohawks against all the De-Lanceys in the province."

"And your boozy fiddler," Captain Warren sighed. "I

believe you have inherited all your mother's whimsy. Why risk yourself for a feckless paddy like Rahilly?"

"Because he reminds me who I am and what I might be."

CHAPTER 19

A SEVERED HEAD

1.

In the Valley, it was a time of new births.

Island Woman watched over her younger daughter as she grew big with child. Her grandsons gamboled about at her heels, sporting with the miniature bows and warclubs their uncle had made for them. Swimming Voices had abandoned the twins to the care of their grandmother when she fled north with Le Corbeau; a new scandal for the gossips at the Upper Castle to twitter about, but a joy for Island Woman, who loved the laughter and energy the boys brought to her lodge.

Now Bright Meadow would bring her a grand-daughter.

Perhaps this was the one she had waited for, all these winters past. The one her dream teacher had told her was coming.

Island Woman walked with Bright Meadow above the limestone gorge. A cloud of butterflies danced above the falls. The water splashed down into the fern-green creek, running fast and cold between walls carved by wind and weather into galleries and colonnades.

Below the falls, the creekbed bulged to form swimming basins. Bright Meadow pointed at the yellow whirr of a flicker. The bird settled on a dead elm and started drilling for unseen prey.

Rainbow trout sparkled in the water.

Laughing, Island Woman stripped off her blouse and deerskin kilt and leggings. Her body was still strong and supple. She shot into the creek, plunged to the bottom and came up next to a conical rock, pushing back her streaming black hair.

"*Kats kanaka!*" she called to her daughter. "Come here."

Bright Meadow's distended belly made her clumsy. She made the *thwump* of a beaver's tail as she flopped into the water.

She floated on her back, watching the passage of birds and butterflies. A redtail hawk sailed above the gorge on silverbright wings.

Island Woman lay on the rock sunning herself, thinking about Snowbird's account of his visit to New York and how Forest Killer had kept his promise. It was a strange story. The newcomers were killing black men because they were scared of their own slaves.

If they do this to their slaves, because they are a different color, what will they do to us, who cannot be slaves, if they become masters of this earth?

It seemed that Forest Killer had opposed the madness and sacrificed his own possessions to save his friends. Snowbird had brought Island Woman a pair of three-point blankets, new cooking pots and knives as her share of the present Johnson had made to the Mohawks on his return to the stone house on the river. The ceremony the white man had held for the chiefs and warriors was the talk of both the Lower and the Upper Castles. Forest Killer had admitted that the lands he worked had been taken from the Mohawk by fraud and had paid for them all over again. This was unheard of.

It was proof—Hendrick Forked Paths had said before the whole village—that this newcomer was to be trusted beyond all others.

He may be the one we have waited for, Island Woman

had agreed. *But we must walk upwind of him. He may be setting lures to draw us into his trap.*

"Ihstenha!" Bright Meadow's shout interrupted Island Woman's reverie. Her daughter's oval face held fear and joy at the same time.

Bright Meadow said, "I think it is my time."

□

Island Woman brewed a tea from the shoots and twigs of the juniper to ease the labor. She sang and told stories while her daughter squatted on a pad of soft, dry moss, her back supported by a maple. The delivery was smooth. Island Woman had already guided Bright Meadow through it, in dreaming.

In a dream visit, the one who was returning to the Flint People had announced her name to her grandmother. It was an ancient name, that had not been requickened for many generations: They Are Sending Her Flowers. It suited the beauty of the newborn and her place of birth.

Island Woman severed the cord and put it away in a little beaded pouch that would be hung from the cradleboard as a talisman. She buried the afterbirth and washed the baby clean.

Then she held up her granddaughter to see the day lilies along the river, the blaze of wildflowers on the meadow above, the carpet of blue phlox under the trees.

Konwatsitsiaienni. They Are Sending Her Flowers.

It was a good name, Island Woman thought. It would be conferred on the child formally, in the eyes of the Real People, in the Strawberry Festival.

In time, Bright Meadow's daughter would own other names. If she was truly the one the dream-prophet had foreseen, her most important name would be the gift of a vision, of a visit from the great ones. This name would be held secret from all but the members of the child's spirit family. This dream-name would be her password into the Real World.

If she is the one.

2.

It was a time of new births at Mount Johnson also.

Little Nancy Johnson learned fast and had her father's gift for words. Billy loved to boast that the third word out of her mouth, after Daddy and Mummy, was "chandelier." Nancy was avid to know the names of everything in the world around her, as if possession of these gave her power over the things they identified. By her second birthday, she was conducting formal conversations in rounded sentences. Soon after that, she had a brother to practice on.

John Johnson gave his mother a harder time than his sister. He kept Cat waiting far into her tenth month, and the surgeon had to use his hands and spoonlike forceps to pull the boy out. Cat tore and lost a lot of blood and the surgeon cautioned that she should think long and hard before trying for another child.

But the rejoicing in the house called her back to health. Denis Rahilly led a musical procession round the stone house, with Paddy Groghan blowing on the warpipes. To the clinking of glasses and the roll of Billy's laughter, Rahilly performed his own version of a baptism over the baby's crib, which cheered Cat more than the cold formalities of frosty Mr. Barclay at the Queen Anne chapel across the river.

"To him that overcometh," Rahilly intoned, "to him will I give a white stone. And in that stone a new name written which no one knoweth but he that receiveth it." Rahilly assured his listeners that the strange words came from the Book of Revelation. But the curious white stone, incised with a spiral design, that he hung from a post of the crib came from another place, one closed to Cat: a place that Rahilly and Billy Johnson shared.

She insisted on feeding John at her breast. She loved the feel of his skin against hers, the eyes fastened on hers over the swell of her bosom. She asked Billy to find her a cradleboard, like the ones the native mothers used, so she could take the infant with her when she tended her garden. She grew early plants, like lettuce and radishes, on the south slope of the hill, to give them a head start. She put in herbs from the old country—thyme and rosemary, yarrow and angelica. She studied the shapes and the uses of plants that were new to her, sharing discoveries with the wives of her German neighbors. Magda Frey showed her the jewelweed, whose leaves turned silver in water, and how it was used to treat poison ivy. Ursula Laucs taught her how to steep the leaves of the coltsfoot and smoke them to relieve coughs and breathing obstructions.

John was still suckling when Cat discovered she was pregnant again. Billy was often gone from her, pleading business or politics; he was now a Justice of the Peace, a Colonel of militia, and an honorary sachem of the Mohawk, an important man in the councils of all the tribes of the Valley. The greater part of his life was hidden from her, including the women he loved and discarded under other roofs or in a snug among the trees. Yet Cat gave thanks for the new life that flowed through her and the peace that reined in her house, saddened only by the lack of news from her mother.

The talk of war she sometimes overheard at Billy's truck house or at the dinner table, when he dined alone with redcoat officers, Crown officials and Indian interpreters, seemed altogether remote. Or that is what she willed it to be. She had seen enough of the violence of men.

3.

Billy Johnson lay flat on his back in the meadow between the house and the river, with the brim of a shapeless old castor hat pulled down over his eyes. The warm breath of the south wind played on his skin, where the neck of his rough osnaburg shirt hung open. He heard the gurgle of the creek that turned his millwheel, the *chk-chk-chk* of a redwing darting over new-planted corn, the chatter of the girls hoeing rows of red cabbage and spinach in Catty's vegetable garden. Then came excited yips, hot panting, and the happy ripple of childish laughter.

"Guess who! Guess who!" four-year-old Nancy screamed, bouncing up and down on his stomach, while Favour, the wolfhound, rammed his muzzle into his master's armpit. Johnson tussled with them until his hat fell off. He smiled into Nancy's bright eyes, vivid as the violet-blue phlox that carpeted the woodlands above the house. Then he saw Cat, framed in the door of the house, with John in her arms, her belly ripening with another child, fertile as the deep loam that filled his dock and his storehouse with barrels of flour and bags of dried peas.

He thought, *I would not trade this place for the grandest estate in Ireland.*

Favour bristled. Then he bolted for the black walnut by the road, barking and showing his teeth.

Hendrick stepped out into the sunlight, bare-chested except for his silver gorgets, his necklace of bones and claws, and the light jaeger rifle slung from his shoulder.

"Serihokten," the warchief barked at the dog. "Stop the noise."

Favour slunk around the Indian on his belly, sniffing and wagging his tail.

Snowbird and White Owl came from the shadows behind Forked Paths.

Billy jumped to his feet, brushing the seat of his cotton breeches with his hands, ready for trade.

Hendrick's response to Billy's greeting was curt, his face somber, but Johnson was not troubled by that. He had rarely seen Forked Paths smile, except when he was reliving the slaughter of an enemy.

Nancy skipped among the Mohawks, admiring their finery.

Hendrick beckoned to Snowbird, who walked up to Johnson and dropped a small sack on the ground between his feet. Flies buzzed around it. The wolfhound ran up whimpering, poking the bag with his snout.

"Out!" Billy growled at him.

The stench from the sack reminded him of salt pork that had rotted in the barrel. He tugged at the rawhide thongs.

"Nancy!" He tried to keep his voice steady and low. "Go to your mother, darling. Go inside the house."

Nancy pouted and dragged her heels as she walked toward the house.

"Take the children inside," Johnson called hoarsely to Cat. "Quickly, now."

None of them must see. His heart banging against his ribs, he carried the Mohawks' gift to the smithy, deserted now because he had sent Gaffney over to the Lower Castle to mend guns for Aaron Hill.

White Owl rambled off toward the kitchen, in search of food. Hendrick and Snowbird followed Billy into the smithy and rummaged around in Gaffney's boxes of files and gun springs as if they had nothing of more consequence on their minds.

Johnson sat the bag on the big anvil, grooved for shaping gun barrels. He slit the sackcloth with his knife and stripped it away.

He was resolved to show no emotion, in the presence of the Mohawks.

He was defeated by the eyes.

"Why did the bastards leave the *eyes?*" he moaned, closing them with thumb and forefinger.

They were not the eyes of a man who died quickly.

Johnson forced himself to make a thorough inventory of this thing that had burst through the peace of his Valley.

The patch around the fontanel, where the scalp had been ripped away, had turned blackish-brown. The lips, the nose and one ear had been pared off like orange-rind. The surviving ear hung in ribbons. Much of the skin had been flayed. Only a bright tuft of red whiskers, and the eyes, confirmed that the head had ever belonged to a man.

"Do you know him?" Johnson asked the Mohawks.

"Hairyface." Snowbird patted his cheek.

The whiskers were the clue. Any number of hairy boatmen had stopped at Johnson's wharf, en route to Oswego, since the ice broke up. He remembered a red-haired brute, one of Van Eps' men, who had rolled down drunk from Fonda's tavern and chased the women round the house until Billy came home and saw him off with a horsewhip.

I would still wish any man a better end than this.

Fights between bateau-men and Indians were anything but unusual, anywhere between Schenectady and Oswego. They fought over women, over drink, over the pay the Indians demanded for helping to lug the flatboats across the Oneida Carry and the lesser portages. They fought for the hell of it.

A terrible thought seized Johnson. "By God, if this is the work of any man of the Six Nations—"

He was silenced by Hendrick's withering stare.

Hendrick nodded to Snowbird, who explained that he had found the severed head at the Oneida Carry, about midway between Mount Johnson and Oswego. The grisly trophy had been impaled on an iron-tipped pole, the kind boatmen used to haul their flat-bottomed bateaux upstream. It must have been left in this public place—visible to fur traders, boatmen and soldiers traveling to Lake Ontario after the spring melt—to make a point. The terror of those open eyes might make the greediest plunger think twice before venturing out onto the lake beach at Oswego to wave a rum bottle at passing Indian canoes on waters the French claimed as their own.

"Who did this?" Johnson demanded.

Snowbird spat on the dirt floor.

Johnson considered the men who stood to gain by scaring trade away from Oswego. The French, the Caughnawagas and the Albany Dutch all resented competition from this quarter. The French agents at Niagara had hired Indians to try to burn down the post at Oswego the first winter after it was opened.

Billy inspected the severed head more closely. He saw that the furrow where the nose had been sheared off was transected by a narrower gouge, forming the crude design of a cross.

"I think this must be the work of Praying Indians," he announced to the Mohawks. "The Caughnawagas come and go as they please in the lands of the Six Nations. Could this be their work?"

Diplomatically, Hendrick allowed the younger warrior to speak. They all knew that his elder sister now lived with the Caughnawagas.

Snowbird weighed his words. He said carefully, "I do not think my brothers from Caughnawaga would make war so near to our castles. I think if they planned to do this, we would have heard about it. Our ears are keen. We hear what is said even in Onontio's house at Montreal."

"Wakaterientare," Johnson agreed. "I know this matter." Onontio—Beautiful Mountain—was the Mohawk name for the Governor of New France.

But Billy was uncomfortably aware that, if the Mohawks were well-informed about the doings in Canada, the Indians from the blackrobe missions had equally good intelligence about affairs in the Valley. And Snowbird could not be trusted to speak candidly to any newcomer about the possible crime of blood-relatives.

"Who did this?" Johnson tried again, shrouding the horror in its sackcloth.

"I think Abenakis from St. Francis did this," Hendrick volunteered. "Abenakis like to kill Englishmen like that."

"Abenakis?" Johnson was skeptical. Lydius had told him bloodcurdling tales of the Abenakis of St. Francis, Eastern Indians who had been driven from their ancestral homes and nurtured a murderous hatred of New England that was useful to the French. But St. Francis was very far away to the north-east, down the St. Lawrence.

"I think maybe Onontio sent Abenakis because they have no cousins among the Six Nations," Hendrick observed.

They will not indict their kinsmen, Billy thought. *But suppose Hendrick is right?*

The implications of Hendrick's statement flooded in on him. If the French were sending Eastern Indians this deep into New York, it meant that the wretched death of a boatman at the Carry was more than a peculiarly nasty episode in the endless contest for furs.

It means war.

"Has Onontio taken up the hatchet?" Johnson demanded. "Has he sent out warbelts? Tell me all you have heard."

Hendrick pleaded thirst.

Billy called Juba to fetch his punchbowl and drank with the Mohawks in the back room of the store, because Cat did not like Indians in the house, and because he did not want her to hear what was said. The talk was mostly in Mohawk; Johnson's command of the Indian tongue had continued to improve, with the help of the native women. Hendrick said he could understand Billy better than Conrad Weiser, the Pennsylvania interpreter, who retained his German gutturals, but not as well as Arent Stevens, the Albany interpreter, who was part-Mohawk on his mother's side. When he shut off the translator inside his head and let himself think in Mohawk, Johnson found that the seemingly endless words moved as easily as water, each syllable lapping over the next.

White Owl must have smelled the rum, because he joined them almost immediately. After a few drinks, White Owl, who rarely had many words for white men, even Forest Killer, spoke freely about his most recent visit to Oswego. The Bear Clan warrior had not liked what he saw there.

"The walls of the English fort are falling down. On the lake, I saw two floating castles, flying the white flags of the Axe-Makers. There were many traders, but not many canoes. One that came carried Red Squirrel, the warchief of the Caughnawagas. Red Squirrel went everywhere, counting soldiers, looking in the powder magazine at the fort, making pictures in his head."

In describing Red Squirrel, White Owl used the old word for warchief, *rohskenhrakehte*, which means "he carries a load of bones on his back."

There is death in the word, Johnson thought.

"I think all the traders from Oswego will soon come running past your house," White Owl continued. "Red Squirrel told them that a great army and a great fleet will come to burn the fort and eat the hearts and livers of the English."

"I think Red Squirrel speaks like a Frenchman," Johnson said. "What message did he bring your people?"

It was Hendrick who answered. "Red Squirrel says if there is a new war between white men, the Real People must stand neutral, or go to live among the blackrobes, because this war has nothing to do with us. He says that when the French take Oswego, the English will all flee from the Valley and leave us to die alone unless we make peace with his father the Sun King."

"What do the Mohawks say to this?"

"There are some who say it is true."

Billy Johnson stared out the glassless window, at the little world he had made on the north shore of the Mohawk: the stone house, the tenant cottages, the fields and gardens hacked out of the forest. In the dancing sunlight, it looked happy and *whole*. Yet this perfect world was as fragile as the cut glass decanter he had shattered when Lydius had brought him fresh proof that the Albany ring had been stealing from his shipments.

Fragile, and isolated. To the west of Mount Johnson, his only white neighbors were the Palatine farmers at Stone Arabia and the Flats, and the traders and the tiny garrison at Oswego. The Germans were a stiff-necked people, used to swimming against the tide. They would cling to their land. But if Oswego fell, the tide would sweep them away. North-east of Mount Johnson were a few white settlers and contrabanders—Dutchman and New Englanders—sprinkled over the Saratoga plains and along the portages between the Hudson and Lake Champlain. If the French sent raiders out from their stronghold at Crown Point, these frontiersmen were all dead. North of Mount Johnson, the Adirondack wilderness of mountains, white-water rapids and forests stretched all the way to Canada.

If the French and their Indian allies came down the Valley, Johnson knew he would not be able to count on Albany for help. The great men of Albany—the Schuylers, the DePeysters, the Livingstons—had done their best to drive the Irish interloper out of business and would shed few tears if French Indians carried his scalp back to Caughnawaga or St. Francis on a hoop.

Whatever the odds, I will not give it up.

Some of his neighbors might flee. But his Irishmen were not the sort to run from a fight. Nor were the Wemps, or the Freys, or the Herkimers.

Above all, there were the Mohawks. Billy looked at the faces of his guests. They had come to him first—not to the Albany Commissioners, or even to Walter Butler at Fort Hunter—with their terrible proof that the French were on the warpath. No doubt they counted on finding generous hospitality at Mount Johnson, and its master took care not to disappoint them. But Billy Johnson sensed a deeper motive.

In part of myself, I belong to them. This is the reason for the trust they put in me.

"By God," he swore fiercely in his own language. "Here is one man who will not leave you or this Valley, not if King Louis comes armed with all the demons of hell! I *am* the frontier!"

CHAPTER 20
WARPATH

1.

The Mohawks were right about the traders. They came fleeing down the Valley, not all at once, but in waves. The slaughter of the boatman at the Oneida Carry scared greenhorns away. But a solitary scalping was not sufficient to induce an old hand to forgo the chance of doubling his money in a single season. Leathery veterans shrugged off Caughnawaga tales of a great army from France; the French and the Mission Indians had been broadcasting scare stories since the English put up their little fort on the lake a generation before, and no one had yet laid siege to its walls.

True, there were reports, months old by the time they filtered up the Valley, that the sabers were out again in Europe. The rulers of Britain and France had broken the paper peace that had been honored—if only on paper—since the Treaty of Utrecht. But this new war was being fought on the other side of the world. It had been sparked by a scramble over the succession to the Emperor Charles of Austria. Both the reasons for this war and the names of its battlefields were obscure to the traders, as to most people in the English colonies. How could the death of an Austrian prince have anything to do with them?

Then Captain Rutherford, the wistful, introspective commander of the Albany garrison—who meditated on Leibniz's monads in his spare hours to console himself for the conditions of his post—sent a military express galloping up the Valley to Fort Hunter.

Billy Johnson went across the river to hear the news from Walter Butler. He found the Lieutenant strapping on his sword.

"It's war, and no mistake about it," Butler told him. "The Frogs have put their ball in the air, the Bostonians have blood in their eye, and I'll be damned if there's any stopping it now. Here, read for yourself."

Johnson scanned Rutherford's dispatch. French soldiers had mounted a surprise attack on Canso, a village of New England fishermen on a rocky cape in Nova Scotia. Now the French were laying siege to Annapolis Royal. New England was up in arms.

Canso—a wretched collection of fishermen's huts huddled against the North Atlantic gales—seemed as remote to Billy as Mollwitz or Dettingen, the European battlefields whose names he had read in much-traveled copies of the *Gentleman's Magazine*. But he grasped its importance. For the first time in three decades, French regulars had attacked an English post in North America, on territory that belonged by treaty to the English Crown. The war for the continent was on.

On the heels of the news of bloodletting in Nova Scotia came letters from London informing the colonies that the monarchs of Britain and France had formally declared war on each other months before.

The toughest of the fur traders at Oswego were now obliged to reflect on the odds of survival. The contractor who had built the new wall around Fort Ontario had billed the government for limestone. But, as White Owl reported to Billy, he had put up only a shoddy clay rampart, so soft you could inscribe your name with a fingernail, so weak a brisk wind off the lake or a cannonball from a French sloop of war might knock it down. The garrison included more ghosts than fusiliers;

according to time-honored custom, the commandant was collecting the pay of dead men and deserters.

The fur traders on the lake calculated their odds and did not like them. When the scalp-yell shattered the morning and a Scots rum peddler was found skinned just outside the fort, the flight from Oswego became a rout.

The traders dumped their barter goods for whatever they could get. Some hugged the south shore as they paddled past Mount Johnson on flatboats or canoes, because they had bought Indian goods from Billy on credit and had no peltries with which to repay him. From his river landing, Johnson watched them run.

The traders' panic infected the settlers. The King's Road filled with families fleeing east.

"Perhaps you should go to Albany with the children," Billy suggested to Cat. "You will be safer there."

"We are not leaving," Cat said firmly, looking at the careworn faces of neighbors who had yoked themselves like oxen to handcarts heaped with their worldly goods.

I know you. I have walked in your shoes.

But the plight of these refugees was far worse, she thought, than that of the Palatine emigrants she had joined on the long walk from the valley of the Klöpferbach to the sea.

We had a dream before us, the hope of a New World. These poor people leave their dreams behind them.

The refugees from the Valley were mostly tenants, unwilling to risk their lives for another man's land. Tenants from Warrensbush walked with them. But Billy's little clan of Irishmen stood with him. So did most of the Dutch and German freeholders, people rooted in the Valley. Johnson set his slaves to work on a stockade, enclosing his house and store and the well. He wrote to Captain Warren, asking him to use his influence to have two companies of regulars assigned to the Mohawk country. He drilled the militia harder and recruited adventurous young woodsmen to be trained in native methods of warfare.

"Will the Mohawks fight?"

John Henry Lydius put the commanding question bluntly. The long, lopsided Dutchmen was one of the rare visitors who traveled westward to Mount Johnson in the first summer of the war.

Lydius squinted at Billy out of his good eye. He had a smile for Cat when she brought him a dish of hard-boiled eggs, the staple of his diet. He cracked one of the shells on the side of his plate, plucked out the quivering contents between thumb and forefinger, and dropped the whole egg down his throat. He washed this down with a gulp of scalding tea and demanded again, "Will they fight?"

"They will wait to see if we fight," Johnson suggested.

"They will not fight for Albany," Lydius reminded him.

"No," Johnson agreed. "They will not fight for Indian Commissioners. They will not fight for Secretary Livingston, who goes about with a deed to the land on which they live in his pocket."

"They will not fight for the Albany Ring," Lydius pressed his argument. "And the Ring will not ask them to fight. Your friend the Patroon has made a deal with the French. He spoke to the Governor of New France face-to-face, at Montreal. He told the Governor that, being Dutch by blood and inclination, the grandees of Albany have no interest in taking sides in any war between England and France. The Patroon promised Albany's neutrality so long as the French and their Indians leave Albany alone."

"But that is treason!"

"The gentlemen of the Ring call it business." Lydius rubbed his jaw. "There were Caughnawagas at DePeyster's house just this past week. I saw them myself. Red Squirrel was there. And that rascal they call Le Corbeau. The Caughnawagas yield second place to no one as intriguers and diplomatists, as you may have observed. I am informed they have made their own arrangement with the Ring. The Ring will supply them with guns and powder so long as they confine their scalping to New Englanders and keep up the traffic in furs."

Lydius paused to swallow another egg.

"It would be strange indeed—" he pursued "—if your Mohawk friends were minded to fight for gentry who have already determined the price at which they will sell the lives of their fellow-countrymen."

Lydius spoke English as he spoke half a dozen tongues, with the fluency of a gifted foreigner. Even when speaking his native Dutch, Lydius sounded like a man who came from somewhere else. As he made his indictment of the Albany Ring, Johnson detected—in the logic, more than the vowels—the flat tones of Boston.

The Bostonians, from Governor Shirley down to the youngest boy on a fishing boat, were as ardent for war as Albany was allergic to it. Massachusetts men were falling over each other to join the colors, spurred by the same combination of interests that had mobilized them against the French in the last war: revenge, religion and codfish. Among the merchant enterprisers who counseled Governor Shirley, the codfish weighed heaviest in the balance. In his first days in the colonies, after landing at Boston, Billy had dined with his uncle at the mansion of a merchant prince that boasted a magnificent staircase, with bannisters of gleaming mahogany and had learned something from the design. At each step, where a pineapple or a scallop-shell motif might have figured, the master of the house had decorated his staircase with a codfish, lovingly carved and gilded—a graphic testimonial to the source of his fortune. New England merchants would fight the French in Canada for the chance of monopolizing the codfish of the great fishing banks off Newfoundland, with as much gusto as the relatives of Massachusetts settlers scalped by Mission Indians would fight for revenge, or a brass-lunged dissenting divine would make war on the Antichrist of Rome.

George Clinton, the new Royal Governor of New York, was a bluff—if frequently inebriated—sailor, who had avowed his determination to "bang the French." But New Yorkers had scant regard for codfish, and few men in Governor Clinton's province shared the enthusiasm of Yankees for killing Frenchmen. While the great men of Albany, like the masters of an independent republic, talked neutrality with the French, the New York Assembly balked at raising taxes to pay for the defense of distant frontiers. And Governor Clinton was flanked on all sides by advisers whose interests lay with the Albany Ring; James DeLancey stood tallest among them.

"For you and me," Lydius said to Billy, "standing neutral is not an option."

Johnson sipped his punch, waiting for Lydius to disclose the object of his mission. He was still inclined to distrust this unlovely Dutchman's confidences. Yet he was struck by how prescient Lydius had proven to be, in assuring Billy—at their first encounter—that they had much in common.

We are both on the front line.

If the French pushed the war into New York, Mount Johnson and Fort Lydius, on the carry between the Hudson River and the lake-roads to Canada, would be prime and early targets.

We are both unloved at Albany.

Our security, and our hopes of fortune, rest on the trust of Mohawks.

Lydius looked at him slyly. "You are a quiet man with me today, Mister Johnson. Especially for an Irishman. I believe you have been studying the arts of silence with the Indians."

"The Mohawk say they do not speak without due reflection because they try to give us their best words."

"What else do the Mohawks tell you?"

"They are divided," Billy reported. "The Confederacy is opposed to taking sides in any war between us and the French, and many Mohawks listen to the Grand Council. The women are especially reluctant. I believe the clanmothers have their own diplomacy with Canada, as well as the rest of the Six Nations."

"I never knew Hendrick Forked Paths to be leery of a fight," Lydius commented.

"There is Hendrick," Johnson agreed. "There are Burned Knives who will get into any fight that is going. And cooler heads that maintain that the Mohawk interest lies with us. If only they can trust us."

"And you, Mister Johnson. You have some pull. I have seen it. Will the Mohawks take the warpath for *you?*"

"Should that be my counsel to them?" Billy evaded the question, and its presumption. "I wonder. Some of their warriors have told me they fear that if they go to war with us, we will lose our nerve and abandon them. There are others who say that if we beat the French, the English will come the next day to take their lands. Can I assure them that they are wrong? When I have seen how the affairs of this province are managed? When I know that Mister Secretary Livingston, of the Albany Commission, has a lying deed in his pocket to half the Mohawk lands?"

"An excellent speech," Lydius commented. "And I am glad to hear you make it, because it confirms my opinion that you have the brain and the backbone for what is required. Let me say one thing to you, and say it plain." He leaned in closer.

"Our sole hope is New England," Lydius declared.

"The Indians will be right to spurn us unless we reward them well, give the management of our relations to men they can trust, and the conduct of the war to men who have something between their legs. As things stand, New York will do none of this. New England will do all of it, given the chance.

"I have sat with Governor Shirley. He purposes great things, and I believe he will bring them to pass. He is the war leader we need. I am in constant communication with Colonel Stoddard, Shirley's man in Northampton. Stoddard is building forts and raising militia all throughout western Massachusetts. He knows there will be no safety for any man's family on our frontier so long as the French sit in their hornets' nest on Lake Champlain. He knows we cannot knock down the nest without the Six Nations. And he has given me the means to draw the Six Nations to our cause."

Lydius explained that Stoddard had promised to raise whatever money was required to buy the loyalty of the Mohawk sachems. It was hoped that they, in turn, would persuade the rest of the Six Nations to take the warpath on the English side. The Assembly at Boston would approve a generous bounty for scalps and prisoners taken from among the French and their Indian allies.

"It is a pretty scheme," Billy Johnson commented. "But I doubt that the Albany Commissioners will tolerate an attempt by Governor Shirley to buy the Mohawk nation away from them."

"We must pull those puffed-up bashaws out of their stirrups before they kill the horse."

"Governors have tried. The Commissioners outlived all of them."

"They will not outlive you and me. If we are clever."

"Am I to understand—" Billy said carefully "—that your Boston friends have a plan for unseating the Commissioners as well as for buying Indians?"

"A man does not send for a stranger to dismiss a servant. This is New York business. It should not be beyond our wit, Mister Johnson. With a little help from your friend Hendrick."

A wink from a one-eyed man was unsettling, Billy found.

He promised nothing to Lydius except to watch and listen.

When the Dutchman crossed the stableyard at his wide-legged, swaying gait—the effect of an accident at his rolling mill—Cat ran after him.

He looked down at the swell of her belly.

"I see Colonel Johnson appreciates a good breeder." He might have been speaking about a mare. "This one will be born in interesting times."

"Have you any word of my mother?"

Lydius shook his head, not without sympathy. "Listen, my dear. There are persons that are made to go native, never mind the age or class. There is a Williams lady from Deerfield way, old enough to be your grandmother, who was taken by the Praying Indians and now thinks herself one of them. She will visit her white cousins at Boston or Stockbridge every few years, in a blanket and beargrease, but will not stay with them. You cannot say the Indians treat women harshly."

"Better than some of our kind."

2.

Island Woman looked at the wooden tally-stick. Notches were carved along the side to show the number of days that would pass before Governor Shirley held a feast for his guests from the Six Nations and the other tribes that were invited to sit with him at Boston. Several of these notches had already been scored across. The tally-stick was garnished with a string of wampum beads, tied in a loop in the proper fashion. In Island Woman's eyes, this was the only thing about it that was proper.

She returned the stick to Snowbird.

She said, "The Bostonians wish us to fight and die in place of their sons. Will they fight for us if the Axe-Makers come into our Valley?"

"When have newcomers ever fought to defend us?" Bright Meadow spat, removing a chewed morsel of deermeat from her mouth to feed to the baby in her lap.

It was a family gathering, in Island Woman's lodge. But in his mother's words and leashed anger, Snowbird heard also the voice of the Mother of the Wolf Clan.

"Forked Paths says it can do no harm to listen to Shirley. We are promised rich presents."

"I hope Forked Paths has not forgotten his own beginnings. His people were once lords on the sunrise side of the mountains. The Bostonians reduced them to wanderers and eaters of bark, until we took pity on them and brought them under our roof."

Snowbird waited for his mother's decision.

She asked, "What does your friend Forest Killer say?"

"He says we must judge the Bostonians by their actions."

"He is honest with you in this," Island Woman nodded. She had made up her mind. "You will go to Boston," she instructed her son. "You will be the eyes and ears of our women. And I will go to Onondaga, to the Place of the Firekeepers. I will take counsel with The Word and the mothers of all our clans."

□

Snowbird rode east on a chestnut stallion lent by Billy Johnson. Hendrick Forked Paths, White Owl and John Henry Lydius rode with him.

Govérnor Shirley feasted them at Boston and showed them an army of volunteers that was massing to avenge the French assault on the fishermen at Canso. Shirley dropped hints of a bolder enterprise he was hatching: a scheme so mad no professional soldier would ever have entertained it. The Governor was planning to send an army of raw provincials up the coast to storm the great French fortress of Louisbourg, on Cape Breton Island. With Louisbourg in its hands, New England would command the sea approaches to Canada. Not to mention the codfish shoals of the Great Banks.

The Mohawks drank Shirley's wine and ate his beef and indicated polite approval when he fulminated against the French. Snowbird watched farmboys drill in a meadow and listened to a sulfurous sermon from a Protestant divine who cited scriptural proof that the Lord of Hosts would march with the warriors of New England.

Shirley and the General Court of Massachusetts wanted the Flint People to guard their borders while the volunteer army went adventuring up the coast. They wanted the Mohawks to warn all the French Indians that if they sent scalpers against New England, the Six Nations would take up the hatchet against them.

"You will see we are generous with our friends," Shirley told them.

The Governor heaped presents on the Mohawk envoys, including a box of doubloons and pieces of eight, because the Flint People had learned the value of dead metal in the world of the newcomers, where everything had a price.

Forked Paths was careful to say nothing to explode Shirley's hopes, even when the Governor asked for something no Mohawk could promise with his heart:

that if Caughnawagas attacked New England settlements, Mohawks should go to war against their own kinsmen.

But the Mohawks gave no definite undertakings.

Hendrick salved the frustrations of his hosts by mounting one of the most remarkable acts of political theater the people of Boston had ever witnessed.

Hundreds of Eastern Indians, including Abenakis from St. Francis—blood-enemies of the Mohawk—had also responded to Shirley's invitation.

In a laced hat and a new ruffled shirt, with King George's pistols in his belt, Hendrick led the Mohawks through the town to a council with the Eastern tribes. In the open field where the Eastern Indians had gathered, Hendrick was informed that their chiefs had not yet arrived. Contrary to the conventions of native diplomacy, Forked Paths refused to delay his speech.

He scanned his audience with a predator's eyes. He had taken twenty scalps from these nations. Mohawks and Easterners had been fighting each other since long before the newcomers came. Facing each other now, above the stir of the assembly, they could hear the spirit-calls of their hungry ghosts.

Looking out across the field of waving feathers, Lydius thought that Hendrick's appearance had the effect of an eagle diving into a flock of sparrows.

Forked Paths spoke over a great black belt.

"We are your fathers," the Mohawk warchief informed the Easterners. "You are our children. If you are dutiful and obedient, if you brighten the covenant chain with the English our brothers, and refuse to take the hatchet from the French our enemies, then we will defend and protect you. If you rebel against us, you shall die by our hands, every man, woman and child that is among you. We will cut you off from the earth, as the ox licketh up the grass."

He flung down his belt in a gesture of cold contempt, leaving the Easterners frightened and angry. Some stalked out of the council. Others wished to answer the Mohawk with hot words. But fear was the ruler.

Governor Shirley was delighted by this drama, and the ministers who quoted Hendrick in their sermons dwelled on the touches of Old Testament fury in the translation.

But the Mohawks left Boston without committing themselves to anything more than bullying words against old tribal enemies. And at Onondaga, where Island Woman sat with the elders and the clanmothers, the Grand Council reaffirmed that the Flint People, as the Keepers of the Eastern Door, must adhere to the longstanding policy of the Confederacy, and stay out of white men's wars.

"We may rule the seas," Lydius observed to Shirley, in a private session that included his paymaster, Colonel Stoddard. "But we can never win on land without the Mohawks and the Six Nations. They own the forest."

"How do we budge them?" Shirley was impatient for action.

"A clear victory over the French will assist. Men are more easily moved when they believe they are on the winning side. The Mohawk have no love for the Albany Ring, and this can become our tool. Above all, we must make this war a matter of life or death for them. If they will not go to war for us, we must bring the war to them."

"How exactly do you propose to do that?"

"Give me enough money, and I will find the way."

3.

Cat delivered her second daughter early that fall, when rumors flew thicker than maple leaves about the Valley. She agreed with Billy that the baby would be christened Mary, which was a family name in both their lines. But Billy thought Polly sounded friendlier, and soon the entire household was calling her that, which irritated Cat because it reminded her of the messy, loud-mouthed macaw—a gift from Captain Warren—that Johnson insisted on keeping inside the house.

Before the first snows, Cat took the baby across the river to the Queen Anne chapel, to be baptized.

She sat in the second pew, rocking Polly in her arms, while Nancy and John fidgeted and pinched each other. Her other company was a friendly Dutch neighbor, Helena Walleslous, the wife of one of the Irish tenants, and faithful, reliable Jamie Rogers, who had folded his long legs into the pew behind.

Rogers swore audibly at the "indaycency" of the rector keeping the mistress of Mount Johnson waiting. Cat half-turned and gave him a conspiratorial smile.

Rogers' presence was a comfort. But it could not make up for the absence of the baby's father. She had not asked Billy to come. She had not expected him to be present; his business affairs had multiplied since he had agreed to supply the garrison at Oswego, abandoned by the Albany merchants because of the risks. And Billy had absented himself from the christenings of both Nancy and John, without feeling the need to offer any excuse.

Cat thought that Billy loved his children as passionately as he loved anything in this world. She also knew the reason he would not stand with her in the stone chapel at the hour when they were named before God. He would not—could not—give her his name. Cat had never asked for that and never would. Happiness, she found, comes easier when you stop reaching beyond your grasp.

But she had set her heart on one thing, and made Billy swear she would have it. Whatever stiff, prideful Henry Barclay wrote in his register, her children would go through life wearing the name of Johnson. One day, she was certain, this name would weigh heavy enough to stifle the names that the mean-spirited might give them.

Mohawks sat across the isle. There was a Mohawk girl to be baptized, who looked to be two or three years old. She was brown as a hazelnut, much darker than her parents. Native children seemed to lighten as they grew older, while Cat's own brood grew a little browner, as sun and wind did their work.

Cat recognized the Mohawk child's father, a towering warrior Billy called White Owl, who had been a frequent visitor at Mount Johnson. She avoided looking at the Indians now and had given them only the most perfunctory greeting at the door. She thought she would never be at home among the natives, not as Billy was, even though she had known kindness as well as terror during her captivity and remembered, as from a dream, the handsome matron who had tended her when she was rolling in the coils of the snake-fever. She was too uneasy about her own precarious station, too deeply wedded to notions of order and boundaries that seemed to mean nothing to the natives, to be able to accept Indians as equals. And perhaps too jealous of Billy's relations with their women, a subject she preferred to shut out of her thoughts.

She regarded Mr. Barclay's decision to baptize a Mohawk child at the same hour as her daughter Mary as a calculated slight—like the fact that the minister was running very late.

Henry Barclay arrived at last, in his surplice and cassock, puffy about the eyes and poorly shaven.

"I see the father once again declines to honor us with his presence," was all his greeting to Cat.

He raced through the formulas in English and threw enough cold water on little Polly's face to ensure that she would howl. Then he repeated the ceremony in Mohawk, for the benefit of White Owl's family.

She looked over Barclay's shoulder as he wrote the names in his register.

He put down, "Mary, Daughter of Catherine Wysenberk."

Cat could not letter well in English, but she knew the spelling was wrong. Not only wrong, but different from what Mr. Barclay had written before. She asked if she might turn back the pages. There: where John's baptism was recorded, the minister had her down as Catherine Wysen Bergh.

She pointed out the discrepancy.

The minister gave her a hard stare. He said, "Be thankful they are in the book at all."

Anger flared in her, but she dampened the fires. To

make further protest would only give Henry Barclay
satisfaction and distress her children. Besides, it was
possible that Barclay's hostility was inspired more by the
absent father than her unmarried estate; she had heard
their voices raised in argument, Valley neighbors. So she
watched in silence as the minister added the names of
the godparents.

In place of hot anger, she felt cold to the marrow. In
that chill season of blowing leaves, with the traders fled
and hearths deserted, and the evil talk of war and
skulking murder, she wanted to invoke God's mercy.

She thought of Conrad Weiser, her strange countryman from Pennsylvania, who had stopped briefly at the
house. Half-madman, half-saint, loved by the natives for
his wanderings in high, stony places. "What is a man?"
he had called to her at their parting. "A man is someone
who weeps, because he yearns to reach the heavens and
can only touch the cover of God's book."

*Conrad Weiser would not deny me grace. He would not
look down his stuffy nose at me because I do not wear a
wedding band.*

Wounded and wary, she waited for Henry Barclay's
blessing.

"This is a sorry business," the rector said frostily. "I
performed this ceremony only because it would be
wrong to attribute the sins of the father to the child. God
knows where William Johnson is going when he leaves
this mortal estate."

She walked out of the church with the baby, looking
neither to right nor left.

I will make no outcry. I can take this too.

To her surprise, the Mohawk mother walked up beside
her and touched her arm.

"In my language," Bright Meadow said to her in
perfectly good English, "the word for priest means
'burned to a crisp.' Because that is what we used to do to
them."

With a ripple of laughter, Bright Meadow swerved
away to rejoin her family. Under the trees, Cat saw
another familiar face: that of the regal woman who had

come to her when she was on her sickbed. Island Woman nodded to her, leaning on the knob of a curious, twisted stick. Cat acknowledged her with a crisp, "Good morning," knocked further off-balance by this unexpected show of solidarity.

"Looks like you have native friends, if you want them," Rogers observed.

He had heard the exchange with the minister and grumbled about it all the way home to Mount Johnson.

"The man's a bully," Rogers declared. "I would sooner earn my bread for twopenny a week than waste my Sundays in his church. It ain't Christian. You mustn't take it personal. Barclay hates Billy because Billy told the Indians they were wrong to give him the land behind the chapel."

"It doesn't matter," Cat said. "I've forgotten it already."

Indeed, by the time she had handed the children into the boat for the river crossing, her mind was on other things. It was time to sow the winter wheat. The household accounts must be put in order. There were provisions to be got in before the rivers froze. And she must talk to Billy about a governess for Nancy and John—if one bold enough to come up the Valley in wartime could be found. She would not let her children grow up like weeds or savages. And she was resolved they would lack none of the armor they would need against the Henry Barclays of this life.

4.

It was a jumpy winter in the Valley. Some of the Mohawks took alarm at rumors—spread by Lydius—that the Albany Commissioners had sealed a secret treaty with the French that would allow them to seize the lands of the Flint People once the French had burned them out of their villages. Burned Knives raised the war-cry at Fort Hunter in the middle of the night, pulling Walter Butler out of bed and scaring Henry Barclay half out of his wits.

Johnson's influence was invoked to calm things down. He promised the Mohawks that he would help them to take their grievances to the new Governor of New York. Reports of Governor Clinton's character and actions did not build confidence. But as Uncle Peter had once observed of a greater dignitary at London, all that is required of a stupid man is that he is ready to be led by the right people.

While Billy and the Mohawks played at shadow war, most men of influence in the province of New York held to the view that King George's War—as it was labeled contemptuously—was no affair of theirs. Returning to Fort Frederick from Manhattan, Captain Rutherford complained to Johnson that the New York Assembly seemed "ill disposed to raise money on almost any account" and that Governor Clinton was completely in the hands of James DeLancey. At Albany, Caughnawagas came and went as they chose, trading silver taken from New England farmhouses for guns and powder.

The real war was being waged far to the northeast.

In the colony of Massachusetts Bay, one man in eight volunteered to join the expedition against Louisbourg, the strongest fort in North America. Governor Shirley picked William Pepperrell of Kittery, the chief merchant of New England, to lead the provincials. Pepperrell was an affable, pumpkin-faced man of commerce whose Welsh father had left him a fortune won from codfish and building ships. General Pepperrell had never heard a shot fired in anger and not one of his officers had greater experience of war than a sham fight on muster day. Shirley equipped them with a precise plan for the siege that omitted nothing except surf, fogs and gales, treacherous reefs and the utter inexperience of farmboys and fishermen sent to fight on rugged, unknown terrain. George Whitefield, the New Light divine, armed the New Englanders with a motto for their flag—*Nil desperandum Christo duce*—which proved to be of more practical use than the Governor's plan.

Even when the good news traveled west that Commodore Warren had left off hunting French prizes and had joined the New Englanders off Cape Breton with the *Superbe* and two more ships of the line, Captain Rutherfurd despaired of the chances of this mad expedition.

"A fortified town is a tough nut to crack," he wrote to Billy, "and the teeth of our provincials are not strong enough to do it, though there are gentlemen who imagine that taking forts is as easy as taking snuff."

Then came the heady news that Commodore Warren had bagged a French man-of-war of sixty-four guns, richly laden with two years' pay for the garrison of Louisbourg and the soldiers of New France.

Billy's clan at Mount Johnson had barely recovered from celebrating this when they learned that the impossible had been accomplished: Pepperrell's green provincials and Warren's little fleet had forced the surrender of the French at Louisbourg. With only enough powder left for one day's fighting, the French governor presented his sword and the keys of the city to Commodore Warren. Parson Moody, the hellfire preacher, stormed through the churches of Louisbourg, bawling that the army of Israel had routed the Canaanites, swinging an axe against graven images.

Peter Warren was made an Admiral; bluff Pepperrell became the colonies' first baronet.

Billy Johnson opened a pipe of Madeira and toasted the victory of Uncle Peter and New England as a family affair. Elsewhere in the colony, the celebrations were more muted. Governor Clinton enviously calculated the value of the rich prizes Warren had taken. James DeLancey sniffed that the pretensions of Shirley and the New Englanders would now become insufferable. And at Albany, Philip Livingston and the Commissioners of Indian Affairs gloomily weighed the prospects that the French would spare no effort to wreak revenge for Louisbourg, and they might be obliged to do something about it.

5.

Governor Clinton detested the climate of New York, and the manners of its politicians, whom he was wont to describe, after a few bumpers of claret and port, as a pack of insolent scrubs. As colonial governors went, George Clinton was no worse than many and an improvement over some. Like nearly all of them, he had been sent to America because he was not wanted at home.

The younger son of the late Duke of Lincoln, George Clinton had been loosed into the world with an annuity of a hundred pounds a year and no obvious talents except vague geniality and a prowess with the bottle that was remarkable even in an age of dedicated topers. Finding no easier road to advancement, he went to sea at twenty-two, an old man among the midshipmen. He managed to sink the first ship he commanded in a squall. He redeemed his fortunes through a brilliant marriage to the daughter of the Duke of Newcastle, the rising star in the government of King George. He pestered the Duke until Newcastle secured for him an admiral's command in the Mediterranean. But George Clinton's luck continued to match his talents. Unlike Peter Warren, he never seemed to be where prizes were to be taken. On dry land again, creditors harried him mercilessly. His wife went weeping to the Duke who, tiring of his importunate relations, decided to put an ocean between himself and both of them by sending Clinton to govern New York.

The new Governor had arrived, two summers before, in a colony where he knew no one. Incapable of writing a speech or of negotiating the thickets of colonial finances, the Governor placed himself in the hands of the likeliest counselor, the subtle, well-connected James DeLancey. He found DeLancey so agreeable that he altered his commission. Instead of serving "at His Excellency's pleasure," the Chief Justice would serve "on good behavior"—which meant as long as he liked. Only as his honeymoon with DeLancey began to sour did Admiral

Clinton realize he had made an error that could sink his governorship.

Governor Clinton's instructions from London ordered him to prepare the province for war. With the conquest of Louisbourg—to which New York's entire contribution had been a few transport ships, lent reluctantly—there was talk of sending an army against Canada. Yet the city merchants in the New York Assembly declined even to increase the peacetime allowances for frontier defense and Indian gifts. The Assembly flatly refused to guarantee revenues for the government—including Clinton's own salary—for more than one year at a time. James DeLancey urged him to dissolve the Assembly and elect a more obliging one. But when Clinton acted on this advice, he found he had been cruelly deceived. The new Assembly was no more accommodating than the previous one. The only difference was that DeLancey's cronies were more firmly in control.

George Clinton withdrew more and more from the life of New York, drinking behind closed doors at the fort that had recently been the focus of the Great Negro Plot, muttering against enemies real and imagined.

The Governor celebrated his sixtieth birthday alone with his family that summer and succeeded in drinking himself under the table. His son Harry helped the servants carry him up to bed. His Excellency woke late, with a vile hammering above his eyes, to find he had gone entirely deaf in his left ear. He inspected himself in his shaving glass, and saw a round, puffy face, moist and pale like unrisen dough, except for the purplish web of broken capillaries across nose and cheeks.

At that moment, something stirred in the Governor.

He summoned his valet. He had him tighten the corset over his dropsical belly until he could fit into his admiral's uniform, the one he had worn when he stalked the quarterdeck of the *Gloucester,* off the Barbary Coast.

His wife came into his dressing room, ready to read him a lecture for the excesses of the night before. Her expression softened when she saw him in royal blue. For an instant, she saw the gallant sailor who had swept her off her feet at a London ball.

"My love," she said to him softly, "whatever are you doing?"

"I am doing what Englishmen are made for. I am going to bang the Frogs."

□

In the affairs of New York, so Cadwallader Colden advised the Governor, there were two constants: self-interest ruled the politicians and the Indians ruled the borders. Victory or defeat in any conflict with the French depended on the Indians. But it seemed the Indians were fast slipping away from the British interest. There had been wild alarums in the Mohawk country. At Onondaga, the Grand Council of the League of Six Nations vowed strict neutrality in the war between two empires of white men.

Governor Clinton determined to throw his own ample person into the breach. He ordered belts sent out to summon the Six Nations to a council at Albany. He wanted James DeLancey and Cadwallader Colden, who explained maps and Indians so well, to go with him. But the two Councillors—who bore no love for each other—made their excuses, DeLancey to intrigue in Manhattan, Colden to correspond with Swedish botanists and Philadelphia savants from his retreat in the Hudson highlands. It was Daniel Horsmanden, the witchfinder-general of the Negro Plot, who escorted the Governor on board the Albany sloop.

□

The chiefs of the Six Nations came to Albany to take the measure of the new Governor and receive his presents, all except the Senecas, who excused themselves because of an epidemic in their country. Hendrick Forked Paths knew the name of this epidemic. It was Joncaire. The sons of the legendary French agent were steadily expanding his influence over the Keepers of the Western Door of the Confederacy.

The Indians camped on the hill above the town, and on the pastures by the river, below the palisades. The Governor invited Canassatego, the bull-chested Onondaga who was the Speaker of the Confederacy, and known throughout the lands of the Longhouse as The Word, to a private reception at sunset, together with Hendrick and other sachems. He presented the Indians with black strouds to condole the recent loss of some of their chiefs and a glass of rum to toast the health of King George.

The following day, the Governor read the Indians a speech prepared by Livingston and the Albany Commissioners. Arent Stevens and Conrad Weiser took turns to interpret. Clinton spoke of brightening the ancient covenant chain between the English and the Confederacy. He said that the French Indians had violated their promises of neutrality by attacking the border settlements of New England and that it was the duty of the Six Nations to punish them. He complained of the commotion among the Mohawks during the winter and demanded to know the reasons for it.

This speech pleased nobody. The Massachusetts delegates thought it was far too mild; the black-swathed Quakers from Pennsylvania—who refused to allow a Yorker to speak for them—thought it too bloody. The Indians were silent and evasive. They omitted the normal cries of approval when the Governor threw down his belts.

Hendrick demanded a private audience with the Governor, in the absence of the Albany Commissioners. "We cannot speak from our hearts when Corlaer sits with men who wish to use us as their dogs."

Hendrick had his way. He told the Governor, "We the Flint People fear we will be treated like our brothers the River Indians. Your countrymen have stolen their lands and driven them from the burial places of their grandfathers.

"We fear that before long we shall not have a dust of ground to set our feet on. There are six gentlemen at Albany with deeds in their pockets to the lands on which we live. They have sent men by stealth to survey our lands in the night. You must know we will not allow ourselves to be brought to the condition of other nations that have trusted English promises."

Governor Clinton promised that all complaints would be investigated. The Mohawk warchief's measured fury gave him throbbing headaches.

"God's daggers," he complained to Horsmanden, "if that savage is our friend I have no wish to meet our enemies."

The following day, Governor Clinton threw down the war-belt, thirty-two rows of wampum with the blood-red design of a hatchet.

A few of the Mohawks raised the *yo-hai*, but The Word restrained them. The Speaker of the Confederacy took the belt gingerly, holding it well away from his body as if it were a poisonous snake that might bite him.

"We will take this hatchet," he said, "but we will keep it under our blanket. We have many friends among other nations, and if we raise this hatchet without consulting them, they will take offense."

The Confederacy would send envoys to Canada, to discuss matters with their kinsmen there and ask satisfaction for the wrongs that had been done to the people of New England.

"Satisfaction?" John Stoddard growled at Lydius. "Do they imagine a few sheep or a few strings of beads can make amends for what we have suffered?"

Stoddard approached the Governor, pressing him to demand assurances that the Six Nations would avenge any further attacks on New England.

The Word's response was evasive.

At the end of the conference, with nothing resolved, the Six Nations collected their presents and raised the *yo-hai*. Governor Clinton doffed his hat and led a chorus of huzzahs. Stoddard and the Massachusetts observers did not join in.

Colonel Stoddard was in a black fury. That morning, in an Albany store, he had discovered a tankard engraved with the initials of a Massachusetts farmer whose house had been burned by Mission Indians.

"There is nothing to be accomplished in this dirty town," he told Lydius. "New York has lost the Indians."

□

Governor Clinton heard speeches. He did not understand reasons. He did not see Island Woman and the clanmothers who had sat silent during the public councils gather round The Word, at the end of the conference, to thank him for upholding the Great Law of Peace while avoiding an open breach with the English.

But through the haze of alcohol and migraine headaches, Clinton could see one thing clearly. If anything was to be accomplished—if he were to avoid being shipped home in disgrace—he needed a man at his side who was held in higher regard by the Indians than the Albany Commissioners. A man with the energy and influence of the French agents who had loosed the Mission Indians against the back settlements of New England and were already eyeing the soft borders of New York.

6.

Fort St. Frédéric rose from the black limestone promontory of Crown Point, commanding the narrows near the head of Lake Champlain. Its stone ramparts were twenty feet thick and twenty feet high, mounted with more than a score of cannon. Above the ramparts, an octagonal tower reared up like the keep of a feudal warlord. This dark tower of vaulted masonry, proofed against bombshells, bristling with cannon and pivot-guns, gave the place its familiar name: The Octagon.

It was four days' march from Albany, but its shadow fell across all of New England. It was here, while Governor Clinton groaned under the pressures of Indian diplomacy and colonial intrigue, that the French were preparing their revenge for Louisbourg.

Governor Beauharnois of New France had better luck with the Indians than Governor Clinton of New York. For this, he could thank soldier-priests like the Abbé Picquet and seasoned bush fighters like Lieutenant

Marin de la Malgue, who won the trust of the Indians by sharing all the seasons of their lives—and by making no attempt to rob them of their land.

Beauharnois had roasted an ox at Montreal and enlisted three hundred Mission Indians, from Caughnawaga and the Lake of Two Mountains, to go with Marin and a body of Canadians against the borders of the English colonies. Marin's orders were to lay waste to the settlements along the Connecticut River. Knowing that the Caughnawagas had few secrets from the Mohawks, he did not tell his warriors where they were headed until they had paddled up Lake Champlain to the mouth of Otter Creek.

Then, in the late sunlight, when their birchbark canoes and bateaux were pulled up onto the eastern shore, Lieutenant Marin called the sachems into a semicircle and drew a rough map in the sand. There were streaks of red in the steel-gray sand. The shafts of light falling over the fir-covered hills to the west lit garnet fires along the beach.

The Abbé Picquet listened as intently as the Indian chiefs while Marin outlined the objectives of his mission. The principal objective—the one the two Frenchmen had spent much time discussing with Governor Beauharnois—went unvoiced. It was to induce the Mission Indians to make war on the English. Everything else was secondary. Once the Mission Indians were fully engaged in the war, the frontiers of the English colonies would become uninhabitable, Oswego and Albany would fall like rotting plums, and the Six Nations would have the best possible reason for staying neutral—their relatives would be in the front lines of the French attack.

The Abbé had the large, intent round eyes of a night-hunting owl. A heavy silver cross hung over the front of his cassock. He carried no weapons, but he held up a staff with the war-banner he had himself designed: it bore the figures of the Virgin and the Lamb of God, woven on silk, cunningly married to the clan devices of the Iroquois by strands of wampum.

The Caughnawagas requested time to consider Marin's instructions.

The Abbé watched them move up the beach, headed by Le Corbeau. He said to Marin, "We must watch that one."

"I fought with him in the west," Marin protested. "He is a born warrior."

"Ah. But he may have less appetite for this affair."

Marin pursed his lips. They knew that Le Corbeau's wife was a Mohawk, the daughter of a clanmother. It was asking a great deal of a man to expect him to swim against the current of his own blood. The Jesuits said Le Corbeau could be trusted, although they had had difficulties with his wife, a woman accused of witchcraft. But the opinions of Jesuits were not a sufficient testimonial for Abbé Picquet, a Sulpician. The Abbé deplored the laxity of the Jesuits at the Sault St. Louis. He was convinced that by tolerating—even promoting—the illegal traffic with Albany, they had licensed the Caughnawagas to act as spies and couriers for the enemies of God and King Louis.

He watched the Caughnawagas return along the beach.

Le Corbeau spoke for all. He said that the Caughnawagas did not want to go to the Connecticut River, where the land was strange to them. They wished to propose a different objective.

"*Tsiron!*" urged Lieutenant Marin. "Say it!"

Le Corbeau took a stick and scratched his own map in the sand.

Marin could not believe his eyes. The map showed the course of the upper Hudson and the approaches to Albany. Le Corbeau added the pear-shaped outline of the palisades around the town.

"The stockade is weak in three places," he said, marking them. "I have seen for myself. Two men can walk abreast through *this* hole. The soldiers are few. There are only two officers, and one is sick. The traders are soft. They will not fight."

It seemed too good to be true. For Abbé Picquet, it *was* too good to be true.

When their force reached The Octagon, he sought to reason with Marin in the seclusion of the commandant's quarters in the tower. Through the slit window, they could see a light moving like a firefly on the water. Indians were spearing fish in the lake by the light of a burning pine torch.

"I know it's a trap," the priest told the soldier. "I know it *here.*" He patted his belly. It was even possible, he suggested, that Lydius, the notorious agent of New England who had lived among the Caughnawagas, was the moving spirit behind this plan.

But Lieutenant Marin refused to relinquish the glittering prospect of taking Albany. The Dutch town at the head of navigation on the Hudson was the key to the whole province of New York. With Albany in French hands, the English would soon be reduced to cowering at the southern tip of Manhattan island, praying for transport ships to take their refugees away.

"Have you ever known savages to attack a fortified town voluntarily?" Picquet challenged him.

"But the Caughnawaga says there are holes in the stockade—"

"Holes that will be filled with English cannon by the time we reach them. If we are not ambushed along the way."

"Our orders are to draw the Mission Indians into total war with the English," Marin stuck to his guns. "They proposed the assault on Albany. We must follow their proposal. Even if we fail, their engagement will be a victory for France."

The priest resolved to deal with a fool according to his folly. After morning mass, he took aside several warriors of Caughnawaga whom he trusted more than the others, and two chiefs from his own mission.

Afterward, they met with their own people. Then they marched in force to Lieutenant Marin to announce that they had agreed on a second change of plan, because of a dream of one of their number. This dream required them to attack the isolated village of Saratoga, where the houses were unprotected and the fort was falling down.

"These savages are as inconstant as running water," Marin complained to Picquet.

The priest smiled politely. He was contemplating a

coup of his own, against an old enemy, one of the most dangerous opponents of New France.

The march from the Octagon followed trails invisible to white men's eyes through virgin forest to the clearing above the upper falls of Hudson's River where, thirteen years before, John Henry Lydius had built a trading post to catch the Caughnawagas before they fell into Albany's net. The main house was built of pine logs. The upper story hung over the lower, loopholed for musketry. Nearby were storehouses, a sawmill and barns for cattle and horses.

In the shelter of the woods, the priest summoned Le Corbeau.

"You know these people," Picquet told him. "You will go to them as a friend. We must not allow them to raise the alarm."

"If you fire too soon—if you give them warning—" said Outchik, the war captain from the Lake of Two Mountains "—your soul will soon join your grandfathers."

Le Corbeau stared at Outchik with cold hatred, but said nothing.

He ambled casually toward Lydius' post, his fusil slung over his shoulder. The white men cutting firewood tensed when they saw him and reached for their firelocks, but relaxed when they recognized a familiar face. They called to the house, and Jacques, Lydius' son— nut-brown as his mother, darker than Le Corbeau— came to welcome him.

"What news do you bring us?" he cried out cheerfully.

"My news is for your father."

"Papa is at Albany, for the winter."

"Then you must hear it alone."

Le Corbeau whipped out his knife and laid the point of the blade against Jacques' throat. At the same instant, a hundred warriors came out of the woods.

"Tell your men not to resist."

"What will you do with us?"

"You will return to the Rapid River, with us. I promise no harm will come to you. Your life is my life."

Abbé Picquet derived signal satisfaction from watching Lydius' house burn. The Mission Indians burned the sawmill, the outbuildings, and the lumber. They slaughtered the livestock, down to the last chicken, and made a barbecue in the blackened ruins of the trading post.

The road to Saratoga was open.

The village on the river-flats slumbered in the cold before dawn until the death-cry went up from a farmhouse at the edge of the woods. Captain Philip Schuyler of the militia, racing for the fort in his nightshirt, was felled by a ball between the shoulders. In an instant, a Nipissing warrior was straddling him, hacking at the top of his head with a hatchet.

Rubbing sleep from his eyes, a farmer's boy came out his door and gaped at a pale, grinning figure in black, with a cross of bright silver in his right hand and a fluttering silken banner in the left, spurring a horde of howling demons into battle.

The faces of his disciples were blood-red, patterned with stars and crosses in white and blue and yellow, with black lines that resembled the phases of the moon.

The most terrifying face was divided like night and day. One cheek shone like the sun; the other was dark as a storm cloud. This devil came dancing toward the boy, tinkling glass and porcelain beads as he shook his head. The child could not understand the savage war-song that rose from his lips—

My mother conceived me in the fire of battle
She brought me into this world with a warclub in
    my hand
She suckled me only with the blood of enemies.

—but there was no need for an interpreter, because another hand laid open the boy's skull.

The priest stepped over his body, mumbling the words of the King of Prophets as he waved his disciples onward, toward the fort: *Anima mea in manibus meis semper*—"I carry my life in my hands."

The boy's sister clambered out the rear window and tried to conceal herself behind the woodpile.

She saw the monster with the divided face peering out through the window frame, looking for fresh prey.

Then another man stood over her. His face was all black, and he was dressed differently from the others.

She opened her mouth to scream, but the African cupped his hand over it.

Ade whispered, "Be still, if you wish to live."

CHAPTER 21
TO CAUSE A BEAR

1.

Island Woman watched a skein of Canada geese winging south across the Endless Mountains. From where she stood, the formation resembled the figure of a headless man, like those the warriors carved to depict the enemies they had killed and scalped.

Snowbird and Dandelion had already brought meat for the winter. They had taken a dozen deer, removed the bones, and dried and cured the venison over the fire at their camp, which greatly reduced the weight, so they could carry the meat from many animals in small bark barrels on their backs. They had dried and packed the skins, and carried them home the same way. It would be easier for the hunters to bring home their game on sleds, when the snow crusted over. But this season, the warriors would stay close to the Upper Castle, because Whirlwind walked through the Valley.

White Owl had returned from a scout, with news of the slaughter at Saratoga.

The French and their Indian allies had laid waste to the newcomers' village. They had taken more than a hundred captives back to the missions. The white men's fort had been taken, after the terrified garrison seized the opportunity to flee under cover of darkness.

Island Woman frowned at the news that her elder daughter's husband had led the Caughnawagas into battle. None of the Six Nations had taken part in the fight at Saratoga, but it had taken place within the traditional hunting grounds of the Flint People. It brought the war a long step closer to the Mohawks, and Island Woman wondered whether this was the result of the bitter darkness in the hearts of Le Corbeau and Swimming Voices as well as the policy of the French.

Island Woman called a meeting of the women's council.

Speaking over the wampum credentials she had inherited from Fruitpicker, she told them, "We must send new envoys to our sisters at Caughnawaga and Oka, as well as among the allied nations of the Confederacy. At all costs, we must avoid a war with our own blood. There are newcomers on both sides who are working to draw us into this war. They long to hear the wind sigh through our empty lodges. They see how our numbers are already reduced by the gifts they have brought us. By the white death and the yellow fever and the hard water that steals the minds of our men. We cannot afford to allow any more of our warriors to be cut down like green corn in a struggle that means nothing to us."

"But our young men love battle," her own daughter, Bright Meadow, pointed out. "They drink the hard water at Forest Killer's house, and at Hard Egg's, and they believe their promises. Our warriors are already half-crazy. They are cutting off their hair."

Many of the women nodded and grunted. Among the Real People, long hair was regarded as a sign of spiritual potency. A man who shaved his head, on the other hand, was probably boiling mad inside, filled with anger and vengeance. That was why men about to go on the warpath cut their hair off, all but a fistful they could shake in their enemies' faces, defying them to come and get it. To go to war, a man needed to be half-crazy. That was why the traditional chiefs—the *rotiyaner*—were made to stand down from their offices if they joined a

war-party. You couldn't trust a man who was shaved for
war to think right, except when it came to killing.

Island Woman looked around the circle.

"We can stop this war," she told the women. "We have
the power to do it, and it is our duty. Men can only take
life. We are the life-givers."

2.

Christmas brought relief from a week of powdery snow,
whipped into high drifts by the cutting winds out of
Canada. Nancy helped Cat to decorate a young fir with
strings of popcorn and gold-paper stars.

After the roast had been served, Billy and the Butler
boys boomed out the chorus of ballads and drinking
songs from the old country, while Denis Rahilly picked
out the tunes on the harp that had been placed in a snug
corner close to the fire.

The smoke from the hearth, compounded by their
pipes, pained Cat's eyes. She needed air. It was so dry in
the house that when she rubbed silk and linen together,
there was a stream of electric fire.

She put on her calf-high, fur-lined moccasins and
called Favour. Men rolling firewood down the hill had
flattened the snow, making a path she followed with the
wolfhound.

It was colder up there, but she had grown accustomed
to the extremes of temperature in this country.

The wolfhound wallowed away into the drifts, to make
his own outhouse. She lost sight of him for a moment,
then heard his low growl of warning. She followed his
tracks for a few paces, then froze at the sight of a tall,
bundled figure working his way around the slope of the
hill. From that angle, he would be invisible to the soldier
at the wooden sentry-post, assuming the soldier was not
already drunk.

The stories of scalping and burning at Saratoga returned to her. Billy had assembled his household and
told all of them they must take special care, because now
the French had brought war into Mohawk country, the
home of the nephew of Captain Warren—who had

inflicted so great a defeat on them at Louisbourg—
would be a special target.

The Indians make total war, Billy had reminded them.
They make no exemption for women and children.

Cat knew this to be true. She had lived it.

Terrified for her children, she waded back toward the
trail, whistling softly for the dog.

The pressure of many feet had made ice slicks in the
flattened snow. In her haste, she skidded on one of them,
lost her footing, and began rolling down the hill.

To break her fall, she tried to shoulder herself toward
the left, into a cushioning drift.

She drove into deeper snow, but her body weight, and
the steep declivity of the hill, kept her rolling downward.

It was not an unpleasant sensation at first, like bouncing around inside a feather mattress.

Then she jounced off something angular and slammed
down into a drift as deep as the house was tall. The snow
closed over her head. She was blinded, gasping for
breath. She felt she was drowning.

She worked her arms, trying to recover the sky. With
each motion, she sank deeper. The snow was inside her
clothes, turning to ice water against her skin. The more
she thrashed, the harder it was to breathe.

She felt she was being buried alive.

She thought, *Men from the house will come looking for
me. They will find my tracks. Favour will lead them.*

She remembered the dark, bundled stranger on the
hill.

If they come after me, they will walk into an ambush.

She tried to rest still, to steady her heart and conserve
what little air filtered through the canopy of snow above
her head.

She could hear no sounds from the world above her.
Only the boom of her own heart.

*It is like being in the womb. Is this what death is like?
Going back to the womb?*

There was a disturbance in the snow above her head.
A big hand, swathed in rags, clawed at her cover.

Prisoned in that cavity in the earth, she had nothing
with which to defend herself.

Her whole body shuddered.

She peered up, to see the face of her death.

A shiny black face, glistening with bearfat, peered down at her.

"Is that you, Miss Cat?"

□

The African half-led, half-carried her to the servants' house, where she told Juba to bring him what was left of the Christmas roast.

Ade said, "I came in case you had not heard."

He added vivid details to what she had learned of the slaughter at Saratoga. The French Indians had taken a hundred captives back to Canada with them. Ade had been able to save a settler's child, but he had lost everything—his forge, his tools, his smithy.

"Stay with us," Cat urged him. "I am sure Mister Johnson can find work for you."

"I'm going back," Ade told her. "It's a good life and a free one. The Indians won't kill a man my color unless he gives them a reason and a half. All I need is someone to stake me."

"I will speak to Mister Johnson," Cat promised. "We owe you more than we can repay."

4.

The attack on Saratoga had broken the rules. Whether the people of New York wanted war or not, war had come to them.

But, as Governor Clinton found, the masters of Manhattan were disinclined to pay for the defense of the frontier.

The alarm had traveled quickly downriver to the city. Cedar logs were hauled across from New Jersey to form a line of palisades across the island of Manhattan. Three log blockhouses were hammered together, portholed for cannon.

At Fort George, Governor Clinton's migraines worsened when he read a letter sent down by the Commissioners of Indian Affairs. They reported that a man could not walk a thousand paces outside the Albany stockade for fear of being skinned by skulking parties of French Indians. Young white men of military age were fleeing downriver for fear of being called up. The Commissioners had failed to carry out the Governor's orders to send out war-belts to the Six Nations, on the grounds that "We thought the sums demanded would be extravagant." And the bearer of this letter was filling his belly in the Governor's kitchen, demanding the extortionate fee of five pounds for carrying a message that was empty of intelligence, even of hope.

George Clinton was in a foul mood when he repaired to Todd's Tavern to dine with James DeLancey.

The Chief Justice kept him waiting. The Governor sought to restore his spirits with a quantity of Madeira that only set him to brooding over the insolence of the people he had been sent to rule. Both the Assembly and the private merchants of New York had refused to accept his bills of credit, telling him to his face that they did not trust His Majesty's Government to honor its obligations. Clinton had taken up his governorship in hopes of making an easy fortune; instead, he had been reduced to mortgaging his own assets to pay for the defense of his colony.

He told his secretary, John Catherwood, to summon the landlord and find out what was keeping Mr. DeLancey.

Robert Todd appeared, notably impaired by drink.

"Beg pardon, Your Excellency. Mister Justice DeLancey sent word he is detained on business."

"Business? This is intolerable! The fellow's house is next door!"

"Begging pardon, Your Grace." Todd leaned in confidentially, "I hear there's a wee drop of money in play at the coffee-house."

The Governor's face darkened.

"By God," he swore, "I shall teach this impudent fribble to attend to the King's business! Landlord, fetch me a case of this inferior Madeira before my head splits open!"

"Would that be a whole case you was wanting, Your Honor?"

"Are you deaf, you insolent loblolly?"

"No disrespect, sir, but was you planning to pay with ready money?"

The Governor stared until it seemed his eyes must burst from his head. "Do you—do you question *my* credit, you dog? By heaven, I'll see you flogged around Gallows Hill!"

Smooth John Catherwood intervened. He would deal with Landlord Todd while the Governor took his ease in the best room. Out of the Governor's hearing, he instructed Todd to charge the wine to the Chief Justice's reckoning.

"It would not surprise me if DeLancey put the villain up to it," the Governor remarked to his secretary after a bumper or two. "While he poses as a friend to my face, DeLancey moves the whole province to rebellion, until His Majesty's Governor and Captain-General cannot command the meanest publican."

The wine flowed again and brought Clinton's frustrations bubbling to the surface. The Chief Justice had proven his disloyalty in a conspicuous way that past week. The Governor had introduced to the Assembly a bill to invoke the full rigors of martial law to punish deserters from the New York regiments. For once—thanks to the support of the country members, alarmed by the murders along the frontier—the Assembly voted as the Governor wanted. Then DeLancey strangled the bill, in the Governor's own Council. The Chief Justice argued that martial law could not be applied to provincial militiamen. Naturally, Horsmanden and a majority of the Councillors backed him; they were his creatures. It seemed DeLancey would stop at nothing to deny the Governor the means to defend the province.

When the Chief Justice appeared in the doorway, with silken apologies and that false, insinuating smile, Governor Clinton was ready for him.

"Do you know, sir, that there are traitors in this province?" Clinton demanded.

"If Your Excellency gives me the names, I shall be glad to examine them myself."

"You may start by examining your own conscience."

"I know no man that loves his country better than I."

"You and the scrubs and fribbles who rule this damnable town love your country as well as a hog loves a feeding-trough. You will not defend the land that made you rich because you see no profit in it. You pay no more regard for our men who are butchered in the wilderness than for a sheep your neighbor kills for a picnic!"

When he raised his bumper, Clinton's hand shook so violently that he spilled half its contents over his neckcloth and flowered waistcoat.

James DeLancey raised an eyebrow at Catherwood.

"I find that His Excellency is unwell."

"So you would wish, sir!" Clinton erupted again. "You will not rid yourself of your master so easily!"

This fresh tirade was interrupted by a rap on the door. It was the landlord's daughter, curtseying low to show off a fine expanse of bosom. She had brought a letter for the Governor from upriver. The bearer would wait for a reply.

"I will attend to it." DeLancey put out his hand for the letter.

"As God is my witness," the Governor bore down on him, "I may be permitted to read my own correspondence."

"As you wish."

"From henceforth, I propose to maintain the dignity of my office. I was brought up in the principle of honor. You may depend on it, sir, I never promise but I fulfill my word."

The effect of this solemn speech was diminished by the Governor's appearance. As the ugly red stain spread down his front, his wig hung down over one ear.

The landlord's daughter, suspended in the doorway, broke into a titter of nervous laughter.

The Governor swore at her and threw the wine that was left in his glass. It splashed over that splendid bosom.

This was too much for the Chief Justice.

"I see, sir, that you are bent on turning the government of this province into low farce. You may do that without assistance from me."

"I am not finished with you, by God. I have not forgotten that you are a Frenchman's son and you bear a Frenchman's name."

DeLancey turned very pale. This was as good as calling him an agent of the enemy. John Catherwood struggled to mend the breach, but DeLancey ignored him.

"Do you dare to call me a traitor?" he challenged the Governor.

"I say that if you was a Frenchman, under orders from Canada, you could not have done more disservice to His Majesty's cause in this colony."

"But for the difference in our stations," James De-Lancey hissed, "I would demand satisfaction. But my word is as good as yours, sir, and you may rely on me for one thing. From hence forward, your life in this colony will be misery."

Wrapping his cloak about him, DeLancey swept out into the night.

5.

In the private account of this incident that Anne De-Lancey sent to Billy Johnson, she said that Governor Clinton realized his folly at once and sent Catherwood running after the Chief Justice to beg that their quarrel might be forgiven. Whether or not this was so, Billy read more into the rupture between the two most powerful men in the colony than either Anne's letter or the common gossip contained. He suspected that DeLancey had carefully fueled the Governor's jealousies and frustrations, counting on the inevitable explosion that would leave Clinton helpless and isolated, a figure for ridicule, while relieving the Chief Justice of any duty to help in a war he opposed. Clinton was too dull to govern by himself, too unpopular to win over the Assembly or enlist a chief minister as able as the one he had lost, too sickly in mind and body to sustain a long battle against his many enemies. No doubt James DeLancey calculated that, in a matter of months, the Governor would feel obliged to resign—leaving him to inherit the spoils.

Billy Johnson could picture the smirk of unguarded satisfaction that must have spread over DeLancey's face when Governor Clinton chose, as his new adviser, a man unlike the Chief Justice in everything but intellectual capacity. The Governor summoned Cadwallader Colden, the prickly, bookish, reclusive philosopher of Newburgh, to return to Manhattan from his retreat in the wilds. Johnson was one of the few men in the colony who liked Cadwallader Colden. He liked him for his imperial vision and his feeling for the Indians, qualities that were wholly lacking in most of the white men of the province. He liked him for his cantankerous readiness to say what he thought, in suitably pithy language, and damn the consequences. He knew what a sacrifice Colden was making in agreeing to place himself in the thick of the political fight in DeLancey's town. Colden hated the parlor games of Manhattan and the smiling deceits of vote-getting. He was far happier writing letters to Swedish botantists and testing Indian roots. Billy had recently sent him some pokeweed specimens; Colden determined that the root was an effective cure for skin cancers.

What was for Colden a sacrifice was, for Governor Clinton, a desperate gamble. The appearance of the pugnacious little Scotsman at his side could add nothing to the Governor's popularity; on the contrary, Cadwallader Colden's ability to make enemies was as notorious as DeLancey's ability to buy friends. Why had the Governor turned to Colden in his extremity? Billy Johnson thought he knew the answers. Colden believed fervently that the conflict that had begun in North America was not just a sideshow in King George's War, a matter of skulking ambushes and disputes over codfish, but the beginning of a vast war for empire that would be ended only with the decisive victory of the French or the English. He believed that this victory required a firm alliance with the Indians, which the responsible officials of the province were patently unable to deliver. He had apparently succeeded in communicating something of this to the Governor's fuddled mind. But shared ideas were not the whole explanation for Colden's rise to the unofficial rank of chief minister. The Governor had turned to him because there was no one else.

All of which made James DeLancey confident that his moment was at hand. Together, Clinton and Colden would succeed in digging their political graves. The success of their war policy depended on two things—money and the support of the Indians. Through his friends in the Assembly, DeLancey could deny them the first, and the Indians were not so blind as to make war on behalf of men who could neither pay them handsomely nor produce an army of their own. At the Albany coffee-house, jolly Oliver DeLancey proposed a wager: that Sailor George Clinton would give up and go home before the summer. The Chief Justice put down ten guineas of his own money.

But there was a flaw in James DeLancey's calculations. He had omitted Billy Johnson.

6.

Cat dreamed she was serving dinner to Billy and his guests. She reached over a man's shoulder to set down his plate and he looked up at her.

He began to change. His forehead bulged out over his eyes. Then the structure of his skull began to shift. She could see the bony plates moving under the skin.

She put his dish down and walked to the head of the table, where Billy had cleaned his plate and was gesturing for more. When she looked back at the man she had served, his skin had changed to a pale green. He had become a snake. There were curious breathing holes on his back. He ate without chewing, and his body swelled as large chunks of food moved down.

Nobody but Cat seemed to notice that there was anything odd about him.

□

In the morning, Lydius arrived at Mount Johnson. The long Dutchman inspected everything: the contents of Billy's warehouses, the swivel guns Captain Warren had sent for the defense of the stone house, the new slaves who were working the fields.

"Very fine, very fine," Cat heard him tell Billy. "But the French will serve you as they have served me unless we hit them soon, and hard. They left nothing but charred earth under my house. If they fancied me, you may be sure they fancy you, Mister Johnson. You are as close as they are likely to get to Admiral Warren, who stung them so bad at Louisbourg. And they know you are the man who saved Oswego from dropping into their lap like a rotten plum."

Lydius gave Cat a narrow look and steered his host into the privacy of the room Billy had turned into his office. Despite the books and prints from London, and the new cherrywood wainscot, it looked like a hunter's trophy room, hung with furs and animal skulls and native weapons. Johnson's household had long since outgrown this house, and Billy talked of building a bigger one. He had made rough sketches, drawing on his memories of his childhood home in Ireland. But such plans would have to wait on the fortunes of war.

Cat knew they were talking war now, behind the closed door.

More than ever, she distrusted Lydius, though her suspicions made her a little ashamed, since she had heard that his losses included a son.

He brings death with him.

She had known Lydius to be calculating and ambitious, reducing others—including herself—to pawns in his games. Now he was vengeful and desperate, which made him twice as dangerous.

He is the snake-man from my dream, and Billy does not see him as he is.

□

She did not know that Lydius had come upriver at Billy's request.

Johnson had received letters from Governor Clinton and Cadwallader Colden, asking him to use his personal influence to enlist the Six Nations for a full-scale campaign against the French. King George and his ministers had paid little attention to the plight of the American colonies, preoccupied with land wars that threatened the House of Hanover's hereditary possessions in Germany, and above all by an uprising in Scotland led by the Young Pretender. Now the Duke of Cumberland had demonstrated the superiority of English field guns over dirks and claymores on the bloody field of Culloden, the ministry had looked more closely at the correspondence from Boston and New York and had formed the conclusion that the proper response to French depredations along the frontier was the conquest of Canada. Governor Clinton had been ordered to raise an army of volunteers and Indians to invade New France and drive its present owners into the sea. But where was Clinton to turn for bold lieutenants in his unruly province? Not to the Albany Commissioners, who had proved their worth at his Indian council the year before. William Johnson's name had been canvassed by many: by Colden, usually stinting in his praises; by Captain Rutherford, the commandant at Albany; by the illustrious Admiral Warren, one of the few heroes the war in America had thus far produced; even by the Governor's wife, who had heard some rare stories from her new servant, Jane Watson, until lately employed at Mount Johnson. William Johnson was young and he was Irish, but young men prosper in wartime and the Governor was assured that the nephew of Admiral Warren must be the *right sort* of Irishman. "He dresses up like an Indian and knows their customs as if born to them," said Mr. Colden. If the Governor still had qualms, they were solaced by the fact that this Johnson was agreed to be a bottle-man of rare stamina and had crossed swords more than once with Clinton's *bête noire,* James DeLancey.

The Governor had dropped hints to Billy—reinforced in more personal missives from Colden—that if he succeeded in persuading the Six Nations to raise the hatchet, great things awaited him.

"You know what this could mean, don't you?" Lydius answered his own questions. "We can depose the Albany Ring. If we can get the Indians to fight for us, the Governor must agree to put the management of our Indian affairs in the hands of men who can deliver. A new regime, Mister Johnson! You could make yourself sole Commissioner, or Superintendent. Write your own job description. Think what it would mean! Three-quarters of the business of this province is with Indians. We could make it law that no trade would be allowed, no land transferred, without your approval. It is a ticket to a fortune greater than the princelings of New York have ever dreamed of."

"You are modest in speaking only of me, Mister Lydius. How do you see your own place in this—new order?"

"As your friend and adviser. I am glad to leave the decorations for them of higher regard. Perhaps you would see fit to name me your deputy."

Billy sat watchful, and Lydius added quickly, "I have made more enemies in this province than you have had opportunity to make as yet. There is no need to encumber our project with all of their grudges."

"It is only a pipe dream unless we can raise the Indians."

"Listen to me." Lydius pulled up his chair, dropping his voice to a whisper. "You need only give a good feast—the Indians will never refuse a party—and put on a good show at Albany. We won't bring the high sachems of the Six Nations around all at once, anyways not without a redcoat army to show them. But that will not count. Indians do not fight because men in high places tell them to fight. Any of their warchiefs—even the greenest warrior—can raise his own army if he can persuade others to follow him, and they will do this for the meanest or highest of motives. I have Shirley's money, for those that will take it, on top of whatever you can get from Clinton."

"Their women are opposed to this war. I have come to respect their power among this people. There is one of the clanmothers—Island Woman—who is most firmly against us. I think I would rather face Hendrick or Snowbird, man to man, than that one."

"You confess there is at least one woman you cannot charm?" Lydius gave his lopsided grin. "I see there are arts you have yet to learn."

Lydius rummaged in his pouch and brought out a scalp, dyed red and stretched on a hoop. The hair had once been a silky, soft brown.

"You must appeal to their hungry ghosts," Lydius told him. "Island Woman lost a husband to scalpers out of Canada. Give this to her in public council, to replace him. If I know Indians, it will silence her mutterings, at least for a time."

7.

"Mama!" Nancy buried her face in her mother's belly, under the sheet, as another explosion rocked the house. It sounded as if the whole china cabinet in the kitchen had come down. The baby kicked and screamed. Cat put her to suck at her breast, though her nipples were sore and her milk no longer flowed freely.

Nancy quivered against Cat's body, which had thickened with childbearing and farm labor. The child's heart flapped like a bird in an attic. She moaned, "Where's my Daddy?"

With her free hand, Cat checked the priming of the pistol on the window ledge and prayed for Billy to come. She had seen him dancing and drinking among the Indian campfires long after midnight, greased and stripped to a breechcloth like one of the Burned Knives.

She snatched up the pistol, trying to hold the long barrel steady, as darkness clotted beyond the doorway.

"It's me, Miz Catherine."

It was Juba, wide-hipped and generous as the earth itself. The slave was armed with a broom handle and the string of cowries she only wore on special days. "There's mending to be done in the kitchen. But nobody's hurt but a chief whose woman bit a piece off of his ear. An' Massa's coming right now."

Johnson ran up the stairs so lightly, in moccasins like a second skin, they did not hear him until he brushed past Juba and caught his children up in his arms. His smile put their fears to flight, though he looked as wild—and smelled as feral, Cat noticed—as any of his native guests who had trampled Cat's flower beds and kitchen gardens to mud. Over his bare chest, slick with sweat and clarified bear grease, he was wearing a savage thing, a circlet of teeth and claws, set with a curious blue stone.

Billy crooned a lullaby to the baby, then handed her to Juba. Cat spoke quickly to Nancy and little John, telling them to go with their nanny. She would check on them later.

"I cannot tarry long," Johnson said, when they were alone. "Or the Indians will seek me out here. Every one of them, drunk or sober, has a thousand things to tell me. I swear, to be master of this people one must be the most abject slave upon this earth."

"Lie with me, Billy."

His eyes moved swiftly from her face to the door. He'd been with one of their women, she could always tell. She did not allow that Johnson's Indian girls were competition, not as long as he kept them outside the house. They troubled her less than his Irish redheads—Molly Finn was the latest she suspected—and the fancy ladies at Albany and New York who imagined themselves his equals and dreamed of luring him into wedlock. Cat denied herself the right to be jealous. Jealousy was not appropriate to her station, and it was not a practical emotion. Can you ask the leopard to change his spots?

"I want to please you, Billy." There it was. It was the only claim she could make on him, except as the mother of the only children he acknowledged as his own.

"Oh, Cat. If you knew how much you have pleased me—"

"Then lie with me."

She had to coax him for a time. But when he entered her, he came with such primal force she had to grit her teeth to avoid screaming her lungs out. His eyes, close to hers, were those of a raptor. He fed on her neck, her breasts. A violent pleasure surged through her blood and set her nerves thrumming. Through his hot breathing sounds older than speech rumbled from the pit of his belly, and she screamed despite herself.

Later, she said, "You are not the man I knew. I do not know whether he is alive or dead. I could never be his wife. Yet you make me feel as his widow."

"I am not the same," Johnson agreed. He smoothed back her hair, with a tenderness he had denied her in their mating. But his gentleness was abstracted, not a thing she could hold to.

"I think you belong to *them* more than us." The frost in her voice made it unnecessary to specify whom she meant.

"I belong to no one. I belong to a destiny."

The quiet confidence with which he said this made the word more terrible. She could forget the other women, even when he returned to her with the smell of their sex in his hair. She could ignore the gossip of her white neighbors, even the contempt of the Anglican minister. But it was hard to live with a destiny. All she knew of it for certain was it would break her and crush her bones like an ox cart if she stood in its way.

He kissed the palm of her hand. "You are the mistress of my house. You are the mother of my children. I shall always cherish you. You will always have of me what I can give."

With tears welling up in her eyes, she had said, "Then will you please keep your savages out of this house?"

His eyes turned cold. For a moment, he lost his lips. "I will not have that word used in my house. Savages, we call them, because their customs are not our own. A Frenchman said that. I wish I could teach this wisdom to our people, who despise the Indians when they do not fear them."

"They are wrecking this house," Cat protested. "They terrify your own children. Think of Nancy and John, if not of me."

"I will see to the guard," Johnson said curtly. "But I cannot risk offense to my brothers of the Six Nations. We have business to do that is a deal more important than breaking dishes. If I fail, Cat, there will be no place for us here—no, nor even for the bewigged traitors at Albany who are selling guns and powder to the French Indians in exchange for the scalps and the silver of our countrymen on the borders of New England."

He wound his breechcloth around his nether parts and added a silver gorget to the jewelry around his neck.

"What is that?" Cat pointed at the circlet of teeth and claws.

"War magic." Johnson laughed. "The Indians go into battle in the company of their gods and hungry ghosts, like the heroes of Homer. To lead them on the warpath, one must heed the same voices."

□

After daybreak, Cat took inventory of the destruction in the kitchen. Her best delftware plates were broken or missing, and a pane of Crown glass, imported from London, was missing from the window, along with a silver salver and a new brass kettle. Through the window frame, between the house and the creek, she saw Mohawks setting a pyramid of logs to burn in the midst of the lawn she had picked clean of rocks and dandelions until her back ached.

Juba mopped up after the baby, who had an upset stomach, and made tea.

"Won't help none worrying about the mess," was her wisdom. "I reckon Colonel Johnson won't have no trouble putting it right, not with him being commissary and all." She noticed the way Cat's mouth set hard as she stared at the native women squatting under an elmbark shelter. "When they's gone," Juba added, "we still be here. We'll tidy up good."

"Oh, Juba." Cat let the tears come when she saw Billy

approaching the fire. His hair sprouted eagle feathers. A
bearskin, lined with scarlet silk, trailed from his bare
shoulder. He had striped his face with charcoal and
vermilion. He gripped a throwing hatchet, daubed with
red, in his right fist. The figure of a red hatchet was also
painted on the long belt of black wampum he held up in
his left hand, the hand—the Iroquois said—that is
closest to the heart.

The Indians gathered into a ragged circle around the
fire. A hush fell as Johnson stepped into their midst.
Then a voice rose in the sharp, barking cry of a war
eagle. *Kya-kyaaa-kyaagh!* Under it came the pounding,
hypnotic rhythm of the water-drums.

The teacup shook in Cat's hand. She said to the slave,
"I don't think they'll ever go away."

□

The Mohawk women sat over toward the east, knees
folded against their flanks. Colonel Johnson saw some of
the girls smiling at him, in his Indian garb. He spotted
Bright Meadow, fetching in her short skirt of white
doeskin and a blouse of midnight blue, hung with silver moons and stars. She affected not to notice him. She
had always disapproved of him, and now she had a
husband—White Owl, already the warchief of the Bear
Clan.

Johnson was glad to see Island Woman, sitting with
other clanmothers. The presence of the Namegivers gave
this assembly the solemnity he intended. But their stares
made him nervous too. What would happen today was
in the gift of these women. With rum and presents, and
Hendrick's help, he could buy the services of Burned
Knives—young men eager to prove themselves, warriors
who killed for sport. Rum and presents spoke louder
than the *rotiyaner,* the traditional chiefs of the Confederacy. Their voices were fading.

But if he were to succeed in inducing the Flint
People—let alone their sister nations—to take up the
hatchet, Johnson must have the approval of the women.
It was a thing that was difficult to explain to outsiders.

George Clinton had stared in blank incomprehension when Billy had attempted to describe the power of women in this people of warriors.

Johnson's eyes ranged over the faces of the Mohawk women, olive and ginger, ivory and soft gold. He had loved the young ones and flattered the old, but he could not predict how they would act when he lifted up the war-song.

He had undertaken an impossible mission. That was what his neighbors whispered, and what the Van Frogs and merchant-smugglers said openly at Albany and New York, where they were already toasting his ruin. Runners had brought word from the Grand Council at Onondaga that the policy of the Confederacy was unshaken: the Six Nations must all stand neutral in the war between Britain and France. The party Billy was staging at Mount Johnson was an incitement to the Mohawks to break with their sister-nations and risk their lives and their independence for him. He was asking them to do something they had refused to do for white men with grander titles.

Island Woman met his gaze. *Wolf woman,* he thought. Fierce and sinewy, a grandmother still capable—he guessed—of taking a man she fancied away from a younger rival. Of all of them, she was the most difficult to know. Of them all, she was the one he needed most.

To the music of drum and fife, Lieutenant Burrows marched up the road with a file of fusiliers from the fort. He looked suitably martial in his red coat, brandishing his hanger, though the state of his soldiers' smallclothes would have disgusted a drill sergeant.

Burrows came smartly to attention in front of Billy and affected to hold his nose. The hazy June sun was beginning to work on the beargrease and pot blacking with which Johnson had slathered himself.

"Whew!" The Lieutenant grinned at Johnson. Billy was not yet a colonel in the eyes of the military. "I'm damn glad you didn't ask me to dress up. You smell as if you were left hanging for three weeks. What do you want us to do?"

"Just pretend you're the Duke of Cumberland with four regiments of foot guards. I have promised them an army."

Burrows whistled. "Better you than me, Billy. I hear they are a rough sort when they are disobliged."

The soldiers formed a line in the shade of the house, and Johnson opened the proceedings by calling for Paddy Groghan. His overseer appeared in a kilt and wound a spiral course among the Mohawks, playing the bagpipes. Their weird, high skirl, which had made the blood of clansmen pump faster in numberless ancient battles, caught the pulse of this audience. Hendrick cried out, delighted, "Macbeth! Macbeth!" while the younger warriors grunted and cawed their approval.

"One tribe of savages greets another," muttered the English officer. He started to repeat this *bon mot* for the benefit of Johnson's bookkeeper, who was idling nearby, but stayed himself with the reflection that the clerk was a Dublin man.

Johnson stood north of the fire, broad as a white oak, stroking the war belt as he began his speech. His command of Mohawk was now almost faultless. In a lilting cadence, gathering strength and depth, he recited the three rare words of condolence, as was required at the start of all Indian councils.

"I wipe from your eyes the tears you have shed for your departed kinsmen, so you may see clearly. I open your ears, so you may hear the truth. I clear the passage from your hearts to your mouths, so you may speak from the heart and not only from the lips, as false men do."

He added his own spin to the familar formulas. Windweaver nudged Island Woman. *"Rateriwatsienni.* This one flowers it up."

As Johnson spoke, Island Woman realized the man she had dubbed Forest Killer was speaking, very directly, to *her.* He spoke of her husband Blackbuck, scalped by French Indians many winters before. Like a Mohawk, Forest Killer avoided calling the dead by their Long-house names; the dead are always listening. But he was calling up their hungry ghosts.

Now he walked toward the clanmother with a hoop of

young willow in his hand. The scalp stretched within it was painted red, but the hair hung down, black and straight as a horse's tail.

"Grandmother," he addressed Island Woman, "I give you this spirit-head to replace those of your family who have gone the long trail. If the Creator wills it, I will soon bring you captives to requicken their names."

After these words, the silence in the assembly grew very deep. Slowly, Island Woman reached to receive the scalp from Johnson's hands. An ululating shriek rose from many mouths.

I came to oppose you, the clanmother spoke to Johnson in her mind. *I will not be tricked by you. I will not allow you to invoke the spirits of my family. What is a scalp to a white man? A strip of skin and hair, signifying nothing. What does a white man know of other worlds?*

"Aksotha," this white man said to her, in the lilting voice of a chief of the Real People, "I give you this life."

She accepted the thing he offered. Johnson's face, as he leaned over her, was half in light, half darkened. He swallowed her sun.

The Mohawks chanted their approval.

When the white man smiled and moved away, Island Woman saw elation in some of the women's faces. She wanted to smack them.

This white man had the gift of the elk-dreamer, the love power. All the women sensed it, regardless of age. He made them shift about and fiddle with their hair. Island Woman felt it herself.

But this was not the shadow that pressed down on her heart. For a moment, when he blocked the sun, she had seen a face from her dreaming.

She tried to shake off these thoughts. *He is only another newcomer, seeking to use us. He has studied our customs to invoke them against us. We must resist him.*

□

Johnson spoke to the Mohawks of a great army that their elder brother, King George, was sending across the ocean. He promised them riches on earth, and better than this, souls to replace all their dead, if they would join the English in a triumphal march on Montreal. He would walk with them. They would be one mind, one heart.

"Brothers, I know very well that the Real People are not as the Sunrise People, or the Axe-Makers we call the French. The white people, English and French, have each a master. When the King their master decrees war or peace, his subjects must obey. I know it is not so with you, because among the Real People each man is his own master and must choose as a man. I know also that war is for you a more serious matter than for white people, because it cannot be ended by a treaty on paper, but must be waged for as long as the spirits of your departed warriors demand vengeance.

"I know you have said harsh things about the English, that they love only your land, that if you join them on the warpath they will abandon you to be destroyed by the French. Brothers, I know that in the past these things were true. But the King has promised to drive the rattlesnakes from your land, and to feed and clothe your families while the warriors are on the trail, and to strengthen your castles so that no Frenchmen will dare to approach them. This promise comes from the heart.

"Brothers—" he swept the earth before him with a white wing "—I carry these words from your elder brother the King. Yet I speak to you as one of your own, as Forest Killer of the Bear Clan. I have run with you and danced with you. I have entered your dreaming. Our lives are joined, for I will never leave you."

The Mohawks had heard many promises from white men before, and they had seen how these promises were kept. Promises from the Governor left them unmoved. What stirred them was the messenger.

The kettles were brought, with steaming chunks of beef and venison, and placed among the rows of warriors.

A low howl rose quickly, gathering strength. Hendrick was singing his war-song. His pounding feet made thunder in the earth.

Now Johnson's voice rose in a high, wordless call that skidded down like the angry cry of a redtail hawk. He joined Hendrick in a furious circle dance. They wheeled and lunged and stamped, evoking battles on land and in the air.

Johnson swerved toward the warpost planted to the east of the fire. He whirled the hatchet above his head and drove it deep into the wood. Hendrick screamed and slammed his warclub against the post.

A weird, whining chorus saluted them.

Some of the women started chanting.

"The eyes of your grandfathers are upon you!"

"Did we bring forth only girls in petticoats?" the Bear Clanmother mocked the young men who remained in their places.

One by one warriors rose to join the dance, bragging of their past exploits, miming the deaths they intended for their enemies.

The monotonous thud of the water-drums, the repetitive syllables of the *HaiHai*, the gloating cries of the women, the slashing arc of hatchets and warclubs, were building a blood-frenzy.

Knowing its power, Island Woman sat still, her mouth set hard, willing her family to avoid this lure. But White Owl rose to join the dance, and even Bright Meadow was chanting. Island Woman glared at Snowbird, silently commanding him to stay in his place. But her son had plucked his hair to a narrow ridge. He was already half-crazy. He loped into the circle.

Hendrick Forked Paths left the dance.

When he returned, he was staggering under the weight of the thing he was gripping by the horns.

Cat saw it from the parlor window and ordered her children not to look. Hendrick was swinging the head of the five-year ox Billy had slaughtered for the feast.

"This is the head of our enemy!" Hendrick yelled. "From this day forward, we swear to drink only his blood!"

He offered the ox head to Billy Johnson, who seized it by the horns and raised it on high.

"Forest Killer will lead us on the warpath!" Hendrick roared. "He is a bearwalker! His steps will make thunder in the earth!"

He fastened a collar of black wampum around Johnson's neck.

Billy danced heavily among the rows of Mohawks, slowed by the weight of the head in his hands. The fever gripped all of them. Snowbird screamed, swinging his killing club in a murderous arc.

When she saw the grayish shades of the hungry ghosts dancing with the living, Island Woman recognized that she was defeated.

I cannot fight Forest Killer here, among the burned bones of our hungry dead. Does the white man see them too? Does he know what he has called among us?

She slipped silently from the gathering. With some hesitation, Windweaver and Bright Meadow followed her.

"Forest Killer has cast a net over us all," she told them. "If we do not stop him, he will make empty beds in our lodges."

Windweaver shook her head. Her husband, Sun Walker, had joined the wardance.

"Forest Killer's power is strong. Your own son is with him. And Bright Meadow's husband. You yourself took the spirit-head from his hands."

The *orenda*—the soul energy—of this newcomer was powerful, Island Woman acknowledged. It was greater than that of the Sunrise People who had come to the Valley before him.

But where did it come from? Did it come from the Dark One? Where would it lead?

CHAPTER 22
THE OLIVE OF LYDIUS

1.

Island Woman called the women of power to the Cave of the Dreamers. They came from all the lands of the Six Nations. Some were gray and bent with age, their faces creased and cracked like withered apples. Some came in the shining flower of their youth. Some were clan-mothers or ancients; Blueberry Song, who came from Onondaga, had counted more than a hundred winters. Some had yet to take a husband. They were joined in the powers of dreaming and healing. And in their self-offering, to the life of the people and the spirit.

They formed their circle around the fire. When the fire grew friendly, they washed their joined hands in its flames, without pain or burning. They brushed away any evil thoughts that may have traveled with them with the smoke of sage and sweetgrass and the real tobacco.

They whistled and sang for their spirit guides, to the rhythms of the water-drums, pulsing in the many-vaulted chamber like the heartbeat of the world. When Island Woman found the face of the dream-prophet in the smoke, and saw the fire in his eyes, she was ready to speak.

"I am a hollow bone," she told them. "Only that

which is empty may be filled. All I can tell you that is true is the gift of the great ones who speak through me.

"We are the burden straps. We carry the lives of our people on our backs. The heartbeats of our grandchildren's grandchildren move with our blood.

"Our great tree of peace is shaking. It is bleeding from the roots. Its leaves are dying from the top downward. This has happened because the newcomers have come to us with soft lies and promises that are worse than lies. They tempt our warriors with glory in battle. They promise us things we never needed before they came and cannot make for ourselves. Among the Real People, there are those who say we must do as the newcomers say because they are stronger and cleverer than us. There are even those who say that the newcomers are the favorites of our Creator, because they make guns and floating castles.

"Those among us who talk this way have lost their memories. We must teach them to *remember*. All true knowing comes through remembering. It comes from the Real World, where nothing in the experience of the soul is lost. It comes from the compassion of our teachers, who are always seeking to call us back to what we are.

"Our great dream-prophet is with me now, to help us remember.

"He speaks to us from the Earth-in-the-Sky, which is as distant from this world as the edge of the maple leaf.

"The Earth-in-the-Sky came close to dying, because of the endless fighting between the Forest People and the Sea People. The Sea People were cleverer than the newcomers. They built ships that could move without wind or paddles. They made metal birds that could fly to the stars. They made poisons that could kill everything that breathes. They had machines that could do the work of men, and move and think faster. The Forest People, who lived closer to the earth, learned their tricks, but they paid for their learning by killing the trees and the animals. Then the sun came low over the earth, a fireball that scorched all the land, so nothing would grow. The waters died from the foul spillage from the towering cities men built, in their pride, to touch the sky. Tiring of the violence and greed of men, the earth turned against its users. It shook them from its back. The towering cities dropped into great cracks that opened in the ground, or were drowned by the fury of oceans and mountains of fire.

"In this way, the people returned to wisdom. They began to remember. They left their wars and their cities. They lived simply again, in the old way, in houses of bark and clay. They sat together around common fires. They gave up their machines. When they remembered how to dream, they discovered that they could travel anywhere in the universe, or bring anything to them, by the power of thought.

"Our dream-prophet wishes us to keep these things in the front of our minds, so we will not be deceived by the newcomers. They have tools we must borrow from them, now they have changed our ways and our desires. But we know the things they have forgotten, to which all of us must return. Or else the bubble in which we breathe will burst and the Mother will shake us from her back."

She paused, stirring the embers with the butt of her fire-hardened stick.

Bright Meadow was the first to venture to break her mother's silence.

"How can we tell these things to the newcomers?"

"We cannot tell them." Island Woman's tone was severe. "These are things that must be held secret, in our hearts. If they are shared with those who are not ready, their power is weakened. The stories that tell our lives lie in wait, like crouching panthers, for those who will know them for what they are."

Windweaver, sitting with her knees folded to one side, straightened her back against the cave wall, alive with the shaman's dream-paintings.

"You give us back our memory," Windweaver said with respect, "and we are glad. But some of us saw you take the spirit-head from the hands of Forest Killer, who seeks to send our warriors against our kinsfolk."

Island Woman nodded, acknowledging that the challenge was just.

She removed the scalp Johnson had given her from her otterskin pouch.

"I took you, from a white man who sees only skin and hair, to deliver you. So you may return to your nation with the words of the women of the Real People." She spoke in the lilting voice of power. Her words were song more than speech.

With slow, ritual movements, she walked counter-clockwise around the circle, showing the dyed scalp to each of the women. Then she cast it into the fire.

The silence of the women became deeper, almost audible, as the stretched skin crackled on the hot coals.

They saw him rise, in the folds of the smoke. Some of them knew him, from the gunpowder tattoos on his chest and over his cheekbones, and the scarred hollow below the bridge of his nose. He was a Caughnawaga who had once lived among the Mohawk.

He was lost and confused, wary of enemies.

Island Woman thought, *He does not even know he is dead. He is hungry for vengeance against those who struck him down in his prime.*

She spoke to the ghost warrior with her mind. *You will go among your own people. You will tell them in dreams that the Real People do not want to make war on their own people. I will come for you, to help you find your kinsmen on the other side. You will walk the path of strawberries with pride, because you died like a man.*

2.

Governor Clinton was ferried by dugout canoe from the Albany sloop to a sodden bog shaded by water beeches, below the traders' warehouses. The boatmen laughed to see him sink up to the knee in his fine silk stockings. The Governor cursed the town and all who were in it.

Only one member of his Council—Mr. Colden—had deigned to accompany him up the river. James De-Lancey had excused himself, on the grounds that the affairs of New York could not be conducted without him. Daniel Horsmanden had demanded an outrageous fee for his services, which the Governor declined to pay.

Neither man troubled to conceal his real meaning, which was that the Governor could go hang himself.

They might very well see their wish fulfilled, the Governor thought.

Clinton found Albany empty of Indians and sickly with smallpox. The Commissioners waited upon him and informed him that the Six Nations were not disposed to take up the hatchet.

Clinton demanded to know what William Johnson had accomplished.

"Johnson is only a sharper and a squaw man," Secretary Livingston said. "His only influence flows from rum. The natives who drink his liquor know they are under no obligation to keep any pledges made, because the man is merely a low trader, with no official position."

Clinton's headaches returned, and he took to his bed.

When Colonel Stoddard arrived, with the delegates from Massachusetts, there was still no sign of the Indian army Clinton had engaged Billy Johnson to deliver. Tossing in his bed, wasted by a slow nervous fever, the Governor told Colden that if he failed this time at Albany, he would leave the colonies forever.

He had wasted more than a fortnight in the town when a rider on a steaming horse brought terrifying news. Less than four miles north of the city, French Indians had ambushed a party of twenty-four whites. Nine men were killed and scalped; another lay on his deathbed.

Captain Rutherford beat the alarm and militia parties were sent out in pursuit of the raiders. They returned at nightfall, protesting that, without Indian scouts, they were in danger of falling victim to a second ambush.

At the Hudson landings, panicky townsmen threatened and cajoled the captains of the sloops, desperate to escape downriver. Nervous of losing his own return passage to York, the Governor sent soldiers from the fort to commandeer one of the flat-bottomed boats. This earned him the contempt of the Massachusetts men and of Captain Rutherford, who remarked to Stoddard, "The cardinal thing, in a time of danger, is never to look as if we are about to jump into a ditch."

Broken in mind and spirit, the Governor announced to Colden, "It is hopeless." He ordered his body-servant to prepare his trunks for the voyage downriver, resolved to abandon Albany—and the colony—to the fate its inhabitants had made for themselves.

□

The morning brought new alarms.

"The Indians are coming!" cried a lookout on the wall of Fort Frederick.

The town jangled again to cowbells as the burghers rushed to bring their cattle in from the pastures outside the stockade. Old Widow Veeder stood on the porch of her house, blunderbuss in hand, shouting, "I'll not give up what I have earned! Not if there's not one man left to defend me from *de wilde!*"

Alarmed by the noise, Governor Clinton struggled into his top boots and climbed up into the blockhouse in the north-west corner of the fort. It was a damnably weak position, he reminded himself, squinting out through a gunport. The engineers who built the fort on the downward slope of the hill, where any attacker from the landward side could fire down on the defenders, ought to be drawn and quartered.

He saw a column of painted savages, brandishing firelocks and hatchets, trooping across the pine barrens.

A nervous gunner crouched over his four-pounder, at the Governor's left hand, his fuse already lit.

The Indians whooped and howled.

"Wait, you damn fool!" Clinton clutched at the gunner's arm. "By God—" he peered more closely at the big savage with the circlet of bear claws who led the advancing party. "By God," he blasphemed again, "that's Billy Johnson."

□

As Johnson and the Mohawks filed through the north gate of the stockade, each man fired his fusil into the ground. Captain Rutherford answered their salute with the cannon of the fort.

For the first time, Albany received Billy Johnson with open arms. Smiling Dutch girls ran out into the street in their short petticoats and bright-colored hose to offer cookies and to crown his warriors with garlands of swamp apple and wild azaleas. Even Cornelius Cuyler and Myndert Schuyler, jealous champions of the exclusive rights of the Commissioners to treat with savages, offered their congratulations.

But it became plain, as a larger procession of Indians —Oneidas and Onondagas, Cayugas, Senecas and Tuscaroras—followed the Mohawks into the town, that Johnson's success was partial at best. These Indians from the farther nations of the Longhouse were not dressed for war. While the Mohawks had marched along the King's Road from Mount Johnson, along the north shore of the river, their allies had followed the south road, to dramatize the fact that they were not in agreement with the war policy.

The Governor took counsel in private with Johnson and Hendrick. They told him that it would be necessary to court the chiefs of the other nations in "little bunches" and to offer them powerful inducements to join the war.

When the Governor asked what these inducements would entail, Johnson produced a shopping list: bags of silver, casks of vermilion, barrels of powder, storehouses of calicos, strouds and calimancoes.

Clinton's headaches laid siege to him again. He protested the lack of money, the stubborn opposition of James DeLancey and the Steering Committee he controlled at New York.

"I will assemble the goods," Johnson promised, "if Your Excellency will sign the notes of credit. In this extremity, the traders cannot refuse us."

The Governor groaned. "I am already in debt above my eyebrows." Forgetting Hendrick's presence, he added, "Are your savages worth this infernal expense?"

Calmly, Johnson reminded him that to ask the Indians to leave their families and take the warpath was to deprive them of their hunting seasons, and their chances of turning a profit in the fur trade.

"As to your debts," Billy continued. "If you have swallowed a cow, it would be strange to stick at the hind leg. Since His Majesty commands us to make this war, he cannot refuse to pay for the expense."

The war was in him.

3.

The man the Six Nations called The Word came with the last party of Indians to reach Albany. He came from Onondaga, the place of the Firekeepers. He was the Speaker of the Confederacy. Island Woman traveled with him, together with the clanmothers of other nations. He had promised to remind the Mohawk of the law of the Peacemaker.

For many winters past, both the French and the English had sent spies and couriers to his green valley among dreaming hills. They had sent killers to take his life, when he had shown that he could neither be bought nor frightened. His heart was not for trade. It belonged to the Real People.

Island Woman had placed her trust in him and in Aaron Black Oak, Windweaver's son, whom they had sent to talk secretly with the Caughnawagas.

Now The Word sat listening to the voice of the crabbed little white man the Governor—still nervous of a second humiliation at Albany—had delegated to read his speech. The Onondaga's eyes slid over the soft, sly faces of the Albany Commissioners to the strong face of the vigorous newcomer the Mohawk called Forest Killer.

Johnson met his gaze.

They measured each other like bull elks, who will lower horns only when neither gives way.

There was no animosity, only this mutual appraisal of strength.

When the Word's turn came to respond to the Governor's martial proposals, he spoke with oriental courtesy —and evasion.

He drew the interpreters and, through them, his white audience, into impenetrable thickets, fogged by native metaphors.

The Governor demanded a clear answer. He showed his native guests the mountain of presents he had assembled for them. Would they now take up the hatchet against the French?

The Word retired for the night to consider his response.

In the morning, he said, "Hitherto we have made no use of the hatchet. But as our brothers now call on us we are ready to use it against the French and their children."

Governor Clinton seized on these polite words as a clear commitment to raise an Indian army to go against Canada, and wrote letters to London saluting a signal triumph. He did not omit Johnson's reward. To the discomfiture of the Albany establishment, the young Irishman was now appointed Colonel of the Six Nations.

□

"You are a chief without Indians," one-eyed Lydius told Billy weeks later, when only a few Mohawks had presented themselves to make war on the French—and only on condition that their duties were confined to daytime scouts.

"The women and the grayhairs have outmaneuvered you," Lydius went on.

Island Woman's envoy had returned from Montreal with an invitation from the French Governor to the Mohawks, to sit in council with him as they had sat with Clinton. He had promised them better food and company, and a friendship that would lay no claims on their lands or their blood allegiances.

The Mohawk elders, urged on by Island Woman and the women's council, had agreed to send peace ambassadors to Canada.

It was a stunning reverse for English policy—and for Billy Johnson's ambitions. His show at Albany was now revealed as cardboard and fustian.

But Lydius told him, "I have a notion how we can turn this about. I will invite Hendrick and a few of our old reliables for a drink at my house. I believe we can send the French an olive branch they will always remember."

4.

Lydius' house stood gable-end to the traffic; the roof was stepped and slated with Holland tiles. The gutterspout ran out over the cobbles.

The night Billy and the Mohawks convened in his parlor, the air about the house was sickly-sweet with the cloying odors from Evert Wendell's chocolate factory. The tinkle of cowbells sounded as Dutch girls in bright woolen hose led their heifers back from the pastures to spend the night in front of their masters' houses.

Hendrick Forked Paths cast a huge shadow against the wall of Lydius' parlor. Warmed by grog, the Mohawk warchief talked faster than his custom, swinging his arms. He was part-drunk and wholly frightened. He explained to Lydius and Johnson that he could not fulfill their agreements.

"The voice of our women is too strong. They say that a body should not fight, one limb against another. And the Caughnawagas are our kin. So we must make peace with Onontio, who sits waiting for our ambassadors."

He did not tell the white men the rest of his fears. He had received a terrible visitor in the night, a thing with a skull for a face and swarming fires in the sockets. This thing had squatted on his chest, squeezing out the air. It had warned him that if he broke the Great Law, his soul would be wrenched from his body and confined in a place of torment, far from the happy lands of his ancestors.

He believed that this ghostly visitor had been sent by Island Woman. It was known to all that the clanmother's daughter was a witch; Island Woman was presumed to have the same power to harm, as well as heal, though she used it more judiciously.

Forked Paths was scared of nothing in human form. But when a shadow passed through his soul, he felt its chill.

Billy Johnson opened his mouth to speak, but Lydius jogged his elbow. *Leave this to me.*

"Is my brother a woman?" Lydius yelled. He seized a

delftware plate from the wall beside the open Dutch fireplace and hurled it to the floor.

Already shaky, stung by the insult, Hendrick violated the first rule of Indian discourse, which is, *Never get mad. If you get mad, you lose.*

The warchief sprang to his feet, clutching at his warclub.

Billy Johnson jumped up and placed his broad shoulders between the two men.

Lydius wiped his mouth. "We must take counsel with foxes."

Hendrick sighed and slumped down on his seat. Lydius' servant refilled his glass. The tension in the other Mohawks—Snowbird, White Owl and Sun Walker—ebbed a little.

"Now that I have considered it," Lydius went on smoothly, "I think the Mohawk women are right. I think you must send people to Canada to make peace with the French. I think my brother Forked Paths and those he trusts the most must go with this delegation, so it will represent the wishes of all the Flint People."

When he explained the rest of his plan, Billy Johnson was torn between admiration and unease, because of the depth of its duplicity. Forked Paths laughed, because of its cruelty.

5.

Forked Paths abased himself within a circle of Mohawk elders. He confessed that he had been wrong. When he had pressed for war, it was the hard water that spoke, not his heart. He was ready to join the Mohawk ambassadors who were leaving for Canada, to make peace with the French, and to commune with their cousins at the blackrobe Mission.

Hendrick's change of heart was welcomed with joy by the old ones and the women.

Island Woman was glad that Snowbird had scoured off his warpaint, and she agreed that it was a good thing for Forked Paths to go with the envoys to Montreal. The Flint People should display unity, and Hendrick—

despite his arrogance and his taste for the newcomers' liquor—was a veteran diplomat.

Bright Meadow whispered, "How can we trust him?"

Her mother responded, "We will watch him wherever he goes. Your brother Snowbird will walk with him. Snowbird will be our eyes and ears."

"But Snowbird's heart is strong for war."

"He is Wolf Clan. He will conceal nothing from the Mother of the Wolf."

She took her daughter's wrist and felt the tremor in the pulse. "I think you fear for my granddaughter's father."

Bright Meadow nodded.

Island Woman closed her eyes, to see better. "No harm will come to White Owl," she pronounced.

But what is this shadow that cuts our path like a blade?
She looked at Forked Paths.
If you break the Great Law, you will answer to me.

□

In the moon of wild rice, Hendrick, Snowbird and the other ambassadors followed ancient paths over the broken spine of the Endless Mountains.

When their rations ran low, Snowbird called the deer:

He searches for me.
On top of the dark mountain
He searches for me.
Among shining flowers
He searches for me.
The finest of bucks
He searches for me.
With his dark blood
He comes to me.

And the deer came to him. The old ones knew that the deer will always come to a man who shares their dreaming, so long as the need is real.

The Mohawk envoys came down at last among the settlements of the French, clustered in a narrow belt along the river. Beyond the cascades, below the point where the Ottawa plunged its muddy yellow water into the blue-gray St. Lawrence, the mountain-island of Montreal shone in the sun.

The French Governor feted the Mohawks with a roast bull and a dozen roast dogs, which the Mohawks declined but the Ottawas and Nipissings devoured with gusto. Onontio heaped praise on the Mohawks for refusing the evil-minded blandishments of the English. He expressed his relief that he would not be obliged to send an invincible army of the Sun King's soldiers, with a host of Far Indians to lay waste to the Valley and cut down every man, woman and child of the Mohawk people—which it would be his unhappy duty to do if the Mohawks should ever take up the hatchet against the French. He reminded the Mohawks that the English colonists had no love for the Indians and that if they ever triumphed in their wars against France—which was of course impossible—they would come to drive the Mohawks from their lands, as they had done to the natives of New England.

The Mohawks applauded these remarks politely, together with medals and dress uniforms, and many liters of the Governor's cognac.

The Mohawks were permitted to go across the river to the mission at Sault St. Louis to feast with their Caughnawaga relations.

As Snowbird climbed out of his canoe, a long shadow crossed his path. It fell from the high cross that stood near the blackrobes' stone church. Hollowed into the main beam was a little niche with mementoes of the sufferings of the Saviour of the Christians—a miniature spear, a crown of thorns. A wooden bird perched atop the cross: a flightless bird, reminding the faithful of the cock that crowed when an ancestor of the blackrobes denied his Great Spirit.

Forked Paths sat with Red Squirrel, the warchief of the Caughnawagas. Red Squirrel was a friend of the blackrobes, who had taught him that the King of France was no ordinary mortal but the elder son of the Mother of God—and therefore could not be defeated by enemies who were merely human. Red Squirrel had sailed with the French in their wars against the Foxes, returning with the heads of vanquished enemies displayed on spikes in the prow of his canoe. He was ready to fight with the French again, in their dispute with the English. But he would never willingly fight his Mohawk cousins.

Hendrick said that it was his belief that the English would eventually win the war, even though their colonies were divided and squabbled like jealous women. He had seen their warfleet at London harbor; its sails blotted out the sun. Therefore it would be wise for his brothers at the Mission to do nothing that would win them the undying enmity of the English.

Having appealed to Red Squirrel's cunning, Forked Paths now said something that appealed to both his cupidity and his fierce devotion to the great Mohawk family that was divided by white men's flags and boundaries.

Forked Paths proposed a secret treaty. Whenever the Mission Mohawks and the Valley Mohawks took the warpath—for whatever reason—they would share the spoils and pledge never to fight each other, even if this meant abandoning their allies under the mouths of enemy guns. White men and other Indian tribes would be fair game.

Forked Paths demonstrated his sincerity by giving Red Squirrel some of the gold coins he had received from Lydius.

The deal was made.

Its sequel plunged the world of the Mohawks—and the Longhouse—back into the dark times.

6.

Forked Paths and a pack of Burned Knives came whooping and hollering down High Street. Forked Paths was wearing a Frenchman's matchcoat, with a wolfskin on top; the wolf's head lolled back from his shoulders. He grinned from ear to ear, making the old tomahawk scar glow white.

The Mohawks threw back their heads. Their tongues vibrated in their open jaws like the reed in a flute, but the sound that came out was not something for music lovers. A Mohawk scalp-cry will unsettle the bowels of the bravest man. Albany householders and servants within hearing set to fastening shutters and doors.

John Henry Lydius left off humping his wife and sprang to the window, in all his naked glory.

"By God!" he cried out. "By God—"

He ran downstairs, just as he was, and threw open the door. He grabbed the scalp out of Forked Paths' hand and held it in his teeth as he clasped the Mohawk in a hug that matched the dead beast on his back.

"By God—" he repeated. "You've done it!"

Lydius covered himself with the breeches and shirt poor Genevieve—outraged to the quick of her New French sensibilities by the spectacle of her naked brute of a husband exposing himself to public view—thrust upon him.

"You were flying the Frenchman's colors?" cried Hard Egg, exultant. "By hyssop and vinegar, I would give my other eye to see the faces of those damned Frogs when you went for their livers!"

Forked Paths had left Montreal, loaded up with presents from the Marquis de la Galissonière, the new Governor and Captain-General of New France. The Marquis was a land-sailor of imperial vision, with a personal dignity that befitted his station as a bastard son of Louis XIV, the original *Roi Soleil*. He believed that his radiance had had a charmed effect on the savages from the Mohawk Valley. To show his faith in the Mohawks who had accepted the peace-belt from him, he fitted them out in the spotless white uniforms of French regular officers. He gave Hendrick, their Speaker, his personal safe conduct, which instructed all French garrison commanders to supply his needs without question.

At the French post at Chambly, Hendrick had his pick of the boats on hand. He chose a sturdy dugout as well as two sleek birchbark canoes that skimmed lake water like a pebble from a boy's hand. Before sunup, Hendrick gathered the young warriors he could count on to follow his pleasure, leaving the old ambassadors on their sleeping-mats. In the darkness, they set off up the lake in the direction of Crown Point, with the lilies of France fluttering over their prow.

Forked Paths found what he was seeking at Ile LaMothe, a ridge of deep woods detached from the green mountains of Vermont.

A party of French carpenters was near the black sand beach, sawing up firs to make flatboats and sleeping-shelves for the outlying garrisons.

Every man on the frontier had a gun. There were no civilians on the borders of New York and New France. But the French carpenters were used to the sight of Mission Indians on the lake, and these savages were flying the French colors.

"Bonjou'," they cried out. One of them waved his tobacco pouch, offering to share.

"Bonjou'," Forked Paths grinned back.

The Mohawk was splitting his sides, as he regaled Hard Egg with the details. The Frenchmen were as helpless as woodcocks, standing out there in the open, with their arms stacked a hundred paces away, beside their sleeping quarters.

The Mohawks fired from their boats, without warning, and plugged five or six in the first volley. When the terrified carpenters ran for their firelocks and the shelter of the woods, Hendrick and his warriors leaped onto the beach to claim their scalps. They grabbed two prisoners before the returning fire from the Frenchmen drove them off. One of these captives was too badly wounded to be worth the trouble of ferrying all the way to Albany. They unwrapped his entrails before they allowed him to die.

In beating his retreat, Forked Paths did not omit to leave a signature on his heroic military action. Lydius had impressed on him that it was very important that the Governor of New France should be left in no doubt that the Mohawks who slaughtered unarmed Frenchmen were the same Indians who had just concluded a solemn peace treaty with him at Montreal.

Forked Paths left, on the beach, the white regimentals of an officer of Guyenne and his safe conduct from the Governor.

"You are a marked man with the Frogs," Lydius said. "You and me both, and Johnson too. But, thank God, you have cleared our paths. It's to be war in earnest. Your women can't stop it now. The Mohawks will have to take up the hatchet. The French will leave you no choice. You will be the greatest man in the Real World, my brother. Throughout the Indian country, your voice will be louder than that of the old ones whose world is passing and the bigmouths who sit by the dying fire at Onondaga. You will be warchief of the whole Confederacy. We will drive the French from their river and hunt together across all of Canada. We will walk with kings. We will hold dominion with the powers of this earth."

CHAPTER 23
THE GOD-GIVEN

1.

It was a clever trick, to make war a matter of deeds as well as words. At least, that was how Hendrick's actions in Canada seemed to Lydius and his New England backers, who were promoting a full-scale invasion of New France.

At his stone house in the Valley, Billy Johnson was not quite so sure. Hendrick fell ill, soon after he had feasted at Mount Johnson and carved a record of his deeds of blood on a blazed pine close to the house. Other Mohawks succumbed to smallpox, which they regarded as a legacy of the Albany council, and took as an omen of what they might expect from their alliance with the English.

Though Hendrick recovered, the tide of opinion now ran strongly against the pro-English faction in the councils of the Six Nations, and even among the Mohawk.

"Have we lost our minds?" Island Woman asked, speaking for the whole women's council. "Have all of us swallowed the green snake? We are slaughtering those with whom we have no quarrel and inviting them to kill our sisters and brothers? And where is the reason?"

When Hendrick was strong enough to reply, he re-

minded his people that the English had promised to send
a powerful army. Even the name of the general who
would lead this army was known. It was St. Clair;
Colonel Johnson would vouch for the fact. No one yet
knew that St. Clair's army would never sail, because of a
rebellion in Scotland. But belief in the promised redcoat
army did not staunch the tide that was running against
the war.

"If this army comes," Island Woman said, "I think it
will hurry the day when the newcomers will swallow up
all our lands, and drive us far toward the setting sun, or
reduce us to the condition of wandering drunks and
basket-makers. Like the people among whom my brother
Forked Paths once lived."

Speaking over her wampum credentials, Island Woman called on the women of her clan to refuse those who
took the warpath the pleasures of the marriage bed, and
the customary rations for the trail.

Her son Snowbird was aghast.

He had promised Johnson that he would guide him on
a scout toward Crown Point. And he had pledged to go
with Hendrick Forked Paths to make war on the island
of Montreal, which would shake the inhabitants of New
France, when the time was ripe.

His mother told him, "You go without my blessing."

□

But Island Woman had to yield a little, because the olive-
branch sent to Canada from Lydius' house had the
intended effect.

In the early spring, the Governor-General of New
France assembled a huge Indian council, at Montreal, to
declare war on the Mohawk nation. When he threw
down the warbelt, all the Mission Indians accepted it.
Even the Caughnawagas.

French agents were promptly sent into the territories
of the Longhouse.

Chauvinerie spoke at Onondaga, the Place of the
Council Fire of the Confederacy, against the perfidy of
the Mohawks and the English warmakers who had sent
them to kill civilians in Canada.

He was well rewarded. The Onondagas brought out
the warbelt they had accepted from the hands of Governor Clinton the previous summer and broke it to pieces
with repeated blows from a jagged rock.

The Flint People were isolated from their sister-
nations, dependent on indifferent—or actively hostile—
traders and politicians in New York, on a King who was
far distant and forgetful about his American plantations,
and on untested friends like Billy Johnson.

Johnson suggested to Hendrick, "We are in deep. I
believe we lose nothing by going in deeper."

Hendrick agreed. He had heard rumors—tomorrow
they might be open taunts—that the women's council
was moving, at Island Woman's instigation, to strip him
of all rights to speak for the Mohawk nation.

Johnson had kept his part of the bargain when Hendrick and his warriors had returned from Canada in the
fall, dressing several of them in fine lace coats, heaping
presents on all. Billy promised greater rewards this time.
And if the women denied the customary provisions for
the trail, the warriors would be supplied, free of charge,
from his own stores.

With these inducements, Hendrick recruited warriors
from other nations to join a new raid intended to spread
terror all along the borders of New France. When the
war-song was raised at Mount Johnson, even Dandelion,
Snowbird's adopted brother—a gentle spirit, close to
children and plants, loved by all—raised the hatchet.

□

Turkey vultures tilted their wings above the steep-roofed
farmhouses, set close together as village cottages on their
narrow strips of land, fronting the St. Lawrence.

In the woods beyond the wheatfields, the Mohawks
moved without human sound, signaling with birdcalls or
hand motions. When Hendrick glimpsed a Canadian
and his boy, working the plow, through a gap in the
trees, he screeched like a bluejay.

The farmer and his son were tame meat, easily taken.
White Owl claimed the old one. He drew a circle around

the fontanel with the point of his knife, then ripped away skin and hair with his fist.

Hendrick looked across the river, to the island of Montreal. The citadel was shiny with brass cannon. There were hundreds of soldiers there, in the white of the Sun King's regiments and the gray of the colonial Troupes de la Marine.

The French had encouraged the Mission Indians to settle on the south side of the river, near the city, as a buffer against Mohawk raiders. But the Caughnawagas were Hendrick's cousins; he was confident they would not betray his movements.

The Mohawks crossed the St. Lawrence in the new dawn, in birchbark canoes, while Montreal slept.

They beached the canoes at a marshy inlet. Forked Paths raised his head, sniffing the air. He smelled the sweetness of fireweed, the sour tang of deer scat, the stale odor of a woman who has not been loved for a long time.

Snowbird's hand moved to the little pouch he always carried on the trail, filled with war medicine: the tiny batons that captured the Thunder power; the miniature warclub, fitted with a stone celt, that helped him to find the heart of his enemies; the snakeskin that made him invisible to pursuers; the maskette that screened him from hostile sorcerers.

The barrel of Hendrick's jaeger rifle, like the barrels of his companions' firelocks, was greased with tallow, so it would not answer the slanting rays of the rising sun.

The whitewashed houses at his left were still sunk in a well of shadow.

Forked Paths put his right fist in front of his shoulder. He opened it suddenly, raking downward, veering towards his heart.

The Mohawks went loping toward the kill.

2.

The Mission Indians called him Dieudonné, the God-Given. The huge brown eyes in the moon-round face belonged to a night hunter, like the great grey owl. The Abbé François Picquet had studied theology at the Petit-

Seminaire of the Sulpicians in Paris, and law at the Sorbonne. He came from well-fed bourgeois stock; his people were merchants of Lyons, a city that could teach even Parisians how to eat. But behind the cedar palisade of his mission fortress at the Lake of Two Mountains, this son of Lyons subsisted gladly on rations that would make his mother weep: a loaf of black bread, a mouthful of oversalted pork. When his Indians brought him trout and partridges, he shared their bounty with the emaciated nomads who came out of the woods in the starving time.

Dieudonné's hunger was not of the flesh.

He made conversions to the music of fife and drum. He sang and composed canticles in his native French and in the tongues of his mixed congregation of Iroquois, Algonquins and Nipissings. He led the Indians on the circling path up the green hillside where seven white chapels of the Calvary shone above the silver of the lake. He schooled his flock in his own conviction, that the purpose of France in the New World was to win the whole continent, from Cape Breton to New Orleans, and westward to the Shining Sea, for the lilies and the cross.

He saw farther than the crooked noblemen the King appointed to govern at Quebec. They saw the American colonies as little more than fortified trading posts, where Frenchmen came to barter with savages for furs, as they bartered with the Congolese for ivory. They did nothing to encourage settlement. When the Abbé first set foot in New France, he found that only sixty thousand *arpents* —ninety thousand acres—were under cultivation in the entire colony. The colonists survived on flour and meat imported from the Old World each spring on the King's ships, and this precarious lifeline could be cut at any moment now the English had seized the fortress of Louisbourg, which guarded the sea approaches to New France.

In this neglect, the Abbé had read the ruin of the French empire in the New World. Year by year, new convoys of immigrants swelled the population of the English colonies that hugged the Atlantic seaboard. They were a farming people, unlike the free-spirited voyageurs and vainglorious seigneurs who ruled the destiny of New France. They could feed themselves and were building a thriving export trade with their wheat and peas. Their goods for the Indian trade were imported from England and Holland, but were of finer quality and lower price than the tawdry *écarlatines* and clumsy kettles the King's ships brought from France.

From the numbers he studied, the Abbé was aware that the tide of history was running strongly in favor of the English. But Dieudonné did not doubt that—with God at his back—he would change that tide. In the cleared fields around his mission, he was training nomads to practice strip-farming. He bombarded the Governor and the Minister of the Marine—and even the King himself—with schemes to encourage immigrants from all parts of the Empire. He lobbied the merchant princes of Montreal with plans for iron foundries and bolting mills.

He had seen this war coming, and he welcomed it. He knew that a war for mastery of the heartlands of North America was inevitable. It was best to fight it now, before the balance of population tilted further in favor of the English, and while their heavy German king was preoccupied with a land war in the Low Countries that he could not possibly win.

Dieudonné knew that the French could win. The French had regular troops, under unified command, while the English colonies sent plowboys and mechanics into battle, and wasted their energies squabbling over who would give the orders and who would foot the bills. Above all, the French could count on the loyalty—or at least the sympathy—of most of the Indians. The Indians saw that the French did not come to steal their lands and make a desert of their hunting grounds. They recognized soul-mates in the carefree land-sailors of New France, who shared their lives and their women, and in black-robe missionaries who shared their sufferings.

Only the Iroquois remained stubbornly opposed to the purposes of the Sun King and Dieudonné, for whom the service of God and a Catholic King were inseparable. The Five Nations of the Iroquois—enlarged by the

Tuscaroras, who had fled from land thieves and Indian fighters in the southern colonies—were a little people. United, the whole Confederacy could field no more than two thousand warriors, and the Confederacy was rarely united. But the Iroquois held the passes between both the French and the English colonies and the untapped riches of the vast interior of the continent.

Before the Abbé's vision of a Catholic empire could be fulfilled, the Iroquois had either to be won over or annihilated. He had little doubt but that, for the Valley Mohawks, annihilation would prove to be the only viable solution. In their policy, the Mohawks had become no better than Englishmen. In their blood-frenzy, they were worse than wolves.

The Abbé had made the solution of this matter a personal crusade.

It gave him high satisfaction that the first Indians to declare war on England and the Mohawks came from his own mission.

The Abbé was a soldier of God. He had already marched with the warriors who burned Hard Egg Lydius' trading house on the carry between Lac St. Sacrement and Hudson's River. He had presided, cross in hand, over the burning of Saratoga. When word came that the Mohawks had fallen on the island of Montreal, his heart leaped up.

3.

Indians from Dieudonné's mission found the place where Mohawks had hidden their awkward elmbark canoes. It seemed the raiders had journeyed on to their killing-grounds in birchbark skimmers bought or borrowed from the treacherous Caughnawagas.

The Mission Indians carried a warning to Montreal. The town bells tolled at one in the morning, summoning the people of the city to arms. Soldiers, Indians and militiamen formed columns in the Place d'Armes, near the huge stone priory of the Sulpicians, landlords of the island. War-parties were formed, under La Corne St. Luc and Legardeur de St. Pierre, veteran Indian fighters.

They paddled by night, above the cascades to lie in wait for the Mohawks when their paths turned homeward.

There were Caughnawagas with the French, even though Dieudonné had warned they could not be trusted and might even be in active collusion with the Mohawk invaders.

When Hendrick and his warriors came upriver, hugging the shore, one of the Caughnawagas fired without orders, alerting them to the ambush the French had laid.

Nervous that their quarry would slip away, the French and the Mission Indians started banging away with their firelocks, into the moonless dark. The first man to fall was one of their own number, a voyageur who had postponed his departure for Lake Michigan in order to join the sport.

Enraged by his death, another fur trader thrashed out into the river and flung himself into the prow of Hendrick's canoe. Hendrick yowled his dragging death-cry, burying the iron celt of his killing club in the Frenchman's neck.

The Mohawks swung their canoes about and slipped downstream, away from the ambush. They had captives with them, pert little mademoiselles from Sennerville, in lacy petticoats, with spindly heels to their shoes no woman of the Real People could walk on. These prisoners would please Colonel Johnson, Hendrick thought. Forest Killer might pay a higher bounty than he had promised.

Forked Paths planned to beach the canoes above the Sault St. Louis and go through the woods that belonged to the Caughnawagas. He was confident that Red Squirrel's people would not betray Mohawk kinsmen to the French. They were family. They had a business agreement. And they heard the same ghosts. Hendrick counted on the Caughnawagas to supply provisions for the trail.

Hendrick saw a pale blur among the spruces that bordered the water. He placed his left arm in front of his chest, using it as a rest for his jaeger rifle. He squeezed off a shot and was rewarded by a yelp of pain.

Hendrick slid his paddle back into the water without

ruffling the surface, guiding the canoe into a narrow channel under the leaf curtain of a lesser island. Here the Mohawks were completely screened from garrison flat-boats and the voyageurs' many-oared *canots-maîtres*.

Willow birch brushed the warchief's shoulder and fell over the canoe, enclosing it. Forked Paths peered into the deeper blackness of the island. This place was uninhabited—neither Frenchmen nor Indians would brave the spinning mountains of ice that were borne down the river each spring, to break over these swampy banks. But something out there in the fog shared the night with the Mohawks. Forked Paths felt it.

Sun Walker, working his paddle in the stern of the canoe, gave a grunting curse as an unseen branch swiped him across the face. As he tried to regain his balance, the prow of the canoe veered toward the shore and snagged among tree roots.

Forked Paths grappled with wet bark, working to get the boat free. The mist seemed denser and whiter.

It hid the men who lay in wait for the Mohawks.

Dieudonné had foreseen the perfidy of the Caugh-nawagas, and the failure of the trap La Corne had set. His inner senses had told him where to find the Mo-hawks. He had become half-Indian.

He had brought only Nipissings to this killing-ground. The Nipissings were the wildest of his Mission Indians, hard to win for the plow or the canticles, slow to re-nounce their appetite for jugglery and human flesh. Other Indians called them *les Sorciers,* the Sorcerers. Their reputation was almost as dark as that of the Mohawks. They had been fighting the Iroquois for generations.

The Nipissings hung in the trees, so still that it seemed their breathing had stopped.

Dieudonné raised his cross of silver.

□

Hendrick and Snowbird escaped the second ambush.

But of the warriors who had set off from Mount Johnson, many were missing. Sun Walker—whose wife

Windweaver was the Mother of the Turtle Clan—was being danced like a captive bear in front of the ladies of Quebec, with fetters on his ankles and an iron collar round his neck.

Dandelion fell under the hatchet of the Nipissing warchief. The Sorcerers were not content to lift his scalp. They butchered his carcass and carried it back to the Lake of Two Mountains. A visiting Jesuit from the Sault was appalled to find Sorcerers feasting on a thick broth boiled from their enemy's flesh. When one of them offered him a drink from the Mohawk's skull, Father Luc descended on Dieudonné, stormy with anger and disgust.

"How can you license these iniquities? How can you celebrate the sacrifice of the Lamb among these demons?"

"Ask him." Dieudonné indicated the Sorcerer who had trailed Father Luc to the Abbe's house.

"Toi avoir le gout francais," the Nipissing told the Jesuit, showing off his Mission French. *"Moi sauvage, cette viande bonne pour moi."**

Dieudonné decided he had best have words with the scandalized Jesuit in private, to discourage him from writing embarrassing letters to Paris.

Abbé Picquet recalled that Moses had demanded the death of every man, woman and child of the people of Midian, who stood against the Children of God.

"Why should Christ's armies in the New World show greater nicety in fighting the wolf-men of the Mohawk, who have martyred your fellow-Jesuits?"

"You make the martyrs bleed anew," Father Luc told him. "I intend to make an accounting of these horrors to my superiors."

"I would counsel you to take care in how you express yourself, Father Luc. It is known to us that members of your own flock not only trade with the enemy, but collude with the savages who terrorize our borders." If the Jesuit complained to the authorities, spiritual or

---

*"You have Frenchman's taste. Me savage, this meat good for me."

temporal, about the behavior of the loyal Indians of Oka,
then the Abbé would be obliged to inform the King that
the Jesuit mission at the Sault was a nest of traitors that
imperiled New France.

4.

The Mohawk survivors brought prisoners back to Mount
Johnson, and one of them stayed behind. Her name was
Angélique Vitry. She was a redhead with an hourglass
figure who appeared to revive from the rigors of her
captivity as soon as she set eyes on Billy. Cat hated her
on sight.

Colonel Johnson, playing gentleman and host, insisted
that Mlle. Vitry must stay at the stone house, where she
would be safe from the passions of neighbors and
Indians who were inflamed against the French, especially after the losses in the fighting that summer.
Johnson said he would write to her father, assuring him
of her perfect security, and that she would be returned to
him as soon as it became possible to arrange a prisoner
exchange.

Angélique Vitry—Cat noticed—seemed in no hurry
to go home to Canada.

She disported herself in the house in lazy deshabille,
exposing more of her generous bosom than Cat thought
appropriate, outside a whorehouse or an exposition of
Greek marbles.

She waylaid Billy at the stables, when he returned
from his business with the Indians or the militia, and
presumed to take his arm on leisurely strolls around the
gardens.

She actually dared to discuss Billy's ambition to build
a grander house, with plans inspired by the armed stone
houses of his Irish boyhood. Cat overheard her lisping
her enthusiasm over Billy's plans to import panes of
Crown glass from London and the finest flowered wall-
papers.

She overheard more than this. Hot groping and gasping. A phrase cooed repeatedly, some endearment she
could not comprehend.

Ma chantepleure.
Was that right?
Something like.
Cat looked for someone to ask, someone who would not snicker at her for eavesdropping. Which would of course be wholly unfair.

How can I eavesdrop, in my own house?

But that wasn't right either. It was not her house. She was only a servant, promoted a neck higher than the others, granted added favors as the mother of the master's children. Those he acknowledged. There were plenty of brown Johnsons running about the Valley, and plenty of people who made sure Cat never forgot the fact.

She became more and more edgy, hot-tempered with the servants that were called servants, and some that counted themselves her betters. Part of it was the shame of seeing Billy going after a bitch in heat, in plain view of all. Part of it—she recognized more soberly—was the fear that this bitch in heat could be the one to claim him as his lady. There was no *de* in front of Vitry; but her father was a man of means, it seemed, with the ear of the Intendant and even the Governor-General of New France. They were enemies for now, but when the war ended—as all wars had to—they were the kind of society Billy might be pleased to consort with.

And there was that business about the *chantepleure.*

She decided to ask Daniel Claus. He was a newcomer to the Valley, but a fellow countryman, an educated young German from Heidelberg. He had been lured to the American colonies by the promise of getting rich fast in the tobacco business in Philadelphia. He had been swindled out of his investment but learned his lesson and made a quick recovery, making himself useful to Conrad Weiser. He had come to the Valley with Weiser, hit it off with Billy and with the Mohawks, and decided to stay. A serious, intelligent young man with a gift for languages. Not one to gossip or question a lady's reasons.

She offered him one of her rhubarb pies.

Daniel loved pastry, and dark bread baked heavy as a brick.

He sighed his appreciation.

"Daniel, my French isn't too good. Do you know what *chantepleure* means?"

He looked puzzled. Then his face lit up. "Of course! You are such a keen gardener! I was wondering why you would ask. A *chantepleure* is that kind of watering can with a really long spout. We had them in the Rhineland. Surely you remember?"

Daniel Claus did not understand why this horticultural information sent Cat rushing from the room with hot cheeks, tears welling in her eyes.

She calls him her watering can.

And she fancies herself Colonel Johnson's lady.

We'll see about that.

CHAPTER 24
MOON OF CRUSTED SNOW

1.

The north wind raked through the woods, driving before it a snowstorm of fine, stinging powder that pricked the eyes.

"The Bear is prowling the sky," Island Woman told her granddaughter Sparrow, as they trudged back to the lodge, dragging wood for the fire on their sleds. The child's Longhouse name was Gift of Flowers, but the nickname Sparrow had flown to her and stuck, because she was small and quick as a bird, and because of her dreaming.

The wind carried a nervous voice from the far side of the river, the voice of a fox that barked like a dog. Seven-year-old Sparrow shivered. This was an evil sign.

There was a stir at the Upper Castle. Sparrow saw the newcomer from the big stone house, muffled to the eyes in his cloak, among a press of welcoming warriors. Forest Killer had come with men and horses and a sleighload of presents. There would be drinking and dancing in the village that night, and Mohawk girls would vie for the attentions of the big white man from Mount Johnson.

Island Woman's granddaughter pretended not to no-

tice Billy Johnson, though she was eager to see the goods
he had brought. She thought that she hated him, even
more than she hated the land-sharks and crooked traders
from Albany. They took the Mohawks' land. Her grandmother and her mother had told her that this newcomer
had made the war that was taking the lives of their
people.

"*Sekon, aksotha,*" Billy Johnson called to Island
Woman, who grunted and nodded.

"Good day to you, little Miss Bright-Eyes!" he called
to Sparrow as she hurried past as fast as she could
manage, encumbered by the heavy load of firewood.

Sparrow flushed in furious embarrassment. How dare
he speak to her!

"Come and see my porcupine!" Billy Johnson
shouted.

Other children gathered quickly. The white man
dropped his handkerchief on a flattened patch of snow
and sprinkled iron filings over it. Then he brought out a
strange, horseshoe-shaped lump of metal, and waved it
an inch or two above the filings. They leaped from the
handkerchief to cling to the magnet, bristling like porcupine quills.

"Here, try it for yourself." He offered the magnet to
Sparrow. Curiosity got the better of her. She set down
her load and went over to him.

He showed her how easily the filings could be stripped
away. "Don't you wish porcupine quills came out that
easily?" he laughed, looking at dyed quills in her earrings, which she had made herself, working by firelight
in Island Woman's lodge.

After a time, Island Woman gave a little barking
cough. Sparrow—shocked at herself for how easily she
had let herself be diverted—ran back to her chores.

When she started to apologize to her grandmother,
Island Woman pinched her cheek affectionately.

She said, "Forest Killer charms all of us. He is death
with a smiling face."

The white man joked with the warriors, and rough
belly laughs gusted after the women.

The child frowned. Everyone knew that her grandmother was not only the Mother of the Wolf, but an *arendiwanen*, a woman of power. People in the village were scared of exciting Island Woman's anger. They thought if they got her mad and her rage got away from her it could hit them like a quartz bullet. Sparrow had learned from her own mother that these things were true and that one day—if she passed all the tests the spirits would set for her—she might inherit her grandmother's gift. This was why she was shepherded away from the games of other children, to spend long hours with Island Woman, learning the medicine plants and the language of birds and spirits. But if Island Woman was truly so powerful, why did she not weave a spell to drive Forest Killer and the other newcomers who brought war to the Valley far from the lodges of the Real People? Was it because the magic of the newcomers was stronger? Or because they had no souls?

□

That night, while Johnson sat with Hendrick and the warriors, Sparrow spied on their council. She heard her uncle Snowbird say that a war party of Mission Indians was on the move. The raiders were coming from The Octagon, the French fort on the Bulging River. They were crossing the drifts on snowshoes. They were as many as the feathers of the pigeon hawk. Snow squalls might delay them; they would also camouflage the invaders' tracks.

Johnson wanted Mohawk scouts to go into the woods with his amateur rangers—Irish retainers and Valley farmers. He said he would pay four shillings a day, plus a bounty for scalps and prisoners. There was no shortage of volunteers.

Sparrow heard her father and uncle join in the *yo-hais*.

Crouched behind the moosehide inner door of Hendrick's lodge, the child again heard the yipping of the fox that barked like a dog and knew a deeper fear.

My father is going to his death.

White Owl and Snowbird rolled back to Island Wom-

an's lodge in the small hours, stinking of Johnson's rum.
Sparrow rose from her place by the fire and took her
father's hand.

"You must not go on this scout," she told him.

White Owl squinted through the fog of liquor and the
acrid smoke from the firepits that made his eyes water
and robbed everything of its familiar form.

"Go to sleep, little one," he mumbled.

"You must not go," the child insisted. "There is great
danger for you. I have seen it."

White Owl's thoughts rose like fish from a murky
deep.

"We are all in danger," he said, as sobriety returned.
"I must lead tomorrow. I am the warrior all others
trust."

Bright Meadow had been pulled from her dream by
the talk by the fire. She sat upright, the beaver blanket
pooling around her middle. The firelight gleamed on her
glossy skin, on the dark cones of her nipples.

White Owl smiled at her.

"Go to bed," Bright Meadow ordered her daughter,
opening her arms to her husband in invitation.

Sparrow went to Island Woman's end of the lodge and
snuggled next to her grandmother, with her face to the
wall. She dreamed of crows, walking through a field of
broken cornstalks.

2.

The French raiders had been seven days on the trail since
they set out from The Octagon across the Adirondack
foothills.

La Corne, their commander, cursed the *poudrière* that
had checked their advance on the Valley. Even on
webbed snowshoes, his men sank six inches down in the
fresh snow until the deeper layers packed firm enough to
support them. Each step—after an hour's walking—
became a painfully slow operation. Each man was
obliged to lift his foot so the toe of the snowshoe would
clear the depression, then swing his leg out in an arc to

avoid hitting his other calf with the frame. After a few
hours of this, rarely exercised muscles tightened up and
screamed their protest. Men failed to lift aching limbs
high enough, snagged the toes of their snowshoes in the
holes they made, and fell flat on their faces. Two of La
Corne's Canadians had been crippled by cramps; when
they could walk no further, he had left them where they
lay, twisting in pain as they fretted their calves.

While La Corne cursed the weather, his Canadians
cursed him. He traveled like his Indians, tireless, indifferent to physical pain. Fur trader, slaver, Indian agent,
officer of the Troupes de la Marine, La Corne St. Luc was
prized by the masters of New France as one of their most
proficient killers. His face did not belie his role. Under
hooded lids, his eyes were as cold as ice shadows.
Exposure to the elements had given his long face—
pitted by smallpox—the color and texture of cordovan
leather. A small, tight mouth was overarched by a cruel
beak of a nose.

His instructions were precise. They had been issued
by the Marquis de la Galissonière, the brilliant hunchback recently despatched to govern New France, but
they bore the mark of more seasoned Indian hands, like
the Abbé Picquet and the Commandant Landriève:

> You will discover the whereabouts of William
> Johnson, the nephew of the pirate Warren who has
> caused such damage to His Majesty's ships, and of
> the Iroquois captain called Tête Blanche, or Hen-
> drick Tehayanoken. You will ensure, by expedient
> means, that these obstinate enemies of France are
> prevented from inflicting further harm on the
> King's subjects. You will exact strict retribution on
> the Agniers, or Mohawks, for their stubborn rebel-
> lion against God and the King their Father.

As he marched, La Corne sheltered the lock of his
musket under his capote to keep it dry. He kept within
easy range of Le Corbeau, the Caughnawaga who led the
march. The Abbé Picquet had warned him of the duplic-

ity of the Caughnawagas, who all had friends or relatives among the Mohawks of the Valley. Despite these cautions, La Corne had resolved to use Caughnawagas for his dangerous assault across the snow, because they knew this country better than any other French Indians, and because they were second to none as fighters, once their blood was up. He had seen that in the campaigns against the Foxes. If the Caughnawagas proved treacherous, La Corne's firelock was already primed, and the target for his first ball bobbed in front of his eyes. It was a spot between Le Corbeau's shoulderblades, *there,* where the Indian had flung back his hood.

As he stared at it, La Corne saw the Caughnawaga crane forward. In the next instant, Le Corbeau threw himself forward, flattening his body into the soft snow. One of the Canadians drooled tobacco juice as his mouth cracked in a wide grin. He imagined the Indian had tripped, but La Corne knew better. He gestured to the others to stay back. He waded forward a few paces, then dropped down on his belly to wriggle up to where Le Corbeau peered down from the spine of a low range of hills, screened by the downward-sloping boughs of a blue spruce.

At first, La Corne saw nothing, except the ragged holes in the snow left by a heavy elk or moose. He tracked them across a frozen creek. He squinted. Half-blinded by the glare off the snow, it was hard to see into the dark among the evergreens on the far slope of the valley. Then a shadow detached itself from the trunk of one of the trees. In less time than it took to blink, it had joined another.

"How many?" La Corne whispered to Le Corbeau.

The Caughnawaga held up the fingers of one hand.

"This many. Maybe more."

"Hunters?"

"Iah." Le Corbeau shook his head. They had not gone after the moose, though its tracks were in front of them and it would be easy game in the drifts.

"They are looking for us."

La Corne looked at the sky. Less than an hour to

nightfall, he thought. They could lose nothing by waiting until then. When they attacked, they must leave no survivors to warn the Valley. There was a chance of taking the Upper Castle by surprise and making Hendrick's stronghold his coffin. It had been many winters since the Mohawks had suffered a direct assault on one of their fortified villages; their sentries must have grown slack. The guard at Johnson's stone house might be more alert, but two well-aimed arrows would take his lookouts silently. Caughnawagas had measured Johnson's walls and counted the number of men about the house who carried firelocks.

"Burn the Upper Castle and Forest Killer's stone house," Le Corbeau had counseled, "and you will cut out the heart and liver of our enemy."

3.

White Owl dug a hole in a snowbank, out of the wind, and crawled inside it like a bear. They had made no fire, for fear of alerting the Frenchmen in the woods.

White Owl lay between sleep and waking, uneasy and wretchedly cold. He made himself *see* a blazing pine-knot inside his belly and feel its heat flow to the surfaces of his skin. Warmth returned, for a time. Then his mind veered away, and the fire died.

He thought about Bright Meadow's embraces on the last night in the longhouse, before he took the trail with the scouts. When she had taken his seed, she had been very slow to release him, holding on to him so tight her fingers dug into his flesh.

He thought about his daughter, quick and curious, probing the reasons for everything. A *dreamer,* the old ones said. Perhaps even a woman of power, a protector of her people. She would need to be watched over in a special way, because such gifts brought special dangers, from the seen and the unseen.

It will be a joy to watch this child grow, White Owl thought. *She is afraid of nothing.*

He tried to picture Sparrow at twenty, then himself, as

he might be when thirteen more winters had passed. He might be raised up to wear the living bones of a chief of the Bear Clan, and sit in the Grand Council, around the Fire That Never Dies.

So you are not ready to die, said an inner voice.

He hesitated for a moment, thinking of his beautiful wife and daughter, looking for the source of this voice. He saw a radiant being with shining wings, a great one who had hunted him during his boyhood vision quest.

"I am ready to die at any moment," White Owl spoke softly but firmly. "I am ready to drop this sack of meat and bones like an old blanket. But I return thanks for the gifts of this lifetime."

It is good you are ready. I will be waiting for you.

White Owl was alone again. When he breathed through his mouth, the cold bit at the lining of his lungs.

He crawled out of his burrow and sat next to young Walter Butler, who had taken the first watch.

"Too cold to sleep?" Butler offered his flask. White Owl took a deep swig, and grunted as the liquid fire burned a channel to his stomach.

In the grainy dark, the Mohawk surveyed the sleeping forms of his companions. There were only six of them, including himself and Butler—three Indians and three whites.

"If we are to fight the French," White Owl remarked, "I think we are too few. If we are sent to die, I think we are too many."

"Once we get the scent, Colonel Johnson will bring up the hounds," young Butler said confidently. Foxhunting was in his Kilkenny blood. "He has already sent to Colonel Schuyler, to fetch the militia."

White Owl took another swallow from the flask. He did not think the men of Albany would come to help either Johnson or the Flint People. His body rebelled against the second dose of brandy, and he spat onto the snow.

"Are you ill?" Butler looked at him with concern.

"It is nothing," the Mohawk said gruffly, returning the flask.

He felt giddy. Something unseen had come at him

through the ether. He felt it bumping and buffeting his second body, the one only dreamers can see.

"Tell me something," Butler said. "Why do you Indians drink? I've watched you. There's not a man among you can hold his liquor."

You give us a craving we never knew before, and you ask why we have it. You put a snake inside our bellies, and you ask why we feed it.

Walter Butler was used to native silences.

White Owl's attention was drawn by the hoot of a gray owl. The sound appeared to come from a stand of white pines, back toward the river.

Whoo-whoo-whoo!

It was echoed by a second call, from the vicinity of an old red oak, ring-barked by lightning.

The Mohawk sat very still, with his firelock across his knees. He had coated the barrel with tallow, to avoid reflecting light. But starlight glinted dully on the brass sideplate, coiled in the shape of a dragon.

White Owl said quietly, "Now they are coming."

When the meaning of the words sank in, Butler jumped up and stared wildly about, searching for movement among the shadows.

He turned to rouse the sleepers.

White Owl saved him the effort, by firing his musket at the blackened face of a warrior who leaped out of the pines, shapeless in his blanket of furs. The blast of swanshot from the Mohawk's gun ripped away the attacker's face and knocked him backward into the slush.

The war-cry went up, from three sides of the camp.

"By God," Butler swore, sighting along the long barrel of his firelock. "There must be a hundred of the bastards."

He aimed at a hooded attacker who was plowing his way up the slope.

Butler gasped as a searing pain scored the flesh of his neck. He squeezed the trigger, but could not hold his aim. His bullet was lost in the snow.

White Owl wriggled close to him and fired at the hooded warrior. He was rewarded by a strangled cry.

The Irishman dabbed at his neck with a cloth, and the cloth came away sodden with blood.

White Owl glanced at the wound. "They only stroked your face. Now we go."

Butler knew the Mohawk was right. They were too few to hold off their attackers, out in the open. They must get away before they were completely encircled. Someone must raise the alarm.

"Scatter!" His cry was only a hoarse whisper.

Moved by a common instinct, White Owl and Snowbird crawled *toward* their attackers, into a thicket of fallen trees.

The waves of French Indians broke at this barrier and flowed round its sides.

White Owl heard the death-whoop. Then the French officer's voice floated back, over the shrieks of the Mission Indians.

"Pursue them! Give no quarter! We will have them all!"

The Mohawks' ruse appeared to have worked.

White Owl slipped his toes inside the loops of his snowshoes and waded toward a grove of cedars. His legs were very heavy. He saw the hollow of the creekbed, the pine thickets on the far side. There was something in the shadows that was not right. He folded his body around the trunk of a cedar and watched. He saw more Canadians and Mission Indians, striking south. Moving that way, they would cut off Butler's retreat.

"Go to the village," White Owl whispered to Snowbird. "Warn our families. Go quickly."

"We go together."

"No. I am tired of wallowing in this white shit."

Snowbird gave White Owl a quick, appraising look. In the next instant, he was gone, over the brow of the hill. Snowbird had heard the exchange, in his mother's lodge, between White Owl and his daughter.

You do not argue with a man who chooses his death at the appointed time.

White Owl stepped out from behind his tree.

"I am White Owl! I am of the Bear Clan of the Flint

People! Who dares to go skulking by night through the hunting grounds of my grandfathers?"

Some of the Caughnawagas recognized him and whispered among themselves.

"Shoot the cur!" yelled one of La Corne's men.

A Nipissing warrior knelt to fire, but the Mohawk's flung tomahawk laid open his skull.

A volley of shots rang out. White Owl felt a burning sensation at the top of his thigh. Then a deeper, stabbing pain in his chest. These caused him only passing discomfort. Control of pain was the first accomplishment of a warrior. Any child could do it. You just put your mind somewhere else. If necessary, you put it out of the body completely.

White Owl raised his war-song. The high notes skirled above the treetops. His body swayed like a dancer's, though his feet were rooted in the deep snow. His enemies seemed insubstantial, wraiths of shadow. He called them into his embrace, but they seemed to flee from him. Perhaps they were going after Snowbird.

"Here I stand!" he boomed after them. "I am a Bear warrior of the Flint People! Who will fight me?"

The attackers moved farther and farther away, dwindling to black specks, vanishing into the grainy dark above the dull gleam of the snow.

For the first time, fear touched White Owl.

He thought of his sleeping wife and daughter, of their friends and kinfolk at the Upper Castle.

What if the attackers had cut off Snowbird and the others?

The village could be taken by surprise, his family butchered while they dozed on their sleeping mats.

I must go to them. I must give the warning. I must fight to protect my people.

He turned his steps homeward, and the trail was easy. Where he had plunged and wallowed before, like a buffalo in a mudhole, he could now walk lightly and quickly, like a man. It seemed the bitter cold had laid down a firm crust over the snow during the fight. He did not question how this could have happened so quickly;

he gave thanks for the fact that the snow no longer crumbled away underfoot. It made a strong surface. He could even run on it.

Spiked walls of spruce parted before him. Fallen logs rolled away.

Soon he was crossing the river, still gathering speed, galloping over the ice.

He saw the palisades of his own village, tranquil under the bitten moon. He leaped from a snowdrift over the sharpened logs, and no sentry challenged him.

He came to the lodge where he lived with all of Island Woman's family except the witch who had run off to the blackrobe mission.

The memory of bubbling corn soup, well-garnished with chunks of bearmeat, lingered near the fire. It made him hungry. He breathed in deeply, and the hunger receded.

He saw Bright Meadow, sleeping with their daughter snuggled in the small of her back. He was filled with tenderness and relief that they were safe. He crouched over them, whispering their names. They did not stir. He spoke louder and laid his hand on his wife's shoulder. She shivered and drew the beaver blanket up to her chin.

Sparrow sat up and looked at him.

It was an odd look, neither loving nor friendly, nor even the cranky face of a sleepyhead child yanked out of dreamland.

The child cocked her head and brushed the air between them with her hand.

"Sparrow?"

Now she was touching his face. His skin had been numbed by the cold. He felt her touch as something insubstantial, a movement in the air.

He reached to catch her up into a bear-hug. And gasped, because his arms cut through her.

Go away, the child said.

The words were distinctly formed, but they did not issue from her mouth, and he heard them with some other organ than the ear.

You do not belong here.

"Sparrow!" he protested. "I have come to protect you! You must listen to me!"

She was shutting him out. Her fear or hostility seemed to blow him across the lodge like a leaf in the wind. He fell across the firepit, but was not burned. He lurched about, angry and disoriented.

Bright Meadow groaned and rolled over. She patted the space next to her. Finding it empty, she rubbed her eyes, looking for her daughter.

"What's the matter?" she whispered to Sparrow. "Can't you sleep?"

"Look at me!" White Owl shouted at his wife. "Talk to me!"

Sparrow said something to her mother that White Owl could not catch, though he leaned in close.

Bright Meadow shuddered and pulled the covers tighter around her. She was naked under the beaver robes.

"You are beautiful," White Owl told her. "Hold me."

Bright Meadow trembled again. She ran her palms over her face, as if to brush away cobwebs. Now White Owl could see she was crying. The beaver blanket rose and fell with the heaving of her body.

He crawled under the covers next to her, trying to press his body against her, to comfort and warm.

Bright Meadow gave a dragging cry of pain and tore at her hair so violently she pulled a whole fistful out by the roots. Then she rushed from her sleeping place to the fire and started throwing handfuls of ash and cinders over her hair and her bare skin.

"Stop it!" White Owl yelled at her.

Go away, his daughter spoke to him with her mind. *You belong somewhere else. You must take the path that is waiting for you.*

At that moment, White Owl realized that he had left his body somewhere else, which meant he was either dreaming or dead.

He followed blood and footprints in the snow back to the place of battle.

He found that a fire had been made nearby. Dying embers glowed among the ash. They had the sweet smell of good oak. White Owl was puzzled by this. He remembered that his own scouts had been forbidden to make fires, for fear the enemy would home in on them.

White Owl circled this place. He saw a dead stump projecting above the snow. Its forks made the outline of a pair of legs, sticking up with the heels in the air. It was somehow familiar.

He drew closer. Now he saw this stump was a corpse, half-buried in the snow. He knew, without searching, that the head was missing. He found it near the fire. There were three of them, impaled on stakes along the line of the summer trail, where the Mohawks would find them easily.

The Mission Indians had enjoyed themselves during the night. They had mutilated the heads of their victims, almost beyond recognition. Noses and lips had been pared away. Skin was crisped and blackened from red-hot knives and axes.

White Owl looked at the bottom half of his head. He knew it by the gaps in the teeth. The top of his skull was missing.

Now he was beyond pain. But, remembering how his child had banished him, and his wife had failed to hear his voice or feel his touch, he knew something worse. He knew desolation.

He was a Mohawk warrior. His whole life had been a training for death.

Yet he was lost in this place of shadows, between the worlds. Was this the work of a soultaker? Of one of the sorcerers among the Mission Indians? Of the man who had taken part of his skull?

If it is not the work of sorcery, why is there no one to guide me?

He began to see what had happened. His spirit had flown out of his body too soon, before he was ready for the journey to the place of rebirth.

He felt a great longing for familiar places, for the warm bodies of his own people. With it came sour anger that they had denied him. Why should they rest easy, if he was doomed to wander?

He turned back toward the Upper Castle, but something stopped him like a wind in his face.

He recognized Island Woman.

She took him by the elbow. She guided him upward, through many tunnels and passages. Landscapes and cities appeared and disappeared. Now she was making him climb a waterfall of light. Narrow ledges broke the vertical ascent. As he climbed, something slid away from him. He looked down, and saw his own shape falling into the abyss.

Up, Island Woman guided him. *Your way is up.*

At the summit, White Owl found himself journeying beyond static forms, into a mind-sea in which forms were ceasely borning and transforming. Lights of many colors, and of colors that had no names, called him different ways.

Wait here, Island Woman instructed him. *Your teacher will come.*

CHAPTER 25
RAGE

1.

The conflict Americans called King George's War ended where it had begun: on the other side of the Atlantic. The treaty the British and the French signed at Aix-la-Chapelle took no account of the American colonies or the interests of their inhabitants, natives or newcomers. In exchange for Madras—of which most Americans knew nothing—England returned the fortress of Louisbourg to the French. Louisbourg, the strongest citadel of New France, had been won with the blood of New England plowboys and artisans, as well as the cannon of Peter Warren's men-of-war. It was the sole conquest of the English colonies in a bloody contest in which the calculated brutality of both sides left everything unresolved.

Bostonians grumbled that the colonies would be better off without a King who left them to fight and die for his empire without a thank you and threw away their victories without consulting them. The reluctant warmakers at New York and Albany muttered, *I told you so*.

By the council fires of the Confederacy, speaker after speaker rose to demand why the English had traded their only conquest in North America for spice houses on the other side of two oceans. If King George was willing to relinquish Louisbourg, he should at least have insisted that the French give up their fortress at Crown Point on Lake Champlain; this was a dagger pointed at the Six Nations as well as the frontier settlers. Why had the English signed a treaty that left the borders of Canada stronger than before? Why had they declared peace in a sleepy French provincial town, while war-parties of Mission Indians still prowled the forests, and Mohawks lay in fetters in the damp cellars of Quebec?

Billy Johnson was hard-put to find answers for these complaints. He was as bitterly disappointed as any man in the colonies.

Governor Clinton could derive some comfort from the fact that he would no longer have to beg money from James DeLancey and the Assembly he controlled to pay for the war and the Indians. The Governor told Mr. Colden, after a bottle or two, "I am tired of filling the bellies of Billy Johnson's hairdressers."

Johnson knew no such comfort. There would be no end to war in the Valley now—he believed—until the French were driven from Canada, or he and his Mohawk neighbors were destroyed. Blood vendettas were not soon forgotten among the Six Nations, and the fight on snowshoes had left fresh ghosts to be assuaged. And whatever papers had been signed in Europe, the rulers of New France were on the offensive. With each week that passed, Billy's scouts and spies brought in new reports of French activity. French soldiers and pioneers were reinforcing and refurbishing the forts at Niagara and Crown Point. Abbé Picquet had been sighted far up the St. Lawrence, searching for the site of a new mission from which he would reach out to turn the Confederacy from the English cause. There was a vigorous new Governor at Quebec, Rigaud de Vaudreuil, who believed that the French must deal the English colonies a devastating body blow before they developed the unity—or the brute weight of numbers through new immigration—to make themselves invincible.

The Irishman in Johnson was no devotee of the cause of empire, of painting more bits of the world pink. But Billy's fortunes were now inextricably linked to those of the British empire in North America. Unless he could recruit the soldiers and the money to beat the French decisively, he would be driven from his lands in the Valley. He needed active support from London to retain any influence over the Mohawks, who were now counting England's unfulfilled promises, along with their dead.

Billy's chances of buying back their affections were slim; his purse was empty. He had bills outstanding against the government of New York for more than £4,000: the cost of supplying Oswego, fitting out rangers and militia companies, recruiting native war-parties and bribing chiefs. The Assembly had flatly refused to pay.

Johnson took a sloop downriver to New York to press his case.

Governor Clinton pleaded migraine headaches, and the ruinous state of his own fortunes, and offered Billy little more than canary wine.

Uncle Peter had sailed home to England, to buy himself a pocket seat in Parliament and a country seat with the immense proceeds from the prize-ships he had taken. He was a doubtful ally for the nephew he had accused of ratting on a business agreement.

For all of a week, Johnson was reduced to haunting the Exchange Coffee House, where James DeLancey habitually held court. It was common knowledge that the Chief Justice was now the master of Manhattan. He had gained from the rise of his friends; his Cambridge tutor was now Archbishop of Canterbury, with the ear of the King and possibly higher authorities. DeLancey played the Assembly like a string instrument. For all his patrician airs, he lost no opportunity to posture as the people's champion against a vain and sottish Crown appointee. He had opposed the war as costly and bad for trade; the wretched peace, after the horrors inflicted on the back settlements, had seemed to prove him right.

In order to turn his bundles of vouchers and treasury

warrants into cash money, or even poor colonial paper, Billy had to find a way to get along with a man with whom he had already crossed swords.

The first difficulty was securing an interview. Johnson called several times at the DeLancey house, to be told that the Chief Justice was not at home. So he kept vigil at the Exchange.

When DeLancey finally appeared, he was surrounded by a flock of courtiers and petitioners.

"Mister Justice DeLancey! I would be indebted for a few minutes of your time."

"I had thought to find you in feathers and warpaint, Mister Johnson. Are you not a chief among our Mohawk hairdressers?"

"They do me the honor of addressing me as such."

"Indebted, is it? From what we have heard, you are in no position to assume new debts."

This brought smirks from the hangers-on.

Johnson held down his rising anger, and gave a brief account of the pledges that had been made to him, and the money and goods he had laid out, on his own account, to defend the frontier.

"I never heard of a commissary that lost money," DeLancey sniffed. He took one of the bundles of invoices from Johnson and weighed it in his hand. "Padded, I fear. Padded as a feather bed."

The smirks became sniggers and guffaws.

DeLancey dropped the papers on a table and brushed on, leaving Billy only one of his vast store of Latin tags: *Non nummis, virtute paratur.* "A man is adorned, not with cash, but with virtue."

James DeLancey's fat, jolly brother Oliver—a prematurely decayed rake—had more time for Johnson. He swept Johnson into a boozy embrace and breathily proposed a nocturnal adventure. He planned to break the windows of a wealthy Jew, newly arrived from Holland, and newly wed to a likely, black-eyed lady.

"Prodigious tits, Billy. Come see for yourself. I know you are a connoisseur."

Billy pleaded fatigue and left drink in his glass, which

was so rare an occurrence that one of the Chief Justice's informers reported to him there could be no doubt that the Johnson sprig was a ruined man.

Johnson returned to the big Dutch house on Saturday morning, and bulled his way past maids and footmen.

Anne DeLancey came down and blushed at his compliments.

"You must leave at once, Mister Johnson. My husband has set his face against you. There is nothing to be accomplished here."

"I will see for myself."

Deaf to her further cautions, Billy rushed up the staircase to the master bedroom. He found the Chief Justice and his bodyservant struggling to get DeLancey strapped into his corset.

"As God is my witness—" DeLancey roared at the interuption. "You have invaded my privacy once too often."

"Forgive me, Cousin. I hope not to disoblige you, but my business cannot wait."

The Chief Justice dismissed his servant and sat, thin-lipped, while Billy presented his case.

"I am not a soldier. I did not seek this war, and most of my friends of the Six Nations did not want it. We drew them to fight our battles with promises that were not kept, and gifts that I supplied on trust. A trust that is not honored. I have lost friends I cherish, because they trusted my word. And the loss of each man falls hard among the Mohawk, because they are a small people.

"I cannot begin to tell you what those who have manned the frontier have suffered, these winters past. Our ordeals may seem small to you, small and remote. But I tell you, with certainty, that what we have suffered is only a rehearsal for the greater war that is coming. It is being waged already in the Ohio country, driven by the appetites of our Virginia and Pennsylvania land barons, and the resolution of French soldiers and priests, who do not answer to conniving assemblies.

"I do not know how this war will end, but I know it goes on as will grow. I do not wish to promote myself above others, but I must tell you that it is my personal interest with the Indians that holds the frontier, so you may sit here at ease, under your pigeon-wings. If you deny me money, the French will consume that interest. It is the Frenchmen's influence with the Far Indians, and the Mission Indians, that made them an overmatch for us in the late war, as we are woefully aware.

"The tame people of these provinces are no match for Indians in forest wars, yet you take no care to preserve their friendship. You court them in time of need and steal from them and abuse them when you think you are safe. The French have more honor, and the Indians see it."

"Are you *quite* finished?" DeLancey dusted his nose. "I find you have gone to school with the savages, Mister Johnson. I am glad you have found a means to promote your education, although I see you have not managed to improve your manners. I thank you for your speech, but I fear it is wasted on me. It is not in my gift to settle your present difficulties, even had I inclination to do it. I cannot concern myself with the troubles of every vaguing Irishman who makes a noise in this province."

In bitter anger, Johnson threatened to abandon his commissions as Colonel of the Five Nations and Commissary of the Indians, and to let the colony and the DeLanceys go hang themselves while he turned his efforts to repairing his own fortunes.

DeLancey smoothed his pearly silk waistcoat.

"You must consult with your conscience. When you find it."

2.

Cat sat on the porch, skewering candied apples with little sticks, for the children to eat. Smells of apples, nutmeg and cinnamon wafted out from the kitchen. She had set a big pot of mulled cider to simmer over the fire. She thought, *Billy will come soon to taste it.*

The hours slipped by, night came down like a black cloth, and Billy did not return. She stabbed at the last apples, more now than she could find mouths for. The little sticks became spears in her hand.

She put the children to bed. Polly would not close her eyes until Cat had made Halloween costumes from scraps of paper and rags for seven of her dolls—her "friends," she always called them.

When she went downstairs, Johnson was shutting the door of the blue room. He had moved in a bed. Most of the nights he spent under his own roof, he now stayed in that room. He was not always alone, since the Indians had brought him the French woman.

"Billy—"

He affected not to hear, closing the door firmly behind him.

She crossed the hall and put her ear to the door. She heard scuffling, whispered profanities, the gurgle of Angélique's laughter. She was ashamed to be eavesdropping, shamed by what she heard.

"Colonel Johnson—" Her throat was congested. She coughed and called louder, her hand on the doorknob.

"God's thunder!" Billy's face in the chink, purple with anger. "Can I have no privacy in my own house?"

Johnson's sanctum smelled viler than a fur trader's digs. The smell emanated from pelts and animal heads, from bearskins and buffalo robes, compounded with old tobacco smoke, sour wine and the peppery, gingerish tang of its master's inhalations and electuaries. Tonight there was something else. The scent of a woman in heat, poorly masked by cologne. Cat always smelled them. In the absence of all other evidence, she *knew*.

She met his eyes. "I must speak with you."

"Dammit, woman. Not now!" But he stepped out into the hall, his clothes in disarray.

"You did not say goodnight to the children."

"I have a thousand things to attend to, woman! This house will be sold from under us unless I can settle my accounts!"

"It means so much to them. It is not so much to ask."

"Tell them I will check on them later."

She looked at his throat. At the door, and what it concealed.

"Oh, Cat." He cupped her cheek with his hand. "Do

not let yourself be hurt by me. God made me as I am. Does not Spinoza say that every kind of being must seek to persist in what it is? Can a rock be other than a rock? Can the tiger live on grass?"

"Don't trust her, Billy."

Why did she have to say it? Because this one challenged her under her own roof? Because the French woman might be the one that did not go away?

His anger returned, stronger than before. Something came down over his eyes like a visor. His mouth became a straight line, and for a moment he lost his lips.

"You are standing in my path, woman."

She could not speak. The force of his anger struck her like a fist.

"Get–out–of–my–way." That voice, slower and quieter, scared her more than the other.

You have no idea of the power of your rage. The words sounded only inside her head. She could not speak or stir.

"Do you hear me?" Billy's voice dropped even lower. "I do not mean to harm you, but I cannot save you if you oppose my path. You are like a mad person standing on Tribes Hill in the thick of a thunderstorm, baring your breast and inviting the lightning to strike. I ask you again, *Will you move?*"

She could only goggle. He swore and lunged at her with the compacted fury of a bull that had been nicked in the ring.

She met the violence of his arms with open palms, limp as flannel.

He lifted her bodily. "Get *out!*" He half-pushed, half-threw her across the hall. She settled in a bruised heap, like a spilled laundry basket, at the foot of the stairs.

When he slammed back into his den, Polly was crying upstairs, her breath sawing like that of a drowning person gasping for air.

Thank God there was always someone else to comfort. At least she had the comfort of giving. She would always have that.

And the dreams.

□

I am spearing candy apples that become faces. Thunder-heads rear up, all along the sky. Billy is out there in the storm, dancing and reveling. He is treading out a compli-cated circle dance, invoking the lightning, exulting in the storm. The lightning strikes him. He lights up. His whole body shines, like a glowworm. He beckons to me.

I do not want to go near him. He is dangerous. But he is commanding me, and I cannot oppose him. I move to him grudgingly, my body protesting every step.

Our fingers touch. Oh, something is breaking far within me. It is an explosion that blows every fiber and particle of my being away from the molten, vanishing core. My parts whirl away from me, air dissolving into air. I am become vapor. I am not here, not there.

3.

Abbé Picquet planted his new mission on the edge of the lands of the Longhouse people, where the Oswegat-chie—the Black Water—joins the St. Lawrence. The warrior-priest had found a deep, sheltered harbor that rarely froze, where sloops could leave on winds from north, south or east. There was plenty of timber for his blockhouses and stockade, his barracks and the steep-roofed church.

The Abbé worked in a fever, building lodges for new converts, clearing land from three in the morning until nine at night.

He made war on sleep, celebrating the Blessed Sacra-ment after midnight.

Picquet was convinced that this mission, dubbed La Présentation, was the key to the destinies of France and the True Faith in the New World. He sat astride ancient warpaths of the Six Nations. If they came again to ravage the strip-farms of the Canadians along the riverfront, they would have to answer to him.

But his principal aim was not defensive; he had al-ready proved that he was no passive soldier of Christ, in peace or war. He had planned his mission for attack. From La Présentation, he was soon dispatching agents and preachers a hundred leagues south and a hundred leagues west, deep into the heart of the Confederacy, to catch the souls of Senecas, Onondagas and Oneidas. He lured them to the mission on the Black Water as the blackrobes of an earlier time had lured Mohawks to the mission on the falls above Montreal. He held out powerful inducements: food in winter, safety under the guns of his fort, release from the green serpent, rum. And the favor of a Great Spirit that marched against witches and Englishmen on heels of thunder.

Mohawks came to kill his carpenters and burn him out. He fought them off and sent scalping-parties to harry their hunters.

At Onondaga, the famous Speaker of the Confederacy, Canassatego—known to the sister-nations as The Word—spoke against Abbé Picquet and his promises, as he had counseled against the pledges of Johnson and the English.

"The priest schemes to steal our souls as well as our bodies," The Word warned.

Confident that all instruments that work the will of God are blessed, the Abbé recruited a Mohawk renegade, a woman skilled in the arts of poisoning. She fed The Word the shredded root of the water hemlock, *cicuta maculata*. The Word vomited blood, when his stomach burst. The songs of the Peacemaker drowned in the hot tides that swamped his lungs.

4.

It was Angélique's turn to weep when the prisoner exchange was arranged.

"But I do not regard myself as your prisoner, *cher* Billy. I am privileged to have been your guest."

And your flowerpot. Cat looked on balefully, remembering the breathy remarks about a certain watering can.

"I will write to you," Johnson said with some embarrassment, conscious of other ears. "I am already in touch with your father."

"I know our people will be friends now. Have you seen the city of Quebec? It is dazzling in summer. I will show it to you."

Will she never leave off?

Cat was glad the children did not respond to Angélique's parting embraces. Except for Polly, who loved everything that breathed.

When the wagon bearing Angélique and the other French prisoners delivered by the Mohawks had vanished down the King's Road to Albany—and eventually, Montreal—Cat bearded Billy in the sanctum from which she had been excluded, on the pretext of the war, while the French woman was in the house.

Johnson looked strained.

"Is Angélique coming back?" Cat asked, point-blank.

"What? Uh. I don't know. I mean, I don't think so."

"I know it is not my place to ask. But the loyalties of the children must not be confused. I must know what to say to them."

"Quite so." He passed his hand across his eyes.

So sad, so tired.

Cat knelt at his feet. "I wish I could do something to help. Would it help you to talk to me, at least?"

"It would only trouble you."

"Try me."

"Well, try this for a start. This wretched war has left me with debts that New York will not pay. And I fear the King will not pay either. I shall have to start all over again.

"I made the Indians promises I could not keep. Or, if I am to be kind to myself, I might say those whose sureties I accepted for these promises have failed all of us. That England would send an army. That there would be no prisoner exchange unless all the Indians of the Six Nations who are held in captivity in Canada are included. Our masters deny me even in this. Can you imagine what this means? Sun Walker, the husband of the clanmother of the Turtle Clan, languishes in irons in Quebec while we swap Frenchmen for Englishmen! The Mohawk will not forgive the insult!"

He reached for the decanter. He reached more and more frequently, Cat noticed.

She listened, grateful that the pain he expressed did not seem to center in Angélique. Or at least, that he did not say so.

"I will start again," he repeated. "I will give up my government titles, because the government that gives them does not honor its obligations, to me or the Indians. I will make my fortune, because in this country only a man with money can win through. I hear the Chinamen are avid for ginseng, which grows everywhere wild in this Valley. I will set the natives to feed them. I will build my big stone house. And it will stand here, in this Valley, as proof of my purpose. When war comes again, as it must, I will be ready. I will not be broken. What I build here will be remembered for generations to come!"

I, I, I.

Cat could forgive him for not including her. But the children?

"You are a good woman, Cat. You must have patience with me. I am quite fatigued. And I have had disappointments heaped on me. I seem to recall you told me once, at Dublin, that something like this will come."

"I believe in you, Billy," she said quietly. "But I think you will always do best when you act for others besides yourself."

5.

The Mohawks had buried White Owl's remains deep in the snow, when the ground was frozen hard as iron. An ice mound served as his burial cairn, until the spring melt, when his family came to wrap him in a beaver robe and carry him to a ground of the ancestors.

White Owl's mother spoke over his burial place.

"I expected to reach the end of the path of life before you. But you were fleeter. You outstripped me and go on before, along the path of strawberries. It is the will of our Creator that I should linger here to drink more of the bitterness of life.

"We part now. You are taken from our eyes. But we will meet again soon. We will sing together in the lodges of our ancestors."

Bright Meadow's lament was a long, ululating shrill. She tore at her ragged blouse, baring her skin to the cold. Her face was gaunt, the skin drawn back against the bones, under the layers of ash and grease. Her hair was rank and matted, the shining plaits brutally hacked off.

Island Woman took her by the armpits and raised her to her feet. "Let him go," she said gently.

"I die this life," Bright Meadow sobbed.

"He journeys on the path of souls," Island Woman told her. "You must let him go where he is meant to go."

She nodded to her granddaughter. Sparrow stepped to the edge of the grave site. She opened the sack she had carried with her.

She hummed to the soft gray bird inside. The mourning dove was yellow under the wings, with a flash of red behind its neck. She had caught it in an angle of the longhouse roof.

The bird did not struggle with her. She raised it to shoulder height and gave it an upward hoist.

The dove sailed into the white sun.

"Your father leaves us," Island Woman said to Sparrow. The dead warrior's name would never be said aloud unless it was conferred on another of the Real People in the rituals of requickening. Because the dead are always listening, and the boundary between the living and the dead is exactly as wide as the edge of a maple leaf.

PART THREE
THE LIVING BONES

━━ ❧✦❧ ━━

I passed some Days at Sir William Johnson's, but no consideration should tempt me to lead his life—I suppose custom may in some degree have reconciled him to it, but I know no other man equal to so disagreeable a Duty.

—Lord Adam Gordon, *Journal of an Officer who Travelled in American and the West Indies in 1764 and 1765*

CHAPTER 26
SHE WHO DREAMS

1.

"Tell me the dream." Island Woman took her granddaughter's wrist.

Sparrow sat close beside her. She pulled her knees up to her chest, inside the circle of her arms, and rocked on her bottom as she spoke. The sweet, earthy smell of the loaves of cornbread baking in the ashes was forgotten.

"I am in the deep woods," Sparrow began. "I am walking into the mist. It is not an ordinary mist. It swirls like a dance robe. Like the feathered robe of an Eagle Dancer. It is full of colors, all the colors of the rainbow. I feel safe inside this mist. It lifts me and guides me.

"When the mist opens, I am in a meadow that is bright with wildflowers. I start to pick them. I am weaving a garland of flowers.

"An ancient man is waiting for me. His white hair brushes his shoulders like horses' tails. His eyes burn like fire. But I am not afraid of him.

"He opens his arms to me, and I offer him my flowers. As I approach him, the flowers become a baby. The baby's skin gleams like the first sap of the maple.

"The old man smiles. He opens his hands to accept

the gift. When I place my baby in his arms, it changes. It becomes a great white belt. The wampum has been formed into many intricate designs. The ancient one teaches me how to read the meanings of the shells of life.

"I do not want to leave him, but he shows me the paths I must follow.

"He speaks to me with his mind. His lips never open. He tells me, *You were an interpreter before your world was born.*

"He says, *Burn tobacco for me.*"

Her eyes closed, her fingertips riding on the pulse of Sparrow's blood, Island Woman saw the shining meadow, and the ancient who had announced himself to her granddaughter.

Island Woman knew this dream teacher as she knew her own heart.

He has summoned her. He concealed himself from my daughters, but he has come for Sparrow. She is very young. She cannot begin to understand the burden of this great gift. She will not be as others. Everything will be different for her. But the gift cannot be refused. This summons comes only to one who dreams true. If it is refused, the soul grows restless and the body begins to die.

Sparrow waited for her grandmother to speak.

Island Woman said, "It is a powerful dream."

"Do you know him? The old one who instructed me?"

"I have seen him. There are places in dreaming where you may look for him again. And for other teachers. You have discovered one of these places. There are others."

"Why did I give him my baby? Why did the baby change into a wampum belt?"

"I think you must dream on this in the woods."

□

Island Woman spoke to Bright Meadow. "Sparrow's guides are calling her. She must meet them alone, at a place of Power."

Bright Meadow was uneasy. Her daughter was so young; she had counted only ten winters. And Panther's breath was on the wind, in the cold moon that beats down the bushes. There was fresh snow on the ground, and dangerous men in the woods, coarse bushlopers who respected neither age nor sex. And the war-drums were beating again, to the north and the west. French soldiers had marched through the Ohio country and sailed down the Mississippi. They had buried lead plates with the arms of the Sun King, claiming all this land for France. They had returned in larger numbers to build forts and demonstrate to the nations that the Sun King had awakened from his long sleep and was coming to take what he claimed on the maps.

"Can't we wait until the sugar moon?" Bright Meadow asked. "I don't want her out in the woods alone in this cold season."

"Her time is now. She has been summoned. This is a great gift, that cannot be refused. Our family is honored. I believe she is the one we have waited for."

Bright Meadow's face creased. *She is aging fast,* Island Woman noticed. Her daughter already had a streak of gray in her hair, which was unusual among the Real People unless they had lived many more winters. Island Woman felt the force of the conflict in Bright Meadow's heart. Of a mother's pride, grappling with a mother's fear. Of old disappointment, that she herself had not been the chosen one—that the gift had skipped a generation—contending with new skepticism about the power of the dreaming to provide a path for their people in the Shadow World ruled by the newcomers and their tools and appetites.

"You are a good mother." Island Woman embraced her daughter, hugging her tight against her chest. "You have always known this time would come. It has come early, because our need is so great. You must release Sparrow to what is calling her. She must fly on her own wings."

2.

Down trails invisible in the deep woods, where the moon was hidden behind the trees, Sparrow struggled to keep up with her grandmother, whose speed and stamina belied her age.

Claws of the forest struck at the child's face, tearing the skin. Sparrow stubbed her toes on a concealed root and bruised her knees in the fall.

When a snowy owl hooted nearby, she began to tremble, because Island Woman had vanished.

Her grandmother's tracks disappeared at an immense barrier of fallen limbs and tree trunks. Some of the trees had been ripped from the earth and flung across the trail. Some had snapped at the middle. Others, still planted in the earth, were bent down by the weight of uprooted trees that leaned against them, sawing and creaking with every blast of cold air.

Sparrow shivered, goosebumps rising on her arms and shoulders.

This was surely a place of Whirlwind, the Dark Twin.

"Aksotha!" The child's voice fluted against the dark power she sensed in every shadow.

She stood very still, willing her heart to stop thumping so she could catch Island Woman's answering call.

The woods were alive with voices.

Sparrow heard the skirl of shifting winds, the cracking of frozen sap, the rustle and chuff of small furry things, the growl of a mountain lion. The high, lonely call of a timber wolf.

She sensed, more than heard, the vibration of something huge. It came bowling through the choked forest, clearing a path by its unstoppable force. Its steps made Sparrow's world tremble.

The child fought with the rank terror of being abandoned in the place, without even the tools of fire to keep night-goers at bay.

She sensed a tremendous force of evil, coiling and uncoiling in the wells of darkness. Its presence sucked out her energy. It made her head go woozy. Her senses blurred. Fatigue began to swallow her. She wanted only to lie down and sleep.

Darkness clotted around her.

She pinched herself hard. She dug her fingernails into her palms until the blood flowed.

I will meet this test, she promised herself. *May the friendly spirits watch over me.*

She forced herself on, willing her failing body to obey her intent. She scaled ridges of broken trees. Through the second skin of her moosehide boots, she felt the smooth furrow of a trail on the other side. She broke into a jog, her confidence rising.

Before she knew it, she was back among the thickets of uprooted trees. She realized she must have turned full circle.

Now she had lost all sense of direction. The night chill slithered inside her marrow. She groped with numb fingers for splotches of moss low down on the tree trunks, to point her north.

The wind dropped. The voices of birds and animals were stilled.

For a long moment, Sparrow heard only the rush of her own blood.

Then she felt, very close to her, the breath of something that thrived only in darkness. She had awakened ancient evil in the deep woods. Her fear was drawing it closer. It had locked onto her.

It knows my life.

She was suffocating in her own fear. The tides of her blood flowed sluggishly now. Her body went limp. It folded under her like a rag doll, and she fell without noticing the bump.

Something squatted on her chest, pressing the air from her lungs.

I must get up. If I stay on the ground, I die.

She dragged herself to her feet. Moving her legs was like walking underwater.

Sparrow battled on. But the forest closed tighter around her, a monstrous womb that would not release its young.

She pleaded for someone to guide her. She called to the ancient one of her dream.

She heard the distant babble of water over stone. She followed it to a rise, and climbed to the top, slipping on wet, dead leaves. Then she was rolling and bumping down a steep rocky incline. She clutched at hanging branches in an effort to break her fall. She fell into icy scum.

When she tried to stand, the spruce bog swallowed her body, up to the eyes. Sobbing, she thrashed around in the cold, sucking mud. It was pulling her deeper. It would not let her go.

Her will to fight was flickering out, because there was no safety even on solid ground. A power of the unseen was pursuing her. She heard it crashing through the bushes, too strong—too confident of its prey—to need stealth.

"Aksotha!" she called again for Island Woman.

A blood-flecked moon rode out from the clouds and showed what waited for her above the bog.

Ohkwari reared like a mountain from the edge of the swamp.

A soft, chuffing sound rose from his belly and blew steam through his lips. He opened his jaws. His canines flashed like white knives. His molars were mortars made for grinding bones to fine dust.

The great dish-face leaned over the child.

The bear was reaching for her. He plucked her from the bog and gathered her into his terrible embrace.

A song from the cradleboard rattled inside the girl's head, mocking the death that had found her:

> *Don't cry, little one.*
> *The bear is coming to dance for you.*
> *The bear is coming to dance for you.*

Ohkwari sniffed her. She met his shining eyes, and her fear slipped away. There was something fiercely protective, and very familiar, in his gaze.

He laid her down gently on a blanket of dry needles.

He pressed his strong paws against her small, narrow hands. He gave her a song of healing. Ohkwari knows all the medicines of the forest.

She knew she had found a guardian.

3.

After this, Sparrow's senses were muddled, and her body became a house of dreams.

When she opened her eyes, in the daylight world, she found herself lying on a limestone ledge, high above the river.

She saw her grandmother tending a fire and smelled burning tobacco.

She was desperately thirsty. She could barely swallow. Her lips were chapped.

Island Woman came to her, nodding as she mimed her need for water.

She thought her grandmother was bringing her ice chips or fresh-fallen snow in her cupped palms. But when she saw that Island Woman was holding a piece of charcoal, glowing dull red from the fire, she took it without resisting. When the fire entered her mouth, she felt cold, not heat, and no sense of pain. Fire touched her eyelids, her ears.

Island Woman—or was it another?—was singing.

"You have changed your eyes and your hearing so you may see and hear in the Real World."

Her grandmother brought eagle feathers. She placed them in Sparrow's mouth four times, while she sang. The fourth time, the feathers disappeared.

She fell deeper into the dreaming.

She sailed on the mind-sea, where forms are endlessly borning and transforming.

She journeyed through night-worlds where the unhappy dead twittered like bats.

She saw things from a time when men were hunted by scaled giants and from a time when men flew beyond the sun inside armored birds.

She fell upward, through a funnel in the sky. She climbed through cloud-ceilings that stretched and parted like membranes. She became a fireball, shooting across starry space. She flew with winged beings across a world that was fresh and beautiful, with colors more vivid than any she had seen with ordinary eyes.

She did not want to come back.

But a loving teacher told her, "You will return to us when it is your time. You are flanked and supported on all sides. You must remember the songs we have given you, to call us in your time of need. Other things you are not permitted to remember."

He blew a shower of crystals into her.

She felt herself expand, growing bigger and bigger. Then she exploded. Pieces of her vital being flew off in all directions, in a shower of particles. When they came together again, she was different. When she came back this time, she was cold and pale as a body left in a creekbed for days.

Island Woman gave her lukewarm water and a mouthful of corn soup.

Sparrow's grandmother asked her nothing about her experiences.

But when she was strong enough to walk and keep down solid food, Island Woman said, "Now it is time for you to tell me my dream."

They sat together again, Island Woman resting her right elbow on her granddaughter's knee.

Sparrow held the matriarch's right wrist in her left palm, her body trembling lightly. Her breathing became rougher, raspier, as if she were asleep and snoring. Her heels clacked against the rock ledge.

Island Woman waited.

"I see the eagle," Sparrow spoke with her eyes closed.

Island Woman said nothing. Wherever she journeyed, the eagle flew with her. This was known. It was no discovery.

"I am flying with the eagle. He is showing me a house of stone. A white man's house, with guns at the windows. There is a fire that burns there night and day. Our warriors are dancing around it. A white man dances with them. He is stripped and painted for war. He is dancing his *oyaron,* like one of the Real People. He is no longer a man. He is beating his wings."

Island Woman grunted. *She sees. She is inside my dream.*

Sparrow gave a sighing gasp. "Our people are vanishing. They are not leaving this place. They are plucked from the dance. They vanish into the air, like wind beings."

"It is the dream," Island Woman confirmed.

CHAPTER 27
WHITE DEATH

1.

The moon of flowers brought hot, sultry days and soft, cold nights. The red maples began to scatter their seeds, and pigeons gathered around them in great feathery clouds. When the wind shook the trees and turned up the silvery undersides of the leaves, the red maples seemed to be full of white flowers.

Mohawk men went out fishing, following the spawning runs of walleye, pike and sturgeon. The women gathered firewood or worked the fields in sociable groups, weeding and burning, getting ready to plant the seeds of the Three Sisters—corn, beans and squash—anew.

Island Woman gathered plants for healing and man-root for trade, ranging the shady hollows with Bright Meadow or Sparrow. Usually, it was Sparrow who accompanied her. The child was quick to learn the medicine ways. She saw the relatedness of things. How the fern whose fronds curl up tight when it is young but unroll and straighten out as it grows is the right medicine for cramped muscles. How milkweed, whose thick juice oozes like pus, is right for skin eruptions.

Sparrow seemed to *know* which roots to pull in the bitten moon, which to take when the moon was full. She knew not to bring the manroot the whites prized so much into the house, because it was in the gift of Tsawiskaron, the Dark Twin. She took nothing from the earth without returning thanks, with words sung or spoken, with little twists of real tobacco.

She is born to it. Island Woman saw Sparrow's vocation confirmed every day. She was both dreamer and healer. In her fullness, she would be truly a woman of power, perhaps the greatest in their line.

When they had gathered more ginseng than they could carry on their backs, Island Woman said, "We will go to The Net."

Bright Meadow was disappointed. "Forest Killer's house is near," she objected. "And he gives fair prices. Everyone says so."

"We go to Albany," Island Woman said firmly.

Bright Meadow was between husbands again, and Island Woman wanted to keep her well away from Billy Johnson. It was bad enough that she was making eyes at old Brant in the Lower Castle, a man who had a wife already. The matriarch wanted no more family entanglements with the Irishman across the river.

Besides, it was likely they would hear something new at Albany. There were fresh rumors of war, reports that the French were sending a great army into the Ohio country. The women should not depend solely on the men for information on matters that concerned the survival of the whole community. Least of all on Hendrick Forked Paths and the Burned Knives.

Women make better choices than men. Island Woman had said this to the women's council after she was raised up as Mother of the Wolf Clan. *We remember what men forget. That we must weigh the consequence of every action down to the seventh generation. We remember because we are the life-bringers and we know that everything is related.*

□

Bright Meadow's skin glistened with oil and smelled of sweetgrass.

In the canoe on the river, Sparrow asked, "Why are the white men so greedy for manroot?"

Island Woman laughed like a crow. "They sell it to yellow men who think it will make their fish jump."

Sparrow was keenly interested, like any girl of her age. It gave Island Woman a jolt, at times, to be reminded that—for all her knowing—her granddaughter was not yet a woman. That time would come soon enough. But for now, she had the innocence and openness of a child.

"Is it true?" Sparrow asked.

Caroline Bigcanoe cackled. She was the fourth member of the party. She was plump and lazy, forever finding excuses to get out of the hardest part of the labor in the cornfields. She had little ginseng to trade at Albany, but Snowbird had given her a few pelts to sell. Island Woman thought her son was too soft on his new wife, but did not say so because she did not want to be accused of talking like all mothers.

"If you find a yellow man," Caroline told Sparrow, "you can ask him."

□

Bright Meadow and Caroline Bigcanoe both loved trinkets. Between them, they brought home a whole sackful of silver bells and brooches and jew's harps from Widow Veeder.

Not long after that, Caroline became lazier than ever. Three days running, she failed to join the other women on the hill where they were planting corn with their digging sticks.

Island Woman decided to confront her. Snowbird and his wife lived with Caroline's mother, in a lodge with the Turtle Clan emblem over the door.

Island Woman was alarmed by what she found inside. Caroline complained of a hard headache and chills that alternated with an itching fever. She could hardly seem to raise her head off her sleeping mat.

Fearing the worst, Island Woman insisted that she should be isolated from the rest of the village. The women carried her on a litter to a shelter in the woods, like the cabins they used in their time of power.

Caroline was so weak the motion of the litter made her swoon.

Island Woman and Caroline's mother took turns to bring her bark teas and corn soup. The fever abated, and she was able to keep a little down.

Then the fever returned with a vengeance. Caroline was on fire. She screamed and clawed at her skin, which peeled off in huge strips, like the bark of the silver birch.

She bled from nose and mouth and the place between her thighs.

Her body shook and kicked as if a whole tentful of bad spirits had gotten inside it.

Island Woman made Sparrow fetch pails of water and washed the sick woman at dawn and at dusk. She knew the skin must be allowed to breathe. If the sickness was what she feared, the ones that died fastest were those whose pores were blocked. She had seen this before.

She went to the elders of the Society of Faces, reserved for men. They agreed to call on the masked powers. The spirits that cause disease are also the spirits that take it away, and the mask is man's link with the spirits.

The False Face, the *kakonsa,* not only summons the spirits that cause and cure sickness. The Face is ensouled. When a man puts on the mask, he *becomes* the spirit, and is joined with its power. Only an initiate, summoned by his own dreams, is permitted to wear a Face. The Face will turn on any other user and drive him to death or madness. Island Woman remembered a man who had abused the power of a Face to make love magic. The mask had cleaved to his skin as if grafted to it. When he finally prised it off, his face was charred.

The Face of the spirit that brings smallpox was a thing of nightmare, more terrible even than the mask of the Divided One, the Face of Whirlwind. The other masks

were black or red, but this one was white, like the white
men who had brought the sickness of spitting sores into
the Real World. The forehead was pitted with ugly holes.
The huge eye-pieces were brass, round and staring like a
great horned owl. The dry, pursed lips were blowing.

The spirits of sickness strike through the air, blowing
evil things into the bodies of their victims. Dreamers can
see them. They look like worms or tiny snakes, like
minute arrows or tufts of hair. If you can *see* something,
you can change it.

But the spirit of the white man's disease was cruel and
unruly. He was an intruder from outside the Real World,
and he was heedless of its laws. He obeyed neither the
shamans nor the white men's doctors. He came and went
at his own choosing.

They fed the Face with tobacco and mush prepared
from the white cornmeal that hunters and warriors carry
on the trail. They rubbed its eyes with manroot, which
has uses traders know nothing about. They sang over it
in high, nasal voices, shaking their turtle rattles. They
followed the Husk Face heralds, brandishing their long
staffs, to the cabin where Caroline Bigcanoe lay shaking
and slavering on a filthy mat.

The masked doctor grabbed her by the hair and
rubbed her scalp violently. He scooped up glowing
embers in his bare hands, suffering no burns. He blew
hot ashes over her head.

Caroline fell into wilder spasms. She mimicked the
whines and screeches of the Face dancer and crawled on
her belly toward the fire. She grabbed at the hot coals
like a False Face hunting tobacco. Island Woman pulled
her back before she scorched herself badly.

They all danced around the fire, to the beat of the turtle
rattles and the water-drum, making the circle of healing.

It is not enough. Island Woman could see it. Already
Caroline's spirit was passing over. It was ready to drop
her body like a worn out set of clothes.

In the days that followed, all of them saw it.

Caroline sprouted spots as dark as blueberries, and
spots as pale and dry as parchment. Her skin whitened
to the color of fading silver.

And Island Woman's fear struck deeper. Sparrow and
Bright Meadow had traveled with them to Albany and
back. They had slept under the same roof. They had
traded and eaten with the same whites, gossiped with the
same Caughnawagas from the blackrobe missions.

Island Woman trembled, remembering the last time
smallpox had ravaged the Valley. And the time before
that, when it had almost destroyed the Real People, and
the gifts of the greatest of all the dream-prophets had
been powerless against it.

2.

*It was in her grandmother's time, at the end of a hard
winter that heaped snow as high as the village palisades.*

*The dream-prophet was ancient and almost blind. He
lived apart from the village, in a cave in a limestone cliff.*

*When the people started dying like rotten sheep, the
clanmothers came to him with gifts of tobacco and asked
him to intercede in the spirit realm.*

*The dreamer fasted for seven nights, taking only water
and the juice of native tobacco. Then the great ones came
to him. They gave him a new song.*

*He made a cleansing lotion, boiled from the bark of the
ash, the spruce, the hemlock and the wild cherry. Island
Woman brought him the ingredients at the times he
instructed.*

*She had been his apprentice from the cradleboard, as
Sparrow was hers. When she was still in her mother's
body, she had heard his singing. He had sung to her when
it was time to leave the element of water. She had always
known him. She knew that when she looked in his eyes.
He scared the other children and many of their elders.
They did not even dare to say his skin name, for fear it
would bring him instantly. They called him Longhair,
because of the storm of white hair about his shoulders. Or
simply Ratetshents. The One Who Dreams.*

*The dreamer told Island Woman to gather the elders
and the clanmothers in the council house. He came to
them, leaning on his oak staff, with a pantherskin over his
shoulders. His hair was dressed with the feathers of the*

*golden eagle and the hummingbird, the heron and the
redtail hawk.*

*He spoke in a lilting voice that was part-human, part-
bird. He whistled for his spirit guides. Island Woman saw
them whirl in the leaping flames of the medicine fire.*

*The dreamer told the Real People to prepare a ritual
feast and to send a white dog to the sky world to atone to
the great ones, because they had strayed from the ways of
the ancestors. He ordered those struck by the disease to
eat only spirit food, the crushed strawberries kept through
the winter for the sacred rituals of the Longhouse.*

*When the villagers kept on dying, he ordered all the
families to hang Faces at the doors of their lodges and to
place straw archers on their roofs to scare away evil spirits
of the air.*

*The people kept dying. The villagers whispered that the
Dreamer's power was gone. The white men's demons did
not bow to his commands.*

*The blackrobe priests said the terrible disease was a
punishment sent by their God, because the Real People
did not follow his ways. They said their God was all-
powerful. Had he not given the newcomers guns and ships
and wagons? Be baptized, the blackrobes said, and you
will live.*

*Many of the Real People listened, and followed the
blackrobes to their missions. They went on dying.*

*The dream-prophet, worn out by his battles, went back
to his limestone cave. Island Woman went with him. She
survived the epidemic that claimed her mother's life and
those of half the village. She learned to journey in the
upper and lower worlds and to hunt lost souls.*

*She saw, in her teacher's heart-sickness, that the white
death came from a different dreaming, into the Shadow
World.*

3.

Johnson was alarmed by successive reports of new
outbreaks of smallpox. First came a letter from Witham
Marsh in New York, reporting that the city was in a
panic and the new session of the Assembly had been

prorogued. Suspicions about the source of the infection fell, as always, on new arrivals by sea—on sailors and slaves off a ship from the islands that had not been duly quarantined. Then came news from Captain Rutherford that a soldier of the Albany garrison had broken out in pustules. Much of the trade of the town had come to a standstill, as the burghers bolted their doors or took flight to country retreats, fearing the night rattle of the death-carts over the cobbled streets. Worst was the news of an outbreak at the Upper Castle. The Mohawks had no resistance to imported diseases. More had died from smallpox and measles than in any war. The new plague would move through them like a wildfire. And it threatened the safety of Billy's own household.

He issued instructions on hygiene and checked for symptoms of disease.

"Sappho has been sick for two days," Cat told him.

Johnson went out to the slave quarters and found the house servant was gone.

He summoned Paddy Groghan, the overseer, and asked what he knew of it.

"Do you suppose she has run away?"

"Not Sappho," Groghan eased his floppy brimmed felt hat back over his forehead. "She's not the sort. Besides, she'd never go without Cuffee. They've been coupling for two seasons, at least. I expect she'll have one in the oven by now."

Johnson spoke to the field hand. Cuffee would not meet his eyes and pretended to understand even less English than he had. Johnson struggled to make his intentions clear.

"I will not punish her, whatever she has done. I must know if she is sick for the safety of all."

He could get nothing out of the field hand. He noticed fresh scars on the man's arm, but thought nothing of it. Men damaged themselves on his estates every day, girdling timber, sawing logs, working the gristmill.

Paddy Groghan came before the week was out, to tell him the worst. "Cuffee's got the pox. I caught him trying to run."

Billy had the field hand isolated from the other slaves. He sent to Schenectady for Doctor Magin.

The doctor rode up the Valley, took a brief look at the patient, and told Johnson he was puzzled.

"Never seen a case like it. It's the smallpox, no doubt about it. I counted eighteen pustules. But they are confined to one arm, his left arm I believe. And though he has the sweats, he remains quite strong. The disease has attacked only one part of the body. A single limb."

Cat listened to this intently. She had joined them in the parlor with the tea and asked if she might stay, to learn how best to safeguard the children.

"I tried to question him about it," Doctor Magin continued. "But the fellow is either defective, or does not comprehend English. I wonder—" he swigged down his tea without ceremony, and held out his cup for more. "Did you ever hear of inoculation?"

"I believe I read something in the *Gentleman's Magazine*. Does it not involve infecting healthy patients with the juice of the disease?"

"Exactly."

Cat grimaced.

"It is a novelty in the practice of British medicine," Magin pursued. "Many of our practitioners consider it a noxious and desperate remedy, as likely to kill the patient as to heal him. It has been generally avoided in the colonies since the Boston riots some years ago."

"The Boston riots? They are unknown to me."

"It was before your time. A surgeon called Boylston experimented on his own son, and some house servants, with some degree of success. I understand that Cotton Mather was at the back of it."

"Cotton Mather? The arch-Puritan? I thought he hunted devils, not germs."

"Perhaps Mister Mather believed they are related. In any event, news of the experiments created an uproar. The Bostonians were not disposed to be thus used. They threw a firebomb into Mather's house. It takes a bold spirit to persist with science in the teeth of public prejudice."

"I could add examples to your case," Billy agreed. "But why this story of Boston and contentious needles?"

"The thing of it is, I think your slave was inoculated."

"That is quite impossible."

"Did you see the scars on his arm?"

"I noticed something. I thought he had scraped himself working my land."

"I presumed the marks were tribal in origin when I first saw them. I have heard that in Africa boys are cut to prove their readiness for manhood. But on closer inspection I formed the judgment that the incisions were made recently, to convey the variola of the pox from another victim to Cuffee."

"It is a strange tale you are spinning us, Doctor Magin. I do not know what to make of it. There is no other doctor in these parts that is known to me. And I have never heard of such practices among the native medicine people. We could of course be dealing with an amateur. The Germans at the Flats are hard to know." He glanced at Cat.

"I read in a paper of the Royal Society that inoculation has been known for centuries in the folk medicine of other peoples," Magin added. "For example, it is well-known in Africa. Indeed, it is said that Cotton Mather first learned of inoculation by questioning an African slave who had the marks on his arm."

"Ade." The word burst from Cat before she could check herself.

Magin looked blank.

"You remember," she said to Johnson.

"Your African favorite. The smith. A useful fellow."

"He saved my life."

"And I rewarded him for it. He must be richer than most of his white neighbors by now, sitting athwart the smugglers' road to Montreal. This Ade," he added for the doctor's benefit, "is a freedman. He was of some service to Cat when she first came to the province. I gave him the gear to establish a smithy on his own account. He lives near Saratoga, with little competition. Respectable tradesmen are too scared of French Indian scalpers to hang out their shingles anywhere near." He returned to Cat. "Why do you connect him with this business?"

"He knows things."

Billy shrugged.

"He is more than a tradesman. In his country, working in metal is akin to religion. And he knows more. Secret things. Mysteries."

Johnson arched an eyebrow.

Cat balled her fists in frustration. "I can't explain!"

"Thank you for your views," Johnson's tone left no doubt that Cat was being dismissed.

"Let me talk to Ade."

"No."

"Then talk to him yourself. I know he can help us."

"Shall we take a turn in the garden, Doctor?" Johnson stood. "Perhaps we will be permitted to converse *without interruption* there."

□

When Billy came in an hour later, Cat was ready for a rebuke. She was not expected to take part in conversations between Johnson and his peers because she was not ranked as one of them. She did not question this. It was as clear, as absolute, as the line of the Helderberg mountains. She had dared to speak up in company because her fear for the children outweighed the conventions of the house. And then because of the depth of her feeling for Ade, which went beyond gratitude and surprised her even as she spoke. She had no doubt she would pay for it, and hoped only that Billy would blow hot rather than cold. The ice was deadlier. It took days to recover from it.

But when Billy strolled into her sewing corner, he bussed her and gave her thigh a friendly squeeze.

"You know, if you are right about your African, we could accomplish something very useful. I have discussed it with Magin. He is quite sanguine about our prospects of success. But you see, he's never done an inoculation. He'd like to see Ade at work and judge the results before he makes up his mind."

She kept her face demurely turned to the cloth in her lap so he would not read her expression.

The amazing, maddening thing about Billy was that, under his own roof, he could change his mind—and his mood—at the drop of a pin. He was utterly immune to any charge of inconsistency. He simply flowed on, a force of nature.

Now he was talking about what it would mean to the Mohawks, and his influence over them, if inoculation could save them from the ravages of a new epidemic.

"Mustn't mention that old fart Cotton Mather," he ruminated out loud. "If the Indians hear there is any connection with the Saints of New England, they will run like rabbits and knock us all on the head first. They are already convinced that some of our people are scheming to kill them off."

4.

Ade worked in a one-room smithy, with a dirt floor and a steep-pitched roof to shrug off rain and snow. The small windows were glassless, but had thick shutters that could be shut tight to keep heat in or curious onlookers out. There were heaps of metal scrap, ready to be melted down and recast, and neater piles of imported barrels and locks, homemade springs, and walnut rifle stocks.

The big fieldstone forge stood in an open-sided shelter nearby. A boy with honey-colored skin was working the bellows when Johnson and Doctor Magin rode up. The boy was pumping the lever that squeezed wind into the banked charcoal.

"Is the smith about?"

The boy pointed to a trail winding back into the woods. The white men tied their horses to the rail and followed it.

Magin started when a cripple in bright clothing jumped out from behind the aspens.

Johnson laughed. "I never thought to see you spooked by a thing of wood, Teddy."

"Lord! I never saw such a thing. What a grotesque! But it looks so *real.*"

They inspected the carving. It was the size of a stunted man, one-legged, leaning on a stick as a crutch. One hand was outstretched in greeting. Or warning.

"Fine woodwork," Billy commented.

"What is it?"

"You must ask its maker. Look, he has peopled the whole woods."

Many of the statues stood taller than man-height. They saw a king on horseback, holding a bird-headed staff. Warrior giants brandishing swords or two-headed axes. Female dancers with swaying hips and enormous, pendulous breasts. There were figures that stood on their own legs and figures that had only been partly released from the trees.

"I wonder what our friend's neighbors make of them." Magin was still uneasy.

"Perhaps Ade's purpose is to keep the neighbors at a distance."

There was a simple log cabin ahead, set on a slope above a pond.

Billy was diverted by the stench of blood. He looked for the source and found he had passed it without noticing. The smell came from a small house of field-stone, no higher than his knee. The size of a doghouse.

He bent to inspect it, thinking that one of the smith's animals had been injured. All he saw inside was a large, rounded stone, slathered with clay, decorated with shells and curious jutting spikes.

"What do you want?"

The African stood in front of his house. He was dressed in a fashion strange to Billy, in flowing white robes with colored stripes. He wore a necklace of cowries and a bracelet of green and yellow beads on his left wrist. He was barefoot.

"Good day to you, Ade. We were just admiring your art collection. You do remember me, I trust?"

"I know you."

"Are all these your own work?"

"They are."

"I wish I had known you are as handy with wood as

with metal. I might have saved myself the extortionate price I paid for my new mantels. Though of course I would be inclined to a different style. Do these statues have some special significance?"

"They are saints."

"They don't look like saints to me," Magin grumbled.

"Come now, Teddy. Each people sees their gods in their own way. If the wolves had a deity, do you think he would look like you or me?"

Ade waited, impassive, volunteering nothing more. He was a fine looking man, Johnson thought. Very hard to put an age on him. He was fine-boned, with strong, regular features. His eyes were amber, startlingly bright against the dark skin. He used his body with natural grace. There was almost a majesty about him, as he stood there, watchful, in his exotic dress.

Billy felt something tense inside himself.

We are animals of different kinds. Wolf and bear, lion and leopard. Meeting at a waterhole, sniffing each other, ready to fight or run. How would he greet me on his native soil?

Johnson did not ask about the stone that reeked of blood. Or how the Indians viewed Ade's forest of saints.

"I come bearing gifts." He held out the bag with the rum and a good new set of chisels.

Ade ignored the presents, so Billy set them down by the step.

"We have come to ask you a favor," Johnson tried again.

"I know why you have come. Please take off your shoes."

5.

Ade *felt* the white men. He watched their eyes, listened to their bodies talk. One of them, the narrow-shouldered one with an Adam's apple that bobbed when he swallowed, was neither better nor worse than other white men who came to the smithy. Magin was surprised to find a black man living at his own whim, in relative affluence, and shocked by the images of the *orishas* in the woods. But he did not see Ade as a man like himself. He saw the African as a specimen and wanted to know no more of its habits than was essential to his purpose. He resented Ade's gaze. He shuffled his feet and curled his toes, embarrassed at sitting on a low bench in filthy stockings, his big toe poking out through a hole.

Now, the other one, the big man with the carefree laugh the whites called Colonel and the Mohawk called Forest Killer, was something different. Johnson was capable of being both better *and* worse than other white men, even in the same moment. He was dangerous. Ade felt Johnson's raw energy, his rage for life on his own terms. He was a rampant bull with women. He was clever and charming. He had the dazzle and mischief of the Trickster. He loved upsetting other people's plans and expectations. But in his raging passions, he was a true *omo-Shango*. A child of Thunder.

It was strange to Ade that he recognized Johnson so readily in the images of his own tradition, of which the white man knew nothing. Johnson was open to learning—at least what he could turn to his purpose. He looked about him with a different vision than the doctor's. He was curious about everything. He met Ade's eyes and looked at him as one man looks at another. Challenging, probing for strength or weakness. But also searching. At this moment, Johnson was slightly puzzled. The white man sensed he was dealing with a force that was greater than he had expected, but he did not know how to account for it. He did not have the words.

He is not a lonely man, Ade thought. *He makes home wherever he chooses to be. He cannot know the depth of my loneliness.*

Ade did not hate white men with the ferocity of other Africans he had known when he was still a slave. He had been sold by a king of his own people, after his father, who led soldiers into battle with a lionskin pelt over his head and shoulders, had been defeated in battle. He had been sold to a hawk-nosed trader in a burnoose, sold again to men who spoke Spanish, captured in a fight at sea, traded and re-traded until a Jew from Amsterdam had given him a chance at freedom. He had fared better than others because of his robust constitution and his flair for languages. And because he had been schooled from childhood in a craft that was valued in the white man's world. The art of the goldsmith and the bronze-maker was no common trade, in the cities of the Yoruba. Gold was the blood of the earth. It was worked with ceremony, in a sacred way. Its secrets were guarded. Ade was admitted to them because the fire of Ogun, the patron of all metalworkers, was in him, and because it was in the destiny read for him by a high priest of Ifa.

The knowledge of smelting gold could be applied to baser metals and lesser purposes. Even those of a lock-smith or an installer of cast-iron stoves.

He had survived. He even lived well, by the standards of the frontier.

But he had been uprooted from his whole world. From the birds and animals whose languages he knew. From trees and plants whose names he could say, from the plains where he had hunted, the mountains where he had dreamed. From a glowing young wife and infant twins who had brought new laughter into this world.

And from the drums.

The drums that carried the rhythms of the saints, the energy of soul.

The white men looked at the *batá,* the talking drums he had fashioned from local woods and skins. The drums were just further curiosities to them. But perhaps Johnson sensed something more, because he had lived with the Indians, and they, too, called their spirits with drums.

Anger flared in him as he watched them drinking their rum, taking their snuff. They wanted him to show them how to stop the smallpox. It was old knowledge in Africa, knowledge Ade had held secret in the New World because the risks of sharing it were tremendous.

The whites saw only with ordinary eyes.

If they saw a black man taking the juice of the pox from one person to another, they would call him a witch if the patient lived, a poisoner if he did not.

The Indians saw with other eyes. But they also believed—not without reason—that the newcomers were plotting to wipe them out so they could seize their lands without having to pay even what they paid to drunken chiefs.

If the red men saw a newcomer—even a black one—spreading the smallpox, they would conclude he was one of their destroyers.

So Ade had kept his knowing to himself. Until the pox struck one of his own. He had encountered none of his own people, the Yoruba, in the back settlements of New York.

But the house slave Johnson called Sappho was a Fon, from the storied kingdom of Dahomey. Under different names, they honored the same gods. She was a child of Oshun, whom she called Erzulie. Generous in body, honey-mouthed, rejoicing in the senses.

With Sappho, and those she brought to the woods at night, Ade had begun to plant the old ways in the New World. It was part of the destiny he had been born with. He knew that now, though he had not understood the obscurities of the last reading the high priest of Ifa had made for him before he lost the world he knew. Across the aching distance, across the terror of the Middle Passage, the *orishas* still spoke to him and reached to others.

Sappho was healthy. She would outlast the pox, though she would bear its marks. When she had asked him to help her friends, Ade could not refuse her.

"Will you help us?" Johnson was asking. "We would reward you handsomely if you succeed."

"Wait here."

Ade parted the curtain that divided his living space from the sanctuary, so his visitors would not see what was inside. From the corner of his eye, he saw Johnson pat the doctor's shoulder—he was always reaching to others, making them his own—and pour him another tot of rum.

In the privacy of his sanctum, on a mat on the floor before his altar, Ade took up the round divination tray he had carved from soft local basswood. The only things there that had come from Africa were the palm nuts he shook out of a bag into his cupped hand.

They left me the palm nuts because they were the only things I possessed that they believed had no value. Yet their value is greater than all I own.

He tapped the edge of the tray with a bone pointer to call the attention of the lord of divination. To wake Ifa.

He gave thanks and praise to the *orishas* and the ancestors. He began, as he did every sunrise, with the Lord of Crossroads, the Opener of Gateways, because if Eshu is not fed he will turn everything upside down, like the trickster he is.

"Eshu, may my paths and doors be opened, and the paths and doors of those I love. May the paths and doors of those who wish to do me, or those I love, harm be closed."

He concluded with the ancient invocation to the master of past and future, who can decipher and help to change anything in a man's destiny except the appointed hour of his death:

"Ifa, moji-boru, moji-boye, moji-boshishe.

"Ifa, awake! Sacrifice is offered. Sacrifice is accepted. Sacrifice will come to pass."

He drew a straight line in the wood dust in the hollow of the tray, a straight path for Ifa to follow.

He grabbed up the sixteen palm nuts, too many for one hand to hold securely, and switched them from palm to palm. Each time, one or two palm nuts were left in the passing hand. These were the numbers he worked with.

With each transfer, he drew lines in the wood dust in the tray, pushing it away from him. He scored two vertical lines for an odd number, one for even. The logic of this inversion was beyond discussion. The binary method for discovering a man's fate—and his character, which is harder to escape—had descended from the realm of the High God, the One behind the many, the One beyond images and forms.

Ade made four-line patterns, in pairs.

Each time a pattern was complete, he recited what he could remember of the *odu,* the poetic scripture of the

Yoruba, passed from the memory of one priest of Ifa to another.

He was painfully aware that he was unworthy of the task. Though he had been admitted to several stages of initiation, he had never been raised up an a *babalawo,* a father of secrets, though he had been told this was his path.

He prayed, "If words are lost, if names are missing, may my sacrifice be acceptable in thy sight. May my heart be true. I am nothing but a vessel for thy purpose. May this vessel be filled with *ashe,* with thy power. Show me the way, Lord."

The white *orisha,* Obatala, spoke to him, reminding him that the way of truth is for all men.

In the last *odu,* he read the signs of both Shango, the power of thunder, and Oshun, the power of woman's love, the beauty of the senses.

The palm nuts spoke of a woman lost in the woods. Of the need for sacrifice and healing.

The woman's children are looking for her.

"We are looking for her, we cannot find her."

"So we cannot sleep."

Ade did not know whether the verses rose from memory or were fresh delivered. But the message was clear to him. The woman must be returned to her brood. Sacrifice must be made.

□

"I will help you," he told the white men.

The doctor looked sluggish, depleted by drink. Johnson, in contrast, was instantly alert.

White men do not know how to feed their spirits, Ade thought. *Johnson can drink as he pleases, more than an ordinary man can bear. At least for now. Because the father of his head, Shango, drinks for him. For the other one, it is different. But it is useless to tell them these things.*

"Is Sappho here?" Johnson asked.

"She is here."

"How should we play this?" Billy addressed Magin. "You are the physician."

Doctor Magin cleared his throat. His Adam's apple bounced. "Do you have—another patient in mind?"

"Not me," Ade said.

"We need—ah—to *verify* your procedures."

"I can show you what is necessary."

"Splendid," said Johnson. "You will of course be compensated for your services."

"Four pigeons and four shillings."

The doctor blinked. Johnson, already on his feet, said, "That seems entirely reasonable."

"That is not all," Ade went on.

"Ah."

He is a trader in everything, Ade recognized.

"Heaven is our home, earth is our marketplace," the African told Johnson.

"I think I can get along with that."

His ease is extraordinary, Ade thought. *He turns as fast as quicksilver. And he feels me, as I feel him.*

"Tell me what you need," Johnson said. "I am not a wealthy man, contrary to rumor. But I make a point of rewarding those who do me a favor."

"You have many of my people on your estate."

"You speak of my slaves? Well, yes. I have above twenty. Some speak in no known language. My uncle shipped many of them to me from his privateering enterprises on the Spanish Main."

Ade had not been certain what he was going to say until he began to speak. Then the thrill of confirmation traveled through his veins, a gentle fire.

"I wish you to let me teach them."

"Teach them what, exactly?"

"Teach them who they are."

"It is an original proposition. You accept, of course, that they are my property? I would not wish them to be inculcated with any—unseasonable thoughts."

"I ask only for the time they have free from their labors."

Johnson reflected. "Was it you, then? The drums in the woods? My overseer said some of the slaves have been keeping unusual hours."

"They have souls," Ade told him.

"Very well. As long as you do not sow any ideas that they might merit a different condition. My slaves may have souls, but I cannot have them going about imagining their bodies are theirs to dispose of."

Ade did not reply.

His long stare disconcerted Johnson. "I will say this to you. I am from Ireland. It is a small land, in the northern sea, off the English coast. My countrymen have been used as slaves and worse. Though I would not have you quote me on this point. I do not judge a man by his complexion or by his estate. If a man offers me his hand in friendship, be he black or white, pagan, papist or dissenter, I welcome him as one of my own family."

Ade took the proffered hand. Who would not?

6.

Uprooted trees and dead limbs lay jumbled together, a field of stiffened corpses, where the Floodwood River had burst its banks in the violence of the spring melt.

Johnson and his companions picked their way up the steep path from the landing to the palisade of the Lower Castle.

"You must go to Two Rivers," Hendrick had told him. "Because their need is most urgent. We will call all the clans to meet you there."

It was a reasonable suggestion. Ogilvie, the minister at Fort Hunter, had confirmed three fresh cases of smallpox among the Mohawks at the Lower Castle.

But Johnson was also uncomfortably aware that Hendrick was distancing himself from any risk that he might be held liable for an unsuccessful experiment. The old fox did it in the native way. He did not say he was unimpressed by Cuffee's quick recovery from the effects of inoculation. He did not say openly that he doubted that what worked on a black man would work for Mohawks.

He said what he thought Johnson wanted to hear.

But he made it quite plain, in his circuitous way, that he had no intention of hosting a gathering to discuss the deliberate spreading of the seeds of the white death in his own village.

Johnson could not blame him.

The old warchief was afraid of no man. But he was wary of the unseen; he believed, like all his people, that the sources of health and illness lie in soul, not body.

And though Forked Paths feared no man, he lived in awe of the older women. They had brought him down once before, stripped him of his chiefly status and even his Longhouse name after he had been feted as "Emperor of the Indians" in London.

Hendrick was moving very carefully since Island Woman had been raised up as the mother of his clan.

□

Island Woman sat with the women, on one side of the council lodge. When Johnson entered, with the doctor and the black men, she watched them with the unblinking stare of a wolf, sifting a strange herd for signs of weakness or danger.

She saw Forest Killer searching for friends among the ranks of chiefs and elders. His laughter was overly loud as he greeted Sun Walker, home at last after his long captivity in Canada. He frowned for only an instant before he turned on more smiles and jokes for a visitor from Caughnawaga.

He felt the suspicion and hostility in the lodge. He was angry and puzzled because Hendrick was not there. He did not like the excuses Forked Paths and his brother had sent. That one of them had a sick wife. That the other had a sore leg and could not travel.

He wore his mask well, but he moved stiffly, knowing now that he was on his own, among possible enemies. He recovered some of his bounce as he greeted the women.

He spoke correctly to Island Woman. He called her Grandmother. He said, "I hope we will come to know each other better."

He left it to the edgy, slump-shouldered doctor to explain their way of fighting the white death.

Magin put on a show with the black slaves. He showed the Mohawks how the pocks on Cuffee's arm had flaked off, leaving him unmarked and now invulnerable to the disease.

He told them that similar results had been achieved with men of other races, many times over. Among the Turks, whose brown skins—Magin claimed—greatly resembled those of the Six Nations, inoculation had been used for many generations.

When he was done, the Mohawks sat in stony silence. It was broken by Sun Walker, speaking for the whole assembly.

"My brother talks of what touches the life of my people. When my sisters and brothers lie down at night, I am afraid they will not live to see the sun. And when they rise up in the morning, I am afraid they will not live to see the moon.

"This evil is blowing on the winds from the east, from the Sunrise People. It is said that what brings disease is what can take it away. But we must smoke together and discover whether this is now true."

□

When Island Woman addressed the women's council, she spoke over a fourteen-row belt, stroking it with her hand.

The white and purple shells had been polished by many hands, those of one clanmother after another.

The belt was the symbol of Island Woman's power. It belonged to the Mother of the Wolf Clan. She used it in public when she raised up a new chief, or de-horned a chief who had abused his office, and at times when the clan was imperiled. The figures of Ohwako and a human couple were joined in the design.

"I have listened to the words of the white doctor," Island Woman told the group. "He is tame meat. His thoughts come from his master, Forest Killer.

"All of us know Forest Killer. Some better than others."

There were a few hot faces, some giggles and snickers.

"But which of us knows his heart?"

She let the silence deepen. The firelight darkened the hollows under her cheekbones.

"Some say the English aim to kill all of us, to take our land, and that Forest Killer is their knife. When my son was at Boston, a minister said in his church that the Real People are creatures of the Devil and should be hunted down like wild animals."

In the breathing silence, the circle tightened. The women of the Wolf Clan were feeling together, communicating beyond and below the words, becoming one heart, one purpose.

"Forest Killer has pleased many, with his gifts and his laughter. Our warriors love him, because his storehouse flows over with rum. Our girls love him, because the elk dreamer walks with him. But he has also brought us hungry ghosts. Our warriors have been cut down like green corn to fight his battles. And what is the value of his gifts, compared to what he has taken from our forests? Where he goes, the trees are dying. We have all heard their pain.

"So now we must know his heart.

"We must look for the wolf trap."

"Skaratons!" Bright Meadow called to her mother. "Tell the story."

"Now I will tell a story," Island Woman agreed. Stories are the shortest path between the listener and the truth.

"It is the Starving Time," Island Woman proceeded. "The white hunter is killing wolves. He is taking their pelts. But the wolves smell him from far off. They see a tiny twig stir when he moves. They feel his movements in the snow through the pads of their feet.

"So the hunter becomes cunning. He buries the hilt of his knife in a crack in the ice. He leaves the blade pointing up. He dresses it with bearfat. It smells juicy and good. It brings on the meat hunger. When the wolf smells it, there is something in her belly that is biting her. She needs to eat right away.

"She grabs at that food without looking for danger.

She licks up the fat until she has ripped her tongue to shreds. She wails and staggers across the snow, bleeding her life out. The hunter tracks her easily, from the blood on the snow.

"We are hungry now," she drew the lesson. "We are dying again. We have all seen many deaths. When I was a child, our lodges were all full, and there were more lodges than the houses of the newcomers that now stand in our Valley. We are dying again from the white death, and our medicine has not been able to stop it. This is not in our dreaming.

"Forest Killer tells us he can stop the white death. This smells good. But we must find out if there is a knife inside before we lick it.

"He has shown us a black man who has taken the seeds of the white death and lived. Let him show us a white man who will do what he asks us to do. Let us take this word to the elders. Let us speak with one heart, one mind."

□

"Let me do it, sir," Jamie Rogers volunteered, when the Mohawk counter-proposal had been explained in formal council. "I got nothing to lose."

"You are a good man, Jamie." Johnson squeezed his servant's shoulder. "Is there anything you would not do for me?"

"Give up drink, sir. That would be hard."

"That's my Jamie. But I fear I cannot accept your offer."

"I will do it," Doctor Magin said firmly.

"And who would make the incisions? Who would suck the damn poison out of the pustules? Not I, if you please, Doctor." He affected the shakes. "Would you trust this hand with your lancet?"

"You jest with me, Colonel Johnson."

"As you will. But this is no jest. They look to me. And, in our present circumstances, only to me. You are to put the damn pest into me."

Magin blanched. "But Billy—" his emotions overrode

the customary formalities "—we cannot risk you. God's thunder, you are our indispensable man."

"That is generous, Teddy. If it be true, it is the reason why no other volunteer will serve."

□

Island Woman watched each phase of the operation. The way the nervous sawbones pricked two big pustules on Lucas Muskrat's chest, transferred the juice to a clean dish, then pressed it into three neat incisions he had opened in Johnson's arm with a narrow, razor-sharp blade. The doctor dabbed at the wounds, making sure the poison mixed well with the flowing blood.

She saw Johnson's servant turn pale and cross himself and mutter prayers to the spirit woman the blackrobes invoked.

She saw the ripple of Forest Killer's muscles, the blood showing through the gaps in the skin like the heartwood of the oak. She saw how his smile never shifted, how his eyes were fixed on hers.

"Are you content, Grandmother?" he asked her.

For the first time, Island Woman began to believe that Hendrick was right about Billy Johnson.

Forest Killer belongs to the Real People, as well as his own.

That made everything different.

CHAPTER 28
MAN OF TWO WORLDS

1.

Caroline Bigcanoe died. So did Lucas Muskrat, and three more at the Lower Castle. But all the Mohawks who were inoculated by Dr. Magin survived.

Island Woman decided that Forest Killer was a man who spoke from the heart. In some things.

He took the white death into himself, to release us from our fears. How many of those who claim to be friends would do this?

She remembered this, in the hard seasons that followed.

They had known boom times in the Valley, while ginseng was in demand. The women and girls earned more in a single moon, gathering baskets of manroot in the woods, than the hunters could earn from a whole winter hunt. The hunters grew lazy, but the women did not mind. They enjoyed the renewed respect that came from their men now they were the ones who were most eagerly awaited at the traders' stores.

Then the ginseng bubble burst.

At his truck house across the river, Forest Killer tried to explain.

Johnson ordered his store manager to open the books

to Island Woman. She could not make out the columns of figures written in Robert Adams' neat, cursive script. She was used to a more graphic system of bookeeping, with drawings of beavers or bucks on each page.

But Sparrow had learned how to read from Hendrick's brother Abraham, who taught Sunday school, and could figure with numbers. She examined the books and confirmed what Forest Killer said. The spring before, ginseng had fetched twenty-two shillings a pound. Now it was hard to find a buyer at two shillings a pound.

There would be no big new cast-iron cooking pot in Island Woman's lodge that summer.

"We are at the mercy of men who live many looks away. They are creatures of fashions that are not ours. It seems the fashion has changed, and so there is a glut." Johnson softened the blow by adding, "I will take your ginseng, and I will give you a better price than you can hope for at Albany, though it will cost me. I have dropped a sight of money on this business myself. Go to Albany if you please. But I fear they will treat you less kindly."

Island Woman's anger flared. How could something the traders had prized and lusted after a year before now be almost without value?

"We are captives of the China trade. It seems the Chinaman has lost his appetite for manroot, or has all that he can use."

"The yellow men's fish are jumping," Sparrow whispered to her grandmother, then stifled her giggles with the palm of her hand, remembering that the joke had been turned by a dead woman.

There was worse to follow.

The demand for furs had fallen too.

The years of half-peace had increased the volume of Canada furs carried down to Albany by their kinfolk at the blackrobe missions.

And the French were again on the move.

Three winters before, a small expedition led by Céleron de Blainville had traveled down the Ohio, burying lead plates that bore the arms of France and the claim that the lands to the west of the Six Nations belonged to the French King by right of prior discovery. Island Woman had seen one of these plates. It had not impressed her. The French claim was nonsense. The smallest child could see that.

The French came yesterday. The Real People were here always. How can white men say they discovered any part of this Turtle Island?

The French could not be serious. That was obvious, she thought, because they had buried these plates instead of setting them up high, for all to see and discuss.

Then the French came again, with an army of two thousand men. They had built a chain of forts through the Ohio territory. Now they were building a stronghold at the forks where the Monongahela meets the Beautiful River.

"It is a leather thong across our throats," Hendrick told a gathering at the Upper Castle. "It is shutting off our air."

Island Woman felt the tightness in her own chest.

The line of French forts stood between the Six Nations and their friends among the Western nations. It threatened to cut them off from the richest sources of beaver.

The Senecas and Onondagas, who lived closest to the French, were yielding to their pressure. Whole families were leaving their villages, to live with the soldier-abbé who had built a mission like a fortress where the Black Water flowed into the Rapid River. Seneca warriors had escorted Marin's army through the Ohio territory.

The encroachments of the French, deep into the hunting grounds of the Six Nations, could tear the Confederacy apart and bring hunger to the villages of those who sided with the English.

Forest Killer saw the danger, but the masters of New York did not listen to him. The Albany Commissioners again ruled in Indian affairs, and Island Woman thought they were no friends to her people.

Hendrick Forked Paths went down the Hudson to New York, with the blessing of all the clanmothers. He spoke to Governor Clinton and the Assembly in white, seething fury. He listed the promises broken, the lands stolen. He told them that the silver covenant chain between the English and the Flint People was broken. It could be repaired only if William Johnson was restored to the management of Indian affairs.

"We trust him because he is half ours and half yours."

For now, the Mohawks would not even permit English interpreters to cross their territory en route to their sister-nations.

Governor Clinton, exhausted by the King's fractious subjects in his colony of New York, was pleased to leave this messy business to his successor. Clinton was going home.

2.

The King sent young Sir Danvers Osborne, a country gentleman whose wife's brother was the ascendant Lord Halifax, to replace Clinton. Sir Danvers was distinguished by the fact that he was the first Governor of New York in recent memory who had not sought public office for private reward. He shipped out to the colonies to escape an asphyxiating mother and the ghost of his beautiful wife, who had died unnaturally young. His family motto was a dangerous one: *Quantum in rebus inane.* "How much in life is inane."

Sir Danvers was reminded of it as he made his viceregal progress from the ship to the waiting carriage along the eastside wharf, the center of a buzzing swarm of would-be courtiers. The subtle James DeLancey applied all his practiced charm, resolved to control the new Governor, or to break him.

Sir Danvers kept his nose in his handkerchief.

His colony stank worse than the Smithfield markets. The stink came in fevered gusts, as wind from a sick man's stomach. It contained the odors of tarpits, skinners' yards, uncured hides, pig slurry, blubber, fish guts, stale oyster shells, fresh dung, the putrid stuffs of the starch makers, hatters' dies, the bloody refuse of the slaughterhouse.

Governor Osborne took in the sights and smells of his

colony for two days. Then he hanged himself by his neckerchief from the spikes of the wrought iron fence around Mr. Murray's garden.

The coroner's jury judged him by his suicide note and branded him a lunatic. The note found on the Governor's body attested both to a misused education and an imperfect sense of the divine will:

> *Quos Deus vult perdere, prius dementat.* Whom God wishes to destroy, he first makes mad. Have Mercy on me God! and blessed Jesus!

James DeLancey became Acting Governor, and now stood unchallenged at the summit of the colony's affairs.

DeLancey inherited Osborne's instructions. These were quite precise. The Governor of New York was required by the Lords of Trade to seek "an interview" with all the chiefs of the Iroquois, and to devise a plan with the King's officials in the other colonies to beat the French, once and for all.

This cut against the grain of DeLancey's previous policy, but he was not a man to allow principle to stand in the way of ambition. If, in order to play Governor, he was obliged to beat the war-drum, then beat it he would. If he needed that Irish coxcomb Billy Johnson to bring the Indians into line, he would find a way to mend fences with him.

"Dance partners change," James DeLancey told his wife. "Policies are made and unmade. But there is always the dance."

3.

The French incursions into Ohio country and the threatened defection of the Six Nations spread fear through the English colonies, and fear gave birth to a rare exercise in unity. The governments of seven of the colonies—egged on by London and by provincial visionaries like Ben Franklin—agreed to meet at Albany to renew the covenant chain with the Longhouse nations and develop a strategy for common defense against the French. Billy Johnson was commissioned to bring the sachems to this gathering. "Responsibility without power," he complained to Hendrick. The Mohawk advised him to take the job. "You will speak for us, and we for you, in front of all these chiefs of the English."

While others talked about talks, Governor Dinwiddie of Virginia—who insisted that the boundaries of his own colony extended as far as the western ocean—commissioned a young planter and surveyor named George Washington to read the riot act to the French intruders in the Ohio territory. Washington was just twenty-two, a year younger than Billy Johnson had been when he first set foot in America. He looked like a soldier: six feet tall, black-haired, with huge fists. His face was pitted with smallpox scars, the legacy of a trip to Barbados with his brother Lawrence, who had inducted him into the ambitious land schemes of the Ohio Company. The previous fall, Washington had jumped at a chance to lead a small party from Wills Creek to Fort Le Boeuf, the new French post on the headwaters of the Allegheny, and deliver a warning message. He had been entertained cordially by Legardeur de St. Pierre, the seasoned Indian fighter in command at Le Boeuf, who politely disregarded the message from Dinwiddie.

For his new mission, Washington had received fiercer instructions. A strong French force under Pecaudy de Contrecoeur had seized a fort the British were building at the junction of the Ohio, the Allegheny and the Monongahela. The French had completed the fortification with the carpenters' tools they had captured, and renamed it Fort Duquesne. Washington was to carry an ultimatum to the French to withdraw and reclaim the fort at the Forks for the Ohio Company. If he ran into resistance from the French, he was ordered to "take prisoners or kill and destroy them."

In the spirit of his age, the young Virginian made a marriage between high policy and private profit. He lobbied to have a new road constructed for his expedition, following a roundabout course so it would pass by Bullskin, his plantation.

French scouts logged his progress toward the Forks.

The commandant at Fort Duquesne sent Ensign Jumonville with a small detachment with a letter to Colonel Washington, requiring him to withdraw. The text was translated into English, so there would be no misunderstandings.

In late spring, Washington's militiamen surprised the French detachment in a muddy meadow. According to French survivors, the Virginians fired while Jumonville's interpreter was attempting to read the letter from his commander. Within fifteen minutes, ten French officers and soldiers, including Ensign Jumonville, were dead.

This incident—which the French described as *l'assassinat,* the assassination—opened a new war between the empires of Britain and France. It was different from previous conflicts. It began in North America. And it was to be waged on several continents and oceans, making it perhaps the first *world* war. By settling the ownership of North America, and removing the threat of French Canada from the English colonists, it was to open the way for the American Revolution.

But no one at the Albany Congress just convening could see this far ahead. As the delegates gathered at the Dutch town on the Hudson, news of Washington's action had not yet reached them. They did not even know that war had begun.

4.

Delegates from seven of the thirteen colonies came to Albany for the Congress that summer. They met in the new courthouse, under the presidency of James De-Lancey. But the real action was played out in taverns and private houses.

The summer heat was broken only by thunderstorms and driving winds.

A Pennsylvania missionary read the sermon at St. Peter's, choosing as his text I Chronicles 19:13: "Be of good courage, and let the Lord do that which is good in His sight." That same Sunday, the river flooded, rising to the height of the lower palisades, drowning wheat and corn in the warehouses.

It was agreed this was not an auspicious sign.

Worse was the poor attendance by the Six Nations. The Mohawks, who lived closest to Albany, did not turn up until two weeks after the start of the Congress.

Hendrick Forked Paths and the Mohawks were preparing two consummate pieces of political theater.

On the eve of the Congress, the elders and matrons of the two Castles asked Johnson to smoke with them. There had been talk of a Plan of Union, advanced by Ben Franklin and others as the model for joint military and political action by the American colonies.

"Many winters before the newcomers came to our country," Island Woman spoke for all, "the Longhouse People had already created our Confederacy and our Great Law of Peace. If the chiefs of the English wish to know how to make such a league, they should consult with us, because we made our Confederacy before the newcomers dreamed of such a thing."

Billy Johnson was delighted by the idea of Indians tutoring some of the foremost men in the colonies. He resolved to carry the proposal, and a copy of Colden's book on the Iroquois, to Franklin as soon as he reached Albany.

The fame of this Philadelphia original had long preceded his arrival at the Congress. Ben Franklin had reportedly invented a metal rod that caught the lightning. The press toasted him as a wizard who stole fire from heaven.

Billy discovered that Franklin was lodging at James Stevenson's house, a few steps from his townhouse on Market Street. He walked over after an early breakfast.

A maidservant received him, pink and flustered, tugging at her apron cords.

"Good morrow, Nellie! Is Mister Franklin in the house?"

The maid's cheeks flushed crimson. She managed to stammer, "The gentleman is dressing, Colonel Johnson."

The girl was broad in the beam, but not without appeal. She had the quality of new-baked bread.

Franklin had an eye for the ladies, it was said. It seemed he missed no opportunity.

"Run along then, Nellie," Billy winked. "I am sure you have things to attend to. I shall find my way."

Johnson found the door to the back bedroom ajar and pushed it open with his stick.

"Mister Franklin?"

He was greeted by a series of grunts and groans, orgasmic in intensity.

"Errrumph! Ah! God be thanked!"

Billy heard the tinkle of rain against porcelain. Then he observed the pale, wobbling posterior of the man he had come to visit, suspended high above a chamber-pot. Ben Franklin was standing on his head. His lank brown hair brushed the floor.

Billy might have spared the man's privacy by beating a quick retreat. But he was transfixed by this unexpected apparition. The tinkle became a steaming hiss. Then Franklin cartwheeled sideways, with remarkable grace, to land on his heels. He did a smart about-turn, pulled down his shirttails, and greeted his visitor with a beatific smile.

"Good Lord!" Johnson exclaimed. "Is this some kind of penance?"

"I see you are not one of our fraternity, Mister Johnson!"

"Which fraternity might that be?"

"Why, the Fellowship of the Stone! The true nobility! An aristocracy of suffering!"

Now Billy could get a proper look at Franklin and liked what he saw. This was no moping Pennsylvania preacher. He was made round and strong, like a swimmer, with the pointed lip of a humorist and alert, restless gray eyes.

Unembarrassed by the invasion of his toilet rituals, Franklin listened to Billy's account of the constitution of the League of Six Nations, and plied him with questions.

"I will tell our commissioners that if even forest

savages can make a federation, civilized men must be able to do the same," Franklin announced. "It will make a nice argument. But I doubt it will win us the day."

He explained his plan for a "general government" of the colonies. The chief executive would be a President-General appointed by the Crown, probably a military man, because of the threat of war. The legislature would be a Grand Council chosen by the provinces in proportion to the revenues that each of them raised for the common treasury.

"Our commissioners have given me the nod," Franklin pursued. "All except James DeLancey, who is neither this nor that but will move where the wind is going. But I think unless King and Parliament take this plan to their hearts, it will not prosper. Our governors all wish to be masters of their own houses, and our assemblies all quiver with suspicion of a Royalist plot to install a woodentop general as dictator of the colonies. It is strange to think that your Indian friends have done something like, without instruction from the Greeks or the Common Law of England. Tell me something of their women."

"They are more formidable than the men."

"Ah, it is always the female bee that has the stinger."

"This is beyond the norm. The women of the Six Nations make and break the chiefs. They choose their husbands and divorce them at will."

Ben Franklin appeared to find this profoundly disturbing. "I am no authority on matters of marriage. Are you a married man yourself, Mister Johnson?"

"Not I."

"Praise God for that. I am not without sympathy for the estate of matrimony, because it seems to me a single man is the odd half of a pair of shoes. But it is surely necessary to try many partners to find the match."

"I am much of your mind, Mister Franklin."

"Are you sure you have had no brush with the Stone? Truly? Well, you are young. You must steel yourself for it, Mister Johnson, for I believe we have much in common. It scratches our soul to some purpose."

□

While Johnson tutored Ben Franklin in the government of the Six Nations, his own mentor—Hendrick Forked Paths—was preparing a political drama intended to change the relations between Indians and white authorities for good.

When Hendrick came into town a fortnight late, dressed in his Court regalia, he demanded an immediate audience with Acting Governor DeLancey, and was given it.

He told DeLancey: "We see that our brother Forest Killer does not sit in your councils. Yet he is the only man here that has earned our trust."

He subjected DeLancey to a long list of grievances. The practices of Albany traders like Livingston Huyck, who kidnapped Indian children as sureties for debt, inflated prices and robbed Mohawks after getting them drunk. The graft of the Commissioners of Indian Affairs, who traded in secret with the French. The crooked land deals.

When the Congress resumed in the courthouse, Hendrick threw a stick behind his back. He told the assembled delegates, "This is how you neglect and abuse us in times of peace, when you think you do not need us. Now you want our help because the Governor of Canada and the Governor of Virginia are quarreling over lands that belong to the Real People. This quarrel may end in our destruction.

"It is three years since we were asked to this place to renew our treaties. It is true there are Indian Commissioners here, but they are not men but devils. They do not smoke with us in friendship. They prefer to smoke with our common enemies from Canada, for the sake of their furs.

"Yet during the last war, it was we who saved you in this town, when you lay about naked and open like weak women.

"We will not do you this favor again unless you raise up the one man we trust to make a true bridge between us.

"The fire here is burned out. We ask that this fire be rekindled at Colonel Johnson's, because he has walked in our skins. He is half ours, half yours."

The Albany Commissioners were aghast. Before the full Congress, Hendrick had hurled the demands he had thrust on Governor Clinton the year before. This time, the echoes would carry all the way to the Lords of Trade and King George II.

"I have never seen anything like it," Franklin remarked to his new friend, over dinner at Billy's house. "The Indians have demanded the right to appoint a King's Superintendent over themselves. And they have named you their man. I do not know if it will come to pass. If it does, you will be *their* agent, more than His Majesty's. And I think they will never let you forget it."

□

Hendrick's public showmanship was undermined by his private adventures during those Albany nights. An Indian council always drew land-sharks and grog-peddlers. On this occasion, they came from all over the colonies with deep purses.

A group of Connecticut speculators had their eye on the choice lands between the forks of the Susquehanna —then called the Wyoming territory. The Connecticut men approached Billy Johnson to speak with the Six Nations, nominal suzerains of this country, offering a handsome commission in cash and in kind. Billy declined to act. There was a competing Pennsylvania deed to some of the land, negotiated by Conrad Weiser.

So the Connecticut cartel turned to John Henry Lydius.

Lydius performed the same trick he had played during King George's War, after Billy Johnson led the Mohawks to Albany, painted for battle.

He invited sachems to his house and plied them with liquor.

And the green snake bit them again. Hendrick too.

Johnson was appalled when he saw the results.

□

Billy remembered his first glimpse of the upper Susquehanna. He had journeyed there with Snowbird, in his second spring on the frontier, to open a trade post at Oquaga. He recalled the joy of open skies after the grueling trek with the pack-train through the Catskills, along the old Indian path strewn with fallen logs and entangling roots, in the perennial half-light of the forest. The Indian longhouses at Oquaga, scattered like jackstraws near the river, flanked by the fields of corn and beans and grazing horses and cows. The Indians were living without a stockade. They believed this land was theirs beyond challenge. That here they were safe from all invaders.

Lydius and his Connecticut partners had changed that.

It maddened Johnson to think of how they had done it.

They must have gotten Hendrick blind, falling-down drunk. The same Hendrick who had stood up in front of the delegates to express the wisdom of hard experience—that the Indians had no tolerance for rum and never would have, because there was something in their bellies or souls that was different from other men. Hendrick had begged the Commissioners to ban the sale of rum in the Mohawk castles. "It keeps our people poor, it makes them idle and wicked. It turns men into devils and causes murder between husband and wife."

All forgotten, over a bottle or three with Lydius, the tea drinker.

How bad was the damage?

Billy reread the deed. As always, the limits of the tract were defined in terms the Indians would have great difficulty understanding, even if they were sober. The grant covered a territory stretching from the 41st to the 42d parallel. It sprawled 120 miles from east to west, starting from a line drawn six miles east of the Susquehanna River.

The price specified was $2,000, New York currency.

A princely sum. A penny an acre? No, more like a penny a square mile.

It was unlikely that any of the Mohawk signatories, or their families, had anything left to show for the deal. The purchase price had already been guzzled. The hangover remained.

□

Johnson called on Lydius.

"There will be all hell to pay at the Mohawk Castles—not to mention Philadelphia—when word of this travels. For your selfish interest, you bring us to the edge of an open rupture with the Mohawk at the moment we most need their friendship."

"The role of moralist does not suit you, Mister Johnson. I remember a time when you were less fastidious about drinking with Indians. And I recollect some deeds you came by in curious ways."

"I have never cheated Mohawks."

"What of other nations, the ones Mohawks claim to rule or represent? If Mohawks have any claim to the Susquehanna lands, it is only that of conquest of other tribes. My partners have bought it on the square. I think we have the better claim. Your problem, Mister Johnson, is now you have got your snout deep into the feeding trough you wish to deny other men their share."

Nothing was settled—except that the estrangement between Johnson and Lydius had sharpened into open hostility.

The music plays, the partners change.

James DeLancey said this, at the private dinner where he informed Billy he would recommend to London that he should be reappointed Colonel over the Six Nations, with wider powers than he enjoyed in the last war.

DeLancey, who scorned me, now declares himself my ally.

Lydius and I went to war together; now we make war on each other.

Island Woman stood across my path. Now she raises me up, as a chief of her people. DeLancey is right.

There is always the dance.

5.

Ben Franklin was right too: It was the Indians who appointed Billy Johnson to the management of Indian affairs.

This was made quite explicit in the formal recommendation from the Lords of Trade to the King, delivered in a letter that fall:

> The reasons of our taking the liberty to recommend this Gentleman to Your Majesty are the representations which have been made to us of the great service he did during the late war, in preserving the friendship of the Indians and engaging them to take up the hatchet against the French; the connections he has formed by living amongst them, and habituating himself to their manners and customs; the publick testimony they have given at the last meeting of their friendship for, and confidence in, him; and above all the request they make that the sole management of Indian affairs may be entrusted to him.

Billy's commission came with a British general and a British regular army, the first Johnson had ever seen. He received the commission from the hands of General Braddock at Alexandria in the spring, when the governors assembled to agree on high strategy and marvel at the sight of redcoats in force.

Billy's Royal commission named him to "sole management and direction of the Affairs of the Six Nations of Indians and their allies."

He was given separate commissions by Governor Shirley of Massachusetts and Acting Governor DeLancey as Major-General of their provincial forces, because Franklin had also been right about the prospects for his Plan of Union.

General Braddock's first step was to divide his forces. The general would lead his regulars and militia from the southern colonies into the Ohio country to take Fort Duquesne and avenge the humiliating defeat Jumonville's brother had inflicted on George Washington at a miserable hole called Fort Necessity. Governor Shirley would lead an expedition against the French at Niagara, with two Royal regiments to be raised in the Commonwealth of Massachusetts, and the New Jersey militia. Major-General Johnson would march against Crown Point, with a force largely consisting of New England provincials and the warriors of the Six Nations.

Hendrick Forked Paths did not understand why the British general was dividing his troops. And he did not relish the prospect of marching beside New England men who might be descendants of the people who dispossessed his family and felt no more warmly about Indians. But the arrival of two regiments of British regulars made a difference. It was proof that King George was awake. Snowbird, who had traveled to Alexandria with Johnson, reported that British soldiers were called bloodybacks not only because they wore red coats but because they were ruled by the lash, like slaves or felons.

"Their chiefs believe their men will fight only if they are more afraid of them than the enemy."

Hendrick had seen this in England. "They are not Real People." There were things about the newcomers that could not be explained.

CHAPTER 29
FIRE THAT NEVER DIES

1.

Johnson stood before the nations, sweating lightly under his scarlet blanket, edged with gold lace. He wore a gorget at his throat and a sword at his hip. He had a file of redcoats at his back and a company of militia, showing off a six-pound cannon and a pair of coehorn mortars.

But Billy spoke to the Iroquois as one of their own, in the formal periods of native oratory, filled with the machinery of clouds and wind. He punctuated each passage by taking up one of the strings or belts of wampum that Daniel Claus and Arent Stevens, the interpreter, held ready for him. The Indians believed that a speech that was not confirmed by wampum was only words from the lips, not the heart.

Runners had gone out to all of the Six Nations and to the peoples of the Ohio country and the Susquehanna Valley. Warriors, elders and chiefs squatted or sprawled full-length in semicircles, halfway up the gentle rise on the east side of the house. Only Hendrick's Mohawks and a few River Indians were shorn and painted for war.

No official of the Crown—perhaps no white man—had ever seen such a large gathering of Indians. By the last count, more than twelve hundred were encamped at Fort Johnson, testing the resources of Johnson's kitchens and storerooms. The warriors had come with their women and children. Island Woman was there, with Bright Meadow and her daughter. They sat in the shade of one of the rough shelters, roofed with elmbark, that Johnson had erected for his guests. They were there not only for the party—Billy was admitted, even by his enemies, to be a generous man, especially when he wanted something—but to keep an eye on their men.

Johnson spoke to the nations of General Braddock, and the British army he had seen in Virginia, and his own commissions: his royal commission as Colonel of the Six Nations, delivered by Braddock, and his colonial commissions as commander of an expedition to drive the French from the hornets' nest at Crown Point.

He spoke across an enormous firepit. The pyre was no ordinary heap of brush and timber. Under Hendrick's supervision, Johnson's slaves and servants had hauled huge trimmed logs—hickory and oak, hemlock and white pine—to the site and laid them row on row, in a grid. The pile rose in steps, each one shorter than the last, until it held the shape of a flattened pyramid.

"Brothers!" Johnson's rolling baritone carried across the natural amphitheater. As he spoke, he stroked a huge belt of wampum, draped from his shoulder, that contained the designs of the great white pine, a sunburst, and the linked symbols of the Six Nations of the Confederacy.

"Our great tree was falling. The silver covenant chain that has bound our peoples in friendship was tarnished and fouled by evil-minded men at Albany. My father the King has cleaned and renewed the covenant chain. The tree you have so often and earnestly desired might again be set up is now raised high. This tree is planted by so strong a hand that its roots will sink deep into the earth. Its spreading branches will shelter you and all our friends. This belt contains my words. With this belt, I invite you and your allies to sit beneath this tree."

Hendrick grunted to a younger Mohawk, and Tekarihoken—the titular chief of the Mohawk nation—rose to accept the belt.

"Brothers," Johnson continued, "at the same time I remove the embers that remain at Albany and rekindle the fire of council and friendship at this place. This fire I shall make of such wood as will give the clearest light and the greatest warmth. I hope it will be comfortable and useful to all who come to light their pipes at it, and that it will be a consuming terror to all evil-minded ones."

Claus stood ready with a pine torch kindled inside the house. The Indians watched in silence as Johnson took it from him.

Billy paused. His eyes moved from Hendrick to Red Head, the Onondaga Speaker, whose face was utterly impassive. Johnson did not trust the Onondaga to keep the promises he had made when he was warmed with rum. He knew that Red Head had been assiduously courted by the French, bribed by the Joncaires at Niagara, baptized by the soldier-abbé at La Présentation. His spies told him that Red Head had played a part in the assassination of his predecessor, Canassatego, who was a more reliable friend of the English cause.

Damn your eyes if you fail me now, Johnson spoke to him silently. *If Hendrick and I must do this alone, it will be enough.*

Billy raised the pine torch above his head. In the failing light, as the sun dipped below the Noses, at the bend in the river, it made a wild, primal sight.

Before he plunged the torch into the bed of punkwood and dry twigs under the pyre, Red Head stepped forward, his chest as deep and sturdy as an oak keg.

"My brother Forest Killer," the Onondaga spoke across the firepit. "We have long been in darkness. We thank you and our elder brother King George for restoring the clear and friendly light that cheered our grandfathers. The fire that was kept at Albany was so low and bad we could not even find a spark with which to light our pipes. We come to assist you now. We bring the Fire That Never Dies."

Red Head motioned to a younger Onondaga, who passed him a bark container that seemed to be filled with dirt. Red Head groped inside and pulled out a coal that glowed dull red under the coating of whitened ash. He laid it carefully on a piece of punkwood. He sucked air into his cheeks until they puffed out like a bellows. Then he blew steadily on the coal until he drew the flame.

He nodded to Johnson, who hurled the blazing torch into the heart of the pyre. Soon flames were leaping high above their heads.

Red Head said, "We will cherish the fire we have kindled here, as well as that at Onondaga. These are the two fires of the Longhouse People. You are our Firekeeper, and wherever you live, the Fire That Never Dies will burn. All other fires we now kick away, as unnatural and hateful to us."

The lords and warriors of the Confederacy shouted, *"Ta'ne'tho!* So be it."

Hendrick raised his voice in the traditional chant, the *HaiHai.* Soon the whole valley echoed with it.

"Do you know what you have done, sir?" Arent Stevens said to Johnson, who was devouring the scene with his eyes.

"What is it?"

"You have made a revolution, Colonel Johnson. There are men who will never forgive you for it. They will kill you sooner than deal with you."

"I have met some of them already. They set their dogs on me in the street."

2.

Billy reminded himself often, in the days that followed, that power lies not in titles but in the ability to move men to action.

He was Firekeeper of the Six Nations.

They had given him the Living Bones, the deerhorn antlers of office of a *royaner,* one of the traditional chiefs of the Confederacy.

"No white man before you has ever received the

Living Bones," Hendrick had assured him. "And, in the times to come, none will do so again. Unless he comes to requicken your name."

The Indians had freighted him with honors. But would they follow him into battle?

The sachems gathered on his estate were slow to make their intentions known. The speech-making continued day after day, and the beauty of native metaphor dulled with endless repetition. In the intervals, from dawn until late at night, Billy was required to sit in private conclave with the chiefs and leading men—and, on several occasions, with delegations of Indian women—all of whom made it plain their allegiance was not to be had without special favors. Johnson exhausted the credit General Braddock had extended to him to buy Indian presents. He dug into his own stock and borrowed from his trading partners. Once again, he was going out on a limb, in the cause of a distant sovereign who might or might not remember his services and of colonial politicians who might or might not deign to cover his expenses.

His Indian guests ate their way through his storerooms, thorough as locusts. Johnson had to set an armed guard, day and night, over his surviving cattle and pigs.

The visitors stripped his orchards and trampled down his gardens and meadows.

"No!" Cat squalled from the kitchen window on Sunday morning, when she saw a group of Cayuga warriors playing a ball game in her walled garden. She ran out with a broom. They laughed when she shook it in their faces and laughed louder when their leader, saucer-eyed, mimicked terror in the face of the lone white woman in cap and apron. They left the garden, but Cat had come too late to save the plot where she had merrily intermingled the tiny blue-white flowers of the flax plants with columbine, hyssop, lemon balm and the native blue lobelia that was so much in demand among Billy's womanizing friends.

That evening, John Ogilvie came up from Fort Hunter to conduct a service, in English and Mohawk. Cat and her children sat on the stairs, because the hall and the parlors were filled with Indians, gaudy as peacocks in the finery of two cultures, wearing laced hats and nose-bobs, embroidered vests, rattlesnake skins, and circlets of bones and teeth.

John was fascinated by them. "I'm going with Papa," he whispered to Nancy. "I'm going to paint my face and fight Indian-style."

"Shut up," his sister whispered. "You're just a boy." Nancy had eyes only for Daniel Claus, the young Indian interpreter, with his knowing dark eyes.

"If I was a Mohawk, I'd be old enough to take the warpath," John argued. "And Daddy's a Mohawk, isn't he?"

"He's no such thing!"

"Quiet, the both of you," Cat hissed. "Tonight, we are in church!"

It was hard to think of the familiar stone house, the scene of so many games and revels, as a place of worship. But, indeed, Parson Ogilvie had set up his altar on the table Billy normally used for a bar, and a remarkable number of Indians knelt to take the wafer and the wine after hearing out a puzzling reading from the Bible that referred to chariots and seraphim and other things rarely encountered in the valley.

Hendrick stayed after service, with his brothers and several elders from the Upper Castle, to talk business. Johnson entertained the Mohawks with a bowl of rum shrub. He had the brew made very weak. Tonight, he hoped not to have to quiet his guests down by adding a few drops of laudanum. Tomorrow, he would need Hendrick's cutting edge in the formal counciling.

Johnson lit his pipe-tomahawk. It passed from hand to hand.

"Red Head is not of our mind," Hendrick cautioned. "The French priests have filled his head with their talk. But his brother will listen. And his wife has a taste for English silks."

"We must serve her appetites." Johnson nodded at Claus, who made a note.

"Our people, also, are divided," Hendrick went on. "At the Upper Castle, our women fear they may be attacked while the warriors are far distant."

"They will be protected. I guarantee it. Redcoat soldiers will remain at my house. They will come to you immediately if there is any alarm. I will send builders to repair your palisades."

"We need cannon."

"Cannon?" Johnson frowned. Who had ever heard of an Indian village with white men's cannon? But this was not an ordinary situation. Canajoharie—the Upper Castle—was the pivot of British influence on the frontier. And the home of his most reliable native friends. "You will have one of my swivel guns," he said quickly. "They were a gift from my uncle. And I will send an officer to show you how to fire it."

"Our women have other fears," Abraham spoke up. "They say our children will go hungry if the men go on the warpath instead of the hunt. Who will bring meat? Who will provide the trade goods?"

"Your women and children will be supplied with all their needs. I have spoken on this matter with General Braddock. The King your father looks after his own."

"There is another thing," Hendrick spoke again. "There is a powerful one at the Lower Castle who speaks against you night and day. He says we cannot trust your promises because you left him to fester three winters in the Frenchmen's jails."

"You speak of Sun Walker."

"Hen."

"I thought I had made it up to him. I thought I had made him understand it was not my doing that he was held captive so long."

"He listens to evil birds."

"Which ones?"

"He has spoken with Hard Egg."

Johnson slapped his temple. *Lydius.* Would he never be rid of the deceiver? He had seen the storm clouds rising when Governor Shirley—against his advice—had given Lydius a commission as Colonel of Indians for the

Niagara campaign. It was intolerable that Lydius was in the Valley, undermining his efforts at the moment he was laboring to recruit the Six Nations for the war, at the expense of his liver, his sleep, and sometimes, he feared, his sanity.

Billy spoke with such composure as he could muster. "What did Lydius tell Sun Walker?"

"He says it wherever he goes. Lydius says we should not follow you, but his master, Governor Shirley. He says he has dreamed you will die beside still water, after betraying those who have placed themselves in your care."

Careful, Johnson warned himself. *I must show no emotion, or else I will lose their respect altogether.* It was possible, after all, that Hendrick was improving his story. *We have trained the Mohawks to reason like us. It is only natural that they should seek to improve their price.*

"Go on," Billy said gruffly. "What else does Lydius say?"

"He says that if we march with you, we will be obliged to make war on our kinsmen."

"You mean the Caughnawagas."

Hendrick grunted.

"Lydius jests with you. But you know this already." *Careful,* Billy warned himself more urgently. *Give them a chance, and the Mohawks will play the game of divide and rule with us that we flatter ourselves we play with them.* New England, mourning the loss of its frontier settlements, regarded all Mission Indians—including the Caughnawagas—as skulking murderers, to be shot on sight. Governor Shirley of Massachusetts shared the sentiments of his colony. He had expressed his outrage to Johnson that Caughnawagas—"French spies"—were seen every day in the trading houses and grogshops of Albany. The Governor wanted the lot of them clapped into irons or packed off to Montreal.

But Johnson said only, "It is my wish, as well as yours, to avoid a fight with your cousins. You must take my belts to them. You must ask them to join our cause. If they will not stand with us, then tell them they must stand aside and not help the French. I have no quarrel with the Caughnawagas. Tell them this."

Hendrick puffed on the calumet and watched the smoke rise. If he was dissatisfied with Johnson's answer, he did not say so openly. But he narrowed his eyes and pointed the business end of the pipe-tomahawk toward the door, which had opened a chink. "I think there is a spy in Forest Killer's house."

"John!"

The door closed abruptly, but Billy bounded through it, chased his son up the stairs, and grabbed him by the ear. "You are supposed to be in bed! What will your mother say?"

"That he takes after you, Billy. Forever putting his nose where it doesn't belong."

Cat stood on the landing, her hair streaming over her shoulders, in a chaste nightgown that buttoned at the neck and came down to her ankles. She looked quite fetching, Billy thought, despite the threads of gray. But his face closed, out of habit. The habit of not seeing her except as an appendage to his house, to his children.

"Go to bed, the lot of you," he said gruffly.

When he returned to the parlor, he found that the Mohawks had wasted no time. They had unearthed the decanters of brandy and Madeira from the depths of the huge Dutch closet. It was going to be a long night.

3.

Cat woke with her heart drumming in her throat. The rush of her blood seemed louder than the interminable drumming and chanting of the Indians camped on three sides of the house. Her breathing was fast and shallow. Her skin was slick with sweat. Her stomach turned over and over, around a tight, unyielding knot of pain.

She did not want to go back into the dream. She wanted simply to pull down a curtain of daylight and shut out the night terror. But the only light outside was the pricking of remote, indifferent stars, and the glow of

the council fires. She saw it again. Saw herself lashed to a
bed like a dying animal, the tight, distended swell of her
belly, grown monstrously huge, ready to burst like a
rotten fruit. She wanted to scream again when she saw
the feet. They were purple-dark. They poked out between her legs where a head should have been, giving no
relief from the dreadful pressure of the hard, ungiving
lump inside her body. She clapped her hands over her
mouth, to silence the audible scream as the dream
sucked her deeper in, and she saw the blood spattering
over the walls, as high as the ceiling.

Billy was somewhere in the dream. But he wasn't with
her. He stood at a window, his hands clasped behind his
back, looking at his own world, not hers.

Dreams don't have to come true, she reminded herself.
Besides, there was no prospect of another child. Billy
had hardly looked at her as a woman—or touched her—
since the Mohawks brought him the French slut as a
prize. And Cat would never look at another man, she
was sure of that. Even though she hungered, as Billy did.
Men could sense it. They looked at her in a certain way,
when they thought they could get away with it. And she
knew that men liked what they saw. She had kept her
figure. She had sprouted a few wrinkles at the corners of
her eyes, and her hands had been coarsened by hard
work in all seasons. Her waist and thighs had thickened
a little with childbearing and a farmer's diet. But her
skin was still smooth, her breasts firm.

Oh yes, there were men who were interested, and they
made her know. Big Gerhard Frey had been less than
subtle, letting her feel his rod when he caught her up in a
country dance at the Palatine fair. Billy would take a
horsewhip to Frey if he knew, just to mark his territory,
in the same spirit—and with no more rancor—than his
mastiff lifted his leg against every tree around the house.
But she would not take another man. She would not risk
her children's birthright. She would not risk losing Billy,
even if he treated her, more and more, as a part of the
furnishings or a faithful dog to be shut in a pen when it
was not wanted.

So she told herself her nightmare could not be about a real child. But it still sat on her chest. It must be telling her *something*. Dreams come for a reason, and if they scare you it is to make sure you pay attention. Maybe the child that was stillborn in the dream was some part of herself that was dying inside. Maybe it was her sex that was dying, unnoticed, unnourished by the only man she could love.

She wanted to go down to the stream, to cleanse herself from head to foot, to scrub off the sweat and the crawling fear that lingered on her skin. But she could not bathe in front of hundreds of strangers, Billy's native guests.

She pulled back the linsey-woolsey curtain she had hung from ceiling rings to give herself a few square feet of privacy, in Johnson's world. Polly, on the low bed next to her sister, was going at her thumb in her sleep like a hungry calf at its mother's udder. One of her legs was thrown out at an angle, threatening to roll her out. The sight made Cat smile. She tucked the errant leg back under the sheet and kissed Polly's hair.

She poured water from the ewer into the washbasin and cleaned up as thoroughly as was possible, dabbing at her skin with a wet cloth.

An animal cry knifed through the darkness.

Her whole body trembled.

She thought, *The Indians are slaughtering one of the cows. Will we never be rid of them?*

The cry came again, louder. It swelled and then shook, like a faltering trumpet.

And Cat *knew*.

"Mummy?" Nancy sat up rubbing her eyes. The long oval of her face was puffy with sleep.

"Go back to sleep, darling. I think Meghan's having her baby."

The little gray mare had looked ready to foal for weeks past. She had swelled up to the point where she looked like an inflated bladder, wobbling about on splints.

"I'm coming too," Nancy announced as Cat buttoned a simple print dress over her petticoat. The mare was the girls' favorite, a natural pacer with an imperturbable disposition, who could be trusted not to bolt. A ride on Meghan's swaying back was smoother than on one of the thick-wheeled wagons that came up the King's Road from Schenectady.

They walked to the barn between the Indian camp-fires. Some of the native women were already up and about, fetching water, setting kettles of corn soup and bark tea to boil. A tall, gaunt Mohawk woman, her face seamed and spotted with age, her iron-gray hair falling in plaits to her waist, greeted Cat with her eyes.

They nodded to each other without speaking. Not at peace, not at war.

"Isn't that Tewatokwas?" Nancy whispered, then corrected herself. "I mean Island Woman?"

Cat didn't like her children to speak Mohawk in the house. It galled her that all of them had become quite fluent.

Cat quickened her stride. The glow of a lightning bug veered toward her face, then vanished.

"Island Woman gave me something, when I was small." Nancy pursued. "A charm. Why wouldn't you let me keep it?"

"You take nothing from a person like that."

"Is Island Woman a witch?"

"Never say that word!"

Cat was now moving so fast Nancy had to run to keep up. And her curiosity about her mother's old feud with Island Woman was quickly forgotten, because there was a gaggle of people at the barn door, jostling for a view inside the stalls. Blanketed Indians, black slaves, a lone redcoat soldier who had drifted away from his post.

Paddy Groghan, the overseer, pushed his way through their ranks.

"It's a devilish bad business, Mistress Catherine."

Behind him, Cat saw Fergus pushing his head out of his stall, ears pricked up at her voice. The old stallion's right eye was milky. He was slowly going blind in the other eye, but Billy would not hear of putting him down. The horse had been with him since his beginnings in

America. Billy had nursed the underfed stallion, infested with botflies, back to health and mated him with a series of mares to produce some of the finest stock in the Province.

Cat was thankful Billy was loyal to his horse, if not by the mother of his children. But, in that moment, she hoped it was Fergus that had screamed and not the mare in foal.

"Who is it?" she asked Paddy. "Who's hurt?"

"It's Meghan, Cat. You don't want to see it."

Already, she was pushing her way through, into the depths of the barn. The scene was lit only by a pair of candles, hung in tin dishes from the posts. Meghan's stall was open. The straw reeked of blood and dung and something Cat could not immediately identify.

The mare was down, lying on her side, her face half-buried in the mess of straw.

Ade was down on his knees beside her. Thank God Paddy had had the sense to send for him. If any man could save the mare, it was Ade. The veins stood out on the African's forehead as he hauled at the slimy, tar-black haunches that hung from Meghan's bloody vagina. The slats of the stall were speckled with dark blood.

It is the dream.

Cat forced back her sickness and fear, waving Nancy back with her outstretched arm. She rushed to Ade and squatted beside him.

"How can I help?"

"You can take her head and gentle her," the freedman said. "She'll trust you." His arms were bloodied up to the elbows.

Cat leaned her head against Meghan's, looking into her great brown eye, stroking her neck.

Ade groaned. "This one don't want to come out."

Then a shock hit Cat like the recoil of a cannon, and Ade said, "It's out."

Cat could hardly bear to look at the dead foal. "I should have known. There must have been something we could have done."

"Don't blame yourself for what's done. There's the mother to save."

But the mare could not—or would not—get up. They coaxed her and tugged her. Paddy Groghan brought five or six strapping men to stand her up on her legs, but she fell as if her legs were straws.

"There's no saving a horse that won't stand," Paddy said grimly.

For hours, Cat watched Meghan thrash and roll back and forth on the barn floor. When the sun came up, a pattern began to establish itself. The mare worked herself, little by little, toward the eastern door. Calling and prodding, Cat and Cicero were at last able to get her settled in a corner of the pasture. They paid no heed to the commotion around them, as the Indians came together for another days' feasting and counciling, serenaded by one of the Butler boys, who marched about playing the bagpipe. They carried out bales of hay and made a protective wall around the mare. Cat fed her by hand, with long-stemmed clover and fresh shoots. She ate sparsely, and the flies gathered around her rump, to feast on the clotting blood.

"Paddy Groghan is right," Ade told her. "There's no saving a horse that will not stand."

"It is the dream."

"What dream?" Ade glanced at her sharply.

"Nothing." Cat bit her lip, resisting the sense of fatality that invaded her heart and mind. *I will it to change. Dreams don't have to come true.*

A shadow passed between her and the orange sun. She looked up. With the light at her back, Island Woman looked like a carved stick.

She spoke in Mohawk.

"I don't understand." Cat shook her head, exhausted, on the brink of tears.

A pretty native girl stepped forward. In the early light, her skin had the soft glow of old gold. She wore white doeskin, and her eyes were huge and liquid, like a doe's. She looked to be Nancy's age, or a year older, though it was hard to say with the Indian girls; they grew up fast.

Sparrow said, "My grandmother knows you are hurting everywhere inside. She knows this because she dreams your dream. She says maybe she can help."

☐

Cat did not talk to Billy about the mare. She saw him
only from a distance, always with native chiefs or officers
of the Indian Department. He had no time for his own.

But she visited Meghan throughout the evening. The
last time, she found Ade had come back.

The African was pressing herbs into the mare's vagina.
The mare raised her long head and snapped at him, but
did not stop his work.

"What are you doing?"

"A Mohawk woman gave me this. She says it stops the
bleeding."

Ade showed her the plant that he had pounded into
medicine. It was bushy, with dark green leaves. It looked
like a common weed, one of the rank growths that were
forever invading her garden.

"Do you think it will work?"

"I don't know this one. This is not my country. I can't
talk to the plants, the way Indians do. But the old
woman is a doctor, a healing woman. I guess she knows.
Maybe you know something too. She says she got this
one from your garden."

"I don't know—" She broke off some of the leaves and
a part of the root. There were herbals in Billy's library
and learned botanical tomes that Mr. Kalm sent all the
way from Stockholm. Maybe she could find something
about it in the books.

"She says something else." When Ade looked up, Cat
could see the pink inside the rims of his eyes, and the
necklace of shells he was wearing inside his leather
blacksmith's apron.

"Yes?"

"She says if you want to heal something, you got to put
power into it. I guess she's right about that."

☐

Cat woke in the night from a stranger dream. She was in
a cave that was full of plants. She was talking to another
woman who knew all their names, and the right time to

gather them, and how they should be used in healing. Cat thought this other person was Island Woman, but when she saw her more clearly, she realized she was talking to a second self. This second self looked as she did, but was wiser, stronger, more radiant. She led Cat out of the cave to a damp place in the woods, and made her feel the spores on the underside of a broad-leafed plant, so she would know them again.

"Where is your body now?"

With the question, Cat woke up with a start. The colors of her dream stayed with her—greens and yellows that were more vivid than anything in the daylight world.

She pulled on clothes and rushed down to the paddock. Meghan was wobbly, but she was on her feet.

Cat pressed her cheek against the mare's neck.

"Thank you, Lord."

The dream returned, with her acknowledgment of the gift. Meghan had been saved, at least in part, by something that had sprouted—unrecognized, unvalued—in her own garden. Something she did not even have a name for, except in the dream. She had looked for the plant in Billy's books, and found nothing like it, except the purple comfrey of the Old World, which was different, because the blossoms of this plant were white.

She owed Meghan's life to Island Woman and her knowledge of plants and healing.

In part of herself—in a dream self—she knew what the Mohawk woman knew. Waking, she was blind and deaf. Surely the message of the dream was that she must put aside old fears and jealousies and open herself to learning.

She looked for Island Woman as she walked back among the Indian campfires. She did not find her. Instead, she noticed a long dugout coming downriver. A tall man, dressed all in black, stood in the prow, shading his eyes against the horizontal rays of the rising sun.

Lydius.

The mare, the dream and Island Woman were forgotten, for the moment.

I must warn Billy.

She had felt the force of hatred in Lydius, focused on Billy. Whatever Lydius claimed to be doing on the river, he had come to strike at Johnson and those nearest to him.

She turned back to the house and saw Daniel, up and about early, as always. He called out cheerily, and she pointed to the boat on the river. Daniel's face tightened. *"Unanstandig,"* he reverted to their native language. "It is indecent." He squared his shoulders and dashed ahead of her into the house. Daniel would know what to say.

4.

When Johnson learned that his most serious rival had been sighted a musket shot from his own house, he gathered the men he most trusted in the Indian Department in the blue room. He still called it the blue room, though the wallpaper had largely disappeared behind shelves of books, hunting trophies and Indian curiosities from as far west as the plains of the Sioux and the swamps of the Cree.

"Lydius is come to buy the Indians away from me," Johnson announced. "He does it in Shirley's name, but he does it for his own ambitions and those of his Connecticut business partners. If they have their way, they will steal the Indians blind, while pretending friendship. They will wreck our expedition and may yet succeed in losing us the war."

"Kill the bastard," John Butler said bluntly. "There are hogs that go missing during an Indian council. Lydius will be no more missed."

"We must blend the serpent with the dove," Johnson said quickly, noting the look of distaste on Daniel's face. "I will not have Lydius harmed or break openly with him during our conference. He holds Shirley's commission. We must seek to win over his master, or at least drive a wedge between them."

He looked at the officers of his department. Young Claus, his mind as quick as a rapier. Benjamin Stoddert, faithful and sturdy as the mastiff that had once dragged him, snowblind, out of a blizzard. Old Arent Stevens, seasoned, sharp-tongued, indomitable.

"By courting the Indians, Lydius seeks to do us a rudeness behind our backs," Johnson went on. "We must encourage the natives—those we can trust, but are not known to be wholly ours—to return the favor in front of our faces, before the whole assembly."

Arent Stevens rubbed his jaw. "An Oneida will serve best," he observed. "An Oneida will stir less jealousy among the other nations than a Mohawk. And the Oneidas are known to have a just grievance against Colonel Lydius. They are suzerains, by tradition, over the Wyoming lands that Lydius and his Connecticut playmates spirited away from them at Albany last year."

"Then find us the man."

"I believe I know the man who will do," Claus spoke up. He talked of a young Oneida chief—Skenandon—adopted from a southern nation that had hunted for generations on the rolling grasslands of the Wyoming territory, between the forks of the Susquehanna. "I heard that he told a dream, in the dream-guessing rite at the Midwinter ceremony, this season past. He said he dreamed the head of the white man who stole the Wyoming lands was cut off and set up on a pole at the Oneida castle, for the children to jeer at and the crows to eat."

"A pretty dream," Butler warmed to the story.

"I believe this Oneida dreamer is the man for the match," Johnson said. He pictured the play that might unfold around his council fire. "We must have Lydius in attendance. The things that need saying must be said to his face. This will lose him all respect among the Indians, surely. Especially if his temper bolts."

Stevens grinned, enjoying the game plan. "I will arrange it," the interpreter volunteered. "Lydius still trusts me, a little. He has hopes that Governor Shirley's purse may sway an old man who will need to rest his legs when this year's campaigning is over. Lydius believes that, at the worst, I belong neither to you nor to him."

"By God, I believe he is right, Arent!" Billy clapped Stevens on the shoulder, then circled the group with the ship's decanter of Madeira, replenishing glasses. "My advantage over Lydius is I value the difference between a man who will sell himself and one who will not."

□

Lydius came to the council, dressed, as usual, in his crow's plumage. The funereal black of his suit and hat was relieved only by a medal and a sash that must have been gifts from Governor Shirley, and a jaunty cockade that looked more French than English to Billy.

The giant prepared to sit on the sidelines, among the throng of traders and tenant farmers. But Johnson beckoned him to take a seat among the officers and interpreters of the Indian Department.

Billy played the genial host. His social poise in all situations—mudwrestling with rough German neighbors or dining with a Governor—was a secret of his rise to power, one of his sources of strength. He knew it, and he practiced it now.

"I did not know how I would be received." Lydius swiveled his one good eye to read Johnson's face. He had substituted a glass eye for the patch he frequently wore over the dead socket. The false iris was a vivid cornflower blue, jarring in contrast with the drowned quality of the true one. Lydius had also acquired a new hairpiece in place of his old-fashioned bag-wig. It was in the military mode, powdered white. It sat up rather high atop Lydius' bald pate, so an inch of boiled skin showed between the ears and the ridges of tight curls.

"A friend of Governor Shirley is always welcome at my house," Billy lied smoothly. "You will take some refreshment, I hope."

"You remember my custom."

"Of course. Daniel—" Johnson turned to the German interpreter. "Will you send for a dish of tea for Colonel Lydius?"

They looked out over the semicircles of Indians. Lydius' arrival on the scene had caused a notable stir among the Mohawks and Oneidas.

"Your sense of timing is exquisite, as ever," Billy

informed his guest. "We have come to the main business. Today I will explain to the sachems what help is needed for each of our expeditions. Then I will throw down the warbelt. I flatter myself that most of our friends will take up the hatchet today. The ground has been carefully laid."

Lydius picked a clump of mud and grass from his shoe. Johnson's meadow looked as if had been pawed by a herd of wild Highland cattle during the rutting season.

"You have been generous with the natives," Lydius commented. "I came by way of your cookhouse. I see you have a five-year ox and six cows ready for the feast. Not to mention a quantity of rum that would make a sailor swoon."

"I fear I am not as generous as some may be, at least in their promises."

"I am not sure I follow."

"There is a rumor among the Indians that Governor Shirley is willing to pay them by the day, at the rate of regular soldiers or even better."

"Is there, indeed?" Lydius fixed his good eye on the bridge of Johnson's nose.

"I, of course, do not have the money to match such an offer. Nor the authorization. Which must come, surely, from Braddock. I think the General would never give it. Our Indians do not fight for individual hire, like Swiss mercenaries. What is given to them must be given for the benefit of all, to the clan and the clanmothers. But I speak needlessly, since I know you are a master of the theme."

"Hendrick is wearing a fine new hat," Lydius parried. "I would not part with it for less than twenty beavers. Do you tell me it is a gift to his nation?"

"A treat is not the same thing as a wage. It is given in a different spirit. If a friendly native says he likes a thing, it is prudent to give it."

"But not to allow him a regular income that might make him a regular fighter, and keep him on the warpath for months instead of days."

"Your view of the Indians has evolved in interesting

ways, Colonel Lydius. I trust the generosity of the
burghers of Massachusetts will disappoint neither you
nor the Indians you cultivate. Ah, Cat. How kind of
you."

Cat moved between the men with a salver laid with
the tea things. She was conscious of their eyes traveling
over her body, lingering at the bust and thighs.

They do not see me, she recognized. They see a piece of
meat, a vessel shaped for their appetites. *They do not
even look at my face.*

Except for Billy, who does not see me at all.

And Daniel, kind, meticulous Daniel. Claus took the
tray from her and served Lydius his tea.

Lydius winked at her. His smile was lopsided, something from a bad dream.

They think I do not see or understand, Cat thought.
*They talk war and high policy in front of me, confident
that I take nothing in, as they speak before the slaves.*

But I see clearly enough, Cat assured herself, inclining
her head to Lydius as if he had paid her a compliment.
*That man is here to ruin Billy. Unless Billy tears his
throat out first.*

□

With his enemy sitting behind his back, Johnson outlined the plan of campaign to the Indians. He requested
that some of the young warriors should go at once to join
Braddock on his march through the Ohio country to
Fort Duquesne. He asked Benjamin Stoddert to stand
and introduced him as the officer who would accompany
this party.

The Indians were not enthusiastic.

Red Head, the Onondaga speaker, complained that
native scouts who had gone with Braddock had been
abused by English soldiers. Some of their women had
been raped. Several had died in a scrap with drunken
regulars.

It was the old problem, Billy recognized. White soldiers thought any woman who traveled with an army was
fair game. They took native women by force, although

there were some who would give themselves freely if they were asked politely.

But Braddock must have guides. In the forest, an army moving without native scouts was blind. Johnson would speak in private with the Western Indians who had come to the conference—Mississaugas, Foxes, Mingoes.

Behind him, Lydius sucked on a clay pipe, untroubled by what was done or not done for Braddock.

Billy spoke of Shirley's expedition, aimed at Niagara by way of Oswego. "I hope and expect that a powerful body of warriors will join our brother Shirley at Oswego and help him to drive our enemies from Lake Ontario. I know that the Governor and his men will be received with friendship and hospitality all along their trail through the lands of the Longhouse."

Lydius bristled, as Johnson knew he would. Shirley had demanded an honor guard from the Six Nations: two hundred warriors to escort him along the Valley. Billy was sure this demand had been inspired by Lydius. Though a Governor's vanity could never be overrated, the only practical effect of giving Shirley his two hundred Indians would be to undermine Johnson's own campaign. The Valley was safe country, at least for the large body of troops that would march with Shirley.

Red Head stood up again.

"Brother Forest Killer, are you not our great tree of shelter? Why do you desire us to shelter under any other tree? Where you go we are ready to follow. Let others go where they will."

Lydius made a sound between a growl and a sigh.

An Oneida chief stepped forward. The Onondaga speaker ceded his place to him.

In place of a belt of wampum, the Oneida held up a dead rattlesnake. He shook it, making the rattles hiss.

"Brother," he addressed Johnson. "You promised us that you would keep this fireplace clean from all filth and that no snake would be permitted to enter our councils. But a snake sits on your side of the fire." He pointed at Lydius, his eyes glinting in a mask of red and blue paint. "That one is *rotkon*—an evil spirit. He has stolen our lands. He takes our people slyly by the blanket, one at a time. He pours hard water down their throats until they are not themselves and wild spirits possess them. They come back to find their marks are on lying deeds. These deeds are in the pocket of that devil and his friends. But we will never suffer them to use or settle the lands that have descended to us from our grandmothers' grandmothers and cannot be exchanged without their blessing."

"Yo-hai!" The hoarse cry of approval issued from hundreds of throats.

Lydius, white-lipped, bit through the stem of his pipe and threw it on the ground in disgust.

Johnson gave a quick sideways glance to make sure that Wraxall—a trusty wordsmith and agile lobbyist— was getting all this down, with the help of the interpreters. It would make excellent reading for the Lords of Trade.

"Colonel Lydius came here of his own accord, without any invitation from me," Billy explained. "I believe that your claims of fraud are just. It will be my pleasure as well as my duty to ensure that justice is done you in this sordid business."

But Lydius did not wait to hear the Johnson version. He hopped across the meadow like a crow after a worm.

5.

When Johnson spoke to the nations the next day, he was no longer dressed as an officer of the Crown.

He had painted his face and chest for war. On his head, he wore the *gustoweh,* the feathered crown of a chief of the Six Nations, a blaze of bright turkey-down inside bands of silver and brass, the tall eagle feathers revolving in the breeze. He wore a ruffled shirt, open to the breastbone, beaded leggings, high deerskin moccasins. He carried a pipe tomahawk, a skin pouch containing tobacco and sumac, flint and steel, and an otterskin bag with the maskettes and dream talismans he had gathered over the years.

He raised the conch to his lips and huffed air into the

shell, breathing from the pit of his stomach. The scream of the conch filled the whole gathering place.

"If you are my brothers, then go with me!" He spoke in Mohawk. He was no longer William Johnson. He was Forest Killer, a chief of the Bear Clan and the Firekeeper of the League. The skin of a huge grizzly lay behind him, in place of the straight-backed chair he had favored in earlier council sessions.

"My war kettle is on the fire. My canoe is ready to put into the water. My gun is loaded. My axe is sharpened and thirsty for the blood of our enemies." He brandished the pipe tomahawk. The blade was red. The wingfeathers of a redtail hawk hung from the shaft.

"My brothers, I desire and expect you to take up the hatchet and risk with us."

He took up a great black war belt, daubed with red figures, and passed it across the fire. Red Head took it from his hands.

The warriors shouted their approval.

Arent Stevens shrieked like an angry seagull and capered around the warpost in a ragged circle dance.

The interpreter danced for Braddock, in Braddock's place.

Billy smiled at the notion of a British general thumping his feet to a native water-drum, stripped to a breechcloth, daubed with vermilion and potblacking.

The rhythms pulsed louder. The women's voices squalled above the warriors' cries. Billy's legs were shaking. He felt an electric thrill rush through his whole body.

He ripped off his shirt and leggings. Stripped to his breechcloth, like Stevens, he hurled himself into the dance. Round and round the warpost, pounding his feet into the earth, miming deeds of battle.

The air became heavy and damp, weighing on his shoulders like a wet blanket. Round and round, times beyond counting. Soon he was gasping for air. His legs ached. Each step drove the pain deeper.

His senses screamed for him to rest. He kept on. His audience respected only that which endures, that which goes the distance.

He did not remember the instant at which the aching stopped and everything became different, because he could see himself as if he were watching the whole scene from a height. His consciousness flickered between separate realities, passing in and out of a light so blinding it became darkness, like the dark of the sun.

By this time, scores of the native warriors had joined the circle.

They danced with the animal guardians and the swift flying birds that would go with them on the warpath. Hendrick, for all his weight and girth, moved fluidly, with the motion of a wolf. Snowbird tossed back his head, his nostrils flaring, kicking and stomping like a bull elk in rutting time.

Billy made thunder in the earth, like Ohkwari, his clan totem. The Mohawks say you can *hear* the footprints of a bear.

The dancers whirled faster and faster, sweat gushing through layers of grease and paint.

The women's voices lifted higher. Island Woman sang a whole forest of birds, sweet music and harsh caws, cooing and whistling.

She whispered to Sparrow, "We are in the presence of the unseen. The spirits are coming to dance with us now."

Sparrow saw it. The ancestors came in an opalescent mist that swirled around the dancers. She saw men she had seen in infancy, warriors who had gone the long trail, and others she had seen in the dreaming. They reveled in the blood-frenzy that was building among the dancers, in the smell of the half-raw meat turning on great spits over the cookfires.

Hendrick Forked Paths saw them too. And Snowbird.

They were singing their songs of power.

Johnson drove his hatchet into the war-post with such force it split the timber and made the heavy beam shudder. Hendrick, close behind him, drove his hatchet in next, and sang of his victories and the dead who called on him for revenge.

Forest Killer threw himself down on the bearskin, but

an unstoppable force was moving through him. He opened his lungs. The first sound that issued was a prolonged, vibrant humming. Then a power song exploded from somewhere deep within him, primal and stirring, carrying heart and belly and lungs. As Billy sang, his whole body flexed and wheeled and craned, a great raptor seeking its prey. He was becoming huge and hugely powerful. Yet he was light at the same time, ready to become airborne. Though part of him squatted on the ground, a larger part was swooping and hunting.

He found he could see in a different way. Among the hundreds of natives who had joined the war-dance—among them and *through* them—he saw other presences. Eagle-men and deerskin-men, bearwalkers and wolf-runners. There was one who stood apart from the others, observing more than participating. An ancient with a snowdrift of hair about his shoulders, and eyes as bright as fire. He looked closely to Billy. He seemed to be checking whether Forest Killer could see him.

Johnson blinked. The apparition did not dissolve into daylight. It was made of smoke, but it had substance. He reached out to touch it. He felt a coldness in the heart of the day. The man of smoke extended a long forefinger and touched Forest Killer's chest. He seemed to be tracing a design. Billy sat quiet, stunned yet utterly without fear.

A more palpable hand patted his shoulder.

"Well done, sir," said Peter Wraxall. "You are a credit to all our tribes. I have often heard it said the Celt has a flair for theater that is second to none. No offense taken, I trust."

The old man and the dancing dead were gone, when Johnson looked again. He sighed. Perhaps he had seen, for a moment, as Homer's heroes did. As he was told the Indians did. On the field of battle, and on other great occasions in their lives, they *saw* their spirits. Switching from that kind of vision to ordinary sight created a moment of confusion for Johnson.

He came back to the useful Mr. Wraxall, slipping into the appropriate guise.

"No offense whatever, Peter. Come, we must see to lunch. I must not allow my people to overcook the meat. Our guests generally want it crawling off the plate."

CHAPTER 30

FIELDS OF WAR

1.

Johnson came to Albany, the mustering place, on a sultry July day of drenching rains that raised steam from the cobbled streets and the cow pastures below the stockade. He found his army stewing with disaffection and resentment.

The New Englanders had rushed to arms eagerly when their Governors issued beating orders to men like Ephraim Williams, the aging border warrior who had raised a regiment from his neighbors in western Massachusetts. Memories of the savagery of scalping parties from Canada still burned strong among New England families. The war on three continents that had been started by a handful of Virginians in a clearing in the Pennsylvania woods was wildly popular at Boston and New Haven. For many New England Protestants, the new war against Catholic France was also a holy crusade. "For such an Enterprise," Colonel Williams was assured by his kinsman, Israel Williams, "there is a Wonderful Spirit in People, and multitudes will heartily engage."

Twelve hundred Massachusetts men had enlisted in the new provincial regiments commanded by Williams,

Moses Titcomb and Timothy Ruggles. The government
of Connecticut had promised a thousand men for Johnson's army. Thirteen hundred Connecticut men joined
up; the extra volunteers were to be paid and provisioned
by New York, and to serve with the New York forces.
Rhode Island contributed a regiment of four hundred
men. And five hundred New Hampshire woodsmen
joined Colonel Joseph Blanchard's new regiment,
though they got lost in unfamiliar woods; by the time
they reached Albany, the rest of Johnson's command
had moved north.

The army Billy found waiting for him was, over-
whelmingly, a New England army. He had only five
hundred New York provincials, against more than six
times as many New England provincials. His immediate
staff were Yorkers or Englishmen—including the fluent
Peter Wraxall and Captain William Eyre, a gunner and
engineer seconded from His Majesty's 44th Foot, the
sole career soldier under Johnson's command. And the
nascent Indian Department was Billy's private fiefdom.
But the eccentric placement of a New Yorker in command of a New England legion might have been calculated to breed jealousy and friction. To many of the men
who would march under his orders, Billy was suspect not
merely as a New Yorker, but as an "Indian lover" and a
"squaw man" whose morals did not bear close examination.

New England volunteers could not be drilled to obey,
like regulars who had taken the King's shilling. Few of
them were impressed by rank or lace ruffles. Some of
their officers—like Seth Pomeroy, the blacksmith who
had been commissioned lieutenant-colonel in Williams'
regiment—had served in the siege of Louisbourg, and
were proudly aware that the greatest victory of the
English colonies in the wars with the French had been
the work of New England provincials.

Billy Johnson would have to earn the allegiance of this
army.

His problems began with his second-in-command,
Phineas Lyman. Major-General Lyman was a political

soldier, with a lawyer's gift for putting a case. A former tutor at Yale college, Lyman was convinced of his intellectual superiority to most men he encountered and held that the command of the Crown Point expedition should have been entrusted to him, not a high-living Irishman from the Mohawk Valley who dressed like an Indian. Lyman's interests coincided with his prejudices. He was a prime mover in the Connecticut land company that was behind the Wyoming land fraud executed by Lydius at the Albany congress the previous summer. Billy was uncomfortably aware that the man who stood a bullet—or a juicy scandal—away from replacing him had everything to gain by removing the prime opponent of this grab for Indian land.

Phineas Lyman would be watching for every slip of his amateur general, while he circulated choice gossip about the whores and native women among the Yorkers' camp followers and the goings on around Johnson's punch bowl.

Lyman was not the only man who would be watching and questioning. This was not an army that would follow orders without debate.

The field officers demanded that the campaign be managed by committee; every command decision must be put to all of them, in what was politely dubbed a council of war.

The New England officers, in turn, were held accountable by their men and often served at their pleasure. Plowboys, schoolteachers and ship's chandlers insisted on deliberating grand strategy. They knew what they wanted: to strike north, hard and fast, against the French and the Indian scalpers who had ravaged their borders, and get home to their families by harvest time.

Though Johnson's intimacy with the Six Nations made him suspect to the Indian-haters in the ranks, his experience of Indian warfare had developed some of the skills required to handle this fractious, undisciplined army. He knew how to bribe and cajole, how to divide opponents, how to play to emotions.

He sent John Ogilvie, the genial Anglican minister

from Fort Hunter, to Albany ahead of his party to appeal to the religious fervor of the New Englanders. The tolerant Rev. Ogilvie delivered a thunderous well-received sermon on how divine providence favored the Protestant cause.

When Billy rode through the stockade the next day, to set up his temporary headquarters at the handsome townhouse he had purchased from Henry Holland, he proceeded to invite his New England field officers to his dinner table in ones and twos, sounding out their characters, plying them with the finest wines, courting them with hints of favor. Ephraim Williams and Seth Pomeroy, at least, were charmed.

But they had long lists of grievances that demanded more than General Johnson's charm.

The Massachusetts men had reached Albany ahead of their stores. They had neither food nor medicine. Many of them had been issued only knapsacks and blankets before marching overland from Westfield and lacked guns and powder.

While waiting for supply ships from Boston, Colonel Williams and his colleagues had turned to local merchants for essentials. Livingston Huyck had sold them barrels of salt pork that proved to be submerged in a thick layer of yellow scum and—when edible at all—was as salty as brine.

"Firelocks and powder are nowhere to be found," Ephraim Williams went on, slicing into a wheel of Dutch cheese at Johnson's table. "Our men have been drilling with sticks and clubs. The bateaux we were promised are not ready. The gun carriages are rotted through and collapse like punkwood under the weight of brass. To top it all, there are no tents for my men. We were obliged to requisition barns and hutches up and down the town, which is an affront to the morals and safety of all. The burghers hate us for camping in their midst and our men fall into low manners. There are many that have the crabs or the blasted French disease. And a third of my regiment is in the grips of the bloody flux."

"It is more than a gentleman can bear," Johnson said with sympathy, breaking the chronicle of woes. He had some affection for Colonel Williams, a man unlike himself in so many ways. Lean, fastidious, principled, his thin fingers steepling without reflection into the angle of prayer.

A man passed over by Governor Shirley for the commission he was promised in a Royal regiment, with a regular's pay and perquisites.

A man who had lost a fort in the last war, through no fault of his own, and would snap at a chance of military honors now.

An elderly bachelor spurned in love, in his Indian summer, by a farm girl who preferred the advances of a surgeon's mate in his own regiment. This scrap of intelligence was the gift of Wraxall, who had a Fleet Street hack's instinct for a story, and plied New England officers with drink at Hogan's or the King's Arms to useful effect.

A man who fancies himself a patrician, better than the plow jockeys under his command, and immune from their gross prejudices against the natives and their betters.

A man, all in all, whom Billy Johnson could get along with.

He said to Williams, "I know a man called Livingston Huyck. I also know where he stores the powder and lead he trades to French Indians under the counter, war or no war. I think we must do this Van Frog a favor to consort with the favor he has done you."

□

Billy sent Jelles Fonda, from his own staff, with a company from Colonel Williams' regiment to Huyck's warehouse above the river.

Their passage was resisted by an overseer called Bratt, who was promptly conscripted as a boatman and laborer for the expedition.

The raid—legalized by the issuance of promissory notes payable by the General Council of Massachusetts—netted several hundred pounds of lead and blackpowder and thirty muskets, which were given to the Massachusetts troops.

Billy's reputation among the New Englanders began to improve.

But the episode did not warm his cooling relations with Governor Shirley, who arrived within the week to assume command of his own expedition to the west.

They reviewed Johnson's army together, at the encampment Captain Eyre had laid out near Schuyler's fortified house outside the stockade. The appearance of the volunteers in homespun and coonskin caps, many of them wilting from dysentery and the fierce summer heat, would have made a British drill sergeant swoon.

"This is not an army," Captain Eyre cursed under his breath. "This is a rabble."

"They have a reason to fight," Johnson reminded him. "That may make up for their manners."

Shirley and Johnson reserved their dueling for a private dinner, with only Lyman and Eyre in attendance.

"You sit where you do," Governor Shirley informed Johnson, "because of your claimed influence with the Indians. Where is the Indian army I was promised?"

"They will be present when they are needed. They are waiting for us to move, and we are damned slow about doing it."

"I wonder if we can trust their promises to you."

"They ask how they can trust our promises to them. Especially when they see our leadership divided, and men sent to woo them who are no friends of the Six Nations."

"Your meaning escapes me."

"I refer to John Henry Lydius."

"Lydius proved his value in the last war. I must have my own Indian agent since you flout my instructions and deny me the forces I require."

"General Braddock named me sole manager of our Indian affairs. Lydius is working in the Valley as we speak to undermine my friendship with the Six Nations. Even if your case were just, you have chosen a poor instrument. Lydius has deeds to Indian lands in his pocket that are an outrage to the Six Nations and have earned him the bitter enmity of our nearest friends."

"I cannot think how you have become so estranged from Lydius, a man who was once your friend."

"I have learned to know him better."

"Or perhaps it is your own ambition that moves, General Johnson." Across the table, Phineas Lyman smirked. Captain Eyre affected to be giving the port decanter his entire attention.

"Know this well, General Johnson. You march at the head of New England men, who will hearken to me if there is any breach between us. General Braddock is our mutual chief, so long as he has the confidence of the King. But Braddock is far away, and we sit here in Albany. I am his second, and one of your commissions comes from me. You serve at my whim, and if it pleases me, I will break you. *Is that quite understood?*"

"Perfectly."

"I will recruit what Indians I choose, for what purposes I nominate. I have ordered Lydius to form them into little regiments of a hundred men. Centuries, if you will. We must have order amongst our auxiliaries."

"Regiments?" Billy echoed. "You expect Mohawks to fight in *regiments?* That is—remarkable!" He laughed so hard his chair shook.

"I am glad you find the theme so amusing."

"Forgive me, Your Excellency. I wish you all the success you deserve."

□

With men in the Valley—Daniel Claus, Matt Ferrall, Benjamin Stoddert—to guard his rear, counter Lydius and bring the Indians in strength to meet him on the road to Crown Point, Johnson applied himself to getting his expedition on the move. In that season of blackflies and rumors, a longer stay in the town or the camp would be fatal to the health, both mental and physical, of his army.

To remove a prime focus of disaffection, Billy sent Phineas Lyman ahead to hew a wagon-road, thirty feet wide, to Saratoga and ferry supplies across the river to Lydius' fortified trading post at the Carry. Lyman's volunteers bristled at being used as construction laborers. Men deserted by the dozen, marching off with clubbed firelocks, sometimes assisted by Albany wagoners who seized the chance to go home.

While he played his own quartermaster-general, drumming up supplies, checking that bateaux were properly tarred and caulked, supervising the carpenters who were building new carriages for the big 32-pound fieldguns he planned to turn on Fort St. Frédéric, Johnson waited anxiously for news from two quarters. For word of General Braddock's fortunes in the Ohio country. And for a report from the Mohawk envoys the clanmothers had sent in secret—at his urging—to talk to their kinfolk at the Caughnawaga mission and to seek to turn them from the French cause.

A rumor in the encampment had Braddock winning a great victory. If true, this could bring many Indian tribes, besides the Six Nations, to the British side. But no one was sure where the rumor had originated. And Billy was not ready to celebrate, because Mohawks had told him that Braddock's officers had insulted their native guides and that his soldiers had abused their women. Johnson knew that a white army was blind and deaf in the forest without Indian scouts.

Snowbird came to Johnson's townhouse with a report from the blackrobe mission that was far from what Billy wanted to hear. Snowbird had spoken with Red Squirrel, and with other Caughnawaga chiefs. "They say they are bound to the French because the blackrobe fathers have sprinkled their heads with holy water. They say they wish us no harm, but must go where their father, the Sun King, directs."

They are upping their price, Billy thought. *There must be a way around this. We will try again. Hendrick Forked Paths will think of a way. It will help if Braddock rattles the Frenchmen's cages to effect.*

Then Matt Ferrall arrived at the house on Market Street, dusty and exhausted from a ride that had worn out two horses, with a courier whose bones showed through his skin.

2.

"It's not true." Billy balled his fist and brought it down on the cherrywood table, so hard the wood cracked and his papers went flying around the room. *"Not—true!"*

Matt Ferrall did not dare look at him. Billy *never* lost his composure before strangers. He boiled inside, like other men. But he had learned to forge his heat into a tool, not an empty blast. He had lost the gift tonight.

"You were there at the end. You saw it with your own eyes," Johnson glared at the messenger, willing him to confess he was the victim of Indian rumors or French lies.

"Hand to God, sir. I saw the General shot off three horses, before the savages potted him."

"Braddock had the heart for a fight, if not the head," Wraxall remarked, as if they were discussing a performance on the London stage.

Billy took a long swallow of canary wine. "Tell me again. Tell me how we managed to lose a whole army."

It was worse than he had been able to imagine. Braddock's regulars, sweating in high summer under their thick broadcloth, powdered wigs and overstuffed packs, struggling through thick forest along the Monongahela, toward the French at Fort Duquesne. A British army advancing without eyes, because the enlisted men's abuse of the Indians and their women and the officers' contempt for them had driven two sets of native scouts away. Braddock had walked straight into a French ambush. To compound the humiliation, it seemed the French all but bumped up against him, with a much inferior force and little time to prepare their positions. What won out was the Indian method of fighting—each man his own fighting force, using every scrap of cover, moving in for the kill when the enemy had fired his musket and was stolidly following his sergeant's barked orders to reload.

Johnson could *see* Braddock, desperately trying to form up his men into tight parade-ground squares, with an enemy behind every tree, beating deserters back with the flat of his sword. That hulking young Virginian, George Washington, was somewhere there in the van, one of the few who got away unscathed. *Beginners' luck—or murderers',* Johnson thought grimly, since it was Washington who had fired the first shots in this war the previous year, gunning down a French reconnaissance party without warning.

"Braddock tried to hold them, sir," the messenger reported. "But the poor devils in the front didn't even have a chance to reload. The savages was on our throats. After Braddock went down, we ran like hares. I ain't ashamed to say it. The officers ran fastest, though Washington behaved like a gentleman. We left our guns and our powder and the stores for the whole campaign. Not to mention our wounded. I don't like to think of it, General Johnson. Them poor bloodybacks on the death-walk." He started shaking again, hearing the scalp-yells.

Billy gave him a whole bottle of rum and told him that would do for the evening. "Mister Wraxall will arrange your quarters." *But not your reception in the town.* Albany was already seething with resentment over the enforced billeting of soldiers and the impressment of wagon drivers, boatmen and laborers for two military expeditions. Word of Braddock's rout would have ugly consequences. On reflection, Johnson called Wraxall back.

"Tell the landlord at the King's Inn he must find room for another body."

The inn was temporary home to the Butlers and Valley men Johnson believed he could trust. Though some would be brooding over their undefended homes when they heard about Braddock.

"A third of our army lost, a third wounded or taken."

"And a third running away like rabbits," Matt Ferrall completed the thought. "And no enemy casualties worth toasting."

"All in the sight of the Indians!" Billy paced the room, pausing to look out over the walled courtyard. If he leaned out, he could see the downspout from Lydius' townhouse, running out into the middle of the street.

"In God's name, how am I expected to keep the confidence of the Six Nations? What can inspire them to honor their pledges after this?"

"If any man can do it, Billy, it is you," said Ferrall. "If not—" he let the words hang in the air. "There's still the old sod," he slipped into brogue.

"Never," Billy said fiercely. "This is my home. I will not leave it."

But Matthew's unspoken thought lay on his shoulders. The British had lost the flower of their army in North America in a few hours of butchery in the woods. A rational man might conclude that the French, with the benefit of better generals, seasoned veterans and a unified command—as well as greater allies among the Indians—would win the present war, despite the disparity in numbers between the civil populations in the French and English colonies. Why should the chiefs of the Confederacy honor pledges to the losing side? Many solemn things had been said and danced around the fire at Fort Johnson. But Braddock's downfall altered everything. Nine-tenths of the Woodland Indians, by a rough calculation, were already on the French side. If the Six Nations turned, Billy would have no home to go back to in the Valley. Even the smug, double-dealing *handlaers* of Albany might soon be obliged to learn French to communicate with their new masters.

There is another blade that threatens me where I live, Billy realized. With Braddock dead, Governor Shirley was commander-in-chief—until (and unless) the Duke of Cumberland shipped out another gold-laced general from an elegant regiment to replace him. Would Shirley resist the temptation to exact revenge for the insults he felt had been done to him and his agent Lydius? At the very least, it would now be exceedingly difficult for Johnson to get reimbursement for a single shilling of his Indian expenses. At the best, Billy faced financial ruin and the calumny of a rival who was now dangerously powerful. At worst, he faced the fate he had hoped to put behind him for good—of becoming another homeless, wandering Irishman, living on his wits.

He would have to sound out the Indians, one by one, lean on old loyalties, offer new inducements.

If they fight now, it will not be for England. It will be for me. Once more, I am the frontier.

3.

Baron Jean-Armand de Dieskau, the new commander-in-chief of the French forces in North America, had never seen anything like the lake beaches below the stronghold at Crown Point.

The sand, in the early light, varied in color from gunpowder blacks and steel grays to pure white or a ruddy, russet shade that flashed with garnet lights. This was the effect, Commandant Landrieve told him, of numberless petrified shells, ground into sand over the millennia, below the black limestone hill on which The Octagon stood.

The walls of Fort St. Frédéric were of black limestone too, bomb-proofed, as thick as a man. Forty guns were mounted in the octagonal keep that rose four storys high. There were more cannon in the stone windmill east of the fort, a lookout that prevented smugglers or at-tackers from slipping down the lake undetected, hugging the shore.

Baron Dieskau inspected everything—the cows the officers of the garrison were permitted to keep in private pastures, the soldiers' kitchen gardens, the young bear, orphaned in spring, that sported with the dogs and perhaps imagined itself one of them. There was a sweet-smelling wildflower that reminded the Baron of a certain lady's chamber at Versailles. Commandant Landrieve called it *cotonnier,* and showed him how the soldiers rolled its petals to make sugar.

Commanding the narrows of Lake Champlain, The Octagon stood athwart the greatest warpath of North America. Indian scalp-hunters and ranger companies, lightly equipped, might avoid it, threading their way through virgin forests. But any regular army of invasion moving overland between Montreal and the populated areas of New York had to contend with Fort St. Frédéric.

There were heights within cannon range. If an active enemy hauled field guns up there, he could fire down into the fort. But he would have to cut a wagon-road through primeval forest—vulnerable to a hundred ambushes—or fight a battle out on the lake, which was commanded by a French flotilla. And The Octagon could be rapidly reinforced and resupplied from St. John's, the wooden fort at the mouth of Lake Champlain.

Baron Dieskau had read Braddock's war plans, harvested from his body in the bloody field along the Monongahela. He knew from these that Fort St. Frédéric was a prime target of the enemy in this conflict. But he was confident that the fortress at Crown Point was safe for now. As a cavalryman, he favored fast, forward maneuvers. His mind was now bent on taking the war deep into enemy territory.

The Baron accepted Landrieve's invitation to breakfast in his quarters, where the light was broken into slats of color—like the patterns in the sand—by narrow panels of stained glass.

The Baron wanted Landrieve's views, as a seasoned Indian agent, of the reliability of his native auxiliaries, who marched in the company of both priests and sorcerers, as well as women and children.

Baron Dieskau wished to know, in particular, the mind and habits of Major-General William Johnson.

A general's first duty, Dieskau believed, is to know his adversary.

□

Johann Dieskau—Jean-Armand to his French employers—was a soldier's soldier, a Saxon recruited by his compatriot, the great Marshal Saxe, to fight in the armies of France. He had unsheathed his saber, as a colonel of cavalry, in the battle of Fontenoy in the last war. He had risen to the dignity of military governor of Brest, the chief French naval base on the Atlantic, before a reckless young Virginian fired the first shots of the new war between the world empires.

Dieskau had been in the New World for all of two months. He had arrived at Quebec in June, on the *Entreprenant,* at the head of the battalions of French regulars that had been sent to reinforce Canada. He chafed under the terms of his new command. He was required to take military orders from a mere civilian— Rigaud de Vaudreuil, the Governor-General—who fancied himself a strategist.

Thanks to Braddock's folly, Baron Dieskau knew his enemy's military plans. When General Braddock had lost his army and his head in the slaughter along the Monongahela, the French had seized the oilskin pouches containing the British plan of campaign. Dieskau and Governor Vaudreuil had pored over them, quarreling over the meaning of English words and above all, over the appropriate French response. Braddock's papers showed that the British were planning two new offensives. On the western front, an army headed by Governor Shirley of Massachusetts was going after the key French posts at Niagara and Fort Frontenac, on Lake Ontario. On the eastern front, a new expedition was being launched against The Octagon.

Governor Vaudreuil had insisted that the threat to Niagara and Fort Frontenac was the most urgent danger. He had boosted the idea of a counter-strike against Oswego, where the English had a small fort and a large trading post. Dieskau had caught a ripe whiff of the corruption he found everywhere in the government halls of New France. He suspected that the Governor-General was being prompted by merchant intriguers like plump, shifty Adhémar, who smelled the chance to grow fatter on contracts to provision the army—and to grab more of the lucrative trade with the western Indians. But Vaudreuil was the Governor-General of New France, and Dieskau was a hired sword, a foreigner whose accent was mocked even by unlettered *Canadiens*. Dieskau had received formal orders to assemble four thousand men at Fort Frontenac and lead them against Oswego.

Dieskau never got to Oswego. The nerves of Governor Vaudreuil and his merchant friends were jarred by intelligence that William Johnson—who had been written off as a pretend-soldier more familiar with the female anatomy than the workings of a flintlock—was advancing north with unexpected speed and resolution. The Governor's despatches suggested to the Baron that his master had succumbed to a *pavor nocturnus,* a fit of the night willies. The Governor imagined all the French posts and settlements between Crown Point and Montreal laid waste by a vengeful army of Mohawks and New Englanders, the *belles dames* of the city ravished in their beds.

The Baron's orders were countermanded. He was to return posthaste to Montreal and march to the relief of Crown Point with all the men at his disposal.

The force he had led up the Richelieu River, to Fort St. John, on a gnat-infested swamp, and up Lake Champlain to The Octagon, was smaller than the army he had been assigned for the capture of Oswego. He commanded fifteen hundred regulars, a thousand provincial militia, and some six hundred Indians, of varying constancy and fortitude. Johnson's column was reportedly larger. But Baron Dieskau did not judge by numbers. Johnson's force was mostly composed of militiamen, who would be fighting away from their home ground, and the Baron had the sovereign contempt of a professional soldier for amateurs on either side. "One savage," he confided to his officers at table, "will put ten provincials—ours or theirs—to flight."

□

Baron Dieskau cracked a gull's egg and ate it in neat, rapid bites. The table would have served for a regimental mess, with fatty slabs of bacon, steaming porridge, blood sausage and generous beefsteaks, fried with onions, and a platter of gleaming brook trout. The Baron's host consumed only bread and milk, like the poorest of peasants.

"You are a mystery to me, Commandant," Dieskau addressed him, making a leisurely inspection of Landriève's high, deep-furrowed forehead, the long, bony jaw, the hooded eyes that gave away nothing. "You speak like a philosopher, a man who would be equally at home at Versailles or in the circle of Monsieur Voltaire. Yet you choose to live here, among fir woods and savages."

"I am content. My wants are few."

"Ah. But can they be satisfied?"

The eyes still gave nothing. The Baron had heard rumors of a personal tragedy, a whole family—wife and children—lost to the Agniers, the Mohawk. Landrieve must have an Indian woman, or a *métive*. Some of them were quite fetching. The Baron had seen them at Montreal, bedecked in lace and hoop skirts, their hair piled up in the latest mode.

Every man has a ruling passion. The Baron was convinced of it. Among the male population of New France, by his observation, there were three ruling passions. The pursuit of glory, which involved the right to put *de,* the signifier of nobility, in front of one's name. Cupidity, aiming at showy consumption, not Calvinist thrift. And living wild as the savages.

But Commandant Landrieve was not easily placed.

"What is it you want?" Dieskau goaded him.

Landrieve's eyes widened a fraction. "There is a Mohawk. We call him Tête Blanche. The English call him Hendrick."

"I have heard of him. A redoubtable old warrior, I am told."

"He destroyed my family. Under a flag of truce. I want his head."

"You jest with me, Commandant."

"I want his head," Landrieve repeated. "Or to see him die."

The Baron felt the man's heat and made room for it. He rattled among the serving platters, replenishing his plate, before resuming the conversation.

"This Tête Blanche—Hendrick—marches with Johnson."

"He *made* Johnson," Landrieve spat.

"That is a large statement."

"It is no less than the truth."

"But Hendrick is an old man, surely."

"He is the pivot of British influence among the Indians. Kill him—inflict a bitter humiliation on the warriors who march with him—and we can control the tide of events throughout this wilderness."

"Are you not over-valuing the importance of a few Mohawks?"

"Baron, you are new to this country. I respect you as a soldier, but you can hardly have had time to learn the ways of the forest. Forgive me if I speak too freely."

"You need ask forgiveness only if you do not."

"There is a law as old as history. The strong hold the passes. The Mohawk are a small people, puny in numbers, wasted by diseases we brought, and the traders' liquor, and the endless wars. And even the incursions of our priests. Half the Mohawk nation is now living at our Jesuit missions."

"Yes. That is something I would like to know more about. Our priests use some clever devices. Cleverer, I believe, than are known at Rome or at Paris. One of the chiefs who accompanies my army told me he was taught that Jesus Christ is the eldest son of the King of France. He has also been assured that, if he falls in battle, the priests will intervene to ensure that he goes to a happy hereafter. Either our heaven or the happy hunting-grounds of his ancestors. The choice, it seems, will be up to him."

Landrième's mouth made a diagonal line. It was scarcely a smile. He said, "We use one demon to cast out another. In a manner of speaking. We must teach the fool according to his folly. Is that not our Lord's counsel?"

"I am no theologian." The Baron felt somewhat uncomfortable. "I suppose General Johnson is no more a seminarist than I am. Tell me about him."

"Johnson has never heard a shot fired in anger. Come to close quarters with him and he will run like a rabbit. He has an army of New Englanders who despise him.

They think he is half-papist and a squaw man. They will not fight for him."

"I hope you are right. Yet this Johnson has an unusual influence among the Indians, I am told."

"Bribes and cozening. And theatricals. Johnson is an Irishman. They make a drama out of taking a piss. Kill enough of them, and the Indians will desert him. They will leave him to twist in the wind. You must understand, Baron. The Mohawks are a tiny people. They cannot replace their dead, even though they pretend to do so with scalps and captives. Kill twenty of them— fifty—and it will have the effect of slaughtering a thousand Canadians or five thousand English."

"You are a relentless man, Commandant." Baron Dieskau was slightly shocked. "Are you sure it is not your personal loss, rather than strategy, that is speaking?"

"I have forged pain into a weapon. It is something that does not bend, a thing you can count on. I ask only to march with you, Baron."

"You are needed here."

"I am needed wherever you find battle. You have expressed your reservations about your Indian forces. I can tell you now that there are Indians in your camp who would rather fight Frenchmen than Mohawks. You need a man who can tell you who to trust."

"I have Legardeur de St. Pierre."

"A good man. A seasoned Indian fighter. But he does not know the Caughnawagas. He does not know their minds or their tongue. You are dealing with rattlesnakes, Baron. The rattlesnake requires special handling."

Dieskau succumbed to the logic of Landrième's argument. Choosing lieutenants for battle was not, after all, like choosing guests for a dinner party. He felt a deepening distaste for this lost soldier of New France, eaten by old hatreds. Yet he could use him. He told Landrième, "I will be honored to have you under my command."

4.

Hauling and hacking, dragging and digging, Johnson's army moved north toward its rendezvous with the French. Up the Hudson to Saratoga, then the cruel portage over and around the falls—where men were crushed under the weight of cannon tearing loose from their moorings—to the blockhouse Lydius had rebuilt at the Carrying Place, after the French burned it in the previous war. Fort Lydius commanded the three paths leading to Crown Point and the empire of New France. One trail ran north, to the narrow, shining lake the French called Lac St. Sacrément. Others ran north-east through sucking marshes to Wood Creek and South Bay, two openings to Lake Champlain.

With fine diplomacy, General Johnson informed his second-in-command that he had decided to rename Lydius' blockhouse Fort Lyman, in his honor, and ordered the Connecticut general to set his men to work pulling apart the trading post and converting it to military specifications.

Lyman, moving ahead of the main force, had already cut eight miles of a road toward Wood Creek. But Billy listened to the warnings of Snowbird and other Mohawk scouts he sent to test the ground: that white men wallowing in the swamps of the drowned lands around the south end of Lake Champlain, or in the horizontal forest of Wood Creek, where dead timber lay across the water, would be easy game for enemy snipers. "Dead meat," Snowbird said, holding his nose. Johnson argued his point with such force in the endless councils of war that Lyman's axemen were diverted to make a road due north, to the narrow body of water the Flint People called simply Kanya:tarokte, The Place Where the Lakes End.

Lyman got his revenge by circuitous means.

□

"Squaw man!"

Billy turned on his heel and walked back through the ranks of Connecticut militiaman. Some of the men were sniggering, but they avoided his eyes. Except the gangling fellow in a foxskin cap, whose lantern jaw was greatly in need of a shave. The militiaman's powder and priming horns, slung from his shoulders on leather thongs, were elaborately carved. So was the stock of the long firelock he handled with confidence. His bold, pale-eyed stare was already an insult.

Billy inspected the musket barrel. "I take it you can use this thing."

"It ain't no thing. I call her Injun Funeral. Ain't a bush nigger who'll get away from me at two hundred paces."

"I hope you can distinguish between our allies and our enemies."

"All bush niggers look the same to me."

"If you learn nothing else in this army," Johnson said quietly, "you will learn that the Indians are men like others and better than many. What is your name?"

"Ezra Stiles."

"Your company?"

"Captain Hall's."

"Captain Hall!"

Hall rolled his heavy gut through the lines, his slowness indicating his degree of respect for his commander-in-chief. Hall was fat and pursy, and stank of rum though it was not yet ten in the morning.

Johnson contemplated him with distaste. "Your men seem to have some difficulty distinguishing friend from foe, Captain Hall. Please repeat my instructions for identifying our scouts."

Hall cleared his throat. "Friendly Indians will wear a red headband."

"What else?"

"The fancy ones will wear a red ribbon in their hats."

Johnson let this new insolence pass.

"And if challenged?"

"They are to call out your Indian name."

"Which is?"

"Warra—" Hall stumbled. "I can't get the hang of it."

"Warragiyaguey!" Johnson bellowed. "Try to remember it."

His glance returned to Ezra Stiles, who was smirking. There was something dangling from his wide leather belt, next to the sheath knife.

"What's that you are wearing, Stiles? A charm?" There was hardly a volunteer in the army who did not carry his personal talisman, a rabbit's foot, a bear's claw, a woman's favor.

Stiles held the thing up, and his grin widened. Johnson saw now it was a scalp, poorly cut, garnished with only a few strands of black hair.

"Injun hair." Stiles patted his firelock. "I told you old Injun Funeral is a sureshot."

"Remove it," Johnson said coldly.

Stiles made no move.

Johnson's sword flashed from the scabbard. With a swing of the tip, he cut the offensive trophy away.

"Pick it up. Now burn it."

Stiles hesitated, then shrugged and walked to the nearest fire. "Injun Funeral will get me another one," he winked at his cronies.

I have been too lax with them, Johnson told himself. *Now they mock me to my face. A British general would have this ruffian stroked with the cat until his back was raw. But I prefer my own way.*

"Squaw man!" another voice bawled as he walked on.

"Captain Hall."

Hall's jowls quivered. He was making little attempt to camouflage his delight with his commander's embarrassment.

"You will identify the man who just spoke and submit his case for court-martial. Pending discovery and suitable punishment, the rum ration for your company is suspended."

"Begging pardon, General. I answer to General Lyman."

"We will see about that."

□

Phineas Lyman argued, in a council of war, that the
sentiments of his men must be respected. They had been
worked without respite, hacking roads through the
woods, plagued by deerflies and gnats, instead of killing
Frenchmen and Indian scalpers, which was what they
had signed up for. Captain Hall was a good man, Lyman
said, with the confidence of his company. And if the
Indians Johnson defended so hotly were worth his
trouble, where were the promised war-parties? Only a
handful of scouts had come with Johnson.

The mood of the committee swung so strongly toward
Lyman that Billy resolved to bide his time.

□

More Indians came in before Billy led the march up the
new road to the lake he had resolved to rename Lake
George, to get rid of the French appellation and please a
King he had never met. Hendrick had met King George,
on his second visit to England, and occasionally sported
the laced hat and sky-blue coat he had received at court.
But Hendrick, and the hundreds of warriors Johnson
had been promised, were still missing.

"Forked Paths will come," Snowbird assured Billy.
"He wants this fight. He knows it will be his last."

Among the stumps of pitch-pines cleared at the south
end of Lake George, Captain Eyre helped Billy to mark
the perimeters of a new camp that might one day be a
fort. It was a good defensive position, protected against
land attack on three sides, by the lake, a swamp to the
west, and rising ground to the east where Eyre put some
of the twelve-pounders. The volunteers chafed at the
notion of building earthen ramparts and blockhouses
after all the navvy work they had been driven to undertake. So Johnson contented himself, for now, with
placing some of the felled trees in a rough breastwork,
little better than a fence, although the news from the
scouts was ominous. It seemed a French army had
reached Crown Point; it was said to be several times

larger than Billy's force, although the details changed in every telling.

Snowbird and the small band of Mohawks that had come with him burned a flat, plate-shaped fungus to keep off gnats and mosquitoes. The pungent smoke fouled the clean night air.

Johnson pitched his tent at a salutary remove from Phineas Lyman.

He sat up after midnight, contemplating the reflections in the lake and the unfinished fleet of bateaux, row galleys and war-canoes with which he hoped to drive the French from their hornets' nest at Crown Point.

His staff officers and servants were asleep. Snowbird dozed outside the flap of the commander's tent.

"The Mohawk seems to have made himself your bodyguard," Denis Rahilly observed. Rahilly was Billy's only company at this hour, and he busied himself plying the bottle between their glasses. As Rahilly grew older, Billy had noticed, he could not finish with a bottle until it had finished with him.

"Do I need a bodyguard?" Johnson asked Rahilly and the night.

"If Phineas Lyman had his wish, sure you would need one. That is a high old name, Phineas. Do you know what it means?"

"It is from the Bible. The saints of New England are great ones for the Book, Denis. Phineas, I recall, was a man rebuked by Moses for failing to slaughter the women and children of the Canaanites."

"And a brave name for a man of war, to be certain. But there is another Phineas. Do you recall the tale of Jason and the Argonauts, Billy?"

"You are full of surprises."

"Now this is an education, General Johnson. This Phineas was plagued by harpies that swooped down to take the food left for him and left a foul stink behind."

"Are you proposing a similar fate for our Phineas?"

"Ah, that is high policy and I am only court jester. Another bottle, Billy?"

Rahilly sounded steady enough—to the extent he was

ever that—but looked unwell. His face was bloated and waxy, like a beached fish.

"I have had enough," Johnson said. "Perhaps you have had your fill too. It is a gift to know when enough is enough."

"Better to drink the stuff ourselves than sell it to the Indians out of the stores, like those pissers in Lyman's regiment."

Johnson was instantly alert. "Have you heard something solid? Or is that another tale of the Golden Fleece?"

"Hall is the man to watch. You should check his stores."

"I will have it done."

☐

Johnson bade Rahilly good night, hoping that his eagerness to probe the actions of the Connecticut officer who had sniggered when his commander was mocked as a squaw man was more than a low appetite for revenge.

He was in no mood for sleep. The Mohawk scouts had brought in a Canadian, babbling in fear of being put through the gauntlet, who claimed that a French general had come down the lake to Fort St. Frédéric, with legions of Abenakis and Caughnawagas in his train.

If this is true, we will be tested as never before. Maybe this challenge will heal our divisions. But I must have eyes inside the French camp. The fog hangs thick between us.

He stuffed a plug of Virginia tobacco into the mouth of the pipe the Mohawks had given him after he was raised up as the Firekeeper of the Six Nations, when they dressed him in the Living Bones of a traditional chief. The bowl, carved from redstone, was embellished with figures of the bear, the turtle and the wolf, the three totem animals of the Flint People.

He felt the same cold fear that had set his hand trembling when the first express came in with the news of Braddock's disaster. He had exchanged many promises with the Six Nations that summer, when they raised him up as their Firekeeper. But would the Indians honor their engagements now? Marching to defeat was no part

of their warriors' conception of military honor. And by
now, every man, woman and child of the Six Nations,
from the Hudson to the Cuyahoga, must have heard the
details of the slaughter of a British army in the Ohio
country, made bloodier by each retelling. Would even
Hendrick stand with him now? Hendrick was a friend,
but he was no fool. He had seen what had followed, in
previous wars—in wars before Billy was even born—
when the British sent woodentops with friends at Court
to command their armies in North America.

It was hard to keep Mohawks away from a fight,
Johnson reassured himself. But fear of the French and
contempt for British military leadership were not the
only tests of Mohawk loyalty. Spies and ambassadors
flitted back and forth between the Mohawk villages and
the Jesuit missions around Montreal. The French agents
were tireless in spreading alarming rumors about how
the English planned to exterminate the Six Nations, or
pen them like cattle, in order to seize all their lands once
the war was done. Unfortunately, a kernel of truth lay in
these rumors—or so any Indian might believe if he
overheard the loose talk at the New Englanders' camp-
fires. Or, especially, at General Lyman's table.

The most serious challenge came from a man Billy
had once regarded as a friend, even a mentor. How green
he had been in those days! Now Hard Egg Lydius had
revealed himself as the snake he must have been all
along.

*It is not easy to know the heart of another human
being,* Billy reflected. Perhaps Lydius enjoyed betrayal
for its own sake. There were those who whispered that
the man was secretly in league with the French, that his
half-French wife, Genevieve, was guiding him in a plot
to turn the Indians against the English colonies. There
was no doubt the man thrived on conspiracy. But what
possessed him, Johnson thought, was raw greed and
envy. Lydius had land deeds he hoped to cash. And he
remembered Billy as a greenhorn, fifteen years his ju-
nior, who had not known the value of a beaver pelt and
let himself be swindled by Albany men and Indians
alike. Hard Egg could not forgive the fact that the

younger man, the tyro, had eclipsed his own influence among the natives.

Johnson rubbed his eyes. They were often sore and dry, the effect of woodsmoke, especially in the native lodges in the shut-up season of midwinter—he believed—more than sleeplessness or diet. In the morning, he would ask one of the Mohawk women for the decoction from the root of the purple coneflower that made a more soothing wash than anything he had found in white men's pharmacies.

Tree frogs shrilled. Then he caught the quaver of a wooden flute, beautiful and melancholy. Among the provincials, or the Albany wagoners, there was a real musician, which no music lover would guess from the performance of fifers and drummers at militia drills.

The clicking of beads, a breath of sweetgrass, very near to him. A native woman dropped to the ground beside him, her arms dangling between her knees, like the wolf's. Billy knew her from the huge, gleaming eyes, the remembered satin of her skin.

She waited for him to speak or move without speaking.

He was tempted. He had gone without female company for three whole days, which always brought on headaches and a surly temper. This was a noisy one. Her baying would make a fine riposte to Phineas Lyman and those that called him a squaw man.

He jerked his chin toward the tent-flap. The woman scrambled in ahead of him, giving him a pleasing view of her firm rump, bounding without restraint under the deerskin kilt.

He was scrolling his breeches down his thighs when he was diverted by a squall outside the tent.

He rushed back out, and found Jamie Rogers—his most faithful servant, left behind to watch over his family at Fort Johnson—struggling in Snowbird's iron grip.

"He's a friend," Johnson barked at the Mohawk.

When Snowbird released Rogers, Billy saw he had an ugly welt under his right eye, and was nursing his shoulder.

"Good Lord, Snowbird has hurt you badly."

"Not him, sir. It happened at home."

"Come inside my tent."

When Johnson had gotten his man wrapped in a warm blanket, with a glass in his hand, he said grimly, "Tell me all of it."

"They pressed me for a boatman. Took me from the Upper Castle, while the gentry was talking to the sachems, plying them with liquor and promises of gold."

"Who took you?"

"Fat Harmanus was one. I don't know the others' names. They said it was Colonel Lydius' orders. I fought them, sir. It was four to one, but I believe I gave them better than I took. One of the buggers must have hit me from behind." His hand moved to the lump above his queue.

"They knew you? You told them you are in my employ?" Johnson was still reluctant to believe the enormity of Lydius' violation.

"I told them. They said you are finished, sir. I am sorry to repeat it. They said Mister Lydius is the second man in this country, after Governor Shirley, and that his word is law."

Johnson's mouth tightened. He spoke very quietly, as he always did when he was at his most dangerous. "How did you escape from them?"

"Mistress Catherine helped me, sir. And old Arent Stevens. You should have seen him. He stripped to the waist and put up his fists when Lydius tried to give him his marching orders. He was dancing around like a cock turkey. Better than a scrapper from home."

"You spoke of Mistress Catherine. What of her?"

"He came to the fort, sir."

"You say Lydius came *to my home?*"

"He spoke to the Indians across your fire. He said Governor Shirley would pay them by the day, good money too. I heard it was ten shillings. But only a few Mohawks came. I guess that made him hot. So he wanted to take from your stores, to supply the expedition to Oswego. But Mister Stevens and Mister Claus came and wouldn't let him do it. Then he said he would take Arent Stevens to be an interpreter for him. That was when Arent got his dander up and offered to fight, in front of the council house. Mistress Catherine used the commotion to speak to me privily. She told me to hide in the barn until Lydius was gone. She came to me at dusk and told me I must hurry to you and tell you the doings."

"What of the Mohawks? What of Daniel and Stevens?"

"Oh sir, I forgot. The pleasure of seeing your honor—" Jamie reached into his shirt and brought out a letter.

Billy recognized Daniel Claus' formal hand. Claus reported that Lydius had bribed some of the Mohawks at the Upper Castle to sign up with Shirley, but that most of them had reneged on their new engagements after sleeping off their hangovers. There had been serious trouble with Nicholas—Sun Walker, the Wolf Clan sachem—who had still not entirely forgiven Johnson for his years in captivity in Canada. Reading between the lines, Billy guessed that Sarah Windweaver, Nicholas' formidable wife, might have been instrumental in his change of heart. The best news was that Daniel expected to arrive with a strong party of the Six Nations within days.

"You have done well, Jamie. You must feed and then rest."

"You'll let me serve with you, sir?"

"You've not forgotten how to mix a rum shrub?"

"No, your honor."

"Then there is no man I would rather have at my side. We have fresh fruit. Tomorrow we shall toast your liberation from Master Lydius."

I shall do more than that, Billy promised himself.

5.

Fires smoldered around the general's tent, on its rocky knoll, and black curls of smoke twisted through the morning haze. The lake behind the camp, which was little more than a rough clearing bristling with tree stumps, shone mirror-bright. Some swore this lake, which Johnson had renamed for the King, had no equal in North America. The soldiers, sapped by the muggy heat, wasted by scurvy and the bloody flux, had no mind to compose sonnets about a lake in a wilderness of miseries.

Now the New England men sweated under a hot sun, swearing under their breath at the Mohawks who strolled in and out of their commanders' tent as if they owned it. Mutiny was in the air that morning. The New Englanders had not joined up to cut trees and dig latrines. They had joined up to kill papists and Indians, and so far the only Indians they had seen were the ones who pilfered their stores and made free with the general's punch bowl. Harvest time was coming on, and farm boys from Deerfield or Lexington wanted to be home with their families.

Not a week before, thirty men from Captain Jones' company had shouldered their packs and started walking home, with their guns clubbed, defying any officer to stop them. Johnson sent Mohawks after them, but all but two got clean away. There were plenty of men in homespun, or in the new blue uniforms with red facings, who had a mind to do the same. Certainly, few New Englanders who would stay for love of a squaw man with the manners of a Tory squire who loved savages better than Dissenters.

A slow drumroll stirred the assembly. With a bayonet at the small of his back, Ezra Stiles was marched through the lines to a pine that had been left standing for just such business.

As the adjutant read the findings of the court-martial—

"Of selling spiritous liquors to His Majesty's Indian allies, contrary to regulations—*Guilty;*

"Of a most heinous attempt at a sodomitical act— *Guilty."* Johnson emerged through the flap of his tent. The sun picked out the gold galloon on his scarlet coat and the bright gorget at his throat, engraved with the King's arms and his own cipher.

Johnson appeared to be engrossed in conversation with his usual coterie—Yorkers and Indians—distancing himself from the grim proceedings the drummers had called his army to witness. Discipline was a tricky business.

Captain Hall, the principal rum-peddler, had been dealt with by his peers and broken to the ranks. The judgment of Connecticut men was a setback for Lyman, Billy's rival.

But not one that will stop his intrigues, Billy thought. *One that will serve only to make him more slippery in his execution of them.*

He had no taste for the business in hand, even though the ruffian who faced the lash had called him a squaw man in front of a whole regiment.

"Sentence!" the adjutant's voice rose higher. "One hundred lashes."

The guards stripped the rum-peddler and attempted sodomite of his shirt and tied him to the tree. The prisoner seemed dazed; perhaps a sympathetic jailer had slipped him a noggin of rum. Two soldiers took turns with the cat, timing their blows to the rhythm of the drum rolls. The knotted cords drew blood with each stroke. After thirty, the prisoner's back was flayed raw. After forty, he drooped unconscious. The guards brought him round with a bucket of salt water that made his wounds sing.

The prisoner was far from popular, a foul-mouthed bully who was not ashamed to make vile suggestions to the youngest boys in his company, even on the sabbath. There were men in his company who believed he had conspired with the commissary to steal food and drink from the soldiers and sell it to the Indians and the Albany Dutch. But the sight of a white man being flogged unconscious in the view of a pack of grinning Mohawks produced ugly muttering in the ranks.

When the prisoner collapsed again, and no quantity of brine would bring him round, Peter Wraxall came trotting down from the hill.

"The General's compliments, sir," he addressed the

adjutant. "General Johnson believes the prisoner has taken all he can bear."

They cut the prisoner down and dragged him away, to be drummed out of the army the next day, with a rope around his neck.

"He's the lucky one," someone observed. "He got his ticket home."

CHAPTER 31
THE WOLF'S THROAT

1.

A cutting wind was gusting out of the north on the last day of August, when Hendrick Forked Paths arrived at Johnson's camp with Daniel Claus and two hundred warriors of the Six Nations.

They were not challenged until they had breached the outer line of sentries and Hendrick broke cover from behind a huge wind-felled tree on a rocky knoll. A jumpy Rhode Island man—seeing the warpaint and feathers, rather than the scarlet headbands that marked these Indians as allies—opened fire in such haste he succeeded in shooting himself in the foot.

Hendrick inspected the camp. Only the placement of Captain Eyre's guns, commanding the corduroy road from Fort Lyman—formerly Fort Lydius, soon to be Fort Edward—seemed to satisfy him. The encampment reeked of excrement; the provincials dropped it like untrained dogs, not even troubling to take a walk into the woods.

The Mohawk warchief told Forest Killer he wished to speak to all the field officers.

He told them:

"Brothers, we are sorry to see the situation of your people. Your sentries fall asleep at their posts and do not see an enemy until he has a knife at their throats. We know the woods better than you and you must hear us on these matters. Our chiefs must sit in your councils. Unless you are willing to study with us and make a union of hearts and minds, you may meet with a sudden and fatal blow. If you follow General Braddock's example, you ask for his fate."

The mention of the slaughtered British general silenced complaints about the impudence of natives who presumed to sit in white men's councils of war.

"I believe Hendrick is right," Johnson spoke up. "The state of our watch has demonstrated that." Though embarrassed, as military commander, by the negligence of his sentries, Billy was delighted by the opportunity to change the balance of opinion on the committee he was obliged to consult over every action.

Now Mohawks would sit with him, across the table from men who suspected that the only good Indian was a dead Indian.

In private, Billy discussed with Hendrick the need for better intelligence on the movements of the enemy and the defenses of Crown Point. And to make new overtures to the Mission Indians.

"If we can only turn the Caughnawaga—" Johnson was convinced "—the French will have no secrets from us. We will have many chances of leading them astray, or taking them by surprise."

"There are bad birds at Caughnawaga," Hendrick observed. "But Red Squirrel has no wish to fight with us. I will smoke with him, if it can be done."

Billy looked at Hendrick skeptically. The warchief was still vigorous, and his iron will carried him farther than many men half his age might ask themselves to go. But he was at least eighty years old and was carrying a gut as big as one of the rum kegs he had emptied along the trail.

"I think you should send a younger man," Johnson suggested. "I need you at my side."

"Red Squirrel is not far away." Hendrick stretched his forefinger along the edge of his nose. "I can smell him."

□

Hendrick went out with several warriors on a two-day scout, while Johnson weighed conflicting rumors and reports and tried to hold his army together. There was a mutiny in Ruggles' regiment, because back allowances of rum had not been paid. The New York militia were restive, demanding silver coin for their pay, something they could get their teeth into, instead of doubtful scrip; to pacify them, Billy was obliged to send Captain Cockcroft back to Albany to lay claim to the small chest of Spanish doubloons and pieces of eight he had brought to the house on Market Street in case of emergencies.

There was some good news. Colonel Blanchard and his New Hampshire volunteers had finally beaten their way out of the Massachusetts woods and arrived at the Carry. Johnson sent orders to Blanchard to stay at Fort Lyman to reinforce the small garrison of Yorkers he had left with Captain McGinniss to guard his lines of communication.

But the enemy remained hidden deep in the fog of the lakes that rose thick as buttermilk in the mornings. Scouts brought conflicting reports. One party reported a large French army at Ticonderoga, building a strong fort; the next saw only a handful of Canadians and no French works. Sightings of French Indians were reported from Schenectady to the Massachusetts line.

Hendrick—from whom Billy expected more—returned surly and winded from his mission. He claimed he had not been able to find the French or the Caughnawagas moving with them.

He is hiding something from me, Johnson thought.

I am his brother by adoption, but the Caughnawagas are brothers of the Mohawk by blood.

Are they brewing something together?

2.

In the morning, Snowbird loomed up in the door-flap of the general's tent while Billy was being shaved. Hendrick and other Mohawks were with him.

Johnson motioned for Rogers to continue his work with the razor.

Can I never have a moment's privacy from the Indians?

"*Katetshens,*" Snowbird announced. "I have a dream."

Johnson groaned inwardly. Peter Silverheels, one of the warriors from the Lower Castle, had come in the day before. He said he had dreamed of a silver armband, and naturally Forest Killer had been obliged to provide it. There was a fine line between Indian dreaming and extortion by Billy's observation. He wondered how it would look in his accounts of the expenses of the Indian Department: "To Peter, a Mohawk, a silver band because of his dream. £1.12." He decided to enter the item, just like that. It would give his paymasters something to quibble about, other than the price of powder and salt beef. And an education in the trials of an Indian agent.

"Tell me the dream."

"I saw death, rising from the Drowned Lands." The sweep of Snowbird's hand indicated the whole expanse of forest and swamp between the camp at Lake George and the mouth of Wood Creek. "No man should go out to the left of this place today."

Johnson was instantly alert. This was the other kind of dream, the kind he had grown to respect.

"You saw this clear?"

"As I saw the bull elk that was chosen to die."

Johnson remembered the hunting party, many seasons ago.

What had Snowbird told him? *Nothing happens before it is dreamed.*

"How many?"

"This is a hundred." Snowbird held up a forefinger. He opened and closed both hands four times. "Some in white coats, some in gray. With many Abenakis and many Caughnawagas. My sister goes with them. She stopped me from seeing more."

"I will send out scouts, to be sure." Johnson felt cold, remembering Swimming Voices and the spells she wove.

"Not today," Snowbird reminded him.

Because of a dream.

Am I to manage an army according to native dreams?

"My brother dreams true," Hendrick interceded.

"Not today," Johnson concurred.

He would tell his officers that this day would be reserved for prayer and fasting. The Protestant divines would love the chance to gab, and the army would conserve its dwindling stores of food and rum.

Snowbird has the sight. The gift seems to run in his mother's line. Island Woman is probably watching us now, in the coals of her fire or the mirror of her looking waters.

But it would be impolitic to try to explain that to a council of war that included men like Phineas Lyman.

5.

I am in the deep woods. It is late in the season. The ground is thickly carpeted with fallen leaves. The reds and golds have dulled. They are sodden and cold. There is a light glaze of ice or frost that crackles underfoot.

I pause at the edge of a rocky creek. Flocks of huge black birds—crows or vultures—are swooping down to attack a bull elk. I am crouched behind a tree, watching.

The bull elk throws back his antlers and bugles. I see the hot breath steam from his nostrils. He trumpets his rage and pain, drumming hooves. Now he is falling under the assault of the carrion birds.

I know his pain. It drives into my heart with the force of a pickaxe.

I turn away. A bird with a huge, knowing head and blue feathers is watching me, as I watched the elk. It might be a kingfisher. It is royal, and other-worldly.

□

Billy cried out as a hand reached into his dream. He sat up staring, clutching the sheet to his bare chest.

"I am sorry," Daniel Claus apologized. "It is news that will not wait."

"Give me a minute." Johnson reached for the ewer, and splashed water over his face.

I have become too close to the Indians. Now I am dreaming as they do.

But what does it mean, the dying elk and the carrion birds?

He rubbed his face with the hand towel, as if this would rub away the dream.

"Talk to me, Daniel. Is it more deserters?"

They had lost more than twenty wagoners and boatmen the previous night, including an Albany river-rat named Andries Bratt, whom Billy counted no loss since he had been spreading sedition among his fellows. The sentries who were supposed to be guarding the perimeter of the camp had joined the deserters, after pilfering from the stores.

"Mohawk scouts are in from South Bay."

Johnson hurried into his shirt and breeches and wrapped himself in his scarlet blanket, like one of the sachems. He stuck a pistol in his belt and joined Claus under the striped awning. The scouts had been served cider and cold venison.

Billy greeted Peter Silverheels.

"The French left their boats here." Silverheels scratched a mark on the ground, next to the wavy line that marked South Bay. "They are walking on three roads." He added the lines, extending them south-west, in the direction of Lydius' house and the Great Carrying Place.

"How far?"

The stick hovered over the rude map. Silverheels jabbed at the place where the scouts had seen the French the previous day. The enemy had already covered a third of the distance from the lake to the Carry.

Silverheels jabbed at another spot. "The French walk quickly. Now they are here."

They are moving to the left of our camp. Snowbird's dream was accurate.

It seemed the French were now less than a day's march from the fortified post at the Carry. If they took Fort Lyman, they would cut off Johnson's lifelines to the south.

This would leave his army marooned in the forest-sea. The French would have leisure to bring reinforcements down the lake and envelop his positions in overwhelming force.

In the scratch marks on the ground, Johnson saw the fruits of the jealousies and delays that had sucked the forward momentum out of his expedition. Without a bold move now, his force would be trapped between the blades of Dieskau's shears—between the French army moving between him and Albany, perhaps already on the road his own men had cleared and abandoned, and the garrison at Crown Point, with all the resources of Canada behind it.

"How many?"

Silverheels threw three bundles of twigs into the circle of candlelight on the ground. There were six or seven sticks in each bundle. Faced by the constant influx of white men, the Mohawks had been obliged to start counting in hundreds. Six or seven hundred Frenchmen and Indians in each of the three columns.

Snowbird was right again.

It was a smaller force than Johnson commanded. But in forest warfare, the advantage did not lie with numbers, but with seasoned leadership, steadiness and surprise.

The scout had another piece of news. "A great chief walks with the French. He wears a blue coat with red facings, and an exploding star on his chest. He carries a little black stick. When he points it, men run."

Billy looked at Daniel.

"Baron Dieskau," Claus suggested.

"I think you are right," Billy agreed. "It seems we are

visited by the French commander-in-chief in person. Marshal Dieskau does us great honor. We must see he is entertained in the proper style."

□

"Baron Dieskau has moved onto our playing field with an inferior force," Johnson told the council of war that convened at midnight. "It seems to me there are two possible reasons. Either the Marshal is supremely confident. Or he is uninformed about our strength and positions."

"There is another possibility," Lyman intervened.

"Yes, General Lyman?"

"That your Mohawk scouts have gotten it wrong. It would not be the first time."

There was a stir of agreement among the New Englanders in the tent, though Ephraim Williams—Billy noted—held himself aloof from the brewing debate.

"It may be this is a trap," Nathan Whiting interjected. He was a confident, thirtyish merchant from New Haven, turned colonel under Lyman's wing.

"Let us know your mind, Colonel."

"It may be a lure to draw us away from the safety of the camp, into an ambush in the woods. I do not trust Mohawks. They are thick as thieves with the Mission Indians."

He did not say more, because Hendrick entered the general's tent, exercising his right to sit on a council of war.

"Gentlemen—" Johnson sought to build a consensus. "I agree that reports from scouts, of whatever complexion, require confirmation. We are caught in the fog of war. But I trust this scout, and I suggest that his intelligence demands immediate action. I know General Lyman will agree we cannot leave Colonel Blanchard and the men at Fort Lyman in the dark, with the enemy advancing at full gait in their direction."

The mention of the fortification that bore his name blunted Lyman's objections. It was agreed that an express rider must be sent to Colonel Blanchard. The only volunteer who could be found was a New York wagoner, James Adams, swayed by Billy's offer to lend him his own horse.

I may have the advantage of numbers, Johnson thought ruefully. *But Baron Dieskau does not have to win the approval of a council of jealous New England men before he sends out a lone rider.*

4.

However, Baron Dieskau, too, was moving in the fog of war, with reluctant or rebellious allies.

"I feel like a man in a blindfold," he complained to Landriève. "You say the Caughnawagas are the masters of this country. Yet I have not received a faithful scout from them since we left Fort St. Frédéric. And now they defy my orders to my face."

Dieskau had ordered his officers to bivouac their forces in the woods, a league from Lydius' fortified house. He had sent Abenakis to report on the state of the enemy defenses. The report was encouraging. There were only five hundred provincials at the post, many of them lounging about outside the stockade, where horses and cattle were grazing.

The Baron called the Indian warchiefs together to announce an assault on Lydius' post at dawn.

Red Squirrel, speaking for the Caughnawagas, asked for time to consider.

He had left Baron Dieskau cooling his heels for two hours. When Dieskau had pressed for a response, Red Squirrel told him the three hundred Caughnawagas would not move against a fortified post in English territory.

"Very well," Dieskau had snapped. "We march without you. You have shown us what your friendship is worth."

The Caughnawagas had requested more time to deliberate. Red Squirrel had returned with a change of policy. Now they were willing to go, since the French set such store by their objective.

They had worn out the Baron's trust as well as his patience.

"The Caughnawaga are meeting the Mohawk in the woods," he told the Sieur de Landrièvre. "Legardeur's Abenakis have informed me of it. They may have used these delays to warn the enemy. And I fear that this change of heart is the preface to the blackest treachery. You have lived with these savages for years. What am I to do?"

Landrièvre listened to the cathedral hush of the forest. Dawn was still hours away. "You have time before you commit yourself," he told the Baron. "There is a man who will tell us what we must know. I will speak with him."

□

Painted and greased like one of the Mission Indians, Landrièvre slipped quietly through sleeping Canadians to the Caughnawaga camp. Thin moonlight caught the white ribbon he had tied around his head, the dull silver of the gorget and double-barred cross that hung over his buckskins.

Something small and feral burst from the bushes and jabbed a knifepoint under his chin.

It was the Mohawk witch's brat, allowed to run wild as any creature of the forest.

The mother separated herself from the shadows. A handsome woman, moving like a cat. But not a woman any man in possession of his faculties would meddle with. Exiled by her own people, excommunicated by the Church, a renegade accused of witchcraft. *Beyond the reach of mercy,* the haunted blackrobe at the Sault St. Louis had said. *Beyond the grace of our Saviour.*

A worthy consort for the man Landrièvre was seeking.

"Sahtenti," Swimming Voices hissed at her son. "Go away." The pressure of the knife was removed. The boy vanished as if he had fallen through a hole in the earth.

"He is waiting for you," Swimming Voices told Landrièvre.

There was blood in the air.

He walked behind her, through dense underbrush. There was no trail Landrière could see, but the bushes parted at her coming. The smell of blood grew stronger.

Le Corbeau squatted on a rock at the edge of a swamp, singing in an eerie, whistling voice. He was feeding a wooden doll. Now he cooed over it like a mother with her infant. His doll would have disappointed a French child. The body was only a stick of greased wood, wrapped in scraps of cloth. The carver had applied all his efforts to the egg-shaped head. Huge eyes stared from under a domed, striated forehead. The mouth was whistling or blowing. A lock of hair and several tiny medicine bundles and tobacco pouches were strung from the neck.

"Say it, French uncle." Le Corbeau spoke without interrupting his work.

"I must know if the Caughnawagas have betrayed us. Do our enemies lie in ambush on the road to the Carry?"

Le Corbeau croaked his laughter. Landrière saw now that the mouth of his doll was smeared red.

"Speak your heart, French uncle. Say what you came for."

The soultaker robs me of my thoughts.

"I have come for Tête Blanche," Landrière admitted. "I have come for Hendrick."

Le Corbeau twitched his lips, sending the Mohawk witch back into the night.

The sorcerer sung nonsense syllables over his doll. He kissed its face and caressed the trailing lock of human hair. He danced with it, rocked it in his arms.

Then he snatched up a staff, the end pointed like a fishing spear. He scratched at the earth, making a crude map that showed a narrow lake, a road and two mountains or ridges.

"Here." Le Corbeau jabbed at the place where the road threaded the hills. He spoke in a high, insinuating, nasal voice, different from his usual one. "You go north, not south. You find the Mohawk here."

Landrière's chest felt tight. It was difficult to breathe. Was this more deception?

Or a cheap performer's trick?

If not, there was something very wrong here. Something unholy. *Beyond the realm of mercy.*

"I want him." Landriève's mouth and throat were dry. He was consumed with thirst. "I want it finished. What must I do?"

The soultaker hooted.

He drew another pattern with the point of his staff. The outline of a man. He swirled his staff above his head, clicking and cawing. When he drove the speartip down into the face, where the right eye might have been, something bubbled from the earth, dark and foul smelling.

Le Corbeau crowed. "You take his body. I take his soul."

5.

Scared men threw themselves on the mercy of Johnson's pickets that night, wagoners who had run off but preferred to face parade-ground discipline than the terror in the woods. Andries Bratt was among them. He said the forest was thick with French Indians. He had seen a rider shot from his horse and scalped four miles this side of the Carry.

Johnson weighed this news at dawn, in a council of war that included Hendrick and Snowbird.

"If we can trust deserters, the enemy has killed James Adams, the courier I sent to Blanchard on my own horse. From the papers Adams was bearing, we must presume Baron Dieskau now has a clear picture of our positions and the state of our defenses. It is a question, gentlemen, of whether we are to wait for him or go out to meet him. I believe we cannot afford to let him take Fort Lyman and cut off our road to the southward. That would leave us as vulnerable as a beached whale."

There was debate among the field officers. It was agreed that troops must be sent to reinforce Blanchard at the Carry. Then Phineas Lyman proposed dividing the army yet again, by sending out a second detachment to capture or destroy the French boats the scouts had seen at South Bay.

"We can take the Baron's fleet while he is thrashing about in the woods. We will be masters of the lake."

Hendrick Forked Paths grunted, and Billy asked the warchief for his view.

Hendrick gathered a handful of sticks. He twirled one of them in front of the white officers, then snapped it between his middle fingers. Then he took up a thick bundle, and demonstrated that it could not be broken even with two hands.

"We weaken ourselves by division, gentlemen," Johnson drew the moral. "Hendrick reminds us in a way that is more eloquent than words."

It was resolved to send a thousand provincials, and the bulk of the Indian warriors, down the road to the Carry to relieve Blanchard and scout out the enemy movements.

Ephraim Williams pleaded for the command of this expedition and got his wish; the Massachusetts colonel announced he would lead the vanguard, with Hendrick and the warriors of the Six Nations. Nathan Whiting was appointed second-in-command and would bring up the rear of the column.

Hendrick dressed for the march in his finest clothes. He brought out the laced hat he had received from the hands of King George, and a fine silver-tipped cane. Then he daubed his face with holy paint, ground from hematite quarried far to the west.

"You look like a man that is going to his wedding," Johnson told him.

Hendrick sniffed the morning air. "Good killing weather," he remarked. "A good day to die."

A cold touched Johnson. "Do me a favor, old friend. Ride one of my horses."

"My brother Forest Killer has lost one horse already."

"Friends count for more than horses, even to an Irishman. Ride Gulliver. He will not shy from a fight. And look after Ephraim Williams. He is driven by the memory of his losses. This can drive him to great things, but it may make him reckless and unconsidering."

Johnson watched the column move off along the corduroy road, through the pickets. He heard Hendrick raise the warsong of the Six Nations, joined by Snowbird and the other chiefs:

The Power of this song
amazes me and all who hear it.
I am permitted to use it
because I am of the Six Nations
and this war song comes from my Creator.
He has made this army
our warriors will be mighty
in his Power.

The warriors screamed and shook out their plumage like great warbirds.

"I don't know if they scare the enemy—" Peter Wraxall began.

"I know," said Johnson. But something was wrong. He felt it in the silences and evasions of his Mohawk friends. Now, as he watched them vanishing down the road that dwindled to a tube poked through the green-black woods, Billy felt it in his bones.

◻

Two miles south of Johnson's camp, Colonel Williams ordered a halt, to rally the stragglers and arrange his men in some semblance of order.

Hendrick cantered past on the general's horse, indifferent to the shouted commands and the chaff of Massachusetts farm boys sweating in the hot haze.

There was a distant crack, like a musket shot. And another. Then a wild thrashing through the trees, between that ominous blue-black ridge to the west and the road.

"Form platoons!" Williams yelled, echoed by his company commanders.

Some of the militiamen obeyed, forming ragged lines among the tree stumps. Others ran for cover. A few rammed homemade bayonets into the muzzles of their firelocks, putting their trust in cold steel rather than ball and powder. If the enemy was on them, there would be no time to get off more than a single shot.

Hendrick leaned on his pommel, squinting ahead down the scarred strip of cleared land to where the valley narrowed between the humped mass of French Mountain and the gentler rise to the west.

Matt Ferrall took aim at a brown shadow springing from cover. His firelock snapped. The shadow quivered in mid-flight, fell on splayed legs, fountaining blood, and toppled over to one side.

"Deer!" Matt laughed his relief.

"Can I mess with you tonight, Mister Ferrall?" one of his men teased.

Ephraim Williams counted thirty of them before he gave up counting. Whitetail deer, bucks and does running together. They kept coming out of the woods even after Ferrall fired. What was driving them to run between armed men?

Perhaps the craziness of the rutting season had come early.

The deer played havoc with the lines.

And Colonel Williams noticed how their behavior seemed to spread a gloomy distemper among the Indians. They were huddling together, talking in their own tongues. Snowbird and Peter Silverheels were consulting Hendrick, urgency in their faces.

Williams joined them, fanning his hand to keep flies and no-see-ems off his face.

"Flankers," Colonel Williams said. "We must have flankers."

Snowbird said, glancing at Hendrick, "I will go."

Silverheels said, "I go too."

"Just the two of them?" Williams did not understand.

"They are Mohawks," Hendrick responded. "They know this country. Two are safer than more."

"Very well." Colonel Williams found Hendrick's face impossible to read. His glance moved from the gunpowder tattoo that showed on the warchief's temple, under his fancy Court hat, to the whitened tomahawk scar that ran from the corner of his mouth to his left earlobe.

Fools did not survive as many battles as Hendrick had, even if they were lucky. Williams must trust that the warchief knew what he was doing. But it troubled him that he could never tell what the Indians were thinking or feeling. All that he could pick up now was a coiled expectancy.

Hendrick dug his heels into Gulliver's flanks and trotted ahead down the corduroy road, tiger-striped by the shadows that lay in the hollows between the logs.

"Form order of march!" Williams shouted to his subalterns.

From the flats where the column was surprised by the deer, the road followed a stony creek south into a narrowing ravine. On the right, above the blaze of goldenrod and the debris of road-making, a steep bank rose thirty feet. Behind it, hemlock woods ran up a gentle slope to the foot of a sharp incline. An army with field guns could camp in there and not be sighted from the road, Ephraim Williams reflected uneasily.

The land to the left of the road was level but swampy, covered with thick scrub and mined with sucking holes.

Half a mile from the mouth of the ravine, the rocky hulk of French Mountain claimed half the level ground. In that constricted passage, a column of marching men would be as vulnerable as chickens in a henroost.

We are going into a funnel.

"It don't look good, Colonel," Seth Pomeroy whispered, at the Colonel's shoulder.

"I believe old Hendrick knows what he is doing."

"It's strange to be walking at the heels of a mounted Indian. Like mother nature turned upside down."

Williams felt a stab of pain above his left eye and slapped at its source. The insect eluded him, but blood trickled over his cheek and soiled his linen shirt.

"It is a plaguey country," Pomeroy observed, keeping pace with Williams' brisk stride. "Only mosquitoes and gnats are at home here. I saw a man in Ruggles' regiment who got a tick in his ear. Overnight, his ear blew up like a cauliflower."

The talk of ticks reminded Williams of the surgeon's

mate—his rival in love—whom he had left attending to sick men while the Colonel hunted the French. The expression on the boy's face when Williams had informed him he would be more useful in camp than on the scout! The resentment in those spaniel eyes!

Colonel Williams was cheered by the recollection, though a pang of Puritan conscience came with it. A man who had been made to attend church meetings three times a day all through childhood never quite recovered from it. Conscience said, *Because Perez Marsh defeated you in the fields of love, you deny him a chance to prove himself in the fields of war. Because he unmanned you, you refuse him the honors of manhood.*

Spurned by Sally for a boy in his teens! The memory of that shame and pain diverted the Colonel from his worries about the march and whether his Mohawk flankers could be relied on. It also tightened a knot in Williams' belly that loosened only when he called a rest stop and ran among the bushes, like half his men, to drop his breeches. It was a fortunate white man in that army who had not succumbed to laxness of the bowels, or the bloody flux.

6.

Snowbird loped through the woods with the fluid gait of Okwaho. He was searching with his inner and outer senses for the friends and enemies concealed in the forest that could swallow armies as fast as a bear eats June berries.

He heard Island Woman's voice. *We may fight the French and the Easterners, but we must not kill our own blood. There must be no more fighting between Mohawks and Caughnawagas, because there is nothing more terrible than a war within one family.*

Hendrick had heard this voice.

Snowbird knew that Red Squirrel, and the grayhairs and clanmothers of the Caughnawaga, heard it too.

He must find friends of the Caughnawaga, in the woods between the armies, before the white commanders or other Indians dragged them into a killing match they could not avoid.

In serving his own people, he believed, he was not betraying his friend Forest Killer. Johnson had been ardent in his own attempts to make a pact with the Caughnawagas. But there were things that were best not said openly to any newcomer. Even the new Firekeeper of the Six Nations.

Snowbird heard a sharp *peent,* like the call of a woodcock in mating time, and answered it, blowing through cupped hands.

Silverheels showed himself among the hemlocks.

He made the sign of crossed arrows, for the Easterners, and pointed to the hilly slope on the far side of the road. The Abenakis concealed there were ancient enemies who would kill a Mohawk warrior on sight.

Silverheels grinned, gesturing to show where the Caughnawagas had hidden themselves, well in advance of the Abenakis, and on the same side of the road as the Mohawk scouts.

It amused Snowbird to stalk a Caughnawaga warrior who thought he was invisible behind a hollow stump. Snowbird jumped light as a squirrel over twigs and fallen leaves. He got his arm around the Caughnawaga's throat, capping his mouth to prevent him from raising the alarm.

"I see my brothers have lived too long with the French. You sleep when you are keeping watch, like the newcomers."

"I think my brother Snowbird has lived too long with the English," came a voice from behind him. "You no longer smell nor hear."

Snowbird turned to find Red Squirrel standing close behind, his killing club raised. The Caughnawaga warchief had streaked his face and chest red and midnight blue. His hair, shaven to a bristling scalplock over the fontanel, was dressed with a silver brooch and the feathers of a bald eagle.

The Mohawk and the Caughnawaga embraced each other, laughing over their game of one-upmanship.

"We smelled you before you left Johnson's camp," Red Squirrel informed the Mohawk scouts. "We don't need to kill your English friends. They will drown in their own shit."

They traded information about the strength and deployment of the rival white forces, and the Abenakis across the road.

The French and their allies had taken up ambush positions, making three sides of a box. Baron Dieskau's plan was to encourage Colonel Williams to march right inside the box before he sealed it up. He had issued strict orders to the Caughnawagas, via Commandant Landrième, that no man was to shoot until the French regulars, who would cut off Williams' route to the south, opened fire.

"We cannot let this happen," Snowbird said.

Red Squirrel agreed.

They discussed the best way to warn Hendrick.

They did not see Le Corbeau, in a mask of black paint and a headband of severed fingers and toes, darting like a flint arrowhead toward Landrième's command post.

7.

The creak of leather, the thud of marching feet, the oaths and whispers of the men as they stumbled along the corrugated road magnified the silence of the enveloping woods. Even the crows were still, roosting in the topmost limbs of the trees.

The wind shifted, now it blew warm in their faces, from the south, providing scant relief from the muggy heat of the day.

The advance party was a hundred paces from the narrows when a deep-bellied grunt sounded from the thickets to the right. It rose to a high-pitched, quavering bugle and then shifted to a wild shriek that carried all the way back to the laggards at the back of Colonel Whiting's companies of Connecticut men.

"It's nothing but an old bull elk, warning us off his cows," a grizzled Northampton farmer reassured a Boston lad, no older than his son, whose hands were shaking. "Old man elk won't abide anything with a pizzle within hollering distance when the ladies are in the mood."

The Boston apprentice smiled back gamely, though fear remained at the edges of his eyes. He had fled from deer. He would not be seen running from elk.

Hendrick spat commands in Mohawk, and the warriors with the advance party raced to cover on both sides of the road.

Hendrick was motioning to Williams to turn back. He made the gesture of tying up a bag.

Colonel Williams blinked, reluctant to give the order to retreat with no enemy in view.

"Form platoons!" he yelled. "Load!"

Matt Ferrall took a thick, paper-wrapped cartridge from his pouch and bit off the bullet. He lifted his musket's frizzen and dropped a pinch of powder into the pan. He stood his firelock on its butt to pour the rest of the powder down the barrel. He stuffed the crumpled paper from the cartridge casing after it, then spat the bullet from between his teeth.

Matt was a practiced shooter. He performed these actions quickly and mechanically, until he saw a man in a mask of grease and paint jump up from a heap of cleared brushwood, ahead to the right.

He saw the silver gorget, the cross of Lorraine. The firelock already loaded and cocked.

Hands shaking, Matt jammed down the mess of powder, paper and lead in the gun barrel with his ramrod and shouldered his musket without waiting for the order to fire.

The Frenchman dressed like an Indian was better prepared. He ignored the threat from Matt. He took careful aim at Hendrick, who was struggling with his frightened horse. Landriève's musket spat lead. Gulliver bucked and screamed and shook Hendrick from his back. The warchief rolled in the dust.

A great howl went up from both sides of the road, followed by a hard rain of bullets. Matt fired his first ball at the nearest enemy who showed himself, an Indian who ran baying at the frightened Massachusetts volunteers.

Panic flowed through the lines. The Boston prentice had never seen a man wounded in battle. He lost control of his bowels when he saw his Northampton mentor take an ambusher's bullet through his cheeks. The ball scored its way through teeth and tongue, coming out the other side.

Despite Colonel Williams' efforts to rally his men to answer the enemy with fire, the van of his column folded in on itself. The churning fear brought by the hellish noise of the enemy and the faces of horror bursting from the woods threatened to take possession of the whole force as maimed and mangled bodies struggled and fell among the ranks.

Ephraim Williams and his officers struggled to steady the men, striking at runners with the flat of their swords. Their shouted orders were lost or ignored in the chaos. Captain Hawley, trying to staunch the flight with his body, was knocked down and trampled underfoot by some of his own men.

From the south, Colonel Williams heard a sound as ominous as the shrieks of the Mission Indians. The hollow thud of kettle drums. Through the smoke, a whitish blur was taking form. French regulars, marching six abreast in perfect order in a line spiked by long bayonets.

A lead must be given—an initiative taken—or else the column would be swallowed up like Braddock's in the bloodbath along the Monongahela.

"To me!" Williams brandished his sword. "Follow me!"

His intent was set on the shelf of higher ground occupied by the Caughnawagas. If his men could take that, they might establish a defensible position and hold the French and their other allies at bay until help came from the camp. Surely Johnson must hear the noises of battle. The wind was gusting stronger from the south.

Colonel Williams scrambled over felled branches, into

thickets that tore his skin. "To the heights!" he yelled, not pausing to see how many followed.

He had seen Hendrick fall from his horse and believed him dead. The Mohawks were caught up in their own battle. The contest for the heights would be a clean fight, one ancient enemy against another.

"Remember Deerfield!" Williams shouted. "Think of your wives and children."

Think of Sally. Would she change her mind if she saw him now? Why did his mind turn at this moment—with death on all sides—to the will he had revised at Albany, from which he had excised his bequest to Sally, leaving the money to a school that did not yet exist, and which he might never see? Would her children go to this school? Would they wear latin-lover curls, like Perez Marsh?

He slashed at a Caughnawaga, crouched behind a pine, who avoided the blow but did not strike back.

"Fight me!" he bawled, his voice breaking.

Red Squirrel contemplated Ephraim Williams from the crest of the ridge. The Caughnawaga warchief respected courage. He admired craziness even more. People who were crazy in the eyes of ordinary men might be favored by the spirits. They saw things others did not.

Colonel Williams stumbled, clawed at loose earth, righted himself and forced himself up a treacherous slope. He had twenty men at his back. The rest of the New England force buzzed and swirled like a swarm that had lost its queen.

Red Squirrel took thoughtful aim. He shot Williams cleanly through the head.

□

Legardeur came loping through high brown grass, barely distinguishable from the Indians under his command, his face smeared with grease from the cooking pot, his buckskins oily from hard wear, a gorget bouncing against his bony chest. He ran with an effortless, relentless speed, remarkable in a white man past fifty.

At his heels ran his personal bodyguard—not *domiciliés* from the Canadian mission settlements, but Far Indians who had fought for him on the borders of Sioux territory and still ate the hearts of their captured enemies.

Legardeur's thin lips tightened into a knife-edged line. Baron Dieskau's orders had been quite specific. No man in the army that lay in ambush was to show himself until the entire English column was inside the box. The regulars concealed beyond French Mountain would cut the road and commence hostilities.

But among the Caughnawagas, treachery was second nature.

And Landrieve, he thought, was no more to be trusted. Among the strange men who had lived with the natives, Landrieve was one of the strangest. A man fighting a private war.

Colonel Williams' column, Legardeur saw, was no longer an army. Small knots of men grappled with Canadians and Caughnawagas, while the rest thronged back down the road to the English camp.

The Mohawks were covering this rout, each of them a killing machine.

Legardeur saw a huge Mohawk warrior, decked out in silver ornaments, drive his hatchet deep into the throat of a Canadian.

He dropped down to take aim at him.

Matt Ferrall, moving close to Snowbird, saw the threat, and fired first, dropping Legardeur with a shot to the heart.

The loss of their leader enraged the Abenakis. A dozen warriors flung themselves at Matt. Snowbird and Silverheels grappled with them hand to hand, but could not break the fierce tide. An Abenaki warrior dropped Matt with a blow that dislocated his shoulder, and hacked off his scalp with such violence he took off the top of the skull along with skin and hair.

The Abenakis laughed when Matt got back on his feet, gouting blood.

"Have to get to Billy," he muttered. "Billy will make it right."

The Abenakis let the walking dead go.

Matt staggered all the way back to the mouth of the ravine, where Colonel Whiting had halted his Connecticut troops, who were wavering between going forward or back. The sight of a white man walking with a hole in his head big enough to swallow an eggplant unnerved the young New Haven merchant. He ordered the retreat, leaving the Massachusetts men who were still fighting—and the Mohawks, who were inside the wolf's throat—to fend for themselves.

8.

To stand and die was not the way of fighting of the Real People. With the flight of the provincials and the death of their white commanders, the Mohawks scattered through the woods, to fight another day.

Hendrick Forked Paths had survived his fall from the horse and hacked his way through a circle of death.

But he had lost his speed. His body was sluggish—a sack of meat and bones he would be grateful to leave behind.

Hendrick had never feared death. How can a man who has journeyed to the other side be afraid of trading one form of life for another? He had dreamed of the friends and loved ones who waited for him.

He feared only what a warrior of the Real People must always fear: to die shamefully, like a beaten cur. To die before his personal allotment of power—his *orenda*—had run out. To die without honor.

He was fighting his way through the woods. He thought the Abenaki camp lay this way. If he was to die this day, he would take more souls with him. Maybe he would even reach the man in the blue coat who drove the French and their allies to battle with a little gold-tipped stick.

A French officer rushed to oppose him. The Frenchman feinted with his sword, then lunged for Hendrick's throat, which was at the level of his eyes. The Mohawk slipped aside with a dancer's grace, something the Frenchman had not counted on.

Hendrick's arm rose, dark against the sun.

The Frenchman parried, but the crushing weight of the heavy burled warclub splintered his wrists and his sword fell.

Hendrick's arm scythed back. He drove the antler prongs that crowned the ball head of his club into the Frenchman's face. The bony points sheared through skin and flesh. One settled in the socket of the Frenchman's left eye.

The Frenchman's body folded under him. His screams drowned in the clamor of battle around them.

Keeyyy-aaaaagh!

Hendrick's scalp-cry soared and slashed down like the scream of an eagle.

He plunged on, through the forest.

But his energy was ebbing fast.

Soon his feet lifted and fell sluggishly, as if he were trying to run along the lake floor, under a hundred feet of water. He no longer heard the screams of battle, only the thunder of rushing water in his own ears. An exquisite pain raced through his veins.

Then a shooting star exploded in his chest.

He clutched at the trunk of a silver birch. His head slumped forward and his stomach heaved. His heart was a great fist beating on his ribs, trying to burst through.

He got a grip on a branch that jutted at shoulder height and checked himself before he slid down the trunk.

A warrior should die on his feet.

He was too old to run any further. Too fat, too tired.

He hung from the tree like a white dog sacrifice, slung from a pole by a collar of red shells.

He told the spirits he was coming. His song began in his gut and rose from his throat in a low hum that got higher and thinner, like a wind that shifted between the trees and set the elmbark roof of the longhouse flapping.

Okwaho was waiting. He was black and tan, his tongue lolling. Wolf would guide Forked Paths on the Path of Souls, to the slippery bridge where the Crusher waited to eat his brain, to the Land where warriors danced for She Who Fell from the Sky. The spirits knew him. He had walked in the steps of the ancestors. He had fed their hungry ghosts. He had made the sky ring with his name.

Hendrick Forked Paths was ready for whomever would come for him.

He missed the warclub that had fought with him in a dozen battles. But he had a good knife in his belt, the long blade fitted to a pronged elkhorn handle, dressed with wolfskin.

He sensed movement among the birches. His enemy came as lightly as a blown leaf, through the circle of dappled light.

Hendrick shut out the pain and fatigue and willed his sack of meat and bones to serve him. He stepped out to meet his enemy, knife in hand, his scalp-lock bobbing, the tattooed sunburst over his left temple throbbing like an open wound.

He saw his enemy. He checked the war cry that had sprung to his lips. He halted the downward curve of Sheffield steel.

He was looking at a boy of eight or nine winters, slight and lanky as a fawn. The child had the fine bones, long oval head and close-set eyes of his Caughnawaga cousins. He wore the Frenchman's barred cross and a fillet of silver in his hair. He was carrying a little bow, hardly more than a toy, a bow for taking squirrels or passenger pigeons.

"*Skenakowa*," Hendrick greeted him. "Peace to you, mighty warrior."

With a single, fluid motion, the Caughnawaga boy fitted a blunt to his bowstring and fired the practice arrow.

It struck Hendrick's cheek, above the ragged white line of the old tomahawk scar. The warchief felt a dull pain, as if a loose tooth had come out.

"Come here, boy, so I can skin you," Hendrick laughed.

A second blunt drove into the socket of his right eye and shut out the sun. A curtain of red steam came down.

He saw forms indistinctly, in the outer world and the Real World that was just behind it. He could not find Okwaho.

He fell straight forward, like a felled tree.

"Tsitak," the boy spat. "Eat shit."

His mother slipped from her place of hiding. Her mouth moved hungrily, the lower lip jutting down in a deep V. As she crouched over Hendrick's huge body, her eyes widened until the whites encircled the pupils, dilated so the irises seemed all black.

Swimming Voices prised the elkhorn knife from Hendrick's fist. She gave it to her son.

Under her eyes, the boy drew a little circle around the warchief's braided scalplock. Blood welled quickly from the incision he made.

Dancer tugged at the matted hair. The scalp was stubborn, taut against the skull as the skin of a talking drum.

Swimming Voices, nervous that Mohawks would follow where Hendrick had come, moved her son aside. She used her teeth to rip the scalp free, and tasted Hendrick's blood on her tongue.

She felt savage triumph. This was one of those who had shamed her.

She passed Hendrick's scalp to her son. The boy held it up to the sun and howled his scalp cry, no fuller than the yelp of a wolf pup.

He was interrupted by a hissing growl. Le Corbeau leaped into the clearing and squatted over the warchief, to steal his last breath. He was whistling for the soul that was leaving. He snapped his fingers at the boy, and he surrendered the ragged circle of skin and hair.

The soultaker thrust it into the pouch he had prepared. It contained a wooden peg, a doll whose features were not yet carved.

The Sieur de Landrieve crashed through the bushes, anxious to confirm that his enemy was dead. Le Corbeau blew into the bag and pulled the drawstrings tight.

The soultaker said to the Frenchman, "What is left is yours."

CHAPTER 32
HUSKING TIME

1.

At Johnson's camp on the lake, the first sounds of the fighting on the road carried back as the soft popping of Indian corn, set to heat in a kettle. As the wind from the south picked up, the noise grew to the harsh crackling of wildfire snapping up dry thornbushes.

Johnson abandoned his maps and papers and rushed out of his tent in his shirtsleeves. Rogers hastened after him, concerned that the general should appear to his unruly troops in the guise of authority. While Billy squinted through the little brass telescope Goldsbrow Banyar had sent up from New York, Rogers dressed him in his silk waistcoat and his new scarlet coat, gaudy with the lace and aiguillettes of a general officer.

"Can't see a damned thing!" Johnson complained, spreading his arms so Rogers could wind the belt and sword-sling around his waist.

"Captain Eyre!" Billy shouted to his artillery officer, who was assembling his gun crews at the battery commanding the road. "Do you have a view to the engagement?"

"No, sir. By the din, they are hard at it."

"How far off?"

"Four miles, I would hazard. Could be more. The wind may deceive us."

The south wind blew hot and hard, a late blast of summer. Johnson's skin prickled under the heavy broadcloth.

He scanned the crude breastwork of sharpened logs and downed branches he had ordered raised in front of the camp. A poor substitute for a fort. This and Eyre's guns were all that stood between his milling, nervous provincials and the unseen enemy.

Our abbatis is damnably flimsy, Johnson thought. *The Mission Indians will find a way around it or over it. Baron Dieskau's regulars will not even break their stride. This will hang on the nerve and marksmanship of our woodsmen. But most of all on Eyre's cannon.*

"You have grapeshot, Captain Eyre?"

"I have made canister by my own recipe, sir. I think it will tax the Frenchies' digestion."

Wraxall hovered at Johnson's elbow, his quill, as always, at the ready. Billy lowered at the ensign that fluttered over Phineas Lyman's tent, like the flag of an independent power. Or worse, of a pretender.

"Peter," Johnson turned to his natty aide-de-camp. "Give my compliments to General Lyman. Remind him cordially that he remains under my command. Tell him it is my pleasure that he detail sufficient men to haul the flatboats up from the lake. Tipped on their sides, I believe they will make a serviceable wall. Good enough to stop Frog bullets, at the least. And we shall save ourselves the embarrassment of raiders making off with our flotilla."

Daniel Claus rushed up the knoll to join them. "Daniel," Billy squeezed his upper arm. "Go over to Colonel Cole. Ask him to make a sortie with his Rhode Islanders. We must have exact intelligence of what goes on the road. I pray Cole will not be too late to be of some service to our friends."

"No council of war this noon?" Wraxall asked slyly.

"I believe the war has found us, Peter. Wars are not won by committees."

□

Baron Dieskau pushed forward, with the white-jacketed troops of the storied regiments of Languedoc and La Reine, cursing the duplicity of his auxiliaries. The opposing force was a shambles. The remnants of Williams' column fled from the steel bayonets, which advanced steadily, relentlessly, to the music of fife and drum.

He was annoyed to see that some of his Canadian provincials, as well as many of his native auxiliaries, had abandoned all discipline in order to strip the dead or dying New Englanders of their boots and hair and personal property. He sent a runner to find Commandant Landriève and instruct him to order the Indians to leave off their scalping and pillaging and move on as flankers for the main column.

Landriève came with his answer in person. "No inducement will make native warriors leave the scalps. They believe that the hair of a dead enemy gives them power. If we wish them to fight for us, we must accommodate their superstitions. And be content when they do not insist on eating the heart or the liver without salt."

The Baron faced a delay in his northerly march. A few of Whiting's Connecticut men punished his force with retreating fire, leaping from tree to tree like the natives. They were joined by a few hundred provincials from Johnson's camp who were soon sent scurrying by the Canadians and Abenakis Baron Dieskau hurled at them through the woods. The ones that made a stand on the road broke before the cold steel of the regulars.

Now the Baron could see lake water, glinting blue as sapphires. Between him and the lake was a wretched encampment, no fort at all, where fleeing men were spreading the contagion of defeat.

"Wenn schön, denn schön," Dieskau said in his native German. "When it must be done, do it well. On to the lake!"

He did not pause to calculate the numerical odds. Numbers, in his experience, were rarely the key to battles. Momentum, luck and leadership were prime. Not one of his regulars had fallen. Hardly a man had soiled his snow-white coat. Ahead was a rabble commanded by a womanizing play-actor. Baron Dieskau smelled victory.

When Montreuil, his adjutant, came hurrying to suggest that they should wait to collect all their native and Canadian forces again, Dieskau said, "The liquor is drawn, and we must drink it."

He drew his saber. The blade flashed in the clear air.

Then the scene was swallowed in yellow-gray smoke as Captain Eyre's cannon belched fire.

Baron Dieskau had not counted on the guns.

□

The south wind blew the smoke back into the gunners' eyes. Captain Eyre darted back and forth between the cannon, the tassel of his Scots bonnet bobbing, yelling orders that were inaudible over the thunder of the guns. The bonnet was a souvenir of his part in the slaughter at Culloden; Eyre maintained it brought him luck.

The noise level was beyond anything Billy Johnson had ever heard or imagined. He could not tell which gun had just fired except by watching the flash from the muzzle. Soon the muzzles glowed red against the blackened barrels.

To the astonishment of Johnson and his provincials, the little phalanx of French regulars marched straight up the road. Their boldness was unnerving, on top of the reports from survivors of the massacre at what would soon be known as the Bloody Scout, and the sight of maimed and mutilated men. One had stumbled in trying to hold his intestines inside his gut with his hands. Matt Ferrall, Hendrick Forked Paths and other friends were not among those who had come in. The time for an accounting would come later.

Eyre's cannon opened up on the French at a withering close range. The lethal hail drove lanes and allies through Dieskau's ranks—and reminded men whose courage had been faltering that French regulars were not unbeatable. Johnson had deployed some of the provincials and the Mohawks who had returned from the scout on both sides of the road. Dieskau's force was caught in a murderous crossfire. But his grenadiers did not give up easily. They charged the breastworks.

Johnson saw several of them, scaling the paltry ramparts of the camp, bent on silencing the cannon. Men wrestled and lunged at close quarters. Then the provincials fell back, and it seemed the French were over the obstacle. They surged forward with a roar—to be blown apart by another blast of cannister.

Billy was hoarse from yelling orders. Rogers brought his punch bowl, and he scooped out half a lemon and sucked it.

He noticed that French, Indian and Canadian snipers had established a shooting platform behind a huge wind-blown tree on a rise to his left, within easy range of the defenders.

He saw Snowbird, moving between the trees, and pointed to the snipers on the crest.

One of the Canadians focused on the big white man in the scarlet coat with gold lace and took a special bullet out of his pouch. A number of the Canadians had learned the trick of notching a lead musket ball and inserting a little strip of leather, soaked in a solution of copper and yellow arsenic. It much improved the odds of sinking an enemy.

Billy fell to his knees as a splinter of fire drove deep into his thigh.

"The general's hit!" Wraxall shouted. "Get him to cover!"

Rogers and Daniel and Wraxall were all pushing and pulling at him.

"It is of no consequence," Billy said, despite the blood fountaining from a place in his leg uncomfortably close to the groin. "Just get me something to staunch the bleeding."

They half-dragged, half-carried him inside his tent.

Wraxall wanted to send for Surgeon Williams, but Billy said, "Let the sawbones stay at their post until we have seen this through." The hospital tent had been shot up, balls whistling in the faces of the surgeons, along with bark splinters and woodchips, while they tried to dress twenty wounds an hour.

Rogers cleaned Billy's wound with raw alcohol and bandaged it with fresh linen.

Johnson was not visible to his troops for perhaps half an hour. When the French assault broke, the best of Dieskau's regulars retreated backward, step by step, choosing to meet death with level eyes rather than a bullet in the back.

2.

Landrième took aim at a Yorker who was showing off on the gimcrack breastworks of Johnson's camp. The fool was balanced on top of a clumsy wagon, brandishing a sword and waving his cocked hat. Landrième's mouth tightened with satisfaction as he saw his target topple from his perch.

The defenders' cannon spat fire and smoke.

Landrième threw himself face down on the earth. It trembled under him. When he raised up, he found Baron Dieskau's adjutant jerking like a hooked fish. A clump of shrapnel had torn a gaping hole in his face and throat. Inside it, the roots of his tongue quivered like a sea anemone in the dark swell of his blood.

The Baron had propped himself against a pine. Landrième did not notice the fresh blood seeping through the Marshal's scarlet breeches until one of the enemy snipers, weaving between the trees, nailed him with a second shot. The Baron gave a little cough and slid down the trunk of the tree into a squatting position.

"There's one of the English that knows how to shoot."

Head down, musket balls whizzing around him, Landrième zigzagged over to the commander-in-chief. "You must keep down. The devils have spotted your uniform."

"I am obliged to you for your counsel, Commandant. I will have no difficulty in following it. I think the opposition has deprived me of the power of locomotion."

"I'll get help."

The remnants of the companies of Languedoc and La Reine were beating an orderly retreat, but they were now an aching distance away. A shadow flitted between the trees, and Landrieve realized that some of Johnson's men—Indian scalpers or white skirmishers—had slipped between their position and the regulars.

To his relief, he saw a party of Canadians, loping through the scrub not twenty yards away, on the other side of the clearing.

He ran toward them. *"Arrête!"* he yelled at a stocky bushloper, who had a pair of powder horns jouncing at his hips. "Baron Dieskau is wounded! You must assist me!"

The bushloper swore and quickened his stride. Landrieve flung himself across the path of the fleeing men. One of them lashed out at him with the butt of his flintlock. Landrieve wheeled away, but the blow jounced off his kidneys and dropped him like a rag doll.

He struggled to raise his head. He let it fall again, into a soft, scratchy bed of pine needles, because it was too late to save his commander. Johnson's provincials had smelled blood. Men in homespun or buckskin, some with improvised bayonets jammed into the mouths of their firelocks, were moving all across the clearing.

□

Zeke Hodges, a Northfield man who had survived the morning ambush, looked at the wounded officer without affection. Zeke was jumpy, more than vengeful. The Frog in the fancy coat—dark blue, with plenty of gold lace and a big gold star on the left breast, over the heart—had juice in him yet. You could see that from the eyes. They were pale and dangerous. Carnivore eyes. And there was no fear in them at all.

That gold lace would fetch a pretty price, Zeke calculated. The Indians were crazy for the stuff. And the boots! They were worth an honest man's wages for a month. Zeke wondered what the Frenchman had in his pockets. Maybe enough to make up for the months away from home, the lost crops, the bloody flux and the damned mosquitoes. Even though he'd have to share with his mates, and the Captain would want a cut if he got a whiff of the prize.

"Don't move!" Zeke's finger shivered against the trigger of his firelock.

The Frog was jabbering. Zeke couldn't make out a word of it. The wounded officer groaned, and tugged at the pommel of his sword.

"Don't do it!" Zeke yelled. He hadn't quite made up his mind to shoot when the gun went off in his hands. He could not miss at that range.

The ball entered the crease of Baron Dieskau's groin and came out the other side.

By the time one of Johnson's officers came running, to prevent outright slaughter, the Marshal had lost his boots and his sash, and was dripping from a nasty rent in his bladder.

His sword was retrieved and carried with the Baron to Billy's tent, for the formal act of surrender.

□

"You will have my bed," Billy informed the Baron, after accepting his sword.

"I had hoped to occupy it under different circumstances."

They conversed, for the most part, in French. When Billy's command of the language failed, or there was need to translate for others, Dieskau lapsed into his native German, with Daniel Claus as interpreter.

The Baron permitted Johnson's servants, under the eye of Surgeon Williams, to roll him from the makeshift litter onto the camp bed.

There was a festive atmosphere in Billy's tent. A table was laid with smoked and boiled venison, oysters and savories of every kind. The punch bowl was constantly replenished. Dieskau, under the threat of the surgeon's knife, announced he would prefer to drink cognac. A bottle of excellent Nantes brandy was instantly produced.

Only then did Dieskau realize that his host was also

wounded and waiting for the doctor's attention. Johnson had a bloody rag wound tight around his upper thigh, and trailed that leg like a dead thing when he crossed the tent, leaning on his stick, to sit between Dieskau and the punch bowl.

"I fear I impose on your hospitality," the Baron said between clenched teeth, not looking at the ravaged flesh that was exposed as the surgeon slashed at his breeches and peeled them away.

"A Marshal of France takes precedence, I think," Billy smiled. "Besides, it is a dubious favor, to be permitted to go first, under the steel." Both commanders knew that more soldiers died in the hospital tents than on the field of battle. "Though Surgeon Williams is of the best. You know that his brother was in command of the force you took by ambuscade."

"My condolences, sir."

"Can you tell me how he died?" the doctor asked.

"It was a clean death, I am told. A bullet through the head. I did not see the incident myself. I had hoped to end the affair otherwise. We were both deceived——" He broke off, clenching his teeth against the red-hot pain that seared through his groin as the surgeon probed the channel of the last ball that had been shot into him. One of Johnson's servants offered him a twist of tobacco to bite on, but he waved it away, preferring another swallow of brandy.

There was scuffling outside the tent, urgent voices speaking in English and Mohawk, then the scream of the scalp-yell.

Snowbird burst through Johnson's aides, swinging his killing club. Fresh scalps hung from his belt. He was accompanied by six or seven Mohawks, including Silverheels and Hendrick's brother Abraham.

Daniel Claus blocked the Mohawks' path. "Forest Killer will hold council with his brothers of the Flint People tomorrow. Tonight, we must all rest and regather our strength."

Snowbird threw his arms around Daniel's chest and moved him aside as effortlessly as a cornhusk doll.

Billy raised his silver goblet. "Mr. Rogers, bring cups for our Mohawk guests. They have fought well today. Their names will be remembered."

Snowbird dashed the cup that was offered to him to the ground. He brandished his warclub at Baron Dieskau. "Give him to us. He has murdered our brothers."

"This is the warchief of all the Axe-Makers," Johnson said evenly in Mohawk, using the old native word for the French. "He is now my captive, and he must stay with me."

"The burned bones are calling for him." The words touched Billy with their cold fire. The *ohskenrari* are the souls that remain close to the bones of the dead, hungry for blood vengeance and the smoke of real tobacco.

"We have lost many brothers." Now Abraham spoke. "They must be replaced."

"They *shall* be replaced," Billy said. "This is my promise to you. But the French warchief will remain with me. This is my promise to him. Any man who touches him touches me."

He took Abraham's hand. "I will stand with you to condole the death of our brother Forked Paths and requicken his name."

3.

Johnson assigned Daniel Claus and fifty men to guard Baron Dieskau from Indian revenge. They shuffled the French marshal from tent to tent, to keep his whereabouts secret from the Mohawks.

The stand of Johnson's provincials at the lake had stopped the French advance and netted their commander-in-chief. Meanwhile, the roar of the guns had inspired Colonel Blanchard, at the fortified trading post at the Carry, to send a small column of reinforcements north. They seized the French baggage train, left under light guard. And on the banks of a stony creek, near the place of the morning ambush, these provincials found Canadians and Mission Indians still engaged in stripping and scalping the dead and wounded. After a short, bloody exchange, they put the looters to flight.

Landrième and the weary survivors of Dieskau's expedition limped through the swamps to the boats they had concealed at South Bay and paddled back to Ticonderoga and The Octagon.

The feasting in Johnson's camp was sobered by the screams of the wounded, the loss of friends, and utter exhaustion.

In the heat of the morning, the dead were already starting to bloat and stink. Seth Pomeroy was sent out with four hundred men who were still fit to bury the corpses before they bred infection. Returning to the place of ambush, they found Ephraim Williams' body where his men had concealed it, and buried him under a white pine. He was one of the few white men slain in the Bloody Scout who had kept his hair.

Billy Johnson counted his losses. One hundred twenty provincials killed, eighty wounded, sixty-two missing. Thirty-two Indians of the Six Nations dead, including Hendrick, and a dozen more likely to perish from their wounds. Four officers of the Indian Department, including Matt Ferrall, killed in the morning ambush.

The French tally was similar. A hundred killed, one-hundred twenty-nine wounded, twenty-four captured.

But the fruits of the fighting on September 8, 1755 were not to be judged by the body count. Johnson's forces had been left in possession of the field. They had captured the French commander-in-chief, whom Billy soon sent away on a horse litter to the care of his bereaved sister, Catherine Ferrall, at the house on Market Street in Albany. The symbolism of Baron Dieskau's capture was as powerful as that of Braddock's death. "We have raised laurels to overshadow our cypresses," Billy wrote.

But in the camp on the lake, there was little fervor for pursuing the campaign into French territory, least of all among the warriors of the Six Nations. They started drifting home with their plunder. Three days after the battle, the Oneida chief came to Billy and announced formally that it was time for all the Indians who had responded to his call to return to their villages.

"You made such a powerful fire under your war kettle that it has boiled over and destroyed our enemies."

Johnson pleaded that while The Octagon stood intact, their mission was uncompleted.

The Mohawks counseled him in private that it was not possible to prevent the warriors of the Six Nations from going home.

"The husking time is coming," Snowbird told Billy. "We must go back to our Castles to cheer our people and help those who have lost a father or brother to mourn. But if you stay here in the woods, I will return to you with some of our warriors before the moon of popping trees."

□

The first blast of cold from Canada sent the redtail hawks flying south. Their wide, rounded wings lifted on the winds that skirled off the ridges of the Endless Mountains.

In the last, hazy days of Indian summer, the hawks struck out across the valleys and caught the bubbles of hot air formed by sunlight on barrens and rockslides.

Riding the thermals, the birds were carried aloft effortlessly, without needing to beat their wings.

They master the air by adapting to it, Johnson reflected, admiring their ease and grace. *I have need of their skills.*

He had ordered the construction of a fort with earthen ramparts, to be called Fort William Henry, that would secure their position at the southern gate of the water-road to Canada. The work was fitful. The men sickened with the changeable weather and the poor hygiene in the camp, while their officers intrigued and scouts snapped at each other in the woods.

Phineas Lyman seeded the story in friendly newspapers, as well as letters to Governor Shirley, that he was the hero of the Battle of Lake George.

Though Shirley had abandoned his own expedition against Niagara, he fired off letters to Johnson complaining because his New Englanders—homesick for their farms and families—refused to carry the war to the black ramparts of The Octagon.

The weather soon put an end to any thought of prolonging the season of campaign. The first snowblasts raked the camp in the second week of October, the men shivered under flimsy blankets, and Billy was stricken with violent headaches that mined his resistance to the poison in his blood.

Though Snowbird kept his promise, returning with a few Mohawk warriors, Johnson was obliged to rely on a handful of white woodsmen who were willing to brave the approaches to The Octagon for his scouts. The most active was an aggressive New Hampshire man called Robert Rogers.

□

"Look ye!" The burly ranger yelled, returning from a foray toward Ticonderoga. "Here is a Frog that will croak no more! And here is another!"

Robert Rogers brandished his trophies. The scalps were imperfectly stripped, the blood caked hard on scraps of skin and flesh. There was a quantity of chestnut hair hanging off one of them. The other had only a few black, wiry strands.

"Got them at Ticondero-gee," the ranger announced. "Smelled the whoresons before I saw them. One of them was taking a crap."

One of the officers gave the ranger his flask, with a low belly-laugh.

Snowbird did not approach, though Rogers beckoned to him, with a flourish of the rum-flask. "Come see how my barbering compares with you Mohawk hair-dressers."

Snowbird moved off, without speaking, toward the edge of the camp. He could never fathom why white men did things without knowing what they meant. The scalp was the *onononra,* the spirit head. It was more than a scrap of skin and hair. It contained part of the soul-energy of the fallen enemy, which could be used to empower its new owner. It could turn minds upside down, or heal them. It could cause lovesickness. It could bring knowledge of the future, success on the warpath, even the gift of fertility.

But this captive soul-power was dangerous. It could get away from its captor and turn against him. Before a scalp could be used as a charm, it had to be ritually prepared. And its taker had to sit apart from the others for a time, like a woman in her moon-flux, until he was cleansed and purified. So he would not spread ghost-sickness among his own people.

The white men who were toasting the ranger with bristles on his face did not know these things.

"What is the matter with the Mohawk?" Rogers asked, puzzled by an Indian who walked away from a drinking party.

"Johnson's hairdressers fear you are cutting into their market," the New Hampshire captain chuckled. "Like doctors hate midwives, or veesy-vicey. Restraint of trade is the interest of any professional association. Besides—" he indicated the pennant fluttering over Johnson's tent "—that's one place a man can always get a drink."

They watched Snowbird strolling through the pickets to the general's tent.

Snowbird said to Billy, "It is time to go home."

4.

Cat dreamed of Billy during the long months of the Lake George campaign. She saw his face over hers, the joy of his smile, the wonder of eyes that feasted only on her. A sensual warmth coursed through her body, flowing and undulating. She exulted in the knowledge that distance and anger—the storms, the other women—had not broken the bonds of the heart.

She woke to the chill of absence, the mildew of doubt. She watched the pale light of morning and listened to fall rain pounding yellow leaves. The rain became snow, blown in drifts that rose above the windowsills. She sobbed in the cheerless dawn, to let out the worry and need, to ease the soul. She wept until the girls came tumbling into her bed, snuggling up against her under the covers, telling her to hush, as if she were the child.

"Daddy's coming home," Polly told her. "He's coming soon."

"Your father is on the King's service." Cat started to explain again why a soldier is not his own master.

"The Mohawks came home two months ago," Nancy objected.

"That is a different matter. Your father is held to a different standard."

It was cold in the bedroom. Cat wound her robe tight around her waist and stirred the ashes in the grate with a poker, hunting live embers.

A dog barked outside. It was joined by others. Their voices rose in a yowling frenzy, through which Cat and the girls heard the rough cry of one of the redcoat guards.

"It's Daddy!" Polly squealed. She led them in a wild rush to the stairs and down to the hall, where John's toy battlements had risen higher overnight. In the half-light, Cat knocked over a bastion.

She found John at the front door, wrapped in a blanket coat, talking to strangers who had come up the King's Road from Albany. They had no news of Billy, not even a letter. They were after winter stores.

Cat dressed and accompanied them to the truck house, where Robert Adams appeared ten minutes later, rubbing sand from his eyes. She was hard with the messengers, though they had a note in Colonel Schuyler's hand. She wanted to see coin, not provincial money or promissory notes. She would part with only a few skipples of peas, a few barrels of flour. It would be a hard season for all in the Valley. There were starving times ahead, since men had been torn from their harvests to chase Frenchmen. Billy had said that this time the fighting would not stop until one side or the other owned the northern frontier.

The Albany men were scandalized by her insistence on hard money. When they made a bid to haggle, thinking to best a woman easily, Cat halved the quantities she was willing to sell.

"You have a trader's soul," Adams told her, not without admiration, when the Albany men were gone.

"I grew up hungry."

"Aye," Adams nodded. His people in Dublin were no strangers to hunger. "And isn't that an education?"

"I don't know about wars." Cat studied the white oak on the knoll above the slaves' quarters. "Women aren't supposed to know, I expect. But I have lived with wars all my life, Mr. Adams. Wars made by men for sport or a line on a map or a prince's pride. I know what war means to *us*. To women like *me*. We do not go about clanging metal. We survive."

She pointed at the oak. The last leaves, turned leathery, still clung to its branches, though the other hardwoods were bare. "Women are like that tree. We hang on."

□

The embers still glowed red, the smells of dinner—venison and pumpkin pie—still hung in the air, when Cat heard muffled hoofbeats on the road. They were followed by knocking at the door, faint but insistent. She was out of the bed in an instant, fumbling to relight the candle. She carried it before her to the stairs, driving back the shadows.

She was annoyed to see that John had claimed even more of the stairhall for his fort, in defiance of her instructions to pack it away. What had possessed the boy to block the busiest path of traffic in the house? She stepped warily around the model palisades and drew the bolt from the door.

She gasped at the caped figures, black silhouettes against the snow, who pressed forward into the hall. The biggest of the men half-lunged, half-fell, into her arms. A cry rose to her lips. He covered her mouth with his right hand, and threw his left around her waist.

"It's all right, my darling."

As her body relaxed, his hand slid away from her mouth. She sobbed his name. And tasted blood on her lip, where his hand had rested.

"Oh, my God! Billy, what have they done to you?"

Johnson laughed gamely and tried to twirl her before him into the cherrywood parlor. But he banged up against the unexpected obstacle of John's fort, and his legs buckled under him.

Daniel Claus sprang after him and spared him the worst of the fall, buoying him up by the shoulders. Johnson's face was white with pain.

"Thank you, Daniel. I will just sit for a moment, in my old rocker. Cat, may we have a drop of brandy?"

When Cat brought the decanter, Billy's officers had removed their outer garb and sat or stood—resplendent in the King's scarlet or forest green—in front of a fire that had been brought to raging life. Instead of breeches, Billy was wearing loose trousers under his general's coat. They were stained with blood that appeared to have seeped through from the inside. Noticing her glance, he draped an arm carelessly over the blot.

He tossed back half a glass of brandy and pink spots reappeared in his cheeks.

Billy made light of the incident in the hall. "I find, gentleman, that my household has not been idle about our defenses while we were freezing our posteriors at the lake. I take it the fortification in the hall is John's work."

"I told him to take it down. The boy has his father's will."

"From what I could observe," Johnson rushed on, his spirits revived by the brandy, "John works with a damned sight more industry than our provincials. I would rather trust my safety to his fort than the one they are building at the lake."

The laughter was forced. All the men were tense and fatigued, and there was no real humor in Johnson's words. Just the effort to deny his pain. There was a physician there—Doctor Dease—who presently insisted on cleaning and re-dressing Billy's wound. He suggested that it would not be a sight for a lady. She might have been glad of this acknowledgment of her status in the house on another occasion; she had no ears for it now.

"I will stay. He is my charge."

She was shocked by the hole in Johnson's flesh, suppurating blood and pus.

"I fear the cold and damp at the lake have not sped the General's recovery," the physician whispered, when she fetched him hot water. "And the bullet must remain. We cannot dare to dig it out."

"Too close to where I live, my pretty." Billy said it with a sudden, barking laugh that did not mask the pain.

Cat stared with horror at the fat black leeches the doctor had brought in a glass jar. "Surely he has lost enough blood already."

The doctor said knowingly, over his little pebble-glasses, "We must relieve the pressure and allow the vapors to rise."

"He thinks the Frogs poisoned me, Cat," Johnson added. "We saw how some of the Canadians wrapped their balls with yellow arsenic. Though the Baron denied it to me on his word of honor."

"It would explain the condition of the wound," Doctor Dease observed.

"That, or the conditions of the camp," Cat said curtly. "I believe you men have little notion of how to tend one another."

Billy and the doctor looked at each other. "Doctor Dease only wishes to help me, my dear."

"He can start by putting those—*things*—away." Cat wrinkled her nose at the leeches. "And I would rather see you drink the Indian teas than brandy."

"God's thunder, but there is fire in your belly this morning!" Johnson winked at the physician. "Would you leave us to talk for a little, John? I will send for you presently."

She washed him and wrapped him and settled him back among feather pillows. He asked for the children, and she fetched them in, one by one. She noticed Nancy talking with Daniel Claus in the hall, hanging on the young German's every word. When Nancy caught her mother's eye, she reddened and looked at the floor. Fourteen years old, already a woman. Had her father noticed?

Billy had souvenirs for all the children. Denis Rahilly and faithful Jamie Rogers fetched them in. For Nancy, a fine piece of French lace, a cameo brooch with nymphs and shepherds. For Polly, a silver bird that sang when you turned a key. For John, a French fowling piece with silver side-plates.

John was eager for talk of battles and the sight of another trophy.

"Is it true you have the Baron's sword?"

"He gave it into my own hand, John."

"Can I see it?"

Out came the bright saber. Billy unsheathed it and allowed John to sweep the blade through the air, lopping off imagined limbs. Cat hated the sight of it. When would the fighting and cutting end?

John wanted to hear every detail of the battle. He brought in some of his lead soldiers, and Billy directed him as he lined them up to represent the rival formations. Billy's face darkened as he recalled the loss of friends and kinsmen.

Cat put up with this for a half hour, then said, "Your father must have rest."

"I'd rather have breakfast."

"Of course. What will you eat?"

"I think a soldier should have a beefsteak and a good mug of ale. That is for John. I will have the same, with a drop of brandy."

"God love us!" John Butler burst through the door. "I told the boys the damned Frogs could never nail a man who was already pickled!"

He rushed to give Billy a hug, followed by a press of neighbors and militiamen hungry for a sight of the victor of Lake George. Cat shooed the girls out to the kitchen with her. John was lost to her, for now.

When she re-entered the parlor, Billy was reliving the scene of Baron Dieskau's surrender.

"I think we gave him a run for his money. The Baron told me he never expected rude provincials to make a stand against the flower of the Sun King's army. They may not thank me for it at Albany or York, but I do believe we saved their hides. The Baron told me that if

he had won at the lake, he would have gone down to
Albany and set up his commissary-general at the fort.
Then he planned to sail down the river and make New
York his forward headquarters. He would have chopped
our colonies in two, and there would have been the devil
to pay."

They were all agape. They all wanted to finger the
Baron's sword. Billy said it must hang over the great
mantel in the cherrywood parlor, where all visitors
could see it.

It was well past noon and Billy was still holding court,
unrested, when Cat took Daniel Claus aside. She could
always speak to Daniel. They had a common language,
in more senses than the obvious one. And she had
watched how Daniel had risen in Billy's favor. Since he
had first walked into Fort Johnson five years before, at
the side of a man Johnson regarded as a dangerous rival,
Daniel had become very nearly the most trusted man in
the Indian Department. Billy valued him for proven
loyalty, as he valued all men who repaid his trust. He
commended him for his command of native languages
and his patience in the often tedious practice of Indian
diplomacy. But he prized Daniel also for qualities that
were not his own—soberness, dogged attention to detail,
the avoidance of passion. Though Cat was not sure
where Daniel would stand in General Johnson's esteem
if Billy noticed the blushes and giggles the serious young
man evoked from Nancy. Billy had not yet chosen to
observe that his eldest daughter was becoming a woman.
When he did, Cat suspected, it would take him any
amount of time to accept that any man was worthy of
one of his girls.

"Mr. Claus—" she softened the required formality by
taking his sleeve "—will you intercede with the General's visitors? He is fatigued, and you see how his
wound grieves him. Rest and quiet will do him more
good than Doctor Dease's remedies."

With Daniel's help, she managed to have Billy carried
into the blue room and secluded for an hour. Then the
Indians began to arrive. By nightfall, thirty of them were

encamped around the house. She bought time with rum and meats from the kitchen, but they could not be kept out for more than a few hours. Billy would not permit it. Soon he was smoking with the chiefs, propped up in bed under the smelly buffalo robe, passing the pipe-tomahawk hung with the wingfeathers of war-birds from hand to hand.

The toasts began, the glory days were recalled, and it was past three in the morning before the house was still and Cat had her man—if only he had ever been truly that!—to herself. She sat beside his bed, keeping the fire stoked up, watching the rise and fall of his chest as he breathed in a fitful sleep.

CHAPTER 33

HUMMINGBIRDS

1.

Johnson was hot and feverish, his lips chapped as if burned by the sun. His bedding was soaked through. Sweat streamed from his armpits and groin and pooled under the small of his back.

He threw off the bearskin and the heaped blankets and tried to ease his bruised body off the bed. A searing pain stabbed through his right side.

He lay back on the wet sheet. Even when he avoided movement, the pain pulsed through him. It was no longer localized. There was a leaden plate pressing down above his eyes. The poison streamed in his veins.

A chill draft blew through the open window. Strange. He did not recall having it opened.

A shadow crossed the thin moonlight.

"Who's there?"

Billy fumbled for the pistol he had kept primed and loaded on the night table since his return from Lake George. Snowbird had come to warn him that the French had put word out they would pay well for Johnson's head. The commandant at The Octagon had specified that he wanted the whole head, not just the scalp.

"Who's there?"

The shadow passed between Johnson and the pale white glow of the buffalo skull between the bookcases.

A trick of the moonlight, he told himself. A breeze ruffling the locust grove.

Then why did he feel a thrill of fear, pricking at his spine? Why did the shadow seem to have a life of its own? He watched it move into the recess where the masks hung. A clotting in the air, taking on deeper color and form. The purple-black gloss of feathers.

A huge black bird, shaking its wings.

Johnson fired the pistol.

The hoarse scream was almost human. Surely it was not inside its head. The thing banged about the room, then dove for the open window.

He groped after it. Again, he had the impression of a great black bird, flapping away across the hill. It flew awkwardly, one wing dragging low.

Johnson closed and latched the window.

He found flint and steel, and relit his candle.

There was nothing in the room now that did not belong there. Except a pair of long black feathers. One of them was wet to the touch. He inspected his fingertips in the light. The liquid was almost colorless.

Tricks of a native sorcerer. They all claimed the power to journey in their dreambodies, and shapeshift into the forms of animal familiars.

Is this what death looks like?

❑

It's late, long after midnight. I am riding on top of a high, covered wagon. The canvas flaps in the breeze.

Below me, in the clearing, hundreds of mourners are gathered, natives and whites. The women have draped themselves in black strouds. Many have smudged their faces with ashes. They seem very far from me, too far to hear me if I called.

The mourners are gathered for a wake, or a burial.

I want to see who has died.

The wagon lurches forward, the crowd parts. I can see

the body laid out in handsome clothes, on a bier. I cannot make out the face.

The wagon rolls on. I can no longer see the corpse.

Then I realize the body has been placed inside the wagon on which I am riding.

I know fear.

The wagon creaks as the horses gather speed. The coachman is hooded. I cannot see his features. I cry out, but he ignores me.

We are up on a high, stony hillside. It is an ancient burial ground.

The native women are wailing and keening. The mourners fan out across the field, moving forward like crows.

I move among them. I am carrying two calumets, puffing on one.

The night chant rises.

I look into the open grave.

I see naked flesh. Many women, bold and inviting, motion to me, shifting their haunches, pressing their breasts together. Their bodies are opulent, but very pale.

Their eyes have no pupils.

□

Cat sat on the edge of the bed, dabbing at Billy's face with a warm cloth, wiping away cold sweat and the yellow pus that oozed from the corner of his right eye.

He told her the dream.

"Shall I send for the doctor?"

"So he can bleed me again? I am too weak for that, Cat. Too weak and too damn tired. I feel something has been feeding on me, leaching the strength out of my blood, leaving only the pain and the French poison. Besides, I think it is too late for doctoring. I have seen my death."

"Don't say that!"

"What else is the dream but death?"

"You did not see the dead person's face."

"True. But the body was put in my wagon."

"Even if the death is yours, the dream does not tell you when."

"You reason prettily." He thought for a moment before asking, "Are you fearful of death?"

He took her hand between both of his. The gentleness —something she had been denied for so long—brought her to the edge of tears.

"I am not afraid to die," she answered him. "But I give thanks for every day I have on this earth. This life is a glory."

"You can say that, after—" He faltered, wondering. "After all you have endured?"

"This life is a glory," she repeated. "And a course in endurance. There is a reason for the tests we are made to take. The Lord knows it, if we do not."

"I envy you your certainty," he said without irony. He lay back against the goosefeather pillows, folding his hands across his chest. So pale and still, his chest barely rising with his breath.

"Please don't lie like that."

"Like what?" He opened his eyes. "Like a dead man?"

"Come back to us, Billy."

"Death is no stranger to me. But I am not in love with him. I have loved life, as you do, but without caution. So I am not sure where death will choose to carry me. The priests give me only the sign of the cross and the sign of crossed fingers. The Indians claim personal knowledge of the other side, because they go there often in their dreams. Hendrick told me something of that."

"Don't talk so much. You must rest."

"It's a good story. I have thought of it often, since I lost Hendrick. There was a chief at one of the blackrobe missions, a hearty pagan who had made the white dog sacrifice and eaten the hearts of his enemies. On his deathbed, the old reprobate agreed to be baptized. No doubt he wished to ensure against a lodging in the hell of the blackrobes. But when the priest came to administer the last rites, the old tosspot had changed his mind. He said he had walked the Path of Strawberries in a dream and found his ancestors living merrily in the old style, around the lodge of She Who Fell from the Sky. He took up his medicine bundle and his pipe, had his face painted red, and died facing the sun."

He chuckled. "But I fear a white man will go some-where else when he dies."

He coughed and fell silent, wearied by the effort of saying so much.

"Can you eat something? Shall I bring tea? Brandy?"

"No brandy. It does not serve me as it used to. Just sit with me, Cat. It is a comfort to me to have company. I have lost so many good friends. Hendrick. And Matt. And all the others. My heart is lonely after them."

She sat by him, clasping his hand. His breathing steadied. Soon he was snoring lightly, as he always did when he lay on his back.

When she was sure he was asleep, she whispered, "I love you."

A salmon-pink dawn was breaking. The light was glaring, through the leafless trees. As Cat pulled the drapes against it, a huge black bird flapped low over the house, cawing. A vast flock of crows rose behind it. She hated the harsh noise of the black birds, so early in the day. She wanted to throw open the window and clap her hands to drive them away, but feared she would wake Billy.

"Can you imagine how much I love you?" Her voice was hardly more than breath as she smoothed his hair, which flowed over the pillowcase. One of Billy's prides. More gray than auburn now, no need of powder. Billy had joked that his gray hair increased his influence among the Indians, who imagined that it signified wisdom.

"I would die this life for you," she whispered. *I forgive you everything. The other women. The terror of your rage.* "If only you will come back to me."

A patter of footsteps in the hall, a scuffle at the doorknob, and Polly skipped into the room, giggling.

"Sshhhh! Daddy's sleeping."

"He has to come see the day! It's so beautiful."

"Daddy's sick."

"I'm going to kiss it better," she promised with a stage hush.

She tiptoed up to the bed and kissed her father's cheek.

Billy opened his eyes and smiled.

"See!" Polly was triumphant. "Come see the morning, Daddy. It's lovely."

"Later, sweetpea."

"And then you have to read me *three* stories."

"Later. I promise."

Polly ran out, a bouncing ball of energy.

"Do you remember what she used to say? 'I see all the parts of the day.' The child has the poet in her."

"And the theater. You make good babies, Billy."

He looked at her, in the grainy light filtered through the scarlet drapes, as if scales had just fallen from his eyes.

"You are a good woman, Cat. I do not know why you have stayed with the likes of me."

He stretched out his hands to her, and she came to him.

"Lie with me, my darling."

"Billy—" Her heart was a bird inside a window, beating wings. He was already folding back the covers, hitching his nightshirt up to his waist.

"I'm not strong, I fear. You will be raising the dead."

She shed her garments slowly, deliberately, despite the chill in the room, which made her nipples taut and sent gooseflesh ripples down her arms and thighs.

You will see me.

When she slipped between the sheets, he kissed her clumsily. She was hungry for his embraces, but he rolled on to her heavily, before she was ready, with a groan that transferred his pain to her own vitals. He made a few awkward thrusts, then groaned again as she felt his desire ebbing. He dwindled inside her. He withdrew without climaxing and flopped on his back, white-faced, his lips sealed tight against the howl he refused to release.

She tried to kiss his mouth, but he turned his head from her.

"You see what I am reduced to," he said bitterly. "They have taken the last thing I could be sure of. Where is the tiger now?"

His body quivered, but he hid the tears.

What is it, in a man, that makes him ashamed to cry, slow to gentle?

Why is his cock the pivot of his pride and fear?

She kissed his chest. "Let me hold you."

He rebuffed her, ashamed and more than a little afraid. The shadow of the night was on him.

He spoke to her as his housekeeper, the woman who fetched and carried and minded his children and did not answer back.

She did not hear him. "Let me love you. There is nothing love cannot make right."

Her hair brushed his temples, a moving curtain. Her breasts swayed against his face.

"You are with the dead," he moaned as her caresses moved lower.

Then he fell silent, his eyelids closed. The only sounds in the room were of their breathing. Her touch was as soft as butterfly wings, as fast as hummingbirds.

She felt a silk flower opening deep inside her. She drew him into it, and he stiffened to fill her completely.

She rocked gently over him. Eyes closed, his arms by his sides, he lay completely inert except for the part she was requickening. She followed the waves and eddies that rolled through her. A pressure was steadily building inside her. It hovered at the edge of pain, deliciously pleasurable. The waves rose higher and stronger. She rolled with them, through peaks and troughs. The pressure was unbearable. She screamed for pure joy when it burst inside her inner core. She would have screamed again, but pressed a hand over her mouth so she would not alarm the children.

At that moment, something glorious took flight within her. A falcon loosed from the jesses.

Billy's buttocks rose and fell with his spasms.

Then he released the howl.

"My God!" She pressed her lips to his glistening cheeks. "I've hurt you."

"No, my heart." He kissed her hands, turning them palm upward, as he had once done in Dublin. "You have performed a miracle. You have raised Lazarus."

He laughed, no longer mindful of the savage pain in his thigh and his gut.

"Where were you?" she asked when they lay quiet together, limbs entwined. She did not say, *Were you with me?*

"I was welcomed by larks."

Her heart smiled, because he had remembered. If only for a moment, they had been together as they were when the world was new.

"You are a gift of life to life. Has any man spoken to you like that?"

"Only one," she remembered. *And he is enough.*

His eyes went to a place where she could not follow. He said, "There is something else."

"Don't say it. Let the moment be enough."

"I wish to say it. I saw the eyes of the Goddess."

"I do not understand."

"It is a thing I had all but forgotten. A thing from my childhood, from the Ireland of my ancestors." He told her about the passage tomb at Newgrange, and what he had seen in the burial chamber, entered for a dare. And what Rahilly and Maire, the wise woman, had told him. That the spiral eyes of the Goddess held the patterns of life and death and rebirth.

"What do they look like?"

"Like the birth of a universe."

Cat was awed. And frightened. After long drought, this was too much for her heart to hold, too much to trust. But whatever came, she would have this morning.

2.

Snowbird was out hunting at dawn in the woods behind the Upper Castle. His dog found the blood on the snow.

It puzzled Snowbird that there were no tracks.

The size of the drops suggested a big animal, or one

that was gouting blood from an artery and would not travel far.

The blood was fresh. Any child could have followed the trail.

He climbed through the hemlocks, the dog bounding ahead.

Then the dog stopped, hackles raised, teeth bared.

Snowbird unslung his firelock. He knew this place. The bald spots on the trees around the clearing were not the work of deer browsing in the starving time. The trunks and lower limbs were charred. People from the village had come here to burn Swimming Voices' cabin when she fled to Canada. The place was forbidden ground.

Yet there was a lean-to against the rocks. A simple hide, scrambled together from fallen limbs and sheets of bark, invisible to anyone who did not know how to look.

The last speck of blood was a few paces from this shelter. There were arrowhead marks in the snow. A large bird must have landed here, carrying its prey. Why so close to human habitation?

The dog ran forward, then whined as if it had been whipped across the nose.

Snowbird took cover behind a tree, watching the hide.

Nothing.

Except the tang of fresh blood.

Snowbird crept to the lean-to. The man sprawled on his back inside was naked, except for his mask of black paint. He had been shot at close range. There were powder burns around the ragged hole under his shoulder. The bullet must have punctured his lungs.

Snowbird kept his distance.

He did not want to mess with whatever might be hovering around the remains of a soultaker.

Remembering what had been done before, he set fire to some dry sticks and threw them onto the roof of the shelter where Le Corbeau had returned to die. The hemlock boughs drank the fire and sent up a pillar of black smoke.

3.

While new armies drilled for battle, and scouts and raiders snapped at each other along the forest borders of the colonies, Johnson was called to face enemies whose weapon was the stiletto rather than the firelock.

Governor Shirley, exercising his authority as interim commander-in-chief, sent Billy a new commission, deleting the vital clause by which General Braddock had appointed Johnson to the "sole management" of Indian affairs. When Billy protested, Shirley hinted that he was fully prepared to replace him with a more pliable Indian agent.

Billy saw Lydius' hand in this.

Daniel Claus had brought him a deed to Susquehanna land, issued by Lydius and his partners. Lydius was printing these deeds like paper money, and selling them to anyone with hard currency. Each deed that he sold was another blow to the trust of the Mohawk and the Six Nations in the English alliance.

Johnson dragged himself from his sickbed and sledded downriver, exhausting one dogteam after another, to confront Shirley in the city of New York. Word of Billy's coming spread fast, and he was given a hero's welcome on New Year's eve. The skies were bright with fireworks, and the streets whirled with festive crowds, brandishing torches and candles.

Billy threw himself into the spirit of the celebration with such gusto that he could not face his morning appointment with Shirley, even after fortifying himself with beer and brandy at breakfast, and put off their meeting until supper.

Shirley was cool and collected, playing the distant patrician.

He sniffed at Johnson's accomplishments at Lake George, observing that the colonies were more vulnerable than before, since Billy had left the French in possession of their fortress at Crown Point.

"I do not know if what you say be true," Billy said

carefully. "I *do* know that I lost some of my dearest friends, native and white, in an engagement in which we licked the French commander-in-chief, the conqueror of more professional adversaries than we could field. What else do we have to show for the first year of this war? General Braddock killed and scalped. Your own expedition miscarried."

Shirley tucked his chin into his stock.

"I fully believe—" Johnson pursued "—that but for our actions at Lake George, Albany would be the commissariat general of the French, and New York city would be Baron Dieskau's forward headquarters."

"You may save your speeches for the rabble and the public prints," Shirley said icily. "It is plain to me that we do not speak a common language and cannot work together. Your partisans are reckless, sir. It has come to my attention that they even presume to use my wife against me."

"I have never impugned a man for his taste in women," Billy defended himself. He was aware that the fact that Shirley's wife was French had caused gossip— especially among a certain type of sectarian New Englander—but he had had no part in spreading it.

"I rule our forces, until His Majesty is pleased to replace me," Shirley went on. "And *you* serve at my pleasure. On my terms. Is that quite clear?"

"I hold a Royal commission, sir. I believe it is as good as your own. It names me sole manager of Indian affairs. If you mean to appoint others to the charge of our Indian relations who have earned the distrust of the Six Nations and may undermine our covenant with them, I am bound by prudence as well as honor to oppose you."

"You had best consider your remarks carefully, General Johnson. I make allowance for the fact that you were drinking half the night."

There are men who are more reliable in their cups than others sober.

Johnson withheld this reply, falling back—very belatedly—on Indian circumspection. He agreed to consider Governor Shirley's proposals.

He left Fort George with the certainty that only one of them would survive this fight.

The huzzahs of the crowd that was waiting for him raised his spirits only a little.

Thanks to Lydius—once his ally against the Albany Ring—he had earned a more formidable enemy in Shirley than he had ever had to confront in the likes of Livingston Huyck. He could imagine the barbed missives Governor Shirley was already shooting back to London, to the Lords of Trade and his wife's noble kinsmen.

To have been cast down at the end of the last war—in the wake of useless slaughter and indecision and skulking treachery—had been hard to suffer. But it was a thousand times worse to be cast down now, at the start of a new war, in the wake of victory.

Shirley is less ready to forgive victory than failure in others, because it reflects worse on him.

4.

In the moon of minwinter, Johnson waited on word from London. The fate of the Valley, the Mohawks—of the war itself—hung upon men who had never seen America.

If they pull me down, I will stand by my people. Billy had made this promise to himself and his neighbors. *I am a warchief of the Mohawk, and the Firekeeper of the Six Nations. If King George disowns me, at Shirley's behest, I will stand in native colors. I will not abandon those who have entrusted their lives and fortunes to me to the likes of Lydius and Livingston Huyck.*

But that evening, he had bolted his door against the Indians.

He sat with Cat and his white children and Denis Rahilly in the cherrywood parlor, with a fire in the hearth.

Chapman's Homer had arrived with the latest consignment of books and magazines from the Adams Brothers in London. He read from it now, pacing between the window and the door. The waves of verse rolled over each other, in Billy's carrying baritone.

It was a story of gods and heroes who lived on strangely intimate terms. Zeus wept from the skies when his son and favorite, Sarpedon, was felled, and had the body magically transported back to the hero's native Lycia for burial. When King Priam walked among the ranks of the strong-greaved Achaeans, the hand of a god was over him, making him invisible to his enemies.

John Johnson, eleven years old and springing up like crabgrass, could not contain himself at the account of Sarpedon's death.

"Is it true?"

"What would that mean, I wonder?"

The boy frowned. "It is a straight question. Did the gods really appear on the fields of Troy? Is it *true?*"

"I suppose it all depends on what one is open to seeing," Johnson smiled. "What do you say, Denis?"

Rahilly stroked the handle of his pewter tankard. "All of it happens in a time when there is no time. That is what the bards would say. It might be it is truer than true."

"You see," Billy carried on, "Mr. Rahilly is a soulmate of the Mohawk. They never ask, *Is it true?* Like Homer's heroes, they go to battle in the company of their spirits. They see things our regulars do not see. Nor our plowboys neither."

"Have *you* seen them, father?" Polly interjected. She was sitting curled up on a cushion on the polished boards beside her father.

"Well, now. I have seen all the parts of the day. That is what you used to tell me, when you were small. I can see all the parts of the day. To speak poetry, now that is truly magic."

Cat could hardly hold her tears back, not because of the talk of dying heroes but because of the perfection—in her eyes—of the scene. It was a simple family gathering: the father reading aloud from a loved book, the children stretched or curled like purring cats, the mother busying herself with her needlework as she watched and listened.

It was nearly three months since the moon-flux had come on her.

This brought her a fiercer joy, though she sensed that this delivery would be hard. The thought of it brought fearful memories of the black blood gushing from the anguished mare in the barn.

She crushed the mocking bluejays of doubt.

She gave thanks for this hour, in this place.

□

When Cat had put the children to bed, Johnson opened another of the new publications from London.

"Listen to this, Denis. It seems they have heard of us in England."

He read aloud the following passage:

Colonel William Johnson lives the life of a Turkish pasha with his complaisant harem of dusky ladies, among the alligators and waving palms of the Mohawk Valley of America. He displays, in all his activities, the unaffected ease of natural liberty. He is opposed to any curtailment of the strongest passion that rules the human heart.

There is scarce a house in any of the tribes about him from which he has not taken a temporary mate, and added a child of his own to the number.

He dwells in a place surrounded by scores of pleasant cottages, each inhabited by a concubine. He has one for each day of the year. Yet the ladies never suffer from jealousy, so equally does Colonel Johnson dispense his favors among them. Each morning of the week, including the sabbath, he makes his rounds in strict rotation, keeping his mistresses faithful by the ardour with which he returns their embraces.

Johnson threw down the magazine with a hoarse laugh.

"I am pleased to note that this report is not wholly fiction!" His face darkened when he added, "But I wonder whether whose cause this notoriety in the bowels of Fleet Street will serve."

Billy brightened again when Rahilly proposed a song.

He picked out the tune on his well-traveled fiddle. Soon Billy was booming the chorus. "I'd like to give a lake of beer to God."

They were disturbed by a violent hammering at the front door.

"Not tonight!" Johnson groaned. He called to Rogers, "If it is Indians, I am not at home! A man must have room to breathe."

"It is an express from Albany," Rogers reported back. He gave Johnson an oilskin pouch.

Rahilly rose to leave.

"No, Denis. You may as well wait to see if you must seek a new patron. For I believe London must listen more attentively to a Royal Governor than to a squaw man who lives among—what did they say?—the *alligators* of the Mohawk."

Johnson unwrapped the papers from London. Together with the letters from the Lords of Trade was a long scroll, inked on sheepskin, made official by a huge red wax seal with the Royal arms.

Billy's hands shook. He turned pale, then flushed to the roots of his hair.

Rahilly watched him with rising concern. A deep rumble rose from Johnson's belly that changed to a barking laugh, but carried the menace of something else.

"Will you listen to what they have done to me, Denis. His Majesty is pleased to name me a baron-knight of his Kingdom."

But there was no mention of the battle of Lake George, or of the Six Nations, or even of America. The fustian prose of the patent of nobility declared that the honor of a baronetcy was conferred on William Johnson as one of those gentlemen who

generously and freely gave and furnished to Ayd and Supply large enough to Maintain and Support

Thirty Men of our foot companies in Our kingdom
of Ireland to continue for three years for the
Defence of Our said kingdom and for the security
of the plantation of our province of Ulster.

The arms Sir William Johnson, Bt., was to bear were the
arms of Ulster, with the Bloody Hand.

"They have translated me into a damned gallowglass!
Into one of our oppressors!"

Rahilly waited for Billy's temper to cool, before
observing that whoever had drawn the patent had simply
borrowed old language. The honor was real, and the
power that went with it was even more real. The letters
accompanying the patent expressed the King's satisfaction with Johnson's accomplishments at Lake George
and announced that Billy would receive a cash present of £5,000. Most important, the letters confirmed
Billy's commission as Sole Superintendent of Indians.

"You have won, Billy," Rahilly pointed out. "Your
friends and enemies alike will not be troubled by the
wording of a scroll you will display only at your pleasure.
You have bested a Royal Governor. The Six Nations will
rejoice. And I rejoice for our countrymen, for what you
have accomplished for all of us."

"You are a good heart, Denis."

He rolled up the patent of baronetcy. It was the start
of a dynasty. His eldest son would inherit his title, and
so on down the line. Only one man before him, in the
history of America—Pepperrell, who had made war at
Louisbourg with Peter Warren—had ever received a title
of nobility from the English Crown. It was not a moment
to be coy about the wording of the gift.

We crown our own heads. Who had said that? It was
the strange, powerful African—a man of mysteries, if
ever Billy had seen one—who had befriended Cat and
watched over her.

"I will be Sir William," Johnson said briskly. "But I
will bear my own arms, and my supporters will bear my
own crest, not a hand-me-down from the users of
Ireland."

5.

Island Woman walked with Cat in the walled garden in spring sunlight. Now and then the matriarch stooped to pull up a weed. But when Cat, following suit, took hold of a mullein stalk, Island Woman tapped her wrist.

"Ononkhwa. That one is medicine. You let that one grow where it wants."

Island Woman's hand closed around Cat's.

It was strange to Cat to be strolling like this, on a patch of ground she had claimed for her own and walled off from the forest, with a native woman she had once feared and despised—a woman whose eldest daughter had attacked her in body and soul.

Yet she felt safe and relaxed with Island Woman's hand on her own. It seemed to her now that she was gliding, more than walking. She became aware of another presence in the garden. Not the young girl Island Woman called Sparrow, who walked ahead of them, communing with her own thoughts.

Cat sensed a presence behind her, at her left shoulder.

She turned. For an instant, she saw a beautiful young man. His face was glowing. She saw him only from the corner of her eye. When she looked at him directly, he was gone.

She felt dizzy.

Island Woman's grip tightened. "You saw him?"

"A trick of the light." Cat faltered. "You saw him too?"

Island Woman led her to the stone bench beside the wall and made her sit with her head in the shade. "Listen to me. I know you are carrying a child."

Cat was frightened now. "But I have told no one. Not even my—husband." *There.* She had said it. Billy *was* her husband, by the customs of the natives if not in the eyes of the church or the law. She had earned the right to call him that, this winter past.

"This child is not meant to live," Island Woman said curtly. "It will grow in your body like a stone. It is one born to die."

"How can you say such things?" Cat moved away from Island Woman, revolted. "Is it not my child I saw now, in the garden? That beautiful, shining youth?"

"It is your death you saw. You are already half in love with it. The child will kill you if you let it grow."

"Don't say those things!" Cat stood up, her chest heaving.

The old woman's granddaughter looked at her oddly, tilting her head to one side, then walked out the gate.

"I can stop the child coming," Island Woman said. "There is time. There is a root I will gather for you, in the dark of the moon. It will cause you very little pain."

"No!"

"This is one born to die," the matriarch repeated.

"It is a child of love." With the words, Cat's face, contorted by grief and fear, became smooth and serene. She saw, with new eyes, the beauty of the day. She heard the laughter of the creek, bubbling down to the green-brown river.

She floated out to where Sparrow was sitting in the shade of the locust grove. She turned a weightless pirouette, and laughed at how her skirts flew out, at the Mohawk girl's doelike, wondering eyes. Where did this happiness come from?

There was a stir among the locust trees. The motion of many wings, making a hum like a swarm of bees, but lighter, without menace.

"Look!" she pointed. *"Look!"*

"Raonraon," Sparrow said respectfully. The hummingbird was a magical creature, a companion of souls.

A whole flock of rubythroats had taken flight from the branches. Forty, fifty, maybe more. They were too quick and too many to count. The sun sparkled on their jewelled feathers.

Cat clapped her hands with pure delight, like a child.

The hummingbirds were all about her now. One hovered in midair in front of her eyes, no bigger than her thumb, no farther away. His companions made a canopy over her head and shoulders.

A man's rich baritone carried from the steps of the house.

"Cat! Come quickly! There is news from London!"

The birds sped away in a shimmering cloud.

"I'm coming," she called back to Johnson. But she could not hear her own voice. It was like waking inside a dream. "I'm coming!" she tried again. She was about to add, "Sir William." The name by which the world they shared would now know him. Baron-knight, King's Superintendent of Indians. A great man with a great name, a man on whom myths would settle.

"Cat!"

"Coming, Billy!"

She looked at the Mohawk women. She took Island Woman's hands. "Thank you. I know you mean kindly. But I must walk my own path."

The matriarch ran her hands up Cat's arms and squeezed her above the elbows. "I have taken you by the hand. Now I take you by the upper arm, which is closer to the heart. We were enemies, but now we are sisters. *Sonkwehonwe.* Now you are of the Real People."

Cat examined the deep, wise eyes in the seared, striated face. "I don't know what to say."

"That is good. Most white people talk for the sake of talking, when they have nothing to say. You are more like us. We don't talk so much because we always try to give you our best words. Sparrow is going to come check on you."

Cat felt a twinge of concern, noticing how the Mohawk girl was ripening into a splendid young woman. How long would it be before Billy noticed too?

"I have to go now. *Ona,*" she practiced the Mohawk good-bye.

"Onen'ki'wahi," Island Woman corrected her. "That's it for now. I'll see you again."

Walking back to the landing with Sparrow, Island Woman said, "I guess it will be soon. You see those hummingbirds? The hummingbird always knows."

CHAPTER 34
THE REAL WORLD

"Forest Killer's woman is young," Sparrow said. "Must she die now?"

"She has chosen her death. She chose it before she came into this lifetime. In part of herself, she remembers this. She is not going before her time.

"Never forget that death is no defeat. Death is the friend who never leaves you.

"A woman of power is always ready to die."

A chill passed through Sparrow, though she knew the words and lived by them. She took her grandmother's wrist. She felt the bones move under her fingertips, light and brittle as a bird's.

She closed her eyes and saw an ugly thing, a thing of waving tendrils, colored in muddy purples and yellows. It looked like something from the bottom of the sea. She willed it gone, and saw black blood flowing. She willed it to stop, as they had stopped the blood of Johnson's little mare, when it was hemorrhaging. She felt the light energy ripple through her, through their joined fields. The blood kept on gushing.

"Stop," Island Woman pulled her arm away. "My

time is coming too. The body gets used up. Then we should be ready to lay it down, as the snake sheds his skin. I'm looking forward to the other side."

Tears glistened in Sparrow's eyes.

"You'll never walk alone," Island Woman assured her. "Trust your guides. Follow your dreaming. Never confuse the Shadow World with the Real World. You know there is a place where you will always find me, in dreaming.

"Come on." She patted the earth floor beside her. "We're going there now. Relax. Breathe with your belly. See it. Smell it. Make it real."

On the river bank below the village, Sparrow saw boys setting traps for muskrats, baited with apples and ears of corn. Downriver, there was a buzz of activity around Forest Killer's docks and gristmill.

Then she shot forward, speeding down the tunnel that opened into the heart of the limestone hills. For a time, she traveled in her own light. Then the glow of flowstone welcomed her into the cave where Island Woman had initiated her into the ways of power.

Where was Island Woman?

She caught a flash of blue, the vivid blue of the talking stone her grandmother always wore.

"Now find me!" Sparrow sensed, more than heard, Island Woman's mocking laughter.

She plunged into one of the passages and ran into a blind wall. She tried other turnings, focusing on the blue stone. One of them brought her back to the place from which she had started. Another took her out among the rattlesnakes in the high grass of the hill.

She found a tiny chink among loose rocks, hardly big enough for a butterfly. She flashed through it like a bullet of light.

She was drawn deeper and deeper into the body of the Mother. She felt the pulse of the river far above her head, beyond a massive canopy of rock and clay. She realized she was now in a tunnel that connected the caves in the Noses, on either side of the Mohawk River. It would be a useful thing to remember, if she ever needed to escape from an enemy, or cross the water unnoticed. She wondered why no one had ever told her of this passage. Perhaps it existed only in the Real World, not in the Shadow World. Perhaps it was taboo.

Another flash of blue.

Island Woman giggled and kicked up dust in her face, blurring her vision while she slipped away in another direction. Sparrow laughed too, beginning to enjoy the game of hide-and-seek.

When the dust cleared, she found she had got down into an enormous underground chamber. The rock floor fell away sharply at one end, where a spout of water plummeted from far above into a well of darkness far below. On the edge of the precipice, a pointer stone stood up like a forefinger. From one angle, it looked like a man with the skin of an animal over his head. From another, it looked like Kenreks, the Panther, reared on his hind legs, ready to strike.

Sparrow began to explore the cavern. Many lesser caves and passages opened off it, through rounded archways. There were shapes obscurely defined on the walls. Scenes of a great hunt, led by a winged figure.

She recognized other images.

A great circle with a cross inside it, with the colors of the four directions and the above and below.

The figures of animal guardians, gathered in a ring around the prone figure of a man. His penis was erect. He was journeying.

"This way," Island Woman hissed.

Sparrow saw the white shadow of a hand, palm outward, outlined by charcoal and vermilion.

Island Woman showed herself. "You must learn this."

Looking where her grandmother looked, Sparrow saw a series of images that intrigued and puzzled her. A tiny figure, neither male nor female, moved on a path with four houses. These were depicted as long rectangles, like the lodges of the Longhouse People. At the entrance of each house, ferocious animals and leering human-like figures waited for the journeyer.

"This is the way of the woman of power," Island

Woman explained. "These are the spirits she must confront and overcome at each initiation." She pointed at spirit bears and rearing snakes. "Each time you do this, the spirits you fear become your allies. You have learned this many times, in dreaming."

"But what is this?" Sparrow pointed to the last house, which seemed to be besieged by hostile spirits of the dead.

"Each test is harder. At the fourth initiation, the woman of power finds the whole house is filled with hostile spirits. She must enter it fearlessly. She must speak with them and overcome them. Only then can you become what you are meant to be."

She indicated the transformation in the little figure once she had passed through the most terrifying of the ordeals. The power centers inside her body—depicted as shells—were now all alive and connected. The lines extending from her eyes and ears denoted the ability to hear and see from a great distance. The wavy lines that extended from her fingers represented the power to heal through the second body, the dream double.

"The path goes on," Sparrow traced the line across the stone with her finger. It no longer ran straight. It zigged and zagged. It forked often, and each time, the wider, easier path proved to be a false trail.

"For one who dreams true, the way is never straight," Island Woman said. "The dreamer's path is the path of the lightning.

"Power brings many temptations." She indicated the false turnings. "The greater the power, the greater the risk of succumbing to these temptations. Your aunt did not learn this. That is why she cannot be at peace. Until she makes whole what is broken. This will require more than one lifetime."

At the end of the shaman's path, Sparrow saw, was a space enclosed by a swelling oval. It reminded her of the womb.

"I know this," she said. "We come back because we have lessons to learn. Or because we are needed."

"The great souls do not have to come back. They come

back because they choose. The true interpreters among us are those who have chosen to come back in the body to serve others. Those who return to us out of love."

"Is this your map, Aksotha?"

"I did not draw it," Island Woman smiled. "But I have walked it for many winters."

"Who made the map?"

Island Woman's eyes widened. The lids closed suddenly, then opened, without dimming the intensity of her focus. She looked like an owl. She was staring at the stone wall of the cave.

She said, "Can't you see him?"

Sparrow looked where she looked. The stone became blurry. Then a mist of particles, not a substantial thing at all. The space between the particles was as vast, proportionately, as the space between the stars.

Sparrow looked through it.

She saw an old man, his skin the color of white ash, his hair draped over his narrow body like a carpet of snow-covered leaves. He was hunched over a rock pool, but his eyes were closed. Sparrow could see the eyeballs moving under the skin.

He was naked except for a skin draped over his shoulders. The skin of a black panther.

"You see him," Island Woman said.

"His eyes are closed but he is watching us."

"He is dreaming my life," Island Woman said. "When he opens his eyes, I will die this life."

The chill passed through Sparrow again. She willed herself to be brave, to be what her grandmother had trained her to be.

"Who is he?"

"He is my teacher. Now he will be your teacher also. You have met him in other forms. Now he shows himself to you as he shows himself to me, because you are chosen. He is The Interpreter. He is Sakowennakarahtats, The One Who Sets Up the Words." She chuckled. "When I was a kid, we called him Longhair. He used to scare us plenty, bobbing up in the woods after dark like a wild spirit."

"Why is he here?"

"This is his place of power. Now it is yours too."

"Has he always been your guide?"

"He came to me when I was a child, when I was passing over. When many of our people were dying from the white death. He made me come back. He showed me what I had to do, to help our people live."

"Will he speak to me?"

"He speaks to you now. *Look.*"

Sparrow drifted closer, no longer conscious of space or the forms she was inhabiting. She looked into the reflecting pool. She saw the panther in it. And—to her deeper amazement—the white man, Forest Killer. The panther was marking his chest with the circle-cross.

"He is marked for you," Island Woman said.

Revolted, Sparrow fled from the cave. She thrashed through a storm of white noise and came back to her body with a jolt.

She lay on her back, her breath coming fast and shallow, the sweat pooling under her backbone.

"You back?" Island Woman asked matter-of-factly.

"It's not true."

"What's not true?"

"What I saw. The thing about—Forest Killer. It's *just a dream,*" she switched into Sunday school English.

"See, now you're talking *his* language. Real People don't say things like that. It's not in our speech. It's not in our nature. I thought your aunt would be the one. But she got off the trail. Took a hard fall. If you use Power for the wrong things, it turns around and bites you in the ass." Island Woman chuckled.

"It doesn't have to come true," Sparrow insisted. "It has not happened. You showed me that what has not happened can be changed."

Island Woman hawked and spat out a thin rivulet of tobacco juice. She said, "In the Real World, there is only *now.*"

CHAPTER 35
MOTHER OF THE FALLS

1.

Cat's child came early, but it strangled in the cord, and the mother did not survive the delivery, for all the efforts of doctors and midwives. The Mohawks came to the stone house in black strouds to condole Johnson. Billy fell into a black dog fit. When he could tear himself from his business—from the constant demands of trade, war and native counciling—he shut himself up in his room. He sent a message to Jacob Glen, at Schenectady, to find him a large gold wedding band of the best quality. He ordered this to be placed in the grave of the mother of his white children.

What I could not give you in life, I give you now.

In the high summer, Billy rode up the Valley, at the head of a column of Mohawks, and sailed west across the lake of the Oneida to the green valley of Onondaga, the ancient place of the Firekeepers, to take part in an ancient ceremony of condolence.

Red Head, the chief sachem of the Onondaga—the man who had brought the Fire that Never Dies to Fort Johnson—had also gone the long trail in that season. At the death of one of the great chiefs of the Confederacy, it was the custom of the Six Nations to come together in the rituals of mourning and requickening. Runners carried tally sticks, each adorned with three looped strings of purple wampum, through all the villages of the Longhouse to call their delegates to Onondaga.

Island Woman was too frail for the journey, and Bright Meadow stayed at the Upper Castle to tend to her needs. But Sparrow traveled west with her uncle Snowbird—who was soon to be raised up as one of the Men of Good Minds—and observed Forest Killer from a discreet distance.

She saw him march to the edge of the clearing at the head of the sachems. joining in the intricate songs of condolence, reciting the whole roll call of the chiefs of the Confederacy, their laws and their customs.

She watched Forest Killer support Abraham, Hendrick's brother—the chief speaker for the mourner—as he chanted inside the longhouse:

> We cover the grave with moss.
> We make the sky clear for you.
> We cause the sun to shine on you.
> We open your eyes and ears and your throat
> for there is something that has been choking you.
> We make the fire new and bright.

She heard Johnson join in the cry of the souls—*Haii! Haiii!*—at the end of the feast.

The white man moved with the solemnity and patience of a native chief. Though this was a political occasion—a chance to assert British influence against the French agents who were more active than ever at Onondaga, with the war never far from anyone's mind—Sparrow saw that Hendrick had been right.

Forest Killer belongs to us, as well as to his own people.

He spoke to her politely, at the Onondaga castle and along the trail, but did not attempt to take liberties. He told her respectfully that he hoped she would not object if he spoke to her mother on their return.

Sparrow said nothing to encourage or discourage him. When she returned to the Upper Castle, Johnson paid a visit to Island Woman's lodge, dressed in scarlet, with a gold gorget at his throat bearing his personal cypher. He brought handsome gifts. He said he was lonely and needed a woman of character to be at his side and help interpret for her people.

Island Woman took no direct part in these discussions.

But she grunted her approval when Bright Meadow said, "My daughter must decide this in her own heart."

Woman decides.

2.

Sparrow knew what she had to do.

She must take Forest Killer to a place of Power, a place no newcomer had defiled, where stones and trees that spoke too slowly for white men to hear would help her to cleanse him of the past and open his heart fully to the spirit guides of the Real People.

In the limestone gorge, green water rushed cold and fast down a giant's staircase to make thunder over the falls. This place had always been part of her dreaming.

She made Johnson fast for a day and night before she brought him here, stripped of his badges of rank, his white man's finery.

They scooped out a firepit before dawn, among the rocks. They gathered sticks of hickory and oak and she showed him how they must be laid, forming the pattern of the four quarters. She sent him out to cut poles to support the hides she had carried on her back for the tent.

When the fire glowed red, she chose rounded stones from the creekbed, to heat in the flames.

When fire lived in the stones, she showed Forest Killer how to arrange them inside the sweat lodge with the aid of cleft sticks. She sprinkled water on the firestones until the tent was filled with hissing steam.

Then Sparrow unwound her belt and let her deerskin kilt fall. She shrugged off her mantle, and loosed the ties of her leggings.

Billy came to help her. His graying hair, freed from its queue, lapped over his broad shoulders. His chest was deep and wide as a drum. There were soft folds about his belly, above the scar of the Frenchman's bullet, but she would make him lose them.

His hands praised her hair, the tight skin over her cheekbones.

She stepped away from him. Creek water splashed about her ankles.

She removed her last garments, and took off her necklace of feathers and yellow beads.

Grinning widely, Johnson rolled down his hose and dropped his breeches.

"Not yet," she cautioned him. "You do not belong to me yet."

She drew him into the tent, through the entry flap on the sunrise side.

She told him, "This lodge contains the universe."

It was dark as midnight inside, and Johnson thought it was hotter than hades. Sweat gushed from every pore of his body. As Sparrow made him shuffle around in a tight circle, moving counterclockwise, all physical desire was sucked out of him—except the desire to catch his next breath. That intolerable heat squeezed the air from his lungs. The back of his throat seemed to fill with hot embers.

When Sparrow allowed him to squat, with the fire-stones between their naked bodies, the heat grew more fierce. Billy could see nothing distinctly.

I might be buried in the bowels of a volcano.

He groaned and started worming his way toward the entry flap.

"Satien," Sparrow growled at him. "Sit. You must become one with the fire. You must *be* the fire."

Billy sank back on his heels, wheezing.

I am an old stump, eaten by flame.

He saw a great white oak, girdled and burned, and felt the scream of the heartwood.

Stranger things reached into his mind. The tent seemed to fill with presences, things with horns and hooves that shuffled around in a circle-dance. He was startled by the hiss of a panther, the rumbling cough of a she-bear, the snuffle of a wolf or wild dog.

He tried to shake himself free from these delusions.

I have fed the native superstitions. I will not fall prey to them.

Twin points of fire came spinning from that searing dark. They pressed close to his eyes, whirling inward and outward in a double spiral. Billy shut his eyes against them, but the lights blazed through his closed lids.

He saw himself as a gawky boy with grazed knees, crawling on his belly along the rubble-strewn passage into an ancient tomb.

He saw the rude carvings hacked by dreamers of his own tribe on the walls of the burial chamber.

He saw death and rebirth in the Eyes of the Goddess.

And found them again in this ordeal by fire and water.

Sparrow called him out to the sunrise and the mercy of running water.

Billy lay in the cool belly of the creek while she sang the words that greet the sun.

His senses began to revive. The firm hillocks of the young woman's body were inviting. In the dawn sun, her skin was smoky red, caressed by gleaming fingers of creek water.

He plunged gaily toward her, diving to catch her thighs between his forearms. At the instant he was sure he had her, she slipped from his grasp.

He saw the flash of copper as she skimmed down the winding course of the creek, toward the falls.

He raced her along the stony bank. As his feet slipped and slithered among loose pebbles, he saw how the white walls of the gorge, streaked red by iron ore, swelled into columns or withdrew into shadowed galleries, like monuments of a lost civilization. In petroglyphs above the falls, he glimpsed faces of birds and animals.

He focused on his quarry. He was overtaking Sparrow.

She was nearing the lip of the falls. She would have to turn back or swim ashore.

In a heartbeat, I will have her.

Sparrow spread her arms wide as a hawk riding a thermal. She trilled a high, flutelike birdsong, rapidly changing pitch. Then she sailed forward, into the cloud of butterflies that danced on the spray of the falls.

Billy splashed out to the place of her dive, weaving to keep his balance in the treacherous current.

Looking down, he saw that the water below the falls was green as weeping beeches. Standing over it was a great boulder sculpted by weather and retreating ice into a squatting female form, belly distended, legs parted.

Billy felt a thrill of recognition.

More delusions from the sweat-lodge, he told himself. Yet what touched him was older. It plucked him back into a man-made cave in Ireland.

He shook off these thoughts, intent on finding where Sparrow was hiding. There was no trace of her down below.

A new fear touched him. She might have injured herself in the fall.

She might have stunned herself on a rock. She might be lying insensate in the shallows, her lungs filling with water.

He leaped over the falls, feet first.

He plunged far, far down, until his feet snagged in something that tightened about his ankles and calves. When he swam for the surface, it dragged him back down. He told himself that he was struggling with creepers or driftwood. But he felt an animate determination in this force that gripped like strong wrists and would not let go.

He fought his way up from the greenblack depths into yellow water, and sucked in a great draught of air under the pendulous belly of the Mother of the Falls.

"I suppose you thought you had me, you fat cow." He laughed at his fancies.

"Kats kanaka," Sparrow called. "Come here."

He saw the shower of the waterfall parted like a curtain. A slim coppery hand beckoning. He swam toward it. For all his strength, the hard spray repelled him. He beat his body against it uselessly until his wits returned.

Then he worked his way round a circling ledge into the narrow air-chamber where Sparrow bobbed between the cascade and the dripping wall behind. It was almost as hard to breathe in here as in the sweat-lodge, but Billy felt wonderful.

He tried to sing, above the thunder of water and the pounding of his heart.

"Mine is the sunlight,
Mine is the mor-ning—"
Sparrow laughed with him.

He found he could speak with her without moving his lips.

"You are different," she told him.

"It is true. I am not the same."

"Do you like it here?"

"It is like being reborn."

She led him up onto the mossy ledge above the Mother of the Falls.

"This place is special to you," Johnson observed.

"I was born over there." She pointed to a high meadow, bright with flowers. "This is a place where Power has rested. A place that is true."

She looked at him steadily. "Your woman loved you. She gave everything to you."

"Yes."

"You will not abandon her children."

"Never. I think they will come to love you too."

"I will not live with you as your German woman did. Or the others. I will not serve you. I will not share you with other women."

Billy laughed. "I will never be tamed. I will not deceive you about that. But I believe you could be many women to a man like me."

He ran his finger from the root of her throat down to her navel. When he reached lower, she slipped away from him. She prowled the difficult slopes above the great rock on all fours. She made him pursue her and mount her as Kenreks, the mountain lion, takes his prey.

Later, she lolled on the head of the Mother of the Falls while he stood on a narrow shelf below, making teasing feints until she slid down and rode him, knees clenched about his thighs, against the hard spray of the falls.

When they began to gather up their clothes, she watched him slip a thong around his neck. She saw the design of a cross within a circle.

She touched the silver pendant.

"What is this?"

"A keepsake. Something from the old country. They call it a Celtic cross."

It was the circle-cross the dream teacher had showed her in the cave.

You were right, Grandmother. It is the dream.

NAMES OF THE
IROQUOIS

Without the names—said the ancient Greek naturalist Isidorus—the meaning of things is lost.

Names have deep importance for the Iroquois, as for all indigenous peoples. It is believed that when the name of a departed person is ritually conferred on a child, an aspect of that person's soul returns to the living. In addition to a birthname, an individual may have several other names. An extraordinary event in a person's life may lead her to take a new name. A dream-name, usually held secret, may be the gift of a guide encountered in a vision quest. A man raised up to the circle of the *rotiyaner* will adopt a traditional chiefly title, just as an English lord assumes the title of his predecessor. As in all societies, people also acquire nicknames that can be very revealing about character and social relationships. For example, one of the Mohawk nicknames for Billy Johnson's most celebrated native consort means literally "they are ganging up on her."

I studied Iroquoian languages, especially Mohawk, in the effort to provide fresh translations of personal names and other expressions, and to get inside the metaphors of the oratory and the dreaming of Woodland Indians.

In writing, Mohawk words look quite impenetrable to most readers. So I have used English versions of most Mohawk names. The full literal translation of many Mohawk names is often hauntingly beautiful. For example, Kawennotie, the name of Island Woman's elder daughter, means "The Words

Are Going Along the Water." But such expressions are un-wieldy, and become tedious with repetition. So I have come up with shortened versions—in this case, Swimming Voices.

For readers interested in language, ethnology and metaphor —and all those who are simply curious about where this stuff comes from!—I have included a short English–Mohawk glos-sary that gives the Mohawk names of the principal characters.

Many of the Iroquois in this book are mentioned in the minutes of Indian councils, in baptismal registers, in Johnson's papers and other documentary sources. Those who are un-known to recorded history are no less "real." Some are remembered and celebrated in the oral traditions handed down by the grandmothers. Some have stepped straight from my dreaming. This is of course highly appropriate, since Island Woman's people are, quintessentially, a people of dreams. "Their cabins are all filled with dreamers," reported Father Fremin, an early blackrobe missionary among the Seneca.

It is the misfortune of many nations of Eastern Indians that they have become known by the names applied to them by their enemies. These are often quite insulting. "Iroquois," for example, is a French garble of an Algonkian word meaning "rattlesnake." The word "Mohawk"—also Algonkian in origin —means "man-eater," i.e., cannibal.

In Mohawk, the first inhabitants of North America are called the *onkwehonwe,* the Real People. The Six Nations of the Confederacy are the *rotinonhsonni,* the People of the Long-house. And the Mohawk themselves are the *kaniekehaka,* the People of the Flint.

The Mohawk language is primarily an oral tradition, and it escapes easy transliteration. However, there is an agreed mod-ern orthography, based on phonetic principles, and I have generally followed this in rendering most native expressions— with the omission of diacritical marks, for which I trust linguists and Mohawk teachers will not scalp me.

There are some exceptions. I've used the older, more familar version of well-known place names (Caughnawaga, rather than Kahnawake) and some other widely recognized terms (like Johnson's Mohawk name). And then there is the shaman-talk.

Shamans—the *raretshents,* the *arendiwanen*—speak a lan-guage of their own, in all traditions. The vocabulary of shamanic practices among the Iroquois, as among other indigenous peoples, is both very ancient and highly individualized. Some expressions (when they can be tracked etymologically) derive from related peoples, especially the Huron, among whom Island Woman was born. I have preserved very ancient words—like *ononhouroia,* the "overturning of minds" in the Feast of Dreams—in the form in which they appear in the earliest missionary accounts, or as they sounded to me when they were used by *dreamers* who helped me explore what Island Woman and her teacher call the Real World.

I am indebted to the authors of three invaluable references, the two most recent by native Mohawk speakers: *A Thousand Words of Mohawk* by Gunther Michelson (National Museum of Man, Ottawa, 1973); *Mohawk: A Teaching Grammar* by Nora Deering and Helga Harries Delisle (Thunderbird Press, Ecowi, Quebec, 1976) and *Mohawk Language Dictionary* by David R. Maracle (Native Language Center, University of Western Ontario, 1985).

ENGLISH–MOHAWK GUIDE TO NAMES

Axe-Makers On'seron:ni. The French.

Bright Meadow *Kahentiwatiseren.* "The meadow is full of sunlight." Island Woman's younger daughter. Sparrow's mother.

Corn Carrier *Kanenhstenhawi.* "She carries the corn." Turtle Clan matron. Hendrick's wife.

Flint People *Kanienkehaka.* The Mohawk nation. Keepers of the Eastern Door of the Confederacy.

Forest Killer *Warragiyaguey.* Literally, "they cut down the forest for him." Mohawk name of Sir William Johnson (1715–1774).

Forked Paths *Tehayanoken.* Literally, "he whose paths fork (or merge)." One of the first Mohawks to adopt a European first name (Hendrick) and later a surname (Peters). Born a Mahican near Westfield, Massachusetts, c. 1680. Adopted into the Mohawk Wolf Clan by 1690. Baptized by Godfrey Dellius, a Dutch Reformed minister whom he later accused of land fraud. Hendrick first lived in the

Schoharie valley, later moved to the Upper Castle at Canajoharie. He made two visits to London (1710 and 1740) as a guest of the Crown. He led his first warparty before 1697 and last led Mohawks into battle on September 8, 1755, when he was killed leading the "Bloody Scout" in the Lake George campaign.

Fruitpicker *Wahiakwas.* Means literally, "she picks the first fruits." Mother of the Wolf Clan.

Hendrick see Forked Paths.

Interpreter *Sakowennakarahtats.*

Island Woman *Tewatokwas.* Literally, "she comes from the water." Adopted Huron captive and woman of Power who succeeds Fruitpicker as Wolf clanmother.

Lake of Two Mountains The Sulpician mission at Oka, on the Ottawa river. Modern Mohawk name: *Kahnesatake.*

Le Corbeau French name for a Nipissing/Caughnawaga sorcerer.

Longhouse People *Rotinonhsonni.* The Six Nations of the Confederacy; from east to west: Mohawk, Oneida, Onondaga, Cayuga, Tuscarora, Seneca.

Lower Castle Fortified Mohawk village of Tiononteroken ("Where Two Rivers Join") near Fort Hunter, N.Y.

Man from the Sunrise *Tiorhenshere.* Englishman.

Peacemaker Mystical figure believed to have inspired the Great Law of the Confederacy, with Hiawentha (Longfellow's Hiawatha) as his interpreter. His Mohawk name is not said aloud outside a ritual setting.

Real People *Onkwehonwe.* The first peoples of America.

Red Head *Kaghswoughtioony* (in the Indian Records). Onondaga sachem, condoled by Johnson in a ceremony on June 19, 1756.

Red Squirrel *Arosen.* Nickname of Caughnawaga warchief.

Snowbird *Ohwisto'k.* Island Woman's son. Warrior of the Wolf Clan.

Sorcerers *Skekwanenhronon.* Mohawk name for the Nipissing, an Algonkin-speaking people renowned for their magical practices.

Sparrow *Tsitha'.* Island Woman's granddaughter and the heir to her gifts of healing and dreaming. Longhouse name: Konwatsitsaienni ("They Are Sending Her Flowers.")

Swimming Voices *Kawennotie.* Literally, "Words are going along the water." Island Woman's elder daughter. One of Johnson's Mohawk lovers, accused of sorcery.

Sunrise People *Tiorhensaka.* The English.

Sun Walker *Karakhtatie.* Also called Nickus. Wolf Clan sachem. Held captive by the French for three years after a battle near Mohawk in June 1747.

Upper Castle Fortifies Mohawk village of Canajoharie.

White Owl *Kwanonneharaken.* Sparrow's father. Bear Clan warrior who becomes paramount warchief of the Mohawk nation. Killed in the battle on snowshoes in February, 1748.

The Word *Canassatego.* Onondaga sachem and Speaker for the Confederacy. Died in 1750, possibly by poison.

MOHAWK–ENGLISH GLOSSARY

ahsha:ra burden strap

aksotha grandmother

anonwara turtle

arendiwanen "she has soul energy"; woman of Power

ascwandics dream talisman (ancient; Huron origin)

ataenneras "she shoots arrows from afar"; witch

Ataensic She Who Fell from the Sky. First Woman, in the Creation story.

atenati elk

atsinahkon "she uses white energy"; exorcist

ihstenha mother

ka'nihstensera clanmother

kahsto:wa headdress

kakonsa False Face mask

kanienkehaka People of the Flint; Mohawk nation

kats kanaka "come here!"

kenreks mountain lion; panther

keriwahontha "I put the matter into the fire"; I see as a clairvoyant

khenoronhkwa "I want your soul"; I love you

kia:tat "I am in my mother's womb"; I am buried

kiheiatha "I die for a reason"

ohkiwe ritual for the dead; ghost dance

ohskenrari "burned bones"; earthbound ghost (ancient)

ohkwari bear

ohseron Midwinter festival

ohskenonton deer

okarita popcorn

okwaho wolf

ondinnonk "secret wish of the soul"; object of desire seen in dreams (Huron)

onen'ki'wahi "that's it for now"; good-bye

ononhkwa medicine

onkwehonwe "The Real People"; the first inhabitants of America

ononhouroia "overturning of heads"; the Feast of Dreams (ancient; Huron origin)

onononra "spirit head"; scalp

orenda soul energy; the Power that is in everything and beyond everything

otkon spirit

otsienha council fire

oyaron power animal; bird or animal whose form a shape-shifter assumes

raksotha Grandfather

raonraon hummingbird

rarenye's "he spreads himself"; charismatic person

ratetshents "one who dreams"; shaman.

Ratiwera's The Thunderers

rohskenhrakehte warchief.

Rotinonhsonni "People of the Longhouse"; the Six Nations of the Confederacy

royaner (plural: *rotiyaner*) "man of good mind." A traditional chief of the Confederacy, chosen by the clanmothers.

sahtenti "go away!"

Sakowennakarahtats "He sets up the words." Interpreter.

Shonnounkouretsi "He has very long hair" (ancient)

skaratons "tell a story"

snekira "drink!"

Sonkwaiathison "He created us." The Creator

Tsawiskaron The Dark Twin (ancient; exact meaning disputed)

tohsa   "don't!"
tsihei   "die!"
wakkwaho   "I belong to the Wolf Clan"
wahetken   shameful
wakskerewake   "I belong to the Bear Clan"
wakaterion tane   "I know this matter."

SOURCE NOTES

"Facts are the enemies of truth," says Don Quixote, and I am much in sympathy. However, my training as a historian dies hard. In writing my tales of the Eastern Frontier, I have adopted the following policy:

Where facts about historical events and the lives of characters known to history can be established from the documents, I have tried to be faithful to these sources. Where the facts are unknown or clouded, I have given myself license to drive a horse and carriage through the gaps. This has resulted in some interesting revisions of the conventional account of many well-known events, including the famous Albany Congress of 1754 and the Battle of Lake George.

Here are some notes on the principal sources—documentary and otherwise—for each chapter.

Abbreviations used:

BARCLAY "Register of Baptisms Marriages Communicants & Funerals begun by Henry Barclay at Fort Hunter." MS in New-York Historical Society

CLAUS Daniel Claus Papers, Public Archives of Canada, Ottawa

CP *The Letters and Papers of Cadwallader Colden.* 9 vols. New York: New-York Historical Society, 1917–35

DCB *Dictionary of Canadian Biography.* General editor: Francess G. Halpenny. Toronto: University of Toronto Press, 1966

DH   *Documentary History of the State of New York,* edited by Edmund B. O'Callaghan. 4 vols. Albany: Weed, Parsons 1849–51

DRIMMER   Frederick Drimmer (ed.), *Captured by the Indians: 15 Firsthand Accounts, 1750–1870.* New York: Dover, 1980

JP   *The Papers of Sir William Johnson,* edited by James Sullivan et al. 14 vols. Albany: University of the State of New York, 1921–65

JR   *The Jesuit Relations and Allied Documents: Travel and Explorations of the Jesuit Missionaries in New France,* ed. Reuben G. Thwaites. 73 vols. Cleveland: Burrows Bros., 1896–1901

LAFITAU   Father Joseph François Lafitau, *Customs of the American Indians Compared with the Customs of Primitive Times* (1724), ed. & trans. William N. Fenton and Elizabeth L. Moore. 2 vols. Toronto: Champlain Society, 1974

LYDIUS   John Henry Lydius Papers, Massachusetts Historical Society

NYCD   *Documents Relative to the Colonial History of New York,* ed. Edmund B. O'Callaghan. 15 vols. Albany: Weed, Parsons, 1853–87

NORTON   *The Journal of Major John Norton, 1816,* ed. Carl F. Klinck and James J. Talman. Toronto: Champlain Society, 1970

OGILVIE   Rev. John Ogilvie, "A Journal of Time Spent with the Mohawk with Some Occurrences." MS in New York State Archives

PAC   Public Archives of Canada

SPG   Society for the Propagation of the Gospel

WARREN   Peter Warren Papers and Accounts, New-York Historical Society

1. WOMEN OF POWER

Iroquois gynocracy: "They say the women court the men when they desire marriage," the Rev. William Andrews, an Anglican missionary, reported from Mohawk country on March 9, 1713, in a letter to the Society for the Propagation of the Gospel. (SPG Mss). Father Joseph François Lafitau, a remarkable early

Jesuit ethnographer, described Iroquoian society as "gyno-cracy," and compared it to that of ancient Lycia (Lafitau 1:285–287).

Jamie Sams' *The 13 Original Clan Mothers* (Harper, San Francisco, 1993) is a beautiful evocation of traditional reverence for women among Native Americans.

For my description of the clanmothers' wampum credentials, I am indebted to Ray Gonyea, an Onondaga friend and scholar who watched over the wampum belts of the Confederacy in the New York State Museum before they were returned to the Place of the Council Fire.

Daniel Claus testified to the influence of a celebrated Mohawk woman, Molly Brant: "One word from her is more taken notice of by the Five Nations than a thousand from any white man." (Claus to Governor Haldimand, August 30, 1779, in Haldimand Papers, PAC)

Hendrick and the Indian Kings: The best secondary source on the 1710 visit by the "four Indian kings" to the court of Queen Anne is Richmond P. Bond, *Queen Anne's American Kings* (Clarendon Press, Oxford, 1952). John G. Garratt, *The Four Indian Kings* (Public Archives of Canada, Ottawa, 1985) contains reproductions of the portrait of Hendrick to which Island Woman objected, as well as many other contemporary illustrations that are an invaluable guide to Mohawk dress at the time.

Dream practices: On shamanic dream practices among the Six Nations and the Hurons, see my essays "Blackrobes and Dreamers" in *Shaman's Drum* (Summer 1992) and "Missionaries and Magicians: the Jesuit Encounter with Native American Shamanism" in *Proceedings of the Dublin Seminar for New England Folklife* (Boston University, in press). Vivid early accounts of the *ononhouroia,* or "overturning of minds" include Father Claude Dablon's report from Onondaga in the winter of 1656 (JR 42:155–65); Lafitau's 1724 account (1:234–36); and *The Journal of Major John Norton 1816* ed. Carl F. Klinck and James J. Talman (Champlain Society, Toronto, 1970), 107–8).

The Midwinter Festival: Other details of the Midwinter Festival, including the ritual dressing of the Bighead heralds, may be compared with William N. Fenton, *The False Faces of the Iroquois* (University of Oklahoma Press, Norman, 1987) and Frank G. Speck, *Midwinter Rites of the Cayuga Longhouse* (University of Pennsylvania Press, Philadelphia, 1949).

2. TARA'S SHADOW

Popular beliefs in the healing properties of the well at Ardmulkin, County Meath, that the pregnant Anne Johnson insists on visiting are mentioned in Maire MacNeill's invaluable work *The Festival of Lughnasa* (Oxford University Press, Dublin, 1962), 25, 636.

William Johnson's birth and bloodstock—including the change of the family name from MacShane, and the kinship with the O'Neills—are traced in a genealogy prepared by his brother Peter Warren Johnson, in a successful bid to adopt the O'Neill coat of arms. This pedigree was recognized by the Dublin Office of Arms on February 24, 1774 (Msc. 14767)

When I visited Johnson's birthplace in the spring of 1987, Smithstown House was the home of a delightfully hospitable horse trainer, Mr. P. J. Beggan; the fieldstone house now has a coating of pebbleash stucco, but is otherwise little changed in external appearance from Billy's time.

3. WOLF CAPTIVE

Running the gauntlet: The treatment of Mohawk captives here corresponds closely with eighteenth century captive narratives, especially *An Account of the Remarkable Occurrences in the Life and Travels of Col. James Smith* (who was taken by the Caughnawagas in 1755); an excerpt appears in Drimmer 25–60.

Island Woman's wagon: Many Mohawk women showed an entrepreneurial streak and contributed to the fact that by the early eighteenth century—contrary to frontier stereotypes—native families in the Valley quite frequently lived in conditions of greater material comfort than the pioneer Europeans. I am indebted to David B. Guldenzopf for his splendid contribution to our understanding of the acculturation process in an unpublished Ph.D. dissertation, "The Colonial Transformation of Mohawk Iroquois Society" (State University of New York at Albany, 1986).

4. STRENGTH OF A UNICORN

Paul A. Wallace, *Conrad Weiser: Friend of Colonist and Mohawk* (University of Pennsylvania Press, Philadelphia, 1945) esp. chs. 1-4, provides an excellent and moving description of the plight of the Palatine Germans in the Rhineland and on the New York frontier.

5. BURDEN STRAPS

The ancient arts used to weave the burden strap, and its importance in the daily lives of Iroquois women, are well described in Lewis H. Morgan, *League of the Ho-De-No-Sau-Nee or Iroquois* (second edition, Dodd, Mead, New York 1901) 2:16-20.

6. A LAKE OF BEER FOR GOD

Rahilly's "hymn" is an old Gaelic song; the beautiful translation used here is the work of Irish poet Brendan Kennelly, and is published in its entirety in his book *Love of Ireland: Poems from the Irish* (Mercier Press, Cork and London, 1968).

The marble slab in the ruined church at Dunsany that Rahilly shows Billy was erected in 1716 by Sir Henry O'Neill, Bt., to mark the burial place of his father, Sir Bryan, his mother, Dame Mary, and his wife Mary, who all died in the same year. I visited the site in April 1987. *These* O'Neill arms contain the salmon as well as the *bras armé*.

Rahilly's romantic conception of the salmon's connection with ancient wisdom is supported by Celtic tradition. The story of Fionn's salmon and its gift of druidic powers is in Robert Graves, *The White Goddess* (Farrar, Straus, New York, 1966), 75, 182. See John Matthews, *The Celtic Shaman* (Element, Shaftesbury, Dorset, 1991) and Tom Cowan, *Fire in the Head: Shamanism and the Celtic Spirit* (Harper, San Francisco, 1993) for lively, experiential approaches to shamanic beliefs and practices in Irish tradition.

After visiting Newgrange—one of the most powerful and mystical places in Europe—I came across *The Cult of the Goddess* by Celtic scholar Lawrence Durdin-Robertson (Cesara Publications, Enniscorthy, Eire, 1974); the scholar's findings suggest Billy may have done more than merely hallucinate when he hit his head in the burial chamber.

7. TIME OF POWER

Charming a Governor's widow: The circumstances of Peter Warren's purchase of the Warrensbush lands from Governor Cosby's widow are described graphically by Recorder Horsmanden in a 1736 letter to Colden; "how she became so infatuated I know not" (CP 2:152–3).

"The place where they got us drunk": Island Woman's version of the meaning of the word "Manhattan" is confirmed by the Rev. John Heckewelder: see his *History, Manners and Customs of the Indian Nations* (Arno Press reprint, 1971), 262. According to Heckewelder, "Manhattan" is a corruption of the Delaware word *Manahachtanienk,* meaning "the island where we all became intoxicated."

Rites of blood and moon: I have discussed the possible ritual uses of ancient Iroquois vessels like the jar Island Woman gives to her daughter with archaeologist Dean Snow of the State University of New York at Albany, who has excavated several important sites in the Mohawk Valley. Father Lafitau, an impressive early ethnographer in so many areas, was not permitted to poke his nose into these matters; cf. Lafitau 1:178–9.

What little I know or can imagine of these things—as a man from a different culture, doubly an outsider—is the gift of the *ka'nihstenserakonha,* the clanmothers, in talk and in dreaming. Hazel Dean-John, a Seneca clanmother, shared with me the inspiring words that have been spoken by mother to daughter at the time of menarche from generation to generation in her line. Iroquois mothers at Ohswehken, Tiyendinaga, Akwesasne and Kahnawake showed me how, to this day, they prepare their daughters to be women with swimming and running and the sacred teaching stories.

Daughters of Copper Woman by Anne Cameron (Press Gang Publishers, Vancouver, 1987) contains a beautiful evocation of women's rites of passage in another Native American culture, the Nootka. For an intuitive and passionate approach to this theme, see Vicki Noble, *Shakti Woman* (Harper, San Francisco, 1991), ch. 1.

8. WELCOMED BY LARKS

Billy's youth and education: There is little reliable evidence on Johnson's upbringing or his reasons for emigrating from Ireland at the age of 23. His correspondence suggests he knew Latin and the books he ordered from London for his library in America reflect the varied tastes of a well-read man, ranging from Smollett to Newton, from political history to theology; cf. JP 1:264–5; JP 3:950, 953; JP 4:358–9. But there is no record of Billy's attendance at Trinity.

On the sexual mores of the Anglo-Irish drinking class, *The Diary of a Young Lady of Fashion in the Year 1764–1765* by Cleone Knox, ed. Alexander Kerr (Appleton, New York, 1926) is most enlightening. On dueling, drinking and other diversions of Billy's crowd, *The Ireland of Sir Jonah Barrington,* ed. Hugh B. Staple (University of Washington Press, Seattle and Washington, 1967) is an entertaining guide. Other details of life in Billy's Ireland have been borrowed from Constantia Maxwell, *Dublin under the Georges* (Faber, London, 1956) and the magnificent "Irish" volume in W. E. H. Lecky's *History of Ireland in the Eighteenth Century* (Appleton, New York, 1878) 2:101–476.

Billy's break with his father: The long silence between Christopher Johnson and his son after William's migration to America may hint at the bad blood between them. Only one letter from Billy to his father survives, written sixteen years after his departure from Ireland. The letter dealt with the legal complications and family jealousies stemming from Peter Warren's will, and though Billy includes a portrait of himself (he complained that it made his shoulders look narrow) the tone is distinctly cool; see JP 1:929–31.

9 . SOUL-DRIVERS

The ruses of the "soul sellers," the conditions of indentured servants and redemptioners on the Atlantic crossing and shipboard auctions like the one on Cat's brigantine are chillingly described in Bernard Bailyn, *Voyagers to the West* (Knopf, New York, 1986).

10 . NEWCOMERS

Balm of Circassia: The advertisement is printed in its entirety in Esther Singleton, *Social New York under the Georges* (Appleton, New York, 1902), 207.

Earthquake in New York: "The houses did shake," the New York *Gazette* reported on December 12, 1737, during an earthquake that started at 11:00 A.M. on December 7 and lasted "over a minute."

The DeLancey In-Laws: Peter Warren married Susannah DeLancey in July 1731. The marriage brought him not only the two trust funds mentioned in the narrative, but an interest in Susannah's later inheritances: from her father Stephen (Etienne), who died in 1741; from her mother (Anne Van Cortlandt), who died in 1743, leaving her a major share in Cortlandt Manor; and from her brother Stephen who died in 1745.

The ambition of James DeLancey (1702–1760), Warren's brother-in-law, was well conveyed by the contemporary historian William Smith, who commented that "he would rather be at the head of a dog than at the tail of a lion" (*The History of the Province of New York,* New-York Historical Society *Collections,* New York, 1829), V:245–7. James' marriage to Anne Heathcote in 1728 had brought him powerful connections in England and a stake in the Scarsdale estate. He was appointed Chief Justice of New York in 1733.

On the faction fights in colonial New York and the pivotal role of the DeLanceys, Stanley Nider Katz, *Newcastle's New York* (Harvard University Press, Cambridge, Mass., 1968) is a consummate work of scholarship.

Cat's escape from New York: The first reference to Catherine Weissenberg in any document found thus far is in the following advertisement, placed in Zenger's *New York Weekly Journal* on January 22, 1739, and reprinted on February 5:

> RUN AWAY from Captain Langdon of the City of New York a Servant Maid, named Catherine Weissenburg, about 17 years of Age, Middle Stature, slender, black ey'd, brown Complexion, speaks good English, altho' a Palatine born; had on when she went away a homespun striped waistcoat and Peticoat, blew-stockings and new shoes, and with her a Calico Wrapper, and a striped Calamanco Wraper, besides other Cloaths.
>
> "Whoever take her up and brings her home, or secures her so that she may be had again, shall have TWENTY SHILLINGS Reward, and all reasonable charge: and all Persons are forewarned not to entertain the said Servant at their Peril.

I am grateful to the late Dr. Milton Hamilton, an indefatigable researcher, for unearthing this advertisement, which confirms the physical description of Cat in my narrative, her proficiency in English, and the fact that when she joined Billy in the Mohawk Valley she was on the run from Captain Langdon.

The rest of my account of Cat's early adventures—including her romantic encounter with Billy in Dublin and her captivity among Mission Indians—is invention. The documents do not tell us how Johnson and the mother of his white children came together.

11. THE OCTAGON

Crown Point: The most vivid contemporary description of the French fort is by Peter Kalm, the Swedish botanist. See *The America of 1750: Peter Kalm's Travels in North America,* 2 vols., ed. Adolph B. Benson (Dover, New York, 1966).

Lake of Two Mountains: My description of the mission, also called Oka, is partly based on a 1757 account by Bougainville; cf. *Adventures in the Wilderness: The American Journals of Louis Antoine de Bougainville, 1756–1760* trans. and ed. Edward P. Hamilton (University of Oklahoma Press: Norman, 1964), 122–4. Paul Lawrence Stevens surveys the mixed population at Oka a generation later in "His Majesty's 'Savage' Allies: British Policy and the Northern Indians during the Revolutionary War" (Ph.D. dissertation. State University of New York at Buffalo, 1984), ch. 1. Today, the Mohawk name for the Oka reserve is Kahnesetake.

12. WINTER GAMES

Colden's history: Cadwallader Colden's *History of the Five Indian Nations,* the first history of the Iroquois in English, was published in two parts, in 1727 and 1747. I have generally referred to the paperback reprint by Cornell University Press, Ithaca, N.Y., 1964. Colden has been much underrated by historians of the Eastern Frontier, perhaps because he was both a diehard Royalist and averse to self-promotion. A scholarly attempt to redress the balance is Alice Keys, *Cadwallader Colden* (Columbia University Press, New York, 1906).

13. THE NET

Kidnapping Indian children: There is an account of Albany traders holding Indian children as sureties for debt in JP 9:36. See also William M. Beauchamp, *A History of the New York*

Iroquois (New York State Museum *Bulletin* 78, Albany, N.Y. 1905), 293.

The Patroon in Montreal: Jeremiah van Rensselaer visited Governor Beauharnois in 1734 with "another influential gentleman"; they offered to use their influence to prevent the Iroquois from making war on Canada if New York was spared from French or Indian attack. See NYCD 9:1039–40.

Father Luc: Father Luc François Nau was at Sault St. Louis (Caughnawaga) from 1735–1743. He describes the public penances he prescribed for drunkenness and other details of mission life in a 1735 report in JR 68:260–85.

Here are his comments on the witch-fear among the Iroquois that drove many—Swimming Voices among them—to seek sanctuary at the mission:

> Others who are accused of witchcraft are obliged to take refuge at the Sault St. Louis, otherwise they would be put out of the way at the first opportunity . . . The devil himself unwittingly becomes the occasion of the salvation of these wretched savages. (JR 68:279)

Father Luc's debate on dreams with Island Woman recalls a questionnaire prepared by one of his predecessors, Father Carheil, to demonstrate the impossibility of soul-flight to the Iroquois; cf JR 54:65–7.

Burials under the mission church: When I visited the stone church at Kahnawake in the summer of 1987, Father LaJoie told me that 301 Mohawks were buried *under* the church between 1710 and 1864; he could not explain why.

14. FOREST KILLER

Fleeced by the Patroon: Johnson complained to Peter Warren that the Patroon had cheated him over horses; Warren counseled his nephew to make no public complaint because the Patroon "is a near relation of my wife and may have it in his power very much to serve you." (JP 13:3)

Snowbird's costume: James Whitelaw met an Iroquois Indian dressed very much like Snowbird at Johnson Hall, Billy's last home, in 1773; cf. "Journal of General James Whitelaw, Surveyor-General of Vermont" in *Proceedings of the Vermont Historical Society* (1905–1906), 132.

Settling Warrensbush: By Billy's own account, he spent his first year "clearing a farm out of the thickest timbered woods I ever saw." (JP 1:907) Edith Mead Fox made a careful survey of the estate—including the location of tenants' and squatters' plots—in "Sir William Johnson's Early Career as a Frontier Landlord and Trader" (M.A. thesis, Cornell University, 1945). Ulysses Prentiss Hedrick, *A History of Agriculture in the State of New York* (Hill and Wang, New York, 1966) contains vivid descriptions of colonial methods of clearing land.

Forest Killer: Joseph Brant, the brother of Johnson's most celebrated Mohawk consort, explained the etymology of Billy's Mohawk name to his friend John Norton, the remarkable half-Scotsman who led Mohawks to battle in the War of 1812. See Norton: 264–5.

Learning the trade: Billy's order of the four hogsheads of rum is noted in Peter Warren's accounts (Warren –19). Johnson's adaptation to Indian tastes is reflected in his own accounts; cf. JP 1:539–40; JP 2:898. The situation at Oquaga around the time of Billy's visit is vividly described by a contemporary traveler, Gideon Hawley; see DH 3:1041ff.

Iroquois spokesmen reported "there are no beaver left in our country" as early as 1671 (NYCD 9:80). Colden wrote an important memorandum on the fur trade that Johnson probably read; see NYCD 5:726–33. Crooked practices like fixing weights and watering rum reportedly drove a Seneca warchief to side with the French; cf. NYCD 7:955–6. For a contemporary account of sharpers in the fur trade by one of Billy's allies, see Peter Wraxall, *An Abridgment of the Indian Affairs,* ed. Charles McIlwain (Benjamin Bloom, New York and London, 1968). Thomas Eliot Norton has written an excellent study of the colonial fur trade that is notably sympathetic to Billy's Albany rivals: see *The Fur Trade in Colonial New York* (University of Wisconsin Press, Madison, 1974).

15. GIFTS OF IRON

Cat's captivity: Some details of my (imagined) account of Cat's Indian captivity have been inspired by the experiences of other female captives in this period, including Eunice Williams— the daughter of a New England minister, taken at Deerfield, who married a Caughnawaga warchief—and such classic accounts as those of Mary Jemison and Massy Harbison. See Rev. James E. Seaver, *Life of Mary Jemison* (Matthews & Warren, Buffalo, N.Y., 1877) and "Narrative of the Captivity and Sufferings of Massy Harbison," printed in William L. Stone, *Life of Joseph Brant* (Alexander & Blake, New York, 1838), 2:Appendix VIII.

The soldier-abbé: My principal source on François Picquet (1708–1781), one of Johnson's most redoubtable French adversaries, is André Chagny, *François Picquet: Un Défenseur de la "Nouvelle-France"* (Librairie Beauchemin, Montreal, 1913). There is a brief but helpful sketch in DCB 4:636–7. Though best known for his activity at La Présentation (near Ogdensburg, N.Y.) after 1749, Abbé Picquet lived at the Sulpician mission at the Lake of Two Mountains (Oka), where Cat meets him, from 1739–49.

Caughnawaga: The origins of the mission at Sault St. Louis— Caughnawaga—are described by Father Claude Chauchetière; see JR 63:139–245. Some details of life at the mission in my narrative, including public penances for drunkenness, are based on a 1735 report by Father Luc François Nau; cf. JR 68:260–85.

The contraband trade: Governor Beauharnois complained in 1741 that "Sault St. Louis Caughnawaga has become a sort of republic and it is only there that foreign trade is carried on at present." (NYCD 9:1071) Successive French governors tried to curb the activities of the Desaunier sisters—the celebrated traders mentioned in the narrative. But they were protected by the Jesuits at the mission, especially Jean-Baptiste Tournois, who succeeded Nau as superior in 1744 and was finally expelled from New France with the trading sisters by Governor

La Jonquière in 1750, after large quantities of English trade goods were found at Caughnawaga.

Hendrick's early life: For Hendrick's account of his family's Mahican origins, see NYCD 6:294. For his protest against a Dutch minister's land deals, see NYCD 4:346–7.

16. BUGLING ELK

Hunters' magic: Frances Densmore, *Chippewa Customs* (Bureau of American Ethnology *Bulletin* 86, Washington, D.C., 1929) describes traditional Woodland Indian lures and other hunting practices. On the habits of mating elk, see Daniel J. Cox's superbly illustrated *Elk* (Chronicle Books, San Francisco, 1992).

Billy's move north: Billy's first surviving letter addressed from "Mount Johnson" is dated February 19, 1740 (cf. JP 1:8–9); however, it seems he did not take up full-time residence on the north side of the river until the following year. He occupied an existing stone house that did not survive the Revolution but probably resembled the Frey house, further up the Valley; Fort Johnson is a later construction.

17. WOLF DREAMING

Lydius: John Henry Lydius (1701–1794), baptized Jonannes Henricus by his father, a minister from Antwerp, is one of the most fascinating and devious characters in the history of the Eastern frontier and deserves a major biography. His account of the assassination attempt at Albany is substantiated by a secret letter in French from his wife Genevieve to her sister, written in 1733 and concealed inside the endpapers of a manuscript hymnal; I discovered this in the McKinney Library of the Albany Institute of History and Art.

Lydius lived at Montreal from 1725–30, and appears to have functioned as a double agent. At the time of his deportation,

Governor Beauharnois described him as "a very dangerous man in the colony" (NYCD 9:1019). He frequently traveled in the company of Caughnawagas; the Rev. Henry Barclay refers to a Caughnawaga chief, Tegeneyachgue, who stayed with Lydius at his Albany house for six weeks in the summer of 1744 (Barclay 69). The key to many of Lydius' intrigues may be found in the deed to a vast tract of land around Lake Champlain that he persuaded ten Mohawks—including Tekarihoken, the senior of the traditional chiefs—to sign in 1732; the deed is transcribed in CP 2:52–4.

Despite some inaccuracies, William H. Hill, *Old Fort Edward* (privately printed, Fort Edward, N.Y., 1929) contains valuable material on Lydius' career and descriptions of his trading post, renamed Fort Edward by William Johnson. I am grateful to Ken Dorn of Johnstown, N.Y. for finding this rare volume.

Cornering the market: In the harsh winter of 1739/40, Johnson made himself the prime supplier of peas in the New York colony (JP 1:10), taking a long step toward his future fortune. In 1740, he went in deep, persuading Peter Warren to underwrite a shipment of goods worth £1,600 from his London suppliers. This was too rich for the blood of the Albany *handlaers*—none of whom had previously laid out more than £300 for a season's trade goods—and no doubt explains much of the subsequent intrigue against Johnson. cf. Charles Roscoe Canedy III, "An Entrepreneurial History of the New York Frontier, 1739–1776" (Ph.D. dissertation, Case Western Reserve University, 1967), 81.

Snakebite: The healing plant used by Island Woman was no doubt *polygala senega,* "Seneca snakeroot," also known as mountain flax. It was also used as an abortifacient and, in modern times, for treating respiratory complaints such as asthma and pneumonia.

Sorcery: For a riveting account of a shamanic battle involving a Mohawk sorcerer's *oyaron,* or power animal, see Lafitau 1:247–8. An aerial collision between bird-shamans of another Native American culture is described in Knud Rasmussen, *The Netsilik Eskimos: Social Life and Spiritual Culture,* trans.

W. E. Calvert, *Report of the Fifth Thule Expedition, 1921–1924,* vol. 8, nos. 1–2, Copenhagen, 1931, 299–301.

18: DEVILS OF NEW YORK

The *"Negro Plot":* The principal primary source on the Manhattan witch-hunt of 1741 is an anonymous account, with minutes of the trials, attributed to one of the principal witch-finders: see Daniel Horsmanden (attr.), *The New York Conspiracy,* ed. Thomas J. Davis (Beacon Press, Boston, 1971). The author made a vehement effort to depict the alleged conspiracy as a "St. Patrick's Day plot" cooked up by "Romish priests" and "papists", including a dancing master, a Latin tutor, and Irish soldiers in the garrison; cf. Horsmanden: 408–10. T. J. Davis has published a recent reappraisal of the affair: *A Rumor of Revolt* (The Free Press, 1985). The anonymous letter from a Massachusetts man to Colden appears in CP 8:270–2.

Johnson on Gallows Hill: Though Johnson left no account of the executions in his correspondence, there is evidence that he was in New York at the time of Othello's trial and execution; he signed one of his three bonds to his Uncle Peter ("I being at New York") on July 15, 1741. Othello confessed to the court on July 12 and was hanged on July 18.

20. WARPATH

Hendrick's speech at Boston is quoted by a visiting doctor from Annapolis; see *Gentleman's Progress: the Itinerarium of Dr. Alexander Hamilton, 1744* ed. Carl Bridenbaugh (University of North Carolina Press, Chapel Hill, 1948). Hendrick's figures of speech are suspiciously biblical; either he had an eye on his New England audience, or his language was "improved" by the interpreter.

The lure of codfish: Benjamin Pickman's house at Salem, constructed in 1740, had gilded carvings of codfish along the staircase.

Polly's baptism was recorded by Rev. Henry Barclay on October 14, 1744 (Barclay 25)

The Mohawk scare: The Albany Commissioners interrogated Lydius on his possible role in inciting the "Mohawk riot" of January, 1745; cf. PAC: Indian Records RG10 vol 1821: 40–6. Governor Clinton asked Conrad Weiser to investigate, and Weiser reported back that the Mohawks told him "the Albany people never spoke from their heart to them" (NYCD 6:292–3).

Albany in King George's War was a little like Casablanca or Helsinki in later world conflicts, swarming with double agents and deceivers. I have drawn heavily on the manuscript *Minutes* of the Commissioners for Indian Affairs for January–August, 1746 in the McKinney Library of the Albany Institute of History and Art (MS #97, vol. 1); the rest of the series is in PAC.

Clinton's Indian council: Hendrick's remarks are based on NYCD 6:294–5. Governor Clinton threw down the war belt at Albany on October 10, 1745; his speech and the Indian response are printed in NYCD 6:297–301. Colonel Stoddard's rage was fueled by a letter he received during the conference from Ephraim Williams reporting an attack on a blockhouse in western Massachusetts; NYCD 6:303.

The burning of Saratoga: My narrative of Marin's expedition is based on his own account (NYCD 10:76–7) and a letter from Robert Sanders to William Johnson describing the destruction (JP 1:43–4).

21. TO CAUSE A BEAR

Bull feast for the Mohawk: JP 9:4.

Saving Governor Clinton's hide: CP 3:228. On the Albany conference of August, 1746, see NYCD 6:317–22.

Scalps and spirit-heads: On the spiritual significance of scalp-taking, see Georg Friederici, "Scalping in America", *Annual Report of the Smithsonian Institution*, 1906, Washington, D.C.

On techniques, see Gabriel Nadau, "Indian Scalping" in *Bulletin of the History of Medicine,* vol X, no. 2, July 1941.

22. THE OLIVE OF LYDIUS

The Murder Plot: Hendrick returned to Albany from Canada on November 23, 1746, bearing a French prisoner and a French scalp. Lydius claimed credit for the Mohawk attack on French carpenters on the Ile La Motte in letters to Stoddard, his Massachusetts paymaster. He added, "I was mostly obliged to do what I have done under a Color of Col. Johnson." (Lydius to Stoddard, Nov. 24, 1746; MS in New-York Historical Society.)

23. THE GOD-GIVEN

Ambush at Chateaugay: French accounts are in NYCD 10:81–3; 89–132. On LaCorne St. Luc see DCD 4:425–9. A striking portrait of the French adventurer is reproduced in Francis Parkman, *A Half-Century of Conflict* (LaSalle edition, Little Brown, Boston, 1902), 2:184.

24. MOON OF CRUSTED SNOW

Battle on snowshoes: The French attack deep inside Mohawk country took place on March 15, 1748. It is described in NYCD 6:422–4 and JP 1:146–7, where the Mohawk warchief is identified as "Gingego, Chief Warrior of all the Nations."

Ghost warrior: The post-death confusion of victims of sudden violence is a recurring motif in Iroquoian folklore; cf. William M. Beauchamp, *Iroquois Folk Lore* (Onondaga Historical Association, Syracuse, N.Y., 1922). Paul Radin reports the native belief that a warrior slain in battle can choose his next incarnation in *The Autobiography of a Winnebago Indian* (Dover reprint, New York, 1963), 72.

Island Woman as psychopomp: For other Iroquoian accounts of shamans guiding the souls of the dead, see my essay "Black-robes and Dreamers" in *Shaman's Drum,* Spring 1992.

25. RAGE

Billy's French captive: Angélique Vitry is mentioned in JP 1:185, 254. At the end of King George's War, her father wrote to Johnson in hopes of arranging a marriage; cf. JP 1:253–4.

26. SHE WHO DREAMS

For further information on techniques of interactive dreaming practiced by Island Woman and Sparrow, see my article "An Active Dreaming Approach to Death, Dying and Healing Dreams" in *Shaman's Drum,* Spring 1994. On working with power animals, see Michael Harner, *The Way of the Shaman* (Bantam edition, New York, 1982). On initiation by dream teachers in shamanic tradition, see Stanley Krippner, "Tribal Shamans and Their Travels into Dreamtime" in Krippner, (ed.), *Dreamtime and Dreamwork* (Jeremy Tarcher, Los Angeles, 1990).

27. WHITE DEATH

African advice on inoculation: Johnson's doctor is right about Cotton Mather; for an account of how Mather and his friend Dr. Zabdiel Boylston learned about inoculation from an African slave, Onesimus, see Kenneth Silverman, *The Life and Times of Cotton Mather* (Harper & Row, New York, 1984), 338–40. It is probable that some of the Africans in Johnson country had also been inoculated.

The Face of smallpox: A whistling mask from the Tonawanda Seneca collected by Peter Furst resembles the Face of the White Death described in this chapter; a photograph of this mask appears in William N. Fenton, *The False Faces of the Iroquois* (University of Oklahoma Press, Norman, 1987), after p. 265.

Shamanic battles against imported disease: The battle of a Iroquoian shaman called Tsondacouané—one of Island Woman's Huron ancestors—with the imported epidemic may be tracked through Father Le Mercier's accounts from Georgian Bay in the terrible winter of 1636–7; see JR 13:227–33; JR 14:51–3.

Epidemics in Johnson's New York: A smallpox scare in 1752 caused the New York Assembly to be prorogued; see JP 9:91, 96. Johnson was sponsoring widescale inoculation against smallpox among his family, his white neighbors and the Valley Indians by 1767, two years before another epidemic in the Province of New York; cf. JP 7:14, 874, 938; JP 12:763, 1019.

The holocaust effect: For sober appraisals of the holocaust effect of smallpox on Native American peoples, see Henry F. Dobyns, *Their Numbers Became Thinned* (University of Tennessee Press, Knoxville, 1983) and Russell Thornton, *American Indian Holocaust and Survival: A Population History Since 1492* (University of Oklahoma Press, Norman, 1987). In 1977, almost two centuries after the discovery of a vaccine, the World Health Organization declared that smallpox was the first of humankind's diseases to have been eradicated. However, modern science is as much in the dark as Island Woman's people over precisely *how* it kills—and stores of the virus have been preserved at guarded laboratories in Atlanta and Moscow (AP report, December 24, 1993).

28. MAN OF TWO WORLDS

Suicide of a Governor: cf. NYCD 6:804.

Washington and l'assassinat: The French side of the story—including the claim that by the terms of his subsequent surrender at Fort Necessity, Washington actually confessed to an act of murder—may be tracked in Fernand Grenier (ed.), *Papiers Contrecoeur et autres documents concernant le conflit anglo-francais sur l'Ohio* (Archives du Seminaire de Québec, Quebec, 1952), esp. 133–81, 196–202.

Ben Franklin's kidney stone is discussed wittily in Richard

Selzer, *Mortal Lessons* (Simon and Schuster, New York, 1976), 88–9.

Hendrick's speech to the Albany Congress appears in NYCD 6:867–8.

The Wyoming land scam: The list of 16 Indian signatories is in JP 1:405. Johnson, asked by Governor Hamilton of Pennsylvania to intercede, was initially evasive (cf. JP 1:134) but later persuaded Hendrick to go to Philadelphia with Daniel Claus to try to put things right. Johnson reported that a Seneca chief who signed the Wyoming deed, drunk, was ostracized by his own community and "obliged to fly to the French for protection"; NYCD 7:956.

Johnson's commissions: The letter of the Lords of Trade was dated October 29, 1754; the excerpt used here appears in NYCD 6:919. Johnson's commission from Braddock is in JP 1:465–6.

29. FIRE THAT NEVER DIES

"All other fires we kick away": The minutes of the momentous Indian council of June 21–July 4, 1755, at which Johnson was formally recognized as Firekeeper of the Confederacy, appear in NYCD 6:964–88.

30. FIELDS OF WAR

The road to Lake George: I have relied heavily on Seth Pomeroy's diary of the campaign and the letters of Ephraim Williams, as well as on Johnson's correspondence; see *The Journals and Papers of Seth Pomeroy,* ed. Louis de Forest (Society of Colonial Wars, New Haven, 1926) and Willis E. Wright, *Colonel Ephraim Williams: A Documentary Life* (Berkshire County Historical Society, Pittsfield, Mass., 1970).

Johnson's feud with Shirley: For Shirley's viewpoint, see his letter to Johnson in JP 1:733–6, written after the Governor had received Lydius' version of the Indian council at Fort

Johnson that summer. For a less Johnsonian appraisal of Shirley's accomplishments, see John A. Schutz, *William Shirley, King's Governor of Massachusetts* (University of North Carolina Press, Chapel Hill, 1961).

Braddock's rout: Johnson's reflections are borrowed from his letter to James DeLancey on July 30, 1755; see JP 1:794–7. For a first-hand French account of Braddock's defeat see NYCD 10:303–4.

Converging armies: Johnson arrived at Lydius' trading post at the Carry on August 14; Baron Dieskau reached Fort St. Frédéric on August 17.

Secret diplomacy with Caughnawagas: Snowbird's report to Johnson is based on JP 2:379.

Lydius among the Mohawks: Matthew Ferrall's account appears in JP 1:807–9.

Discipline in Johnson's army: Pomeroy reports the punishment prescribed for a soldier condemned for "profane swearing and a Sodomittical attempt"; Pomeroy *Journals:* 106. For Johnson's account of the arrest of Captain Hall on charges of selling rum rations to the Indians, see JP 2:7.

31. THE WOLF'S THROAT

Hendrick's speech is printed in full in NYCD 6:998–9.

Dreams and scouts: A sachem's dream on September 6, which led Johnson to order that no man should go out to the left of the camp, is described in a letter by a gunner under Captain Eyre's command that appears in NYCD 6:1005. Johnson's accounts of military expenses provide further evidence of his respect for native dreams during the Lake George campaign. He made the following entry on September 3, 1755: "To Peter a Mohawk warrior to fulfill his dream a silver band £1.12" (JP 2:593).

Eyewitness accounts: Johnson's official account of the Battle of Lake George, addressed to "the Governors of the several

Colonies," appears in DH 2:691–5. Three Massachusetts men associated with Ephraim Williams left accounts of the battle: Seth Pomeroy (*Journal*); Dr. Thomas Williams (cf. Arthur Latham Perry, *Origins in Williamstown* Scribner's, New York, 1894, 366–7); and Perez Marsh (Wright, 147–9). Other important sources are Daniel Claus' *Narrative of his Relations with Sir William Johnson and Experiences in the Lake George Fight* (Society of Colonial Wars, 1904), and, from the French side, Baron Dieskau's report in NYCD 10:316–8, which complains of Caughnawaga double-dealing. Samuel Blodget's invaluable *Prospective Plan of the Battle of Lake George* (Richard Draper, Boston, 1755), based on participants' reports, gives a clear view of the sickle-shaped ambush line; it is reproduced in DH 4:opp. 259.

War-song of the Six Nations: My version is adapted from the translation in Parker's *Constitution of the Five Nations,* 52–3.

Spoiled surprise: Baron Dieskau ascribed the loss of surprise to the treachery of Caughnawagas who showed themselves to Mohawks prematurely: "Had my orders been followed, not a man of them would have escaped." (NYCD 10:342). John Burk, an officer in Williams' regiment, wrote to his wife after the battle that an over-eager Canadian Indian had fired too soon; cf. William A. Pew, *Colonel Ephraim Williams: An Appreciation* (Williams College, Williamstown, 1919), 22. The Claus *Narrative* contains a theatrical exchange of speeches between Hendrick and a Caughnawaga sachem, but Claus was not present. A more plausible version of a Caughnawaga–Mohawk dialogue was supplied by an anonymous New England survivor; see Epaphras Hoyt, *Antiquarian Researches* (A. Phelps, Grenfield, 1824), 274.

Hendrick's death: Claus reported that Hendrick was killed and scalped inexpertly by women and children in the French Indian camp; this version may have come from Mohawk survivors. (Claus *Narrative,* 16) The artist and illustrator Rufus Alexander Grider (1816–1900) inspected thighbones identified as Hendrick's at the Lake George site a century ago and made a sketch of them that is in the New York State Museum (Grider Scrapbooks, 6:8).

Whiting's retreat: Perez Marsh—a surgeon's mate in Ephraim William's regiment and the colonel's rival in love—accused Colonel Nathan Whiting of "disgraceful behaviour" in his prompt retreat but was not present. Whiting's reputation is defended in John W. Krueger, *A Most Memorable Day: The Battle of Lake George, September 8, 1755* (Center for Adirondack Studies, Saranac Lake, N.Y., 1980).

32. HUSKING TIME

Poisoned bullets: Surgeon Williams wrote that "many of the poisoned balls we brought in out of their bullet pouches, taken among the plunder"; cf. *The Historical Magazine* 7:213. The *Boston Gazette* reported on September 29, 1755 that French musket balls were "chew'd" and appeared "surprising green" when extracted from wounds.

Indians after the battle: The remarks of Aguiotta, the Oneida sachem, on September 11 are reported in NYCD 6:1011. Johnson reported on October 22: "I have now but four Indians with me . . . They seem to be infected with the epidemical disease of our troops, home sickness" (JP 2:238).

Robert Rogers' scouts: cf DH 4:259–61; Pomeroy *Journal* 120; JP 2:258, 294–5.

33. HUMMINGBIRDS

Title of baronetcy: The patent issued to Johnson was boilerplate, originally devised to encourage English soldier-squires to settle Ulster. The text is in JP 2:344–7. For the effect of Billy's London honors in immobilizing his colonial opponents, cf JP 2:462.

Lydius selling Susquehanna deeds: Claus sent a specimen deed to Johnson; JP 9:162.

34. THE REAL WORLD

The shaman's dream-map resembles the birchbark scrolls of the Mide priests of the Ojibwa more than distinctively Iroquoian material; cf. W. J. Hoffman's seminal work, *The Mide'wiwin or "Grand Medicine Society" of the Ojibwa* in the Seventh Annual Report of the Bureau of Ethnology (Smithsonian, Washington, D.C., 1891), 143–300. However, the tribal affiliation of Island Woman's dream teacher is unclear and, as a master shaman, he would undoubtedly have drawn from more than one tradition. More light is cast on this subject in my narrative *The Interpreter*.

35. MOTHER OF THE FALLS

Condolence: Johnson's leading role in the condolence ceremonies for Red Head, or Kaghswoughtioony, the great Onondaga chief, is described in NYCD 6:133–4. This is also the earliest detailed account I have found in English of an Iroquois condolence council.

ACKNOWLEDGMENTS

Many people helped in the making of this book.

I am grateful to friends of the Six Nations and other First Peoples of America who gave me a window into the world of Island Woman and her people: especially to Ray and Fred Gonyea, Tom Porter, Jake Thomas, Tom Hill, George Abrams, Oren Lyons, Hazel Dean-John, Pete Jemison, Eva and Don Maracle, Phil Montour, Marilyn Johnson, and to the teaching and example of Jamie Sams, the late Frank Fools Crow, Johnny Moses and Medicine Grizzlybear Lake.

In my forays into Billy Johnson's world, I found a wonderful guide in Wanda Burch, the curator of Johnson Hall (Billy's last home in the Valley) who is not only a Johnson scholar but a *dreamer*. In Ireland, P.J. Beggan, the present owner of Billy's childhood home at Smithstown, was a gracious and genial host and Helen Marry was a wonderful guide to the back roads and ancient mysteries of County Meath. In England, Billy's lineal descendent, Sir Peter Johnson, Bt., offered sage advice and encouragement, and Bill Tower unearthed a "lost" portrait. On native lands in Canada and New York, I met many other Johnson descendents, and was delighted to find that there is a lively oral tradition concerning the King's Superintendent of Indians and his consorts—though on the Six Nations reserve (near Brantford, Ontario) Billy is sometimes confused with a more recent Mohawk namesake who shared his love of high living.

Among scholars and historians who offered advice and encouragement along the trail, I am grateful to William Fenton, the great ethnographer of the Iroquois, Dean Snow,

Barbara Graymont, Gunther Michelson, Charles Gehring, George Hamell, John and Mary Webb, John Demos, Constance Crosby, Peter Benes and the members of the Dublin Seminar for New England Folklife, Rosemarie Manory and the Hudson-Mohawk Institute, Isabel Thompson Kelsay, Robert Allen, Brian Leigh Dunnigan and Christina Johanssen Hanks. I benefited greatly from the industry of an indefatigable researcher, the late Dr. Milton Hamilton, whose papers now reside in the McKinney Library of the Albany Institute of History and Art.

I am indebted to the dedicated staff of many libraries, museums and historic sites, including the Public Archives of Canada; the National Museum of Man in Ottawa; the Woodland Indian Cultural Centre in Brantford, Ontario; the Field Museum of Natural History; the Hamilton College Library; the Iroquois Indian Museum; the Rochester Museum and Science Center; Ganondagan State Historic Site; the New-York Historical Society; the Massachusetts Historical Society; the Albany Institute of History and Art; the New York State Library; the State Historical Society of Wisconsin; the Montgomery County Historical Society; Fort Ticonderoga; Fort Plain; Fort Klock; Old Fort Niagara; Fort William Henry; Fort Johnson; and Johnson Hall. I owe special thanks to Bill O'Connor and the staff of the Albany Public Library, which fielded many esoteric requests and gave me an early forum for some of my discoveries.

I am grateful to many friends in the Mohawk Valley who share my passion for frontier history and helped me bring Billy Johnson to life on stage in the premiere of my one-man theatre, "Conversations with Sir William Johnson," in Johnstown, N.Y., on June 11, 1993: especially Hugh Carville, Rod and Chloe Correll, Dr. Jacqueline Taylor, the former president of Fulton-Montgomery Community College, Dr. Anna Weitz, Robert Schultz, Peter Betz, Dorothy Fraser, Dale Higgins, Arlene Sitterly, Brian and Anita Hanaburgh, Martha Wood, Mark Rettersdorf and Laurel Corby of the Fulton County Regional Chamber of Commerce, the Rev. William Small, the late Rebecca Evans—a generous patron of many Johnson causes, including Fort Johnson—Morris and Geraldine Evans, and Pastor Barry Murr and the parishioners of First Presbyterian Church. Among the many devoted re-enactors who help to bring history alive for new generations, I give special thanks to Jack Barton Frost and the Brigade of the American Revolution, Noel Levee and the Tryon County Militia, and Louis Decker. Ken Dorn, the paragon of Valley booksellers, was a guide to the arcana of wild birds as well as rare books.

Congressman Sherwood Boehlert, Dean D'Amore and other moving spirits in the Northern Frontier Heritage project helped to broaden my interest in the frontier on which—in many senses—America was born. John Jermano, the director of the New York State Office of Canals, was an engaging guide to the water-roads of New York, then and now. Senator Daniel Patrick Moynihan was a living reminder that erudition, eloquence and the Celtic flair for theatre did not vanish from New York politics with Sir William Johnson.

THE FIREKEEPER is a journey into the Dreaming, even more than a journey into history. My fascination with dreams began in early childhood, and the first person to confirm my boyhood suspicion that "the dream world is the Real World" was an Aboriginal friend in my native Australia, as explained in the personal note that follows.

In my practice and teaching of dreamwork, my principal teachers have been in the dreamworld itself, including the native shaman and the *ka'nihstensera* (clanmother) of long ago who appeared to me, night after night, when I first set out to explore Iroquois country. It was these dream encounters, more than any event in outer reality, that led me to study the Mohawk language—to decode some of my dream messages. Much of THE FIREKEEPER springs straight from my dreams, and my greatest debt is to my dream teachers.

But I have also learned a great deal from other dream-workers, including Stanley Krippner, Jeremy Taylor, Patricia Garfield, Rita Dwyer, Strephon Kaplan-Williams, Jessica Allen and Aad van Ouwerkerk, all gifted teachers and generous spirits.

In my understanding of shamanic practice, I am greatly indebted to Michael Harner and Sandra Ingerman, as well as to Ginny Black Wolf and the members of my Active Dream circles. Thanks also to Peter and Jill Furst, for sharing the marvelous fruits of their scholarship and adventures; to Tom Cowan, whose shamanic practice honors his Celtic ancestors; to Jeanne Achterberg, who has helped to bring the shaman's way of healing into modern homes and hospitals; to Holger Kalweit, Roger Walsh, Joan Halifax, Fred Alan Wolf and the late Mircea Eliade, for their splendid books; to Timothy White of *Shaman's Drum,* for editorial acumen grounded in experience; and to Philip and Vassa Neimark, whose luminous work has made Ade's tradition—the way of Ifa—accessible to a new audience in the West, and helped many to clarify their natural energy paths. Most of all, I thank Philemon, who called me to this path; Marshall, who reminded me when I had forgotten; and Gabrielle, who recalled me when I had strayed again.

Many others encouraged and sustained me, dreaming and waking, during the adventures that resulted in this book. Maurice Sonnenberg, a consummate New Yorker, was a friend in all seasons and helped me keep my sense of humor. Pat Model shared in the oak dreaming. Bob and Barbara Willner followed their dreams to the point of loaning their wonderful country retreat for some of our adventures in consciousness. Willard Vine Clerk, a magical artist, lent some of his magic at propitious times. Susan Novotny, Grover Askins and Dan Driggs—magical booksellers and generous friends—were willing accomplices for that benign spirit Arthur Koestler called the Library Angel.

I was graced to find in Tom Doherty a publisher who is equally at home in the realms of history and imagination and whose personal enthusiasm for this project helped me rediscover my wings. I am also grateful to three lively and supportive editors—Bob Gleason, Ed Breslin and David Hartwell—and to my agent, Stuart Krichevsky.

I give thanks, finally, for the love and laughter of my family: to my daughters Pandora, Candida and Sophie, to the memory of my father and mother, who shared in the dreaming, and to the spirited companionship of my wife Marcia, who helps me to join sun and moon, earth and sky.

A PERSONAL NOTE

I was six years old when I met Jacko, an aboriginal boy a year or two older than me, in Brisbane, Australia. My family did not approve of me hanging out with "blackfellas"—an attitude typical of white middle-class families then and probably now. Jacko's father was in jail, and he lived with his uncle Fred, who made a fair living painting gum trees and koalas for the tourist trade when he wasn't drunk. But I'd find a way to slope off with Jacko. We'd start off on a tram (there were still city trams in those days) and end up out in the bush.

During these adventures, Jacko talked about the dreamtime. He was the first person I knew who lived inside a dreaming tradition. His family taught him that dreams are the most important source of information we have.

"Uncle Fred went into the dreamtime last night," Jacko would say. "And he brought back this picture. It's not for the tourists. It's powerful." Or: "Aunt Beryl visited my grandma last week. Grandma's been gone five, six years, but Aunt Beryl says she's doing fine. She told my aunt what to take for her lumbago."

I don't remember what tribe Jacko belonged to. I haven't seen him in forty years. Except in dreaming.

But I owe him a debt I need to acknowledge here. While my own society—my family, my schools, my church, the whole popular culture—was telling me that dreams are "only dreams," Jacko was telling me that the dream world is the real world.

I haven't forgotten, Jacko.

If I have come anywhere near presenting a true picture of the dreaming of Island Woman and her people in this book, it is not only because I have immersed myself for seven years in the study of Native American traditions.

It's because of Jacko. In the simplest way possible, without any fuss, he was saying to me: Just do it.

So I've worked with my own dream journals since I was a teenager. (Some Native Americans say white folks need to write everything down because they have such poor memories.) And at my family breakfast table, as at Island Woman's, the first question we ask each other is, "What did you dream?"

ABOUT THE AUTHOR

Robert Moss was born in Australia of Scots, Cornish, Irish and French ancestry. He now lives with his wife and daughters on the edge of Mohawk country in the upper Hudson Valley of New York.

He has pursued various careers: as a college professor of history and philosophy, as a war correspondent in Vietnam, magazine editor and syndicated columnist; as novelist, actor and storyteller; and as a teacher of dreamwork, creative visualization and other methods of personal empowerment. His previous novel, *Fire Along the Sky,* is the first of his narratives of the Eastern Frontier. In the course of researching this cycle, he studied the languages, oral traditions and spiritual practices of Native Americans—especially the Iroquois and their neighbors—with elders, healers and clanmothers. He also conducted extensive research among manuscript sources in Canada, Great Britain, France and Ireland as well as in the United States. He walked the scenes of William Johnson's boyhood in County Meath, as well as the battlefields of the French and Indian wars and the places of power used by Island Woman and her lineage of dream-healers.

An active member of the Association for the Study of Dreams, Moss has published ground-breaking studies of the shamanic dream practices of the Woodland Indians as well as articles on dream precognition, healing dreams, and dreams of death and possible afterlives. He teaches and practices Active Dreaming, an approach to dreamwork that incorporates shamanic techniques such as drumming for dream re-entry. His workshops are popular both nationally and internationally. His book *Conscious Dreaming: A Spiritual Path for Everyday Life* is both a personal odyssey between the worlds and a practical guide to dreamwork and shamanism.

He has also published six popular suspense novels, including *Moscow Rules* and *Carnival of Spies.*

The next of his narratives, *The Interpreter,* follows the story of Island Woman's lineage of *arendiwanen,* or "women of power," back into the time of first contact between the Real People and the newcomers.

Historical fiction available from **TOR**
FORGE

PEOPLE OF THE LAKES • Kathleen O'Neal Gear and W. Michael Gear

The spellbinding tale of pre-Columbian North America by the bestselling authors of *People of the Sea*.

FIRE ALONG THE SKY • Robert Moss

A sweeping novel of America's first frontier. "There is not a single stuffy moment in this splendidly researched and wildly amusing historical adventure."

—*Kirkus Reviews*

THE EAGLE'S DAUGHTER • Judith Tarr

War and romance in the Holy Roman Empire! "Seduction, power and politics are the order of the day."—*Library Journal*

THE WOMAN WHO FELL FROM THE SKY • Barbara Riefe

The ancient nations of the eastern forests come to life in this novel of early America by the *New York Times* bestselling author.

DEATH COMES AS EPIPHANY • Sharan Newman

"A spectacular tale made even more exotic by its rich historical setting. Newman's characters are beautifully drawn."—Faye Kellerman, author of *The Quality of Mercy*

NOT OF WAR ONLY • Norman Zollinger

"A grand epic of passion, political intrigue, and battle. History about as vivid as it gets."

—David Morrell